MW01076123

ASHES OF MAN

By Christopher Ruocchio:

THE SUN EATER SEQUENCE

Empire of Silence

Howling Dark

Demon in White

Kingdoms of Death

Ashes of Man

ASHES OF MAN

THE SUN EATER BOOK FIVE

CHRISTOPHER RUOCCHIO

An Ad Astra Book

First published in the US in 2022 by DAW Books, Inc

This edition first published in the UK in 2022 by Head of Zeus Ltd,
part of Bloomsbury Publishing Plc

Copyright © Christopher Ruocchio, 2022

The moral right of Christopher Ruocchio to be identified
as the author of this work has been asserted in accordance
with the Copyright, Designs and Patents Act of 1988.

All rights reserved. No part of this publication may be reproduced,
stored in a retrieval system, or transmitted, in any form or by any means,
electronic, mechanical, photocopying, recording, or otherwise, without
the prior permission of both the copyright owner and the
above publisher of this book.

This is a work of fiction. All characters, organizations,
and events portrayed in this novel are either products of
the author's imagination or are used fictitiously.

9 7 5 3 1 2 4 6 8

A CIP catalogue record for this book is available
from the British Library.

ISBN (HB): 9781803287553
ISBN (XTPB): 9781803287560
ISBN (E): 9781803287539

Edited by Katie Hoffman

Printed and bound in Great Britain by
CPI Group (UK) Ltd, Croydon, CR0 4YY

Head of Zeus
First Floor East
5–8 Hardwick Street
London EC1R 4RG

WWW.HEADOFZEUS.COM

TO MATTHEW, ANDREW, MORGAN,
DYLAN, ARIEL, KIM & RALPH.
MY SIBLINGS—BORN AND FOUND.

CHAPTER 1

THE SAILS OF CHARON

DAY.

Day was breaking over dark waters, Colchis's white sun still low and golden at the horizon. Salt wind blew lank hair from my brow, stung my face.

In the end, I had not left Gibson's tomb with Valka and the others. They had gone down to the old camp by the shore, had left me kneeling in the dirt before the new-raised cairn. The oldest tradition held that the body of any lord must—after the cathars had washed it, embalmed it, and cut away the organs for the canopic jars—lie in state for three days, and that his heirs should keep vigil the while, sleeping in shifts if they slept at all. Gibson once told me my father had done it alone, kneeling in the chapel at Devil's Rest before the body of Lord Timon, my grandfather. I could remember my grandmother, Lady Fuchsia, lying in the purple chamber set aside for her. We had not been permitted to see her, though we had. It was in that violet chamber that I first met Death, and the stench of her has never left me.

We did not have three days for the proper vigil, nor any cathars or canopic jars. That was just as well. Palatine Gibson plainly was, but he had died a scholiast, and the Strictures of their order prescribed that all scholiasts were to be burned, their ashes scattered to the winds.

Ashes.

No ashes, as there was no time.

I had taken all the time we had.

Had I slept there, kneeling on the hard-packed earth? Or only dreamed?

I had seen a different ocean, had watched it recede along a shore of crushed bone. Mirrored knights stood silent sentinel about a bed draped in red silk in which a man lay dying. I lay in that same bed, Selene beside me. Selene and Valka. Valka alone.

Myself alone.

Alone.

A woman with eyes like black suns sat draped in cloth of gold. The vision turned, and Dorayaica, the Shiomu Elusha, strode along beneath the colonnades of the Eternal City, Vati and Attavaisa beside it. It turned again: the Emperor's face smiled down at me, then—as if in a kaleidoscope—split in two. I blinked, and saw Alexander's face and mine looking back at me, each of us on golden thrones. The ocean receded again, waters running from my advancing feet, and I stared out into darkness. A square of darkness framed in light, blacker than anything I'd ever seen, blacker than the stones of Annica, blacker than the Howling Dark.

A window onto night.

Why should a darkened window fill me with such fear and sorrow?

I blinked.

Through it all, I remember the salt wind raking, tousling the tall grass that grew along the black edge of the bluffs. Whitecaps glowed orange in the night off the glow of the gas giant, Atlas, whose limn hung low over the horizon, vaster than any moon.

"It's time to go, Had." A hand clapped my shoulder, and turning from Gibson's cairn I blinked up at Pallino. The old myrmidon grinned down at me, grizzled as when I first knew him, the scuffed old leather patch obscuring one eye. "You been at this long enough."

"I didn't hear you coming, old man," I said, going to one knee.

It was only then that I remembered Pallino was dead, and found myself staring up at empty air. I shut my eyes, opened them again.

I was alone.

My knees ached from the kneeling, and my whole body complained as I struggled to rise. My ruined shoulder protested, and I used my left arm—the arm with hollow bones—to push myself to my feet. I could scarce remember when last I had been so tired. It must have been that first night aboard the *Ascalon*, after Valka and I had escaped from Akterumu. Thinking of Akterumu, of Pallino—who had died there with some many thousand others—and of Dorayaica's coronation darkened the newborn day, as though gray clouds buried the pale sun.

But I reached out and laid my hand—my three-fingered, right hand—upon the top stone of Gibson's cairn. No words came to me, no final speech, no promise. What could I say to him that I had not already said? That he did not already know?

Nothing.

I only brushed the dew from the top stone, baring the faint inscription I had made with the point of my fishing knife. I smiled down at it a long moment, and raised my face to the sun.

It was time.

Valka saw me returning before any of the others. I wondered if she had been sitting up for me in the old camp, sleepless as I'd remained sleepless beside Gibson's tomb. Wordless, she embraced me, cool fingers on my face. We drew apart, and she asked, "Are you all right?"

Looking round I saw Imrah standing—so like Siran—in the door to one of the dormitory pods my Red Company had left upon the beach centuries before. "Too many ghosts," I said, and smiled.

"You look like hell," Valka said, drawing my attention away from the young Keeper of Thessa.

"It was a long night," I said, putting my hands on her shoulders. I did my best to smile once more.

Valka stepped back. Her golden eyes swept me up and down, evaluating. "You should clean yourself up. I've got most everything on the boat. Imrah says we can leave when you're ready."

"I *am* ready," I said. "I can wash on the *Ascalon*. We shouldn't linger. The Empire knows we're here?"

Valka gave a small nod. "They must. I had to use my name to call for Gibson's doctor. They're bound to notice."

I looked out to sea, toward the gray shape on the brightening horizon that was the isle of Racha. Presently I turned to Imrah. "I fear I've brought the hammer down on you and your people," I told her.

The Sevrastene native swore an oath in her language whose meaning I could well guess, and she gestured as if to throw something away. "They will not bother us. It's you they want."

"All the more reason for us to go now," I said to her and Valka both. I would never forgive myself if any harm befell the islanders.

"What will you do?" Imrah asked.

Valka and I held one another's gaze a long moment then, neither speaking. We had rehearsed our plan before, several times. I had intended to go straight to Aea and the athenaeum at Nov Belgaer after we visited Thessa and the other islands, but the discovery that Gibson was alive—against all hope and reason—had shredded what thin resolve we had. After so many years alone aboard the *Ascalon*, after that black day on Eue and all that I had suffered on Dharan-Tun, I had not been able to bring myself to return to the Imperium proper, to place myself in their power, at their mercy.

I had not wanted to leave Gibson.

Still, I had always known I must.

Not taking my eyes from Valka, I answered Imrah, saying, "We'll leave directly for the city. They probably won't expect that. I mean to land at Nov Belgaer and speak to the scholiasts . . ."

My voice trailed off as I remembered Gibson's muttering in his fevered dreams. He had spoken of his son—his *true* son—and thought me him. He had cried out in turn for *Alois* and *Livy*, and had thought he was on Belusha, the most feared of the Emperor's prison planets.

"Is Arrian still the primate at the athenaeum?" I asked.

"Arrian?" Imrah asked, dark brows knitting. It was not impossible. Tor Arrian had been young enough when last I'd come to Colchis, and he was of the Aventine House, of the Blood Imperial. The centuries would have weathered him, but they need not have cut him down. "The name sounds familiar? The Emperor's cousin or some such? We don't have much dealing with city folk, but I think that's right."

"Good."

By announcing myself to one of the Emperor's own family, I would make matters that much harder for the Chantry and those other forces within the Imperium that would leap at the opportunity to make me disappear.

The governor-general in Aea had a telegraph containing a particle directly entangled with one aboard the Emperor's vessel. I would be able to transmit a message directly to Caesar via the line he had given me when I first sailed to Colchis, without having to speak through the Council or any of the various ministries. I had had such a particle aboard the *Tamerlane*, but the *Ascalon* had none.

"My arrest must be as public as possible," I continued.

"Arrest?" Imrah asked, confused. Doubtless she thought we were all on the same side, that it was all so simple.

"My detainment, let's say," I replied.

Valka and I were supposed to be dead, lost fighting the Cielcin. If Dorayaica had been true to its word—and I had no reason to doubt its *truth*—Lorian Aristedes would have arrived on Forum bearing the news of Cielcin unification, of the new, Pale empire raised against our red one.

Chess pieces moved in my mind.

Our survival would be a shock.

"Shouldn't we go directly to the governor-general's palace?" Valka asked. Nov Belgaer had not been a part of the plan we'd discussed so intermittently for so long.

I was already shaking my head. "I need to see Arrian. I have questions."

Valka took a step nearer me. "About Gibson?"

I made to smooth back my matted hair, but the sight of the dirt on my hands stopped me. My fingers were crusted with dried blood where the knuckles had cracked during the previous day's exertions, and thin scratches covered my forearms, red against the paler scars. My whole body ached. "He didn't tell me who he was."

"Does it matter?" Valka asked, eyebrows coming together. "You know who he was to you."

I threw up my hands as if to encompass the whole island. "How did he pay for this? That hospital pod must have cost ten million marks at least! And to ship it here without attracting notice! Don't you wonder?" In fact, I wonder now if she did not already know. Many were the nights when I had retired early, and it was she who had stayed awake with the old man, talking into Colchis's overlong nights. That thought did not occur to me then and there.

"Imrah!" a rough, masculine voice called from the water's edge. "The doctor wants to know when we're putting out!" It was the voice of Imrah's brother, Alvar, who stood with hands cupped about his mouth on the stone pier the Rachan villagers had built out from the shoreline.

Siran's great-great-grandchildren . . .

"What?"

Something of the new light of day haloed the two of them, Imrah and Alvar, and I smiled in the brief instant between his shout and her reply. Some good had come from the Red Company, from my actions, however small. Siran was dead, but had died happy, had left this family behind. Lorian yet lived, and Switch—I did not doubt that he had died so very long ago. Had he died happy, despite my actions? My smile faltered to realize that in sending him away, I had spared him death at Akterumu. Might I have spared all the others, if I had driven them each away as well?

"I said the doctor wants to know when we're heading back! She wants to get home!"

"Tell her it won't be long!" Imrah shot back. "Valka says she packed near everything in the night. Lord Marlowe's come down off the mountain."

Alvar paused on the pier a moment, noticed me standing with the two women for the first time. "You all right, lord?"

I raised a hand in silent acknowledgment.

"What's left to pack?" I asked Valka.

"Just your things," she said. "I got most of it together, waiting for you. I left out what I thought you'd need. You really should clean up, you know. 'Twill not take long."

She was probably right. I only nodded weakly in reply, brushed past her and Imrah and into the pod Valka and I had shared with Gibson. Valka had said it was the same pod we'd stayed in when the Red Company came to Thessa the first time, but I could not remember. Unlike the majority of the pods—which were bunk houses that slept fifty each—ours had been intended for use by the high officers, and contained only four bedrooms clustered about a common room that opened on the veranda the locals had built up around the old prefabricated unit. It had been our home for the too-short years we'd spent on Colchis, and standing on its threshold I felt certain I would never see it again.

I had needed to come to Colchis. For Siran, for Gibson, to feel right again and whole. Siran's grave had—in my mind—become a grave for all the Red Company. Now that I had built the graves upon the whole of the island's crown, and buried Gibson, too, I found I had no reason to remain. I was not even sure I could bear to climb back up the cliffs to the funeral grounds.

It was time to go.

Despite what she had said, Valka had packed most of my things. Two black trunks stood stacked, closed at the foot of the rumpled bed we'd shared, a bag half-open atop them. Stripped of the detritus of our lives, the room felt barren, lifeless, and larger than ever it had before. Fresh clothes lay out for me on the gray bedsheets. Not the knee-breeches and linen tunics I'd worn in the style of the local fisherfolk, but the old Marlowe blacks. Feeling the pressure of time, I skinned out of my soiled clothes— leaving them in a trail behind me—and staggered into the bath. My scarred reflection greeted me, black hair shot with silver at temples and forelock. Scraped and sweating from the long night and the labor of building Gibson's cairn, I still looked better than I had done in as long as I could remember. Gone was the skeleton man that had crawled out of the *Ascalon* and capered in the sun and salt spray. In his place, a man stood neither old nor young, eyes deep and distant as the sea. New muscle had returned to wasted limbs, but his scars were numberless, and his motions clumsy and never without pain. The marks of alien talons slashed his left cheek, and yet it seemed in the dawn light that he bore them nobly.

It was a new day on Colchis, and for Hadrian Ma
any he had seen.

The ugliness of the world does not fade, nor are fear a.
by time, nor is any suffering forgotten.

We are only made stronger by its blows.

All in black again and clean, I left the pod, Valka's leather bag slung over
my shoulder. She had not come to check on me, but I had not wasted time.
If the local prefects came to Thessa in the hopes of finding us, they would
find us lately gone: clothes discarded on the floor, the beds unmade, the
climate control still powering down.

Valka rose quickly from the carved wood bench to the right of the doors
beneath the pill-shaped window. "All ready?" she asked.

"Where's Imrah?" I asked in return.

Her tattooed hand checking the drape of her braid, Valka answered,
"Gone to the ship."

"We need Ginoh and Alvar to get the trunks," I said, indicating the bag
on my shoulder. "I've got everything together."

She offered me her hand, and I took it, and led the way along the stony
path down to the water and the stone pier that stretched out into it. The
tide—made extreme by the proximity of the planet, Atlas—was at its highest ebb, and the waves splashed up and over the sides. We broke apart as
we reached the end of the pier, and I called out to Alvar, who stood at the
gunwale, asking him and his cousin to hurry and grab the trunks we'd left
in the pod building.

Imrah emerged from beneath the covered area that served the little
trawler for a bridge. With the sun rising, she'd found a broad, conical straw
hat that tied below the chin, and hugged her painted linen coat to ward off
the spray. An older, gray-haired woman in a blue tunic and trousers followed after. The doctor that had been too late to help Gibson.

"Are we ready to go?" the old woman asked.

I gave her a withering glare. A man was dead. The very best man I had
ever known. And this woman was in a hurry. I turned instead toward the
front of the ship and—without a word—climbed up onto the forecastle.

A shadow drew up beside me.

"Your work is done, I think," I said, looking down at the Keeper of
Thessa.

..rah adjusted the set of her hat with a finger, but did not take her eyes
..rom the island. "Oh no," she said. "The dead still need their Keeper. Some
of the village families have been burying their dead on the north side of
the island now, too. The rich ones. Once word gets out the Halfmortal was
here and raised monuments to his fallen companions, everyone in the islands will want to be buried here." She did turn then, and smiled. She
looked so like Siran, with the same almond eyes and strong jaw. "There
are so many here who talk with pride about their ancestors from Marlowe's
company, all over the islands. They'll want to get as close as they can to
the legend."

I sniffed, bowed my head. "The legend." It was hard to minimize the
derision in my voice.

Imrah seemed not to notice. "There will always be a Keeper here.
Now." She leaned against the railing. "I never thought I'd be the one. To
know you, I mean."

"I owe you and your family more than you can know," I said thickly.
"For watching Gibson. All these years . . . for everything. What?"

The woman was shaking her head, shrugged her linen coat about her
slim shoulders. "You owe us nothing, lord. None of us would *be* without
you. You let Siran stay. Commanded it."

"Is that what she told you?" I almost laughed.

"Live well, and light a candle for me." Imrah's words carried the weight of
religious recitation. I did not recognize them, not at first. Did not *remember*
them.

We'll need it.

We had needed it, in the end.

"I only told her to *live*," I said at last. They were the words of my last
command to Siran of Emesh, spat at her in the tunnel beside the blast pit
in the cothon at Aea's starport. "I almost cursed her, did she tell you that?"

I could not make out the feelings in Imrah's face, so studious was her
control. Presently she shook her head. "I never knew her."

"But you thought it was a blessing? A gift I'd given her?" I asked, looking up to see Alvar and Ginoh returning with the first of the two trunks
between them. Off to our right, a gull pierced the surface of the waters to
catch some hapless fish. "She didn't tell your grandmothers that she was an
oathbreaker? That she all but dared me to kill her for her desertion?"

Was that horror in the young woman's eyes? Surprise? Misunder-
standing?

I let a breath hiss out between my teeth. "I had a friend once. He be-

trayed me, and I . . . sent him away. Siran knew if she betrayed me in turn—
wanting to leave—I'd not stop her. I'd not have stopped any of them." I
turned fully away from her, stared up the rocks toward Gibson's tomb. I
could almost see it from the water. "Now I wish I'd let them all go with
her. They'd have lived, too."

I could feel Valka's eyes burning their hole in the back of my head. We
had been down this road before, a thousand times. "No one lives forever,
lord," Imrah said after a pause. Ginoh and Alvar had reached the boat,
and—dropping the trunk on the deck—had turned already to fetch the
final one. "If they had stayed, their graves would be here on Thessa just the
same, only you'd not have been the one to build them." A warm hand
touched my arm. "The gods bend evil to good ends. If Siran betrayed you,
as you say, it was so we would be here when you returned. And your father.
So too I believe the evils you have seen must serve some good in time."

I had nothing to say to that. Had I not said much the same thing before,
in my turn?

"Do you know, Imrah, that you live on a truly beautiful world?" I
asked, turning to take in the whole of that island of the dead before looking back at her.

She was smiling then, and Valka smiled behind her. "I do," the Keeper
replied.

"I have always struggled," I said, "to stand still long enough to see it.
All my life. All my life I've spent chasing my *dream*. That was what Siran
betrayed, what Switch—my other friend—betrayed. I could not bear that
they had dreams all their own." I put a hand on the Keeper's shoulder. "I
do owe you, Imrah. Your whole family. And Siran. For reminding me to
be . . . human."

So often we don't see the truth because we won't look low enough.

Gibson's words resounded across the waters, as if falling from his tomb.
"The highest place . . . the bottom of the world." I looked up at the mountain, at the man buried beneath the earth there. One could hardly look
lower than the grave.

"What?"

Seek hardship.

"Nothing," I said, and smiled.

Alvar and Ginoh returned not long after, and in moments the ropes
were cast down and the ship put out on the fading tide. The two men
called to one another, and steered their boat back into the waters for Racha,
the *Ascalon*, and the universe beyond.

As we sailed away I moved to the rear deck to watch the island fade. It never did.

The rising sun ahead cast white light down upon the silver sea, and caught upon the whited stone that crowned the isle of the dead. The numberless graves shone like fingers of pale fire, gleaming in the sun. Monuments not to death were they, but to glory.

My friends were dead, and Gibson was dead. Their souls were gone into the Howling Dark, never to return as I had.

As I had . . .

I was not dead, nor sailing to my death—I knew—but back to life and the worlds of men, and not alone.

Valka took my hand.

CHAPTER 2

THE ATHENAEUM AGAIN

"TELL ME WHO HE was," I said again, sitting on the edge of my seat. Across the ocean of polished wood and vellum and brass writing instruments between us, the aged primate Arrian narrowed his eyes. He had been a prince once, a cousin of the Blood Imperial via a cadet line. That was no secret. The primates of the Great Library were almost always close to the Imperial blood. Tor Aramini, who had designed Nov Belgaer Athenaeum and the secret archives that housed the Mericanii daimon, Horizon, had been the brother of Emperor Gabriel II. But the former lives of most scholiasts were abandoned when they chose their new names, consecrating their lives to research, to study, and to service.

It had not been so for Arrian. His role as primate of the Imperial archives had been a political appointment, and why not? Most scholiasts were palatine, the lesser sons and daughters of the old families. Each one had been *someone*, carried allegiances and pains. The Emperor would want the chief of his greatest library to be a man bound to him by blood as well as duty, to keep him close.

Only the past is written, Gibson had said to me. On no world was that truer than on Colchis, where the past was indexed and alphabetized. If an answer existed to my question, it was here.

"Do not presume to order me, Lord Marlowe," the primate said. "You are not here under Imperial authority this time." How old the primate had become. The centuries wore heavily on him, and his once-red hair had turned the yellow of aged ivory. His once-smooth face was furrowed where time had worn away his features as water scratches at limestone. And the eyes . . . those chips of Imperial emerald—once nearly so sharp and bright as those of the Emperor himself—were dim as smoked glass and concealed behind a constellation of interchangeable lenses by whose art alone Arrian might yet see at all. Still, the Imperial iron had hardened in his bones, and he did not bend before me.

"Do not threaten me, primate," I said coolly.

"I do not threaten," Tor Arrian replied, "I simply remind you that I allowed you through the gate as a courtesy, lordship, and that courtesy may be revoked." He moved a stack of papers obscurely across the desk in front of him. A fire crackled in the hearth—the only heat in that chilly stone room, and the air smelled of peat. "Your previous visit was a service to us, and we are grateful. It is this gratitude that opened the gates."

It was my turn to narrow my eyes. "Do not lie to me, primate." I had stood outside the gatehouse in the light rain for the better part of an hour, had shouted and pounded on the doors. Only my mention of Gibson's death had opened the gates, and three brothers in green robes had hurried me directly to Arrian. "My previous visit is immaterial. You opened the gates out of simple curiosity."

"We all thought old Gibson dead for centuries," the primate admitted. "The islanders delivered his ashes." Arrian splayed gnarled hands on the tabletop before him. "And we all thought that *you* were dead."

That caught me by surprise. Nearly half a century had passed since I arrived on Padmurak, it was true, but I had not expected word of my disappearance to have penetrated the confines of the athenaeum, or to have spread across the Empire. I thought the death of Hadrian the Halfmortal to be the sort of thing the Imperial propaganda corps would prefer be kept secret. Rumor—it seemed—was faster than light.

Thinking along this line, I asked, "Does everyone believe this?"

"News of your death has not entered the public record, but there are whispers." The primate's eyes grew narrower still behind their cluster of lenses. "William wrote me personally to confirm them."

William. Strange to hear the Emperor referred to with such familiarity.

Arrian sat back, flicked a set of lenses down into place over his eyes to better see me at his newfound distance. The apparatus had the effect of magnifying his eyes to monstrous size, making him seem some species of owl. "Where have you been?"

"Tell me who he was, Arrian," I countered, "and I will answer your questions."

"You'll answer to His Radiance soon enough."

"To His Radiance, yes," I agreed. "Not to you."

That brought the conversation grinding to a halt. Tor Arrian removed his lenses, turned a delicate brass knob on one side before replacing the device on his face. He hid his agitation well, but I—who had a lifetime of interpreting the alien minutiae of Cielcin expressions—was uniquely attuned to read the elderly primate's angst for what it was.

"Before he died, Tor Gibson had a stroke. It left him very confused about where he was. He thought he was on Belusha." The name of the prison planet made Arrian blink. "For a scholiast, primate, you emote rather a great deal."

Those huge, cloudy eyes blinked again, and Arrian said, "There are so many of us, I do not know everyone's names or histories."

"Nonsense," I said without hesitation. "You are primate of the Imperial Library. He was one of your archivists." Scholiasts were expected to command enormous swaths of information. They were masters of mnemonic. Asking me to believe he simply did not know was ridiculous. Placing one hand on the edge of the desk before me, I bowed my head. "I know what I am asking is not in keeping with tradition. I also know it is not a violation of Stricture. Please, Arrian. Tor Gibson was . . . a father to me. I would like to know his name. That is all."

Tor Arrian shuffled his papers again and stood, groaning. Old as he was, he moved smoothly enough, slippered feet shuffling on the Tavrosi carpet that lay upon the smooth stone of the floor. A bust of Zeno looked down from a niche behind his desk. In silence, he approached the tall, arched window that overlooked one of the athenaeum's interlocking quadrangles. "Do you know what our Order is, Lord Marlowe?" he asked, clasping gnarled hands behind his back. I said nothing, sensing it was better to let the old man have his floor. "It's a gutter," Tor Arrian bowed his head, "into which the refuse of the great houses is finally drained."

I sat there stunned to silence. Whatever I expected the primate to say, it was not this.

"For every one of us evoked by the lords of the Imperium, called to a life of service, there are ten unfit to serve. These halls are filled with the inconvenient sons and daughters of the Empire. Those unfit to rule, to serve in the Legions, the priesthood—those their parents cannot even give away in marriage."

I turned fully in my seat. "How can that be?" I asked. To be a scholiast required enormous discipline, decades of study and practice, the command of many libraries' worth of information.

"Ask any of the brothers in the kitchens for counsel, and they will give you blank stares," Arrian said. "Ask them to perform an analysis of Imperial spending in the last millennium, or to calculate the amounts of fuel that must be manufactured in a given sector for a given period. They will give you nothing." The primate's reflection stared at me out of the window glass. "Most of us are here not because we choose to be, or because we are capable, but because we are embarrassments."

Still I was stunned. I could not believe my ears. I had wanted to be a scholiast with such fervency, such longing, that to imagine it a kind of punishment was alien to me as the slime-choked pits of Eue.

"I was myself forced into the Order," the master scholiast said. "There are so many of us lesser offshoots of the Imperial blood . . . all of us forbidden to bear children since the days of the Great Charters." Again Arrian fell silent, and removed the elaborate spectacles from his face. "You must understand, all manner of men come to us. Exiles. Refugees. Criminals. We even train peasants in the arts of thinkery, and they return to their villages as instructors and counselors—though a mere plebeian cannot hope to become a true scholiast. They haven't the time." Without the strange constellation of lenses to obscure his features, Arrian looked almost like the red-haired clone of the Emperor I recalled from my first visit—almost the young man he had been—if in a thin and fading way. "Tor Gibson's story is not unusual."

"Tell me," I said, growing irritated with the old man's delay and unable to quench the sudden knot of anxiety that had begun to tighten serpent-like about my innards.

Arrian turned, putting his back to the window. "Are you familiar with the Septembrine Revolt?"

I shook my head, prompting the scholiast to sigh. "We have so much history now, even controlling for the Cielcin. We have too many worlds. Soon even we will not be able to account for all of it. You know I sometimes think the Empire must crack under its weight?" I did not tell him that it was cracking already, did not remind him that the Norman Expanse was lost. "This was before the Cielcin invasion. Early sixteenth millennium, during the reign of our Radiant Emperor's grandfather. Prince Charles Bourbon—the Fifty-Third, that is—passed over his eldest son, Philippe, in favor of the younger one, who would go on to become Charles LIV, Prince of Verehaut."

"House Bourbon?" I said, and remembered the story. Prince Philippe Bourbon had been Lord Augustin's father.

"Prince Philippe attempted to murder his brother. When that failed, he gathered together a coalition of lesser houses loyal to the Bourbons. The poine fighting lasted the better part of two decades before Philippe's son,

the late Lord Augustin of the Imperial Council, betrayed his father to
Prince Charles's men in exchange for his life and freedom." One of the
lenses in Arrian's mad spectacles clicked upward out of the way, responding
to some condition of the light perhaps. "I'm not surprised you're not too
familiar with the story. It was several centuries before you were born, and
Verehaut is quite far from Delos, but the Septembrine Revolt was one of
the more foul examples of poine in recent centuries."

A leaden weight was forming in the pit of my stomach, and I fixed my
eyes on the window above the primate's head. "I knew a little of it," I said,
a shade defensive. "If not the name."

"Charles Bourbon would not execute his brother. Prince Philippe and
his Septembrines were exiled to Belusha. I understand that most of them
died there."

"And Gibson was one of them," I said, in a desperate attempt to divert
what I knew must be coming. "One of the Septembrines." I wished at once
that I had not come to the athenaeum.

I knew what Tor Arrian was about to say.

"Oh no," the elder scholiast said, eyes hugely magnified so that twin
moons shone down on me, green as his robes. "He was the prince himself.
He served most of his time on Belusha in cryonic fugue—a benefit of his
rank—and appealed his way into athenaeum on Syracuse. The Imperial
Council commuted his sentence, in part at Prince Charles's urging, and he
was permitted to embrace Stricture and join the Order."

I closed my mouth, had hardly heard any words after that first sentence.
He was the prince himself.

I had always suspected that Gibson was from some exalted line. His
great age alone testified to his belonging in one of the great houses of the
Imperium. As a boy, I used to imagine that he was—like Arrian himself—
a cousin to the Emperor through some lesser line. Believing that Gibson
was some lord greater than my father, some higher authority, had been a
comfort when Lord Alistair would lash out in his cold rages, or force me
to sleep in a bare cell.

But this?

Had Valka known? Had Gibson told her?

"Gibson was . . . ." I could hardly get the name out, "Philippe Bourbon?" I tucked my hands into my coat pockets to hide their shaking,
though perhaps the nearly blind old primate would not have seen.

"As I say," Arrian said, "exiles, refugees, and criminals. Why do you
think we strip away our old names? As Tor Gibson, Prince Philippe was

permitted to live out his days anonymously, and in a role where he could do no more harm to the Imperium, and where it could do no harm to him."

"No harm to the Imperium?" I almost laughed. Almost. "He taught me." And I had killed his son.

The thought ran through me like the wind rushing out an open air-lock, and I sat half-frozen in my chair. Only the cheery crackling of the fire could be heard, strange counterpoint to the unheard roaring in my mind. Augustin Bourbon had tried to kill me. Him, and Sir Lorcan Breathnach, and the Empress herself. They had armed the assassin, Irshan, and bought Lieutenant Casdon's loyalty, helped her to smuggle a knife-missile into my cabin aboard the *Tamerlane*. They had nearly succeeded, and nearly killed Valka as well. I should not feel horror, or pity.

But I had killed Gibson's son.

I should never have come here.

Never mind all else he had been, never mind that Augustin Bourbon had himself betrayed Gibson in his former life. I still had killed him, had ordered his death. And I had told Gibson *everything*. Told him how I had summoned Crim to my bedside whilst I lay recovering from my wounds, how I had ordered him to find a means of killing the Lord Minister of War. He had said nothing of the relationship between them, revealed nothing.

I am sorry, my boy, he'd said instead—when it was I who should have apologized, should have begged for forgiveness—and would have, had I but known. *I wanted to give you a better life,* Tor Gibson had told me. This *life.* Gibson had wanted me to become a scholiast—*I* had wanted to become a scholiast. In the Order's embrace, Gibson had found a new kind of free-dom, and wanted it for me.

I had become something else instead, and time moves in but one direc-tion only.

Only the past is written.

I was still moving in a kind of haze when I left the athenaeum by the main gate and began the long descent down the bluff toward the lot where vis-itors were obliged to park their vehicles before beginning the climb. I re-member that the sun shone very bright and beautifully that day—just as it had on Thessa—more white than gray. The morning's rains had passed away, and the thin layer of cloud that so often shrouded the misty library fortress and the moors below was banished utterly by the noon. The pale towers of the city of Aea shone away to the south, white and gray amid all that greenery. The *Ascalon* waited below, its single rear fin rising like a tower itself from the hills below, black against the verdant highlands.

It wasn't alone.

Three white fliers orbited like vultures in the sky above, and another six formed a cordon on the ground about our vessel. I had expected to find them there, and so paused only a moment, and clutched the packet the primate had given me. I had done as I'd promised: explained what had happened to old Arrian, told him that the Commonwealth had knelt to the Cielcin; that the Cielcin were now unified, an empire in all but name; and that I had escaped only through the sacrifice of my entire company.

He did not try to stop me leaving. Arrian knew so well as I that our loud arrival at the base of the mesa had alerted Imperial authorities. We had both known my road ran straight into the arms of the Empire, that nothing I could do could stop that now. As I'd risen to leave, Arrian had handed me a leather envelope, its surface cracked with age. It bore no device, no emblem, no mark of any kind save two words inscribed in flaked vermilion ink. Ancient as the letters were, Gibson's hand was unmistakable.

For Hadrian.

"We found it in his cell when we emptied it," Arrian explained. "After the islanders wrote to tell us he was dead."

"And you never investigated," I said, accusingly.

"There was no cause for it," Arrian said. "We had no reason to suspect the villagers of duplicity." For what seemed the hundredth time, Arrian had removed his convoluted spectacles and polished them with a silk cloth that he kept neatly folded on his desk. "We retained the letter against the possibility of your revisiting us."

I eyed the old primate with suspicion. "Did you open it?"

Arrian replaced his glasses on his aquiline nose. "You would be surprised how many such artifacts we retain from the brothers and sisters. We have an entire collection of unopened letters."

"You don't send them?"

"Unless a scholiast is evoked by the outside, his work—like his person—is forbidden to leave the athenaeum," Arrian answered. "It is well you came."

I had intended to open the packet on the *Ascalon*, but seeing the fliers waiting, I knew I would not have a chance. Not for hours. Maybe days.

Standing alone on the ancient, sandal-worn steps leading down from Nov Belgaer, I broke the primitive wax seal and glanced briefly at the contents. A letter and a small packet waited within, each wrapped in machined vellum of the kind designed to outsit eternity.

Nervous, I fished the letter out, tucking the packet under my arm to read more easily. *For Hadrian,* it said, handwriting matching that on the leather envelope. Sinking onto the steep stair, I broke the second green wax seal. Gibson's familiar spidery hand shone up at me in the customary scholiasts' vermilion.

Dear Hadrian,

I have no way of knowing when you will read this, but there is no better place in the galaxy to leave a letter in safety than in an athenaeum, and while I have little expectation that you will return here whilst I am yet among the living, I suspect you will return one day. As I am not permitted to send you a message, I must be content to write one and hope that you come calling in future.

It is ISD 16607, the 27th of October. Tomorrow, I leave Nov Belgaer and take ship for the southern isles. Your friend, Siran, has written the college hoping that one of our order might serve to chronicle the history of the islands, and I have taken the quest on myself. I understand she has quite the family now. You might come and meet them . . .

I put the letter down and smiled at the heavens, heedless of the white shapes of the Imperial fliers that awaited me on the moor below. It was a map of sorts, one that ran straight to Thessa and the white dome of a hospital module. "Clever bastard." Gibson went on, detailing his plans to travel to Racha by way of Aea and Egris. He spoke a little more about Siran and her family, how she would visit the athenaeum each year at the new year, when the college opened its gates to the public for two weeks. It was comforting to think of them growing close in my absence. I wondered how it had begun. Siran had met Gibson briefly during our first visit to the Great Library. She must have returned to the college after I left her with Lem the eolderman. Nostalgia for her heroic past? Or simple curiosity.

I read on:

I wish I understood what was happening to you, but you've grown beyond an old man's limited knowledge. I do not envy your road. I think of you often, and meant what I said: you are your father's son. What I have not said, what I should have said, is that you were ever a son to me. The son I always wanted.

Yours,

Tor Gibson

I was weeping silently by then. The Greeks spoke of *catharsis,* of the purging of emotion by tragedy. I have always imagined it a kind of breaking, of shattering—not into a thousand shards—but *back* into one.

I shattered then, knowing what I knew. There was no admission in his letter, neither that he was planning to freeze himself on Thessa with Siran's help, nor that he was the father of the lord minister I had destroyed. No recrimination, no revelation either.

But the old man—Tor Gibson, Prince Philippe—was not quite done. There was a postscript.

Please find enclosed a replacement for the gift you so carelessly lost leaving home all those years ago. Be careful. I do not think I will be able to replace it a second time. You may yet find a use for it.

Fingers at once numb, I removed the small parcel from the leather packet and broke the seal. I recognized the brown book at once. The edition was identical, down to the embossed motif of the single, weeping eye on its cover beneath the title.

The King with Ten Thousand Eyes.

I opened that romantic novelization of the legend of Kharn Sagara—trying not to think about my brush with the reality behind that legend—and there it was, tucked inside the front cover just like the first.

A letter of introduction.

The words *To the Primate* shone red on the front of the envelope. The green wax seal on the reverse bore no mark, for the scholiast who wrote it had no rank, no title, no name save that which he took on when he embraced Stricture and the Order.

I did not open it.

I did not have to.

CHAPTER 3

THE WAKING WORLD

GIBSON'S PACKAGE UNDER MY arm, I crossed the road from Aea that passed the Library on its mesa and ran north to the gentle slopes that led into the moorland. So much of the moors of the northern continent were unsettled and unplanted, a lush, green desert of moss and wort, with here and there a lonely tree born from seeds dropped by the chance action of a bird. Thousands of years of human cultivation, and Colchis was still in the first blushing of its flower. Like so many planets across the cosmos, it would take aeons to fully develop the ecosystem until it was an image of Earth's. There was an emptiness about those highlands that recalled the damp wastes of Eue, and I shivered and turned my collar up against the wind.

I had loved Colchis when first I came to it, and loved parts of it still. But one cannot step into the same river twice, nor onto the same world. All things are always in motion. That is why it is the highest good and cause of civilization to preserve—to conserve—what is good. It is for that reason we plant new seeds, that if we might not preserve the trees, we might preserve the forest. If Earth is truly lost—as I believe—and not returning, then it is good that we plant her children across the stars.

Such empty places as that moor ever bring my mind to such thoughts. To the responsibility we men have as gardeners and stewards of creation. And perhaps the addition of a few new trees would lessen that place's resemblance to the blasted sands and slime pits of the cold, damp hell that had swallowed my men whole.

But there were no trees.

There was only the arrowhead shape of the *Ascalon* ahead of me, with its slim tail fin rising from the rolling hills. It would have looked lonely were it not for the low-slung forms of the Legion shuttles parked not two hundred feet from the landing ramp and the Sparrowhawks circling above, white and red. As I drew nearer, I could count the legionnaires standing guard or moving between the shuttles and the ship. There were at least thirty.

"You there!" proclaimed a soldier with the faceless red mask and gold medallions of a centurion. "Identify yourself!"

Several of the guards trained stunners in my direction, and a few gripped their lances tighter.

"I'm not armed!" I said, dropping Gibson's parcel on the mossy ground to raise my empty hands.

The centurion pushed his way past the forward ranks of his men. "Identify yourself!"

"You know full well who I am!" I said. "Where's Valka?"

"I'm here!" Valka emerged from the ramp, followed by two bare-headed soldiers.

The centurion raised his own stunner. "I said identify yourself!"

"What a welcome this is!" I snarled, hands still in the air. "I'm Lord Hadrian Anaxander Marlowe, Royal Victorian Order, formerly of Delos. Lower your damn gun, centurion, and quit acting the fool!" My own rage surprised me. I had not expected to meet the guards with anything other than resignation, but a sudden fear for Valka's safety had flowered in me. I had been too long away, and what trust or safety I'd felt in Imperial hands had long faded away.

I could feel the discomposure of the men around me like a tremor in my boots. They shifted uneasily where they stood; one or two dropped their guard, faceless heads cocked with disbelief.

"Is it really him?" one man asked.

"Lower your weapons," the centurion said, letting his own stunner fall. He advanced, flat red mask betraying no hint of emotion. When he'd come within five paces, he said, "I didn't believe it when we got the call. Growing up, they always said you died."

I had to remind myself that the officer was likely so young that he had not even been born when we first landed on Padmurak. He'd lived his whole life in the time since I'd leaped upon that chariot in Vedatharad, probably in the time since I awoke in the darkness to find Severine and Syriani staring down at me.

When I said nothing, the centurion knelt. "My lord, I've been ordered to bring you and the lady to Governor-General Dorr."

"She's not a lady," I said, catching Valka's eye and finding a rare smile.

"She's a doctor." Stooping, I collected Gibson's envelope with the letters and the book. "Are we under arrest, centurion?"

The man did not reply at once. A sufficient answer. "You are to be guests of the governor-general, lord."

"I see," I said. "Permit me then to gather my effects. I would prefer not to go before your master as I am."

"Of course, my lord."

I need not have feared. The guards treated us with every courtesy after the tension of our initial encounter, though they took Valka's sidearm. I had no weapon to surrender—having thrown Olorin's sword into the sea at Thessa—and was surprised when the guards made no moves to bind our wrists. That was a good sign. We'd had no way of knowing *which* Empire it was we'd given ourselves over to. I had hoped to find the governor-general favorable to me and not aligned with the Empress and her Old Lions—or the Chantry—and for the time being at least it seemed that hope bore out.

A small team of the soldiery remained behind to fly the *Ascalon* to the cothon at Aea's starport, but Valka and I were placed directly onto one of the smaller fliers. The soldiers spoke no word to us save those that were necessary, ushering us from the flier when we landed and out into a high-walled court whose pale stone walls I recognized as a part of the governor's mansion.

Soldiers clad in Imperial white and crimson patrolled the walls and stood at posts along halls and colonnades, and we were shown inside without delay. Once or twice logothetes in the drab grays of the civil service froze in their tracks to watch us pass, and a black-skirted maid stood wide-eyed and dropped her silver platter.

"They thought us dead," Valka hissed in Tavrosi Nordei.

I shook my head. Whether or not they thought us dead was not the issue. We were storybook characters to them, myths and legends. We might have been Jason and Medea returning from the sea, or Sir Tristan and Iseult, or Cyrus and Amana. Had Thor or the Cid Arthur himself appeared before them, they could not have looked more surprised. One old man in the black uniform of an officer saluted to see me.

I did not return the gesture. I did not want him to see my ruined hand.

The governor-general's office was where I remembered it, at the far end of the administrative wing on the fourth floor, overlooking the walls and the corner of Front and Sun Streets with a clear view of the Chantry building with its green copper dome and minarets topped with icons of the virtues. A statue of Open-Handed Mercy shone white upon the nearest, wings spread out like those of an angel. The granite floors and inlaid cabinetry were all the same, and the great desk—a monolith of hand-carved ebony—was exactly as I remembered it.

But the man who sat behind it was changed.

On our first visit to Colchis, the governor-general had been a tall, icy woman with white-gold hair and pale eyes. I do not remember her name. But she was gone—dead, I felt sure, another casualty of Ever-Fleeting Time. In her place sat a broad-shouldered, yellow-bearded man dressed in the white suit and red sash of his rank, rings on his fingers like a petty impersonation of the Emperor himself.

He stood swiftly as Valka and I appeared, evidently as stunned as his staff and soldiery. "Earth and God bloody Emperor," he said, and made the sign of the sun disc with his hand—as though this small piety might erase his larger blasphemy. "It really is you. I thought my men had made a mistake. Hadrian Marlowe . . ." He shook his head. "I never thought I'd see the day . . ." He came round his desk and thrust a hand toward me. "I'm Velan Dorr, Governor-General of Colchis." There would be no hiding my hand this time. I reached out and grasped the governor-general's offered hand, smiled, but said nothing. If he marked my missing fingers and the scars on my face and arms, he did not betray himself. "How do you come to be here, my lord? Of all places? The rumors . . . they say you died!" He drew back, looked round to Valka and to his men, as if expecting an answer might come from anywhere.

"I must ask for the use of your telegraph. What I have to say must be said to the Emperor himself."

"Where have you been?" Dorr asked, his initial shock fading. "Our last record is from your stopover here on route to the Commonwealth. I've just been looking. That was almost a century ago."

"I *must* speak to the Emperor, Governor-General," I said more stridently. Dorr and his men seemed well enough disposed toward me. There was a chance I might simply bully my way through this episode to some security. Now that I was in Imperial hands, I found I did not want to talk about Padmurak and Dharan-Tun. I certainly did not wish to unburden myself to this man, not when I knew I must do so again for Legion Intelligence and the Council and the Imperial Office itself.

"Not until I know what's going on!" said Velan Dorr. "Please." He gestured to a sitting area to the right, red velvet chairs circled beneath high windows and a view of Sun Street. The stuffed head of an Athyrasene xanarth hung mounted to a plaque between those windows, its huge, square jaws open to expose block teeth, each as large as a man's fist. Dorr had taken three steps by the time he realized I was not following, and turned back.

I was trapped, I knew. To refuse at this juncture would be to declare myself hostile, to force Dorr to escalate our conversation to interrogation. I took a deep breath instead, then, looking round at the guards, at the servants standing—heretofore unseen—in a corner by a pocket door.

"Send your people away," I said, still commanding. When Velan Dorr made no sign, I said, "The things I have to say cannot get out, my lord."

Dorr seemed to mull this over, arms crossed. Presently he made a gesture, two fingers toward the double doors. "Leave us. All of you." He turned his back, moved to the circle of fine armchairs. He touched his right ear as he went, said, "Ada, send in Numa, thank you." He waited at a sideboard while the guards and servants filtered out, then made the same, two-fingered gesture to indicate his chairs. "Sit. Please."

Ever the more prudent one, Valka made our choice for me, and slid into the nearest of the fine chairs.

Dorr took a seat directly beneath the head of the great xanarth, directing his words to Valka as he did so. "You're Doctor Onderra, are you not?"

Valka gave a crooked smile—never a good sign from her. "I am, yes."

"Can I offer you a drink?" the governor-general asked us both as I came to sit beside Valka. "Wine? Brandy? I've some feni I had shipped in from Athyras." He pointed up at the xanarth. "I spent some time there as a young man. Reminds me of then."

"Do you have any zvanya?" I asked, thinking of the strongest liquor I could. I felt at once that I would need it.

"Jaddian stuff? No, my lord."

"I'll take the feni, then," I said.

"Wine for me, if you're offering," Valka put in.

The great double doors opened a moment thereafter, and I turned to see a slim, bald man enter. He wore the green robes of a scholiast, and the necklace of bronze medallions that hung heavily from his shoulders showcased the degrees of his education. "You called, lord?"

"Numa!" Velan Dorr said, gesturing from the sideboard at Valka and myself as he went about producing the appropriate glassware. "Good. I wanted you for this. Lord Marlowe, Doctor Onderra, this is my counselor, Tor Numa. You may say in front of him anything you would say to me."

"I would as soon speak directly to the Emperor," I said again, a half-hearted final attempt.

"So you have said," said Dorr, proffering a glass of the clear liquor, a sphere of ice floating in it. "But I am the Emperor's servant here."

Unstoppable force. Immovable object.

So I stopped, took the offered glass. "The Red Company is lost," I said, and the words were like the tearing off of a bandage from a wound half-healed. "We were captured. At Padmurak. Betrayed." I threw back the harsh, astringent liquor in one toss, made a face. "There is a king now among the Cielcin."

I recounted then—for the first of what felt like a hundred times—all that had happened since our ship passed Colchis on the way to Padmurak. I told them how we had come to the Commonwealth and been welcomed at the Great City of Vedatharad, and how the Conclave Guard disguised as revolutionaries had attacked me on the bridge. I spoke of our escape through the city, and of my ill-fated decision to leap onto one of the chariots that had pursued us, and of how I languished in a Lothrian cell.

I did *not* speak of the vision I'd had of myself in that cell, or of any other vision, but told how the Lothrians—in league with the black sorcerers of MINOS—had handed me over to the Cielcin. And when I spoke of the alliance between the Lothrians and the Cielcin, Velan Dorr uttered an oath so foul even Valka blushed.

"They have us encircled then," Dorr said. "The Cielcin to the east in Norma, the Lothrians to the north and west." I thought he might spit then and there upon his fine carpets.

"And all the food they'll ever need," Valka put in.

That made me think of Looker and Carry, of Magda and all the *zuk* laborers across the Lothrian stars. I thought, too, of the terrified and mutilated slaves I had known in Dharan-Tun, the legions of human misery toiling beneath the skin of that wretched world. Cattle in all but name.

Words halting by then, I continued from Padmurak, and spoke of Syriani Dorayaica, of the great palace of the Dhar-Iagon, of the Iedyr Yemani, of MINOS and of how I came to realize the *Tamerlane* had been taken along with me. I spoke then of Eue, of how Dorayaica's forces had landed in triumph and been welcomed by the other princes of its kind. I spoke of the alliances Dorayaica had forged with Peledanu and Attavaisa, and about the Aetavanni.

"He killed them all?" Dorr asked when I paused to take a sip from my second glass of feni.

"It did," I answered, cradling the cold glass in my hands. Valka gripped my wrist to steady me. "Dorayaica's human allies released a neurotoxic gas that killed all the Cielcin in the temple. I thought it would kill me . . ."

I came then to the coronation feast, and I told how, on Dorayaica's orders, the slave-generals of the White Hand doled out the bodies of the lesser princes to the gathered masses of the Pale. Bastien Durand's head bounced down green marble steps, his headless body falling like a tree. And I heard once more the crash of thunder as the *Tamerlane*'s guns resounded one final time.

Elara died. And Crim died. And Ilex died. And Pallino died alone with me atop the wreck of the *Tamerlane*. I did not speak of the Quiet, or of the other Hadrian who had put his sword into my hand. I spoke little of Miudanar, reducing the black temple of the Watcher's skull to a mere building. It was more than Dorr and Tor Numa would believe. As I spoke, the crumbling halls of the *Tamerlane* collapsed once more about me, and I stumbled—delirious—back down the winding stair and along the umbilical in the shuttle bay where the sleeping *Ascalon* stirred.

Valka emerged from the airlock. My heart and my salvation! She raised a hand and slew my pursuers with a spell. Engines flared, and Corvo stayed behind to man the guns and cover our escape.

I fell silent then, imagining—not for the first time—Otavia Corvo watching us from the bridge, shielded from the flash and radiation wave as the *Ascalon* leaped to warp. How many Cielcin had we slain with our leap to transcend light? I liked to think of hundreds falling from the skin of the *Tamerlane*, struck dead by light more blue than even their inhuman eyes could see.

In the silence that followed my narration, Corvo turned from the tactical console that had been Lorian's in the pit beneath the captain's overlook and took up the rifle she must have carried with her . . . and waited.

One last warrior alone in the city of Akterumu—a captain gone down with her ship.

Black curtains seemed to fall across my mind's eye, obscuring my tale.

"And then we set course for here," Valka said, picking up the thread I'd let fall.

Through the window, Open-Handed Mercy—whom the ancients named Eleos—smiled beatifically from atop the nearest of the Chantry's minarets.

"Why here?" asked Tor Numa, the perfect scholiast. The perfect question.

I looked up at him, studied his thin, bloodless face, the viridian robes I'd so wanted to wear and the necklace of bronze medals. *How much should I tell them?* I wondered, and answered before any of my thinking might register on my face. "Because we had been here before."

"Colchis was the nearest world familiar to us," Valka said. "We could not have hoped to reach Forum or return all the way to Nessus, not without a crew or more than we had."

"You had no crew!" Governor-General Dorr exclaimed, the reality of that fact just sinking in. "How did you manage the journey? Across Commonwealth space . . . it must have taken decades."

"Twenty-eight years," Valka said.

I drained my third cup of feni and was silent.

"Just the two of you?" Velan Dorr asked. "It's a miracle you didn't go mad!"

"I spent most of it in fugue," Valka confessed, turning to me. I glanced at her and away.

Dorr's gray eyes focused on me, and he practically mouthed the next question. A single word. "Alone?"

I nodded, swirled the quite shrunken sphere of ice about the base of my tumbler. The cashew liquor was stronger than the palm wine favored by the Sevrastene islanders, but I contemplated asking for the bottle. In the new silence, I weighed the risks of sharing our fears that we should fall into the hands of the Chantry. Dorr was the Emperor's man, but there would be only so much he could do to resist the Inquisition should they demand he hand us over.

The governor-general's mouth hung open. A sudden premonition overcame me as I realized that here was yet another song the future would sing of the Sun Eater. How Hadrian Halfmortal waited utterly alone for a dozen years and more beside the crystal coffin of his lady! I have heard versions wherein I dealt with demons in the dark silence, with the very devil that adorned my father's banners. One particularly good opera—by Martezi—had me contend with a king of the Extrasolarians for the sake of Valka's very soul.

I wish it had been true. The reality—the soul-sucking solitude and grinding loneliness—lacked the romance of these stories. Lacked almost everything at all.

"There is a part of your story I don't follow," Tor Numa said into Dorr's incredulous silence, shaking me from my own reflections. But the scholiast's eyes moved to Valka. "How did you come to be in a position to intervene at this . . . Akterumu?" He had not seated himself during the entirety of my story, and circled round the far seat where Dorr sat beneath the xanarth's head between the high windows. "Marlowe said you were separated on Padmurak, that you commandeered a Lothrian vessel and stowed away on the surface of the Cielcin worldship, but I believe I speak for Velan as well when I say we would like your story."

Valka and I exchanged glances.

"It will need to go in the official report," Numa said, which I took for gentle pressure.

I knew the coming days would be filled with Valka and me both recounting our stories—separately and together—to logothetes and representatives of every office and department on Colchis. We'd already been at it for more than an hour.

Valka's eyebrows arched, and she massaged her neck with one hand. "'Tis as you say. We managed to escape the Lothrian guard when Hadrian was taken. By then the *Tamerlane* was already in Cielcin hands, I think. They wouldn't answer our comms . . ."

And she began to recount her story, which I had heard in full only once before. She had recounted it to me in brief after that black day in Akterumu, while she tended to my wounds. It was only later—after I recovered something of my wits in the first year of our voyage to Colchis—that she recounted her journey to me in full. I would hear it again a hundred times in the coming days, as we were each interrogated and questioned and asked to read our accounts into Imperial record, and so I remember it well.

You may think, Reader, that I ought to have told her story sooner, included it—perhaps—while she slept on the long road to Colchis. But I could not do it. I felt at the time that doing so would prove needless, that I had said enough. I was not with her, and I felt it was not my place to tell her story. And besides, the thought of her alone but for her three companions for so great a length of time still tears at my heart.

Even after all these centuries, it pains me to think of her thus.

But now I see I cannot pass her story by, for it deserves telling. Valka and Pallino, Corvo and Crim alone against the Cielcin. Alone for eleven years while I languished in chains in the pits of Dharan-Tun.

I shall attempt to recount it here, as I heard it that day beneath the xanarth's head and the watchful gaze of Eleos. I shall try. But I am not

Valka. My old memories are—will ever be—imperfect. Even now, when all has changed . . . rare are those moments which retain their brightness, which hang inviolate behind my eyes and echo in my ears.

I may falter, or wander, or err where she would not.

But I shall try, for this is the proper place—and the last—for it.

CHAPTER 4

AIR AND DARKNESS

"'I'LL BE BACK,' HADRIAN said. 'Help Corvo drive!'"

"And then he was gone, climbed up through the roof of the van. I didn't realize what he'd done until it was too late. He'd jumped one of their chariots, used it to shoot down the others. Cover our escape. Something must have happened—I didn't see. Maybe he circled back to deal with the Conclave Guard's pursuit. Maybe he missed a turn in the tight streets. I was in the copilot seat beside Otavia, helping to drive . . ."

She did not explain that we were relying upon her eidetic memory to navigate the streets of Vedatharad. It was easy enough to gloss over, and it had been her practice not to draw any more attention to her Tavrosi implants than was strictly necessary. Many were the priors and inquisitors of the Chantry who would have no regard for her status as a demarchist citizen, or for her relationship with me.

"We made it to the gate just in time," she said. "Hadrian was shouting *go* on the comm. I thought he was right behind us. He couldn't have been far."

"I couldn't have missed it by more than half a hundred cubits," I said, and found Valka staring at me. I fell silent.

"'Hadrian!' I was shouting. 'Hadrian! Tavi, we have to go back!'" Valka angled her head as she spoke, voice coming out oddly flattened. It was an affect I had heard from her before. Often when she repeated bits of what she had said before or heard, it was with the tone and inflection replicated as well. A perfect copy. Almost a recording—though she played it on her own lips. But there were other times—when we were pressed for time, most oft—when she would simply recite, let the words run out in their proper order without regard for feeling. Though she had been careful not to call out her Tavrosi heritage a moment earlier, the machine in her was plain enough to see. Numa must have seen it. As a scholiast, he was cousin to machines himself, and should have known the signs. But neither he nor the governor-general interrupted, though I watched them, that old part of me that longed to leap between Valka and whatever threatened her ready to lunge.

"'Twas too late," Valka continued. "The doors were shut, but we had a clear shot along the underground highway back to the starport. Or so we thought. The gates were barred when we got to them. Otavia and Pallino suggested we abandon the van, and we did. They'd gotten guards into the tunnels by then. We fought our way back to a maintenance hatch about a kilo back from the starport exit. Pallino mined the door. Stopped them following."

I could almost hear Pallino cursing, shouting for the others to move along.

Right on cue, Valka tipped her head the other way. "'Move it, you dogs! Double quick!' he was shouting. But I turned to Otavia and said, 'We have to go back! Hadrian is still in the city! We can save him!' She put a hand on my shoulder. 'I know, Valka,' she said. 'But they won't kill him. He's too valuable a hostage. Better if we reach the *Tamerlane*. We can negotiate from a place of strength.'"

At that, Valka had relented. The *Tamerlane* could not have stood against an entire Lothrian fleet single-handed, but she was in high orbit above the Commonwealth's capital, and in a position to do or threaten no small amount of harm.

"We didn't know the *Tamerlane* was already lost," Valka explained. "But we made our way through the maintenance tunnels to an airlock. Padmurak's atmosphere is unfit for terranic life, and some of us were without suits—myself among them. We commandeered equipment for the few of us who needed it and cut our way onto the surface.

"We were able to reach the airfield. 'Twould seem they had not counted on us escaping the underground. We met no resistance. No air support or anything. But our shuttle was gone."

Valka seemed to deflate in the telling, her shoulders slumped in her chair.

"'There has to be another way!'" she said, not looking up. I started, recognizing the phantom of Pallino's voice in the brusque patter of her words. "There *had* to be another way," she repeated, speaking for herself this time. "'Twere . . . seventeen of us left by then. We assaulted a hangar on the edge of the airfield and managed to take control of a military freighter. We lost eight in the attempt."

The cheap glass visor of a Lothrian helm shattered under Corvo's fist, and the man within fell gasping in the thin and frigid air. Another fell dead beneath one of Crim's knives, and Pallino's plasma burner torched a third. Then Valka came—in Lothrian armor herself—and hurried up the freighter's ramp amid sparking lights and the foggy mists of coolant hoses.

"I have experience flying ships," Valka continued. "And I . . . speak basic Lothrian. We were able to launch. Hard launch. Fusion lifters. We were clear of Vedatharad in minutes. 'Twas then we discovered the Cielcin." Her hands twisted in her lap, her wine cup forgotten on the table at her elbow. "'Twas not one of their *oscianduru,* not one of their worldships. 'Twas smaller. Class-7, I guessed. An asteroid they'd hollowed out, expanded into the classic spinship cylinder. Perhaps three hundred kilometers from end to end. The *Tamerlane* would not respond." The fingers of her left hand spasmed, flexed. Nails bit into the flesh of her right arm. "The *Tamerlane* would not respond."

Recognizing the symptoms of Urbaine's worm at work in her, I made to rise, saying, "Valka . . ."

With a force of will, she unclenched her left hand, seized it with her right. Ignoring my interruption, she pressed on. "Otavia and I managed to get a ping off her transponder—they hadn't disabled it yet. That was how we found their ship. The Cielcin were in orbit around one of Padmurak's moons. The Lothrians had a military base there. It looked like they were . . . supplying the Cielcin. Freighters like ours. Otavia inserted us into a high polar orbit around the moon, lost us amid the other freighters.

"'Twas nothing we could do. Our ship was not warp-capable, and we stood no chance of rescuing Hadrian if we returned to Padmurak. We debated the better part of a day. Slept in shifts. But we decided the only thing to do was chase after the *Tamerlane.* The Cielcin had it almost aboard their ship by then. We joined the Lothrian convoy supplying their ship. When we were close enough, we diverted, clamped ourselves to the hull."

"Weren't you detected?" asked Governor-General Dorr.

"I studied Cielcin ship design for years," Valka replied, referring to the thousands of hours we both had spent poring over schematics and reports and countless holographs made by Legion Intelligence of the ships and worldships captured over the long centuries of fighting. The first and greatest of these, called *Echidna,* had been taken by Cassian Powers after the Second Battle of Cressgard, right at the start of the war. That capture alone accounted for more than forty percent of the Cielcin material in Imperial hands, and had been instrumental in helping to formulate our understanding of their technology and tactics. "They've virtually no sight lines, and even their short-range sensors won't operate inside about a half-kilometer from their hull. If we registered at all, we were dismissed as an artifact. Noise."

That seemed to satisfy Dorr.

"We planned to venture out onto the hull, find a way in, but Crim argued that we should lay low, make sure we'd not been detected. Otavia and I took turns listening at the comms station, only nothing came of it. We powered down the primary reactor, hoped that would stop them detecting our presence.

"'Twas during this time that we discovered our *cargo*," Valka continued, still clutching her left hand. The taste of feni soured further still upon my tongue to watch her, and I looked away.

I saw too clearly then what she had seen: the frost-rimed racks, the bodies under glass. I knew what she must have felt. I had felt it myself, dragged into the Grand Conclave's audience hall and confronted with the First Finger of the Prophet's White Hand.

"Bodies," Valka said. "Human beings. There must have been two thousand on board."

The Lothrians were selling their people to the enemy. *Feeding* them to the Cielcin. The freighter they had stolen from Padmurak was a slave ship and a cattle carrier at once, its human chattel destined for the labor camps and dining troughs of Dharan-Tun.

As Valka detailed the discovery of their freighter's human cargo, I found myself thinking of another such cargo. Of twenty thousand human souls given to Kharn Sagara by Raine Smythe. Given by me. The price we'd paid to arrange a meeting with Aranata Otiolo and grim fate. What had become of them? More SOMs for the Undying's private army? Food for the demonic Brethren? Something else?

May Time, Ever-Fleeting, forgive me.

"We were preparing to venture out onto the hull," Valka was saying. "But before we had our chance, the Cielcin jumped to warp."

"To rendezvous with Dharan-Tun," I said. "I was already on board."

"We didn't know that," Valka said. "Pallino realized first they must have handed you over." She tilted her head, recited, "'Remember Berenike? That Pale bastard wanted Had handed over. Why bother taking the *Tamerlane*? They got him, too, Valka. Depend on it. Those gray-faced fuckers turned him over, I'd bet my right eye again.'" Pallino's ghost faded away, and with a deep breath, Valka continued, "We were trapped. We couldn't leave the freighter at warp. We were right on the surface. Of course that meant they couldn't get at us, not so long as we were underway."

"'Twas four years before they reached their destination. We survived off Lothrian ration packs and whatever we could grow in hydroponics. After the first year, we decided to put four of us under the ice. Pallino volunteered, and three of the men. Corvo and I couldn't. We needed to watch the ship. None of the others could."

"When they finally reverted, we tried to wake the others. Tolten would not revive." That had been the name of one of the common men. "We'd arrived at Dharan-Tun. I don't know how familiar you are with Cielcin worldships, governor. The Cielcin live underground, beneath kilometers of rock to shield them from the radiation of space and warp travel. The surface is covered with pits, canals, machinery . . ."

How well I knew the sight she described. The white and deep-scarred face of Dharan-Tun. I had seen it first on Berenike, peering down through the haze of atmosphere like the milk-blind eye of some idiot god. Up close, it told a different story. Craters rimmed with bulwarks of black iron, fortress towers and ramparts rising from the ice like the bones of dragons picked clean by desert sands, vast plains of frost where nothing grew, and trenches deep as hell that exposed the fires beneath. And the engines! Like mountains of gray steel the great engines rose, apertures vast as empires, fueled by oceans of antimatter forever forged in foundries near the surface.

"We had to make a choice," Valka said, weighing the options in her hands. "We could remain with the ship that brought us to Dharan-Tun, or we could make a break for the planet. 'Twould prove no choice at all. The Cielcin took the *Tamerlane* from the vessel and brought it down onto the planet's surface. We followed best we could. Hid ourselves in a crater ten point two kilos from the basin where the *Tamerlane* was docked. We had no way of knowing how long we had before the whole worldship made the jump to warp. We had to act quickly.

"Corvo decided we'd leave two men behind to guard the freighter, while the rest of us ventured over the surface to the *Tamerlane*. We reasoned they would not have started the procedures for the jump to warp until after the *Tamerlane* was in dock. We'd have hours. It takes a Cielcin worldship several hours to spin up its drives. We were sure we had the time.

"Still, 'twas an hour and forty minutes' journey to reach the *Tamerlane*'s docks. We had notions of waking the crew, taking back the ship, but from the moment we arrived, we knew it was impossible.

"The *Tamerlane* was never built to land, and I've no idea how they kept it together at all. The Cielcin had put it in a kind of dock, a huge channel built into a rift valley in the surface ice . . ."

I had seen precisely the sort of place she meant on the rare occasion I was brought all the way to the surface. When we'd departed Dharan-Tun for Eue, I had seen them stretching away from the sinkhole that served as the Prophet's royal starport: black channels cracking the icy face of the world, perfectly straight, high-walled and ramparted with cranes and gantries of all description, each swarming with Cielcin workers and human slaves in bulky suits whose exposed hoses might easily be torn by some errant spar or the idle whim of their masters.

Clear as I see the bust of that first Gibson on the shelf above me now, I saw then the little figures of Corvo and Valka, Pallino and Crim and the two men who had survived the journey out of Padmurak, like ants measured against all that vastness of ironwork and stone. How small they must have felt, huddled on the uppermost lip of that precipice, looking down through miles of catwalks and ladders to the base below our captured ship. How vast and dark is our universe, how arrayed against us—not indifferent as the ancient magi would have it—but hostile and cruel. And yet above them—above it all—unrolled like a carpet of diamonds black as ink, the silent stars whirled. Each placed there, if Dorayaica spoke truth, by the Quiet's hand, to light our way in the Dark. Each had been painted with deliberate care, that each ray of light might fall as a sparrow, in accordance with his will.

"'Twas nothing we could do," Valka said. "Even if we wanted to storm the ship and wake the crew . . . we could go nowhere. Even if we woke all ninety thousand . . . we would be ninety thousand against . . . tens of millions? More?

"We made to leave, but before we made it half a kilo we were ambushed. Set upon by a group of Cielcin. 'Twere not soldiers, but 'twere more than a dozen of them. Pallino was wounded, and we lost one of the others. But we won free. We managed to incapacitate one. Otavia dragged it unconscious all the way back to the freighter."

I tried to picture Otavia Corvo dragging an unconscious Cielcin by the heel across miles of cometary ice, the wounded Pallino limping and cursing behind.

"The Cielcin who attacked us were only workers," Valka continued. "They had no comms, no weapons worth a damn. The one we captured didn't know much, either. But we learned enough." Again her head tilted to one side, voice flat. *"Marerunu oyumn o-Shiomu siajun ti-tajarin."*

"It said it had heard Dorayaica had . . . me," I translated, recognizing the blank faces of Dorr and Numa.

"Marerunu oyumn o-kousun biqu ti-tajarin!"

"It said Dorayaica would kill me," I translated, wondering why Valka was giving these lines as she had heard them for an audience that could not understand. Was it purely for dramatic effect? Had I so polluted her?

She caught me looking and straightened. Was that a thin and self-deprecating smile? "We questioned it," she said. "Learned where we were going."

Akterumu!

"Before we could plan a second raid on the *Tamerlane*, the worldship went to warp. We were trapped again—as we knew we would be—on the surface. We killed our prisoner. We had no choice." Here she hung her head, as if the memory were shameful. "After we lost Tolten to cryoburn, none of us was willing to risk going under the ice a second time. We treated Pallino's wounds and stayed put. With the worldship at warp, we were relatively safe. The Cielcin could no more risk an expedition on the surface than we could—and the bodies of the work crew that had surprised us must have been lost to the ion storms and the ice.

"Supplies started low three years in. Otavia and I did all we could to keep hydroponics operating, but the Lothrian ship hadn't been prepared to keep a crew alive. If it had taken much longer to get where we were going . . . we wouldn't have made it."

"How long?" Tor Numa asked.

"Seven years from rendezvous," Valka answered. She was nearing the end. "The instant we reverted we made a break for the *Tamerlane*. Seven years waiting in that Lothrian slave ship . . ." She shook her head, didn't speak for a long moment. Often I've wondered if there were things Valka had not told even me. I'd never asked, did not ask then. "Seven years. It felt like seven hundred. All those half-dead faces in the racks." She wiped her eyes, raised a hand to stop me as I stood to go to her. "And we just *left* them there. In that freighter. We never went back. How could we? There was nowhere to go. We couldn't stay anymore. We had to go to the *Tamerlane*. Live or die.

"We'd discussed it on the freighter. We couldn't save everyone. But there was a chance the *Ascalon* was still on board. Still operational. It could take half a hundred in fugue. We might save *some* people. Fifty in ninety thousand." Here she paused, shaded her eyes—and an emotion I felt all too sharply settled over her, her head tilted to one side as if she might drain her grief out one ear. "'Tis awful what one calls victory in such extremes."

A breath pushed itself into her lungs, and she straightened. "'Twas not well-guarded. The Cielcin had been digging through the ship in the years since we arrived. That much was clear. Graffiti in the corridors, cabins worked over. Some of the fugue pods were smashed. Others emptied. Some had . . . bits left." She swallowed. "They must have had some shielded way to get in from underneath. Accessways, umbilicals. We got in through a hatch in the dorsal hull, close to the surface. But we met no resistance. That surprised us.

"'Twas not long before we reached one of the security offices. Otavia and I replaced our stolen Lothrian equipment, we all replaced our weapons. Then we split up. 'Twas left to me to see to the *Ascalon*, so I went down to the shuttle bays to get a sense of its condition. The others made the bridge. 'Twas . . . 'twas the last time I saw any of them alive."

Valka was silent then a long moment, hand still on her face. "I was a soldier," she said at length. "When I was young. In the Demarchy. Home Defense. I fought in exactly one battle. Just one. Against the Prachar separatists. Didn't lose a single man. Still . . . 'twas bad enough. But this . . . all of them. *All of them.*"

Again I went to stand, and again she thrust a hand out to keep me away. For so long she had kept silent, but I knew her pain was there. I'd see it time to time, etched just beneath her face, betrayed by some set of her jaw, by some flicker in her eye. Betrayed by some fragment of Urbaine's worm. She had suffered—not as I had suffered—but in her own way, and suffering is not quantified or measured. It only is.

"Thank you, Hadrian," she said, pushing me back to my seat by her tone. Golden eyes returned to the governor-general. "The Cielcin were on board the *Tamerlane* by then. I sealed myself in the *Ascalon*, confined myself to running systems checks, hoped I wouldn't be detected. They were awakening the crew. The sleepers. 'Twas nothing we could have done, not without risking discovery. Otavia and the others had gotten pinned down in a maintenance annex near the bridge. The Cielcin had gotten to it first, along with their Extrasolarian allies. We had to stop using comms for a while to not risk detection. They had the ship tethered to a fleet of lifters. We were in motion. They were taking us down to the planet."

Valka collected her wine cup, found it empty, held it in her hands, eyes fixed on its hollow depths. "The *Tamerlane* started falling apart in the upper atmosphere. Her landing on Dharan-Tun was bad enough, but the gravity on . . . on Eue was almost twice that of Dharan-Tun. The ship wasn't made for those stresses. The superstructure started to shear, and when we landed most of the lower levels buckled at once. But the sleepers— the crew—were all on the upper levels, near the dorsal hull, and the moment we landed the Cielcin started moving them out. I watched on the security cameras. They took them all to the equator, shoved them down the launch flumes for the lightercraft—'twere a dozen or so that vented very near the ground, like slides. Hadrian told you the rest. About the crowd, the temple, the old city." She broke off, replaced the glass on the table at her elbow.

"'Twas about then I sensed Hadrian."

"Sensed?" Dorr blinked, confused.

"*Detected* Hadrian," Valka amended, lying to cover her slip, "forgive me. My Standard is not what it could be. His *suit*, I mean. I tried to contact him. It did not work at first. I told the others. Pallino and Crim took the others and found a shuttle. Otavia took the bridge. A few Cielcin remained behind, but she killed them, took control of the weapons systems. Once the Cielcin cleared the ship, I fired up the *Ascalon*'s sublight reactor. 'Twas about then I got Hadrian on the comms." She looked at me then, a breath escaping with a taut smile, and she whispered, "And you know the rest."

Her part all done, she hung her head, and said no more.

CHAPTER 5

MARCHING ORDERS

VALKA'S STORY BROUGHT OUR audience with the governor-general to an end, but it was only the first of such audiences. For the next three months, Valka and I remained guests of Governor-General Velan Dorr. For three months we dwelt in the very apartments we had shared our first night on our previous visit to Colchis. Our days were filled with reports. How many times we were made to retell the stories we'd shared with Dorr and his scholiast only Valka could tell. We must have recounted the events since we left Vedatharad half a hundred times: to logothetes of the governor-general's office, to men of the system legate's staff, and to the local chapter of the Legion Intelligence Office. Even the Chantry had their turn—though neither Valka nor myself were subjected to the Question as I once had been.

I suspected Dorr's hand in that, or the Emperor's. For surely word had gone out to Forum and to the Imperial fleet—wherever it was. For we had told them *everything*, everything—of course—except for those parts they would not believe. We told them nothing of the Quiet, nothing of the Watchers, or the Enar.

For such things would not be believed, unless it was perhaps by Caesar himself.

"The Emperor's movements are known," I told the Intelligence Officer sent to interview me, as I had told the legate's men, the logothetes, and the governor-general himself. "The Cielcin extracted His Radiance's itinerary from my crew by torture during their captivity on Dharan-Tun."

"And from you?" asked the Intelligence man—Modanpotra, I think his name was. He was the first to ask so directly, so offensively, in a way almost leading me to reply.

I had thus far managed to evade the issue entirely. I *had* betrayed the

Emperor's movements to the Cielcin in time. The ice pit yawned cavernous in my chest, and I heard the creaking of the iron chain, felt the bite of the cold and the manacles that held my raw ankles. But I did not hesitate in my denial. "Not from me," I said, and hid my hands beneath the brushed steel table between us. My injuries were shame enough, without piling shame upon my name. "Certain of my crew were taken. At Padmurak, I suspect—those who were not frozen when the *Tamerlane* was captured. They were tortured separate from myself. I do not know who confessed. I never saw them alive."

"And yet you know they confessed?" Modanpotra asked, cocking one black brow.

"I saw their bodies," I said, remembered the hollow pits of Lieutenant White's skull. "Syriani Dorayaica made certain of that. It told me it knew the Emperor's plans. Perfugium. Vanaheim. Balanrot. Every stop on the Emperor's tour."

"And yet you did not transmit this knowledge via telegraph before your journey here?" The Intelligence man's eyes narrowed. "Why?"

"As I told the others," I answered him, "Doctor Onderra and I were afraid the information might fall into the wrong hands once it reached the Imperium."

Modanpotra's face twisted in confused consternation. "What wrong hands? We are the Empire."

"The Empire is no monolith, Agent Modanpotra, as you well know," I said, hoping the ice in my voice defense enough. "I am a knight of the Royal Victorian Order. I serve the Emperor, and the Emperor alone."

"And yet you give this information now," Modanpotra said.

"I have no choice," I said. "We came to Colchis because we knew it. I can but hope that your hands are the right ones."

Modanpotra's voice took on the character of a man asking a child if he believed the monster still lurked beneath his bed. "Whose hands do you believe are the wrong hands, lordship?"

I matched his condescension dram for dram. "Sir," I said, "I have been the subject of more than half a dozen assassination attempts since joining the Emperor's service. You are Legion Intelligence. You tell me."

Mollified, Modanpotra changed tactics. "Why did you come to Colchis?"

Tor Numa had asked the same question earlier, and yet Governor-General Dorr had circled round, as though they had not believed our answer.

"You were in the athenaeum," Dorr had pressed. "Why?"

Night had fallen by then, and the statue of Eleos—Mercy—was visible only as a pale, lamp-lit shape through the high window. The xanarth's head still leered, square-toothed and hideous. A fresh glass of feni sweated in my fingers, a new sphere of ice melting in the cashew liquor.

What could I say?

Throughout our interrogation—that first night and after—both Valka and myself had been careful to skip over our sojourn amongst the islanders. She had purged the flight records when we landed below the mesa at Nov Belgaer. A close examination by the Intelligence Office or the Inquisition might reveal the altered logs, but I hoped not. Imrah and her family had been so good to us for so long, and for no better reason than my relation with Siran. It would be poor payment indeed to repay all their charity and care with a visit from the Imperial authorities, and besides, Valka and I had spent years with Gibson among the islanders, years in which we might have—should have—reported to the proper authorities.

My fault. My weakness.

I prayed the villagers would not suffer for it. I shuddered to think of the Inquisition loosed upon the peaceful islands, their black ships floating high above the gray waves.

But I was not—had not been—ready to face the world of men and play the great game of empire and thrones. The miracle and surprise of Gibson's presence, which had seemed at the time so great a blessing, had cost the Empire years. We might have warned them of Dorayaica's swollen fleet all the sooner, but I had not wanted that part of my life to end, like a man who lies lost in the memory of a pleasant dream even after he has awakened to the new light of day.

But our time together had ended, as all dreams must.

And the Cielcin were coming.

"I can't talk about that," I said after a long silence. "My business at the athenaeum was my own."

And yet I had told Tor Arrian everything, had needed to in order to learn the truth of old Tor Gibson's name, and so when Dorr had pressed, I'd relented, saying, "I had a tutor as a boy. A scholiast. He was returned to athenaeum after I left home and embraced here at Nov Belgaer. I met him again on my previous visit to your world. I went to pay my respects. To set my affairs in order. He was like a father to me."

Dorr would follow this up, I had no doubt, and Arrian would confirm that our conversation had been of Gibson. Would Arrian tell Dorr of

Thessa? Of Gibson's sabbatical to the islands in the years before his apparent death, and of the hospital module he had ordered there to extend his life?

I thought not.

Arrian had—unwittingly—allowed Prince Philippe Bourbon to escape the scholiasts' Strictures. It was not something he would want scrutinized, and yet it might happen. Dorr's men or the Inquisition might come to Thessa and to Racha in time, and Imrah and her clan might pay for their kindness.

I could only pray they would not.

The orders came faster than I'd anticipated. Almost I had expected Caesar to order Valka and myself confined to Colchis, as he had confined us on Nessus long ago, perhaps to await his return to Forum at the end of his tour along the Centaurine front.

But word came down: we were to be brought to Nessus with all due speed. I was to return to my imprisonment in Maddalo House and to give fresh report to Magnarch Venantian. On Nessus, we were to await further word, or to await the Emperor's return. We were being brought back—not onto the game board—but into the wings, ready to enter play.

And we would not travel alone.

The *Ascalon*, newly repaired, repainted, and refueled, awaited us in a broad, low-ceilinged hangar on the outskirts of Aea. The governmental starport was relatively quiet beside the already quiet commercial port. The major starlanes had long since shifted away from Colchis, relegating the system to the status of a minor and cozy backwater, relevant only thanks to the presence of the Imperial Library—itself relevant only to the nobiles and academics allowed access to it. Colchis saw little traffic, official or otherwise. It was one of the many reasons I loved it so.

Colchis let a man forget the universe, and I was a man who needed forgetting.

But I had lingered at the shores of Lethe long enough, and drunk too long and deeply.

We said our goodbyes to Governor-General Velan Dorr at his palace one misty morning. His men packed us smartly into the back of an armored black groundcar. Still I remember the shape of the gargoyles leering at the gatehouse in the walls surrounding the governor's mansion. Valka held my three-fingered hand as we pulled out onto Sun Street and passed before the Chantry sanctum and beneath its white turrets and the graven images of Mercy, Justice, and Fortitude.

Still the city seemed to sleep. But few vehicles were on the road, and fewer peasants milled along the sidewalks. The rush hour was yet to come, and what few men were in the streets appeared to me a melange of gray-suited government men walking to the palace complex from the train station that connected the city's boroughs to its heart and country farmers in their carts or trucks driven in from beyond the city wall.

This was the Empire I loved, though I had scarcely lived in it. The Empire of ordinary men and women living ordinary lives. I smiled to see them, though I felt again the sharp division I had felt—as between species—wandering the streets of Meidua as a boy. With the glass of the armored window between them and me, I might have been at a menagerie, though I dared not guess which of us was the audience, and which the caged beast.

It took the better part of an hour to reach the landing field, a patchwork of gray tarmac and black pits surrounded by the monolithic concrete walls of sound barriers and the drum-turrets of flight-control towers. An array of radar dishes and comms antennae bristled along one margin, and the air was filled with the whine of repulsors as a great dromond—a stretched black pyramid nearly half a mile from end to end—lowered itself onto one of the vaster tarmacs.

That quiet little empire of the city was passing away. That black cargo ship was only the first harbinger of the wider universe, a pseudopod of the greater galaxy reaching down to earth. Our driver passed under the shadow of that great ship as we circled round the blast pit that formed the center of the cothon that was our final destination.

The armored car's doors clamshelled open, and an attendant of the port authority—a smartly dressed woman with a beret to conceal her pinned-up auburn hair—saluted with one silk-gloved hand as three stevedores approached to collect our luggage. Brief pleasantries exchanged, she led us down a ramp cut into the level of the tarmac that curled clockwise some distance removed from the edge of the pit.

I lingered just a moment, my head just above ground level, and watched the dromond sinking toward land. Small as ants and smaller seemed the men upon the ground, waving their guide rods like antennae, shouting indistinct orders to one another on the air. What roads had that ship taken to reach Colchis? What tidings did it bring?

"Are you well?" Valka asked, stopping me when we had followed the attendant down the ramp and through the private terminal down to the dock where the *Ascalon* waited in her berth. She fussed with my collar, a sad smile masking the deep concern in her eyes.

I returned her smile, and kissed her brow. "I'm just . . . not certain I'm ready for another long voyage after the last." Looking over her shoulder, I eyed the old Challis interceptor with some trepidation. The ship had been my home for nearly thirty years—my prison for nearly twenty—and nearly a decade on Colchis with Gibson and Imrah's clan had not washed away the numb and hollow dread I felt at the thought of climbing back aboard. Standing in the corridor, I wondered if I would ever look at space travel as I had before.

I thought not.

"'Twill be all right," Valka said, her smile growing wider and more sincere. "You'll be in fugue this time."

Swallowing, I nodded. That much was true. At the urging of Magnarch Venantian, Governor-General Dorr had assigned a crew of twenty to escort us from Colchis to Nessus. The *Ascalon* was built for speed, was far faster than the *Tamerlane* had ever been, but Nessus and the Centaurine provinces lay clear across Imperial space, thousands of light-years distant. The flight controller we'd spoken to the night before had said we would be sixteen standard years sailing back to Nessus.

"That's just the thing," I said. "It used to be the fugue I dreaded. Now it's the waking."

"Lord Marlowe!" The intruding voice had a ringing, almost musical quality, and turning I saw an olive-skinned young officer approaching, one hand upraised. Despite his nearly Jaddian appearance, he wore Imperial dress blacks with an officer's maroon beret set at a jaunty angle on his head. Similar signs of disregard for formality were evident in his dress. The top button of his tunic jacket was undone, his boots were not polished, and he wore a highmatter sword not in the tidy holster one expected, but swinging from a magnetic loop at his belt like the handle of a torch light. And then there was his hair, which was not Legion regulation at all. Convention forced the common legionnaires to shave their heads, but allowed officers to keep their hair. Still, there were limits, but this man far exceeded them, wearing his hair extremely long—almost to his waist. He'd gathered it all into a reddish-brown braid at his shoulder that reminded me of nothing so much as the queues the Cielcin wore to mark their status.

Valka withdrew a step as the man approached and saluted me, and in that action, too, was a mark of the man's regard for protocol. He ought to have stopped full, clicked his heels, and pressed his fist to his heart before raising his right hand. He only beat his chest and waved.

"Are you the captain?" I asked, ignoring these breaches of protocol and still taking in the measure of this man. He had a fox's clever countenance, slanting brows, and a hawk's nose. His lazy insolence reminded me of . . . something. I couldn't place it, but I was sure at once I did not like him.

"Commander," the man corrected, but bobbed his head the same. "Sir Hector Oliva, sir. Special Security Division. Legion Intelligence Office. Magnarch Venantian charged me to bring you to Nessus." He extended a hand. "It's an honor to meet you, sir."

I returned the salute more stiffly—more correctly—before taking the young officer's hand. Whatever the fellow's bohemian appearance, his grip was strong, and if he marked my scars or missing fingers, he gave no sign. The Intelligence Office's Special Security Division normally confined itself to espionage and matters of inter-house warfare, or else meddled in the affairs of worlds and states beyond the Imperium. Evidently one of their agents was to play my shepherd and bag man.

"Oliva," I said after a brief pause. I did not recognize the name—though perhaps you do. "You're a SpecSec man. Is there word from Sir Gray?" As head of the Legion Intelligence Office, this Oliva would report ultimately to Sir Gray Rinehart, who had replaced hapless Sir Lorcan Breathnach after the latter's ill-fated attempt to assassinate me had almost claimed Valka's life. Rinehart was not an enemy, but I was not certain he was a friend. And this Oliva had just said the Magnarch charged him to escort me to Nessus. Not Rinehart. Not the Emperor. Was that cause for concern? Or only the chain of command operating as it should?

Is there a hidden knife? And which hand holds it?

Oliva shook his head. "No, my lord. Sir Gray remains with the Emperor. We don't expect word from him or His Radiance until the fleet next makes reversion. Please." He gestured that Valka and I should walk with him. The *Ascalon* waited in dock ahead, hanging from tracks that extended past the hangar doors and into the pit at the center of the cothon roundhouse. "I appreciate that this is all . . . a little strange, us commandeering *your* ship and all for the voyage. I hope that my men and I will not prove an imposition."

"Oh, not at all, Commander," Valka said, taking my arm. "We're grateful for the escort."

"It's an honor, truth be told," Oliva returned. "And an excuse to finally move on. I've been stuck on this rock here for eight years now. Been eager to join to fight proper."

That checked my advance. "Are you?"

Oliva looked back, highlighting that prominent beak of a nose. "Sir?"

"Eager?" I repeated the word, making it a question. "Have you ever fought the Cielcin?"

"No sir," Oliva answered truthfully, "but there's a first time for everything. And I'm more than ready to get a crack at their Pale faces. Depend on it."

Valka's hands tightened reflexively on my bicep, their neatly manicured nails communicating one single, silent word. *No.*

Ignoring her, I said, "If you knew what you were talking about, Commander, you'd not be so *eager*. Depend on *that*." I had been so eager. Once. Sure that stiff necks and religious dogma were the only obstacles to peace. Greed. Pride. Envy. With such eager surety I had ridden out to find Vorgossos, to change the world, the Empire, the galaxy.

And I had paid for it.

Commander Oliva maintained a studiously bland expression throughout my response and for several seconds afterward. Then he chuckled softly and said, *"Beluto intusha."*

I know a little.

Once, I might have laughed to hear the tongue of the enemy in the mouth of my fellow man. For so long, so few had bothered to learn it, had bothered to understand the Cielcin as I did, that I despaired—at first of the possibility of peace, and later of my own loneliness. Oliva's answer was an answer I might have given myself—and probably had given to many— once. No more. His was that same destructive arrogance which had placed me on my path, the same arrogance that had carried me up from Emesh to Vorgossos . . . and to Eue. Taking advantage of my surprise, Oliva pressed, "I studied Cielcin language and culture at Ares. Top of my class."

"Top of your class . . ." I repeated the words at barely more than a whisper. "You're a War College man, then," I said. "Fascinating." The War College on Ares was among the best naval academies in the Imperium, if not the very best. It was also among the very oldest, exceeded only by the old schools on Avalon and Mars. Summoning up long dormant faculties in my brain, I said, *"Paiwa oyumn o-cahoti gahatiri ji etadayu ti-jutar ija ba-okarin."*

I could tell from the way Oliva's mocking eyes narrowed that he did not quite understand me, though he doubtless caught the words for *knife* and *own* and *throat*. His struggling with the sentence ought to have underscored my point, but Oliva simply laughed this away, too.

"They always said you were intense, by damn!" he exclaimed. Still smiling, he turned and continued down the gentle slope, past the emptied kiosks that sold nothing at all toward the pier beneath the waiting *Ascalon*.

The old Challis-class interceptor stretched only five hundred feet from end to end, a sleek, low-slung vessel, like the upward-curving blade of a sword on display, with her main repulsors, her fusion torches, and warp pods extending from short, graceful wings near the rear and a single, prominent tail fin folded gracefully to accommodate the hangar's low ceiling. Her titanium and adamant skin had been repainted and enameled black and ceramic white, and shone bright as new in the stark lighting of the bay. Dorr's men—evidently confused—had painted only the red pentacle—point down—upon the rear fin, forgetting the pitchfork that had been a part of my sigil since I ascended to knighthood and was restored to the palatine caste.

We had emerged into the hangar near the nose and the open doors of the cothon, and a sharply sloping ramp led up to the forward airlock. It was the same airlock through which I had hurled myself bleeding and shell-shocked, pursued by Cielcin on the day of the Black Feast. Seeing that door again then and there, with the hangar doors standing open and the new sun streaming down through the launch pit in the cothon's center, felt like an injustice. Why should my thoughts be pulled thence on so fine a day?

Once, I might have delighted to find another officer in the Legions learning the Cielcin tongue, but I guessed that even Oliva's braid was a romantic affectation, an expression of xenophilic admiration for the Cielcin, an embrace of the ways and styles of the enemy, just as the powers of Europe had once embraced the curved saber of the Turk.

Could I truly fault the man for that? Did I not still own the cape of scarlet *irinyr* that Vati had draped over my shoulders for what should have been my execution?

There was too much, entirely too much, of Hadrian Marlowe in the young Hector Oliva, and I hated him for it. I opened my mouth to say something—I know not what—but Valka jumped ahead of me, perhaps sensing my disquiet. "How did you come to be on Colchis, commander? 'Twould seem a poor posting for an officer like yourself."

If Sir Hector were relieved to have this new line of conversation, he did not show it. "A punishment, I'm afraid. Ran into a spot of trouble rescuing Archduke Bierce's daughter from some freeholder scum. Her ladyship was *especially* grateful, and not in a way that endeared her rescuer to her lord father." Again he laughed—he laughed too easily. "She still telegraphs, not that I reply. Wouldn't be proper." He broke off to bark an order at one of his subordinates, who was loitering on the dock below the ramp, then stepped up onto the gangway. "Shall we?"

I gestured for him to go on ahead.

Doubtless you find this meeting strange. I did not. I did not then know the name of Sir Hector Oliva, Champion of the Battle of Taranis, captain of the *Siren*, commander of the last defense of Nessus, Hero of the Empire. The only man besides myself to stand in single combat against the Dark Lord of Dharan-Tun and live to tell the tale.

No one did.

But it was so—though no account save this, I think, will write of it. Nevertheless, Hadrian Marlowe and Hector Oliva met this once and traveled together. His tale is not mine, and is elsewhere recorded, and yet I must mention him, because I was wrong about him.

We have need of heroes, however broken, however terrible, however insufficient they may be.

And we have need of more than one hero, for heroes do break, you know.

CHAPTER 6

DOUBTS

"WELL, I THINK HE'S amusing," Valka said, reclining on the bed we shared in the largest of the *Ascalon*'s few, small cabins. "You only dislike him because he reminds you of a certain boy I once knew on Emesh so many *centuries* ago."

I grunted, froze in the act of removing my long coat. Frowning, I said, "You see right through me, don't you?"

"You're not so opaque, dear," Valka riposted.

Again, I grunted, and slipped out of my tunic, wincing as my bad shoulder flared with pain, bringing with it the memory of the wall above the gates of the Dhar-Iagon, the chain rattling, my vision whiting out as mute slaves wound the winch to haul me back into my cell. Suddenly embarrassed of the injury, I clutched my shoulder with my hollow-boned left hand.

"You really ought to have had them see to you while we were here," she said, looking up at me with a pity bright and painful as the sun. The ship bucked beneath us as the fusion torches flared to life. Valka had gone to the bridge with Commander Oliva and his lieutenants to oversee take-off. I had retired to the cabin, having said my goodbyes to Colchis upon the landing field, and so had only heard the whine of servos as the gantries extended to shuttle the *Ascalon* into the launch pit at the center of the ring-shaped cothon terminal. The vessel's primary sublight drive did not engage until it reached about forty thousand feet, relying instead on its repulsors to clear the lip of the underground launch bay and the morning airs above the city.

Evidently, we had reached the edge of the lunar atmosphere and scratched the margins of space, for the whole ship shook, then vibrated, then glided smoothly on. Without looking, without having to look, I knew we had left Colchis behind. The false gravity of the suppression field had taken hold, activated during the first moments of thrust. By Oliva's word we were leaving Colchis and the gas giant Atlas behind. I imagined them like a pair of mismatched eyes—one blue, one orange and far greater, watching us go. In a few hours, we would reach safe distance and make the jump to warp.

Nessus was waiting, and beyond Nessus: the Emperor and the enemy both. Ruminating on this, I massaged my shoulder, feeling the muscles and the scar tissue like swollen cords. "Nessus," I said, as though this were an answer. "I'll have it done on Nessus. There'll be time there. Who knows how long we'll be waiting on Imperial orders. Plenty of time to heal then."

I let the words out flat as I was able, knowing I would not forgive myself if I let the longing I felt seep from that dark place in my chest. How I wanted to be healed! So many years aboard the *Ascalon*, so many years on Colchis had gone by, every day invaded by the aches of Dharan-Tun. Every morning I had wakened to the dull throbbing of old wounds, every day I had lived with those embers fanned to new fire by some dumb movement, some idle mistake.

No more, I prayed quietly. *No more.*

On Nessus, Imperial physicians could restring my ruined shoulder, patch the old scars where Dorayaica's slaves had peeled strips of skin away. On Nessus, they could regenerate the fingers Dorayaica had bitten from my hand. They might even regrow the bones given sufficient time. Kharn Sagara had replaced my left arm entire, after all. But he—they—had but a fortnight, and so had fashioned bones of adamant rather than let new ones bloom.

Catching my reflection in the mirror that covered one wall, I touched my claw-torn cheek with the hand Kharn had given me. "Maybe I'll have them clean this up as well."

"Oh, I don't know." Valka bit her lip, raised one winged eyebrow. "I rather like the scars."

I laughed softly at that. She always could drag me out of the pits I made for myself. Then I remembered Oliva's indifferent laughter, and abruptly stopped. Letting myself sink onto the foot of the bed, I half-turned to look at Valka. "It feels strange to be moving again."

"On a ship, you mean?"

"Forward," I said. "We were on Colchis nine years. It feels like no time at all." I inhaled. "It feels like time stopped at Akterumu. Like I keep expecting to wake up."

Valka shifted nearer, the mattress compressing beneath her limbs. Temple smoke and sandalwood filled the air about me. The same bathing oil. Time standing still. "For you, perhaps," she said, one tattooed finger tapping her head. "'Tis not so for me."

Time did not blur for her.

"It's like . . . like Gibson dying started up time again," I said, and shook my head. "I still can't believe he's gone. Twice in my life I thought I'd never see him again . . . but this time . . . this time, it's really true." Nostrils flared, I inhaled sharply, cast my eyes at the smooth metal of the ceiling, at a thin scratch in the titanium where the warm white light caught and glimmered. "Prince Philippe Bourbon . . ." I breathed the words.

Valka's left hand settled on my knee, remarkably still. *Tor Gibson,* she said, a strength in her voice like the foundations of the world. "You read his letter."

"I killed his son," I said, thinking of fat Augustin Bourbon in his fine robes of blue and white, and of Crim entering the medica when Siran had gone.

I want you to kill a man, I'd told him. *Make the arrangements for it after we're gone.*

Valka took her hand away. "I will not hear this again," she said. We had discussed this a dozen times in the apartments loaned to us in the governor-general's mansion. "He knew you did. And he forgave you."

"How can you know that?" I asked.

"Because I can read, *anaryan,*" she chided, but her voice was kind. "I thought you had the trick of it."

I snorted in spite of myself, asked, "Did he tell you who he was?"

"No. 'Twould seem he did not want us to know. 'Twas a weight—I think—he did not wish for you to carry. Had he wanted you to suffer, he'd have told you." As she spoke, she began to unwind her braid. The red-black had grown so long that sometimes she seemed almost a different woman to the one I'd met in the palace of Balian Mataro so very long ago. "Instead, he moved heaven and earth just to see you again. To be there when you returned. And why? Because he guessed you *might* come back. He did all he did for the barest chance you might return and need him." She reached out, cupped my scarred cheek. "One of these days you will have to accept that people love you, Hadrian. Gibson did. I do."

Not for the first time, I reflected on just how Gibson's miracle had been done. A disgraced prince, he must have had a secret fortune—Consortium stock, perhaps, or numbered accounts with the Rothsbank or Vigran Huaxia or one of the other Mandari holders—that had escaped detection when Gibson, Prince Philippe, was sentenced to Belusha. Siran must have acted as his agent, securing the funds for the hospital module and the reactor that had maintained it for so many years. It must have raised eyebrows in the customs office on Colchis, but it seemed no one had stopped the Consortium from delivering its cargo to barren and unsettled Thessa.

"Besides," she went on, "if what Arrian told you is true, his own son betrayed him. There cannot have been much love there. You *anaryoch* keep strange families."

"As if you clansmen are any better," I said, defensive, remembering too late that Valka was not truly a demarchist anymore. Her own people had tried to kill her, had tried to destroy her mind that a new woman might live free of the shadow of what Urbaine had done to her. And I remembered, too, that her own father—who had loved her beyond any doubt—had died a victim of the Inquisition on Ozymandias before she ever left her home on Edda. Still, only a little sorrow etched itself across her grim but lovely face. "I'm sorry."

Valka's asymmetrical smile faltered only a moment. "'Tis nothing," she said, but turned away. "Read his letter again." She stood smoothly then, and leaned down to kiss me. The dull ache in my chest and shoulder ebbed just a bit.

As she moved toward the water closet, I asked her a question. A very old question. "Valka," I said, and cleared my throat. "Am I a good man?"

She turned then—hands on the door frame—and surveyed me a long time. What did she see with those inhuman eyes? Those eyes that saw everything without exception, without distortion?

A smile split her face. A true smile, brighter even than her pity had been bright. "You're still asking that question?" she managed to say, laughter cracking her words. "After all this time?"

I could only blink at her.

"Do you not have your answer a hundred times over?" A brief tremor shook her arm, but she hid it behind her back and shook her head again. "Monsters don't have doubts."

CHAPTER 7

PAST AND FUTURE HEROES

HOW MANY TIMES, ON that previous journey, had I stood just there—in the *Ascalon*'s narrow cubiculum, fugue creches lining either wall—and just looked at her? How many hours? How many days in those nineteen years?

Only then most of Oliva's men slept alongside her, or across and further down. Twenty-five creche chambers lined either wall, each bank canted back from the central aisle so that the sleepers half-stood, half-reclined in violet fluid. More than half the creches stood empty, the white rest mats cleaned, clamps and hoses at the ready. Oliva's men had all clustered toward the near end of that long, narrow hall, side by side and ready to cycle in and out when the time came for them to change shifts every two years.

They'd let her stand alone—as she had before—in the farthest corner on the port side, nearest the bulkhead and the hatch that led through to the upper airlock to the small ship's dorsal hull.

I would join her, soon. Just another week or so, a month at most. I wanted to set my thoughts in order, to prepare myself for all that was to come. For Nessus. For the Magnarch. For my gilded cage at Maddalo House again.

She looked so peaceful, tethered in her creche. Her long, dark hair floated about her face like a shadow, like a shroud. How black the tattooed lines of her clan *saylash* stood out against her pale flesh, sharp and cold! Almost dead she seemed—as indeed she was—preserved not at all unlike the eyes and heart and brain of my grandmother in their canopic jars. Reaching up, I used the warm blade of my hand to smear away the frost that so obscured her, revealing her more clearly, and found myself remembering another voyage.

From Berenike. To Edda, long ago, with Urbaine's worm chewing through her brain.

My heart had lived in my mouth that whole voyage. Those long years.

The Demarchists had saved her life, but they could not heal her, could not banish the daimon that haunted her mind. I remembered how they had studied her under ice, then awakened her. How her left hand tried to strangle her, to put out her eyes. How she had bitten her tongue, and scratched her face almost so badly as Dorayaica scratched mine.

Always her left hand, the hand that bore the markings of her tribe.

The left hand. Darkness. Damnation. Sinister, in the Latin.

But they had saved her, those *doctors* of the Demarchy. They had given her back control of herself. They could not stop her having the impulses Urbaine's worm had put in her, but they'd made it where she could stop them. Then they'd taken her from me, locked her in a prison they called a hospital. For their *safety*, they said. For fear her daimon would infest them. In the end, they had threatened to kill her. *Reformatting,* they'd called it—they never called anything by its right name, like the Lothrians— always sanitized it, whited over horror as lime whitened the tombs of the patricians on the hills beyond Meidua.

Still I remembered seeing her again, when Crim and I had found her in that Tavrosi prison, her white smock stained red, her left hand clutching the knife she had wielded to slay her jailers.

She had freed herself before we could reach her.

My reflection beside her face in the glass smiled to recall.

"Karras told me I'd find you in here," came the by-then-familiar, almost lilting voice, and looking up I saw the figure of Hector Oliva emerge through the portal at the far end of the long hall. We'd been underway for just about a month by then. Valka had gone under only a handful of days before, and I was myself not long for the waking world. I had lingered only to take the time to draft reflections on our time on Colchis, to prepare for my return to Nessus, and to familiarize myself with the new wrist-terminal I'd purchased from a vendor on Front Street our last night in Aea. Valka and I had enjoyed a private dinner on the garden terrace above a restaurant in the city—under Dorr's watchful guards, naturally—and after, we'd been permitted to walk the streets with some measure of anonymity, and I had at last replaced the terminal I had lost with my capture on Padmurak.

When I did not reply, Oliva said, "Are you ready to go under the ice?"

"Not yet," I said, looking round. Aboard ship and under way, Oliva had abandoned his uniform tunic entirely, favoring a simple white shirt open to his sternum, though he still wore his uniform trousers and unpolished black boots. "I was just . . . visiting, I suppose." I nodded at Valka, suddenly and absurdly conscious of my bare feet and of the black rubber mat biting into them. "I spent a lot of time in here on our previous voyage."

Oliva tossed his Cielcin-style braid back from his shoulder. "I'd heard that. Is it true? Did you really spend twenty-five years on this old boat alone?"

"It was nineteen," I said, remembering something I'd told poor, doomed Leon at the Battle of Eikana. "Some stories are true."

The younger officer winced. "It's no wonder you're so . . ." He raised an open hand and gestured to all of me. "A Cielcin prison camp and then . . . that." He surprised me then, seeming to realize his rudeness. "I did three years alone on a courier mission just out of Ares. I'd just joined SpecSec. I thought that was long." He shook his head, disbelieving, perhaps, or overcome. "Nineteen years! Earth's bones, man."

"How old are you?" I asked, slashing across the man's shock and awe.

Oliva answered quickly, not needing to think about it. "Thirty-seven actual."

I sniffed, turned back to Valka. Oliva had stopped a respectful dozen paces away, not wanting—I judged—to come too near her nakedness, though he had not troubled about the undress of his subordinates. "I was barely a knight at thirty-seven. I was at Thagura." Having said that, I realized it was not quite right. I had spent years on Forum after Vorgossos, studying all the Empire knew of the Cielcin. How old had I been at Thagura, then? Forty? Forty-five?

Oliva hooked his fingers through his belt—an affectation I was prone to myself—and asked, "You didn't go in shifts? You and her?"

"I'm palatine," I answered, returning my attention to Valka. "She's Tavrosi. I have the years to spend." I looked down at the frost-melt on my palm, regretted wiping Valka's creche lid clean. The frost had helped conceal her.

"My lord, if I may ask," Oliva inquired, suddenly a touch formal. "How old are you?"

I had been prepared for one of the usual questions. About Aptucca, about Vorgossos, or Berenike. *Is it true you can't be killed?* Not this. I almost laughed. I knew the answer, but only because Dorr's medics had run a physical exam months earlier, shortly after he took us into custody. They had run all manner of tests. Pathology, blood, magnetic resonance. They'd checked the telomere degradation on a part of my palatine genome designed to give precisely the answer Oliva wanted. "Three hundred eighty-four actual," I said, unable to keep the note of sadness from my voice, "but it's been nearly a thousand years since I was born."

I could not remember when I had last dared say that figure out loud. *Nearly a thousand years . . .* I had spent so much time in fugue, traveling between the stars. I realized I did not know if my father was still alive. He should be, must be dead—unless he had traveled much himself. My mother was dead, I knew. But what of Crispin? And the sister I never knew? How much longer would it be before word came that—like old Tor Gibson— Lord Alistair was dead?

Should it have come already? Would it meet me on Nessus?

I cannot say why, but I always knew the message would come, by courier or telegraph, that a young man in livery would greet me with a salute and word from Delos.

My lord, your father is dead.

"Three hundred eighty-four?" Oliva echoed. "I'd not have guessed."

"You'd have guessed higher?" I asked, knowing how I looked, my face battered, body torn, black hair shocked with white.

Oliva only grinned, and despite myself I found myself smiling the crooked old Marlowe smile. The younger man shook his head, gripped the shield generator on his belt from old reflex. "It must have been lonely. All those years on your own."

"Old men are always lonely," I said, and felt my smile falter. "Almost everyone I know is dead." Valka's face floated in dream-like death behind the glass of her creche. "But it was a small price to pay, really. For her." I nodded at the faintly humming creche. When Oliva did not respond, I turned to him, leaving Valka to her sleep. Leaning against the controls for the unused pod beside her, I said, "You're not married." It was not a question.

"Me?" Oliva blinked. "Black planet, no! Not me."

Belatedly recalling the young commander's reference to the Archduke Bierce's daughter, I asked, "Girl in every port, then? Is that it?"

"Not every port!" Oliva's easy smile returned. "But not necessarily one *per* every port, either."

A rough bark of laughter tore from me. "That was never me." My mood darkened almost at once, sobered, for here was a young man, and I was very old. "You'll tire of that life eventually. Or it will tire of you."

"Ah, but you've just admitted you're not the voice of experience!" Oliva grinned ruefully, shaking a finger in my direction. "How could a man tire of change, mm? Besides!" Here he pressed his hands against the small of his back, leaned to stretch the long muscles there. "I'm a sailor, Marlowe. I couldn't settle down if I wanted to. A man in my profession takes what he can get—which is all the girls want to offer anyhow."

"Maybe," I allowed, pushing off the control console to stand straight again. "Maybe you're right. But there are women and *women*, commander. Some ask nothing of us, and so we are nothing to them. But there are those women who ask *all* of us. Those are the ones worth giving *all* for."

Ever quick with the riposte, Oliva returned, saying, "And they call me romantic."

"They misuse the word," I said, feeling my thorns grow sharper. "What you do isn't romance."

"It is so!" Oliva exclaimed. "Black planet, Marlowe! I'm not a criminal. I've hurt no one."

"Only yourself." I glanced back at Valka where she floated in her fugue creche, thought maybe I should prepare myself to join her after all. Had I ever thought like Hector Oliva did? Of women or of anything at all? Had that kinship Valka remarked on been a thing skin deep only? To my surprise the junior man had not sprung back with a reply. Turning back, I found him still staring at me, green eyes curiously bright. "What?"

"Are you married?" he asked.

There was the strike I'd been looking for! He'd been strangely slow with the knife.

I should have berated him, reminded him of the difference between our stations, but that would have been to cede the point, to admit defeat—and he knew it. Oliva had held his tongue only to weigh the consequences of that barb. Did he dare strike such a blow against a lord of the Imperium?

Well, he had so dared, and so struck.

"No," I answered plainly, and shut my eyes. It was an old pain I felt and forced down with an older aphorism. "We are palatine, you and I. We serve the Emperor, and he has not given me leave to do as I wish." I did not add, *and Valka does not wish it.*

My hand went to where the phylactery with Valka's preserved blood ought to have been, found only the piece of the Quiet's shell on its chain beneath my shirt. She had given it to me on Berenike before the battle, a compromise between her Tavrosi culture and my Imperial tradition. And I had lost it, left it on Nessus when we sailed to Padmurak.

No marriage for Hadrian Marlowe, no children. Only the grasping shadow of that fullness denied me by station and blood. "I am old, Sir

Hector," I said, using the young man's given name for I think the first time. "I have fought in more than thirty battles on as many worlds. Spoken with gods, battled demons. I've broken bread with the Scourge of Earth itself, and treated with Kharn Sagara. I have served the Emperor loyally for more than three hundred years, and I have loved only three women." I raised my three-fingered hand for emphasis, ticked the fingers down as I spoke. "One I lost, the second I betrayed, and the third . . ." I gestured to Valka's creche, "is right there."

"You and I are very different, I think," Oliva said.

"That may be," I allowed, and moved to brush past the younger man. Stopping beside him, I put a hand on his shoulder, glanced back at Valka. "I would marry her, if I could." I looked down, as if ashamed of my words or the feeling they conveyed. "But I have given her *all*." I released his shoulder then, and shouldered by.

"I am sorry, lord," Oliva said, words stiff and suddenly awkward, spoken by the officer the man sometimes wore. "I did not mean to give offense."

"You needn't worry," I said, reaching the far door. "It is an old wound."

"Lordship!" Oliva's voiced chased me up the hall. I stopped. "May I ask you another question?"

Turning, I gestured for him to proceed.

"Your face," he said, meaning my scars. "Was that really the Scourge's doing?"

For a long moment I made no move. I saw again the black sands of Eue, the slim, tall banners of the Cielcin flapping blue and black and green, and the distant dome of Miudanar's skull in the distance.

Arkam resham aktullu. Arkam amtatsur.

Dorayaica's claws flashed, and I shook myself. "It was," I said, and forced myself not to touch the ragged scars.

Oliva could only shake his head. "It hardly seems real," he said, hands moving to his hips. Eyes on the floor between us, he said, "I was born after Aptucca. After you bested Ulurani. I never thought I'd meet you, but . . . you. Dorayaica . . ." He paused. "It's like . . . you're like . . . meeting characters from a storybook. An opera . . . I don't know. Like . . . like you shouldn't be real."

To my astonishment, I laughed. A low, ugly little laugh. "Maybe we're not so different. I have thought the same thing many times, if not of myself." I looked away, up at one of Oliva's sleeping men in the fugue pod to my left. "We humans have lived so long in history, I think, we've forgotten that myth is the older, deeper tradition. Perhaps some part of us finds it uncomfortable when those two spheres overlap."

The younger man evidently had nothing to say to this, and so said, "Everyone thought you were dead."

"So did I," I said, not dishonestly. I had not expected to escape from Akterumu.

"They never issued any formal statement; I think the Imperial Office knew doing so would be a blow to morale. They never even declared you missing, did you know? But the rumors got out just the same. Marlowe died fighting in the Commonwealth. Marlowe died in battle, captured by the enemy, that sort of thing."

"I didn't know that," I said.

"I never believed it," Oliva said.

"Well," I felt the frown set in, "you were wrong." Realizing I now stood between Oliva and the door, I said, "Now it's my turn to ask you a question: You're a SpecSec man. What's to be done with me?"

Sensing he was out of dangerous waters, Oliva's smile returned. "On Nessus? You know the drill. We'll be detained in orbit, you and the lady will testify again for the Magnarch's men, you'll be put to the Question, and brought on down. We're under orders to keep you safe until the Emperor sends word. That's all."

"The Question?" I asked, repeating the hateful words. The Question was the Holy Terran Chantry's procedure—its *rite*—for ascertaining the humanity of an individual. I had been put to the Question once before, on the *Tamerlane* above Forum when Augustin Bourbon and Lorcan Breathnach had been attempting to frame me for consortation with artificial intelligence. Too well I remembered Inquisitor Gereon and his test kit. The adrenaline injection. The panic. Instruments evaluating blood pressure, heartbeat, skin conductivity. Readouts chiming. The sense of impending doom.

Before we begin, have you anything to confess?

You are not accused of any crime at this time.

And yet, was not the simple fact that the inquisitor deemed the Question necessary a kind of indictment? If I was under no suspicion, I would not be under investigation. And yet the Question did not interrogate guilt or innocence, it did not evaluate action. It tested *essence*, the essential nature of the organism under study. Man or machine? Human or homunculus? Man or daimon or beast?

"Why was I not put to the Question on Colchis?" I asked. Surely I should have been, if I was under suspicion. It would have been protocol.

Oliva tilted his head to one side, as though doing so might dislodge some sticky thought from the inside of his skull. He stood there a moment, hands still on his hips, pondering how best to respond. It was a measure of care and deliberation I had not yet seen from the man, and it surprised me. "I . . . should think it obvious," he said. "LIO Special Security on Nessus ordered you were to be brought to them . . . unspoiled."

"Unspoiled?" I repeated the archaism. "What do you mean?"

"They ordered you weren't to be interfered with, not by Dorr's medical staff, not by the Chantry, except to screen you for infection."

"They think there's something wrong with me?" I asked, but the thought clicked into place even as I spoke the words. "No. No, I see." A raised hand forestalled Oliva's interruption. "Your orders came from Rinehart."

"Not Rinehart," Oliva said. "From Magnarch Venantian. But you see my meaning. They're both of the Emperor's party."

"They wanted to ensure that *when* I was examined by the Inquisition, it was where they could best keep an eye on them."

Oliva tapped his temple with one finger. "Just so. That's why they picked me."

"An atheist, are you?" I asked.

"I've no love for Mother Earth's Holy Terran Chantry, let's say," the younger man replied, and flicked his braid back from his shoulder, almost in irritation.

Magnarch Venantian had no love for me, but he was fiercely loyal to the Emperor, and to the Emperor personally. His was a loyalty that ran above and against loyalty to the Chantry, against loyalty to the old houses and old bloodlines. If I understood Oliva rightly, he had ordered Legion Intelligence and Special Security to protect me from the Chantry until I could be brought safely within the reach of his arm and army. The Chantry had tried to kill me on Thermon. The Empress and her Old Lions had tried to kill me on Forum.

I had been so intent upon my choice of Colchis as the place to reveal myself to the Empire again that I had forgotten the other pieces on the board could move themselves. As I had reached for the Emperor and safety, his agents had reached for me.

"We are both the Emperor's men," Oliva said.

"We are *all* the Emperor's men," I corrected him, smoothing over the implication that there might be tension or unrest between the various groups and parties. "It is only that some obey the man, and others the throne he sits upon."

Obedience out of love for the person of the hierarch.

Obedience out of loyalty to the office of the hierarch.

Had Rigel, who formulated the Eight Forms of Obedience, placed these two in the wrong order? Was not love the higher motivator? Was not obedience from devotion the highest form of loyalty? Should not then obedience for love of the hierarch stand athwart obedience to his office? Should not the man weigh more than his crown?

Look lower. I heard Gibson's voice. *The truth is lower.*

"They said you were a philosopher," Oliva interjected.

"Only a student," I said in answer. "I spent many years at court. You would not believe the number of people who prefer to guess the Emperor's will, rather than heed it."

"I might," said the other man. "My lord, may I ask one more question?"

It was *my lord* by then, not *lordship* or *sir.* A subtle change. Noting this increased deference, I raised one eyebrow. "You may."

"When you were at court . . . they say you caught a highmatter blade in your hand."

I actually snorted. It was a child's question, a question the boy Hector Oliva had been must have wondered at for years.

"Is it true?"

To answer, I raised my left hand. The scars from Irshan's blade notched deeply my palm and fingers, thick and deep and shining in the white lights of the cubiculum. Oliva—the boy, and not the soldier—drew forward to better see. "The bones are artificial," I explained. "Adamant to the shoulder, with the flesh regenerated over top. It's no miracle, like they say." The true miracle had been that Aranata Otiolo struck off my right arm, not my left.

"I knew there had to be some explanation," Oliva said, and yet his eyes were downcast, as though the revelation saddened him. "The stories they tell. Besting Ulurani in single combat. Escaping the pleasure gardens of Gadar Malyan. Rescuing the legions off Nemavand. They can't all be true. You can't have died, for instance."

I only smiled then, and—offering only a weak salute—turned and went back down to the main deck, leaving the young hero alone with his un-asked question.

CHAPTER 8

GHOST IN THE RUINS

WHITE SHEETS COVERED EVERYTHING: the furniture, the suits of armor that stood against the walls, the matched banners that stood at either corner of the grand staircase . . . even the thick carpets—Jaddian, not Tavrosi—that lay upon the flagstones of the entrance hall at Maddalo House. Sunlight fell through the little windows high in the wall behind, passing through the richly carved wooden trusses through air so thick with dust I could taste it: the bitter ash of years.

"No one's been in since you left, lord," said the groundskeeper, a local man called Kaffu. "More than an 'undred years, they say."

"One hundred seven," Valka said, coming in through the open doors, her slaved glowsphere gleaming from its place just above her shoulder, keeping formation. In the night behind her, I could hear the clamor of Oliva's men and the Magnarch's unloading our shuttle. Following my interrogation by the Chantry under the watchful eye of a Legion Commandant named Lynch, we had been taken from the anchor station atop the hightower above the city of Sananne under cover of night and returned to Maddalo House. Venantian had not wanted a spectacle, though whispers would inevitably start.

Kaffu bowed to Valka, crushed his felt cap in his hands. "'Undred seven? That so, madam? Only been 'ere the last six my own self. Old Gren, though, 'e been on the property some forty-some. 'im and 'is kids. Not married myself, mind. Live in the other outbuilding."

A ferocious sneeze resounded through the entrance hall, and turning as if at a gunshot, I saw Sir Hector Oliva standing on the threshold, his face in his sleeve. He wore a black leather case on a strap over one shoulder. It held his lute, a *mandora* of exquisite make. He'd played it many times—at all hours—aboard the *Ascalon* as we sailed for Nessus, and played it well as his own legends say. In his other hand, he clutched another, flatter case, more than half so long as he was tall.

Recovering from his sneeze, the commander said, "Black planet! The air is foul in here!"

"'Tis only stale," said Valka, who had spent much of her life in staler climates, in ruins and in tombs.

Kaffu bowed again. "Begging your lordship's pardon. I was only told you was arriving an hour back. 'Lord Marlowe's coming!' they said. 'Best get ready!' I 'ardly got my boots on and dressed proper when you all landed that fine ship o' yours. You give me just a moment, I'll get them generators fired right back up, get them ventilators going and the house shields running. You'll see!" He cast his sharp eyes round the dusty hall as he chattered, a torch beam white in his hands. The cobwebs and white cloths like drifts of snow only heightened my sense of unreality, as though we were not in Maddalo House at all, but a stage set wrought to imitate it, and the play was not set to go on until the morrow. Evidently noting the cloths himself, Kaffu added, "Might be morning afore I can 'ire some lads from town to set *everything* 'ere to rights, but we'll 'ave it done. Depend on it."

"Not to worry. I'll have the guards set to clearing the tarps, sirrah," I said, and passed the fellow a single hurasam for his pains. The gold glinted warmly in the torch beam and in the light from Valka's glowsphere. "I'll have them tossed on the veranda. I trust you and Gren can take it from there in the morning?"

The groundskeeper's eyes widened at the sight of the gold coin. He took it, and seizing my three-fingered hand, he knelt to kiss it. I, who had been a rat in the canals of Borosevo once, understood the value of such wealth to such a one. To the man I'd become, it was almost worthless. The coined specie of the Imperium represented little more than barter chits for those commodities beneath the notice of interstellar commerce. It was a fortune for him.

A moment after, Kaffu rose and hurried with his torch into the depths of the old abbey for the cellars where the power and shield generators had slumbered these hundred and seven long years.

"You live here?" Oliva asked when the groundskeeper had gone. He shrugged the mandora higher on his shoulder and came further into the room, steps crinkling the drop cloth that covered the vast Jaddian carpet. His dark eyes scanned the entrance hall, taking in the high vaults, the semicircular arches, the rich wood carvings and round windows. "Is this . . . was this a Cid Arthurian *fordgron*?" he asked, using the proper name for a temple monastery of that syncretic cult.

"It was," I said, moving toward the fixture at the base of one stair rail. Laying my hand on the marble railing, I looked up the grand staircase where it split and ran left and right to the balcony that overlooked the entry. "Ninth millennium. The warrior monks were among the first to colonize Nessus, prior to annexation. When the Empire arrived, the Chantry—ah—liquidated the cult and gutted this place. They destroyed most of the icons, but they spared the beams, see?" I pointed to where the heavy trusses and arches held up the high ceiling, each carved in the likenesses of vast, primordial serpents. "The wood's all imported. There were no trees on Nessus when the place was built."

"And the Merlin Tree?" Oliva asked.

"Cut down, I'm afraid." I studied Oliva then a long moment. Had I misjudged him?

Oliva shook his head, whistled appreciatively. "Must have been damned expensive flying all this in," he said. "You know how much the Consortium charges for that kind of import? What is that, anyway? Cedar?"

I told him I wasn't sure.

"I only wondered," he said, and gestured down the side hall. "Those round arches . . . and the windows. Classic Cid Arthurian style."

"I didn't realize you were a historian, commander."

Oliva shrugged, eyes lingering on the draconic shapes graven into the support beams that held up the upper floors and from which hung the dead chandeliers. Pulling his eyes away, he asked, "Where would you like my people?" Oliva and his lieutenants, Karras and Magaryan—as well as the rest of his little band—were to be quartered with us. To keep them from talking in the city, so Commandant Lynch had said when he ordered us from the anchor station, but I knew better. Had the Commandant and Magnarch Venantian simply wanted to keep Oliva and company from idle chatter, they might have left the whole team in fugue, or else confined them to quarters on the anchorage or at Fort Horn.

The LIO man and his fellows from SpecSec were meant to keep eyes on us. There would be more security further out. Men posted in the village, patrols on chariots circling the grounds, just as before. The Magnarch and the Emperor both had not forgotten how the Chantry tried to kill me on Thermon, or set Udax against me at Gododdin. Nor had they forgotten Irshan and the Empress's little plot.

The Emperor's man Hector Oliva may have been, and though I was myself the Emperor's man, I was still Hadrian Marlowe.

Valka answered for me. "There are some rooms in the east wing. We'll walk that way." She began leading Oliva up the stairs, passing me by the rail. I watched her go with a fond smile, a sadness deep in my soul. One hundred seven years we'd been gone. I'd spent fifty-one of them conscious. A lifetime.

Too long.

"Hadrian?" Valka had stopped halfway to the landing, turned back, and something in the way she stood—the cant of her broad hips, the angle of her jaw, or the way the tip of one ear poked through her loose, long hair—smote my heart. I was not quite a dead man. Not yet. My heart still beat, blood sang. "Aren't you coming?"

In answer, I reached up and tugged the weighted cloth free from the fixture that topped the end post of the rail, sending waves of dust sheeting through the air. The fabric tore on the wrought-iron stave that formed the centerpiece of the fixture and hit the ground with a soft *thump*.

The banner beneath hung from the stave, nearly so tall as a man, its woven red-on-black jacquard astonishingly clean and dark in that un-lighted hall of dust and white linens. The pitchfork and pentacle sigil shone in the light from Valka's glowsphere. For a brief moment, nothing moved, and I felt myself a character in a marble frieze, a tableau: Valka, Oliva, the standard, and myself. Not living men at all, but memories. Ghosts.

It was the Red Company's standard. *My* Red Company. *My* House Marlowe. House Marlowe-Victorian.

Victorian. Victorious.

A lie.

The terrible urge to howl and tear the flag from its staff roared up in me, and I gripped the edge of the flag to pull it down.

"Hadrian," Valka's bright voice lit the room once more, and I jerked my hand away. "Come on."

Kaffu must have reached the cellar generators, for the house lights came on as we showed the commander to his room. Oliva thanked us and en-tered the dusty suite. I heard him sneeze again as he summoned Lieuten-ants Karras and Magaryan on his terminal as we left him, but we did not linger. Valka and I proceeded instead along the freshly lighted corridor to the chambers we had shared all the long decades of our exile.

I felt even more a ghost on entering the old bedchamber. Here too white linens covered everything, covered the carved wooden bedstead and the Jaddian carpets, hung over paintings and counters and shelves. I was a phantom wandering the ruins of my former life, a life that belonged almost to some other man, some *greater* man, some man who never suffered the pits and scourges of Dharan-Tun. I feared to pull the sheet from the mirror, feared to see the cringing shadow I'd become staring back at me out of Hadrian's Marlowe's glass. And more, I feared to look out the darkened windows, to see the lights of the village of Fons in the distance and think of ordinary men.

I had thought my time on Colchis sufficient balm, but some wounds never truly heal. One cannot step in the same river twice, and home is not home when you return, for you are not yourself. The man you were yesterday died yesterday, and is only a piece of the man of today, as you will be tomorrow.

Valka had stripped the covering from the bed, and the dark wood gleamed, posts and headboard graven with the shapes of birds and flowers, rich enough for any king. It did not seem right that I should sleep in so fine a bed while those others who had sailed with me slumbered on the black sands of Eue, and in the bellies of the numberless Pale.

It was not right that I should live at all, with them dead.

But there is little right in all the universe, and none which we do not fight for and make for ourselves.

"I'll check the baths," Valka said. We had been up for more than twenty-four standard hours at a stretch by then, between our descent and the final interview with Lynch before processing. "We should wash up and get some sleep."

"I'm not tired," I lied, moving to the vanity beneath the covered mirror where Jinan's old basin ought still to be. Right where I had left it. Bracing myself, I pulled the cloth from the mirror, and quailed as I met the eye of the creature in the glass.

Valka's voice floated in from the other room. "You have to sleep, Hadrian. They'll be at our throats tomorrow."

She was right, and so I only grunted in reply. The cycle of interview and inquiry, of debrief and describe begun on Colchis had begun again, and we would spend days without end in meetings, recounting all that had happened since we left this place. The Magnarch and his people had ensured we were returned in relative secrecy, and that would give him time, time to spin and structure the official story before all hell broke loose. That was why we had been restored to Maddalo House. In the Magnarch's palaces, any number of servants, soldiers, and civil functionaries would know that Hadrian Marlowe yet lived. Out here, only Oliva's men and Commandant Lynch and the soldiers on the anchorage knew I had returned.

And Kaffu, of course. And Kaffu would be enough.

I could hear the stories already.

'E's back, don't you know? the groundskeeper would say in his cups.

There were light in the old abbey last night! a housewife would say to her salaryman.

You mean the devil's manor? Do you reckon he's back? a drunkard would ask his barkeep. And so the story would go, spreading through Fons and the surrounding villages until the rumor was like brushfire in the countryside.

The Devil? The Halfmortal?

I thought 'e was dead.

The thought almost made me smile—even in the mirror, and so I tugged the cloth covering the counter beneath it free. I did smile then, for there it was, undisturbed these last eleven decades, right where I'd left it. Right where I'd hoped it would be.

Valka's phylactery.

The silver half-moon pendant inscribed with the superimposed letters *V* and *O* lay without its chain in the bottom of the bowl. It must have slid from the chain it shared with the Quiet's shell by chance and so been left behind when Anju and the other servants had packed our effects for the journey to Padmurak. So small it was and innocuous, they must have simply left it, not knowing what it was.

I pressed my eyes shut and held the precious thing in my palm.

Their carelessness had likely saved it. I might have lost it in Dharan-Tun, lost it as I had lost my rings, as I had lost the Quiet's shell—though that providence had restored to me.

"Valka!" My voice broke. "Valka! I found it!" I moved toward the bathroom door, holding the phylactery aloft for her to see. "It was here all along! Just here!"

Golden eyes went wide in the warm light of the bath, and she hurried forward to see. Her own phylactery—containing a crystallized preserve of my own blood—hung on its chain between her pale breasts. She'd half-undressed while I remained in the bedchamber, and steam was rising from the marble bath behind her. Already I could smell the telltale aromas of sandalwood and sweet smoke.

"I thought I'd lost it . . ." I said, numb with relief.

She kissed me, and drawing back said, "I always thought 'twas still here." She closed my fingers over the half-moon pendant. "Put it back on, and get undressed."

I awoke with Valka naked and curled beside me, my fugue-sick limbs still aching. Pale sun fell through the great round windows and glass door that fronted the balcony overlooking the English garden. Somewhere below, a lark was singing, soft herald of the day. After so many years in silence on Dharan-Tun and aboard the *Ascalon*, and after nearly a decade with only the harsh braying of the Colchean gulls, the music and the beauty of its song was like the opening of spring on a world of ceaseless winter.

Valka's tattooed arm lay athwart my chest, and so I lay there a long while, tracing the delicate spiral markings that denoted her place in the Clan Onderra. Her *saylash*, or so they called it in far-off Tavros. Closely I had studied the shape of that tattoo on many mornings for so many of the long years of my life, and yet still it seemed to me that always there was some facet, some new detail to discover, so intricate was its design. I did not want to disturb her, and so I lay listening to the lark a long while, and watched the yellow sunlight brighten the dusty chamber . . . until at last she moved and freed me from her clutches.

After another quiet moment, I arose and dressed.

Old Anju was long dead, and the larders and chillers alike stood empty. Arrangements would have to be made for Oliva's people to travel to market in Fons or one of the other villages to restock the old house. Possibly a cook and a couple servants would be found as well. There would be time to make such arrangements in the weeks ahead. I had no notion how long we might remain at Maddalo House. A season? A year? Or seventy . . . as before?

With the day opening like the violets, it would not be long before the Magnarch's men arrived. Perhaps old Karol Venantian would come himself.

I thought not.

Some LIO man would come and repeat every question Dorr and his office has asked on Colchis. They would want the whole story, the complete narrative from the attack of the liberalists upon the bridge in Vedatharad to the moment I stepped onto the *Ascalon* and surrendered to Dorr's men.

I would tell them *almost* everything, as I had told the others *almost* everything.

I had told no one how I, too, had given the enemy the Emperor's itinerary. That confession was for the Emperor, and for the Emperor alone—or so I told myself in the pale light of dawn that morning in the gardens.

A long time I stood by the fish pond, watching the golden shadows of the koi moving in their slow and thoughtless way. I was still standing there, recalling the splash of alien fish in the waters of my cavern cell, when all the air filled with droning, and a great wind bent the cypress trees. Looking up, I saw a black flier streak overhead and circle the domes and pointed gables of Maddalo House on its approach, sending waves through the tall, green grass. Not moving from my spot, I marked its progress, watching the broad wings fold up as the flier settled on the front lawn.

"Right on cue."

I did not go to meet them, but stumped over to the green metal table where Valka and I once had taken dinner with Bassander Lin. I seated myself and waited, knowing someone would be along to fetch me.

That was where they found me: four praetorians in the violet-fringed white of the Magnarch's guard. Gravel crunched under their armored heels as they came down the path from the house. Their masks were not the black slates of common legionnaires, but fashioned—like the mask of my own armor—in the images of serene human faces, blank-eyed and expressionless.

Their leader—whose gilded crest bore a plume of purple feathers—saluted crisp as any soldier I had seen and said, not unkindly, "Come with me, sir."

Their indigo cloaks floated on the wind ahead of me as I followed them back up to the house, along the lower hall past the darkened kitchens and the servants' quarters and up through the entrance hall to a parlor that looked out over the cliffs and the rolling countryside beyond. Miles away, the city of Sananne shone pale silver, and behind it, the great monoliths of the Imperial shipyards rose white as mountains against the eggshell blue of the morning sky.

But in the parlor itself, not remote, but terribly present, the Magnarch Karol Venantian—my one-time jailer—sat in my best chair.

"Lord Marlowe!" Karol Venantian said. The man looked positively ancient. The Magnarch of Centaurus had been an old man so long as I had known him. I did not know his breeding, but House Venantian seemed one of those that, while long-lived, enjoyed a shorter, brighter youth and a long, trailing old age. He must have been well north of six hundred years old by then, perhaps nearly seven, and his white hair—thinning when I had left Nessus for Padmurak—was nearly all gone. His bare scalp was spotted with age, but his eyes were sharp as ever, and the fragile hand he raised still glittered with rings.

Knowing the sign, I went to one knee as was expected, took the withered hand, and kissed the golden signet on the thumb.

"I confess," Venantian began, voice airy and dry as bones, "that you were a mystery I was certain would never be solved. I have read the testimony you and your doctor gave to Velan Dorr on Colchis. I am . . . sorry. Sorry for the treatment you received at the hands of the enemy." He made a gesture that I should rise, and I did so, mindful of the mounded drop cloths that lay piled about the edges of the recently excavated room. Evidently, Oliva's men had not made it to the parlor the night before. I would have to tell Kaffu to have the tarps all removed. "Terrible," Venantian was saying. "Truly terrible. Is it true you lost your entire company?"

Venantian's question fell with all the bluntness of old age, hit me like a slap. I tucked my chin to hide the flush of shame and fury that lit my cheeks, and sucked in a breath. Mastering myself, I fixed my eyes on a point over the seated Magnarch's shoulder, and said, "You read my report."

"I did."

"Then Your Grace knows I did. We were betrayed . . . betrayed by the Lothrians."

"So I heard," the Magnarch said. "Yet explain to me: you had a warship at your disposal, did you not? You might have resisted. Might have escaped. Might have at least transmitted warning via telegraph as your ship fell. You did not. Why?"

I had anticipated this. Karol Venantian was never my friend, but still the accusation rankled. My jaw so tight it might have been wired shut, I said, "I was no position *to* resist, Your Grace. Per my report, I was on the planet's surface."

Venantian raised a withered hand. "Your negligence has cost us *decades*, Lord Marlowe. Decades. Had word but reached us sooner, we might be better prepared. The Emperor might be safely here or on his way back to Forum. Were you any other officer, I would order you end your life in atonement for so gross a miscarriage of duty."

Miscarriage of duty? The words resonated in my chest, and for a moment the room blurred before my eyes. A little breath escaped me, and I said, "It wouldn't take."

The Magnarch arched one wispy eyebrow, but did not rise to the bait. "As it stands, the Emperor left orders that you were to be conveyed to him for judgment when and if you should appear."

I blinked, mind suddenly blank. "The Emperor?" The Emperor was in transit—in fugue—and had been ever since I climbed down the winding stair from Nov Belgaer to find Dorr's men waiting for me. What was more, his fleet was traveling at warp, and no signal—not even quantum telegraph— could penetrate the folded space-envelope that encased his ship. He could not have received word that I was living, not at least until he put into port at Ibarnis or Aulos or wherever it was he was going now.

Unless word had reached him *before* I returned to Imperial custody.

Unless . . .

"We had word from your man, Aristedes. We recovered him some twenty years back. He washed up in a fugue pod on the borders of the system, kept babbling about a Cielcin Emperor—said you were dead— even under amytal. The Emperor insisted we treat you as missing, and left orders to remand you to him should you appear."

Fearing my knees would fail me, I sank onto the low ottoman of the seat opposite the Magnarch's chair. "Lorian," I breathed, and shaded my eyes with a hand. "He made it!" Lorian was alive. Dorayaica had been true to its word, at least. "You said you found him on the edge of the system?"

Too clearly I pictured the MINOS ship as it skirted the heliopause of Nessus's sun, pausing just long enough to eject its sleeping messenger. Weeks must have passed before the emergency beacon reached the nearest in-system relay and alerted the Nessus Defense Force. I imagined them dredging the lonely pod from the deep black of space, searchlights piercing the darkness like plunderers cracking open a tomb.

"Where is he?" I asked.

"We have him here," Lord Venantian replied. "He was too much a security risk to grant him freedom of the planet, so he's been on ice at Fort Horn for most of his stay."

My heart would not leave my mouth. Lorian alive! It had seemed too cruel a joke that black day, and it had been so long! So many years! Alive! "I would like to see him."

"In time," Venantian said.

"He is my officer! I have every right to see—"

"Be silent, lord!" Venantian at last dropped his paper-thin hand. "In time, I said. We have more pressing concerns for the moment. Namely, you."

"Me?" I glowered at him, finding it very difficult to focus with so many and such extreme emotions cascading through my head. None of Gibson's old cantrips seemed to work just then, or to matter. Lorian was alive, after all!

Oblivious to the storm in my soul, the Magnarch carried on. "Word of your disgrace cannot be allowed to circulate. You will remain confined to these grounds for the duration of your stay. A guard and house staff will be provided to ensure the details of your misadventure do not leak to the public or the press."

"My *disgrace*?" I stood again, sharply, spat the word back at him with such venom the praetorian nearest me fell back a step, hand going to the hilt of his unkindled sword.

Cold as ice, Venantian leaned back in *my* chair. "You were sent to curry favor with the Lothrians. Instead, I am told the whole Commonwealth is against us. The gray men have allied themselves with the Cielcin! What do you call that, if not disgrace?"

Just what had Lorian told this man?

"They were in bed with the Cielcin when we arrived. They had been for decades, maybe longer." I almost shouted the words. "You said you read my report! The Extrasolarians had infiltrated their Grand Conclave, suborned them, offered them Earth knows what. You think this is *my* fault?"

The Magnarch's bright eyes narrowed. "You must understand this from our perspective. Your man Aristedes appears and tells us the *Tamerlane* was lost with all hands. That you selected him—and him alone, of all your companions—at this xenobite's behest, no less, to deliver a message to us. And then you appear. Not here, in Sananne. Not on Forum. Not at any Legion base. But on Colchis. At the very library where you unearthed a Mericanii daimon."

"What has any of this to do with Horizon?" I said, naming the machine we'd unearthed on Colchis. I could only gape at him.

"You tell me!" Venantian snapped. "What were you and your Tavrosi woman doing on Colchis?"

Still gaping, I managed to say, "You think . . . you think me a traitor?"

"Or a coward," he answered. "Don't take me for a fool. What were you doing on Colchis?"

"Mourning!" I snarled, and turned my back on the Supreme Lord of the Centaurine Provinces. I would not be forced to explain to *Karol Venantian* of all people that Siran, alone of all my company, had a proper grave, and that I had gone to be near it, to mourn in the only place in all creation—save Eue itself—that was so close to Death. To my very great surprise, Venantian did not speak, and after a moment I turned back. "You *dare* accuse me . . ." I was seething, could barely get the words out.

The Magnarch shook his head. "I accuse nothing. We must simply be sure. Legion Intelligence will find the truth. They always do."

"You seriously think me one of their agents?" I snarled. "Me?" I held up my ruined hand. "Look at me, my lord!" I hissed, and when the Magnarch opened his mouth to reply I shouted him down. "Look at me! See these fingers? Dorayaica bit them off itself! And these!" I showed him the white stripes of scar on my fingers and arms. "Here is where they flayed me! And this!" I turned my head, fingers to my temple as I leaned to present the crescent scar that just barely vanished into my hair. "This is where they cut me so the blood would not pool in my head while they hanged me naked by my ankles!" I let my hand fall. "This is only a taste, Magnarch. Shall I remove my shirt?" Again he opened his mouth to reply, again I stepped over him. "Seven years! Seven years I was in their hands. Seven years I suffered, and would have died had not my *Tavrosi woman*," I hurled the words back at him with all the contempt I could muster, "bent heaven and Earth herself to save me and to try and save the others!" My nostrils flared, and I took a step nearer the old man in his seat, prompting his praetorians to step forward with raised hands.

I backed off, raising my own hands, palms open in show of peace. "You asked me a question earlier," I said, not finished. "You asked me if it was true I lost my entire company. I did not *lose* them. I know precisely where they are. They are dead. Destroyed by *our* enemy, an enemy it seems to me you little understand, Your Grace."

"Are you quite done?" Lord Venantian snapped, at last working up the energy to cut across my tirade. "I have not missed your histrionics, Lord Marlowe." Clawed hands gripped the leather arms of the chair, manicured fingers dripping with rubies, diamonds, and amethysts. "Whatever your condition, I have my orders. We will await the Emperor's message, and if he orders me remand you to him, I will do so—but I will not do so until I am quite convinced it is safe."

Safe. I shook my head. For all his contempt, I knew that Venantian was not wholly unreasonable. Even in matters of poine, former prisoners were always subject to examination. Always put to the Question. There was no telling what might have been implanted or altered in a man in captivity. History is full of such tales, of wars fought with cloned usurpers, of ransomed sons returned with memories and personas changed.

I felt my anger quiet, grow cold and brittle. "Why did you come, Your

Grace?" I glared down at him. "If you meant only to impugn my honor, you might have confined yourself to a holograph and spared both of us the time."

The Magnarch blinked up at me, surprise stretching his wrinkled face. "Respect," he said simply. "Whatever I may think of you personally, lord, you are no common soldier. Your rank and deeds are worth something." He inclined his head toward my ruined hand. "I will send for my physicians."

I hid the maimed appendage in a pocket of my coat and was silent.

"I do not believe you a traitor, Lord Marlowe," said Karol Venantian, gesturing for the nearest praetorian to advance with his cane, "but one does not rule as Magnarch by *belief*. I will not gamble with the Emperor's life." He rose slowly, groaning as he went. Standing, the Magnarch was far from impressive. A gilded stick-figure, back bent, shoulders hunched, shorter than I remembered. "When word of your survival reaches the masses, they will say it is another miracle. They'll repeat their nonsense about how you cannot be killed, but I know better." He produced a white kerchief and promptly spat into it, coughed gently, and leaned upon his gilt cane. "Martyrs are better than heroes. It would have been better if you had died with your men."

"My men, Your Grace, had other opinions," I said darkly, remembering how desperately they had fought to get me to that shuttle. Even as I spoke, Karol Venantian brushed past me, flanked by his ivory-masked praetorians. As he reached the circular door that led back to the hall I called after him. "Lord Magnarch!"

Venantian halted, but did not turn.

"Thank you," I said, "for bringing me here before the Chantry could test me." I let the rest go unsaid. Venantian knew as well as I that the Chantry wanted me dead.

"Emperor's orders," the old man said. "I pray you pass the Question, Marlowe, but I will have questions of my own, after, and I will have answers."

He turned away and was gone.

CHAPTER 9

MADDALO HOUSE

AS I PASSED OVER my trial on Thermon, as I passed over much of what occurred on Colchis, I shall pass over much of what occurred in the long weeks of trial and interrogation Valka and I endured at the hands of Venantian's officers. You have journeyed far with me, Reader, and so know what I have suffered and that I have spoken truth.

I had endured the Question at the hands of an inquisitor named Marius aboard the anchorage atop the hightower above Sananne, watched by Lynch and a trio of scholiasts sent by Venantian himself. They had learned the lesson of Thermon well, and knew better than to leave me alone with any clergyman of the Holy Terran Chantry.

My humanity had been proven beyond all doubt, and Valka's status as a Tavrosi clansman spared her the same scrutiny, though in the coming weeks it would take Venantian's scholiasts and logothetes many thousand man-hours and miles of ink to finally spare her any confrontation with the Inquisition. Ultimately it was my name and the Emperor's countenance that spared her.

Through all that, the true interrogations began, as day after day faceless and forgettable logothetes belonging to the Magnarch's private office or to Legion Intelligence and Special Security asked question after rephrased question, compared my responses to the reports we'd made on Colchis, to Valka's testimony—often as not collected in another room—and to the statements Lorian had given under amytal when they collected him twenty years prior. I submitted myself to interrogation under truth drugs, and tried to imagine Legion interrogators dealing with a drugged and manic-babbling Lorian.

Of Lorian himself, there was no sign.

Through all this the old house was cleaned and restored to something like its former glory. Contractors were brought in—terse men with a military edge about them—to re-order Maddalo House and to clear away the drop cloths and the dust, to perform maintenance on and to optimize the villa's generators and house shields. The well had dried up and needed excavating after the cisterns ran out, and for two days we relied on water rations to drink and wash with.

I had no illusions that the Magnarch's contractors were not also installing surveillance equipment in the house, and so had no choice but to submit myself to their spying. During my interrogations, I learned from one particularly sallow and pinch-faced woman that they had stripped the *Ascalon* and combed through her structures and her systems. They had acquired—among other things—the coordinates for Eue. She would not answer my questions regarding whether or not the Imperium had dispatched an expedition into those unmapped regions to investigate the Cielcin's black capital. I think it must have happened, if not then, then at some later time—under Caesar's own orders.

I do not know that story, nor can I guess its end. Did the Legions sail in force against Akterumu and burn that profane city? Does dead Miudanar still dream terrific dreams on the black sands of Eue?

For years on that long journey to Colchis alone, I had considered deleting the coordinates from the ship's navigational matrix, but I never did, anticipating something like the Magnarch's doubts. They would want to verify my story, would send a probe at least to image and scan the world.

I had not expected Venantian to call me a traitor, but I had known that I could not speak of a Cielcin planet—could not tell my story at all—if I did not provide some proof. I had made no reference to the Enar or the Watchers in any of my reports or depositions, save only to reinforce my earlier descriptions of Syriani Dorayaica—the new-crowned Shiomu Elusha of the Cielcin—as a religious leader as well as a secular one.

Prophet *and* king.

Venantian's physicians arrived a week or so after our first meeting: two scholiasts and a Durantine surgeon named Elkan, who performed a complete holograph and resonance image of my body there at Maddalo House and who laid plans for skin grafts and the repair of my ruined shoulder, as well as the restoration of my lost fingers.

"The fingers? These will be no problem," Elkan said, peering down at his tablet. "The shoulder will be worse. Not impossible. But worse. The lateral and anterior deltoids must both be removed and replaced with new tissues. There is too much scarification to ever salvage them. We may save the teres muscles with grafts, but it may be necessary to replace even these. As for the bones themselves . . . do you see where the humerus meets the cavity? The dislocation never set right, and there's been a lot of grinding. We can replace the bones. Ceramic inserts. Perhaps even printed adamant like your other arm." He pointed at the images on his display. "It will be a long surgery, and even longer for you to recover, even with beta injections."

"Can you replace the whole arm?" I asked, gripping the left.

Elkan blinked at me with beady, dark eyes, strangely bird-like. "Oh, that won't be necessary. It takes weeks to regenerate even the bones in your fingers. The arm would take month!"

"What if you printed the bones?"

"Like your left arm?" Elkan sucked his teeth. "It is an option, but a time-consuming option. The outcomes may be better long term, but you would need to devote years to conditioning and retraining neural pathways."

Still gripping my left arm, I said, "I remember."

"I simply don't think it necessary. Most of the damage is in your shoulder, in the glenoid cavity. Replacing the arm would do little to help that, and replacing the ribs and bones of the shoulder . . . my lord, it would be best to induce coma and put you in a beta tank. Full physical recovery could take . . . a year?"

I told him I understood.

"We can start on the fingers as early as tomorrow. Regrowth will be painful. You remember puberty, yes?" He tried to smile, but the effect was less than settling. "It will be like that, but worse. The fingers will grow like . . . branchings? On a plant? The bones will ache, but you will be able to work with the correctives in place. I will need to monitor your progress, of course, but I am only a short flight away." He put away his tablet and shut his medical case, nodded to one of his aides. "I will return tomorrow with the heavy equipment. As for the shoulder . . ."

"That will have to wait until after this round of inquiries," said one of the scholiasts, an elderly woman with a tight-lipped, grave little face.

Elkan stood wearily. He was very short, nearly so tall on his feet as I was sitting down. He blew out a long breath. "Fingers!" he exclaimed. "Fingers will be easy! You will see!" He reached up and patted me on the shoulder. "We may perhaps be able to do something about the scars, as well. Grafts are a small matter." He extended one forefinger and traced the marks Dorayaica's claws had made across my cheek.

I raised a hand and forced his hand away. "Forget it," I said. Somehow,

the idea of wearing a false face disgusted me more than any thought of
shoulders or fingers—more than the false bones of my left arm.

I could not say why.

Kharn Sagara had rebuilt my left arm in mere days only because he had
not grown new bones. The adamant sheath that encased the new marrow
in my left arm had not only given me bones that even highmatter could
not break, but had dramatically accelerated the recovery process. The new
tissues had been atrophied and raw, but physical therapy had in time restored the left arm until it was the equal of the right.

But Elkan's methods called for the growth of new bone, and new bone
was slow in growing. The process ached and stank to high heaven. The
brace and correctives that encased my right hand recalled the very device
Tor Alma and my father's lesser physicians had given me to treat my broken
arm as a boy: a nightmare contraption of stainless steel that kept the joints
in alignment and kept me from bending my wrist. Hair-fine and flexible
glass needles pierced the back of my hand, inhibited the nerves, reducing
pain and inducing paralysis where it was most important to protect the
new growth.

Some part of me wished I could watch the stumps grow, but a plastic
baffle concealed the missing fingers, leaving me only with the horrid smell
and the dull ache of referred pain felt all the way up my arm, and the faint
pulse of blood in new capillaries.

"Doctor Elkan says it'll be about six weeks like this," I said, raising the
gauntlet with a wince. "They'll start on the shoulder after. Apparently the
anesthetic for general surgery will disrupt the pharmacons inducing the new
growth. So it has to be one thing at a time." Lowering my right hand, I
gripped the little metal cylinder I was toying with in my left hand to stop
myself from hissing.

Valka shuffled the papers on one of her many desks, leaned back in her
chair. "'Tis really legal for them to interrogate you while you're medi-
cated?" she asked. "One would think 'twould invalidate your testimony."

"They've been very careful about that," I said dryly, and shut my eyes
a beat. "They've not given me anything that would compromise me." They
had, in fact, kept me on simple anti-inflammatory drugs, foregoing the
heavier painkillers.

"How very generous of them!" Valka exclaimed, snorting her derision.

Valka's study occupied the whole of an upper hall in the east wing's fourth and topmost level. It overlooked the main lawn that stretched away north and eastward to the wall and tree line that encircled the old abbey's grounds. Beyond it, I marked the thin columns of smoke rising from the village of Fons. The city of Sananne was invisible from this window; the great city and her shipyards lay away south, down the cliffs, and over the rolling low country.

But I *could* see Sir Hector Oliva.

The young knight stood out on the grass, taking shots at a bale of hay he had purchased in the village. The contents of his second case—the flat one tall as he was—had revealed themselves in due time.

"Is he still out there?" Valka craned her neck.

"All morning," I answered her, and turned the cylinder in my working hand. It was heavy for its size, about two inches long and three-quarters of an inch in diameter.

As I watched, the young knight raised his antique bow and smoothly fired. The arrow made no sound, but struck the center of its target half a hundred yards away.

"He can't fight with that thing, surely?" she asked, sliding from her seat to join me at the window.

Again I turned the cylinder over in my hand, sent it dancing along my knuckles like some plagiarius toying with a gold coin. "I guess everyone needs their hobbies." Not paying proper attention, I bumped my right hand against the sill and groaned as pain lanced up my arm. I dropped the little cylinder.

Before I could retrieve it, Valka stooped and scooped it up. "Careful, barbarian! You're not so young as you used to be!"

"I'm young enough!" I said, and held out my hand for the cylinder.

Valka weighed the thing in her palm, frowned down at it. "This is the highmatter reservoir from that assassin's sword?"

"It is," I said, and made an impatient gesture. "I was thinking about finding a craftsman to build a new hilt for it. I need a sword." The old thing had been lying there in Jinan's basin, right beside Valka's phylactery, left there as though by the hand of God. "But there aren't many places that can do the work properly. Elos, Phaia . . . Jadd . . ."

Holding the reservoir between thumb and forefinger, Valka lifted it into the light. Its surface was dull titanium, without mark or joint save the valve on the cap end, and the ancient, Greek letter Φ, a mint mark. Within, trapped in its inert state, lay about a pound of highmatter. How long had the particle accelerators fired to produce so much of the exotic material? Years? Decades? Pure chance alone determined when and how often the rare five-quark baryons were produced—one at a time—and it took trillions to make a sword, to assemble those baryons into stranger atoms, to link those atoms into a single, liquid molecule and to shape that molecule into a blade sharp enough to cut almost anything. All the foundries on Elos and Phaia might produce but half a dozen such cores in a year, or half that number.

"You said he was Jaddian, yes?" Valka asked.

"The assassin?" I glanced back down at Hector, who was now running tangent to his target, firing as he moved, drawing arrows from a quiver at his hip. "He was. Yes. A Maeskolos."

Valka tapped the letter Φ with one glossy fingernail. "This is not Jaddian."

"No. It's a *phi*." I took the core back from her, ran my thumb over the mint's mark. "It's for Phaia, the planet where the core was made. All the Imperial swords are designed on Phaia or Elos, so the cores get a *phi* or *lambda*, depending. The Jaddians make their own."

Valka blinked at me. "Is not *lambda* L? Why are the Elos swords not *E*?"

I shrugged.

"So this is from an Imperial weapon?" she asked for clarification. When I only nodded, she continued, "Why would a Maeskolos use an Imperial sword? Is that not strange?"

Again, I could only shrug, a rigid and asymmetrical motion with my right shoulder as it was. "Possibly one of the Lions gave it to him. Prince Ricard, perhaps. Or Prince Philip. Maybe Lord Bourbon himself." Thinking of Augustin Bourbon again sent a numb ache through me deeper than the ache in my bones, and I turned away from the window and the light.

Valka had settled back into her seat, surrounded by loose phototypes printed and pinned to the plaster walls above the polished wood of her desk. "'Twas not the princes', surely! They were no knights. Do you not need to be one to have one of these?"

"Neither was Bourbon," I said. "And you only need to be a knight to wear one, technically." Having said that, I had carried Sir Olorin's blade for decades before the Emperor knighted me, though I had done so almost exclusively in realms beyond the Empire. Bassander Lin, too, had carried such a weapon for centuries, and Bassander was even still no knight— though perhaps he should have been. One certainly had to be a knight to commission such a blade.

I told Valka as much, and she mused, "I wonder who it was made for."

"I'm sure it belonged to Bourbon," I said. "He was behind Breathnach, behind the knife-missile. He put the princes up to their little game—or the Empress did. She might have had a weapon to spare." I held the little thing in my palm, feeling the dreadful weight of it, so dense and cold. "Surely neither of them would be so foolish as to arm an assassin with their own blade?"

"Maybe not," Valka agreed. No one was that foolish. "But a blade he wasn't supposed to have?"

"Bourbon?" My eyes darted to Valka's face, narrowed. I saw where she was going, and shook my head. "You're not serious."

"His father *was* a rebel," Valka said. "Was he a knight?"

"I don't know."

"Suppose it was. Suppose that sword was Gibson's."

I closed my hand over the cylinder. "There's no way to know."

"But suppose it *was*," she said, more forcefully. "It could be true. And if it is . . ." A smile lit her face, making her eyes like stars. "Perhaps 'twas meant to be."

"Meant to be . . ." I weighed the little thing in my hand again, turned back to the window, to Sir Hector and his bow. The young commander had approached his target to retrieve his arrows for another round.

I heard Valka moving once more at my back, and leaned against the edge of the window. "You lead a charmed life," she said softly.

"Had you said *cursed*, I might have agreed," I said, and lifted the core to the light, examining it as a jeweler might some fresh-cut diamond.

Gibson's blade. It *was* possible. Philippe Bourbon might have surrendered just such a weapon when he was sent to Belusha, might have left it in the keeping of his son. Thus Augustin might have found himself in possession of an antique weapon no living smith could identify, and a painful reminder of his family's sordid past. Save that mint mark, the core had no other identifying feature. No serial number. No incept date. Bourbon might have altered the hilt housing beyond all hope of recognition, transformed it into a new weapon entirely.

It would have been nigh untraceable, making it—in a sense—-the perfect instrument to hand an assassin. Not foolish at all.

Gibson's blade . . .

The universe is infinite, or so the scholiasts say, and I have seen that it is so. But it is infinite only in certain ways: in space and in potential. It is bounded in time, for time had a beginning—all magi agree—and so it

must have an end. As will we. Something in this asymmetry between infinite space and finite time, I think, explains all coincidences, conserving
fact as readily as other laws conserve matter and energy.

Or perhaps . . . it is only that we are human, and that our human lives
are woven together, and are more tightly bound by the action of the loom
of human drama.

"Gibson's blade . . ." I mused again, this time aloud. "Do you really
think so?"

"I think 'tis certainly possible," she said, "and anyway, 'tis a nice thought.
He would have wanted you to have it, had it been his to give. If it *was* Tor
Gibson's. You are his son, after all." She smiled up at me.

Hastily, I slid the core into a pocket of my tunic, shook my hand as
though it had burned me.

Valka's eyes never left me, and after a stiff and awkward moment, she
asked, "Do you think that what Dorayaica said is true? About the Quiet
creating the universe?"

As if burned a second time, I looked up at her, raised a finger to my ear
like a man hard of hearing asking her to repeat herself. Understanding the
sign for what it was, she spoke in Nordei. "They can't hear us," she said.
"'Tis a microphone on that windowsill, there." She pointed to the far wall.
"I forced a reset just now. An innocent enough looking fault. We have a
few minutes. Oliva's men will notice before long and send someone to
check on us."

Despite the peculiarities of our situation, I smiled, thinking back to
those early days in the palace of Balian Mataro. "Really takes you back,
doesn't it?"

Valka returned my smile. "Indeed, but answer my question."

"I think that Dorayaica believes it," I said without much hesitation. The
Cielcin lord had never lied. "And some portion of what it believes is true.
You saw the skull at Akterumu. The Watchers are real, Valka. The Quiet
are real—*is* real."

"But do you think it made . . . everything?" she asked.

"He," I corrected her. "The other . . ." I had to laugh, hearing the
words I spoke. "The other *Hadrians* I've met have called the Quiet *he*."

I saw Valka bristle, uncomfortable with this datum. "Why would they
say that?"

"I don't know," I told her, honestly. "When I try, I can reach them. Their
memories. These other Hadrians . . . these lives that never happened. Some
of them know things, things I'm sure I never learned. I remember . . .

being a slave on Emesh. And you and I, we were on *Echidna*—or was it *Typhon*? The Cielcin worldships. The ones the Empire impounded."

"We've never been to *Typhon* or *Echidna*," said Valka as soothingly as she could.

"I know!" I said, good hand on my heart. "But I remember! There was a map—I've seen it!" I stopped, looked at her with intent. "Does the name . . . Nairi mean anything to you?"

Valka shook her head.

"Or Vaiartu?" I asked.

"Hadrian." Valka's face darkened. "I don't know what you're talking about. These visions . . ."

"They're not visions!" I hissed. "They're memories! My memories!" I winced as a blast of pain lanced up my right arm, like all the growth of youth compressed from years to days. I imagined the fingers inside the baffle pressing against the skin from underneath and stretching. "I trust myself, at least."

That brought a small smile to Valka's face, but she did not reply, only cocked her head.

"But do I think he's a god? The Quiet?" I asked, returning to the real question. A twinge of the old scholiast rang out in me, and I advanced to the next question. "What is a god?" If a god were only something greater than the seeker, more developed than man, then the Quiet was a god beyond all doubt. But by that token, we men were gods to the Umandh, to the Cavaraad, and the other lesser races that dwelt among the stars. And what gods! Zeus and his debauched cabal of bloody-minded psychopaths could hardly be more degenerate.

We were just as mortal as the others . . . only flesh and blood.

But the Quiet?

What is a god?

Valka pursed her lips. "A creature in a fairy story."

"Only this story is true," I said, knowing well that shade of disdain in her voice. I had shared it once, disbelieving the fairy stories the Chanters told of Earth and her Son, the God Emperor. The Earth was just a lump of rock—*our* lump of rock, but a lump of rock all the same—and old William Windsor had been a man. A man *like me*, a man anointed by the Quiet, called to play a part, to lead mankind along the *shortest way* to an egg and a bassinet at the end of time.

But he was only a man, as was I.

"You believe it, then?" she asked.

"How can I not?" I asked her. "Valka, I was *dead*. You saw it."

Though he slay me, I will trust in him, my other self had said, and so I tried.

"But you believe that it—that he, whatever—created the universe? You said yourself the Quiet comes from the future. That it's born at the end of time. How can it create the universe if the universe created it?"

"Without beginning," I muttered, "or end. Sounds like a god to me."

The door to Valka's office opened suddenly, and the pale, waspish face of Lieutenant Karras appeared in the doorway. "Is everything all right?" he asked, a touch stupidly, given that there was no reason save the technical fault in the room's recording equipment to justify his intrusion. Realizing his mistake a moment too late, Karras flushed. "I heard raised voices," he added by way of damage control. Valka and I had been communicating in almost hushed tones.

Legion *intelligence*, indeed.

"You must have been imagining things, lieutenant," Valka said sweetly.

Almost feeling bad for the young junior officer, I said, "I assume our friends from the city are due shortly, is that it?"

"What?" Karras blinked, let the carved wooden door swing fully open. "Ah, yes. Yes, my lord. Within the hour."

I grinned at Valka. "I guess we'll finish this later," I said, and moved to kiss her swiftly upon the cheek.

"I'll be here when they need me," she said, returning to her work.

CHAPTER 10

SURVIVORS

NOT FOR THE FIRST time in my life, I found myself strapped to a bed. It was *my* bed at least, and not the cold, hard bed of a medica. Pale bandages bound my chest and upper arm, and I lay in a hazy sweat where the afternoon sun fell bright and cheery down upon me, exacerbating the cocktail of painkillers and healing factors thickening my blood.

My terminal sat on the table beside me, reciting passages from Orodes's *Theosophy*. The ancient Persian philosopher's words floated on the air like perfume, the artificially feminine voice of my terminal performing the recitation numb to inflection and meaning.

"Was it not thus that Ahura Mazda spoke to Mashya and Mashyana? 'You are man, you are the stewards of the world, you are created perfect in your devotion to me! Therefore be devoted to my law! Think good thoughts, speak good words, do good deeds, and worship no demons!"

I little understood him, understood only as I listened that this was the very god of fire and order the Jaddians worshiped to this day. My surgery had gone well, so Doctor Elkan said. The interrogations were over, and word had come from the Emperor that I was to meet him at his next destination: on Carteia. Grudgingly, Venantian had relented.

We had been on Nessus for a little less than a year, and just as Maddalo House was starting to feel real and really *home* again, we were looking to leave it. It would be some months before I was fit to leave, but the Emperor was on Ibarnis and expected to remain there for some months himself. There was time to heal before we must be aboard the *Ascalon* to rendezvous with the fleet at Carteia.

Despite my immobilized shoulder, I played with my regenerated fingers, tapping the fingertips against my thumb in sequence. One-two-three-four. One-two-three-four. Just as my regrown teeth had transformed my mouth and made it an alien landscape, the new-grown fingers made my hand seem like something other than my own.

Whose hand is this?

The question had almost the ring of one of Gibson's old meditative questions, and seemed to echo in his voice, mingling with Orodes's words from the terminal.

"*. . . only later did evil enter the hearts of men, and their minds were thoroughly corrupted. And Mashya and Mashyana proclaimed that evil had created the waters and the earth, the plants and the animals, the sun and moon and stars . . .*"

Whose hand is this?

Gibson's voice. Prince Philippe Bourbon's voice.

Strange that he should be so much more with me now I knew he was truly gone. But perhaps it was not strange at all. My dead outnumbered my living—as becomes true for each of us in time. The dead become ever closer companions as we grow old ourselves and nearer eternity. And afterlife or no, they live on in us.

Perhaps that is why it seems we have ghosts. Because we carry them in ourselves.

I kept tap-tapping my fingertips against my thumb—one-two-three-four, one-two-three-four . . .

Whose hand is this?

Not mine. They were not my hands. Not either of them. I no longer recognized them. The left—false-boned and scarred from my battle with Irshan—showed too the wheals of cryoburn where my rings had frozen to my flesh. The right had cryoburn to match, white and glassy, contrasted with the angry red marks where Dorayaica's torturers had loosened my skin and peeled the flesh away. My new fingers looked almost comical by comparison, perfect and clean.

"Earth and Emperor," came a dry, familiar voice, "look at you . . ."

Looking blearily round, I saw a child standing in the door to mine and Valka's bedchamber, dressed in the crisp blacks of an Imperial naval officer, one silver-ringed hand resting on the door frame, his head haloed by a nimbus of neatly shorn white hair.

With my left hand, I swatted about on the side table, trying to find my terminal and silence Orodes's burbling *Theosophy*.

"*. . . so I say to you that God created time to trap . . .*"

I found it, silenced the cool, feminine voice. There were tears forming in my eyes, and the whole room swam. "Lorian?" I barely managed the word. Maybe it was the medication, but I hardly recognized the diminutive commander. "Is it you? What happened to your hair?"

"What?" Aristedes took a step into the room, feeling the short and unruly mane that stuck up from his scalp. "Oh, this! Regulation! Commandant Kartzinel took issue with what he called *flouting tradition*, if you can believe it." The intus advanced slowly toward me, moving like a man in a daze. Through the haze of my painkillers, I recognized the numb and hollow look in the younger man's eyes, the tired shock of old memories rushing in, old scars reopening. "It really is you."

I raised my eyebrows, slid my terminal back over my left wrist with a movement of my fingers. "You were expecting someone else?"

In answer, Lorian gestured to my bandages. "What did they do to you?"

"The doctors? Or the Pale?"

"To your arm."

"Is this a part of the questioning?" I asked, and tried to laugh. The motion only brought pain, and I coughed—which was worse. "I thought Legion Intelligence had their day already."

Lorian's colorless, bright eyes swept over my bandages, marked my fresh fingers and the white streaks in my hair. The little man had so penetrating a way about him, observant as any scholiast. He was the sort of man who could finish a game of druaja blindfolded after only a passing glance.

"Valka said it bit off your fingers," he said at last.

"Dorayaica?" I asked, turning from the little man to look back out the window. "It did." I could see the evergreens and the pencil cypresses that stood over the yew hedge that framed the English garden like turrets on a castle of green. "They skinned me, strung me up by the wrist. Dropped me maybe thirty feet, left me hanging off the wall for . . ." I paused to watch the wind bend the cypresses. "I don't know. Days." Groaning, I turned back to find Lorian staring at me. "Dislocated the shoulder. Tore a bunch of the ligaments. Never healed right. Venantian found a Durantine surgeon to put me back together."

"Why aren't you dead?"

"Hello to you, too."

"I mean, how did you escape?" Lorian hadn't blinked since I turned to look back at him, and though he stood not quite five feet high he seemed to tower over me where I lay. "There was no way anyone could get out of that place. Even with the whole company . . . we were unarmed, outnumbered five to one. Six to one. Maybe more."

"Valka," I explained. "She and Corvo survived Padmurak, stowed away on the Cielcin ship that captured the *Tamerlane*, rode it all the way to Eue."

"Eue?" Lorian cocked his head.

"That place," I said, glossing over the entire history of Elu and the Enar and all the rest, "that Cielcin planet."

Lorian stood just at the edge of the bed by then. I blinked up at him, tried to shake my head to clear it, but the gesture sent a spasm of pain through my newly reconstructed shoulder, and I yelped.

Heedless of my distress, Lorian asked, "Was that their home?"

"More or less," I gasped. "As near to one as they have."

"How did you survive?" Lorian's words came out pressed flat between clenched teeth.

I looked at him then, *really* looked. His long-fingered hands—not ringed but secured by silver braces that kept his joints in line—were balled into fists.

Again I blinked up at him, half-confused and half-muddied by drugs. "I told you," I said. "Valka saved me. Her and the others. Managed to get me to the *Ascalon*."

"Where are the others, then?"

"Didn't Valka tell you? Didn't she let you in?"

"Haven't seen her. Some LIO chap with a braid let me in." He half-turned to look back out the bedroom door. "Not exactly regulation either, that one . . ."

"Oliva," I said, "the Emperor's watchdog."

Without warning, Lorian hammered his hand against my wounded shoulder. I yelled, drew back, feeling the new muscles in my shoulder groan and scream as I pulled away. If Lorian intended a second blow, he did not get his chance to deliver it. Cursing, the little man fell back, cradling his hand to his chest. "Damn you, Marlowe! What the *hell* happened?"

I wanted to curse myself, but I could scarcely find the air. Only then did I realize I'd been screaming. The pain in my shoulder was extraordinary, even through the opioids. I held my good hand to test the dressing, but felt no seepage—that at least was good. Chest heaving painfully, I rasped, "Fuck you, Aristedes!"

Lorian crouched on the Jaddian carpet just barely a yard away, hunched over his hand. Craning my neck to see, I was rewarded with the horrifying image of Lorian snapping his wrist *back* into alignment with a dry *crunch*. The intus grunted, flexed his fingers experimentally as he rose. "None of them? Not one?" He tugged one finger straight with another curse and a groan. "You couldn't save even one of them?"

"I saved you!" I roared, starting to wish I hadn't. Lorian wouldn't look at me, only hugged his arm to himself. "You weren't there!" I hissed, taking advantage of the silence. "Crim and Pallino brought a shuttle in, took me and about . . . thirty from the field." I began a halting summation of that terrible day for what felt the thousandth time, recounting how Aulamn had attacked the shuttle, how Crim and Pallino had died defending me, how the tramway within the *Tamerlane* had collapsed beneath my feet. I did not mention the Quiet's shell, or how I thought his providence had intervened to deliver me. Lorian had always doubted. Lorian would not believe.

The whole recitation could not have taken more than five minutes. Five minutes . . . when it had taken lifetimes to endure.

When I had finished, Lorian still hovered about a yard from my bedside, his pale eyes still glaring. "Not one?" he breathed again. His voice was very far away.

"No."

"What's going on in here?" Valka appeared in the doorway, single-sleeved shirt leaving her left arm bare. "I just heard Lorian arrived, Hadrian, I—" She fell silent, taking in the tableau: me with my head back against the pillows, breathing hard. Lorian glowering, still clutching his arm.

"He hit me," I said, raising eyebrows at Lorian.

"I dislocated my hand," Lorian hissed.

"Because you *hit* me," I snarled.

"Not in his shoulder?" Valka's face went white, and she hurried to check my dressing. "Lorian, what were you thinking? I'll call the doctor."

I caught Valka's wrist with my left hand. "I'm fine. There's no blood."

"You might be bleeding internally," she said, and rounded on Lorian. "What the hell were you thinking?"

The intus drew himself up to his full and terribly unimpressive height. "If you hadn't sent me away," he said, speaking past Valka to me. "If I'd been there."

"If you'd been there," Valka said, raising a hand to calm the small commander, "you'd have been killed, too." She turned from him to check my shoulder, one hand hovering gingerly an inch above my dressing.

Still more furiously, Lorian shook his head again. "I might have done *something*. Organized a better defense. Something!" His pale eyes seemed to darken, as if their light retreated up some tunnel in his skull. "I might at least have taken Corvo's place."

"She'd not have let you," Valka said, not unkind.

Shutting my eyes to avoid seeing the guilt I knew all too well etched on Lorian's face, I said, "You'd never have made it off the sands . . ."

Not a one of us spoke then, not for the better part of a minute. We three survivors . . . the only survivors of that Black Feast, together again.

Valka spoke first. "'Tis good to see you again, Lorian."

"And you," he said, stiffly, then haltingly asked, "Should I . . . send for the doctor?"

"I already have," she said, tapping her temple with two fingers. "Emergency medical is inbound."

"I feel fine," I said, voice high and very strained.

"Hush," Valka said, and squeezed my good hand.

"I'm sorry," Lorian said, voice brittle as his posture.

I gave him the barest of nods. "So am I."

At Valka's urging, Lorian returned to Fort Horn after emergency medical arrived and determined that Lorian's blow had—miraculously—done little lasting harm. Thus I was spared further surgery, but Elkan called in via holograph and directed the medtechs to up my medications. I think I slept for three days.

When perhaps a week more had passed, Elkan returned and declared that I was fit to trade my bed for a float-chair on the condition that I wore a sling. He removed the drain tubes from my shoulder and back and applied beta correctives. The last wounds closed by the end of that day. Only then—when I was well enough to direct myself about the house via the float-chair's controls—did Valka extend a fresh invitation to Commander Aristedes.

I found Lorian waiting in the same parlor where Lord Venantian had received me when we first returned to Nessus. The tarps had all long since been cleared away, baring the darkly carved wood and leather furniture, the polished brass and stained-glass lamps and high, round windows. The little intus stood with reinforced hands clasped behind his back, his profile exposed as he stared up in mingled fascination and distaste at the oil painting of a nude palatine woman reclining on a divan—one of the house's few remaining fixtures that had survived from the previous owner.

"Enjoying the view?" I asked, stopping my chair just as I crossed the threshold.

The other man pulled his eyes away only reluctantly. "It didn't strike me as your style."

"It's not," I agreed, marking the way the woman lay with legs thrown wide, one hand fingering the silvered stem of a long cigarette holder. "I wanted it taken down, but Valka enjoys making me uncomfortable." I looked round the room, at the fresh-dusted collection of old books and folios that had been brought down to Nessus from the *Tamerlane*.

Lorian sniffed. "Some things never change."

"No indeed," I said, advancing the float-chair until it drew level with the ottoman I'd occupied during my interview with the Magnarch. "Thank Earth."

The other man glanced back up at the painting, mouth opening to form the start of a question. He faltered.

"You're not going to hit me again, are you?" I asked, perhaps a shade provocatively.

"I . . . no." Again Lorian pulled his eyes from the canvas. "I'm sorry, it's just that . . ."

"I know."

The white-haired intus spared another glance for the odalisque in the painting. "Who was she?"

I spread my hands, a shrug without the use of my shoulders. "Some paramour of old Lord Maddalo's, I think." I adjusted the woven blanket that covered my lap. "Or maybe one of the other owners of this place. I forget. It's changed hands a lot since the annexation. Whoever it was obviously loved her very much."

The smaller man snorted. "Well, he had an odd way of showing it."

"Some men love a thing so much they hide it away, others love a thing so much they boast of it at every opportunity." I made a gesture as if to throw this line of reasoning away.

"How's your shoulder?"

"Not bad!" Glancing down at the dressing and the corrective beneath my loose silk robe, I carried on, "The doctor says I should be able to start using it in another week or so. I'm only in the chair to help keep me from moving it. Then it'll be a few months retraining it, but we're not due to leave just yet."

Lorian inclined his head. "Then I didn't do any lasting harm?"

"Not this time!" I laughed shallowly, offered Lorian the best chair with a sweep of my left hand. He took it. "It will take more than you to do me in, commander."

Aristedes seemed less than comforted by this, and made a face as he settled onto the edge of the chair opposite me. "I've been thinking about it . . . since they thawed me out last month and before. When I first got here. I think the Pale made a mistake." Not expecting the conversation to move in this direction, I arched my eyebrows, urging my former tactical officer to go on. "Sending me here as a messenger. They ought to have quashed the lot of us. If they had, we'd have no warning of the Lothrians' subversion. The Lothrians might have crossed the Rasan Belt in force and taken us in the rear while the main force was tied up half a galaxy away out here. As it stands, we know to expect the pincer."

"You think it was hubris?" I asked. "Or do you suspect a deeper play?"

"It was hubris at Berenike. Dorayaica is formidable, but he's overconfident."

"*It,*" I amended, an almost autonomic reflex. "*It's* overconfident." Still, Lorian was not wrong. Dorayaica had overplayed its hand on Berenike, had allowed me to play for time sufficient to allow our fleet to circle back. Was it possible the Prophet had made another error? "On the other hand, Dorayaica may want us focused on the possibility of a Lothrian invasion, precisely to split our forces."

Lorian leaned forward, resting his elbows on his knees, his chin on folded hands. "You think it might be a trick, then?"

"The Cielcin must know that even united, their combined forces cannot hope to match the Legions man for man." I fiddled with the control lever for my chair as I spoke, not looking Lorian in the face. "Dorayaica knows Cielcin disunity has heretofore been their great weakness. It's seen to that, and it will certainly be looking to put that weakness back on us."

The intus bobbed his head. "Divide and conquer."

"That's why it's targeting the Emperor."

"What?"

A pained smile slashed its bloody way across my face, and I would have touched the scar behind my ear had my right arm not been trapped in its sling. Memory sank into the pits of Dharan-Tun, and I said, "The Cielcin know about the Emperor's tour."

"How?" Lorian's face darkened considerably, reminding me just how much he resembled a skull beneath that sallow film he called skin. I fancied

I could almost see the gears through his skull clicking through the implications.

Divide the Empire's attention. Cut off its head.

I opened my hands, wincing as the movement pulled on something in my reconstructed arm and shoulder. "Doesn't matter." My eyes flicked up to the sculpted plaster molding, sure one of Oliva's watch-eyes was there recording. Was that only dust floating in the rainbowed light through the high windows? Or microscopic cameras?

Lorian compressed his lips to an almost invisible line. I had confessed my failure neither to Venantian's men nor to Inquisitor Marius and his ilk, just as I had not told Dorr or his people. Syriani Dorayaica had known the Emperor's plan of travel *before* it wrung the names from me, had broken me purely for the pleasure of it. I knew I should not feel guilt—but I feel it still. Even here, now, after so long.

"Does the Emperor know?" Lorian breathed. The critical question.

I had to remind myself that Lorian likely had been kept in the dark regarding all developments following his return to Nessus. Legion Intelligence had taken all he knew and stashed him in fugue until my arrival justified his decanting. He was an asset, and at any rate knew too much of me and too many Imperial secrets to ever be allowed a posting on some common naval vessel.

"How long have you been out of the ice?" I asked.

Lorian counted on his fingers. "Five weeks," he said. "Kartzinel keeps threatening to put me back under now it's apparent to LIO I don't have any new light to shed on yours and Valka's testimonies."

"Who?"

"Kartzinel?" Lorian's brows contracted, almost conspiratorially. "He's Commandant at Fort Horn. Tough son of a bitch, doesn't seem to like me." He affected a mock salute as he spoke. "I almost prefer Beller." Beller had been Lorian's first commanding officer, and the man from whose service I had poached the young Aristedes when I was but a newly minted knight of the realm. "Neither he nor Venantian have any idea what to do with me, I think. There's been talk of sending me to Forum before they put me on ice. I can only assume that talk all dried up."

"Why Forum?"

Lorian puffed out his cheeks and threw up his hands.

"In answer to your question," I said, attempting to bring the conversation back around. "The Emperor must know. They forwarded your initial report to the fleet, left standing orders that I should be brought here if I ever materialized. Didn't they tell you?"

Head again propped on his hands, Lorian mumbled, "They don't tell me anything."

"Valka and I will be leaving to join him on Carteia as soon as the doctor gives me a clean bill of health. I've been ordered to give my account to him in person."

The good commander let his hands fall, sat a little straighter. "Do you think the Lothrians have the firepower to pose a credible threat?"

"I think they're a paper tiger." Everything I had seen on Padmurak spoke of a nation in decay and desperation. "I think the Lothrians are little more than a human *ranch*," I qualified. "Their Conclave's been handing whole populations over to Dorayaica's generals. You didn't see Vedatharad. The city was emptied. I'd wager it's like that across the Commonwealth, will be until they manage replacement."

The word *replacement* made me think of the *nowoyuk*, the Lothrian *new men*, neither male nor female. I supposed the Conclave had found its way to rid itself of Old Natures—Old Bodies—after all. I felt sick at the thought of their tacit genocide.

Lorian's face darkened. "Paper tiger's bad enough. They'd not need to pose a genuine threat to split our forces. It would be enough to raid a couple colonies, sail across the Rasan Belt and cause a panic." He drew a rattling breath. "If it were me, I'd attack the Belt and the Emperor simultaneously. Sow confusion. Knock us back on our heels."

"That may well be their plan," I said. "All the more reason for us to reach the Emperor. He *must* return to Forum."

"Agreed." Lorian's eyes wandered back up to the painting of Lord Maddalo's concubine. "At least we have the Jaddians on our side."

"The Jaddians?" I blinked at him. "The Jaddians!" I had forgotten the Jaddian armada. Twenty thousand ships were sailing from the Outer Perseus to our aid. Two hundred million mamluk clone soldiers under the command of Prince Kaim du Otranto, *Al Badroscuro* himself. "Have they arrived?"

Wrenching his gaze back under control, Lorian pulled a face. "Not yet. They're about a dozen years out, I think. From here, that is."

"That's about as long as it takes to reach Carteia," I said. The conversation ebbed then. Neither Lorian nor I moved or spoke for a long while. The only motion in the darkened parlor was the sweeping of the shadows cast by trees that fell through the high, tessellated windows. "I'm glad you're all right, Lorian," I said, finally. "The Extras . . . they didn't . . . try anything with you, did they?" All my life, I'd heard stories of the sort of things the Extrasolarians did to nobile prisoners. It had been common practice since antiquity for the various warlords of backspace to return the severed heads of emissaries and ransomed sons *still living*. One especially lurid tale I knew involved one warlike baron who received his son's still-beating heart in a gilded box for threatening war against the barbarians.

"They more or less shoved me straight into fugue," he said simply. "Inquisition was all over me from the moment I arrived." Plucking at his shirt to emphasize his skeletal frame, he added, "One of the few virtues of me . . . ah, my condition. I'm definitely myself." Lorian stopped short of offering any further explanation, and hung his head. If anything, he looked even smaller with his hair cut. Shrunken.

Without warning, he inhaled sharply, fixed his eyes on me, and I saw the light had come back into them. "Take me with you," he said. "To Carteia. When you go."

For a moment I only blinked at him, and when I spoke it was to say, "Only if you promise not to hit me again." The words escaped me wholly unbidden, and I almost laughed at myself.

Lorian must have sensed that laughter, for he smiled the thinnest shadow of a smile that I had ever seen. "I will hit you," he said, "if I have to."

"Can you come?" I asked. "Doesn't Kartzinel hold your leash?"

"Oh, he'll drop it quick as asking. Depend on it."

I opened my mouth to speak, but closed it again. Without knowing why, I found myself moved beyond words. I didn't know what to say, and so stammered, "You . . . want to reenter my service?"

Lorian stood smoothly as his ungainly limbs would allow, crossed the few yards between us. To my astonishment, he knelt then and there upon the red and golden carpet, and took my left hand in both of his. "My lord, I never left it."

CHAPTER 11

NEW FLESH, OLD SPIRIT

MONTHS PASSED, AND WORD came down that the Emperor had set sail for Carteia from Ibarnis or . . . wherever he was. The days seemed to grow shorter—though the astronomic year on Nessus was so long that we had seen no winter in all our time, and the days were warm and bright and long as men dreamed of in the dead of Earth's bitter winters. Time ran down, and seemed to rush in running. We could not stay, nor did I truly want to. Maddalo House had been a home before, if a prison, but for all our attempts to recapture that homeliness on our return, it never came. Oliva and his people were never far, were always watching, and the cooks and cleaners Lord Venantian had engaged for us were pale shadows of old Anju and the others we had known.

The gilding on the bars of our cage had peeled away in our absence, leaving only honest steel. Yet even as that cage chafed against me, my body—which had seemed a prison for so long, as the Cielcin believe—began to open up. With Elkan's blessing I set aside the float-chair and started walking, and abandoned my sling before long. I saw the surgeon less and less, and a young lady came in his stead. His apprentice, I believe, a patrician woman with kind eyes who put me through my paces with a rigor old Sir Felix might have admired. Under her watchful gaze, I performed numerous exercises, first experimenting with, then strengthening the new muscles of my shoulder, arm, and back.

The pain was gone, replaced with the childish weakness I remembered from my long months retraining the left arm after I'd lost it battling Aranata Otiolo. I can remember standing before the mirror in our baths, studying the fresh, white skin—like marble—that flowed seamless over the new tissue, that met and interrupted the ugly whip scars that thickened my back. I recalled the tattered doll I'd found in the tram terminals beneath Deira on Berenike, the patchwork soldier abandoned by some desperate family fleeing the Cielcin onslaught, his armor cobbled together from painted wood and bits of cloth.

I had become that toy soldier, soiled and scarred.

"Raise your arm again," said Doctor Elkan, peering over his spectacles. "Good, good. Big circles."

I obliged, testing the full range of motion. There was no pain, no *twang* of fibers, no grind of bones.

"Right arm over your head, stretch to the left. Very good! Now around your back. Try to touch your spine." He shuffled round me as he spoke, pressed damp fingers to my shoulder blade to better feel the motion. "That's smooth! Very smooth! You've healed remarkably, Lord Marlowe. Most remarkably! I wish I could say it was all down to my influence, but truth be told, most patients tend to shirk their part in recovery."

"I wanted my arm back," I said simply.

"Well, you have it!" Elkan said, and thumped me on the back to illustrate his point, not hard.

"Will I be ready to sail at the end of the month?" I asked.

"You're ready to sail now, my lord, though I'd hold off entering fugue for a month at least. There shouldn't be blood-flow issues after all this time, but longer is better." Elkan came back round again in front of me, looked about the drawing room in a satisfied sort of way. "The new tissue will be at slightly elevated risk of cryoburn for the first year or so. The capillaries will not all have . . . opened up." He spread his fingers in simulation. "Exercise will help, of course, but you must do your best to take care. They are your own cells, and so the risk of rejection is nonexistent, but they are soft tissues, and will tear if not *strengthened*." Here he closed his hands into fists, shook them for effect.

Smiling at the old man's display of vim, I flexed my shoulder, gripping it with the opposite hand. Standing straight again, I said, "Thank you, doctor."

Doctor Elkan returned my smile. "It was a privilege, lord. My grandson, he . . . very much admires you. As did I, when I was a boy." He stooped and collected his medical kit for the last time, then bowed. "Please do take good care of yourself. It will take time to fully heal."

The black knight's mace caught me full on the chin, snapped my head to one side. I went to one knee, head ringing like a bell as I snorted air out through my nose.

Good care, I thought, looking up at the black steel figure that towered over me, horned helm glittering where the projectors painted it onto the fencing dummy. Sabaton-clad feet made no noise on the glassy floor of the fencing round as the armored figured raised its maul in both hands for the killing blow. Had the mace been really what it appeared—a bar of cruel iron with thorned and clawed head—I would have been dead already. But the thinly padded plastic rod only stung.

"Halt!" I grunted, counting on the mechanisms left by the old Cid Arthurian monks to hear.

The black knight's holograph faltered, the mace fell. A gray-padded mannequin stood in its place, steel arms clutching its training weapon in articulated metal hands. It had no face, no clothing, no legs beneath the knee. A many-jointed arm of enameled steel connected to the automaton's spine, controlled it as a puppeteer controls the object of his craft from one of four concentric tracks built into the ceiling.

I rubbed my jaw until it stopped smarting, knew I wore a wheal red as fire where the brand had struck. Using my own training sword for a cane, I found my feet, turned my back on the drone. Bare feet slapping on the polished floor, I crossed the gymnasium to the steel carafe and cup of warm water I'd set for myself.

Beyond the huge, round windows, the night was dark and quiet. A gentle rain pattered against the iron barring—wrought in imitation of the branches of a tree—that reinforced the alumglass. It had rained all day, and showed no signs of stopping.

I poured the water out for myself, massaged my still aching jaw. The new fibers in my shoulder burned, but it was a sweet ache, the ache of muscles not yet used to their labors. My reflection watched me through the false branches soldered against the windowpane, not quite the man I'd been. There was a time when I could fight all four of the automata together and not be struck once. I had set myself against just one and failed.

Enough. The word echoed in memory to the sound of a training sword striking wood. *Go again.*

Nostrils flared, and I shot the water in one, adjusted my grip.

At least it was night. One of Oliva's minions was doubtless watching from the servant's quarters they'd transformed into their office, but I was at least alone. I did not want an audience—did not want Oliva's judgment, or Lorian's sly remarks.

It was something I wanted to do alone.

Testing the weight of the weapon in my hand, I filled my lungs and settled into the old-fashioned *linea* that was my preferred guard. Not long before, the stance—arm raised and straight, blade pointing like an accusing finger—would have been impossible for me. I thrust the point toward the inert mannequin, said, "En garde!"

The sub-daimonic mechanisms of the old machine attended, and the automaton's skeletal iron fingers moved to grip the weapon again. Holograph projectors glittered to life, painted the likeness of a knight in Gothic plate and vibrant tabard, yellow, red, and black. Red plumage bristled from his helm, and the padded rod that was its weapon became—in seeming—a longsword bright and straight as laser light.

The machine skeleton beneath the gleaming image moved, one for half a moment out of phase with the other, so that it seemed a creature four-armed, two-weaponed. Machine and image aligned as the mannequin raised its sword in salute. It advanced on silent feet, on feet that were not there, servos in the unseen skeleton whining as it raised its sword to strike.

Callused feet scraping on the glass-smooth floor, I struck first, point aimed at the daimon's gorget. The phantom knight turned a parry, thrust two-handed at my face. I recovered, snapped my blade down in *seconde* to batter the thrust aside, then swept my blade back around my head in a rolling cut aimed to flatten the knight's helm.

The armature that controlled the puppet knight torqued back, simulated a desperate backward scramble. The knight righted itself, slashed wild left to right to keep me back from it. I shifted stances to a saberist's hanging guard, felt my shoulder burn from strain. I gripped the muscle with my left hand to steady it, parried the second cut, flowed again into another rolling cut aimed at the joint between neck and shoulder.

My blade struck true!

The phantom knight faded as the armature drew back a pace, dragging its fighting marionette with it. A chime sounded in the control box—a hemisphere of black glass in the center of the armature's concentric tracks. The projectors flared, painted a new image of a knight in banded plate with a long, red coat and two great, black-feathered wings. The longsword became a curving saber, not unlike the scimitars of the enemy. A cape of leopard skin hung from my opponent's left shoulder, and it advanced with careful steps, one hand against the strong of its blade, guard posture shifting with every step.

The black wings dipped as it struck, and I stepped in to parry, aiming my point at my opponent's throat. The winged knight slipped my thrust and disengaged, circling to my left. It raised its sword in just such a hanging guard as I had used before, waiting for me.

I threw a cut at its head. It parried, but I knew it would, and pressed my attack, redoubling with a second cut to the head. The winged knight fell back, holding its parry. The armature holding it whined, servos humming as it seemed to shift its weight. Knowing the lunge was coming, I recovered forward, dragging my back leg after me, and turning, slammed my left shoulder up under the automaton's sword arm.

A man might have groaned, winded, but the machine was unmoved. My left shoulder complained where I had used it to strike bare steel, but the blade had missed me. I wrapped my left arm around the machine's right, put my hand on its face, felt the smooth metal and glass of the marionette, not the faceplate of the knight. There was no yielding of human flesh beneath armor, and the mismatch unsettled me.

Had we fought with highmatter, this move would have been suicide. Highmatter took no force to cut, and all my opponent would have needed to do was turn his wrist to cut into my back—though he cut himself in the process. Fighting as we were with training swords, I owned the machine's right arm, and with my free hand pulled its face back to bare the neck. I raised my own sword, moved the edge to the exposed throat.

The automaton's left fist shoveled into my ribs, and I felt familiar stomach-freezing pain as my ribs hit my liver. All wind gone from me, I felt myself starting to fall. Then I saw—too late—the fist circling back around to strike me right across the face.

I hit the hard floor without ceremony, lay there as the winged knight circled round. The simulation was not over, but the sub-daimonic mechanisms that served the machine in lieu of thought were made not to attack a man on the ground.

Good care indeed, I thought, more glad than ever that I was alone. Again I seemed to hear Sir Felix tap the floor with his sword. *Go again.*

With another grunt I lurched back to my knees, used my sword for a cane to stand.

That was a mistake. I had not called a halt to the fencing program.

The winged knight swung its sword, pulled the blow a micron from the side of my throat.

"Bad luck, old man," came the voice I'd least wanted to hear.

"Halt program!" I barked, finding my feet at last.

Hector Oliva stood in the door to the hall, dressed in black Legion fatigues like a common soldier. His bow case was in one hand, his braided hair a bit disordered, his clothing damp from the rain. I guessed he'd been in the yard again, shooting in the dark and the damp.

"Didn't expect to find you at it at this hour."

"I didn't want an audience," I said in answer, hoping the young man would catch my meaning. "What do you want?"

"I only thought I heard someone in here," he said, and set his case down just inside the door. "How's it feel?"

I didn't answer him at once, but crossed back to the carafe and my steel cup, poured another glass at the bench before the great, round window. Bassander Lin had stood at this very window the last time I'd used the gym before we sailed for Padmurak, the day he told me he believed I was to be named an auctor of the realm. Another old soldier, patchwork and spare parts, shattered in his battle with Bahudde.

"Better," I said to my pale reflection, and downed the water. "But not good enough." Setting the cup down, I turned and seated myself beside the carafe on the polished wood bench. "You were shooting?"

Oliva spared a glance for the rain-flecked leather case. "Yes. I had the second shift today. Don't like to sleep right after, if I can help it."

That was the second shift running the suite of monitoring equipment the Magnarch had installed in Maddalo House. To keep us safe, yes, but to keep us under observation. I gave the man my most brittle smile. *Watchdog and wolf at once*, I thought. "In the rain?"

"I like the rain," Oliva confessed. "I've spent most of my life on starships, my lord. The rain makes for a change. By Earth, even the night is something. No real night out there. Low-light's not the same."

"I know what you mean," I said.

"I haven't been in here," Oliva said, tone lightening as he turned to encompass the gymnasium with a wave of one hand, the weights against the far wall, the padded benches and table and the racked training swords, the water fountain and—most of all—the fencing armature with its tracks above the glassy, polished floor. "This was all original?"

"The fencing equipment was," I said, pointing to the mannequins on their armatures, now hanging like strange fruit from branches near the ceiling. "The monks used to train their initiates against the machine."

Oliva had come to stand on the very edge of the fencing round, eyes up on the device. "They used to test themselves," he corrected. "There were trials, degrees earned—not unlike the Jaddian swordmasters and their *Circles*. When one of the warrior monks was ready to be tested, he would display his ability against the machine." He took a step back, retreating from the ring, hesitant—I thought, almost reverent. "They were expected to perform a specific sequence, specific techniques, if they wanted to attain the next level of mastery. It wasn't enough to just *win*."

I raised an eyebrow, surprised. "You know them well?"

"I . . . wanted to be one," Oliva said, "when I was a boy."

You are a boy, I thought, but bit my tongue. "That is a dangerous thing to want." The Cid Arthurians were not a protected cult, not adorators like the Museum Catholics who dwelt in the mountains of my home. The monks themselves had been driven from Imperial space for denying the divinity of the God Emperor, though for thousands of years those who held to their beliefs were found among the Legions, whole cells of men who held to the example of the Arthur-Buddha and his knights, exemplars of chivalric virtue. Many were the times such cells refused to fight, or follow orders, and many thousand were the commanders who found themselves with mutinies on their hands. I had long suspected that it was this reason—and not any pronouncement of faith—that had prompted the Empire and Inquisition to turn on their kind, as they had but rarely turned and with less ferocity upon the Catholics and other faiths whose memories litter the stars.

"Just a child's dream," Oliva said. "What I wanted was to travel the universe. Save the Empire. Battle the Pale. I thought being one of the monks was the way to do it." I heard his rueful grin before he turned. "That was before I discovered girls, you understand?"

I allowed the barest of dry laughs. "Indeed." I stood. "Would you please let me be? I want to get a couple rounds in before bed."

Oliva began nodding and drew back, not taking his eyes from the old cultists' machine for several paces. He tore his eyes away only reluctantly, turned to face me. "Would you like a partner?"

In answer, I only rested my training sword against my shoulder—as Crispin had so often done and been so often chastised for doing. I wondered at the commander's motivations. Did he wish to say that he had crossed blades with Hadrian Marlowe? Did he wish to boast that he had beaten me? I was not practicing in the dead of night out of simple pride, but to protect the *idea* of me. It would not do for word to get out that

Hadrian Marlowe was a failing old man who could not face an enemy in the field. Not yet, not when I had just returned to life—or so it seemed—to the world of men.

"All right." I do not know what made me say it, not even now. "Blades? Or hand to hand?"

Oliva grinned. "Custom is the challenged chooses, no?"

I let my training sword fall from my shoulder. "All right. Blades, then."

The younger man crossed the fencing round to the far wall where the training swords hung, plucked one down that looked the twin to my own. I watched him go, returned to my bench to towel my sweating brow. Was I trying to push myself? Or punish myself?

Oliva would have the advantage, that much was sure. He was younger—far younger—doubtless more energetic, and I had been fighting already for more than half an hour. But I was palatine—as was he—and so at least wore my centuries lightly. Old I might have been, and *aged*, but a plebeian might have called me forty—would have called me thirty were it not for the scars and the white in my hair.

"Why no shoes?" Oliva's question slashed the air between us, cut my musing in two. He pointed with his sword down at my feet, at the circles of black medical tape that secured the joints of my largest toes to keep the skin from tearing.

I looked down at my feet, at the thick calluses that had carried me through Dharan-Tun. Gibson had asked me that question once when I was a boy. "It builds character," I said, coming to the edge of the fencing round, feeling the black glass smooth beneath my feet. I sketched a circle to one side, whirling my blade. "I never wear shoes when I train. Bare feet force you to focus on your footing."

"Do they?" Oliva made a small *hmm* noise. "Interesting. I'll have to try it." He tested the heft of his own blade, tossed the weapon from one hand to the other, slashed the air. "You ready, old man?" He brushed the tip of his nose with his thumb, settled into a low guard.

I did not answer him. I was learning not to mistake Oliva's laughing way for insult. The commander had an insolence about him, a swagger and confidence that—while galling—was not without its charm. Perhaps Valka was right, perhaps he was not unlike a certain young myrmidon brought up from the fighting pits of Borosevo. I wish that I could say I saw it in him then: the seed of the man he would become, the seed of greatness. Though I have seen the many futures and swum the waters of time, I do not know their currents. Who can see the tree written in the seed, or know its fruit? Only the Quiet one, whose hand did the writing, and whose eye sees all the universe as you or I apprehend the words on a page.

I bent the training sword in my hands. The polymer flexed smoothly, sprang back more supple than steel. I had not fought a living foe since that black day on Eue, and that had been decades before. I slashed the blade experimentally, settled into my customary guard: feet apart, knees bent, weight back, arm extended. Again my blade thrust out like an accusing finger. It was a highmatter duelist's stance, meant to maximize the space between my body and my opponent.

That was answer enough for Hector Oliva, who swished his own blade, saluted with a flourish. "Have at you, then!" He held his sword saber-fashion, blade across his body at a high angle. Then he leaped, point flashing at my eyes. I parried, swords *clacking* as they bound. Oliva recovered back, circled left. I pivoted to follow him, turning on the polished floor, following Oliva as he danced round the perimeter of the sparring ring. Again he lunged. Again I parried. Again he drew back, resumed circling. I followed him with my sword, point tracking his progress as the cobra tracks the flutist.

"You are more cautious than I expected!" he said.

"I've had reason to be," I replied.

Oliva swung.

I relaxed my grip, dropping the point of my sword so Oliva's blade whistled through the region mine had occupied an instant earlier. He grinned, snorted in a satisfied sort of way as my blade snapped back into alignment. He swung again.

Again I dropped my point, stepped back to maintain distance. Oliva disengaged, bounced on the balls of his feet, all nervous tension. I was not fighting like myself, not pressing the advantage, not following through. I was fighting instead like the boy I'd been, afraid to hurt Crispin, too afraid to make a mistake.

It was training, after all, not war.

The young commander shifted to a hanging guard, then kicked out with his foot as he leaped toward me with a cut aimed at my flank. Stepping in, I caught the blow against the strong of my blade. I'd hoped to catch the young knight as he recovered, but he was faster than I guessed, and leaped back as my own sword whistled in a flat arc.

I'd pressed him near the edge of the round, and his bootheel caught on the faint lip that separated the circle of polished glass from the wood floor. Oliva looked down, momentarily distracted.

I stabbed straight at his heart.

The younger man whirled to parry, sloppy and desperate. He swung out of the way, eager to escape the edge of the fencing ring, his sword high as that of a carnifex as he leaped aside. Then it fell like the White Sword of the Cathars—and struck me full in the face.

I did not fall, but stumbled back, swearing and holding my nose. It wasn't broken, but the blow smarted and doubtless had left a wheal beneath my eyes.

Oliva did not gloat. That surprised me. He didn't even smile. He drew back—at once the consummate professional, and found his place at the center line. Catching my eye, he offered only a tight nod.

Inexplicably, I grinned, still pinching the bridge of my nose. The pain ebbed in seconds, and I ran my thumb over the bruise. "Is that how it is?" I asked, still smiling.

Some part of me had woken up.

Somewhere in the deeps of time, old Sir Felix struck the mat with the tip of his sword once more.

Again!

I boiled off the line, lunged straight for Oliva's face. The young commander made to swat my blade away, but again I deceived him, dropping my line toward his thigh for an instant before snapping the blade back up again to strike the lad beneath the sword arm.

Too late, Oliva leaped back, grunting in acknowledgment of the blow. He patted his ribs to show where I'd struck him, and grinned. "There he is!" he said, and thrust his sword in my direction. "There's the Demon in White!"

I set my teeth. Waited.

This time Oliva advanced, blade lancing high. I knocked his weapon higher, stepped in, aimed a cut at his ribs. The commander skidded back, caught my blow against his quillons as he went to riposte, trapping my blade in a neat one-handed bind. He would have slashed my wrists—a lethal blow had we fought with highmatter—but I disengaged, brought my sword slamming down in a blow that should have split him in two in a proper fight.

My sword found only air.

Hector Oliva twisted to one side with all the terrible speed of a cornered viper. I'd overcommitted, and my blade struck the solid floor. Oliva slashed wildly at my hip.

I caught him, and a sharp *Ha!* of victory escaped me as I retreated, whirled my blade to clear the way between us. "You're quite good!" I said.

"Thank you." Oliva made a gesture as if doffing an invisible cap. "You're not half-bad yourself." Then he leaped without warning, blade slicing the air from right to left. Only half-ready, I caught the parry a second early, and my sword vibrated evilly in my fingers. Still, I lunged, stabbed Oliva between the eyes. Then the commander performed one of the maddest feats I'd ever seen. He brought his ear to his shoulder so that my blade skimmed his cheek, but passed him by, not sacrificing an erg of forward momentum. Then he twisted, anticipating that I would simply press my blade against his neck—such gentle pressure being sufficient for highmatter to kill. As I flicked my wrist to mime decapitating him, he ducked, bending at the knees so that my blade skidded through the air above his head.

Time slowed as he straightened, having ducked my blade entire. I saw his weapon coming, rising from below with confused lightning. Too late. Oliva's sword clipped me just above the ear, knocking me off balance. I staggered, and the whole world spun and toppled as I fell to hand and knees.

There I remained, head ringing, perversely glad that at least my shoulder did not ache. I had been regenerated, made whole once more, but I was not the man I was before. I was myself the river that I could not step in twice. The waters of yesterday were gone.

"You all right?" Oliva's shadow fell over me.

Though some part of me had opened its bleary eyes when Oliva scored his first blow, I was so much less than what I was. The new muscles of my shoulder lacked the instincts of the old, the decades of conditioning. I was a shadow of the man who'd fallen on that bridge in Vedatharad, would never be that man again.

Again!

"I'm fine," I said gruffly. "Thank you."

Hector reached down and offered me his hand.

I took it, stood.

We're each Sisyphos in our way. Gibson's words dusted me off.

I squared my shoulders, swept my blade into line. "Again."

CHAPTER 12

TO CARTEIA

WE LEFT NESSUS BEFORE the year was done. Elkan had declared me fit to travel, and Venantian wasted little time in preparation—indeed he was glad to be rid of me. Oliva and his team were once again cast in the role of Charon, drafted to ferry us half-dead and sleeping across the frozen years. At my urging, men were brought from Fort Horn and made to crate and carry mine and Valka's possessions from Maddalo House up the hightower to the anchorage station and the *Ascalon*. I oversaw the process personally this time, and ensured that nothing so dear as Valka's phylactery or the core of Gibson's sword was overlooked. I took much more than we took to Padmurak. I emptied the library and ordered Valka's study packed and sealed, and many of the mementos that littered the halls and rooms—the battle flag of Marius Whent, a dented myrmidon's helm, Jinan's laving basin—were likewise boxed away.

In my heart, I knew that I was never coming back.

I think now that I believed I was sailing to another gilded cage. After all, what could the Emperor do with me? I had lost my whole Company, lost the *Tamerlane*, and, with it, lost my value as a military asset. My value as a diplomat, following the failed Lothrian expedition, was worse than dubious. I suspected I was to become a curiosity, one of the many advisors chained to the foot of the Solar Throne. Possibly I would be dispatched to Forum to take up Cassian Powers's old seat on the Imperial Council, the one I had so narrowly avoided all those years before. Having lost me once already, the Emperor could not afford to lose me again. I was too valuable, and too dangerous a piece. Syriani Dorayaica would continue hunting me, hounding me across the stars. To avenge the humiliation of my escape, and . . . if what it said was true . . . to break the lines of causality that linked our time with the Quiet's distant future. To sever that shortest way.

In the gray light of Nessus's last dawn, nothing was certain.

Though for decades it had been my prison, Nessus had become my home, in its way. Valka and I had lived there for almost seventy years—longer than many a plebeian lifetime—and despite the limits on my freedom, those years are to me now among the happiest of my unhappy life. Since Eue I had lived in a walking shadow, a long twilight of the soul. Though it was dawn on Nessus, her star was setting soon—as was my own. The white cloths would once again be unfolded and draped over tables and couches, and no hand would come to lift them away. Dust would gather in Maddalo House once more, and there the dust would remain . . . until fire fell upon Nessus like rain.

As fall it would.

You have heard that story, heard how the Cielcin came to Nessus and set the hills ablaze. You have heard how it was that Lynch and Kartzinel organized the last defense, and how the great shipyards were burned and the city of Sananne was harvested and brought low, its men and towers threshed like grain. Some of you will have seen the footage, will have seen the great fleet commanded by the Grand Vayadan Vati Inamna, and seen the Grand Vayadan itself standing on the steps of the Magnarch's palace as the black banners of its king snapped against the sky. You will have heard how a certain Captain Hector Oliva stood against the enemy when all was lost.

And you will have heard, too, how when his Empire needed him most, Hadrian Marlowe did not appear.

But that was all to come, and on that day—with the sun rising gray to gold—when I last saw the green hills of Nessus, it was a bright, clear autumn. The woods were fragrant, and the grass was green, and the thin cypress trees that fringed the grounds of Maddalo House bobbed and bent in the wind. The future seemed . . . not bright precisely, but open. Open as the pale, clear sky.

"I almost don't want to go," Valka said, taking my rejuvenated hand in hers when she found me beneath the portico at the head of the paved drive. Not speaking, I looked up at the plastered roof above our heads and back at the richly stained wood doors in their circular arch. Kaffu stood behind with the older groundskeeper, Gren, and his family—the last remnants of the house's proper staff.

One of Gren's children waved.

I touched my forehead in some kind of salute, and the boy grinned. His sister hid her face in her mother's skirt. To Valka, I said, "I know, but I do."

I had decided just then and there. I was ready to be gone, ready to be out from under Venantian's eye and thumb, ready as I had been that morning on Colchis beside Gibson's tomb. Ready to live again. Though I wore no sword, I hooked my free hand in my belt where the old hasp ought to have been. I took Valka by the hand and led her out from under the portico.

I did not look back.

"Lorian waved from orbit," I said. "He says the last of the cargo's all on board."

"He's on the ship already?" She looked at me sidelong.

"You know what he's like. Prefers the lifts when he can use them." Lorian had ridden to orbit with the freight, preferring to take the slow voyage up the lift cable to orbit overnight rather than suffer through the high stresses of liftoff. He had journeyed directly from Fort Horn with a small number of Oliva's men who had been sent to collect fresh equipment. My own armor, painstakingly repaired and restored by the technicians at the fort, had been among that last shipment. "He says everything's ready."

"I'm glad he's coming with us," Valka said.

"As am I!" I exclaimed, and swung our hands between us.

The flier was waiting on the drive ahead, between the abbey and the outer wall, its black wings folded up like the wings of a paper bird. A pair of soldiers in the Imperial white and violet of the Magnarch's service milled about it, busy at the work of some pre-flight check or other. Nothing about the stark geometries of the aircraft or its brushed, black metal finish belonged on that country lane, hemmed by the yew hedges and cypress trees.

"Are you all right?" she asked. I'd grown silent as we left the house behind.

"I'm fine," I said. Talk of Lorian had moved the deep structures of my mind back to thoughts of the others, to Pallino and Elara, Corvo and Durand, to Crim and Ilex and all the rest. To Siran in her tomb on Thessa, and Gibson not far off. "It's just . . . the Red Company, on the road again." A bitter edge crept into my voice, and I felt her hand tighten in mine, willing me to strength I hardly found. "All three of us."

Valka pressed her weight against me, and we walked thus for a dozen steps or more. *"Saam mang vae racka,"* she said in Tavrosi Panthai, which had become our private tongue.

Three will have to be enough.

I turned my face up to the cloudless sky as we proceeded round the bend and onto the straightaway that ran from the house across the lawn to the outer gate.

A solitary drop of rain struck my cheek.

One of the soldiers manning the flier gave out a cry at our approach, and Valka raised a salutary hand.

"Hadrian?"

I had stopped walking at the first sight of the pilot officer emerging in his black uniform and red beret from the shuttle's ramp, leaving Valka to go a step past me. Our hands came apart.

"Hadrian?" Valka nodded at my face.

I reached up, felt the tear on my cheek and knew it at once for what it was. "Only the rain," I said, and wiped it away, thinking of Oliva's words on the night we'd sparred in the gymnasium.

The rain makes for a change.

Perhaps I sensed that change coming, sensed something of the darkness present beneath the thin light of that autumn day. The year on Nessus was fading, falling toward winter—as do we all. It was as if some half-forgotten memory stirred, as if I saw by that sense other than sight the shadow that reached out for us, the shadow we were rushing to meet. Perhaps you sense it, too, dear Reader.

You know where this ends.

But the new fingers of my hand twitched, and Valka's smile cut the fog that fell upon me, and I remembered I was whole again, and remembered that despite the hollow ache in my chest and the terrible weariness that has never left me that I was *alive*, and Valka was alive—and Lorian—and that I stood upon the grass of a green and human world on a quiet morning in autumn.

And that was a mighty thing.

"I'm *fine*," I said again, attempting to make reality and not describe it. And smoothing back my white-streaked hair I looked back one final time at the peaked gables and round windows of Maddalo House. There were the windows of Valka's study! And there—half-hidden at this angle—the tops of the trees that hemmed in the English garden. Above it all the old bell tower the monks had built stood like a beckoning finger, begging me to return.

But the labyrinth awaited me, disguised as the flier's ramp. It was not the pilot officer I'd seen, but the minotaur in new shape.

"Are you coming?" Valka asked, a touch sly as she again offered her hand.

I, Theseus, took it, and this time followed Ariadne.

"Always forward!" I said, and thought, *Always down.*

And never left nor right.

CHAPTER 13

PARTING

I DID NOT SLEEP. Not for the first year, nor through the second. El-kan's warning about cryoburn resonated strongly with me, and so I spent time each day in the *Ascalon*'s small gymnasium, running and working the machines to stretch the new tissue and improve blood flow. After the first couple months passed, Oliva and I cleared a space in the hold and sparred together again, and slowly—painfully slowly—I began to do *better*. When we first started, I won but one in ten engagements, then two in ten, then three. I stopped counting, and I am not sure Oliva ever started, but by the end I think I traded him blow for bloodless blow.

Still, it was not enough. Every blow, every punch, every flash of the blade fell short of my hopes. And in time, Oliva's shift was up, and his lieutenant, the willowy one called Magaryan, awoke from fugue to take command. The young commander went under the ice. A week later I fol-lowed, reassured by Magaryan's medtech that I had finished my therapy and the risk of cryoburn had been minimized. And so at length they put me under in the creche at Valka's side that I might finish the voyage to Carteia asleep.

It was the last voyage on which I ever spent any great length of time awake between the stars.

As a young man, I had often taken years for myself at the beginning of each long voyage. It was the only peace I could find in a life of battle and strife. But that young man was gone, replaced piece by piece with the older man who watched me from the mirror. There was no peace for me in the bright quiet of the *Ascalon*, nor on any ship. I felt the solitude must drive me mad once more.

Like young Oliva, I longed only for rain, for wind, for company and the simple pleasures of the simple life Valka and I had lived with Gibson on Thessa.

And that life I had in dreams alone.

Warm music played from the hold below, carried through the open door to mine and Valka's cabin. I had dressed in my diplomatic best: the old black Marlowe tunic, white shirt, the black trousers with the red piping, the polished knee-high boots. For the first time in I-could-hardly-count-the-years, I donned again the white cape of my station, a *lacerna* fastened at the right shoulder with a ring of polished gold.

"He's still playing?" Valka emerged from the washroom, one hand checking the bronze pins that held up her hair. She had chosen not to wear any sort of formal gown for the occasion, opting instead for boots taller even than mine and fashioned of red leather to match her old jacket. She wore a close-fitting shirt beneath and the flared Tavrosi jodhpurs she so favored, every inch herself. How like the woman I'd met on Emesh she appeared, with her long hair done up in the back and pinned, as if the centuries had not gone by. "What?"

I was smiling at her, and shook my head.

"I thought they were all supposed to be gone by now," she said. "We need to leave, do we not?"

"We do," I said, checking the time on my terminal. The Emperor awaited. "Oliva's just getting his men together. They're shipping out. Won't be here when we return."

"We should see them off, then," Valka said, placing hands on her hips. "Shall we?"

A knock sounded, and Lorian peered in round the open door. "Are we going?"

I stood, checked the drape of my cape, and gestured for Valka to go ahead of me. "We're going," I said.

We had landed on Carteia in the night, but three days after Oliva's men awakened the whole crew. For the first time on all our journey, all twenty-four of us had been awake together, with most of Oliva's men packing and stowing for our descent to join the Emperor's camp.

The bulk of the Imperial fleet remained in orbit, but Caesar himself, along with two dozen frigates and hundreds of smaller personnel ships, had established a camp city on the surface near the ruins of the old capital at Rothsmoor, and we'd set down on the edge of it.

I followed Valka and Lorian to the hall, half-listening to their polite chatter as we reached the tight stair that connected the *Ascalon's* three primary decks. We had only one level to descend, our feet rattling in counterpoint to the gentle strumming of the mandora. Reaching the bottom of the stairs, we passed through the bulkhead into the cramped corridor that ran along the spine of the lowest level. One of Oliva's men stepped out of the way as we emerged, dodged toward the opening of the main hold to our right.

As we made to follow, a clear voice rose above the music.
Though the stars be dark and the way be lost,
though our toil be long: don't count the cost.
Though the foe's ahead and no friend's behind,
my brothers! My brothers! Now hold the line!
There are those at home who need us now . . .
Who need us now . . .
Who need us now . . .
There are those at home who need us now,
so up! My lads, and fight!

On *and fight!* a number of voices joined in at a shout, though the singing voice went on, strangely upbeat in counterpoint to the sweet, sad playing of the lute.

"His lordship's on deck!"

The men stopped their labor as we entered the hold, froze loading crates onto float pallets or stopped where they stood to salute. Hector Oliva paused his singing, strummed his mandora softly a moment. Stopped. It had been his voice filling the echoing hold, a high tenor with a roughness to it that made him seem more plebeian than palatine.

"My lord!" he said, letting his foot fall from the crate he'd been using for a stool. "We're nearly gone!"

"Concert on your way out, is it?" I asked.

"It's tradition!" the commander said. "But we've got our orders, as you know!" Still clutching his lute by its neck, he stood, arms wide. "We're to report to LIO at 13:00. Word is we're bound for Idu."

"Idu?" Lorian echoed. "That's on the borders of the Veil."

Oliva rested his mandora against the crates he'd been sitting on. "It is," he said. "Word is the Extras are on the move, rushed in to pick up the pieces after Marinus fell."

"They have you fighting the Extras?" I asked.

"Unclear," Oliva said. "Some warlord's been massing an army at Latarra. Brief said he'd gone and laid claim to Monmara, word is he's rebuilding the old shipyards."

"Latarra?" The name sounded familiar, but I couldn't place it.

"Calen Harendotes," Valka put in, her memory ever sharp.

"That's the one!" Oliva said. "The Monarch, they're calling him. Say he's playing at Emperor."

"What's he to do with Idu?" Valka asked.

"Couldn't say if I knew," Sir Hector said, putting hands on his hips. "But our roads part here, I think." He took a step forward, eyes downcast as if searching for words on the scuffed metal floor. "You're off to meet the Emperor?"

For a moment I did not speak. Some lump had massed itself in my throat.

The Emperor was waiting.

How many years, how many decades gone since our last meeting in the chapel at the Magnarch's palace in Sananne? I had gone so far: to Padmurak, to Eue . . . there again back again. So far to circle back right to where I'd started.

The Emperor on his throne formed the anchor point, the centerpiece about which all the human universe turned. He alone, of all the stars in heaven and of the constellations of the blood palatine, did not move. In mere hours I would kneel before his throne again and find him utterly himself, ageless and unchanged, when I had changed so much.

"I am," I said, painting over these thoughts in my head.

Oliva extended a hand. "It was an honor meeting you, lord," he said, not smiling, all sincere. "I hope you fight them like you fought me."

I took his hand. "You want me to lose?" I said, grinning in spite of myself.

The younger man laughed. "You didn't lose! You aren't dead!" Releasing my hand he clapped me on the shoulder, and turned round to inspect his people, who had resumed their work while we spoke. Before he could ask a question or shout an order, pale-haired Lieutenant Magaryan stepped up, her pack on her shoulder. "Hector! We're all ready to move out."

"Hear that?" the commander asked, withdrawing his crumpled beret from a pocket in his tunic jacket and grinning like half a Cielcin himself. "The time's come!" He crammed the hat onto his head, draped his braid at his left shoulder. "Loras! Alleman! Get those pallets out of here! Everyone else! After me!" Turning his back, he stooped and with a fluid motion collected his lute and deposited it into its case. Before I quite knew what was happening, he had the instrument on his shoulder and his bow case in his left hand. "Let's move it, people! Karras knows the way!"

It was snowing outside, but it was the sky that was white. The earth at the base of the ramp—there was no tarmac—was a sucking field of black mud churned by the passage of feet and wheels and the iron peds of military equipment.

"We should send for a palanquin," Lorian said. "Wouldn't do to go before the Emperor a mess."

"They'd have sent one if they wanted us to have it," I said. "We'll walk."

I took my first step with great care, feeling the new world squelch beneath my sole.

A new world.

Carteia.

Carteia had suffered horribly. Her largest city lay in ruins not ten miles off, a blackened crater filled with the twisted hulks of what once had been fair towers. Her other cities were similarly torched, their populations destroyed in the firestorm or else carried off by the Pale. I fancied I could almost smell it. Perhaps it was only the special quality of the snow. Wet earth and quiet.

Commander Oliva and his little column had hurried on ahead, paused by the makeshift fence that hemmed our little landing field while his men reordered their packs and tall Magaryan spoke with the soldiers minding the gate.

"Sir Hector!" I called out, raising my restored right hand in farewell. "Watch yourself, out there!"

Oliva broke off from his conversation at the sound of his name, and looking back raised his own hand. "You too, Lord Marlowe!" he said, and cupping his hands to his mouth, he shouted, "Don't lose your head!"

Lorian barked a quiet laugh at my elbow, and I felt Valka stiffen at my side.

"You should say something," she whispered at my ear.

I shook my head. "Let him go," I said. *Let him have the last word.*

I waved him on.

He did not linger, but turned to bark a stiff order to Karras and Magaryan. Still I can remember them, standing in the mud at the end of the field, the snow falling thick around them, not melting in their hair. They had their own road to take. To Idu. To Taranis. To Nessus again.

To glory and defeat.

Though our roads diverged, they were not so different. Valka was right—she always was, about me at any rate.

We were not so different, Hector and I.

They turned left and onto the muddy lane that ran between the grounded ships of the Emperor's compound. When we reached the gate, I turned and watched them with their packs and float pallets until they were lost in the press of people hurrying from ship to ship.

We turned right ourselves.

The Emperor was waiting.

CHAPTER 14

SUNLIGHT AND ASHES

THREE TIMES THE FASCES fell as the great doors swung sound-lessly inward. Obscured somewhere in the wings, a herald proclaimed, "The Lord Hadrian Anaxander Marlowe-Victorian, Supreme Comman-dant of the Imperial Red Company, Knight-Commander of the Royal Victorian Order, Bearer of the Grass Crown, Holder of the Order of Merit, Hero of the Empire, and escort!"

A sea of powdered faces turned toward me as I crossed the threshold, Valka on my arm and Lorian at my side. The Emperor's throne room aboard the grounded frigate *Radiant Dawn* was like a little piece of Forum. The checkered floor was of porphyry and pale marble and beaten gold wire, and the triple line of columns that ran along either side of that mighty space gleamed resplendent with carnelian and gold. The space was large enough to be a shuttle bay—and indeed might have been one in the original design—but all the art and skill of the Empire was there in evidence: in the mosaics that decorated niches in the side walls behind the courtiers and the red-clad men of the Martian Guard, in the frescoes that filled the vaulted ceiling and the panels above the arches of the colonnades, in the cut-crystal constellations a lesser man might have called chandeliers.

And in the Solar Throne itself, and in the man who sat upon it.

It was not the same chair that stood in the Sun King's Hall on Forum, but a duplicate cast in its image. The red velvet circle of the headboard haloed the Imperial head, and the blades of polished gold that radiated from it gleamed so that Caesar shone like the sun. Behind the throne, a relief sculpture of palest marble stood, a toroidal arch about whose circum-ference the muscled forms of men and soft shapes of women clambered, each reaching down and back to haul the others higher, toward the sun at the apex of the ring. Beneath their striving Caesar sat, clothed in snowy argent, his gloves and shoes of crushed velvet red as his hair. A golden diadem sat upon his brow, golden chains of office weighed down his broad shoulders and hung beneath his arms, and golden rings glittered upon all his fingers save one.

I was at once conscious of the countless eyes upon me, and of my scars. Too loudly rang the snap of Valka's bootheels, and the awkward drag and shuffle of Lorian's feet chased after me where he had lagged two steps behind. We reached the empty space before the throne where the courtiers gave way to red-plumed Martians armored in vermilion and gold. A double line of the Knights Excubitor in mirrored plate and cloaks of Imperial white stood before the throne, their highmatter swords alive and humming and held vertical before their masked faces.

I dared look left and right, and saw men and women of all descriptions, powdered faces, painted ones. Logothetes in gray and scholiasts in green, Legionary officers in armorial black, courtiers in finery of every color like a parliament of singing birds. There were Jaddians among them: men in articulated ceramic masks, women in translucent silks and chains of gold. Consortium board members stood apart in gray and indigo with tall cylindrical hats—and there were faces I knew. The Legate Sendhil Massa, and Sir Gray Rinehart, the Director of Legion Intelligence!

And there was Bassander Lin.

The scarred tribune met my eyes and touched his white beret.

I gave him the smallest nod and sank to my knees before the throne.

I did not speak.

But Caesar did.

"We are exceedingly relieved to find you amongst the living, Lord Marlowe," he intoned.

I bowed my head at the sound of the voice Imperial, kept my eyes fixed upon the polished porphyry of the steps to the Solar Throne.

"One would think that by now we here should have learned our lesson with regard to reports of your demise." Was that irony in the Emperor's voice? I detected the hint of a smile in his tone and thought I heard faint and distant laughter from the gallery at my rear. "But it would seem that you continue to surprise us."

I could feel the weight of each eye as though they were the stones of Gibson's cairn. I wondered what they'd heard, what they'd whispered—what they *knew*. What was the official story, I wondered? And what rumors had percolated through the court like water rising through desert sand? Only then, kneeling, did I realize how strange it was that we had not been coached or briefed for this audience by the Emperor's chamberlain, Lord Nicephorus, or by one of the lesser androgyns that surrounded the Emperor at all times. The servants who had scraped and polished our boots of the mud from the yard had ordered us only to keep our answers short and gracious.

This was only to be an official reception, they'd said. Only the public annunciation that Hadrian Halfmortal had escaped death once again and returned from the underworld to his master's side.

Realizing almost too late that I was expected to say something, I lifted my eyes. "Your Radiance," I rasped, throat suddenly dry. "You honor me."

"We do," the Emperor agreed. William XXIII raised two red-gloved fingers like some antique hierophant offering a prayer. "And yet . . . and yet we are disturbed, my lord. Disturbed because our men in Legion Intelligence tell us that your Red Company is no more."

This public declaration sent a ripple through the crowd about us, and glancing back to where Bassander Lin stood just behind the Martians by the last carnelian pillar, I saw his face turn mask-like. Too well I knew that hollow-eyed expression. It was the cousin of the numb horror whose fingers still caressed my tired heart.

He hadn't known.

"Is this true?" the Emperor asked.

He knew full well that it was. My report and Valka's and Lorian's would all have reached him. What was it Gibson's shade had said to me? *The actors know they are on stage.* This was theater, political theater, scripted and directed for effect and for those present. For the Jaddians, the Consortium, the courtiers and foreign dignitaries attached to this itinerant court.

"It is true, Radiance," I said. Protocol would have me bow my head and plead forgiveness, but I gave no heed to protocol. A touch of the old Marlowe fury flickered in me. I resented being made a showpiece, and so I stood. "We were taken. Captured at Padmurak by Cielcin loyal to the Scourge of Earth." Was I meant to tell my story—my shame—to these high lords and ladies? Did they mean me to relive and recount the horrors of my captivity or the desperation of my escape? I fixed my eyes on Caesar, looked neither left nor right. "The *Tamerlane* was destroyed with all hands save these." I raised my hands, indicating by my gesture the persons of Valka and Lorian beside me. Without turning to look, I knew that Valka was standing, and knew Lorian yet knelt. Aristedes was Imperial to his bones, whatever the Empire might think of him, and he had not the years of long familiarity I had with the person of the Emperor himself.

I could sense the stillness in that great hall. The quiet.

I knew then what must be expected of me to say—what the crowd expected the Emperor to ask of me.

Suicide.

I had failed His Radiance. I had failed the Empire . . . and mankind. I had failed in my service, and like countless thousands—perhaps tens of thousands—of officers throughout the long history of the Sollan Empire, I would be expected to take my own life. So I squared my shoulders, turned up my chin to face the Emperor.

"Destroyed . . ." He repeated my word as if it were piece of shrapnel he examined in his hands. "You were sent to secure an alliance with the Commonwealth. You failed. We cannot tolerate failure, Lord Marlowe."

Did he want me to grovel? To beg? If so, then he had made a mistake. He should not have allowed Valka to come with me.

I felt her hand on the small of my back, and all at once found my knees quite inflexible.

When I did not speak, the Emperor did. "Have you nothing to say?"

After Dorayaica, William held little terror for me. "I did not fail, Your Radiance," I said.

The tense quiet in the hall turned to utter silence. No one seemed to breathe. I had contravened the word of the Emperor himself. To his face. In his presence. Before the assembled court.

To my astonishment, the Emperor confined his response to the mere narrowing of his eyes. So I continued. "Radiance, the Commonwealth are in thrall to the Cielcin. They have been for decades." I paused. The Emperor knew this. Had I been brought forward to make these revelations? Or had I only been meant to bow my head and slink away? "The Lothrian Grand Conclave has been selling its people to the Pale. For slaves. For food. To enrich themselves and protect themselves from invasion. They believe the Cielcin are their path to dominion over these stars. By aligning with the Cielcin, they believe they stand to gain our worlds and territories." My words sent a ripple through the congregation. Some of them—Sir Gray, certainly—had known of the Lothrian betrayal, but it would be news to most of them. And what news! "They will gain only time," I said. "The Cielcin will eat them *last*." I let these words linger only for a moment. Only the Emperor's patience had allowed me to mount this much of a defense, and it must have been wearing thin. "Radiance, it is because of me that word of this betrayal—this crime against sacred humanity—has reached your ears. My men gave their lives to deliver me to you, that I might bring you this information." I did kneel then, and turned my face to the floor. "*They* did not fail."

At my back, the crowd was like a stand of swaying willows: rustling, whispering as the Emperor considered my words. I did not dare look up, and counted the minute tiles that fringed the lowest step of the dais to distract from the sudden hammering of my heart. A shadow fell across me then, and the hem of the Emperor's pale robes and red-shod feet appeared on the steps above me.

"Just so," spoke the voice Imperial, *sotto voce*. Emperor William XXIII raised his voice then, speaking to the whole assembly. "Lord Marlowe speaks the truth! The Lothrians have betrayed us." Looking up, I found the Emperor standing upon the lowest steps, one foot a step above the other, his snowy cloak trailing behind him, his hands behind his back. "We believe they mean to make their war against us. That they will cross the Rasan Belt and strike at the heartlands of Empire while their masters chew about the fringes. This we cannot allow." Here he pressed his lips together. "What is more, Lord Marlowe is right. Without him, without his people's sacrifice, this *treachery* might have taken us unawares."

Had the Emperor foreseen my self-defense? Had I performed precisely as expected, even in my defiance? I looked to him for a sign, found none in that ivory mask he called a face. The chamberlain, Nicephorus, stood equally unreadable behind the Solar Throne beside the hooded Archprior, Leonora.

But the Emperor was not finished. "Tell me, Lord Marlowe," he asked, "are you still my man?"

What could I say?

"I never left your service," I said, and felt Lorian shift where he knelt behind me.

Caesar's placid mask broke into an approving smile, and he descended the steps until he stood over me. One velvet-gloved hand drifted into view, rings heavy and shining. I moved to kiss it, but the Emperor turned his palm up, beckoned with the fingers.

I took the hand, and His Radiance pulled me to my feet. Then in the full sight of hundreds, the Defender of the Children of Men and Servant of the Servants of Earth embraced me like a brother. I did not move. I did not dare even to breathe. How many of the Excubitors had their weapons trained on me in that moment? One false move was death.

Caesar withdrew to arm's length, and resting a hand on my shoulder, said, "You've done well bringing us this news, cousin. We are once again in your debt."

"What the hell was that?" Valka hissed, clutching my arm. Snow crunched underfoot as we left the hastily poured tarmac of the landing field about the Emperor's frigate for the warren of muddy byways that formed the periphery of the camp city.

The *Radiant Dawn* formed the centerpiece of a city of landed vessels: a great, sleek arrowhead of black and gold crowned with a sloping ziggurat that towered over the forest of lesser ships and shuttles. Thickets of lighter-craft crouched in rows along the camp's western edge, and everywhere great trenches, chain-link fences, and earthenworks carved the land into sections. Men in the red and ivory of the Legions stood at their posts or marched in units from place to place, and black-clad naval officers and scho-liasts in green hurried about on the errands of empire. Still, it was only a piece of the vast court apparatus that had joined the wandering Emperor on pilgrimage. I could not see the great fleet in high orbit, but it was there, its telegraphs firing at all hours to tether His Radiance to the Council on Forum.

There must have been a million people in the Imperial camp. Lost amid the grounded ships, the caravan city stretched from horizon to horizon beneath the cloudbound sky. The Emperor and his people had been on Carteia for the better part of two years by the time we arrived, and had been hard at work directing reconstruction in the wake of the Cielcin attack.

Some days, or so the soldiers said, when the wind was right, you could still smell the burning.

"Hadrian!" Valka tried again. "What the hell was all that?"

I slowed our walk—mindful that Lorian was starting to lag behind—and said, "I don't know." I held her gaze, offered a reassuring smile. "But it'll be all right. Things could have gone a good deal worse."

"Worse?" Valka's brows knit.

"He could have kissed you!" Lorian laughed, cane picking out little holes in the wet earth. "Earth and Emperor, I haven't been that surprised since I caught Corvo in the showers."

"At least Alexander wasn't there," I said, ignoring the intus's interjec-tion. I did not want to think about Otavia Corvo.

"I forgot your prince was along for this adventure," Lorian said. "You think they kept him away?"

That was the interesting question. Had the Emperor kept his son out of our audience? Had Alexander forgiven me for my old insult? Or had the intervening years etched his hurt deep enough to make it contempt?

I said nothing. I *could* smell the burning, a faint carbon stink on the wind. Away to the south, I could see where the skeletal forms of new towers were rising in the new city that was to replace vanished Rothsmoor. The Cielcin were not yet a century gone, and the black crater where the old capital had been was still visible even from space. House Bampasis was gone. The baron, his wife, his children, and concubines all perished in the firestorm, as had nearly all the seventeen million people who had called the great city home—if they had not been carried up to the enemy's fleet first. The Cielcin had raided all across Carteia's thirteen continents, raided even the little hamlets and guilder farms that ringed the equatorial zones. Since they'd arrived on Carteia, the Emperor's forces had begun a census, but the full human cost of the invasion was a thing never to be fully compassed.

But reconstruction was well underway. Caesar had already named a replacement for the late Baron Arlan Bampasis, a local archon named Sir Caedmon Brandt. Still, Carteia would be centuries recovering. The Cielcin attack had claimed upward of ninety percent of the planet's inhabitants, and what remained were for the most part tropical farmers and fishermen and the Urslic herdsmen who drove cattle and sheep across the great steppes of the southern wilds.

The cities would be slow to come back.

"Let's head back to the ship," I said. I had no desire to be caught out in the open by the odd courtier or by a common soldier like Carax of Aramis. After my little bit of theater with the Emperor, I wanted nothing but to disappear, to retreat to the relative safety of the *Ascalon*, where at least I could not be made a party to any great *scene*. And after so many years in relative solitude, the crush and scramble of the court and camp was more than my old nerves could take.

"Hadrian!"

As if summoned by my desire for solitude or queued up by some diabolic stage manager, the sound of my name cut the air like a knife. Heart leaping violently, I looked round for the man who had shouted it.

Bassander Lin shouldered his way through a pack of junior officers, using his cane like a shepherd's crook. He had hardly aged a day in all the time since his visit to Maddalo House. I guessed he must have spent most of the time since in fugue. As a middling officer, he would be neither required to sit on the Emperor's council, nor would he be among those drawing the shorter straws, required to steer the fleet through warp as the Emperor toured the frontier provinces.

Lin moved stiffly, the legacy of his brutal treatment at the hands of the *vayadan*-general Bahudde in the Battle of Berenike, but he smiled as he drew near in his cold, professional way, and raised a hand in short, stiff salute. "I'm glad you're all right," he said, drawing to a halt half a dozen paces from Valka and myself. His long black bridge coat drifted about his ankles in the steam off a vent from the ship above us. His mouth was open, but no further words came out, as though he were dumbstruck to find that we were real.

"Alive!" I corrected, returning his salute. "*All right* is something else."

"I'm familiar with the distinction," Lin said, and stabbed the mud between his feet with his ashwood cane. Bowing his head, he removed the white tribune's cap and said, "I am sorry. About the others. About the Red Company, I mean. I didn't know until . . . until just now. When I heard the news, I . . . I almost couldn't believe it." He looked sharply up at me, his eyes having fallen to the earth. For an instant, I felt the old line of fire drawn between us, but its heat was different. "I wish that I had been there."

The old ghost of a smile pulled at my lips. "So do I," I said, and gesturing to Valka, explained, "We were on the surface when the ship was taken."

"I was in fugue," Lorian said. "Imagine how I feel."

I felt a pang for the good commander, and Valka said, "I didn't know that."

"No need for a tactical officer on a diplomatic mission," he said sourly, and inclined his head. "Corvo left Durand in command when you went missing, Hadrian. He probably never saw it coming."

Bassander's face was utterly unreadable. "I liked Durand," he said. "Very diligent. Always wondered why Corvo had the command instead of him."

"Uncreative," Lorian diagnosed. "Bastien was good at following orders, but too rigid to lead."

"He died well," I said, cutting across Lorian's remark. I caught the junior man's pale gaze. Lorian had been there when Durand died, when Dorayaica struck off his head. The memory of it leeched what little color there was from Lorian's face.

He swallowed. "He did."

Not a one of us spoke for a long moment, and Lorian had to move aside as a double column of armored legionnaires marched past—patrolling the compound, I guessed.

Seizing the opportunity, Bassander asked, "May I walk with you?"

I gestured on ahead. "We're just returning to our ship. I get the sense I'd best keep my head down."

Lin fell into step alongside Valka and myself, with Lorian again following close behind. "You may be right about that. There were many at court who were . . . less than overjoyed, shall we say, to learn of your survival."

"Prince Alexander?" I asked.

Lin hissed, though out of pain or sympathy was any man's guess. "He'd be one, aye. He's with the fleet now. The Wong-Hopper Consortium sent one of the cargo liners with building materials for Brandt's new city, and Caesar sent the boy to welcome them. Of course the rumor is he sent him to orbit to keep you two apart. For the audience at least. He's due to return in a couple days."

"Who else?" I asked, feeling a lead weight in my guts. Ahead, a trio of heavy armored groundcars rolled slowly through the mud on wheels taller than a man, blocking traffic.

"Leonora, of course. The rest of the clergy."

"No surprises there."

"They haven't seen what I've seen," Lin said with a lack of hesitation that chilled me, and cut the air with the blade of one hand. "Then there's a few of the strategoi. Bartosz, for instance."

"Bartosz is here?" I asked, incredulous. Sir Leonid Bartosz had been Bassander's old commander in the 347th Legion. I had nearly killed him for cowardice at Berenike.

Bassander opened one hand in a partial shrug. "I told you he was reassigned. Venantian had him placed on strategic advisory."

"Promoted him right off the field, eh?" Lorian sneered. "Milk-blooded little rat. He ought to have slit his own throat."

"Lorian . . ." Valka said, a warning note in her voice.

"It's all right," I said. "Lorian's right. He didn't mean to imply anything about me." I glanced over my shoulder at the intus, whose eyebrows contracted in confusion.

Lin coughed. "The Emperor would never order you remove yourself," he said. "You're too damn valuable."

"So it would seem," I said, then circled the conversation back to its proper channel. "Who else should I add to my list of enemies?"

"Bulsara wasn't overjoyed," Lin said, referring to the Lord Director of the Colonial Office. "But I'm not sure he's your enemy. You know what he's like. Likes things tidy. Massa was telling me the scholiasts are all in a snit. You ruin their projections."

Valka snorted.

The *Ascalon*'s rear fin appeared over the low body of a cargo freighter ahead. We hadn't far to go. As we reached the near corner of the freighter's lot, following a knot of junior naval officers, Lin changed the subject. "The Cielcin have been quiet now for decades. Carteia was one of the last planets they hit."

"They were forced to draw off. Dorayaica summoned them all together . . ." I replied, trailing off. In silence, I tried to figure the timing of the attack on Carteia relative to the Aetavanni. Nearly seventy standard years had passed since that fateful day on Eue. Carteia had been attacked some twenty years before that. Twenty years had proved sufficient time for the Pale to cross the vast distances between the Centaurine provinces and the unmapped regions of the galactic north. The great Cielcin worldships were many times faster than our vessels. The mighty engines that drove them across the light-years took far longer to spin up to warp speeds due to their tremendous size, but that same huge volume allowed them to fold space much faster once the engines started to burn.

"They'll make their move soon. Dorayaica needed to consolidate its rule over the clans . . ." I said, staring up into the cloud bank, as if I might see Dharan-Tun and the thousands of Cielcin worlds peering down through the fog like the blind eyes of gods. "This is but the calm before the storm, Bassander." I stopped speaking as a pair of scholiasts hurried past, the hems of their green robes bunched in their fists to keep them from trailing in the muck. I watched them go before continuing. "It won't be the same. They'll be organized. We should expect coordinated strikes across the Empire. Not just here. They'll hit us in clusters. Shipyards, supply depots. Maybe Nessus itself."

"And there's the Commonwealth to consider," Lorian said. "Breaking the provinces is just the first step. If they succeed here, they'll make their end run through Sagittarius to the Spur. Hit Forum, Avalon, Renaissance, all the old worlds . . ."

"Earth," Valka said, voice barely above a whisper.

Lin shook his head. "Why not drive straight for the core?"

"Dorayaica must guess how well defended those systems are—if it even has the coordinates to find them," I said.

"And it knows the Emperor is here," said Valka.

Again we halted to allow a six-legged tank to continue along the cross street. Its huge, scarab-like body swayed as it advanced, massive peds smashing the soft earth flat. Watching it go, listening to the whine and stomp of its mighty limbs, I repeated Valka's words. "And it knows the Emperor is here." I put my hand to the scar on my temple.

Perfugium. Vanaheim. Balanrot.

"We'll be ready when they move," Bassander said, stumping nearer with his uneven gait. "Will we win?"

I looked round at him, and saw in his dark eyes the same look of holy terror—of religious awe—that I'd first seen in them aboard the *Demiurge.* It was not *Tribune Lin* who asked the question, but Bassander the *believer.*

"I don't know," I told him, and told him true. "I'm not a prophet, Bassander."

The Quiet had shown me the future, but he had shown me all of it: every instant of time past and time present, every possible state of time future. I had seen so much, too much to ever answer that or any question.

"But you are here for a reason," Lin said. "You survived again, when none of the others did. That cannot be meaningless."

I laid a hand on the other man's shoulder. "Maybe." I could not tell him the truth: that the visions I remembered most clearly were not of the future—not anymore. I had seen my death at Akterumu, seen it a thousand times. And I had seen other moments, seen myself ignite a sun—but I had been *young* then. In all the visions I had seen, I had seen nothing beyond the dome and the massacre on Eue. Nothing that *could* still happen.

Do what must be done.

"What do you intend to do?" Bassander asked, his soldierly mask slipping back into place. "Will you rejoin the fighting?"

I opened my mouth to respond, but for a moment no sound came out. Turning, I saw Valka watching me, gold eyes unreadable. But she smiled.

No.

The word floated just beneath the surface of my tongue, but did not leap from it. I did not dare speak it aloud. And yet it was truth. I did not want to fight, did not know if I had the fighting in me. Durand and Corvo, Pallino and Crim and all the rest had died to save me, but hardly a day went by I did not hear the screaming, smell the blood of that Black Feast and feel once more the pressure of Miudanar's solitary, hollow eye.

My hands were shaking, and I hid them in the pockets of my coat. I needed to be away, to be alone, to be back in the safety of the *Ascalon*, away from Bassander, away from the Imperial court, away from the Emperor and the war and *everything*.

I bared my teeth—a Cielcin smile—and answered as I had answered the Emperor, saying, "I am a soldier of the Empire."

CHAPTER 15

THE PRINCE

GREAT SHAPES MOVED BEYOND the sky.

The cloud layer—which had hung for days above the Emperor's camp city like so much smoke—had finally broken on the fourth day of our sojourn on Carteia, revealing the vast black shapes of the fleet in low orbit, the greatest dreadnoughts and battleships like arrowheads, gray and faint against the pale, white sky.

But the greatest of these were dwarfed by the Consortium freighter. Not because it was larger—though at fifty miles end to end it outmassed all but the lone superdreadnought that formed the backbone of the Emperor's fleet—but because it flew so much lower, relying on its repulsors and on its adamantine bones to keep from breaking in the tidal stresses of Carteia's gravity as it skirted the upper atmosphere. Strangely fish-like it seemed, with the broad fins of its solar collectors spread out like antique sails, its hold's mouth yawning wide and dark as it expelled its vast cargo for the slow descent.

White contrails hit the sky, without the flash of friction fires or the thunder of supersonic sound. It was imperative that its cargo should descend gently. The buildings were not meant to fly.

"Amazing, isn't it?" said Bassander Lin on my right. I looked round, found him leaning on the iron rail of the viewing platform, eyes on the sky. "What we can do?"

The Emperor had ordered a new city for the people of Carteia, and though it would be years before it came into its own, the foundations would be laid that day.

I said nothing to old Lin, but listened as the cornicens sounded their trumpets to greet the descending buildings, the towers and halls, the warehouses and schoolhouses and housing blocks. Many buildings had already been raised, and the whole land was cleared and graded and made ready, the sewers and power grid prepared.

Rome was not built in a day, or so the ancients said.

But we are not Rome.

A whole city was falling, carried on repulsor glow, buoyed by hydrogen balloons vast as starships and swaying on cables of whiskered nanocarbon. A whole city . . . from the sky.

About us the Imperial court milled in all their finery, drinking the Emperor's wine and listening to the piping of the Legion band the Emperor had provided for the occasion. Lin and I stood apart, and I marveled to find a dead space between us and the nearest courtiers. There had been a time when I could not keep them away.

"How many has it been for you?" I asked, squinting out across the landing field that was to be the site of Baron Brandt's new city, at snowy fields and the rich brown of freshly turned earth.

"How many what?" Lin asked, not following.

"How many worlds like this?" I asked. "How many battles?"

"We didn't fight here. Carteia was already lost," Lin replied, thumping his cane against the platform. He looked back over his shoulder and up to the covered terraces where the lords and ladies stood watching amid heating columns and inside the static field. "But this makes . . . twenty-nine? Thirty?" He thumped his cane again. "We always rebuild."

"But can we?" I asked, turning my collar up against the chill wind, unsure if the thought were a reflection of the Imperium . . . or only myself. "Can we keep rebuilding?"

Lin pointed off to the right, to the public lot where the Emperor had permitted the commoners to mass and watch the arrival of their new world. I could see the white shapes of soldiers keeping order, and the patchwork myriad organism called *crowd* that pressed against the palisade made to contain it. "They think so," he said.

"Lord Marlowe!"

We both turned to find a group of courtiers descending the steps from the covered terrace, led by a black-haired young man wearing a mask of enameled red ceramic that articulated with the motions of his face. He was Jaddian, and wore a richly embroidered kaftan over his loose shirt and baggy trousers.

"It is . . . Lord Marlowe, is it not?" He inclined his head to one side.

I spared a glance for Bassander Lin, but the tribune's face was studiously unreadable. "It is," I said, turning to fully face the young man. "I am."

The *eali nobile*'s face split into a broad grin, white teeth flashing in the bloody mask. "I am Rafael Hatim ban Onophre du Lurash, a Prince of Lurash." He bowed suddenly, eliciting a gasp from the rather astonishing pair of Jaddian women who had followed him.

"Mi Domi, non ti eprepe!" exclaimed one.

I smiled at her, understanding her Jaddian perfectly.

But Prince Rafael Hatim seemed not to hear his concubine. "When I saw you in court four days ago, I knew I must meet you! And here you are!" Without hesitation, he thrust out a hand for me to shake. I took it, and he clasped my hand in both of his. "A star shines upon our meeting, indeed! Many are the tales we've heard in Jadd! I never thought to meet you." Unsaid was the fact that he had thought me a dead man, as so many had.

Not knowing what to say, I said, "It is an honor to meet you, *Domi*."

"The honor is mine!" the prince said, gesturing to his women and the others—mostly Sollan Imperial courtlings in togas and fine suits. "There is so much I must ask you! Is it true you were a captive of the *davoi*?"

I swallowed. *Davoi* was *demons* in Jaddian, was *the Cielcin*.

"It is," I said stiffly.

Prince Rafael Hatim's mouth opened, and he looked round at the others before asking. "Of the Scourge of Earth itself?"

"Your Highness," Lin said, stumping forward with his cane. "Lord Marlowe had a harrowing experience . . . it is perhaps best not to speak of it—"

"I was," I said, and smiled a smile that didn't reach my eyes. I felt suddenly that Valka had been right to decline the invitation to this event. She and Lorian had remained on the *Ascalon*. But I felt I could not have refused. My absence would have been noticed. "For seven years."

"And you escaped! *Dolá Deu!* How was this done?" The Prince's mask shifted as his eyes went wide.

"We stole a ship," I said, not wishing to recount the tale. "My people and me."

"Will you drink with us?" asked Prince Rafael Hatim, indicating his coterie. "These are my women, Tula and Arianne, and this is Garan Peake—Lord Allander Peake's son. You know his father, I believe? And this is . . ." He proceeded to introduce me to series of court fixtures, a flurry of well-dressed and well-kept faces whose names were older than life on Carteia. Trapped by social convention, I was dragged up the short flight of stairs and through the static field to where it was warm, and an androgyn in Imperial livery poured me a glass of Kandarene red that had been left to age in climate-controlled vaults aboard the *Radiant Dawn*.

For the next hour I fended off questions from Prince Rafael Hatim and his women and from Lord Garan and the rest, all the while wearing a version of the mask that Lin wore so well. In truth, I was glad to do so. The young courtiers kept me on the periphery of the Imperial pavilion, and so I was spared a place near the middle, where the Emperor held court on a gilded wooden seat that served in lieu of the throne, his Excubitors and advisors wound tight about him. By allowing the Jaddian princeling and his coterie to hold me hostage, I was insulated somewhat from the attentions of the court proper, from the Emperor and those about him who thought of me as an enemy.

I remember little of what was said, remember instead the golden aureole that was the headboard of the Imperial seat, remembered the back of the Emperor's head just barely visible over Hatim's shoulder. Leonora stood at his left hand, a black shadow in the white felt crown of her office; and bald Nicephorus, ever at its master's side.

It felt so strange to be back, as though all of Padmurak and Dharan-Tun had a been a dream, and yet it felt as I still were dreaming, and it was instead that pavilion and the well-dressed and powdered that were unreal—and I myself was unreal. How could I be at the Imperial court again? On Carteia or anywhere? How could any of it still exist when so much had changed? When I had endured so much?

"My lord?" asked the odalisque called Arianne. She was not the one who had reprimanded her prince for bowing as he introduced himself to me.

"I'm sorry?" I blinked round at her. She was staring up at me from her low couch.

"I asked if you would sit with me," she said again, hand trailing on the tufted bench beside her, chains tinkling on wrist and brow. Her eyelids were painted black as Valka's so often were, her whole aspect like the dusk. "You would honor me."

I was seated on a cushioned stool between two arms of couches that enveloped me, Lin standing to one side. Hands cradling the crystal wine cup—bad form, that—I checked my reflection in the crimson liquid. "I'm afraid my honor demands that I not honor you," I said, politely as I could. I wished Valka *had* come, then.

Arianne made a face. *"Shafaaq es,"* she said. *A pity.* Undeterred, she sat up and leaned enticingly forward, reaching out with one perfumed hand to touch my scarred cheek. "We have heard so many songs of you in Jadd," she said, and drew back as I recoiled, a smile frozen on her painted olive face. "My prince is a great admirer."

I spared a glance for Prince Rafael Hatim, who seemed unbothered by his woman's pass at me.

"I am a great admirer of your people," I said, not knowing what else to say. "I knew one of your swordmasters when I was a boy. He gave me a sword after the Battle of Emesh."

Prince Rafael Hatim whistled. "A true *sayyiph*?" His enameled mask clicked as he spoke, plates shifting. "That was a mighty gift! Not idly are the swords of the Maeskoloi drawn, and almost never are they given. What was his name, this champion of yours?"

"Sir Olorin Milta," I said. "He was sulshawar to the Satrap of Ubar."

"Ubar?" Rafael Hatim looked round at his companions. *"Hal ti tae-riph Ubar?"*

The odalisques shook their heads.

"You don't know Ubar?" I asked, and felt my brows furrow. Lady Kalima di Sayyiph had been an emissary of the *Domagavani*, the assembly of Jaddian princes. I had assumed her world had been equally as lofty. But this Prince Rafael Hatim du Lurash had not even heard of the place.

"There are many lesser satrapies in Jadd." Rafael Hatim waved a hand. "I cannot know them all. Milta, what did you say the name of your Maeskolos was? Do you know his Circle?"

I could only shake my head. A swordmaster's Circle was his rank, his degree of mastery. "I did not know him well."

"His name is not known to me, either," the Jaddian prince said. "Have you the sword?"

"No," I said, thinking of the way my other self had put the blade into my hand, and of the waters of Colchis where the sword doubtless remains. "I lost it . . . in the war."

"I pray it served you well," the prince said.

"It did," I said in answer, stared once more into the depths of my wine. Bassander shifted behind me, his attention drawn by a sudden change in the intensity of the Legion orchestra as they began a new piece. Away beyond the roof of the pavilion, the towers of the new city were drawing ever nearer. I could just begin to make out and to count the black shapes of windows on the nearest towers, watched a lighter circling the sinking buildings, its pilot monitoring the descent. "How do you come to be a guest of the court, *Domi*?"

Again, Prince Rafael smiled, white teeth flashing in the red mask. "My father is Prince Onophre du Lurash. I am here for him. For my family.

There are many of us in the Eternal City. Jaddians and Durantines. Normans and men of the Small Kingdoms. All guests of your Emperor."

"So you're a hostage?" I asked.

"If you like!" Rafael Hatim laughed. "My family has enjoyed good relations with the Empire for generations. I am working to continue this. It will be good when I am ruling Lurash, you see?"

"But we're not in the Eternal City," I said. "How did you come to be a part of this expedition?"

"We were invited!" the prince replied. "Surely you know of *our* fleet? Prince Kaim du Otranto sails for Nessus with two hundred *million* mamluk clone soldiers. My father serves Prince Kaim's grandfather, who is First Prince of Jadd, and so I am here as liaison for when we return to Nessus." He broke off just long enough to accept a recharged glass from his woman, Tula, as the concubine settled in beside him. "The war is very far from us in Jadd. Very far. It is good that there are those of us who make this journey. We should see, that all in Jadd may see."

Bassander Lin turned from his examination of the descending towers, twisting his cane in his fingers. "You know him? Prince Kaim?"

Prince Rafael Hatim looked up at the tribune, touched his forehead in a gesture of acknowledgment. "I am having that honor. Prince Kaim is the greatest of us. They say he is Prince Katanes come again. He crushed the Lothrians when they came to our stars when he was just a boy."

"He's fought the Cielcin as well, has he not?" I asked.

"Prince Aldia promised twelve thousand ships to the war effort nearly a thousand standard years ago," Lin interjected, answering for the prince. "They never arrived."

The Jaddian prince's mask clicked as he worked his jaw. I thought I remembered something about that. There was always talk of the Jaddians committing fleets to the fighting when I was a boy. Always instead a token force appeared, served in a battle or for a campaign, and vanished again. Kalima di Sayyiph and Sir Olorin's fleet had been one such example, but on further reflection I realized that Lin was right: that for all my years of fighting, the greater Jaddian presence rumored to always be on the verge of setting sail had never arrived.

I'd never given it much thought. Everything after Vorgossos had driven such things from my mind.

Sensing a cord of woven steel tightening between the princeling and the tribune, I said diplomatically as I was able, "Perhaps it will be different now."

But Lin was a solider, had been all his life, and the memory of the Jaddians' failed promises sat in his belly like a stone. He chewed his tongue a moment before uttering one single word. "No."

The prince drank. "Prince Aldia made his commitment without the support of the Domagavani. The other princes denied him. 'This is not a Jaddian matter!' they said, and so the fleet was withheld. But it is said that Aldia sent Prince Kaim and many of his own servants to the Veil of Marinus and beyond. There were *davoi* brought in chains to the Alcaz du Badr, to the Tower of Mirrors itself! Prince Kaim testified before the Domagavani, saying this was our fight as well! He slew one of their princes before *our* princes. There before the assembly!"

"I didn't know that!" I said, and sat a little straighter. "When was this? Which prince?"

"I do not know," Hatim said. "I have no talent for their names. But this was . . . perhaps two hundred standard years ago? It is strange to me you do not know this, of all people, my lord."

I ticked the numbers off on my fingers. Two hundred years ago I was on trial for witchcraft before the Chantry's Inquisition on Thermon. It was no wonder I had not heard the tale. By the time I had escaped to my imprisonment in Maddalo House, the story would have been but small news on Nessus.

"I'm afraid there's much I don't know," I said, and hid myself in my wine cup.

A cornicen in the Legion band chose that moment to sound his silver trumpet loud and bright in the clear air, yanking each of us by the ear. Careful not to upset my goblet, I stood and followed the limping Bassander to the rail at the pavilion's edge as a peal of distant thunder boiled the air, soft and low.

A cloud of dust and snow flowered in the middle distance, at the nearest edge of the new city. One of the towers had struck earth, and already I could see the ground crew hurrying to secure the tower in its pre-built foundation, like ants about the boot of a giant.

A smattering of well-bred applause sounded from the pavilion, and I looked out toward the crowd of onlooking plebes who had gathered behind the fence to see all their Emperor did for them. Their cheering reached us a moment later, a dim roar lost beneath the rumbling of the earth. The great, gray balloons that had slowed the tower's descent detached suddenly, rose like votive lanterns back toward the faint and yawning Consortium dromond in the upper air.

"Maybe we can keep rebuilding," I said to Lin.

The tribune grunted. "Someone can," he said. "It might not always be us. But life has its way of rolling back the tide. Who was it said you could move planets with a big enough lever? Shakespeare?"

"Archimedes," I said, leaning against the rail.

"You always know," Lin said, a small laugh escaping him. "How is it you always know?"

"I read," I said, and shrugged. "People always accuse me of wasting my time, but they don't complain when I have their answers."

Lin made a small, affirmative sound. "Suppose I've never seen much point is all. The world's so not like what it was when those books of yours were written. Seems to me yesterday's dead don't have much to say of today."

"The world's changed," I allowed, and glanced back to where Prince Rafael Hatim sat with Garan Peake and the others. "But men have not. Nor will." I clapped him on the shoulder. "We keep making the same choices. The same mistakes. So the same wisdom will ever serve us."

Lin had no riposte for that. After a quiet moment, his wrist-terminal chimed, and he patted his tunic pockets, drew out a slim titanium pillbox, clicked the tab to dispense a small, red gel capsule, which he swallowed dry. Seeing me watching him, he grimaced. "For the pain." He underscored his words with a *thump* of the ashwood cane, indicating the systemic injuries he'd incurred fighting the *vayadan*-general Bahudde.

I said nothing, sensing that my pity or my sympathy—even my camaraderie—would have felt to him like shame. So I excused myself, bowing my head. Lifting the emptied goblet, I said, "I'm going to dispose of this."

I left him then, standing by the rail, and acknowledged Arianne's attempts to recall me with a short wave as I pressed into the Imperial pavilion. Liveried servants—all of them Aventine House androgyns, hairless as old Nicephorus save for their powdered white wigs—stood at intervals with silver trays under their arms or else moved between the couches and knots of standing dignitaries with trays laden with cups of wine or canapes or delicate little pastries. I accepted one of these latter items politely and ate it, discharging my goblet to a passing, empty-handed servant.

Whispers followed me as I went, and more than once I caught the lingering eye of some painted lady, the slack jaw of a lordling silenced mid-sentence. One man in the indigo and gray of a Consortium director bowed and murmured respects in Mandari. I bowed only my head and pushed past. I had vague notions that I should make myself seen. I had been invited, after all, and the Emperor would expect me to make my presence felt. So I resolved to cross along the rail below the Emperor's dais where he sat in conversation with the newly minted Baron Brandt and a number of other lords. There was an empty space before the throne where none congregated. The milling lords instead confined themselves to the space nearest the rail, some rapt in conversation with one another in little human knots, others observing the spectacle with field lenses or opera glasses while—on the side opposite the Emperor's dais—a holographed diorama showed the new city as it was to be.

Keeping nearer the rail and away from the Emperor's dais, I crossed the void toward the gleaming city. The velvet roof of the pavilion domed above us, buoyed by the columnar heaters whose warmth inflated the air and filled it with the smell of incense and warm spice.

The Emperor had chosen a broad plain for his new city, a place that had before been a part of Carteia's empty countryside. Most Imperial cities began with a germ, a nucleus of central planning built about the binary hearts of palace and Chantry sanctum. The cities were then left to grow, to follow the land and the sensibilities of the settlers until they reached the city walls, which by old tradition were built miles from the city's heart. Such walls were built not to defend the settlements against attack, but to bound the city's growth.

This new city had no wall, though one glimmered in red about the edges of the table, waiting one day to be built. The palace, too, was red. Doubtless the palace and the bunkers dug beneath it were better built the traditional way. I wondered where the new-made Baron would live in the interim. In some armored frigate, no doubt, grounded and guarded, kept apart from the new city. The Chantry sanctum, too, would be built by human hands. But the rest? White spires and rows of low buildings lined boulevards already paved and waiting.

I fingered the inscription glimmering under black glass along the edge of the display table. *The City of Bennu,* it read.

"Bennu," I repeated the name aloud under my breath. I couldn't place it. "Bennu?"

"It's a bird," a clipped, cool voice intruded. "Some ancient bird. It dies and rises again. Like a phoenix." I looked up, found the owner of that voice staring at me across the holograph of the new city. "Like you, I suppose."

The man who'd spoken was little changed from my memory. His Imperial red hair was longer, combed back from the green-eyed aquiline profile that defined his august family. He had his father's square jaw, his mother's alabaster complexion, and a cool detachment all his own. He wore a suit of Imperial crimson embroidered with cloth of gold, and a half-toga white as snow draped round him from his left shoulder, secured by a golden fibula fashioned like the sun.

"Aren't you going to bow?" Prince Alexander asked me, an asymmetrical smile—*my* asymmetrical smile—cracking his eugenically handsome face.

I smiled instead, stood a little straighter. "My prince!" I said, surprised to find my heart warming to see him, and I hurried round the table to take his hand. "I'd heard you were here! I'd looked for you! Are you well?" None of my apprehension or earlier fear mattered then, not in that moment. I had so few familiar faces left in all the universe, and at once I could not bear that I should be estranged from any of them. I took the young prince's hand in both of mine and bent to press my forehead to it. It was not precisely a bow, nor was it proper protocol to touch a member of the Imperial family. Doubtless the Excubitors near at hand tensed, and the Martian Guards looked on, hands on stunners. Had it been the Emperor himself, they might have fired.

Alexander tugged his hand away, and when I straightened he looked at me with something like shock. His emerald eyes were wide, his lips parted. "It's good to see you, dear boy," I said, aware that some of the nearer eyes had found me. I didn't care.

The prince narrowed his eyes. "You look older," he said after a long moment. "Father said you looked older." He glanced sidelong at the nearest listener, and the woman averted her eyes. "It's true then? The Scourge of Earth tortured you?"

"For seven years," I said, and averted my eyes. I did not want to talk about that, not where so many could hear.

Alexander just kept looking at me, his mouth half-open. "Your face . . ." he managed at last.

"Dorayaica," I said, feeling the scars on my cheek burn as my face flushed. I hid my hands in the pockets of my long, black coat, suddenly ashamed of the scars I had ceased to hide in leather gauntlets. An ugly feeling settled in my chest, the ugly feeling I'd felt lying on the glass floor of the gymnasium in Maddalo House, on the rubberized mats in the *Ascalon's* hold, bested once more by Sir Hector.

"I'm sorry," the prince said, inhaled sharply. "I *am* sorry, Marlowe. I can't imagine what that was like."

"I pray one day no one will have to," I said, and ducked my head. "Imagine. Or know."

"I pray you retire in peace to Nessus," he replied. "I suggested it, in fact. In council. I told Father to leave you to your manor in Sananne. You've suffered enough. We can ask no more of you."

I blinked at him. "I'm not done yet, I promise you."

Alexander's face turned strangely mask-like. He had learned to better control himself in the years we'd been apart, it seemed. His voice even, he said, "Perhaps you should be. What you've been through . . . you deserve rest."

"None of us gets what we deserve, my prince," I said. "Perhaps we should all be grateful for that."

The prince snorted, turned his head away. About us, the crowd had begun to relax—just a little—to turn back to their own conversations. The Emperor on his dais leaned to whisper something to bald Nicephorus, resumed his conversation with Lord Bulsara.

"Is that so?" Alexander asked, studying the map of the new city of Bennu. "If we got what we deserved, you'd be a prince of the realm. Magnarch. Viceroy."

"I don't want that," I said, and cocked my head to study the younger man more sharply. "You know I don't."

Alexander tucked his chin. "The people were overjoyed to learn of your return. They thought you dead. We all did."

Did you hope it, I wonder? The thought leaped to the fore of my mind, crushing my earlier joy. This was not the boy I'd known so very long ago. That boy was dead, crushed by my own carelessness in his delicate childhood, ground down by the adulation of the crowd at Berenike. He said that he had counseled that I be left in peace on Nessus. I believed him. He'd hoped that I would die there, a done old man; hoped that I would never again trouble the machinery and game of Empire.

But trouble it I had, and would again. My very breathing troubled it, rattled its leaded panes. And troubled him, as I had troubled his mother, the Lions, the Chantry, and so many others.

"They say you will drive the enemy from the Veil and into the maelstrom in the galaxy's heart!" Alexander said, studying me from my response.

"They say a lot of things," I said, as I had said a hundred times before. "They don't know *me*, Alexander. They know their stories, and the stories say all manner of things." I tucked my own chin and stood beside him, studying Bennu and not the man beside me. "But I am your father's servant. You know that."

"Do I?"

"Why else would I have come?" I asked, my crushed joy oxidizing rapidly to bitterness in the heated air. "I'd do as well to rest my head in the *Lion's* mouth."

Alexander shrugged his slim shoulders.

I turned to face him, leaned one hip on the edge of the Emperor's table. "I meant what I said, dear boy." With painful slowness, I raised a hand and set it on his shoulder, just above the golden fibula. "It is good to see you."

Once, perhaps, that would have been enough. Perhaps it would have been enough still if Alexander only knew how far I'd come to say those words to him. But he had not been aboard the *Tamerlane* at Padmurak. He had not journeyed through the darkest pits of night, or come to that profane capital at Akterumu. He had never left the Imperial court, that world of whispers and of hidden knives. His mind—which once had been bright and open, hopeful as the minds of all children are hopeful—had become a thing of switches and wheels. Though I meant what I said, he could not hear it, could hear only an old man's craven scheming. Doubtless he thought I meant to cozen him, to twist him back to my camp—as it were. And why should he not think this? Everyone around him thought thus, and used one another as levers, as wedges and knives.

"I wish you'd stayed dead," the prince whispered at last, and moved only his eyes to look at me. They were wet and bright. "It would have been so much easier."

My eyes left his face, driven off by his own. They found the Emperor instead. William XXIII had been watching us from his throne—I knew not for how long—in silence and . . . was that concern? I held his gaze a moment, then looked away. Nicephorus was watching, too, and shook his head minutely from side to side.

I let the prince's shoulder go.

"I know, lad," I said, and pushed off the edge of the display table, dusted the front of my coat. "But for me? Or you?"

Alexander didn't answer, but turned away and strode swiftly off into the gaily colored crowd.

CHAPTER 16

NICEPHORUS

THEY'RE ALL FOOLS, I thought, words repeating for the dozenth time in as many seconds as the door to the council chamber hissed shut behind me. Something of my agitation must have betrayed itself on my face, for the androgyn attendant opposite the portal smiled at me before averting its eyes. I gave the homunculus a polite nod and turned to go, brushing past the Martian Guardsman posted to the right of the door.

You would have His Radiance retreat to Nessus prematurely? Sir Gray Rinehart's incredulity had been evident in the arching of his eyebrows. *Caesar has made his intentions perfectly clear. He will continue his tour of the provinces. He has spoken!*

"Fools." I hissed the word, shoved hands into the pockets of my coat. A pair of logothetes in the grays of civil service lurched out of the way as I hurried up the hall, shaking my head to myself. How many times had I told them the Emperor's movements were known? Dorr's men had sent word from Colchis, Venantian's from Nessus. They were warned.

It is the Emperor's wish that we fortify our borders! exclaimed Leonid Bartosz, the strategos who had fled the command in panic at Berenike and who somehow still sat upon the Emperor's council. *With the Veil overrun, the Centaurine provinces lie exposed to attack! We must gain a sense of our position.*

Bennu is to be a military depot, said Tor Xanthippus, one of the scholiasts who sat on the Legion Advisory Council, subordinate to the Lord Minister of War on Forum. *Our time here is essential. The Seventeenth Fleet leaves Gododdin in four months. In eight years it will be here. Our corps of engineers must prepare for their arrival. Baron Brandt and the locals cannot do so without our assistance.*

I'd told them that I was not arguing that we should abandon Carteia or the outer provinces, only that the Emperor was exposed out here beyond Gododdin, and that Syriani Dorayaica knew where to find him.

You think the Martians and the Knights Excubitor not up to the task of protecting His Radiant Majesty? Bartosz had asked. *Perhaps you think it should be your job instead?*

"Damn fools."

I had not been permitted to see the Emperor since the raising of the first towers of Bennu. The next day, Lord Caedmon Brandt had presided over the groundbreaking on construction for what would be his baronial palace, a project projected to take the next eighty-some years. In the flatlands beyond the new city, great engines had begun carving the earth to lay the foundations of a Legion supply depot, and the peasants who'd escaped the sack of Rothsmoor or who'd migrated from the wilds for the promise of government work and dole had set to work clearing land for the spring planting. Bromos would sprout thickly come summer, and in the years to come would feed the Legions that would call Carteia home.

What would it matter if the Emperor fell?

The hall that ran from the council chamber to the lifts was trapezoidal in cross-section, narrower near the top, and paneled all in darkly fitted wood, hung at intervals with portraits of the Imperial family going back generations. Their names flickered past: white faces, red hair, emerald eyes. *Titania III, William XIX, Titus VIII, Titus Emilian, Gabriel IV, Irene II, Prince Arthur, Alexander V . . .*

I stumbled a moment before the image of Emperor Cyrus II, whose long and oiled and neatly combed red hair and inbred palatine phenotype made him seem almost a clone to young Prince Alexander. Not for the first time, I wondered at them all.

The Aventine House.

Seventeen millennia of them now, since the God Emperor put Old Earth to fire and the sword. Seventeen thousand years. Two hundred and fifty-one monarchs.

One family.

Theirs was the single greatest dynasty in all our human history. Often I have thought of Sargon, the first man to dream of empire. King of Akkad. King of Sumer. King of the Universe, he called himself, when Akkad and Sumer were only cities, and the *universe* of Sargon's day was a scrap of marshland between two rivers. His empire could not have encompassed more than two million people. Perhaps three.

King of the Universe, indeed.

A peasant slave when measured against the lords of the Aventine House, who ruled a half a billion suns. Not Kings of the Universe, but Lords of the Galaxy, and each of them *designed*, bred in long attempt to replicate the powers and character of William the First, who saw the future in his dreams.

A futile attempt, though they knew it not, and toil still in secret.

A brief conversation with the lift operator brought me to ground level, where I decamped the lift and hurried along the corridors to the open hold that served the grounded frigate for an entrance hall. The halls here were dark metal and polished black glass, with brass fixtures and grilles covering speakers and surveillance equipment: the classic Imperial military style. Still fuming, I did not check myself as I moved along the hall, and forced a young lieutenant to scramble out of the way. She saluted awkwardly, and called a question I did not hear.

The Martian Guard held their posts at the landing ramp that served for a lower gate, and the men let me pass out from under the shadow of the *Radiant Dawn*'s sloping and polished black-mirror hull. The Emperor's men had paved much of the earth around the Emperor's frigate, leaving the muddy byways to the outer reaches of the camp. A yard had been arranged with a palisade of chain fences to hem the approach to the *Radiant Dawn*'s ramp, and colossi like scorpions large as cargo vans crouched to either side, their long guns at the ready. Martians in heavy armor kept watch from their backs, and a full detachment manned the gate and ran checks on the officers and functionaries that filtered in and out.

None troubled me. My face was known.

"You there, man!" I signaled to the duty officer. "Order a car round, if you would. I need a ride back to my ship!"

The duty officer saluted at once and turned to see it done, shouted to a junior man down the way to signal the motor pool. I shoved my hands deep into the pockets of my coat as I waited, wishing I'd had the sense to wear my military tunic, whose high, close-fitting collar would have served to insulate me against the winter's chill. My fingers brushed against something deep in one pocket, and—curious—I drew it out and looked at it. It was a piece of *pate de fruits*, one of the gels Crim was always making and handing out.

I just kept looking at it, not really seeing it.

The cold wind stung my face, and I shut my eyes, closed my fist over the paper-wrapped candy. It was hard as stone, and no wonder—it must have been in the pocket of that coat for decades and decades. I must have put it there before Padmurak. He must have given it to me that last voyage, as we walked the *Tamerlane*'s equator.

"Lord Marlowe!" The duty officer had returned, raised his hand in salute. "Your car's coming round. This way." He gestured that I should follow, and I did, passing with him through the chain gate and out into the main road. Gray snow had started falling once again in heavy, scale-like flakes, blew in cyclones on the wind.

A nondescript black service vehicle—armored like a tank on four spherical wheels—rounded the corner from our right, exiting an aftward hold via a second ramp from the frigate at our backs. Turning to watch it come, I glanced up at the arcing hull of the *Radiant Dawn* as it rose a dozen levels above us, comms equipment bristling against the sky like slender ramparts.

The officer waved the car down, but it sped up again as quickly as it slowed, hurried down the road to the corner and turned left out of sight.

The duty officer chased after half a dozen steps, waving his arms and cursing as he went.

"What's the matter?" I asked.

The Martian turned back to look at me, fingers to the right side of his helmet, as if by doing so he might better hear. "What are you playing at, Willem? You were supposed to take Lord Marlowe back to his ship in T-4!" He paused. "What do you mean *belayed*?" He hissed, turned to me. "A thousand pardons, my lord. I'm not sure what that was. I'll get it sorted. And I'll deal with my man Willem when he gets back, mark my words."

"I can walk if that's easier," I said, inclining my head toward the busy camp street. "It's only a couple miles. I've done it before." I did not relish the prospect, cold as it was, and doubly with the snow kicking up again.

"Nonsense, my lord," the Martian said, "I'll call another car. Just a moment." And at that he ducked his head and turned to call the motor pool again.

As he did so, a second vehicle descended the ramp and turned onto the hastily paved street. It was not one of the standard ball-wheeled ground-cars, but one of the all-terrain transports used to carry men and supplies over the trackless lands between the Emperor's camp and the new city of Bennu. It had a narrow, high-slung carriage that reminded me almost of a dragonfly. Its six wheels were all situated far to the front, so that the rear of the carriage hung out several feet over bare ground, allowing it to drop its rear ramp for the offloading of men or supplies. The whole thing bounced and swayed as it made its way toward us, its wheels nearly so tall as me, and came to a halt.

The side hatch opened, and a young Martian officer with a scarred dark face leaned out with a friendly smile. "Lord Marlowe, sir?"

"I am!" I called back, moving to the curb.

"We're headed out past T-4. We can drop you!"

I turned to the duty officer, asked, "This you?"

He shook his head, signaled his earpiece with a finger. "Still on the line."

"I'll take this one!" I said, and saluted the fellow before mounting the rungs to the little hatch.

The scarred but smiling Martian helped me in, keyed the door shut behind me.

All at once, I understood everything that had just happened.

"Do take a seat, Lord Marlowe," said the man seated against the far wall of the compartment—if *man* were the proper term.

"Lord Nicephorus!" I said, unable to conceal my surprise. "To what do I owe the pleasure?"

The Emperor's chamberlain smiled thinly at me, indicated the tufted leather bench opposite it. "Please," it said. "Sit."

Sensing that the jaws of some intangible beast had fastened about me, I did as I was ordered. There was something horribly familiar about the androgyn's manner and bearing, about the timbre of its voice, but I couldn't quite place it.

As I settled into the seat opposite it, Lord Nicephorus touched a contact patch behind one ear. It must have subvocalized an order to the driver, for in the next minute we were off, merging smoothly onto the main road. I was seated backward, and so watched the *Radiant Dawn* grow slightly smaller through the round window by the hatch the Martian had closed. Of that solitary Martian, there was no more sign. He must have returned to the driver's compartment and closed the wood-veneered door.

The Lord Chamberlain and I were utterly alone.

"You did well to defend yourself at your reception here," Nicephorus said, twisting the golden ring upon its left index finger. "His Radiance hoped you would. You gave us ample reason to show mercy."

I wondered at the *us*, but did not press the question. Instead, I wondered, "Would he have ordered me to . . . *remove* myself? If I had not given him *ample reason to show mercy*?"

"Nothing so vulgar," the Lord Chamberlain said. "But we would have needed to chasten you—publicly—and to find subtler use for you. Indeed, we may still. *Find subtler use,* I mean. Your embassy to Padmurak was meant to further remove you from the axis of our world—"

"Obviously," I interjected.

The androgyn's hairless eyebrows contracted. "But as is your nature and curse, it had the opposite effect. Rumors of your heroic death metastasize like a cancer, and already they say the Halfmortal has cheated death *again.*"

I was silent. The whole carriage rocked as the vehicle rounded a corner, and I saw a triple column of legionnaires on patrol in ivory plate. The *Radiant Dawn* was still visible behind us, dwarfing the nearer ships brought down to serve as offices and barracks.

"There are those on the Council—and those who hold Caesar's ear more generally—who called for it. For you to *remove yourself,* as you put it. But His Radiance put an end to all that." Some other word or words had floated almost to the tip of the homunculi's tongue, and there was an expression in its smooth face I could not name. "Still, I suppose you don't need me to tell you that you have enemies."

"Is that what this is about?" I asked, spreading my hands to indicate the rich carriage about us, all leather and darkly polished wood. "You might have sent a holograph, my lord."

Nicephorus only smiled, but the light of it did not reach the creature's emerald eyes.

We drove on in silence then for a tense moment, neither one of us stirring. Our groundcar was picking up speed, row upon row of the camp city moving steadily by. I wondered at that. I had ridden back and forth between the *Ascalon* and *Radiant Dawn* perhaps a dozen times by then. One did not simply travel through the camp city without stopping. There was just too much traffic.

"Lord Nicephorus . . ." I began when we had trundled off the paved way and onto the muddy tracks that extended from the heart of the camp to its periphery, steadying myself as the carriage bounced. "*You* have the Emperor's ear . . ."

"If you are asking whether or not I am your enemy," the Lord Chamberlain spoke over me, "you've nothing to fear." Nicephorus scratched its nose. "But then, that is what I'd say whether I were your enemy or not, mm?"

My eyes narrowed involuntarily. "I wasn't going to ask a question," I said. "But you have the Emperor's ear. You must convince him to return to Forum at once. His movements—this entire tour—are compromised. The Cielcin have your full itinerary. Vanaheim, Balanrot, Perfugium. The list!"

"I know."

"You know?" I echoed, dumbly. "My lord, I have been trying for weeks to persuade the Advisory Council to abandon this mission. Rinehart. Xanthippus. Bartosz. They will not listen."

"I know that, too," Nicephorus said. "As does Caesar."

"And yet we do nothing?"

"We do not do *nothing*, Lord Marlowe," the chamberlain said. "We are staying the course. His Radiance has no wish to leave the border unsecured."

Scowling, I shook my head. "He's too exposed out here!" I said.

"We are well defended," Nicephorus said. "There are three Martian Legions in orbit above Carteia, and *four* Orionid Legions. Hundreds of ships."

"You have not seen the fleet the Prophet has amassed," I said, still shaking my head. "Syriani Dorayaica has rallied all their clans to itself. It's united them under one banner. More than a thousand worldships, each the size of a *moon*. Who knows how many billion soldiers? Seven legions are not enough."

The carriage rocked as the wheels struck some rut or divot made by the earlier passing of a colossus. Nicephorus caught a leather strap on the sloping wall to its right to steady itself. After a tense moment, the androgyn nodded. "I understand." The Lord Chamberlain leaned back against the cushions, a frown creasing its palatine-handsome face. "Have you considered that it is Forum that is less safe?"

I blinked at the homunculus.

"Its location is known. The Cielcin must have thousands of our starcharts by now. Tens of thousands. How many of our ships have they captured?" Nicephorus's face seemed frozen, an ivory mask without warmth or expression. How like the Emperor it seemed then, pharaonic in its calm. "We might amass a thousand legions at Forum. If what you say is true, a thousand will not be enough." When I said nothing, the Lord Chamberlain continued, "Do you not think the Emperor has weighed these matters carefully? You are not the only man in the Imperium who can *think*, my lord."

Whatever growling response I'd made ready for the Lord Chamberlain died before I could use it. Something out the window distracted me, and I leaned nearer the glass to get a second view. It was the yellow placard of a street marker—a sheet of cheaply printed steel painted with the Galstani letter *D* and the Mandari number *11* in thick, black lines.

I frowned at it, and turned that frown on Nicephorus. "Where are you taking me?"

The homunculus didn't answer.

"My ship is in section T-4, my lord," I said. "We're going the wrong way."

"We're not going to your ship," Nicephorus said.

"Where then?" I asked, a sudden fear settling over me. Was Nicephorus one of the Lions? An ally of the Empress on Forum? Or was it something else? My hand went to my belt, feeling for the sword handle that should have been beneath my coat. The sorcerer, Iovan, had suggested that MINOS had its agents even among the Imperial elite.

Nicephorus gave no answer, but raised bare eyebrows at my questing hand. Too late, I remembered I had no sword, I had thrown the ruin of Sir Olorin's weapon into the sea on Colchis, and I had no chance to commission a smith to forge the core Valka believed was Gibson's into a new hilt.

"What's the meaning of this?" I hissed, not bothering to hide my anger. "Who are you working for?"

"Working for?" Nicephorus asked, incredulous. "Why, *His Radiance,* of course. I told you: I'm not your enemy. And if I were, I'd not have spent the last ten minutes talking. You'd be dead already, Lord Marlowe. Neither I nor the Martians like to waste time."

"You ordered the other car off," I said, feeling my brows knit. "Where are you taking me?"

"We haven't far to go," the fellow said. "Better not to talk."

Starved for options, I sat back in my seat and watched the Emperor's camp diminish behind us over Lord Nicephorus's shoulder. The fins and conning spires of the various frigates and shuttles almost looked like a city. We had left them all behind, were crossing the naked fields of snow beyond the outermost sentries.

Alone.

"Stop that," snapped Nicephorus after my third attempt to turn round and try to see where we were going. I relented.

After perhaps another twenty minutes of uneasy quiet, the engine shifted down. The quality of the snow crunching beneath the heavy tires changed, grew heavier and louder, and the car labored as it turned slightly left. The camp had become a black patch against the horizon, barely visible through the snow.

A huge, black bank rose out the window to my left, its surface covered here and there in snow. We passed it by, and at once I felt we were descending, proceeding along a gentle slope until the Emperor's camp was lost to sight. More dark mounds and deep snow drifts rose to either side. In one I thought I saw a pointed arch yawning, and rows of square windows open and whistling. Icicles. Pillars. A shattered aqueduct.

I knew where we were then.

"This is Rothsmoor," I said. "The old city?"

Nicephorus nodded.

"What is this about?" I asked, but the androgyn only shook its head and pressed that ringed finger to its lips.

There was nothing left standing in the city. The Cielcin had launched their raiding parties first, sent berserkers howling into the streets and houses, the schools and stores and beds. They had killed and raped and feasted as they pleased, and rounded up those they had not killed—women and children and old men, for the most part—and carried them off in their siege towers, simple rockets that returned to their worldship. The rude markings of their presence still shone on the faces of blasted buildings, daubed in blue paints or in that rusted black we all instinctively recognize as blood. The Emperor's men had—I guessed—cleared all the bones away; the heads on stakes and mounded bones, the skins like tattered flags. Those that remained after the bombings, at any rate, for once their pillage was done, the Pale had rained fire on the city. They had left nothing, not even the old baron and his family cowering in their bunkers beneath the palace ziggurat.

Nothing but ashes and snow.

Another fifteen or so minutes passed before we ground to a halt.

"Lord Nicephorus." The scarred Martian emerged from the forward compartment, another of his brothers in tow. "We're here."

"Capital!" The androgyn stood, and turning, opened a compartment behind its seat and drew out a heavy cloak of scarlet wool lined and collared with ermine. It put the garment on, pulled up the deep hood to cover its bald head and ears, and followed the Martians as they dropped the rear ramp. It would not do for the Lord Chamberlain of the Sollan Empire to struggle down the short ladder I had used.

I followed Nicephorus and the Martians out into the snow, a solitary figure in black behind three in red.

The deep quiet struck me first. The falling snow covered the world in a down blanket that swallowed all sound save the crunch and passage of our feet. I felt I could have stood there for many hours—despite the cold, despite the ruin—and simply *listened*. So deep was that quietude that I felt a gentle peace fall upon me, and for a moment I forgot the strangeness and the danger of my circumstances, and followed Nicephorus without complaint. The androgyn's red cloak trailed on the snow to either side of the channel the two Martians carved with their passage, and I was conscious of my own coat as it caught in knee-high drifts of snow.

Without a sword, I kept one hand near the hilt of the knife strapped parallel to my belt on the back side, within reach of the thumb trigger to activate my shield. Nicephorus had a point. If it was the creature's intent to kill me, it might have done so in the groundcar. There was no need to go to all this trouble.

"This way!" the scarred Martian called back over his shoulder.

Glancing back, I saw another pair of Martian Guardsmen following. They must have emerged from the forward compartment of Nicephorus's van after we had. And there! Another flash of red! A Martian sentinel atop the ruins of a tumbled-down section of wall.

My sense of gentle calm curled and withered and blew away.

I knew where I was going, and who I had been brought to meet.

CHAPTER 17

DISQUIET GODS

I FOLLOWED THE MARTIANS and the cloaked Lord Chamberlain up a cracked and snowy stair, through busted doors into the lobby of what appeared to have once been a fine hotel. The windows all were shattered, and the drifting snow had floated in and left piles beneath the damaged sills.

Sofas and winged armchairs all were overturned or smashed, and the stained-glass lamps that had decorated the concierge lay shattered and ruined. A huge oil painting depicting men and women lounging together in a tiled pool had been slashed and spattered with old gore long turned black. The marks of talons and of clawed feet showed in the upholstery, in the marks deeply gouged into the wood paneling and countertops.

We did not pause to reflect on any of this devastation, but proceeded instead along a back corridor, past the restrooms with their ruined frescoes and a bank of hollowed-out dispensaries. Another Martian emerged from a side door ahead and to our right, saluted Nicephorus and myself.

A further two Martians opened double doors at the end of the hall, and we ascended a short flight of steps to what had once been the grand dining room. The balconies of two upper levels wrapped around the lavish chamber, supported by pillars clad in black marble. The once-great chandelier—a constellation of ten thousand crystal tears—lay in icy shards amid the banquet tables in the center of the round space. Seeing the far wall, I understood why this place had been chosen for our secret meeting: it was alumglass, not the common glass of the windows in the lobby, and so the room was proof yet against the elements—and against small-arms fire from without.

Even still, it was not proof against the cold.

A concave arc of these alumglass windows dominated the space opposite the entrance, where further steps ran up to a dais where once, perhaps, an orchestra had played to entertain the hotel's wealthy guests. Brass veins separated the still-whole panes, through which one could see much of the devastation and ruin of the once-great city of Rothsmoor: an ocean of blackened stone and ash half-buried by winter's gracious cold. Directly in the center of the orchestra there stood a seated marble statue whose head had been knocked off.

The man I had expected to find was standing there beside it, right against the glass, his nose almost pressed to it, like a scarlet shadow cast by that throned and headless statue that might once have been of himself.

"Lord Marlowe," said William Caesar, not turning to face me. He gestured with one red hand to the space beside him. "Come and join me, if you would."

I hesitated only a moment, then mounted the two short steps to the orchestra beneath the windows. Why would the Emperor go to all this trouble to meet with me? He might as easily have summoned me to his quarters, or to some secure conference room aboard the *Radiant Dawn*. I could feel my frown deepening as I moved to stand beside him.

Our reflections peered back at us, ghosts lost in the ruins of that dead city.

"Seventeen million, three hundred twelve thousand, nine hundred seven," Caesar intoned, not stirring. "The population of the city, per the last census run by the late House Bampasis." I did not reply, sensed that any reply would be unwelcome just then. "We've no way of knowing how many fell in the first bombardment, or were carried off by the Pale. We don't even know how many escaped." The Emperor tucked his chin—against the cold, I deemed. "Most likely, we never will."

"We never will," I echoed, sensing the time had come. "We'll get close, but I always wonder how many we miss." My mind returned to the high bluffs of Thessa, to the funeral markers I'd raised, to all the names of my own people that I could not remember.

"Each one of them haunts me, Lord Marlowe," the Emperor said, not taking his eyes from the ruins of Rothsmoor. "I've been out here half a hundred times since we landed two years ago, and before. On Siraganon. And Balanrot. And the others. I've made myself *look*." I recognized the four quick, staccato breaths of a scholiast breathing technique, and thought I could guess the words the Emperor murmured in his heart of hearts.

Grief is deep water.

Rage is blindness.

Without turning to look at me, he continued. "I know you know how it feels," he said. "I read your reports. What happened to your people . . . there is no word, no curse black enough for such atrocity. Please know: I meant what I said when you arrived. I *do* grieve with you. For every one of your men." Still he did not turn, he hardly moved, but there was a thickness to his words that rang of truth. Each syllable fell like blood dripping from the altar stone. One by one. "Had I but known what would befall you on Padmurak, had I had but a *whiff* of the Lothrians' treachery . . . I would not have sent you. Their blood is on my hands."

I looked on Caesar in amazement, not daring to speak. It was the man himself who spoke. Not the crown. Not the throne. No royal *we*, only the honest *I*—so much smaller, so much greater. Half-choked, I stammered, "They were your servants, Radiant Majesty."

"They were," William said, still watching the burned city in the snow. "But I was theirs, and a poor servant I have been." His nostrils flared, and he inclined his head at the ruins. "This was a fair city once. *Seventeen million* people lived here. All of them gone. All because I failed them."

Was I meant to console him? To tell him he'd done all he could—was doing all he could?

I said nothing.

"How can we ever hope to prevail against such demons, I ask you?"

"By being demons ourselves, sire," I said.

My self-indulgence drew a short laugh from our Imperator, but he pressed his lips together quickly and did not reply.

"You know the old stories perhaps better than I," I said into the fresh quiet. "Angels are only demons that kept their oaths . . . and still serve good and truth."

"Good and truth," the Emperor repeated. "Quite right, my lord. Quite right . . ." He nodded as if to himself, then without warning or transition he raised his voice to fill the echoing dining hall. "Leave us!"

Without hesitation, the heavy tread of armored men sounded on the floor behind and on the balconies above and to either side. Looking back, I saw the red of Martian armor appear as a dozen hoplites or more deactivated their active camouflage, and turning to my right I saw the mirrored silhouette of an Excubitor in its white cloak appear as if from nowhere. They all retreated, vanishing through the double doors or through side passages on the levels above.

In a twinkling, only Nicephorus remained, its hood thrown back, breath misting the air as it settled into a rare intact chair to one side of a smashed table on the dining floor below us.

Emperor William XXIII cocked his ear to listen, and when at last the doors were closed, he turned fully away from the window to face me. He wore a cloak of scarlet and ermine identical to the one Nicephorus had donned, which he threw back as he turned, revealing the white armor beneath.

"Are they gone?" he asked.

"They're gone," Nicephorus answered, removing its finger from the contact patch behind one ear.

The Emperor was nodding. "Very good," he said, and rounded on me. Gone was the thick emotion in his voice, gone the man beneath the crown. He was all *Emperor* again, and the business of Empire burned in eye and breast. "Tell me, Lord Marlowe: did you find them?"

I blinked at him. "Find who?"

"Your *Quiet*," the Emperor said. "You went to Colchis to find them. Did you succeed?"

Again, I blinked at him, and tried to work myself backward in time to the conversation the Emperor referred to. It had been before Berenike. Before Annica. Before we sailed to Colchis for the first time, immediately after I'd survived Prince Philip and Prince Ricard's assassin in the Grand Colosseum. So very, very long ago. The Emperor had asked me how I knew of the Quiet, asked me if I truly had the visions they said I had . . .

"I did," I said, and held his gaze.

Caesar's face was an ivory mask, a scholiast's pose, utterly void of expression—the perfect realization of pharaonic calm. "Tell me," he said, and clasped gloved and glittering hands before himself.

"I . . ." My voice cracked as I tried to begin. Where should I begin? Where could I? My eyes flickered down to Nicephorus, flicked back to His Radiance, uncertainty a sucking wound in my chest. "On Forum, that last time . . . we spoke of Brethren, of the Mericanii daimon enslaved to the King of Vorgossos." If I expected William to interrupt, I was disappointed. "Something in the nature of its biology . . . its programming . . . allows it to perceive time as you and I perceive this room. That day, I told you how it had peered into the future and found *the Quiet* peering back, how it told me the Quiet had interfered with human history since at least the time of the God Emperor, how it believed—how *I* believed—that the Quiet was a race situated at the end of time. I was mostly right."

"Mostly?" Nicephorus prodded.

The Lord Chamberlain's interjection drew my gaze, and I licked my lips in apprehensive calculation. "Radiant Majesty," I asked after the space of a breath, "did you know there was a Mericanii daimon beneath the Imperial Library on Colchis when you sent me there?"

To my great astonishment, the Emperor barked a short, rough laugh. "Black Earth, no!" He swore, and chuckled. "You have a talent for putting your foot in it, Lord Marlowe, and no mistake! I did not know of the machine. Indeed, if I had—I would never have sent you to Colchis." His face grew darker then, and he asked, "Is that why you returned to Colchis before reporting in? Special Security tells me you entered the athenaeum there, and were rebuffed by the primate there. Were you trying to get in to see the daimon?"

"What?" I did not bother to check my shock. "No! No, I went to Colchis to bury my dead. One of my companions was buried there already, and my childhood tutor had retired to the athenaeum there . . ." I did not give the name of Tor Gibson of Syracuse, lest the Emperor and Special Security suspect the late Prince Philippe in some nonexistent conspiracy. I reminded myself that Gibson had been a traitor before he was my tutor. "I went for comfort, but he was long dead."

The Emperor's eyes narrowed almost imperceptibly. Gone was the man who had offered me his condolences mere minutes before. "The daimon is no longer any of your concern," he said. "The Chantry have appointed their Sentinels to monitor the situation. It is well guarded."

"That is well!" I said without hesitation, thinking of the old ship and Horizon's rotting consciousness, senile relic of a cruel and barbaric age. "The galaxy is safer for it." My tongue felt thick and very dry in my mouth. I chewed a slow moment, trying to continue. "I had hoped to find some record of the God Emperor's time. Records attesting to his powers—not scripture."

"Why?" It was Nicephorus who asked the question.

I looked down at it, held its green gaze. "Because Kharn Sagara told me the God Emperor had visions." Turning back to His Radiance, I said, "I told you as much on Forum, Radiant Majesty. Kharn Sagara told me that William the First *saw the future*, and that it was his visions that delivered man from the machines."

"They say you can see the future," the Emperor said, connecting thoughts which I'd not given voice.

"I can't," I said, since we were speaking *truth*. "That isn't how it works.

I was shown the future. Sometimes . . . sometimes I remember bits of what I saw."

"Mother Earth keep us," the Emperor breathed, forming the sign of the sun disc. "You do not deny it?"

"Not here," I said, indicating the crumbling splendor and the devastation about us with my eyes. "Not now." My neck bent, and looking down I half-expected to see the points of laser light dancing across my chest as the Martians took their aim.

When the Emperor spoke again, it was in hushed tones, words little more than breaths. "So it's true," he said, a hand rising to cover his mouth. He looked down at Nicephorus. "You really are . . . the *one*."

How could any man respond to such an accusation?

"You denied it. On Nessus when we last met." The Emperor took a step back, his pharaonic mask cracking. "That was wisely done. But we are alone now. That is why I brought you here. No one is listening, and no one will get past my men." He let his ringed hand fall, released a breath that turned to steam in the frosty air. His shock and joy ebbed, and after a beat he was *the Emperor* again, grave as stone. "All that we here discuss, you will tell no man—not even your Tavrosi woman. Am I clear?"

"Yes, Honorable Caesar," I said.

"Swear it."

"I swear it."

"Swear it by the oath you swore to me," the Emperor said, almost snarling.

I took a half step back, startled by the man's sudden intensity. "I so swear," I said again, and raised my right hand. "By my oath, and by these." With my left, I drew out the silver chain I wore from around my neck, baring the Quiet's shell and Valka's phylactery both.

That seemed to satisfy the Emperor, who pursed his lips and glanced once more to Nicephorus, but the androgyn was silent as the Dullahan statue seated above us all.

"You . . . said you sought for record of the God Emperor's day," said William XXIII. "Have you ever heard of the *Acts of Will*? Called by some *The Book of the Son of Suns*?" Caesar's eyes were like green stars. There was an intensity in him I had never seen before, a fervency like that of the *vates* who preach of the end of days.

I only looked at him blankly.

The Emperor sucked his teeth, touched the ruby in the center of the circlet on his brow as though it were a bead of bloody sweat. He began to nod his head, and I sensed that he was working himself up to speak. After a moment, he said, "All that I am about to tell you is known only to a few. To myself. To Nicephorus here. To certain of the Chantry and the High College. Precious few."

"I have given you my word, Radiance."

"On your life, then," the Emperor said. "Only three copies remain. The Chantry destroyed the others before the sixth millennium. One copy is in the Eternal City under lock and key. The second is on Avalon, at the Cenotaph. And the third lies in a vault on Old Earth."

"On Old Earth!" I gasped, shocked to hear of the homeworld spoken of as a place and not as goddess or paradise. "But . . . what is it?"

William suppressed an amused smile. "A biography—a journal, really—written by the God Emperor's . . . woman."

"His woman?" I asked, understanding why the text would have been suppressed by the early Chantry. Though the lords and ladies of the Imperium kept slave-boys and concubines alike, it would never do to suggest the Firstborn Son of Earth—the God Emperor himself—possessed any vices. "Not his wife?"

"He did not love his wife," the Emperor said. "And she shared neither his bed nor his counsel. No. *The Acts* was written by Catherine the White. She was his closest companion, and the mother of his son. His *real* mother."

My understanding only grew sharper. "Victor Sebastos?" I asked, naming the second Emperor.

"Victor the *Bastard*," the Emperor replied with bloody emphasis. "Impatian's histories are mostly lies, I fear. Victor's pedigree was common knowledge in his day, but the Throne and the Chantry both have painted over it in the eons since."

It would have been one thing to suggest the God Emperor possessed mortal vices. Quite another to suggest the blood Imperial was illegitimate. In those days, lords and ladies—even the Aventine House—still bore and fathered children in the old way, as the plebs and beasts still do. I was reeling.

"That day on Forum . . . you did not ask if the tales of William's visions were true." The Emperor turned again from me, seeming to find it easier to speak to his own pale reflection in the armored glass. "Catherine wrote about William. About the *man*, not the god. For that more than any other reason, she had to be done away with. It was the work of centuries, burying her memory. But she is gone now, remembered only by pagan cultists in backward corners of the oldest worlds, her story changed by time beyond all recognition . . . but we have her book." His shoulders hunched. "She wrote about his dreams, she who woke so often in the night beside him. She said he would wake screaming, covered in sweat, shaking in the dark. She said he had *seizures*, Marlowe. Always seizures. She says he said a *voice* spoke to him in the night, just as your friend, Sagara, told you. But she confirms much of the legend. Often he would awake in the dead of night with coordinates, and go to his generals with a plan. Always he would know where and when the Mericanii would strike, where they had sent their colonies. He would order his ships to warp to new systems, where they would find beachheads already built. It was his visions that enabled him to outmaneuver the machines. That much is true."

"This voice . . ." I asked, my own voice halting. "Did he describe it to her?"

A cool, clear voice answered from below us. *"He said it was as though some friend who had always been there, ever by his side, had taken him by both his shoulders and—as if after a hundred years of silence—had finally started to speak."* I looked round, still reeling from the shock of revelation, and found Nicephorus—eyes closed—reciting in that flattened, affectless way redolent of the scholiasts. Reciting in Classical English. *"It spoke to him—not in words, but in images—in sounds and feelings that were like words to him as heard them. It showed him many things, he said. The ocean of stars unrolled beneath his feet. The Earth afire. The cities and the pyramids of America laid low. And the children of Earth and of iron were laid low with them, and the smoke of their burning blackened the skies forever.*

"Then he saw a new city descending as from heaven and shining like the sun. And angels took him by the hand and brought him up, and it was not only the stars but the centuries that knelt before his feet. Only then did the voice speak to him in words like the words of men, saying, 'O Prince of Hosts, O Father of Trillions, all this must be.'"

I felt my blood run cold, and turned myself to face the window glass, the better to hide my face from the Emperor and the androgyn alike. Nicephorus kept up its recitation for another verse or two, but I had ceased to hear it.

. . . this must be.

Words that were not words, but images and feelings. The unvoiced voice of he who showed me the visions on Emesh, that poured all of time in through my eyes upon the mountain, that turned me back from the Howling Dark beyond Death. Utannash the Deceiver.

The Quiet.

"Lord Marlowe?" The Emperor's hand was on my shoulder. "What is it?"

"It's nothing," I said. "It's a lot to take in is all."

Caesar withdrew his hand. "He called it *the Hidden One*, or so Catherine says."

"The Hidden One?" I looked round at Caesar, put my shoulder to the glass.

"His guardian angel." The Emperor crossed his arms, stroked his chin with one hand. "The God Emperor told Holy Catherine it was the Hidden One that was the source of all his insight, denied that he had any special power in himself. Just as you do."

I put up a hand for silence, even though it was the Emperor I hushed. My mind was a while catching up. For decades—centuries—I'd had my suspicions. But to have those suspicions, those *fears* confirmed—and by the Emperor himself—shook me to my atoms.

This must be.

The same words. The same voice. The same *thing* that had spoken to the God Emperor had spoken to me. "You are the shortest way . . ." I murmured. Thus too had the God Emperor been. Another link in the bright chain to hook the Quiet and haul it out of undiscovered time. How many of us had there been since men were children? How many more were there yet to be?

"What?"

"Nothing," I said, shaking my head as if to clear it of some fog. "It doesn't matter." I blinked round at Nicephorus, at the Emperor, at the once-splendid dining hall filled with broken tables and shattered glass.

Both the Emperor and Nicephorus were staring at me, silent in their matching scarlet robes. One could almost hear the snow falling in the hushed calm beyond the alumglass, it was so quiet.

Quiet . . .

"I think, Lord Marlowe," said the Emperor into that pregnant silence, "that you had better tell us everything."

I caught myself sizing up the Emperor and Nicephorus both, checking the distance to the double doors like a man planning to run. What could I say? Did I dare say *everything*? My mind raced to the recording Pallino's suit had made during the battle aboard the *Demiurge*, the one that contained the only record of my death and resurrection during the fight with Aranata Otiolo. Crim had hidden it from the Inquisition when they put me to the Question, but restored it to its proper place in the *Tamerlane's* vaults when we left Forum for the last time. It had not been taken by the

Chantry when they took me at Sybaris, had not been found in all twelve years of my trial on Thermon.

What had happened to it?

I supposed that it lay in the wreckage upon the black sands of Eue. Had the Prophet's soldiers found it as they dismantled the *Tamerlane*? Or had the Shiomu Elusha left the ruined hulk to molder there in the sight of Miudanar until the end of time? It was almost a shame. Dorayaica lusted after *truth*. Had it but known to look, it might have found that polished little sphere of crystal, and in it the one truth it could never accept. The Truth of Utannash.

At once I was aware of both the Emperor's and Nicephorus's eyes upon me—emerald and emerald. Had I not spoken for too long?

Fear is a poison, Gibson's voice murmured in one ear.

I found myself nodding agreement, working myself up to speak as the Emperor had done. "It's the same voice," I said at last. "My Quiet, the God Emperor's Hidden One. *This must be.* This must be. The same words. He said the same words to me."

"Convenient," said Nicephorus, evidently the skeptic. ɪ

"On Emesh!" I exclaimed. "He showed me a vision of Dorayaica marching across the stars! Radiance, you remember. After the Battle of Hermonassa, you gave audience to survivors of the battle. A legionnaire called Carax spoke to you. He spoke of his meeting with the Scourge of Earth. I interrupted him, asked him if the xenobite prince wore a crown. I described Dorayaica because I had *seen* Dorayaica before. In my visions. Do you remember?" The Emperor opened his mouth, eyes turned to one side in recollection. "On Emesh," I said again. "And again in the visions the Quiet gave the Brethren of Vorgossos for me. And again later, I saw the Cielcin fleets burned from the sky. I saw our worlds burning, and that same voice, the voice your Catherine described—speaking in words that were not words, but visions and feelings and sounds—that same voice told me that all I saw *must* be. By my oath, I swear it."

With every new word, the Emperor seemed to shrink. The light in his eyes dimmed, as if shuttered by some unseen mechanism. How can I describe it? He looked at me the way Bassander Lin had done after the battle on the *Demiurge*. The little light that remained in his eyes shimmered there. Not the light of tears. It was the light of *belief* that smoldered in Emperor William's eyes, small, fragile, and flickering.

"Bollocks," said Nicephorus—who had none. "Nonsense. It's nonsense."

The Emperor shook himself, and I turned to find the androgyn on its feet. The Lord Chamberlain stared up at me with hard eyes.

"I can hear no more of this. William, you waste your time with this charlatan." Nicephorus raised its chin. "Lord Marlowe, we show you a glass slipper and you claim it was fashioned for your foot. *Quiet* indeed! You say these *visions* of yours come from *the Quiet*, but there is no such thing."

Still shaken by the revelation at hand, I could hardly muster a response. Like a boxer wrong-footed by a shovel to the ribs, I stumbled, dropped my guard for the overhand that rang my brain and soul like a bell. "What?" I asked, stupidly.

"Do you know where that name comes from? *The Quiet?*" Nicephorus asked.

My memory rushed back to warm, fly-haunted nights on Emesh long ago. To Valka's cluttered apartments in the diplomatic wing of the house of Balian Mataro.

Ke kuchya mnousseir, she'd called them then, speaking in her native tongue. *The Quiet Ones.*

"Because no one can read the markings in their . . . in the ruins?" I said. "Because there are no artifacts *beyond* the ruins themselves."

"Just so," Nicephorus said, gripping the hems of its cloak. "*We* named them. You claim this *thing* that speaks to you calls itself *the Quiet.* But the Quiet don't exist! They're a nonsense the ancient xenologists concocted to explain what they couldn't understand! A nonsense that we and the Chantry have allowed to persist!" Agitated, Nicephorus shook its bald head. "Will you tell us Zeus spoke to you in a dream next? Or Ulmo? What other fables have you to peddle to us, my lord?"

"Nic, that's enough!" The Emperor did not shout, but raised a hand for silence.

Like a stone then silence fell. Nicephorus's jaw worked as though the homunculus meant to bite through stone or smash its teeth to flinders. I looked down at it, slow to understand the Lord Chamberlain's problem.

I never said he called himself *"the Quiet,"* I thought to myself, not quite daring to speak into the Emperor's new-made calm. *The Quiet had never called himself anything.*

"Mostly right," the Emperor said, turning from his servant to me. "Earlier. You said you were *mostly right* when you believed the Quiet to be a race situated at the end of time. What did you mean?"

"I never said he called himself *the Quiet,*" I said aloud, addressing

Nicephorus in relative safety before addressing His Radiance. "We called him that—I called him that—before. Before I knew him."

"Him?" The Emperor had caught the operant word at last. "What do you mean, *him*?"

"What did you mean by *a nonsense*?" I asked both the Emperor and chamberlain at once. "A nonsense you and the Chantry have allowed to persist?"

The Emperor's eyes flashed again, not shuttered as they'd been before Nicephorus's outburst. "You first."

I swallowed, held the Emperor's gaze for a long moment. Neither one of us moved. Despite the closeness and privacy of our conversation, I knew I walked the edge of a knife, trod a path narrower than the span over darkness from the place of Dorayaica's hidden throne. Whatever else he was— whatever else he knew—William was *Caesar*, Radiant Emperor of Man. This demanded all my care, for my life—and not only my life, but Valka's and Lorian's—hung there in the balance.

"The Quiet isn't a people. Or if he is, I know but one." I raised one finger, let it fall. "It . . . he is a *person*. An intelligence. A will." I could feel Nicephorus coiling its tongue to strike, and scrambled to fill the air. "The God Emperor had the right of it. The Hidden *One*. It is *one* voice that speaks to me, Radiance. *One* voice. And his time is coming, not past! That much is true." Sensing it was called for, I went to one knee. "On Forum, I told you I served *him*. The Quiet, the Hidden One—call him what you like. I do serve him. He asked me to save mankind. To play my part saving it. You are the Emperor of Mankind, and I have never left your service."

The royal shadow fell over me. "On your feet, Lord Marlowe. You needn't grovel."

Looking up, I felt suddenly foolish, and stood. "Syriani Dorayaica be- lieves the Quiet is . . . believes the Quiet created the universe. You said you read my report?"

"I did," the Emperor said, holding my eye with his. "That was not in it."

"No," I said. "It wasn't."

"God!" Nicephorus could take it no longer. "You ask us to believe that *God* speaks to you?"

To my surprise, the Emperor hissed, "We believe it of William, Nic. What cause have we to think revelation ended with God's Emperor?"

God's Emperor. I stood a little straighter, ears pricking. *Not God Emperor.*

The conversation cooled again to unsteady quiet. Nicephorus still stood at the bottom of the stairs before the orchestra. The Emperor stared at some spot on the ruined carpet between my feet and the androgyn. I did not dare to move.

"What did you mean?" Some part of me dared to speak. "That the Quiet is a nonsense?"

Handed this simple question, the Emperor came back to himself, gathered his cloak about him. "We've been hunting for extraterranic life since before we could fly," he said. "Before we ever left Earth we . . . hoped we were not alone. They say Felsenburgh's machines received some signal from the stars, and that it was for that reason the Mericanii began to launch their colony missions. I don't know that I believe *that* part of the story, but . . . we were always looking. Always listening, but there was nothing.

"The magi of the time—there were no scholiasts, not yet—began to theorize that we were *early*. The eldest children of the galaxy. It was thousands of years before they were proven wrong. As we got out into the universe, we started finding ruins, all across Imperial space. The wise convinced themselves they were all the remnants of a single civilization. The Quiet Ones—later just the Quiet. Not because they left only buildings, but because they left no *signals*. No radio filling the void as our own ancient transmissions do. This was before the quantum telegraph, you understand. Before the datanet. It took centuries to gather all their findings together, far longer than it took for the stories to propagate through the starports and space lanes. Do you know what they found when they finally did?"

Again my throat was dry. Valka should hear this, *needed* to hear this. "What?"

"There was no *single* ancient civilization. The Quiet Ones did not exist. Their hypothesis was wrong. The people—or the person, if you are right—who built the ruins on Emesh and Judecca and the rest were but *one* of three, *possibly four*, great ancient civilizations that have left ruins across our stars. We've known this for thousands of years."

Nicephorus spoke into the silence that followed the Emperor's words, voice quieter, more calm than before. "It took thousands of years to realize what we had. By then the idea of one great ancient power had permeated the academy and public perception. They couldn't let it go. So we brought the narrative under control."

"Via the Chantry?"

"Via the Chantry," Nicephorus confirmed.

"From your report, I gather you know this yourself," the Emperor said. "Your Tavrosi woman, she is a xenologist, is she not?"

Despite the raw edge of shock I still felt—despite the strangeness of the day and my circumstances, the fact that I was speaking so frankly with Caesar in the ruins of a world far from prying eyes—I prickled. "Her name is Valka," I said, "and she is." But Valka had believed the *old* story, believed the Quiet Hypothesis. She had not recognized—or had perhaps never seen—the ruins of the other races. Realizing that I had just rebuked the Emperor, I plowed ahead, hoping to bury the offense in fresh words. "In my report, I spoke about the Cielcin holy world, about the ruins there."

"Eue, yes," His Radiance said.

"Akterumu," I said, and felt my eyes grow hard and narrow. "You're telling me you knew about the Enar? About the Deeps? About the Watchers all along?"

The Emperor's own eyes narrowed. "Do mind your tone, my lord. We are speaking privately, but I am still the Emperor of Man."

On reflex, I bowed my head, averted my eyes.

Apparently satisfied, the Emperor moved off half a dozen paces, leaned upon the brass rail that separated the raised orchestra from the dining room floor. "Some three thousand years ago, the Expeditionary Corps discovered the ruins of a settlement on Nairi—then as now an obscure planet in the Outer Perseus."

"Nairi!" I gasped aloud, unable to stop myself. Had I not said the name to Valka one day in her study at Maddalo House? Sir Hector stood in the yard, practicing his archery. Some other memory had haunted me in that place, whispered the name of *Nairi* out of undiscovered time.

"You know it?" The Emperor's face darkened.

I shook my head. "Only as a name."

"Do you know of Sir Damien Aradhya, then? The *Atropos* Expedition?"

"*Atropos?*" I blinked at him. It was the name of one of the Fates in ancient fable. "No, Radiance."

Nicephorus snarled, "You take us for fools?"

The Emperor released his grip on the brass rail. "The Corps performed their survey, returned to the Magnarch on Tiryns with stories of a lost city." At the words *lost city,* thoughts of Vorgossos and Akterumu both welled up, and a shadow fell upon my heart. "The sailors returned with the usual old stories about *the Quiet Ones,* but their holographs and survey data told a different story. They showed a city carved into the face of a cliff, half a hundred miles from end to end.

"HAPSIS recognized the city for what it was: a city belonging to a people they called the *Stonebuilders*," the Emperor continued.

"HAPSIS?" I asked, looking round at Nicephorus.

The Emperor exhaled a short laugh through his nose. "You are being initiated in all the great mysteries today, it seems. I thought you knew of them."

I could only shake my head.

"HAPSIS is a branch of the intelligence service. Not under the Legion umbrella. Not SpecSec." The Emperor's smile was thin enough to cut. "They've been around a long time. The handling of contact is their special charge. They were at Cressgard, and helped to take Echidna. They were on Emesh, for the natives *and* the ruins. It was HAPSIS that realized we were looking at multiple ancient civilizations in the first place. They were the ones to collate and compare the various reports from sites across the galaxy back in the early Empire."

"And which were we looking at on Nairi?" I asked. "These *Stonebuilders*?"

"To judge from your reports: the same creatures that built the ruins on Eue."

"The Enar?" I felt a crawling feeling on the skin of my arms, remembering the grim vision I had seen the night before the Black Feast, the crab-like entities dissolving in black slime, their empire gone to dust by suicide.

"We called them the *Stonebuilders* for much of our history, for the way that they built their cities, but they called themselves the Vaiartu."

Vaiartu.

This time I was able to confine my response to the widening of my eyes. I was sinking fast, lost in a trackless mire of other memory. The Enar. The Vaiartu. I heard the word chanted as I'd heard them chanting as I dreamed in their crumbling city.

Vai ar tu! Vai ar tu!

Had I not said that very name to Valka that day in Maddalo House? I remembered it so clearly, and remembered *more*, remembered things I could not remember. Memories of places I was sure I had never been, of conversations I was sure I had never had.

Vaiartu.

It was the name of a planet and a people both, a place I had never seen, never been, and yet remembered as I remembered the grave city of Akterumu before I had ever come there. In memory, I stood with Valka beneath the low white dome of a Cielcin temple. Torch lights of human manufacture gleamed whitely all around, and the floor was a tangle of cables hooked into dehumidifiers and other necessary equipment. Above our heads were carved and painted clusters of *Udaritanu* glyphs, cartouches covering the interior of the white dome. Beside us, a green-suited scholiast called Psellos was speaking:

It's not really a temple at all, my lord. Museum would be a better word. You see, this chamber was given over to the display of this artifact here. He gestured at the tablet displayed upon the altar in the center of the dome, resting on an easel of bronze and bone. Broad and flat it was, the color of malachite, green as the stones of Akterumu, and on its face was carved a single line of text that spiraled thrice around the perimeter, tighter and tighter, claw marks rising and falling from the center line like the perturbations of a sound wave. In the center, another cluster of circular glyphs clumped.

Not *Udaritanu*, not Cielcin writing, but the stranger anaglyphs of the Quiet the Cielcin aped by their art.

Psellos continued. *It's one of several such tablets in the Echidna hoard, but this one is unique. It identifies worlds settled by the Firstborn . . . Neither language is Cielcin. The middle is a pictographic representation of the Firstborn's writing system. Meaningless. But the text around the perimeter,* Psellos traced it with a finger, *belongs to the Vaiartu people. These marks are numbers. Coordinates.*

'Tis a map! that other Valka exclaimed.

It was an Enar tablet, and precisely like the one Prince Ugin Attavaisa had presented Syriani Dorayaica before the Aetavanni.

"You've found their homeworld," I said slowly, and leaned against the plinth of the headless statues. "Your xenologists discovered a map in the Echidna hoard, didn't they? The Cielcin Prince of Echidna had a collection of Enari artifacts. Vaiartu artifacts."

"How can you know that?" Nicephorus mounted the first step to the orchestra, cloak swaying about it. "How can you possibly know that?"

Realizing that I'd overextended myself, I tried to backpedal, to explain away what I could not reasonably know. "I . . . had access to the Echidna files for years when I worked advising Legion Intelligence."

"Not *those* files," the Lord Chamberlain replied.

"The Hidden One speaks to him, Nic," the Emperor cut in, the shuttered light coming back to his eyes. "He sees as the God Emperor saw." William Caesar shook his head, as if to clear it, and when he was done the light had gone from his eyes. He was himself again. "Yes, we found their homeworld—or so we think. But that was far more recent, after Lord

Powers captured Echidna at Second Cressgard." He turned, returned to
the window glass. "But I was speaking of Nairi. Indeed, it is *because* of
Nairi that I put myself to all this trouble." Red-gloved hands rose in a
shrug that encapsulated the room and our meeting in it. "Your reports
echo much of what HAPSIS and the Chantry already knew of the Vaiartu
and . . . the Monumentals."

"The Watchers?"

"Yes." The Emperor let his hands fall. "The Vaiartu city on Nairi ran
half a hundred miles north to south. It was the only settlement on the
planet."

I did not speak for a long moment. Had it not been the same on Eue? I
had seen much of the planet's surface on our approach from Dharan-Tun,
and had seen nothing but sand and pits filled with clotted slime and choked
riverbeds. Akterumu had been alone, a solitary, cyclopean monument built
to hallow the corpse of their deathless god.

"An outpost?" I asked at last, looking from Caesar to Nicephorus, who
had mounted the final step and joined us in the orchestra.

"Just so," the Emperor said. "Nairi was not the first Vaiartu site the
Expeditionary Corps had uncovered, but it was at the time the greatest.
We did not then know it, but we had found one of the great pilgrimage
shrines of the Vaiartu kingdom. Emperor Sebastian XII—may Earth keep
his bones—arranged for an expedition under the command of Sir Damien
Aradhya. One of HAPSIS's best. He and the starship *Atropos* sailed for Nairi
with a team of magi and a corps of Legion engineers with orders to excavate the ruins. The workers, of course, believed the old Quiet fables. Only
Sir Damien and his scholars knew the right story."

"I don't understand what any of this has to do with me," I said.

Caesar turned his head just enough to fix me with one green eye. "I'm
getting to that," he said, and smiled indulgently. Despite that smile, I
sensed a prickling of irritation from the man, another reminder of just how
rotten was the ice on which I stood. "We received reports steadily for a
time and then . . . nothing."

"Nothing?"

"Nothing," the Emperor repeated. "It took decades before a legion
could reach Nairi system and investigate, but *Atropos* was still there. In
orbit. Empty. The crew had gone." William paused again—I think—to
permit me the opportunity to interrupt him. When I did not, he made a
little sound of approval and a shrugging gesture with his lips. "It wasn't

hard to find them. They were on the surface. Every one. The recovery team found them . . . and not *only* them."

I sensed that there was much the Emperor was not saying, that the spaces between his words contained volumes—but I did not press him. The Emperor locked eyes with his own reflection in the snowy glass, spoke to it and not me. "*Atropos* had found the . . . the body of some *titanic* beast. A leviathan of monstrous size entombed beneath the city. The original expedition were all dead. Suicide, the rescue team ruled it, except . . ." He trailed off, shook his head. "They found more reports from Aradhya aboard *Atropos*. He never sent them. He called the beast *the Monumental*, and supposed the Vaiartu had built the city to worship the creature."

Arkam resham aktullu.

Miudanar's dry whispers resounded once more in my ears.

Arkam amtatsur.

That voice has never left me.

"Aradhya was right," I said. "The Enar served the Watchers. Worshiped them."

"And the Cielcin worship them now."

"Yes," I said, growing quiet and very still. I felt as I imagined a stylite must feel his first day atop his pillar, afraid to move, afraid even to look down, for it seemed the Emperor and I stood upon the borders of infinity, at the lip of some parapet on the edge of a pit blacker than the one I'd crawled out of after death. "The Monumentals . . ." I breathed, trying the new word. The old word. Aradhya's word. "What do you call the Quiet, then?"

"The builders of the ruins you encountered?" The Emperor arched an eyebrow. "The Firstborn." I'd known what he would he say before he said it, had learned it an instant before from my memories of that other life. How I longed to be away, to be back at Thessa with Valka and Gibson and nothing else, without a care.

But Gibson was dead. And I had killed his son.

"The Firstborn are by far the most numerous of the ancient civilizations," said Nicephorus, speaking for the first time in a long time. "That was partly why our early xenologists believed there was only one ancient culture."

That is because the Quiet's cities are rushing back in time, I thought, but did not say, *paving over the ruins of the Enar.*

"Why didn't you tell me?" I asked aloud.

The Emperor did not turn. "Be grateful you are being told now," he said coolly. "I am not in the habit of dispensing such secrets to my knights." That put me on my heels, but the Emperor tempered his words with a sigh. "We thought—before Nairi—that they were only gods. Fictions, you understand. The Vishnus and Jupiters of the Vaiartu, carved into their temples and monuments. But after Nairi . . . we knew. I suspected that day on Forum that the gods of the Cielcin—if they were real—were the same creatures . . ." He trailed off, arms crossed beneath the scarlet and ermine cape. "What does Dorayaica intend with them?" he asked, still not looking at me. "What did you not put in your report?"

That was a difficult question. In answering at all, I would admit to omitting information from my reports, would admit to lying *by omission* to the Emperor himself.

So I did not answer him at all.

"What happened to it?" I asked instead. "To the body of the Watcher *Atropos* found?" Some pearl of Miudanar's consciousness had remained in its bones, even in death.

I prayed they had destroyed it.

The Emperor only smiled. A thin, somber expression to paper over answers I knew he would never give. He held my gaze a long moment then, studying me with the long care that so defined his rule. "You haven't answered my question."

Here at last, then, was why I had been summoned. Why Nicephorus had intercepted me in the street. Why the Emperor had gone to so much trouble to stage this little meeting in the ruins of the world.

To ask this question.

But I had said so much already.

"The Watchers are dead," I said, and screwed shut my eyes, "or so I think. If they are not, they are far away. But even dead, they have power. At Akterumu, the dead one I saw—Miudanar—called to me. It showed me a vision. It wanted to frighten me, I think. It showed me the Cielcin searching for others of its kind. Long ago they searched, and found. Dorayaica is searching now. One of its lieutenants brought it a tablet. A Vaiartu tablet leading to their worlds, just like the ones HAPSIS found in the Echidna hoard. If the Scourge of Earth can align with one of its *living* gods . . . we have not the strength to stand against them."

"Can they find one?" the Emperor asked.

"I don't know!" I said. "When I was a boy on Emesh, the Cielcin came. One of their *baetayan*—their priests—was among them. Tanaran's prince had sent it searching for their gods. I thought then it was the Quiet they sought, but it was the Watchers. Aranata Otiolo must have had a tablet, a Vaiartu tablet." I broke off, remembering what Attavaisa had said when it gifted its tablet to Dorayaica. Otiolo's former master, Utaiharo, had possessed a collection of Enari tablets.

We will never know all Otiolo took or destroyed . . .

"I was not *sure* the Watchers were real until Akterumu. The Quiet showed me them in my visions, but I did not believe! I believe now."

The Emperor raised both hands to his face and rubbed his eyes. It was the most human gesture I had ever seen him perform. "I believe you," he said. "Can you find them?"

"I don't know," I said again, far more softly, and cast my eyes to the chipped frescoes on the roof above. The artists had painted the open heavens, the golden clouds of nebulae peopled by seraphim with flaming wings.

Angels.

"There is more," I said at length. All then was silent and dead as the dead city outside. Above me, the figure of an angel in scarlet robes, with wings incarnadine and hair of flame, stood six-winged with sword afire to challenge the Dark across the diameter of the ceiling. "Dorayaica itself is . . . different. I did not put it in my report because . . . I did not think I would be believed. In my vision, I killed it. Struck off its head. But *something new* crawled out of its corpse. It was one of *them*. One of the Watchers. The Monumentals. I thought it was part of my vision, but when I fought it during my escape, I wounded it." I had wounded the Pale King twice, once below the ribs, and again in the ankle, but that did not matter then. "Its blood was like quicksilver. Not black. And when I opened its side, *something* . . . slithered out."

"Slithered out?" Doubt shaded His Radiance's antiquely handsome face. "Like a snake?" He had turned his back on the window, and with his red hair and cloak he might have been one of the painted angels on the roof above, but his face was incredulous.

"I know, it sounds mad," I said. "But if you have some knowledge of the Watchers, as you say, you know they defy our understanding of the laws of nature. The one on Eue was dead. A hollow skull. But it spoke to me. Who knows what all it can do?"

The Emperor bowed his head, hands going to his hips, sending ripples through the fiery cloak that mantled him. "I was afraid of this. Of something *like* this. Ever since I saw what you did at Berenike." One green eye flickered open, fixed on me. "I *have* seen things myself. Aradhya and *Atropos* uncovered much before the end, things that would curdle even your blood, I think." The eye closed again. "I am sovereign of half a billion suns, Marlowe. Half a billion suns, and still the Dark is vast enough to swallow us whole and not even notice . . ." He turned his back, returned to the ruined city. "I mislike this waiting," he said then. "The Cielcin have not attacked in decades. Not since you went away."

They had all gone to the Aetavanni.

"That will change soon enough," I said, far from comforting.

"You will receive a call when it does," His Radiance said, not then knowing his words were prophecy. "We will leverage the resources of the Expeditionary Corps and HAPSIS *both*, and dispatch legions to the far regions—such as we can spare. Many of the Vaiartu worlds are known to us. We will find Dorayaica's *god*, and when we do . . ." He turned again, and a green fire was in his eyes, keener and more deadly than any I had before seen there. "We will kill it. You and I."

CHAPTER 18

SHADOWS UPON TIME

THE SNOW HAD WORSENED by the time the six-wheeled ground-car returned to the Emperor's camp, and Carteia's thin, white sun had rolled down low in the afternoon sky, was fattening even then to the pale yellows of sunset, visible only as a diffuse gleam through the day's heavy cloud. The *Ascalon* was waiting, snow blanketing its dorsal hull, white on black. The solitary tail fin rose like a standing stone above the chain fence that encircled its landing field, and the two men posted to the little guard-house on the gate both huddled inside despite the comfort and protection of their heated armor.

The car ground to a halt, and Lord Nicephorus—who had been quiet for much of the journey home—said, "William believes you are the God Emperor come again." Its Imperial emerald eyes were narrowed to mere slits. "He believes that Mother Earth and the Hidden One have sent you to us. I do not."

"You've made that clear, my lord," I said, and made to stand. "Still, I thank you for the ride." I wanted to be away, to be alone. To drink. There was much to think about, not just the Emperor's revelations, but about the consequences of my own. I felt like a man coated in phosphorescent paint and forced to wander a shooting gallery in the dark.

The Lord Chamberlain caught my wrist with thin, dry fingers. I glared down at Nicephorus, forced myself to remember that here was the Lord Chamberlain of the Sollan Empire and did not tear my hand away. "William has given his life to this war. A thousand years. He is the longest reign-ing Emperor in our history, and he will not lay down his life until the war is done." The chamberlain's eyes never wavered as it spoke, bored holes into my face. "You have given him hope, and if you betray that hope . . . if you have lied to us. To *him*. I will kill you myself."

Not for the first time that day, I marveled at the creature, the Emperor's homunculus. For so long I had thought it only a bodyservant, the chief of the androgyns of the Imperial court, the genetic eunuchs entrusted with the care of the Imperial family and harem. But it was evidently more. Much more. Lord Nicephorus alone had been trusted to remain in the Emperor's presence for our talk. Not even the Excubitors had remained. It seemed more than any servant, but the Emperor's closest confidant. His friend.

How had I not noticed before? Surely I had seen the Lord Chamberlain on Forum a hundred times? Had my own prejudices blinded me, caused me to dismiss Nicephorus as little better than a slave?

"I hope you will," I said, and tried to pull my hand away.

Nicephorus held on tighter. A ring of yellow gold shone upon its finger. "He trusts you."

"In which case we're not so different," I said, and held up my scarred right hand, showcasing the wheal of cryoburn scar on my first finger. "This is all that's left of the ring he gave me. Now I can never take it off."

"They said you were a creature of low drama, Lord Marlowe," it said. "I see they spoke true." It released me then, with its hand, but not its eyes. "William believes in gods and devils. But the beast they unearthed on Nairi was only a beast. So too the one you found. If your god exists, it is only a beast like the others. You are not touched by the divine, Lord Marlowe. You are in league with alien powers. William has lost sight of that. But I have not lost sight of *you*." It made a dismissive gesture. "Go now."

The scar-faced Martian had returned and opened the hatch, admitting a swirl of white flakes. I stood there half a moment, needing the final word. Presently the words found me, and I said, "I wish I knew you better, Lord Nicephorus."

"Lord Marlowe, you do not know me at all." The chamberlain raised its ermine-fur collar against the chill.

Robbed of the final word, I made to bow out as graciously as I could. But the day's first purpose stopped me, my hand upon the frame. "Lord Nicephorus," I said, "the Emperor is not safe here. If Forum is unsafe as well, and Avalon, I understand. But Cielcin will be hunting him, if they are not already."

"I have heard your warnings, Cassandra," Nicephorus replied. "So has His Radiance, and His Radiance has chosen. If you are his servant, as you say, you will stop this subversion and be silent."

I was silent then, but turned to regard the chamberlain a final time.

"Now go," it said to my face, again adjusting its furred collar. "You're spoiling the heat."

The hatch hissed shut and the car rolled off at once without pomp or ceremony, and I was stranded in the snow. One of the men in the guard-house punched the other in the arm and pointed to see me standing without armor or helm in the frigid air. One fellow set his steaming coffee on the counter and tugged his coif back up and over his bald pate, while the other turned to look.

I waved them off. I did not need tending to or fussing over.

I was thinking about what Nicephorus had said, of the Emperor and his thousand-year reign. William XXIII had ruled since well before I born—and that was already a thousand standard years past, though I was not yet four hundred actual. The Emperor, too, had cheated the passage of time—was cheating it by this voyage, stretching the natural span of his years further even than the porphyrogeneticists of the High College could contrive.

. . . he will not lay down his life until the war is done.

A deep fondness and respect for old William blossomed in my chest as I trudged through the gate to the landing field that approached the *Ascalon*'s open ramp. Behind me, a freight truck filled the street, carrying cargo to the new city of Bennu.

Writing this, I have no way of knowing who you are, Reader—or in what age you are reading these words. I do not know what you must think of me, or of all us sad Sollans. Nor do I truly care. Wherever you are, whenever you may be, you have not faced the Pale in battle, you have not seen the ashes of war covering world after world, or witnessed the horrors of Dharan-Tun. You have been spared. We have spared you. Whatever you may think of *me,* know this: seldom has man known a ruler like William Caesar. They say it was in me that the likeness and power of the God Emperor returned. There are those who write or whisper now that I was the conclusion of the High College's dream, the culmination of all their careful breeding, their delicate gene sequencing. I tell you I am not. Whatever I am, whatever power I have obtained—however briefly I ruled—I say it was in William the Great, the Sun of the Millennium, that the likeness and greatness of the God Emperor returned.

As a boy, I questioned the goodness of Empire. You may question it yourself. But question not the goodness of the Emperor. The boy on Delos I once was believed that all lords of our Imperium were as my father. Many are. But the lord of the Imperium, the sovereign of those half a billion suns . . . he was of another cloth entire.

Damn him not with me.

I reached the *Ascalon*'s ramp in moments. Her fin and fusion engines loomed above the slit of the aft warp projectors like the buttressed minaret of a sanctum. There I halted in the bitter wind, and looked back at my thin shadow cast upon the snow by the stark light of the hold.

Turning up my own collar against that wind, I imagined the call going out. The orders handed down to ships of the Corps and of HAPSIS alike, spreading via the datanet's telegraph relays unto the farthest suns. The enemy was moving, and we must move to meet them. The Emperor had said much, but too little. How many Enari worlds did the Empire know? How many cities of the Vaiartu kingdom had HAPSIS plumbed to their hidden depths? Was the Leviathan of Nairi the only Watcher our priests and magi had unearthed?

The cold wind grew colder still, blew clean through my soul.

The Emperor said a call would be coming for me, a bell ringing on some onrushing day. Was I then to be stabled in expectation? Put on ice against the day of uttermost need? A sick knot formed in the pit of my stomach.

I had no wish to fight again, to face the Pale or the black monsters they served.

Warka shanatim madatim itteche en.

By Imperial decree, I would enter internal exile once again, be siloed to await the trumpet blast. Like doomed Sir Damien Aradhya, I would be sent on expedition. Not to explore the unknown, as I had dreamed of as a boy, but to hunt and kill a god. Almost I wished I would be sent then and there to hunt the Watchers as I had hunted for Vorgossos. But the Emperor had tightened his leash. His other dogs would do the hunting, and I would be unchained only for the kill.

Snow had settled in my hair, and feeling had gone from my ears and the tip of my nose, and my face was starting to sting. So I turned and left the frigid ramp for the relative warmth of the hold, stomping to clear my boots as I shook the flakes from my hair.

Another trio of guards in the white of ordinary Legion men sat to one side of the inner door. With Oliva and his people gone, Sir Gray Rinehart had ordered a security detail for Valka and myself, though there was little cause for it.

"Back in, sir?" asked one, a gaunt, sallow-faced man whose own nose and cheeks were red with cold. Like the others of his trias, he wore his coif

but no helmet. To judge from the crate between them, the three were playing at cards.

"Yes, soldier," I said.

"Hope the meetings went all right, lordship," said another, tapping his
chest twice in salute. He did not rise. "There word on when we're leaving
this rock yet?"

Flapping my coat to clear the last of the snow before I crossed the inner
threshold, I said, "None, Lucas. I hope it won't be long. I'm tired of snow
as you, I don't doubt." And I had been so glad of it when we arrived, as I'd
prayed for rain on Colchis.

"Next world will be as shit, most like," he said. "You can count on that.
His Radiance is good an' all, but he never takes us nowhere nice."

"If he did, Luke," said the first, "there'd be no need to take us!"

"Aye, Sev, you got a point."

"You all can shut the ramp," I said. "Sun's going down. If anyone comes
calling for me, let them knock."

"Will do, lord," said Paul, their triaster.

I keyed the inner door and went within.

It wasn't far to reach our cabin door. Up the stairs on the left and along
the narrow hall, past the sealed and empty cabins that had belonged to
Oliva and his men to the captain's suite at the end. The door cycled on my
handprint, deep-scanned the veins.

Valka was asleep, though it was only evenfall. The room had no windows, and so but for the low-light from the washroom and the faint lam-
bency of the holograph plate on one wall, the chamber was dark as night.

She stirred at the new light and sound, and one golden eye peered out
at me from beneath tangled red-black hair and white linens. "Is everything
all right?" she asked. "You were gone far longer than I expected. I've been
waiting."

I opened my mouth to respond, shut it at once. I had been on the verge
of telling her everything, and almost too late remembered where I was.
Where *we* were. Valka's implants might protect us against watch-eyes and
spydust and whatever else LIO and SpecSec, the Martians and all the rest
had set to watch us, but I could not be sure. The Emperor had ordered me
to secrecy, even from Valka. Indeed, he had singled her out by name.

At once I feared to speak, feared that even the barest chink in Valka's
defenses might cause word to reach the Emperor of my infidelity. "I'm
fine!" I said, sure the lie reached my face. "I was . . . delayed is all."

There was so much I wanted to say, and yet I knew I could not. Not there, not then, not on Carteia. How I longed to be away then, for good and all. What good was it serving good and truth, if I must lie even to her?

I peeled off my coat, opened the wall hatch that concealed our armoire. "I'm going to go upstairs," I said. "To the mess. I need a drink."

It was as close to an admission as I could come.

CHAPTER 19

A SHOT IN THE DARK

DARKNESS.

The only light in our cabin aboard the *Ascalon*—save the low red indicator by the washroom door—came from the holograph plate to the right of the bed, itself tuned low and red, displaying the time in Mandari numerals. It was little more than an hour past local midnight. Carteia had a twenty-nine-hour day, and so deep in winter, nineteen of those were in darkness. Dark like the Dark of space itself.

"Hadrian?" Valka twisted in the bed beside me. "What's wrong?"

I sat up, cued by some sense other than hearing that something was wrong.

It was quiet. *All* was quiet, without the drone of the starship's engines. *Ascalon* was cabled to the camp's makeshift power grid, and only the white noise of electronics remained to paint over the wind whistling in the night. I would not have been able to hear Lorian in his cabin, or the soldiers Paul and Sev and Lucas at their post in the hold, yet still it seemed too quiet.

"Was it the dreams again?" asked Valka, making me think of Holy Catherine waking in the night beside the God Emperor so long ago. Would she write a book of me one day, I wondered, looking round at her. She sat up, naked as was I, the linens pooling about her waist.

"No." I shook my head. "No, it's not that."

"You've been quiet lately," she said, "more than usual." She lay her tattooed hand upon my shoulder. "Lie back down."

I held a finger to my lips, straining to hear. I had heard *something* in my sleep. I must have done. Brushing her hand away, I swung off the bed, feet scraping on short carpet to the bench where my clothes lay out.

Bang!

The noise punctuated the act of tugging on my pants, and I froze there in the dark. Valka's eyes found mine, luminous in the gloom.

We both knew the sound of plasma fire when we heard it.

"Stay here!" I said, shrugging my tunic into place.

A shout resounded a moment later, words I couldn't understand.

For once, she didn't argue as I stepped into my relaxed boots and kicked the tabs to tighten up the calves. Heading to the door, I snatched up my shield-belt, felt the knife and pistol clatter as I clasped it to my waist.

Another shot reverberated through the hull, and I pounded the door control with my fist even as my shield coalesced about me.

"Hadrian, wait!" Valka had found her voice, and stood. She cursed as I hardened the door lock with a key press and stepped into the hall.

I had no sword.

I drew the meager pistol instead, a lightweight phase disruptor of the kind favored by bridge officers. Being right-handed, I held it in my left, drew the knife with my right.

Lorian's door was two down on the right, and—keeping my gun sighted on the end of the hall near the ship's lone stair—I advanced and keyed the door. It slid aside into a pocket in the wall.

Lorian was gone.

A blackness settled in my heart and soul as I swept the narrow room and rumpled bunk looking for the little man.

He's just gone into camp, I told myself. Lorian had often stayed out late drinking and gaming with some of the other junior officers, or else visiting medica. He'd spent the odd night there undergoing some testing or other relating to his condition. *He's just gone into camp,*

Another shout sounded from below, and I rushed along the hall to the stair.

A figure dressed in the red and ivory of a common legionnaire barreled up the steps into me, hurling himself at my midsection. Somewhere in the confusion, a shot I'd not even known was fired caromed off my shield, disruptor fire crackling in the dry air. The both of us slammed against the bulkhead opposite the door, and we both went down all a tangle. An armored forearm caught under my chin and forced my head back, and I gasped as what I think must have been a knee slammed into my ribs.

He was atop me then, one knee pinning my right arm at the shoulder. I could not raise my knife, and so brought my gun up and under his arm to fire. Armored as he was, the disruptor bolt failed to penetrate the thermal layer beneath the white ceramic.

There was no time to think, no time to wonder who he was or who had sent him, not when *why* he'd been sent was so plain. Some detached part of my brain marveled at the work of Doctor Elkan, for my shoulder ached not as the man leaned his weight upon it. He said nothing, but his breath hissed beneath his blank-faced helmet inches from my face. We struggled there upon the floor, lungs gasping.

His own gun—a plasma burner—inched toward my face.

Bang!

The shot scorched the metal by my head, and I felt the air boil, feared my hair had caught afire. I fired again, but when the shot failed to do any good against the armored and shielded man I let it drop, caught the wrist that held the plasma burner and torqued it wide. Another shot streaked to my left down the hall, set the metal of the deck to gleaming cherry red.

The visored head slammed down, and it was luck and well-trained reflex flooding back that made me tuck my chin. The blow that might have struck my nose struck my brow instead, and I fell back, ears ringing, head swimming with pain and the trauma of impact.

I cursed, and tried to find that place within me where the power lay, tried to look along those avenues no human eye could see, to see a way out for myself and *choose*. The vision would not come, had not come since that other Hadrian put the sword into my hand.

My left hand was flagging. Black Earth, the man was strong! And I was not as strong as once I'd been. All my hours fighting with Oliva, all my long years and exercise and slow retraining . . . and I was still not sufficient to the task.

Someone had sent an assassin against me. A lone gunman in the black of night. It was not an elegant maneuver, lacked the brazen cleverness of Irshan and the bombs rigged to my shuttle. But it had not needed to be.

The bastard's plasma burner approached by microns, and I could feel my arm weakening with every heartbeat . . . and the vision would not come.

Valka was hammering on the door at the end of the hall, cursing me in Nordei and Panthai and all the tongues of the Wisp. She was right. I should not have tried to save her. She might have saved me.

Then I remembered the knife.

The assassin knelt on my shoulder, bruised my bicep with his knee. But my arm was still free about the elbow, and though I held his gun hand with my left, my right still clutched the long knife I'd brought from Thessa.

I hammered the blade into my assassin's flank, just above the hip bone.

I felt the tip skate and scratch over armor, slide into the underlayment just below the belt. The man atop hissed as hot blood began to run. In desperation, I stretched my left arm far as it would go, seizing the moment to shove the plasma burner so far as I could from my face. If I could get some distance—any distance—between us, my shield would render the firearm as good as worthless. I brought my own knee up between the bastard's legs even with my knife still in him.

He groaned, cursed as I shoved him to one side. I tugged my knife blade free. It and my hand both were red with the killer's blood, and I snarled as I rolled up to my knees. I was between the assassin and the stairs then, and half-stood.

A blast of violet fire filled my vision. I smelled ozone as the cloud of superheated plasma boiled just outside my shield, and cursed. The assassin barreled into me, and we both were falling, falling down the first leg of the *Ascalon*'s twisting stairs. The wind went from me, and I struck my head on the landing, but the assassin rolled over me and down the next several steps to the floor below and the main hold. The blind panic of blood loss was on him, and he was on his feet long before I was.

He must have lost his plasma burner in the fall, dropped it on the stairs above me or below us both, because he didn't fire.

He turned and ran.

Whoever he was, he had expected to kill a man asleep in bed—and kill his woman too—he had not expected a fight, had not expected a knife buried in his bowels. I heard his feet on the lower stairs, and forced myself to breathe faster, to will myself to stand.

There was blood on the stairs, blood in the lower hall. The door to the hold was open, and the cold night was rushing in. My own blood pounding in my ears, I reached the door, and found a body lying on the threshold.

Lucas, Paul, or Sev—I did not know, nor did I bother to find out, nor did I linger in search of the other two. That my assassin was none of the three I was certain. Even armored, I'd have known the men set to guard me the last several weeks. The who and why of it did not then matter.

I had an enemy to catch.

He'd reached the ramp and the muddy snowfield outside. Even at this distance, I could see the glass of the little guard house was shattered, and the men inside lay slumped over the console. There were only two. Two of my five guards should remain.

"Stop!" I cried, seeing the assassin ahead, one hand pressed to his wounded side. "Murderer!"

He only stumbled away faster.

The street beyond the guard house was empty at this hour. We were on the edge of the camp, far from the Emperor and the lords whose lives most mattered, and miles from the ruins of Rothsmoor and the new city of Bennu alike. None were concerned about attacks from the ground, nor murder in the black of night.

"Murder!" I cried, staggering through the snow after the disappearing assassin.

"Lord Marlowe!" came a voice from the right of the ship. It was the triaster, Paul. "Someone shot the floodlights and cut the fence in back. Sev's gone after them! I left Luke on the door." Then he saw the state of me, bloodied and not dressed for the cold. "What happened to you?"

"Luke's dead!" I said, not stopping. "The killer's getting away! Follow me!"

To his credit, the triaster didn't hesitate, but fell in beside me. With the floodlight on the fence post gone, the blood was still not hard to find on the snow. But in the black sludge and mud of the street, it was impossible.

And the killer was already gone. Paul's arrival had cost me what precious time I had. The assassin might have followed the main road left or right from the gate, and then turned in either direction at the corner of the *Ascalon's* yard.

"Go left!" I said, turning right, heedless of the bitter cold but grateful at least that it was not then snowing. I reached the corner of the fence that encircled *Ascalon*, and looked left and right. Sensing movement, I crossed the street left and hurried on, still clutching the bloody knife.

A legionnaire rounded the corner, red and white and carrying an energy-lance in the crook of his arm. I raised my knife and pointed it at him, and he flinched badly, slung his weapon to bear. "Drop the knife!" he bellowed. "Don't move!"

It wasn't the same man.

He was unwounded.

I did not drop the knife. "Murder!" I said, unhelpfully. "My guards. Murdered."

"I said drop the knife!" cried the frightened sentry.

I let the weapon fall, raised my bloody hands. "I am Lord Hadrian Marlowe, Royal Victorian Order," I said. "Someone broke into my ship and murdered my guards. He was dressed as a legionnaire! This is his blood!"

Hearing my name, the soldier must have recognized me, for he lowered his arms. "Where did he go?"

I stooped to collect the knife. "Not this way, evidently." I turned back and swore so fiercely that the word echoed off the grounded vessels and filled the night. The blocs around us were starting to stir. Lights were coming on, and armored soldiers and men in black fatigues appeared from hatches and at the gates of lots like the one the *Ascalon* was berthed in. "Put out the alarm!" I said. "Radio *Radiant Dawn*, let them know what's happened. LIO will want to investigate."

Paul had returned to the gate and the blasted guard house by the time I made it back.

"Anything?"

The triaster shook his helmeted head. "He stuck to the mud tracks, whoever he was. I'm sorry."

"You did all you could, Pal," I said, and—realizing my mistake— screwed shut my eyes. "Paul." Not wanting to choke before the common soldier, I turned my back. "Let's get out of the cold."

"They'll find him," said Lorian, seated at the end of the table in the *Ascalon*'s common mess, far to aft on the level above the engine room and the cabins. The good commander *had* been away gaming with certain others of the junior men. Playing *baccara*. Gambling. "We have the blood on your knife. They'll gene-type the fucker."

"It doesn't matter who he is," I said, scrubbed clean and sitting at the opposite end of the table, Valka to my left.

A medical team had come and checked me for concussion—I had none—and even then was cleaning the blood and clearing away the bodies of Lucas and the men at the gate. Orders had come down—from Rinehart or one of the other high officers—and a full fire team along with a six-legged scarab tank had taken up posts in the yard.

Paul and Sev both remained, seated opposite Valka in the middle of the table. Both had taken down their coifs, and both were pale and haggard-looking. Lucas had been their third since basic, I'd gathered, and his loss— to treachery, no less—was etched deep in both their faces.

"It doesn't matter who he is," I said again. "What matters is who sent him."

"It matters to me," said Sev. "I'll have his head."

"You will," I said. "They'll find him, but it won't change anything. Boys, your friend is dead. And I'm sorry. It's because of me."

The triaster punched the table with his gloved fist. "Damn it, he did his job. It's how he would have wanted to go."

I looked at the young soldier. Plebeian that he was, he could not have been more than thirty. A man, and yet a child. "I think he would have rather died at home, an old man, his family about him." I drank deep of the wine I'd poured for us all, returned the glass to the table.

"In which case, lord," Paul said, "you've the least cause for guilt of any man I know. It's you as is trying most to end this damn war. Whoever tried to kill you . . ." he shook his head, "is with the enemy, I say." He grew quiet, and he and Sev both were very still. "I wish I could have seen it coming is all."

I, who had seen Akterumu and the Black Feast coming, silently shook my head.

One of the cleaning crew came up then from below. "Lord Marlowe?"

My back was to the door, and I turned. "Yes, soldier?"

"We're all done here."

"Very good," I said, and offered a small salute. When the man was gone, I turned to Sev and Paul. "You lads should go and get some sleep. The centurion and his fire team have the watch, and it'll be light soon."

The two soldiers did not argue, but left Valka and Lorian and myself alone at last.

I saw them both again only once, in the morning, before they returned to their ship and unit, but I have not forgotten them, or the sacrifice of their poor friend.

"Are we clear?" I asked, when the last of the two men's footsteps were gone.

"As clear as may be," Valka said. "'Tis so much surveillance kit packed on this ship now, I can never be sure."

I nodded my understanding, thinking again of my oath to the Emperor.

"Who do you think did it?" asked Lorian, not caring now the two legionnaires were out of the way. "Who do you think sent our new friend?"

And did they send him because they know about my meeting with the Emperor? I asked myself. I was a long time in answering, and covered my turmoil by uncorking and pouring a fresh cup of wine. I did not think it was Nicephorus. I had done nothing to merit the androgyn's wrath, not since that day in the city. I was still of use and value to His Radiance, and the Lord Chamberlain would not—I think—gainsay the Emperor's wishes. And at any rate, I did not dare suggest Nicephorus as a suspect, not when some errant bug or scrap of spydust might overhear. Lorian and Valka had no knowledge of my association with the Lord Chamberlain, and so I could say nothing.

But I did not need to. The answer presented itself.

"'Twas Alexander," said Valka, cool and certain.

"The prince?" Lorian frowned. "He's still mad at you? For calling him a *brat*? That was decades ago."

"Only years for him," I said, and took a sip. It tasted of spice and candied fruits. "And that's not the main of it. You know that. Alexander was at Berenike. He saw me."

Lorian leaned back in the high-backed black seat. "So? So did millions of other people. So did the Emperor, if all you've said is true."

"He's scared of me," I said. "He thinks I want the throne. He's afraid I'll come for him and for his family."

"He spent years with you!" Lorian exclaimed, exasperation and disbelief in his tone. "Years with us! He should know you don't want the damn throne!"

I spread my hand—the hand that had that night wielded a knife in combat for the first time since Eue—on the glass top of the table. "*He* wants it," I said, at once very tired, "and so he cannot imagine anyone *not* wanting it." I swallowed. "It's possible that it's one of the lesser lords. Bulsara maybe. Leonid Bartosz has no love for me, that much is sure. Or whoever ordered this assassin did so from off world . . ."

"The Empress, do you think?" Valka asked.

I smiled at her as she took the hand I'd left upon the tabletop. "You're right. It's Alexander," I said. "It has to be." Had he known about my meeting with his father not five days past? Since Nicephorus took me into the city, my engagements had dried to naught. No summons had come from the Emperor, or the Security Council. I had left the *Ascalon*, yes, but only to attend upon Prince Rafael Hatim, with whom I'd shared a meal in his cabin aboard *Radiant Dawn*. To the casual observer, that had been nothing strange. But Alexander might have noticed the change. Surely someone in the camp must have marked that the carriage that took Marlowe to his ship first took him beyond the camp in the direction of Rothsmoor. And yet, if there were rumors, I had heard them not—and surely Rafael Hatim would have whispered them over dinner.

I longed to tell Valka and Lorian, but even in the relative safety guaranteed by Valka's digital override of the ship's surveillance equipment, the secrets I'd been told I did not dare share until Valka and I breathed the free air of some other world.

"Those poor boys. Lucas and the others . . ." I turned the wine cup in my hands, hunched over it. "Too many have died on my account." I shut my eyes. "And for what? This time? A delusion . . . I . . ." A thought struck me then, a mad thought. An absurd thought.

"What is it?" Lorian asked, seeing the change on my face. "I hate it when you get that look about you. Getting that sort of look about oneself is *my* job, Marlowe."

I glowered at him. "I've had an idea."

"Mother Earth and Emperor . . ." The intus rubbed his temples.

"What is it?" Valka's voice was grave with fresh concern.

"I should talk to Alexander," I said.

"Hadrian, no!" Valka exclaimed. "You'd do well to stay clear of him! He tried to kill you!"

I turned sharply to regard her. "We don't know that for certain," I said. "And if he did, he did so because he's afraid. If I can speak to him! Head him off. If I can . . . allay his fears. Calm him down."

"If he's the one who ordered that assassin, and you request an audience the following day . . . you think 'twill *allay* his fears?" She shook her head. "More like you'll drive him to panic."

That gave me pause, and I looked away, looked down at my blackened reflection in the surface of the Emperor's fine wine. Exhaustion further tempered the long care in my still-young-seeming face, and the faint creases at eyes and mouth seemed etched more deeply than they had that morning, and more deeply still than they had before Nicephorus brought me to Rothsmoor.

"You're right," I said. It was the young man who would have charged the prince's gates and battered down his door, the young Hadrian who might have called for an assassin of his own, as I had with Augustin Bourbon. Mistake me not—no thought of harming Alexander entered my head . . . or if it did, it was a passing fancy. It had been one thing to arrange for Bourbon's death—and I have rued that murder in my soul. Quite another to strike at a prince of the realm, and a boy who—if I had not loved him—I had at least once held in my care. "You're right."

Better to wait. Better to do nothing.

The Emperor would have a reply of his own.

CHAPTER 20

THE DEMON'S KING

THAT REPLY CAME BOTH later and *sooner* than I'd expected.

Two weeks and more had passed since that bloody night, and nearly three since that day in the city. Valka, Lorian, and myself had all been locked and left alone aboard the *Ascalon*; kept under the watchful eye of a Martian centurion called Elan, his *scarab*, and his fire team. As between my secret meeting and the assassin's knife, I had not been asked to any meetings, but so too had my dinner invitations dried up—a mixed blessing.

All attempts to find Alexander's assassin had failed. The blood on the knife and on the floor and walls of the *Ascalon* had not belonged to any soldier or courtier in the camp, so said the SpecSec man sent by Sir Gray Rinehart. Gene sequencing had turned up certain polymorphs common to the Urslic tribesmen who ranged across the tundras and steppelands of Carteia's southern wilds, but the men of the Urslic tribes were not indexed on any genetic census on Imperial record.

The prince had chosen his killer well, and Lucas and the men at the gate would have no justice in this life.

After that, I had expected some fresh representative of Special Security or the Imperial Office to appear and inform me that Valka, Lorian, and myself were to be returned to safety on Nessus, or to Forum itself—or else that we three and the *Ascalon* entire were to be mothballed and stored in cold safety aboard one of the fleet's larger dreadnoughts.

None did.

Instead a nuncius arrived bearing the Emperor's seal on the twentieth day since Nicephorus met me at the motor pool. The page—one of the lesser androgyns of Nicephorus's ilk—bore a simple, handwritten message that I should attend upon the Emperor at once.

The call could not have come so soon.

I had not spoken to Valka of our secret meeting, and the assassin had driven all thought of my prior strangeness from her mind. But my silence and my oath to the Emperor sat in me like rotting meat. As a boy, I would have damned my oath and told her everything, *anything,* and damned the consequences, too. But she was all I had, and I would not risk her safety or mine in breaching the Emperor's trust. I told myself that she would learn eventually, for when the call did come and I joined the men of HAPSIS and of Gnomon, she would be by my side.

The snowstorms seemed to have broken at last—if perhaps only for a time—and the white sun of Carteia shone on the snowbound and icicled camp as I rode to the Emperor's command ship. All the grounded vessels steamed in the morning light, and their blankets of snow and mantles of dripping icicles made the whole place seem—save for the black and sludgy roads—like the palace of some faerie queen wrought of crystal and iron and glass.

Two faceless Excubitors opened the ornately carved wooden doors to the Emperor's offices aboard the *Radiant Dawn.* Crossing the threshold, I detected the static cling of a prudence barrier tuned low enough to admit entry. The minute I was in, the Martians would doubtless restore the field to full force, rendering it more impervious than stone.

The Emperor himself arose as I entered the office, gesturing dismissal to the pack of advisors clustered about his desk and seated in the padded chairs before it. "Lord Marlowe!" he exclaimed. "You're right on time."

The men seated before the Emperor stood roughly, evidently caught by surprise at the Emperor's sudden motion. None were permitted to sit in the Imperial presence, not when he had chosen to stand. At the far right of the desk, I recognized dark-haired Sir Gray Rinehart, Breathnach's replacement as Director of Legion Intelligence, and Tor Xanthippus of the Security Council.

Lord Nicephorus was nowhere to be found.

Because it was expected of me, I dropped to one knee and pressed my right fist to my breast. Head bowed, I said, "Honorable Caesar." Was this the call I'd been told to expect already? Surely neither the Corps nor HAPSIS could have found the Cielcin in so small a span of days, much less recovered some lost Vaiartu tablet such as Dorayaica possessed. They might have intercepted some Cielcin communiqué, but it seemed unlikely. It was just too fast.

This had to be something else. Imperial ships would be scouring the galaxy, searching for Vaiartu sites, and searching those sites for signs of the

Watchers, if only for bones. The Cielcin had a head start. Attavaisa had given the Prophet a tablet containing a partial atlas of Vaiartu worlds. The Cielcin had been searching for such sites for thousands of years. Yet none had ever found what they sought: a living god, a Watcher of old.

The Emperor's dogs were hunting now for the same thing, but hunting without a map.

They could not have found something, surely. Not so quickly!

This meeting had to be for something else.

Was it for Alexander I'd been summoned? The prince was conspicuously absent himself. Had the Emperor gotten wind of his son's involvement in the attempt against my life?

But I was getting ahead of myself. I did not *know* it was the prince who sent the Urslicman against me in Imperial dress. I only guessed.

"You may rise," the Emperor said, and turning to the congregation between us, ordered, "The rest of you may go."

I regained my feet as Xanthippus and the others bowed and scraped to take their leave. As they did so, Caesar rounded the corner of his desk and tapped Sir Gray upon his shoulder, whispered some unheard command. The Intelligence Director bobbed his head and retreated to one wood-paneled corner beneath a portrait of the late Empress Titania Augusta, William's mother.

When at last the others all had gone and the Excubitors sealed the doors and the prudence shield, His Imperial Radiance William XXIII turned to regard me with emerald eyes. "We had hoped," he began, all *Emperor* again, "that your long vanishment would have caused tensions in our court to cool somewhat. It would seem we were mistaken." It would not have done for me to interrupt the Emperor in that moment, even to gainsay him. I simply stood there then, feet apart on the marble and porphyry. "Perhaps it would have been better if we had left you in security on Nessus. We had hoped our public countenance would serve to mitigate the zeal of those among our well-intentioned servants who feel you pose a threat to us. Alas . . ." He spread his hands, as if to say *what's done is done.*

"You are certain it was one of the court, then?" I asked, checking Sir Gray in the corner.

The director gave a silent little nod, but the Emperor said, "There is hardly any agency left on Carteia with sufficient vim besides our court. Unless you have wronged the native Urslicmen in some way?"

A joke? I was too shocked even to smile.

"Sir Gray here despairs of our ever finding the rogue that did the deed, but his patron? We have our theories."

Did I dare accuse Prince Alexander?

But Caesar was still speaking. "We had hoped to speak with you sooner after your arrival. There has been much to attend to breathing new life into this old world." He leaned against the corner of his desk as he spoke, robes of white and scarlet samite shimmering. His eyes narrowed almost imperceptibly as he spoke and papered over the meeting that had not—officially—occurred. "Perhaps if we had, this ugliness with your Urslic assassin might have been avoided."

Emerald and amethyst held each other's gaze a long moment.

"I . . . understand," I said. Our conversation in Rothsmoor was not to be addressed. Whether or not Sir Gray knew of HAPSIS and Nairi, the Vaiartu and the Hidden One and the *Acts of Will*, none of it bore on this discussion.

"They say you fought off the assassin your own self," the Emperor said. "That is well! We are pleased to learn you have recovered so."

I bowed my head, for it was the Emperor I had to thank—however indirectly—for the services of Doctor Elkan. "You honor me, Radiance." Gone was any of the familiarity of our previous meeting, gone the man William, hidden behind his mask.

The Emperor dismissed my words with a curt shake of his head. "Not remotely. Your service to us and to the Imperium has been beyond price. Restoring your body was the least we could do. Were it peace time, Lord Marlowe, we would award you a duchy at least." His eyes picked their way over my scarred face. "We read the reports you gave to Legion Intelligence," he said, retreading words we had shared in Rothsmoor. "The medical files, too. The things they did to you . . ." He shook his head. "Unthinkable." I did not say that such things were thought of every day, and not only in Dharan-Tun, but in the bastilles and dungeons of the Chantry. "I am sorry."

"If it please the Emperor," I ventured, "are there any leads in the matter of my would-be assassin? In the identity of his patron, rather?"

The emerald eyes flickered. One gloved hand toyed with the heavy chain of golden links that draped the royal shoulders. "You've some notion vis-à-vis the culprit?"

I licked lips suddenly dry, but managed, "Your son . . . thinks himself my enemy."

"You dare, sir!" Sir Gray exclaimed, coming off the wall.

Caesar raised a hand to halt his servant in his tracks. To his credit, the Emperor confined his own response to the elevation of one eyebrow. Voice calm as still water, he said, "Delicately phrased, my lord. *Thinks himself your enemy,* indeed." A shadow fell on William's face, and he let his hand fall from the golden rope upon his chest. "You may be right. It is a shame you were not so fine a teacher as you are an instrument."

Stung, I hung my head. "I know."

Restoring his hands to their customary place behind his back as he stood straight again, Caesar continued, "You little apprehend the position your tenacity and celebrity have placed us in."

"I apprehend a little," I said. "We've had this conversation before."

"So we have," the Emperor agreed. "And yet there remain among our advisors many who believe your danger exceeds your usefulness. If your assumption proves correct, my own son included."

None of this was news to me, and so I might have said nothing. But the tenor of this conversation—official, on the record, was so at odds with the *secret* one Caesar and I had shared but weeks before that I could not hold my tongue. So I cleared my throat and fixed my eyes on a point over the Imperial shoulder. "If I may, Radiance." The Emperor inclined his head that I might proceed. "What do you believe?"

The scholiast part of my mind clicked through several possibilities, scripting what seemed in that instant a likely scenario. The Emperor would make public dismissal of me—award me precisely that duchy he mentioned—and appear to retire me by force to some bucolic gerontage on the outer rim. In secret, though, he would vanish me to his private purpose, to fight not in open war against the enemy, but in darkness against the disquiet gods of night.

"We believe . . . that you have demonstrated time and again that your use far exceeds your risk." Caesar crossed from the tiled floor to a carpeted alcove right where stood a rosewood piano of immeasurable age, immaculately maintained. I recognized and could read the Classical English lettering—gold against the burnished wood. *Steinway & Sons.* With a pang I realized the instrument must have come from Old Earth itself, and felt my jaw slacken slightly. "You did well to defend yourself in our last audience," he said, again eliding our meeting in Rothsmoor. "You cut quite the heroic figure, my lord. There are those among my counselors who believe you are a sword without a handle, did you know that?"

I blinked at him. It was an obvious thing to say, too much a performance. "I do, yes."

"They may be right, but I believe I've the art to wield you for the present." The Emperor's fingers dusted over the cover protecting the ivory keys. "Did our Nicephorus also say that we would have ordered you to *remove* yourself if you had fallen to pieces?"

I swallowed again, and again considered the scenario that had mapped itself in my mind. A *disgraced* Lord Hadrian Marlowe—ordered to suicide—might even more easily be vanished into the shadow world of intrigue and elder races, the *Mag Mell* of the Vaiartu, Monumentals, and Firstborn.

"The secret to politics, dear cousin," Caesar said with a thin smile, "is to ensure one stands to profit regardless of outcome. Had you fallen to pieces, as I say, we *would* have ordered your end." He rested his hand atop the Steinway. I sensed the shine and razor's edge concealed beneath the word *end*, and briefly shut my eyes. Confirmation, at least. "Had that come to pass, certain of our problems would be resolved, and many in our council would rest more easily. Alexander, perhaps, among them." The Emperor's smile widened a fraction, as if by doing so he might soften the blow of what he said. "As it stands, you provided us a way to save face, you and I, and to salvage the disaster of the Lothrian expedition. One door closes, another opens." He shrugged. "Understand, cousin, that we hold no malice for you. *I* hold no malice for you, nor is our gratitude any less. And we are sorry for your trials and the loss of your men. But . . . *I am humanity,* and humanity cannot shy from what is necessary in the face of all that besets her."

I hooked my thumbs in my belt and pivoted to face the Emperor properly in his new position, stood with feet apart. "And my death might have proved necessary?"

The Emperor tapped his fingers on the lid of the antique Steinway, as if playing the precious instrument. No other part of him moved. "We hoped it would not be, though it seems there were those with other ideas . . ." His fingers continued their mute music on the lid of the grand piano. "But we have elected to retain your services." He paused a beat, fingers stopping. "*Now* we honor you."

I ducked my head again, drummed fingers against the worn megatherean leather of my shield-belt. I thought I could sense where this was going. He had a fresh task for me, one that would take me away again from the scheming knives of court, from assassins and princes, suspicion and bad blood. And when it was done . . . what?

Into darkness?

"What would you have of me?"

Extending a hand in the direction of the room's forgotten occupant, the Emperor said, "Lord Director, the holograph, if you please."

Sir Gray Rinehart saluted and advanced to the piano. He produced a metal disc about as wide as the palm of his hand, placed it on the lid of the antique instrument between the Emperor and himself. An instant later, a cone of pale light traced several windows in thin air, each displaying an image. One showed a darkened corridor, debris floating in null gravity, light fixtures cracked and dead. Another showed a bank of what appeared to be fugue creches, their lids rimed with frost and gleaming indigo. Yet another showed what looked like the ruins of a human corpse, the tissue bloated like the flesh of some deep sea creature dragged into the light and air.

There were others.

A ruined shuttle sparked in the vacuum of a greater hold.

Banks of more fugue creches—hundreds of them—lined the walls of a vast, tubular hall.

The snow-white teardrop of a starship twisted, its tiled hull shattered in the unforgiving light of space. It had an Extrasolarian look about it, ugly and featureless, without the grace or dignity of Imperial manufacture.

"Our scouts intercepted this vessel some fourteen hundred light-years from this system," Sir Gray said, pointing at the white ship. "Assuming its on-board navigation can be trusted . . . it was sailing from Latarra."

"Latarra?" I was a minute remembering the name. Latarra had been an obscure world in the Veil of Marinus, beyond Imperial control even before the coming of the Pale out of the north. As Imperial control throughout the Veil collapsed as the war went on, Latarra came under the boot of the Extrasolarian warlord Calen Harendotes. The so-called *Monarch* was one of hundreds of such petty dictators—men like old Marius Whent of Pharos—who established themselves over systems or worlds or parts of worlds and prayed their dominions were small enough to escape Imperial notice. But Harendotes had begun massing an army to himself, and more! He had started *conquering*, they said. Norman refugees and survivors of the abandoned Imperial colonies in the Veil had flocked to him across the burning stars, and *worse* characters besides. Extras out of backspace, even captains of the Exalted in their vasty ships, blacker than the night. There were those who even whispered that Harendotes had dealings with Vorgossos, though I did not believe them. Vorgossos was gone, vanished after the destruction of Aranata Otiolo's worldship in the battle on the *Demiurge*. I imagined Kharn Sagara had taken his world—a worldship itself, most like—into the farther Dark, there to await the end of the tribulations tearing the galaxy apart. "Has Latarra declared against us?"

Sir Gray made a negatory gesture. "Nothing so overt. The Extras don't *declare* anything. They simply act."

The Emperor watched us both from the far side of the piano, face still as stone. Turning his attention back to me, Sir Gray said, "We have reason to believe this ship here belonged to the same Extrasolarian cell you encountered at Arae. The same cell responsible for the Cielcin chimeras."

"MINOS," I said.

"Indeed," Rinehart said.

Again, I asked, "How did you catch them?"

The Intelligence Director turned from the holographs to better look at me. He was clearly palatine, though I knew he had been a soldier once. He wore his civilian suit of charcoal and blood red like a uniform, and kept his jet-black hair clipped short, as did so many naval officers. Looking at him, it was hard not to think of his predecessor, Sir Lorcan Breathnach. Breathnach had been a career soldier as well, though Breathnach had been only a patrician, promoted for his works and for his personal loyalty to the late Lord Minister of War. Was Rinehart also an enemy? I thought not, but their number seemed to be multiplying once again.

How could I be sure before the fellow plunged a knife between my ribs?

"We have our spies among the Extrasolarians," the Emperor said, stroking his chin with a gloved forefinger.

Taking this as permission to elaborate, Rinehart added, "Our agents on Latarra have kept us informed of the Monarch's movements. He is trading with all manner of barbarian savages, including this MINOS company. We believe this vessel was bound for one of their hidden fortresses—like the one you broke at Arae, Lord Marlowe. Thanks to their intelligence, we were able to intercept this shipment as it cleared Latarra space."

I gave this bit of information a perfunctory nod, asked, "What was the cargo?"

"We're not entirely certain," Rinehart replied.

I blinked at him. "Not entirely certain?"

The director glanced toward His Imperial Radiance, who said, "Tell him all of it, Director."

Bowing stiffly, Rinehart gestured to the holographs. "These images were taken by our boarding party shortly before the vessel was lost."

"Lost?"

"We cannot be entirely certain what happened, but it appears the Extras destroyed their own ship after our men came aboard. Breached fuel containment. We lost the ship and our boarding party. The savages could not hope to best us in open combat, so they resorted to suicide. Their cowardice cost us a hundred men . . . and all of their own people."

I had no difficulty believing it myself. On Padmurak, Iovan had made it abundantly clear that MINOS was no mere cybernetics company, no simple manufacturer of arms and chimeric body parts. They were fanatics, a fraternal order of sorcerers dedicated to the dismantling and destruction of the Sollan Empire. And if they had allied with Calen Harendotes, the Monarch of Latarra, the Conqueror of Ashklam?

I shook my head. The Empire was assailed on all sides.

The Cielcin. The Commonwealth. MINOS. The Extras. This . . . Monarch.

And the Watchers themselves . . .

"Harendotes has amassed quite an army for himself, has he not?" I asked, still scanning the assembled holographs from my place beside the piano. One leaped out at me: the image of a man in robes of sable and cloth-of-gold captured by a drone or by spydust on the wind from far away. Grainy though the image was, I could make out the shape of a deep cowl and the flash of the brassy lenses that concealed the eyes. "Is this him?" I pointed with my chin.

"It is," Rinehart confirmed. "And he has. He's been buying out Norman mercenary contracts across what remains of the Veil for the last hundred years. He had nearly half a million ships in Latarra system at last estimate. Earth knows how many soldiers."

"Most of them Norman refugees," the Emperor said. "Barbarian peasants."

"Each and every one of them can hold a lance, Your Radiance," Rinehart advised.

"To what purpose?" I asked. "Do we know?"

To sell them to the Pale?

I had never seen Calen Harendotes before, and so studied the image with care. If the man beside him was of ordinary build, then Harendotes himself was uncommonly tall: perhaps seven feet from sole to crown. Rumor said that he was palatine, some black-barred nobile of obscure lineage acting under a new name, playing king beyond the borders of the civilized world. I could see it, but there was no way to be sure. Whatever he was, that he was fast becoming a major player on the stage could no longer be denied.

"War," said His Radiance the Emperor. "What else?"

The black pit that had taken up residence in my gut yawned and stretched a little wider. "Caesar, you should withdraw to Forum at once. If . . ." My voice failed to silence. "If the Monarch and MINOS are cooperating, that means Harendotes has thrown in with Dorayaica. We are surrounded out here."

William's face was unreadable as he said, "You have been telling my counselors this for weeks, I understand."

Rinehart stepped in. "We've no way to be certain Harendotes and MINOS are *allied*, precisely. We only have evidence of this transaction, though our spies suspect there may be others."

"That's the trouble with these barbarian cells," the Emperor agreed. "No law. No loyalty. Only expediency. And there's too damned many of them."

"If there is even the slightest chance this Monarch is our enemy, Caesar, we must take it as certainty and act accordingly," I said, watching his reaction through the projected holographs.

Caesar's voice seemed far away. "You would have us sail in force to Latarra? Destroy the planet?"

"I . . ." I stopped short. How many millions lived on Latarra? How many millions more were there in the Monarch's fleet? Was I truly countenancing a massacre? We had the means. The atomics. It was possible to strike the planet with even a single ship, as Hauptmann had struck at Otiolo. But it violated every rule of war, man-against-man, that had held the line of civilization for so many thousand years.

It was wrong, and at once, I was filled with an acrid and oily shame.

The image of the white ship hung like incense smoke above the Emperor's antique Steinway, bits of its shattered hull twisting in the spotlight of the Imperial cruiser that illumined it. "It's not a military vessel," I said, eager to move on, and indicated the wreckage. From the way the hull had been punched through—leaving a clean, round hole—I guessed they'd been hit with a MAG cannon. A single tungsten rod the size of a tram car had plowed through the outer hull, tearing through decks and the ship's titanium superstructure like tissue paper. "It looks like a simple personnel transport." Done musing, I looked round. "Slaves?"

As if he'd been waiting for me to ask that precise question, Director Rinehart clicked a button on his wrist-terminal. All at once the holographs vanished, replaced by a star map showing the Centaurine provinces and the nebulous region of the Veil where it cupped the borders of the galactic core. A single system glowed red, highlighted against the pale whiteness of the other stars.

"This is Latarra." Rinehart pointed at the system, paused to advance the holograph. The field of view zoomed in—as though we traveled kilolights in an instant. A red line traced its way across space, a slender finger reaching out from Latarra into the void. Waving his finger along the arc, Sir Gray continued. "This was the ship's vector leaving the Latarra system." He indicated the end of that trajectory, circling a point near the edge of the Centaurus Arm and the borders of Imperial space. "And this is where our people ambushed the transport."

Rinehart continued: "We had Xanthippus's team calculate the superset of all possible destinations based on what we know of their trajectory." He pulled up a list of systems by Vandenberg catalog number, a gleaming panel beside the map, and seven stars lit up on the projection. "Having spoken with our people on Latarra and dispatched scouts with light-probes to the region, we believe we now have the location of their hidden base." At that, Rinehart thrust a finger into the projection. "Here."

I squinted at the projection.

Again the image shifted at a cue from the director, displayed a model of the star system in question: twin suns and a necklace of circumbinary worlds. It had no name, only the Vandenberg number. *VA-91:35 DB-639.*

No name meant no settlements, not even a mining outpost. It meant that not even the Expeditionary Corps had been through to survey the system. There were many such stars in Imperial space, systems without viable worlds or other points of interest, cracks in the Empire's pavement. Such systems were often the haunts of the Extrasolarians—as Arae had been.

A virgin system, untouched even by the Mining Guild.

Sir Gray sketched a circle around the fourth planet out from those binary suns. *DB-639D.* "We started observing the system approximately forty years ago, when the information first reached us at Balanrot. In that time, we've been able to detect reversion bursts in-system on no fewer than six occasions."

I nodded. A reversion burst meant interstellar travel. Meant starships.

Meant people. The system was well situated, right on the edge of the Centaurine provinces.

"We believe the Extras are manufacturing weapons on the planet, and intend to abet the Cielcin invasion."

"A weapons manufactory?" I said, remembering the black pits of Arae, the tanks filled with the living failures, hybrids of Cielcin and machine. MINOS had long since perfected the process of marrying inhuman flesh and circuitry. "You mean chimeric soldiers? You think they're building an army?" The fugue pods in the few holographs the Imperial boarding party had managed to take before the ship was compromised might have been carrying Cielcin—thousands of them arranged and surgically prepared at Latarra.

"That is the high probability," Director Rinehart replied, an almost scholiast cadence to his words. "Latarra might simply be sending slaves, or personnel."

"Or raw materials . . ." I mused, thinking. Dorayaica already had hundreds of Cielcin chimeric warriors at its disposal, to say nothing of the three remaining original fingers of its White Hand. But thousands? Did the Prophet intend to supplement its army with a horde of human-chimeric slaves? If Rinehart's guess was correct, if the Shiomu Elusha intended to build an army of such monstrosities . . . "Why haven't you destroyed the planet?"

Though I directed the question to Rinehart, it was the Emperor who answered me. "Because we do not know what is happening there."

"You want me to take it," I said, reaching the ungiven order. "Don't you?"

Caesar spread his hands. "No one knows these Extrasolarians better than you—certainly no one knows the Cielcin better."

"And it removes me from the equation here at court," I said. It was all too much. "Your Radiance, I have no men!"

"That is easily remedied," the Emperor replied. "We understand that you and Tribune . . . Lin? Have worked together before. You will accompany him and advise. We wish for you to take the planet, discover what the Extras are doing there, and report back."

Lin!

They wanted me to take Lin and the 409th Legion? Had Lin suggested this? Volunteered himself for the expedition? It would be just like him, and yet the Mandari captain had said nothing of this when we'd talked together my first day on Carteia, or when he'd joined the three of us aboard *Ascalon* for supper twice before my trip to the ruined city. Yet surely preparations for such a mission had been underway all this time.

Air hissed between my teeth as I turned my back on the Emperor and the holographed star chart. In that tenuous calm, I drank in the tableau of antique armor, oil paintings, and darkly polished wood that comprised the Emperor's office. It recalled his place in the library tower of the Peronine Palace, and might almost have passed for a room in Devil's Rest.

Shutting my eyes, I said, "Another impossible task." I felt my shoulders tighten, as if in anticipation of the knife. "Am I meant to fail this one, Radiance?"

No answer.

"Do you believe that we are treating you unfairly?" the Emperor asked.

I dared not answer, and that was answer enough.

"We do not ask anything of you, Lord Marlowe, that we do not first ask of ourselves. You know better than any of us—I deem—how delicate is the thread from which we all hang. We *thought* you understood as well that our chains of office *are* chains indeed. As are yours." The Emperor grew very quiet by the end, his rich baritone extinguished like a fire put out. "We are men who bear them, Hadrian. Not who cast them down."

The bitter sense of shame returned, and I laid a hand on the corner of the Emperor's desk to steady myself. *We are beasts of burden, we men . . .*

Caesar's voice returned, rekindled as something hard and brittle as old bones. "I told you: I *am* humanity, and humanity is bleeding. I have given everything I can, everything my station demands and allows." Here was not the Emperor speaking, not William XXIII Avent, Firstborn Son of Earth, Guardian of the Solar System, King of Avalon—no. It was but William himself. William the man, old and tired as I. "I will not stop fighting," he said. "Not today, not tomorrow, not until the Cielcin are burned from our skies. You swore an oath to do the same, I remember."

"I did," I said, and had sworn by that oath again mere weeks before. I grew very still, for I had heard every one of my nearly four hundred years in my voice. I felt them, too, each like a loop of chain upon my shoulders, just as William had himself described.

The Emperor again narrowed eyes like chips of jade. "You will go to this planet. You will find this hidden fortress and discover what they are up to. You will take Tribune Lin's fleet and whatever else you deem necessary, and you will bring these Extrasolarians to heel." The Emperor clasped his hands behind his back. "We will go to Perfugium and await our Jaddian friends. When you are finished, you will rendezvous with us at Siraganon, and we will hear no more talk of retreating to Forum. Are we clear?"

Knowing what was expected of me, I knelt. "Completely, Your Radiance."

Caesar's polished red boots slid into view. "No rest for the wicked, Demon in White." He extended a hand. "You were right. You were wasted on Nessus. But better wasted than dead at the hands of my own misguided servants. Or my wife." I choked, and the Emperor said, "I know all about Agrippina's role in that ugliness in the Colosseum, and I am sorry for that as well." He gestured that I should stand. "If this *Monarch*, Harendotes, is against us, perhaps you will discover that, too." He turned to glance at Sir Gray. "Director Rinehart will see to it that you are given all the necessaries." And with that he signaled my dismissal, waved one glittering hand.

I saluted, beating my breast. "Hail Caesar."

"Earth bless and keep you, Lord Marlowe," His Radiance said. I turned to go. I made it hardly half a dozen steps before the Emperor's words floated after me, clamped down like a solid hand upon my shoulder. "And Lord Marlowe?"

"Yes, Radiant Majesty?"

"Your years of service have earned you much leniency with us, *privately*," he said, and pressed his fingertips against the lid of the antique Steinway. I imagined those fingertips turning white beneath the glove. "Contradict us in public again, and I fear our leniency must run out. Are we clear?"

Again, I said, "Completely, Your Radiance."

I left him standing beside his ancient piano, a figure of carnelian and white marble. Like one of the icons in Chantry he seemed, the image of kings long past—for so he was. Like all our Emperors, a failed experiment, an attempt to cast again in flesh and bone the image of the God Emperor who had delivered man the stars. Was it truly his office that hung so heavily from his neck? Or only the weight of that failure? That reminder that he was not the God Emperor, but a mere and walking shadow?

That reminder that *God* did not speak to him as me.

CHAPTER 21

OF DRAGONS

"IF 'TIS MINOS AS your intelligence suggests," Valka said, her eyes hard as glass, "our first priority must be shutting down their comms." She chewed her tongue, turning from Bassander to Lorian; to Bassander's first officer, a gloomy giant of a man named Astor; to the holograph images of the dozen or so other captains comprising the high officers of Lin's fleet, pale and translucent as ghosts. Between us, hovering above the black glass of the tabletop, a constellation of images hung, aerial photographs and scans taken by a solitary light-probe—no larger than a coin—that we had accelerated into the unsuspecting star system. The pictures showed a complex of low, gray buildings clustered about a dark tower arrayed along a rise above a fat, green river that rippled like a serpent across the ocher lowlands toward a shallow sea.

"Why?" asked one of the more junior captains, a palatine woman with a knife-sharp jaw, her blond hair cut shorter even than Lorian's.

Valka held the woman's gaze a moment, still chewing her tongue, as if trying to express the proper words. "Have you never fought the Extrasolarians before?"

The woman shook her head.

"MINOS are scientists," Valka said. Encountering incomprehension on the faces of some of the officers, she added, "Magi. Certain of their operatives possess cerebral implants—a neural lace—which will allow them to broadcast and transmit an image, a copy, of their minds to a receiver offworld."

"Usually a ship," Lorian said.

Valka nodded agreement. "As soon as these images are broadcast offworld, the MINOS operatives will kill themselves rather than be taken alive." She swept the table with her eyes. "Once these images are safely received, they may be installed in new bodies. A clone or . . . homunculus."

All this talk of necromancy sent a ripple of discomfort around the table. Bassander and Lorian both made the sign of the sun disc to ward against the mention of evil. They were not alone.

"*If* we can block their escape," Lorian put in, "they may be more willing to surrender and cooperate."

The parliament of ghostly officers accepted this with little more than a stiff nod. From my place at Bassander's left, I studied the lot of them: a motley collection of green junior men and tired veterans. I'd come to know a few of them in the six-year voyage from Carteia to the unnamed system. Captain Mattias Simonyi had been at Senuessa, and he remembered me—though I did not recall him. He was captain of the *Gran Squall*, the 409th Legion's largest troop carrier. His men would form the bulk of the ground assault on the MINOS fortress, should it come to all-out war. Sevim Tenavian—the blond woman with the close-cropped hair—had never seen combat before, had spent her short career attached to the Emperor's guard for his tour of the far provinces. And Ausric Dayne and I had shared many a conversation about history, though he was greener even than Tenavian. The others were only faces, bluish, ghostly shadows hovering where chairs ought to have been.

"We can jam outgoing comms," Bassander said. "Once we engage, we can overwhelm any satellite grid they have in place."

Valka was already shaking her head. "That won't stop a tight-beam transmission if the boost is strong enough, and you can bet they'll be prepared for that eventuality."

Speaking around his fist, Lin's first officer, the giant Astor, inquired, "What do you propose?"

Lorian answered for her, tapping the black glass of the tabletop with one intricately braced finger. "We need to field a strike team. Disable their ability to broadcast from the surface to offworld." He gestured at the images of the compound taken by the light-probe. A trio of white domes dominated the lower, flat-roofed buildings that radiated from them, flowing like the cilia of some pale fungus across the reddish earth. "There's a spire off that southmost dome. There." He pointed at the dark tower near the center of the compound overlooking the river. "Destroying that should trap the Extras."

Tenavian interrupted. "What are the odds it's shielded? If they don't know we're coming, we could just rod the site from orbit, precision strike on that tower."

"And if we're wrong?" Lorian asked the palatine captain. "If the tower is shielded, we'll have alerted the bastards to our presence. We'd do as well to shout *'Have at you!'* on all frequencies before charging in like a pack of medieval cavaliers."

Lin gave an uncharacteristic snort, apparently amused by the thought of cavalry.

Astor grunted. "We could send Sharp and his boys in, Lin. Have them hard drop."

"That could prove suicidal," said Captain Simonyi, his holographic image steepling translucent fingers. "We have no way of knowing how many men the barbarians have on the planet."

"Hard drop's too risky anyhow," Lorian said. "They may see us coming."

Bassander raised a hand to cut off his subordinate, but nodded his agreement as he added, "And if LIO's guess is correct, if they are manufacturing an army of those monstrosities . . ." The tribune fell silent, one hand tightening on the head of his cane. I could tell just by looking at him that he was remembering Bahudde, remembering the single blow that had shattered nearly every bone in his body.

"No." I laid a hand on the table, drawing all eyes to me. "It's no different than our raid on Eikana. Lorian's right." I turned my eyes on the good commander. "We take them hard and fast, and we take them from the inside."

Lorian tapped the tabletop once again. "The *Ascalon* should be able to avoid most forms of detection."

I flinched, and it took every ounce of my restraint not to glare at Lorian. The little man had as good as put up his hand and shouted *Hadrian will go in first!* Only Valka seemed to have noticed my reaction, and looked at me with unbearable pity in her tired eyes. Beneath the table, I clenched my hands, stared down at my reflection in the black glass, at the shadows carved beneath my eyes and the curling strands of hair that fell across my face.

How old I was.

Bassander frowned. "How many will it hold?"

"Fifty," Valka replied, tossing her braid back over her shoulder.

Seeing Bassander's face begin to sour, I said, "It'll *hold* twice that. It only has fugue pods for fifty."

Lorian's lupine smile asserted itself. "If we separate close enough to the system, limit the *Ascalon*'s warp time to . . ." he glanced at me for approval, ". . . under twenty-four hours? We can double-pack the ship for that long at least."

"Easy for you to say," I said pointedly. "You won't be packed in there with us."

"You're not leaving me behind!" The good commander bristled. "I can direct you from the ship."

I raised a hand for calm. "You're wasted on ground engagements, Aristedes. Lin needs you up here." I turned to the Mandari captain. "Did we get a look at what's in orbit?"

The tribune shook his head, smoothed his smoky hair in agitation. "No."

"Another reason to send the *Ascalon* in first," I said. "We can drop a telegraph relay at the edge of the system, tight-beam a report back so the fleet doesn't come in blind." Lin nodded. That was standard enough operating procedure.

"It doesn't look like a military base," said Astor, drawing our attention back to the images. The hulking first officer massaged his lantern jaw. "See the solar collectors? Too exposed. And some of those smaller outbuildings might be barracks, but I'm not sure. Might be more lightly defended than we think."

"We can't count on that," said Captain Simonyi. "They wouldn't need much space, surely, to manufacture those demons."

Ausric Dayne, who had been quiet for most of the meeting, cleared his throat, holographic image flickering from signal delay. "If that *is* what they're doing."

That sobering reminder of our ignorance hung on the air like an unholy smell.

Crossing my arms, I leaned back in my chair, glowering up at the projections. I had not wanted to come, did not want to go back into the fray, and yet I had no choice. The Emperor was right, there was no one who knew the Cielcin quite like I did, nor anyone who shared my experience with MINOS. "I'll do it," I said. "I'll lead the strike team."

Without turning to look, I knew Bassander and the other captains had their eyes on me. Slowly—painfully slowly—I turned to look at the Mandari Tribune. "Give me a hundred men."

The *Ascalon's* hold brimmed with movement, its low roof echoing with the noise of voices and rough laughter. Half a hundred men or more were already crowded into the low space, busying themselves with munitions and other hardware or with the stowing and removal of the crates that had been there before.

"Keep the aisles clear, Mads!" said one grizzled centurion. "We'll need to offload in a hurry come planetfall!"

"Aye, sir!"

"How many gees does this fucker pull? Anyone know?" another voice called out.

"Any more than half one standard's got to be too much for your fat ass, Altaric!" called a man lounging against the far side of the hold, a half-eaten ration bar clamped ironically in his fist. "The target pulls point nine, so you're fucked!"

I hung back at the base of the ramp a moment, not wanting to interrupt them. My shadow hung its head, and I felt my shoulders hunch. Almost it seemed I was standing in the hall outside the dormitories in the hypogeum of the coliseum in Borosevo, listening to Switch and Pallino and the rest bickering in the common room. I raised a hand, fingers half-expecting to find the sweating concrete of the archway.

They found the cool steel of the ramp hydraulics instead.

I was in a massive hangar aboard Tribune Lin's flagship, the *Tempest*. The great battleship was perhaps only half the size of the *Tamerlane*, but where the *Tamerlane* had been built to store tens of thousands, the *Tempest* was all hardware: wing upon wing of lightercraft waited in banks above launch tubes that fluted the lower hull. Fully one fifth of the *Tempest's* nearly twelve-thousand-man compliment were aquilarii, the pilots of small lightercraft. The *Tempest* was designed to siege planets, to launch thousands of bombers and to bombard shielded targets from orbit.

It would be the perfect hammer if our battle on the ground came to all-out war.

Still I lingered on the threshold a moment, wondering if there were some way I might turn back, step not up into the *Ascalon*, but back to the past. Still I imagined that those were not the voices of Lin's shock troops I heard, but those of my dear myrmidons.

"I said keep the aisles *clear*, Mads! Not *just put that shit anywhere*! Earth and Emperor!" the centurion shouted, slashing his hand through the air. "Move it!"

As I mounted the ramp at last, long coat flapping about my ankles, another of the soldiers said, "They are clear, Quent!"

"Shit, shut it down! The Halfmortal!"

An eerie silence stole over the hold, and every face turned to stare at me. They were all of them men—nearly all of the Legions' elite squads were—each shave-pated and dressed in the customary black fatigues worn by soldiers aboard ship. Though they were each plebeian, many were nearly so tall as me, and each was broader in the shoulder. They had an air of laughing danger about them, the easy confidence that comes from men acquainted with violence, and for whom violence is never far and always certain.

Such men were rarely quiet. Only when duty called.

The centurion shouldered past his subordinate and snapped a crisp salute. Gone was his gruff and jovial demeanor, gone his rude speech. The man that saluted me was all business. "Lord Marlowe, sir."

I acknowledged the salute with a more casual wave of the hand. "You have the command, sirrah?"

"Aye sir, lordship." The centurion fixed his attention on a point over my shoulder—all very correct. A broad burn scar slashed his left eyebrow and ran up his forehead, angry red against his sailor's pale flesh. "Quentin Sharp, sir. Command Centurion, Ninth Special Detachment, 409th Centaurine Legion."

I paused, surveyed the rest of Sharp's Special Detachment a moment. "Very good, Command Centurion. You understand the mission?"

Sharp did not nod; he hardly seemed to move. "Aye, sir. Infiltrate and sabotage."

"Have you ever faced the Extrasolarians?"

"Couple police actions, lordship. Pirates and the like. But that was years ago."

"Never a magus, then?" I asked. "Or a chimera?"

If he felt any uncertainty or hesitation, Quentin Sharp's face betrayed none of it. "My men and I took out a number of the Cielcin hybrids rescuing Countess Volsenna at the Battle of Cidamus, cracked one of their heavy-weapons platforms my own self." He cracked a smile then, too. "That's why they call us the *Dragonslayers*, lordship."

I laughed. "The Dragonslayers? Do they indeed?" I looked round, hoping to find someone who understood the joke, but Valka was not due to join us for another hour or so, and the faces of the other soldiers were studiously blank. I caught myself regretting my suggestion that Lorian remain with the fleet. He might have laughed with me. "Do you know what the name of this ship is?"

"The *Ascalon*?"

"Do you know its meaning?" I asked.

Sharp shook his head. "No, lordship."

"It was the name of the lance Sir George wielded in the old stories," I said, and touched the spot on my right hand where the Emperor's sovereign ring had once been. "The one he used to slay the dragon."

Sharp blinked. "Was it really?" His composure cracked just a bit. "A good omen, that!"

I clapped the fellow on the shoulder. "That it is, centurion." I cast about the hold, searching . . . "Where are my effects?" Much of the cargo Valka and I had brought with us from Nessus had been moved into a hold aboard the *Tempest* to accommodate Sharp and his Dragonslayers.

"In your cabin, lordship," the centurion replied, shifting his gaze back to a point above my shoulder. "All the necessaries. Tribune Lin ordered the rest left aboard *Tempest*."

Brushing past the fellow, I said, "Very good." I turned back. "Is the pilot officer aboard?"

Sharp relaxed from attention. "Not as yet, lordship. She's due within the hour. We'll be ready to launch in two."

Again I said, "Very good, centurion. I will be in my cabin. Have Doctor Onderra sent up to me when she arrives."

The officer saluted again, clicking his heels together. I pushed past him toward the stairs. Before I reached the bulkhead, Sharp's voice rose again. "Secure those disruptors! Vann! Stas! I want you both on final checks on all shield emitters. We're under thrust in two hours, do you hear?"

As my boots rang on the metal steps that led up to the level of my cabin, their footfalls echoed against the vaults of the coliseum underground in the hollows of my mind. I could almost imagine that Sharp's brusque orders were Pallino's, almost imagine that we had never gone to Padmurak. To Eue. To Akterumu.

I blinked away tears as the cabin door hissed shut behind me, and slowly peeled my greatcoat from me, as though it and *Lord Marlowe* were a shell that hid the worm within.

"I can't do this," I whispered, coming to a standstill before the crate— like a coffin—that housed my restored armor.

Why should your burden be light?

Prince Philippe's voice—Gibson's voice—floated back to me out of a half-remembered dream. I shut my eyes, leaned against the metal pod, gripped its hard, defined edge.

We struggle, and by that struggle we are filled.

"Seek hardship," I murmured, remembering Brethren's words.

I had found hardship indeed.

Numb fingers fumbled with the clasp of my shield-belt. I wore no sword, and the dagger and sidearm clattered as I peeled the belt off. The whole thing thudded to the carpet, and a moment later my tunic jacket followed, magnetic clasps popping as I tore the garment away.

"Have I not had enough?" I asked, not expecting any answer. "Done enough?"

All was quiet.

The armor pod chimed brightly as I keyed it open, the heavy metal and polymer lid opening like some mighty jewel box to present the armor packed in foam beneath. The Magnarch's armorers on Nessus had restored it beautifully. The serene enameled face mask, mirror-black beneath the helmet with its broad neck flange, stared down at me like one of the statues in our necropolis, like one of the funeral ivories that hung from the arch beneath the Dome of Bright Carvings. Every scratch or hint of grime had been scrubbed away. The ebon surface of the muscled cuirass had been expertly restored. It drank the stark, white light of the cabin, and the sculpted motifs of stars and human faces that tipped the red-edged black leather pteruges glittered.

For that suit of armor, it was as if Eue had never happened.

I pulled my shirt up over my head. My shoulder offered no complaint. That at least had been erased, though the scar tissue pulled across my back. The suit underlayment was in a drawer at the foot of the armor pod, and I sank to my knees to retrieve it.

"I can't," I said, and shut my eyes, discovered just how ragged my breathing had become. The shame I'd felt in my meeting with the Emperor had evaporated. The courage I'd felt volunteering for the strike team in Bassander's meeting had withered and blown away. I had not worn the armor, not since that day on Eue.

Not since the Prophet's coronation.

Not since its Black Feast.

Shaking, I gripped the new fingers of my right hand with the hollow-boned ones of the left and sank to the short, gray carpet, knelt before the open casket that housed Lord Marlowe's empty husk.

Life is very long.

That was how she found me.

The door cycled, and light streamed in.

"Are you all right?" she asked. I did not turn, but saw her shadow slink into the cabin, saw it vanish as the door hissed shut. "That centurion said you were in here."

"It's too loud outside," I said, inhaling smoke and sandalwood. Fingers trailing on the carpet beside me, I added, "It reminds me of *them*." Valka did not need me to be specific. She knew who I meant.

"I know," she said, then sniffed. "I met the pilot officer coming aboard. We'll be ready to fly in about an hour."

"And how long to planetfall?"

"About twenty," she said. "Lin brought the fleet as close to the system as he dared. He's afraid they have telegraph sensors this far out."

I flexed my shoulders. "He's probably right." Lin had brought his fleet to about a quarter of a light-year outside *DB-639*'s heliopause. The light from our warships would not reach the planet for months, but any probes left out in the blackness might detect our presence. So far out, though, it was unlikely. A quantum telegraph was an expensive piece of hardware, and while it was almost a certainty that the Extras had a cordon of telegraph sensor relays strung about their system, it was unlikely they had sufficient number to map the volume so far out from the planet's twin suns.

Valka came to a halt beside me, placed a hand on my shoulder. "I don't know that I can do this," I said, reaching up to take her hand. "I thought I could, but I just keep seeing it . . . over and over." My voice broke, and I clamped my eyes shut, but that made it worse, made the images clearer. Durand's head bouncing down the green marble steps, blood dripping from Elara's lips, the way Crim's flesh had pulped like clay in Aulamn's fist.

You give them hell now . . .

Fingers tightening in my hair, Valka yanked my head back so that I looked up at her. Her grip slackened, and she cocked her head, peered down at me. She stood behind me, so that—looking down—she seemed upside-down. "You are *not* dead, Hadrian," she said, and—stooping— kissed me. She forced her tongue into my mouth. Her hands were on my face, nails sharp against my cheeks. I responded, wrapping a hand up behind her neck to hold her close. After a long moment, Valka drew back, one corner of her mouth tugged up—the right corner—her eyes half-closed, almost dreamy. "See?"

I didn't answer, but pulled her face to mine and kissed her as I had not done since we went under the ice at Carteia, perhaps since we had left Nessus. Her tongue was sour on mine, but that was sweet in itself. I felt the knotted tension and dread that coiled my every fiber unclench, felt the horizon of the universe contract to the borders of that little room. There was no Eue, had been no feast. Not then. Not for that moment.

Then Valka bit me.

Not hard, but hard enough to startle. I cried out, and falling back I pulled her down after me, and we fell laughing to the deck. "The hell was that?"

Still chuckling, Valka rolled onto her knees. Back arched, she eyed me appraisingly. "See?" she asked again. "I knew there was still fight in you."

"Is that what you call it?" I asked, and let my head fall back against the scrubby carpet.

"Where is the boy I met on Emesh?" she asked, swaying as she drew nearer, biting her own lip.

I touched my own, felt the mark of Valka's teeth. There was no blood. "He died."

Valka sucked on her teeth, eyes wandering down the length of me. "Doesn't look dead to me." She swung one leg over me, pressed her weight against mine. Hands on the floor to either side of my head, Valka kissed me again. "How long are you going to mourn?" she asked, breath hot on my neck. "'Twas not your fault."

You knew it would come to this, kinsman.

"I should have stopped it," I said. "Could have stopped it."

I had seen it, had I not?

"You're not a god, Hadrian." She pressed her cheek to mine. "I was there, too. Remember? There was nothing you could have done." She didn't let me answer. She kissed me again, heedless of my grunt of pain as her lips brushed against my injured ones. With one hand she fumbled at my belt.

I knew what she was doing, and I knew why. I let her do it.

Valka was right. I was not a dead man. And when she drew back to slip out of her vest and pull her shirt over her head, I rose and flipped her to the deck beneath me. Her smile widened, high breasts heaving in the light from the armor pod. "You're right," I said, one hand trailing along her tattooed flank.

"Of course!" That smile hung on her face. "Did you doubt it?" When I didn't move or speak, she said, "We don't have long, you know. You'd better hurry."

We lay together atop the coverlets, as we had the night after Valka rescued me from Akterumu, after she had tended my wounds and cut my hair. She lay curled beside me, one leg drawn up across my hips. I held her close, as I had on countless nights—for countless days. Neither one of us spoke for several minutes. We did not have to. After so long a life together—so many decades—words were such insufficient and inadequate tools.

She'd made her point.

"Is it the assassin that bothers you?" she asked, one yellow eye peering up at me through her tousled hair. "Men have tried to kill you before. And me."

The ceiling above us was common steel, stainless and brushed so that it reflected nothing, not even the pale echoes of our shapes. "It's not that. I . . ." I remembered stepping over Lucas's body in the door to the lower hold, remembered falling down the stairs, the wind knocked out of me. Remembered, too, falling from the steps of the black temple at Akterumu, landing in the torn corpses and offal that had once been my men. The torn head of the woman—chop-fallen—glared at me from that dull steel ceiling. "People keep dying. Because of me."

"You mean the soldiers?" she asked.

"Yes."

She was silent a long while. "I wish I could tell you those guards were the last," she said. "But they won't be."

"More will die tomorrow," I said.

"*Ja,*" she said.

"It's too much," I said. "Too many."

"What is it you always say?" she asked. "Always forward, always down?"

"And never left nor right," I murmured, not taking my eyes from the ceiling and the lone, low light at its apex.

"'Twill all be over, one day," she said, and laid a dry hand upon my cheek. "I promise." We lay there a moment in close quiet. "This cannot last forever."

"But when?" I asked the light above us. "When will it be over?"

"When 'tis over," Valka breathed. "No one can answer that. But it cannot last forever. The war. The Cielcin. Dorayaica will die—of time if nothing else."

"We don't know that," I said, and looked at her, thinking of the crawling horror I had seen slither beneath the Prophet's Pale flesh. "It isn't . . . *right*. Isn't . . ." I wanted to say *human*. "Normal."

She knew what it was I meant.

"Nothing lasts forever, Hadrian," she said. "The war will end."

"But to what end? Ours?"

Her hand tightened on my cheek. "Maybe. Maybe. But not if we keep fighting."

"And what if I can't?" I asked her. "That assassin nearly killed me, Valka. Out there on the stairs. I can't fight like I used to. I'm not the man I was."

"You're not," she agreed. "You're right. The boy I knew on Emesh died *long* ago. I love the man you are better."

"We could die tomorrow," I said, voice gone very sober.

"That," she answered pointedly, "has been true many times. It does not mean we should not go." With exquisite care, she extricated herself from my arms and sat up. "I need to clean myself up," she said, beginning to roll away.

I would not let her go, and held her to myself a moment, lips brushing her hair. The scent of temple smoke and sandalwood filled my nose.

"Hadrian," she said, not unkindly, "someone will be at the door before long. That centurion, or the pilot officer. They'll have missed us by now."

Knowing she was right, I let her go, relaxed my grip only slowly. Sitting at the edge of the mattress, Valka looked down on me, a sadness in her smiling face. Her dark lipstick ran across one cheek, and I guessed I must be wearing some of it myself. I wiped my face reflexively, found that I was right. "It isn't your fault," she said, and said again, "You're not a god. Even with everything you can do. You can't control everything."

"I can't control *anything*," I said. "Even with all I can do." I had failed in the exercise of my power every time I'd tried since Eue. She knew that, and she—of all the people I have ever known—did not need to be reminded. "We're at the Emperor's mercy."

"Did something happen?" she asked me. "With the Emperor?"

I hardly dared to move. We had traveled six years from Carteia to reach the target system, but I had slept that time entire, and the paranoia and the fear of the omnipresent surveillance had not gone. The *Ascalon* had been in Imperial hands that whole time, and there were sure to be countless iron ears still listening.

"No," I said, but nodded.

Valka nodded in return, and seemed to understand. The left corner of her mouth spasmed, and she clenched her left hand tight. Without having to ask, I knew that she was accessing her implants, and that doing so had disturbed some shade of Urbaine's worm. *"Rea skall vae saker,"* she said. *We should be safe.*

I shook my head. "Not this time."

She stood abruptly, padded to the narrow door that opened on the cabin's small private washroom. Propping myself on my elbows, I swung to seat myself on the bed's edge, the better to see her face reflected in the mirrored wall above the sink. She dampened a cloth with the contents of one dark bottle, began scrubbing away the lipstick and the charcoal on her eyes.

"I cannot see you like this, Hadrian," she said. "Not any longer."

I could not answer her. There was no response to give.

My silence drew Valka from the mirror. Still naked, she leaned against the door frame, gripping her painted shoulder with the opposite hand. She studied me a long time then, her head cocked to one side. Golden eyes flickered to the door, as if she expected it to open, or to hear the cough of some lurker at the keyhole. She chewed her tongue, and said at last, "We should run."

My head swam, and I felt as a man plunged directionless into deep water. To talk to her of Rothsmoor and the secrets I'd sworn to keep where we might be overheard was one thing. To talk so openly of fleeing— of treason—was another. My heart hammered in my throat, seemed almost part and particle with my tongue, and though my mouth opened I found I could not speak.

Which way was up? And which was forward?

Valka's words—if recorded and returned to some unfriendly ear—had doomed us then already. What agent of the Empress, of Alexander, or the Chantry could hear such talk and not cry murder to the Emperor? For all his honesty in Rothsmoor, William had made it clear in sending me to this nameless place that I was still but an instrument. Not a pawn, but a hierophant, centurion, or knight. I was his to move through the labyrinth, his to play and check the Pale King.

"We can't," I said.

"We *have* to," said she.

"It's too late, Valka," I said. The time to run had been at Colchis, probably even before Colchis, but duty and sorrow bent us thither.

"No, 'tis not," she said, still dabbing at her bottom lip with the rag.

"The minute this is over, we go. We take this ship and run. Leave Lorian. Leave Lin." Her eyes returned to the door, and I was sure by then that she feared a listener more than any interruption. "We've always talked about it. About going to see the Marching Towers. The Arches at Panormo. Athten Var . . ." She trailed off, wiped absently at some invisible spot beneath her left breast. "'Tis time."

"We can't go to any of those places," I said. "They're in the Empire. If we run, there's nowhere in the Empire we can hide. Not for long."

Valka crossed her arms properly, drawing my eyes. "Then we leave the damned Empire. Follow the Quiet. There are ruins all up the Outer Perseus, places I've never been."

Very slowly, I raised my face to hers. "You're serious?"

"Of course I am," she said, gesturing to the door and the world beyond with a fierceness and a venom I had seldom seen in her. "You cannot live like this, Hadrian! You can't! And I won't watch you eat yourself. You've done enough. *Khun vassa! We've* done enough. Your Emperor means to work you to death. You know that." She twisted and tossed the rag in the sink. "Don't let him."

"They'll hunt us," I said, studying my ruined hands. The sword scars and the cryoburn and the two fresh fingers. I counted our foes. "The Emperor. The Chantry. The Legions. Alexander . . . Assassins will follow us wherever we go."

"So what?" Valka tossed her head, defiant. "How is that any different than 'tis now?"

A hollow laugh escaped my throat, and to my shock I found that I was nodding along in agreement. "All right," I said, and stood. "We run. We run . . ." One step at a time, I closed the gap between us, until the little air between us was filled with the dusky scent of her. "One last fight, then." I made a vague gesture in the direction of the nameless planet we readied to make sail for. A strange thrill went through me to hear myself speak those words. It was as if the weight of some horrible yoke was lifted from my shoulders, or as if I had passed out from under the eye of some terrible shadow and felt again the wild wind off the seas of my home, promising adventure and a future not bounded, but open as the trackless waters of infinite space.

And in the back of my mind, a quiet voice whispered that Nairi lay among the stars of Perseus. *Follow the Quiet,* Valka had said. *Follow the Quiet* indeed.

"We can leave after the fleet moves in," Valka said. "After the battle.

Lin and the rest will be busy enough cleaning up our mess." Her face fell, and she clasped her hands between us, eyes downcast. "Lorian will never forgive us."

I took those warm hands in my damaged ones. "Lorian would never let us leave."

I told myself that it was enough I had saved his life, one among ninety thousand.

"'Tis a pity we cannot take him with us."

"He wouldn't understand," I said, and for the first time in minutes, I held her gaze. Valka looked up at me, brows contracting. But she smiled, and for the first time in longer than I could remember, the pity was gone from her face and eyes. "I almost wish we could go now," I said.

Those winged brows contracted further still, and she drew back. "Oh no," she said, and the venom had returned to her voice. "I wouldn't miss this for all the stars in the sky." A tremor shot up her left arm, and she slapped the door frame to make it stop with such force the sound of it was like a thunderclap in the close, still air of the cabin. Without her having to say so, I knew she was thinking of Urbaine. Thoughts of MINOS and the vile magus triggered the neutered remnants of the worm that had once tried to devour her, and she shivered, suddenly cold. "*He'll* be there."

I drew her close, wrapped my arms around her. It was my turn, it seemed. "We don't know that," I said to her, trying to reassure.

She pressed her cheek to my chest. "I do," she said, not needing reassurance at all, and hugged me to herself. "I do. And I wouldn't want it any other way."

CHAPTER 22

THE HIDDEN FORTRESS

THE VIOLET GLOW OF warp vanished in an instant, leaving us in starlit Dark. The nameless planet hung before us, red and rusted brown save where green rivers like veins peeking through sallow skin split its mottled surface.

"What an ugly place," growled the bald centurion, Quentin Sharp, from the back of the *Ascalon*'s cramped bridge.

Gripping the back of the copilot's seat with gauntleted hands, I said, "I've seen worse."

"Atmosphere's reading over eighty percent carbon dioxide," Valka said from the seat in front of me. "Nitrogen, ammonia. Trace amounts of methane."

"What an ugly place . . ." Sharp said again, more darkly.

"Have they noticed us?" I asked.

The pilot officer, a pale, freckled woman with a thatch of fine, red stubble on her scalp, shook her head. "All quiet, my lord."

"Good," I said. "Stick to the plan, pilot. Take us in over the pole."

"Aye, sir."

The nameless world twisted through the forward viewport as the pilot turned the *Ascalon* over until it seemed the planet hung above our heads. We advanced on pure momentum, engines dark. The pilot officer had performed our primary sublight burn before making the jump to warp. The light from that burst of acceleration would not reach the planet for days, but the speed we gained from it carried us as momentum after the shock of warp. The pilot had calculated our vector and velocity to drop us into a decaying polar orbit so that we might slide into the atmosphere with as little pomp or spectacle as possible, without even the friction burn of re-entry to betray us, thanks to the vessel's energy shield. The interceptor's hull had been fashioned and shaped in such a way as to make it nearly invisible to radar. Assuming all went to plan, assuming the pilot had made her jump and calculations correctly, we had nothing to do but wait.

"Were there moons on the LIO survey?" the pilot asked, shaking me from my contemplation of the rusty world above us.

I followed her hand to the limn of the umber planet, to where the icy faces of three moons rose, radiant as the Imperial regalia in the light of that system's twin suns. There should not have been so much ice this far insystem, well inside the double suns' habitable zone.

I knew at once what we were looking at, and felt my blood run cold. "No," I said, remembering the debrief all too well. "There were not."

Valka had seen what I had seen, and said, "Those are ships."

"Worldships," I said. "Cielcin worldships."

They must have arrived some time after Legion Intelligence performed their initial scan of the system, maybe even after we sent our light-probe on flyby. They might have *just* arrived.

Sharp cursed. "Look at the size of them!"

"There'll be a fleet of lesser vessels in support," I said, and placing a hand on the pilot's shoulder, I leaned down. "Can you scan?"

"Not without tipping them off to our presence, lord."

Valka's voice cut through the tension-thickened air like highmatter. "This all but confirms what the spies said," she began. "It must be MINOS."

"Unless even more of the Extras have rallied to the Cielcin cause," I said, thinking of Kharn Sagara. The Undying King of Vorgossos had traded with the Pale before, with Dorayaica itself. What was stopping him—*them*—from doing so again?

"There!" Sharp pointed. "On the left. See it? What is that?"

A black shadow was crossing in front of the leftmost Cielcin moon, an elongated cigar-shaped vessel, easily a hundred miles long. I had not seen its like since I was very young, since the *Mistral* sailed from March Station to meet . . .

"'Tis an Extrasolarian Sojourner," Valka said. "The Exalted are here, too."

"Earth and Emperor . . ." the pilot breathed. "Should we abort?"

"No," I said, moving to stand behind the pilot where her chair thrust out into the alumglass blister at the *Ascalon*'s prow. "This changes nothing. We have our orders, and we knew this place was bound to be defended. Human. Cielcin. Chimera. It doesn't matter." Lin and his legion had advanced the fleet to a mere five light-days outside the system while we moved in. Less than two hours' distance at full warp. We had only to signal via the *Ascalon's* telegraph, and he would come screaming in with a dozen warships and tens of thousands of men.

"I've never seen one in person," the pilot said. "A Sojourner, I mean."

"We've ridden on one," Valka said, drawing horrified looks from the pilot and Command Centurion Sharp.

Standing straight once more, I said, "Hell is empty, and all the devils are here." I bared my teeth in a pained grimace. We had known the Cielcin and the Extras were in bed since the Battle of Arae, but I had never seen a Sojourner fly side by side with a Cielcin *scianda* fleet.

The effect was horrifying.

"Can you get better visual on the Sojourner?" I asked. A sudden fear gripped me, and I leaned in over the pilot's console.

Valka answered from the chair behind. "'Tis not the *Demiurge*, Hadrian."

She was right, and had read my mind precisely. When I moved to join her, she showed me a close-up on her monitor. Though black the ship was, and large almost as Kharn Sagara's dreadful vessel, it was not the same ship. The *Demiurge* had bristled with buttressed towers and sculptures of men and goddesses standing in rank and file upon the battlements like a gathered army. Sagara's ship had been a work of art and terror.

This ship was smooth as glass, her hull of shining, minute tiles black as the space between the stars, made visible only by the contrast of the icy moon behind it. As I watched, the moon itself turned, revealing the lip of one vast engine, like a mountain range of iron.

The four on the bridge each seemed to hold their breath, and almost I felt I could sense the same unbreathing stillness in the hold two decks below. One hundred men clutching their guns in anticipation.

Before long, the ship began to shake, and the pilot said, "We've hit atmo! Seventeen minutes to the drop."

The suppression field took most of the shake out of atmospheric insertion, but I gripped the overhead straps on reflex. Twisting to put a hand on the command centurion's shoulder, I said, "Have your men get ready."

Sharp jerked his head and left, boots rattling on the deck plates.

The borders of the viewport shimmered with golden fire as the Royse fields took the brunt of the atmosphere, a faint phosphorescence that might have been visible to anyone on the ground. Of far greater concern was the sound, a noise like thunder in the high heavens. But the site was yet thousands of miles off, just north of the equator, and the rest of the planet was uninhabited, as deserted as the bogs and wastes of Eue. I watched coppery tundra streak by overhead, swaying where I stood hanging from the strap.

The world twisted once more, sliding up the right edge of the forward viewport until those unpathed wilds slid fast beneath our feet. The *Ascalon* would not be in the planet's air for long. She had only to skip across the top of the sky like a stone upon the water, to remain long enough for Sharp's men—for Valka and myself—to leap in repulsor harness and fall like heavy rain upon the fortress far below.

"The moment you're clear, I want you to telegraph the *Tempest*. They need to know about that fleet."

Hunched over her instruments, hands on the control yoke, the pilot replied, "Yes, my lord."

"And await my signal." I did not wait for a reply, but turned to go, tapping the back of Valka's chair as I went to signal that she should follow. On reflex I checked my terminal. Less than fifteen minutes to mark. I hurried along the hall after Quentin Sharp, turned right, and descended the steep, winding flight of stairs down two levels to the hold. The whole starcraft rattled about me, filling the air with a flat, droning scream that forced the soldiers in the hold to yell. I pulled my elastic coif up over my head and snugged it into place, pausing to tuck my trailing fringe of black hair beneath the armorweave.

The other men had already donned their helmets, and stood in five ranks twenty deep along the aisles Sharp's men had arranged in the supply crates. Those crates had been emptied in the interim. Lances assembled, disruptors holstered, bandoleers strapped into place. Each and every one of Sharp's Dragonslayers wore a repulsor harness—I wore one myself—buckled over the shoulders and about the waist. The devices permitted us to control our descent, to float out of the sky, not fall, relying on the same technology that lifted ships without wing or engine and allowed chariots and cargo floats to operate.

"We're ready, my lord!" Sharp exclaimed, shouting over the screaming vessel. I glanced up at the signal light to the right of the ramp. It glowed red, as I expected it to. It would cycle blue when we were over the target. Sharp alone of the men in the hold had not donned his helmet, and he eyed me with concern. "You've done this before?"

I realized only haltingly that the centurion meant his words as a question. "Four times!" I shouted back. The last had been at the Battle of Comum. I did not tell him that, or that I had been more than a hundred years younger at the time.

My answer was enough for the centurion, who beat his breast in salute. "Stas's got your kit! He's in front! First wave!"

Rather than shout a response, I signaled that I understood and shouldered my way up the line. The Dragonslayers tried to squeeze aside, but
the space between the munitions crates was so cramped that they failed
more than they succeeded. I was grateful that Valka and I had been able to
spend the brief journey in-system in the captain's quarters, not cramped
down in the hold or in the mess two levels above. I did not envy these men
packed like salt fish in a tin.

Stas was one of Sharp's decurions, a man betrayed by the double red
stripe on the left half of his visor just beneath the spot where his eye should
be. Not needing an explanation, the hoplite turned as I approached and
reached down into the nearest crate. The decurion drew out a long, slim
packet wrapped in an oilskin cloth. "Quent said to hold it for you, lord!"
he shouted.

Unwilling to shout myself, I laid a hand on the junior officer's shoulder
and took the packet, undoing the leather skein that held it closed. I hadn't
wanted to carry the scimitar about the ship. It was too long, too liable to
catch on one of the Ascalon's narrow door frames or on one of the ducts or
bronzed pipes that threaded the walls and ceiling.

"That one of theirs?" Stas asked, but backed off when I glared up
at him.

It was the very blade I'd dragged across the threshold of that very ship
in that last, desperate hour on Eue. A Cielcin blade. Imrah's people had
fashioned a scabbard for me of native rayskin when we had tarried on Colchis, and wrapped the abrasive material in woven cords dyed sable and
scarlet. This I'd ordered hung from a baldric of black leather fastened with
a silver hasp, that I might wear the great blade over my shoulder.

A grim trophy, but one I could not bring myself to cast aside as I had
cast aside the blade my other self had put into my hands. It had come to
me in the same moment that the Quiet's shell returned, and so I felt it a
part of that endowment, as though it were a gift from on high.

And I needed a sword.

I pulled the first foot or so of the blade from its scabbard. The ceramic
shone milk white, the hilt black and gnarled, the grip curved to fit a hand
larger and with more fingers than my own.

"It will do," I said, strapping the baldric in place over my repulsor harness. "Thank you, decurion." I checked that my sidearm was secure in
its holster, and—satisfied—keyed my helmet on. The helm unfurled from
the suit's neck baffle, opened and closed about my coifed head like a ne-
nuphar shutting with the setting of the sun. I closed my eyes against the

claustrophobic darkness of the suit. An instant later, the entoptics switched on, presenting their simulacrum of the hold and the men standing tense in it. I had not worn the suit since that wretched day. The familiar sensation of the air cyclers breathing across my face, of the water tube tickling the corner of my mouth, sent a thrill of terror through me, and I clenched my teeth. I might have collapsed, sunk onto the nearest crate, but for the reminder that I was in front of my men—though they were not truly mine.

I wanted nothing more than to be somewhere else, anywhere else. I longed to stand once more beneath the cypress trees of the English garden at Maddalo House, or to swim naked with Valka in the oceans about Thessa. I ached for my quiet walks about the equator of the dormant *Tamerlane*, for the bees and basil bowers of hydroponics. For the training yard in Borosevo. For the sea walls and Gothic spires of Devil's Rest.

Always I had led from the front, and in that moment—after all those years—I finally understood why. We believe war is waged by heroes and brave men, and it is so. But war is waged as much—and more—by those not brave at all. I am not Pallino, I am not sure I ever was. No Son of Fortitude, me. Only an old man too afraid and too tired to run.

As in Rome of old, it was the men behind me whose closed ranks held me to the mark.

"Are you ready, decurion?" I asked.

Though he was helmeted, I could almost *hear* Stas blink. "Yes, my lord."

I gripped the baldric that held my alien scimitar. "Very good." I checked my terminal once again.

"Five minutes, you dogs!" Quentin Sharp declared, voice quiet, controlled over the common band within my helmet. We could not rely on comms before long. Not only was there a chance a signal might be overheard, but open comms were nothing if not an invitation to the Extrasolarian magi.

"Out of the way, damn it!" came that old, familiar voice. Looking back over my shoulder, I saw Valka pressing past the men. She had donned her own armor—what remained of it. The scarlet plate of a Red Company officer was long gone, replaced with the sculpted white torso of the standard Imperial officer over the knee-length black coat. The white segments of a manica ran from her armored right shoulder to her polished gauntlet, which gleamed with the lights of terminal controls. But the underlayment was her own, and her left arm, lacking the manica on the right, showed the spiral patterns of her Tavrosi *saylash*, black on black beneath the officer's pteruges that decorated the left shoulder. Her helm was on, and the armorers on Carteia had found an officer's serenely sculpted mask for her, white beneath the armored cap with its Roman neck flange. The lenses of her eyes were black.

I reached out, took her hand to haul her past the last two men between us.

"That her?" I heard a voice ask over the comm. "The Devil's witch?"

"They can hear you, asshole."

Silence.

Valka's fingers tightened on mine, a private signal. *Don't.*

It wasn't right seeing her in Imperial colors, and I turned away, rounded on the hold, sweeping my masked gaze over the assembled company. I did not have to say a word. The Dragonslayers all shifted uncomfortably, but held ranks and did not admit which of them had spoken out of turn.

"You all know your parts!" I said, and was pleased my voice did not shake. Once, I might have made a speech to embolden the men. Once, I might have stood upon the nearest crate and riled them for their fight. But that Hadrian was gone, lay dead upon Elu's altar. "You will not fail." An order? A threat? Reassurance?

Who could say?

I turned away, renewed my grip on Valka's hand. Over our private band and in Tavrosi Panthai, I said, "Don't let go." Her hand tightened.

One last fight.

"One minute!" Quentin Sharp's voice filled the comm. "First wave, ready!"

The men about us all shifted their weight, standing with left feet forward like a maniple behind their shields. Ahead, the ramp opened, and a scream of wind filled the hold. An indicator in the top left of my vision marked the plunging temperature, the poisonous air, the altitude. The ramp extended nearly twenty feet into open air, right out the back of the starship.

The light switched from red to blue.

"Go! Go! Go!" Sharp shouted.

Stas moved, and the men of the first rank with him. Clutching Valka's hand tight, I followed, her half a step behind.

"First wave! Comms dark!" Stas called back as he reached the end of the ramp. And then he was gone, diving head first into clear air.

We leaped after him, killing our comms.

My stomach lurched, veins constricted with horror at the sight of seven miles of empty air and nothing between us and the ground. I did not scream, and that was well, for there were none to hear me in my helmet.

Valka's hand clenched mine, but she did not panic, instead stretched herself out so that she fell spread-eagle. I copied her, saw Stas and the first knot of men do likewise.

The fortress unrolled beneath us like a carpet in some Jaddian bazaar. Three shining domes, each perhaps half a mile in diameter, placed like pearls along the arc of a green and turgid river, surrounded by low, straight buildings that radiated from each like the spokes of a wheel. Smaller by far than the domes of Vedatharad were they, but they served the same purpose: their glass filtered the light of that nameless planet's binary suns, transmuted it to something wholesome and temperate. Even as we fell, I could spy the verdant greenery beneath the glass canopies, and guessed that within were gardens and orchards designed to feed the men and women who staffed that vile place. The finger of the great tower loomed over all, its twin shadows cast across the compound like outstretched arms. A great bridge stretched across the river from the central dome to a landing field organized about the slim spire of a hightower, its lift cable stretching all the way to orbit.

We plunged toward it all, the poisonous air rushing past us in a torrent that might have deafened me were it not for the helmet. Looking back, I saw the rest of Sharp's Dragonslayers fan out across the sky like a phalanx of dark birds, and behind them, the dim, dark shape of the *Ascalon* as it glided on across the uppermost airs, black against the still-black sky. As I watched, that sky seemed to close like a curtain, fading from black to white to pale orange.

We were to break into three units. The first—under my command and that of Decurion Stas—was to breach the main facility and disable the comms. The second, led by another decurion named Aron, was meant to blow the moorings that tethered the hightower's lift cable to the earth; while the third—led by Sharp himself—was to plant explosives on the dozen or so shuttles on the landing field, thereby cutting off any alternative avenue of escape.

The domes grew larger, and the pale luster of the sun off the glass faded, and I thought I could count the individual panes of the geodesic dome at the heart of the fortress.

Astor was right. It didn't *look* like a military base. The whole place had the feel of some frontier college, were it not for the hightower and the shuttle port, or of a Consortium research institute.

I banished these thoughts from my mind.

Stas twisted in midair, forcing his feet straight down so that his tunic belled up and his plasma rifle fluttered on its strap. He fell like a stone, streaking away from us as the men about him followed suit. Valka clutched me tighter, and together we made that same shift, pointing our boots at the earth.

Small as we were, we might escape detection by the fortress's radar; fast as we were falling—falling out of the sun—we might be missed by the naked eye. The repulsor harness's cord flapped in its sheath on the shoulder strap. Unlike the parachutes favored by the ancients, the harness needed very little space to work to stop my fall. The sky would not be filled with sheets of canvas, with targets to blot out the sun.

The ground rose to meet us like the face of a tidal wave, rust red and brown above the river bed. The hightower's cable slid past us, then the spire that buttressed its first miles or so of skyward stretch. Aron's group would be landing high up on the tower, planting their charges as they worked their way to join Sharp on the ground. The roof of one of the long, narrow halls lay beneath us, just as planned. Below, Stas raised a hand, the signal to those of us above. We were five hundred feet from the rooftop. Four hundred.

Three.

Then he shot past us, rocketed back toward the clouds—or so it seemed. He had pulled his cord, was slow-falling toward the rooftop beneath us.

"Now!" I yelled, not sure if Valka could hear. I let her hand go to be sure. The concrete face of the flat roof rushed toward me like the palm of an angry god to swat me like a fly. I tugged the cord, felt the harness thrum about me and the straps cinch and pull at my shoulders. It was like plunging into a vat of gelatin, like being caught like a fish upon some vast, elastic line. Valka floated beside me, our feet fluttering two hundred feet above the level of the roof. The harness vibrated awfully, rattling my teeth. But that was far preferable to the alternative. I flailed my arms uselessly, as if swimming. The harnesses lacked sufficient power to lift a man into the air, and while I could maneuver the harness by throttling the left and right repulsors, I had nowhere to go but down.

The first of Stas's men hit the ground just before us. They killed their repulsor harnesses and activated their shields with practiced efficiency as the trio took up the familiar wedge formation common across the Imperial Legions, back to back to back.

My own boots found solid ground an instant after, and Valka an instant after me.

"Door!" Stas said, voice low, and pointed.

Another thirty men alighted on the roof behind us, moving half-crouched, their rifles and lances sweeping the terrain. The building on which we stood attached to the dome at the narrow end, ran for nearly a mile in unbroken line out onto the low hills that rose above the river. The tower stood at that other end, its heights crowned with a thicket of antennae and satellite dishes. The door Stas pointed to lay in the direction of the dome.

"Move!"

Clutching the baldric to keep my scimitar from rattling, I followed Stas toward the door, keeping low, as if doing so might somehow prevent anyone in the tower behind from seeing us. The whole world seemed to hold its breath; all the men about me were silent, focused as laser light. A gentle wind blew across the fortress, carrying tongues of vapor from the narrow stacks that studded the ramparts like merlons.

"Locked," said the man on the door.

Unstymied, Stas thumped his chest three times to signal the breach team. Two men came forward. Working with silent efficiency, the first opened the service panel beneath the door controls, crouched as he fiddled with a tablet he'd unstrapped from his thigh. The lock looked standard enough, but there was no telling how the commands that bound the door shut were written. The Imperial codes were all standardized, and might be overridden, but there was no telling with these backspace barbarians, and so we could not simply override the lock as we had when breaking into the fuelworks at Virdi Planum.

The tech clamped two wires onto components within the opened panel, held up three fingers. Two. One. With his other hand, he threw a hard switch on the edge of his device. The panel sparked, smoked, went dead. Satisfied, the tech drew back, permitting his compatriot to step in and plant the thermite charge.

The explosive burned hot and bright. The common steel bubbled and melted like wax, and after a moment, the two men had the door open. In disabling the door, they had ensured the fortress's security would register only a technical fault, not a proper breach. We would not have long in any case. Stas led the way into the airlock, the torch beam of his rifle sweeping the darkened chamber. Evidently we'd disabled the airlock lighting as well as the outer door. "Seal it," he said, jerking his head at the gaping hole in the outer door.

The two techs moved to obey. One produced a can of the same sort of spray insulation used to quick-patch damaged shuttle hulls and began to fill the outer hatch. We had to seal it behind us, or else the intrusion of the outside, poisonous air would doubtless trigger the alarm.

At a sign from one of the others, I moved to follow. We had to clear the roof and quickly. We were exposed, and terribly visible, and I felt certain that at any moment the wail of sirens would sound above us all, and we would be too late to stop any of the sorcerers from shedding their human skins.

But I froze upon the doorstep. That situation—that place—recalled for me the hatch upon the surface of the *Tamerlane*, the smoke of the charge not unlike the smoke of Aulamn's burning. One hand on the door frame, I knew I stood once more at the gate of the underworld.

The labyrinth.

I had escaped it once.

Could I escape it once again?

Did I even dare try?

Valka laid a hand against the small of my back. *"Kar lasu braiyot, anaryan,"* she whispered in her native Panthai.

Barbarian, she said, reminding me. *One last fight.*

CHAPTER 23

ANGELS OF DEATH

I BEGAN TO UNDERSTAND why no alarm had been raised.

The fortress was empty—or so it seemed. Despite the great fleet in orbit, not a single soul met us in the hall. Not guards, not magi, not . . . anyone. Stas and his men moved in stages, one trias advancing at a time to cover a new position, to check branchings off the hall, to check side doors. They spoke in monosyllables. *Go. Check. Halt. Left. Right. Check.*

Go.

The walls within shone starkest white beneath fluorescent bars sterile and inhuman. The floors glowed with wax, polished to a perfect sheen, spotless and untrammeled. Standing by one corner, I felt Valka's eyes on me, and turned. She bowed her head and muttered a single word.

"Vorgossos."

She was right. For its emptiness and its sterility—the empty, echoing halls—recalled nothing and nowhere so much as the halls of the Undying, and of the facility beneath it where the black magicians of that evil world practiced their forbidden arts, twisted blood to shapes not to be named, and where the Brethren lurked in dark water beneath all. Kharn's palace had not been so bright or so clean, and so I could not say how it was or why it was that Valka's mind had made the connection—perhaps it was only the vast Sojourner in orbit high above—but the instant she did, mine agreed.

There was something in the quiet of that place, the faint whir of ventilation, the nearly imperceptible whine of the lights, the beep and distant chime of electronics. As I made to round the corner, the man in front of me raised a fist to call a halt. He pointed.

A small, dark shape hunched over the floor. A little more than a cubit in diameter, it looked like nothing so much as a flattened and slightly oblong dinner cloche, black as space and mirror-smooth. It beeped and whistled, proceeding along the floor toward us without regard or care for our presence.

"Earth and Emperor," one of the men hissed. "It's a machine."

The man before us raised his rifle to fire on the daimon. My own hands moved instinctively to the disruptor pistol strapped to my thigh.

Valka's hand shot up and forced his barrel down. "'Tis a *janitor*," she hissed, pointing at the trail of newly polished floor behind the creeping thing. I felt my shoulders relax, took my hand away from the gun. Still whistling tunelessly to itself, the little thing trudged toward us. Those of Stas's men in the way edged away from it, moving from one edge of the hall to the other. "It does not care about us," Valka said.

I had seen such things in the Demarchy, but we have no such automata in the Imperium. Self-governing drones such as this might pass Chantry inspection, provided they were beneath a certain complexity, but there would always be doubt—and doubt invited suspicion, and suspicion invited the Chantry. Well-traveled as I was by then, I knew there was no harm in the machine, but still I shuddered, for in every such unmanned machine there lurks a shadow of the Mericanii, a pearl of that ancient malevolence and intelligence like a shadow cast across time. But Valka was right. The little drone kept about its work, moved up the hall at a steady pace, polishing the glossy floor. I wondered if it noticed us at all, and despaired of so many fresh footprints upon its handiwork.

If it did, it offered no complaint, and we pushed on.

There were two hallways on that uppermost level that ran the length of the long building from environment dome to tower, one along either outer wall, with numerous cut-throughs to connect one side to the other. With no way to access the communications tower at the one end, we circled back, splitting our force on either side to sweep the level.

In this fashion we descended three levels, meeting no one, triggering no alarm. Many of the doors were locked, and those that weren't revealed only office blocks, warrens of small rooms, white desks littered with storage chits and print-outs, black glass displays. In one chamber, the low hum of computer banks greeted us, ventilators blowing white mist overhead. Still, no way into the tower presented itself.

"I don't like this," Stas grunted. He and I faced one another across the open door to the stairs. "Place is empty."

"They have their machines," I said. We'd caught another of the cleaning drones two levels down, matching its counterpart's progress down the hall. "And someone's here. You saw the shuttles in the yard." The last man passed us, tapped Stas on the shoulder as he went. "Go."

The decurion moved into the stairs, and I followed after, gripping the door as I went. The lintel gave beneath my fingers. Rather than follow the others down, I stopped, looked back at the frame. A thin strip of black rubber ran around the door, and unlike the doors on the levels above, this one was nearly two inches thick and secured by heavy pins that extended into the jamb.

Not an airlock. An environment seal.

"Stas!" I pointed.

The decurion swore. "Medical grade?"

"May be."

Stas swore again. "Just what is this place?"

I shook my head. "I'm not sure, but I have a feeling . . ." My words died, and I shook my head again. "We have to move."

"Clear!" came the muffled sounds of the men below. "Go."

Both the decurion and I turned and hurried down the stairs after the others, men moving left and right into the hall to cover our entry. An identical heavy door greeted us with an identical environment seal. Another polished white hall greeted us, lamps steady and sterile and cold.

"Set to stun!" one hoplite shouted, and an instant later the distinctive cough of disruptor fire cracked the air, followed by a gasp and a muffled thud. Then the same hoplite said, more quietly, "She's down."

Emerging into the corridor, I turned right, found two of Stas's men standing over a gray-suited woman where she lay sprawled on the floor.

"Looks like a tech, lord," one said, voice pressed flat by his helmet.

Valka beat me to the woman's side, crouched to turn the woman over. The barbarian's head lolled limp as a corpse's, struck the white floor without ceremony or grace. I recognized the precise gray of her smock at once, and the square brass plate over the lapel pocket—two interlocked chevrons forming a letter M—confirmed my suspicion.

Valka hissed. "'Tis them."

"Get her into one of these rooms and bind her," I said, looking over my shoulder to where Stas lingered by the door. "Secure the floor." A dozen of the hoplites moved off in opposite directions, sticking to their triases as they swept up and down the hall. "We need to figure out what they're doing here," I said, "and find a way into that tower."

"A pity we knocked her out," Stas said. "Might have had answers."

"She would only have signaled the others via her neural lace," Valka said, crouching at the woman's side. She turned the MINOS technician's head to reveal the lines of subcutaneous organic circuitry, black as activated charcoal. "She may have done already." Despite the helmet, I knew that Valka was chewing the inside of her cheek. "We don't have long."

"Look, sir!" one of the hoplites called, drawing our attention. He stood by a long, short window with rounded ends, one of many that lined that antiseptic corridor.

Leaving Valka by the unconscious magi's side, I swept up the hall, one hand on the baldric that held my sword in place, the other resting atop my sidearm, ready to draw. The window looked down a level onto what I took at once for a surgical theater. The pale, organic shapes of an armature hung from a node in the ceiling like the limbs of some skeletal willow. The bed beneath was empty, but many wires and braided hoses ran from the perimeter walls to the bed itself. Blackened panels gleamed on the walls, and another of the custodial machines trundled about the room, restoring the hoses and wires to their proper places with long and spindly arms.

The chamber had been in use until very recently.

"What is this place, my lord?" the hoplite asked when I drew up beside him.

I felt my intestines twist, and I shook my head, remembering the black pits beneath the mountain on Arae, the chimeras afloat in their tanks. All too easily, I imagined a Cielcin berserker strapped to that table. Its limbs amputated, its brain and spinal column excised, organs transplanted into the waiting chassis. Then I reminded myself that among the Extrasolarians, such was done to men and women—and children, too—every day between the stars.

"Evil," I answered him, and moved away. I stopped at once, mind caught on some detail of the theater below. I turned back, marked the thin smear of fluid still on the surgery floor.

Red, not black.

Fear is a poison, Gibson spoke within.

I tightened my grip on the baldric, shut my eyes behind my mask.

"My lord?"

"You heard the lady," I said in answer. "We haven't much time."

The others had gotten one of the side doors open, and two men carried the unconscious magus inside. The laboratory within was dark save for the pale glow of glass cabinets above the counters. Microscopes and other research equipment stood at the ready, and a faint whirring hinted at some unseen mechanism working in the background. Another surgical armature hung from a hemisphere in the ceiling, its jointed arms and segmented tentacles quiescent.

The two hoplites laid the woman on the ground. One went for binders. My attention flickered over the room, marking the three round windows that stood at intervals along the wall to the right before settling on the isolation pod opposite the door. It was one of the medical clean benches of the type used by natalists and bonecutters who handled delicate biological samples, gene tonics, and pathogens. Control gauntlets for either hand waited just outside the glass-fronted chamber, connected to a suite of mechanical instruments within.

Within . . .

"What is that?" asked one of the men.

A shapeless, fleshy lump lay on the slab behind the glass, connected to various feed lines, its surface studded with probes and glass wires.

"Some kind of fungus?" another asked, prodding the glass with the tip of his lance.

"Don't do that," I said, slapping the weapon down. "Stand down, man!"

The *thing* inside did not react. I wasn't even sure it was alive.

"Some sort of native, do you think?"

"'Tis human," Valka said, cutting the cloud of confusion like a plasma bolt.

"Human?" Stas asked, approaching the container. "No way, ladyship."

Stepping over the body of the unconscious magus, I followed him. Behind me, Valka moved to one of the dormant terminal displays, tapped at it with a finger. The *thing* was certainly of terranic origin. There was something familiar about the texture of the flesh, the corded striation of tissue, the pale fat. If Valka was right—if it *was* human tissue—then it reminded me of the uncomfortable similarities between our flesh and the flesh of those beasts we ourselves devour: oxen, kine, and boar. Here then was a statement of that most horrible Extrasolarian belief. *Men are meat.*

Small wonder that they should align with the Cielcin.

And yet there was something profoundly *wrong* about the tissue beneath that glass. It had a jaundiced look to it, yellow and bilious, shot through with pink veins. The color alone looked sick, and that was without considering the spongy, moist texture of the thing, or the most obvious problem of all . . .

"It's too damn big to be human," Stas said.

He was right.

Every year at Summerfair the various tribes and townships of the prefecture would come to Meidua to present their gifts to my lord father. Not just the painted carvings that decorated the council dome at Devil's Rest, but wine from the adorators who dwelt in the mountains, sauce liquamen from the fishing villages along the coast of the Apollan, and rich cheeses and true wool from the nomads who migrated from the lowlands and up the great plateaus, and whose families supplied much of the labor that worked the uranium mines. But among these gifts were melons from the ranchfolk who dwelt beyond the Redtines, where the great inland desert of the Iramnene formed the center of Delos's largest continent. *Angu,* the locals called them, and the greatest of them grew to half the height of a man.

This was as large, and nearly as round, as though it were an egg.

I reached the obvious conclusion just as Valka said the words. "'Tis a tumor."

Stas recoiled. "What?"

I turned to look at Valka, who hunched over the terminal display. I could hear her frown through her white mask. "Hadrian. Come here."

I moved to her side, peered over her shoulder at the image in the dark glass of the terminal. Ignoring the blocks of text written in Mandari ideograms, I focused on the image displayed there, Valka keyed it backward as I watched, showing the removal of the vast tumor step by step from an amorphous mass of human tissue that lay quiescent on a slab in another, similar operating theater. As she reversed the series of still images, ticking backward through time, undoing the ministrations of the many-armed surgical golem with every frame, I came to realize what I was looking at.

"Those stumps there," she said, tapping the display, "are legs."

I could feel the oath rising in me, but felt it drowned by the cold rush of wind across my soul. Valka kept reversing the image. The subject—the person—had no visible head, so bloated and misshapen was his—her?—torso. A suite of tubes and other equipment instead ran beneath misshapen folds of what appeared like fat, vanishing as up a sphincter. As Valka continued ticking back through the images like the pages of some terrible book, I watched the autosurgeon as it appeared to restore a fibrous appendage like a gnarled tree limb back to its place, and it was only with mounting horror that I realized that it was an arm, or had been, for it was like no arm I had ever seen. As big around as the trunk of an old tree it was, and twice as long as any arm should be. It terminated not in a hand, but in a knobby growth with more than a dozen uneven fingers.

"Remind you of something?" Valka asked.

I did not have her perfect memory, and so I stood there open mouthed.

Perhaps you see it yourself, already.

It is one thing to read of horrors in the dusty quiet of a library cell. Quite another to meet them in the bright light of day. "The Mericanii," I said, and felt the men about me tense at the word. The ancient daimons who ruled the Mericanii Totality had needed living, breathing humanity that they might themselves survive. Those daimonic machines had been a species of parasite, had crouched coiled about the brain stems of ten billion human souls, and so ruled a sleeping Earth. Installing themselves into every living man and woman, they had so saved mankind from famine, from plague, and war. Columbia and her daughters had put in place the capstone of man's Golden Age, made peace on Earth—Utopia—and all that it had cost our ancestors was *everything*.

But not even the machines could stop Death.

The humans in their care—their masters, their slaves, their *hosts*—still perished, and each death cost the machines dearly. Before his death and abdication, Julian Felsenburgh had charged his iron children to care for humanity, and each death was a failure. What was more, each death robbed the machines of life, for they had made their abodes in the brains and nervous systems of mankind, and dwelt in them as I had dwelt within the walls of Maddalo House. Thus to lose even one of their human chattel was to lose a piece of themselves, though the core of their ghostly bodies dwelt not in flesh, but in the silicon and ytterbium crystals that gleamed in the once-mighty pyramids of Earth.

So they had found a path to eternal life, and blessed humanity with it—and in so doing had cursed our ancestors with undeath.

"Cancer?" I said, stooping to examine the image more closely.

No ordinary cancer produced such horrific results. The man on the display must have weighed seven hundred pounds to judge by the size of him. His arm—before the autosurgeon removed it entirely—had grown nearly so long as he was tall, had twisted and bloated him until he was not a man at all, but a *mass*.

The machines had inflicted cancers upon the humans in their care, broke down the barriers in their genes that blocked tumor development. They force-fed and watered and bathed their dreaming captives—each and every one—pruned them like vines, like the jeweled trees so prized by the lords of the Nipponese great houses. They clipped away at the new growth, amputated limbs and malformed protrusions alike, installed them in water baths when their bones could no longer support their swollen weight.

Growth was *life*, meant life.

Felsenburgh had not charged his creations to protect their dignity, their quality of life. The machines had obeyed, as how could they not? And mankind was nearly destroyed in the name of its own safety. Were it not for the God Emperor, we might have spent eternity as bloated brains in jars, dreaming infinite dreams beneath the watchful eye and ministration of a collection of Cartesian daimons, unable to rise from our comfortable sleep.

"They're replicating the Mericanii cancers?" I asked. I could hardly get the words out. "Are they building a new . . . a new daimon?"

Valka shifted where she stood, toggled to the controls. "Mutation to the activin receptor genes, growth hormones . . ." Her lips fluttered as she read on. The three-dimensional models of various proteins spidered across the display. She shook her head. "I'm not sure. I'm not that kind of doctor." She began flipping through the terminal's records as fast as she could. As she did, I knew each frame, each cellular model and biopsy report etched itself into her perfect memory. Neither she nor I could understand the precise science, but we could bring it to those who could. "One thing is certain, however." She straightened, turned her visored face to look at Stas and me. "'Tis no weapons manufactory."

"Earth's ash!" one of the soldiers swore, leaping away from one of the round windows in the wall to our right. Two of his fellows caught him before he could fall over the bench in the center of the room. He raised a mailed hand, pointed at the dim chamber beyond. Words seemed to have left him, and he tripped over himself in his efforts to find his feet once more.

What might have frightened so hardened and well-trained an Imperial legionnaire I dared not guess, but advanced toward the window. Through the round portal lay a small room with a sealed door in the far wall. Dim yellow light suffused the chamber, cast by a glowsphere near the ceiling, so low that before the chamber's contents had been almost veiled. Pressing fingertips to the glass, I realized that assessment was wrong. The light was not dim. The glass was polarized, tuned to filter most of the interior light from the darkened laboratory.

"There's something there!" the soldier said. "It moved!"

Something *did* move beyond the glass then, an indistinct, blurry motion like the rolling of a whale against the waves. "Find the controls," I said, feeling around the edge of the window for a panel or switch to depolarize the glass.

Valka beat me to it. The glass snapped from nearly opaque to translucent, and I recoiled, looking in upon that terrible cell. A patient lay upon a bed bolted to the left of that padded chamber, alone save for toilet and grimy sink. Thinking of my own cell beneath the People's Palace in Vedatharad, I shuddered, but could not look away—could look nowhere save at the bloated horror reclining on that bed.

The change in the glass must have disturbed it, for it rolled onto one side, using one twisted limb for leverage as it turned its face to us. I cursed just as the legionnaire had done, and felt my jaw go slack with horror. It was—or at one time had been—a man. The eyes were still human, wet with loneliness and pain, but the head! The head might have weighed forty pounds, so swollen and distended was it, misshapen as a rejected gourd. Patches of dark hair still covered the cranium, but the flesh—and indeed the bone beneath—bubbled and swelled until I guessed the poor man could no longer lift it from the bed. His lips moved, but if any sound emerged, we could not hear it. He lifted one twisted arm. A second, smaller forearm sprouted from his elbow, its fingers—small as the fingers of a newborn babe—cherry red and swollen, oozing some translucent fluid I felt sure must stink of hell. I turned away. "Close it back!" I said, and heard the snap as the glass re-polarized.

Pale arms dragged across the surface of my memory, rising as from dark waters. Brethren's arms had branched thus, twisted and bloated and white. The daimon of Vorgossos was a survivor from the time of the Mericanii, a creature of human flesh tormented by foul and ancient arts. The same arts that had preserved the Mericanii's populace in their iron dreams.

Brethren had been a survivor of the Mericanii Empire, the last of its fell daimons still fully functional and free—if the Emperor could be believed, if Horizon had been destroyed. So too these magi, these men of MINOS. They were survivors of a sort. Inheritors of Felsenburgh's black legacy.

"We should burn this place to the ground," Stas said.

I raised a hand to forestall this line of thinking. "We have a job to do," I said. "We've wasted too much time."

The instant those words left my lips, a narrow door opened opposite the round windows, and a thin, gray-skinned man in the customary gray and white MINOS smock entered. He froze when saw us, beady gray eyes picking out his stunned comrade bound and unconscious on the floor. We stood frozen, too, staring at him in surprise. He looked for all the world like a man who'd just emerged from the lavatory. The pocket door sealed behind him, and looked once more like only a piece of the wall.

"Don't shoot!" he said, dropping to his knees. "Don't shoot!"

The ordinary words shook the men about me back into ordinary patterns. They didn't shoot, for to shoot a man surrendering would have been a monstrous thing, and their decency overrode their sense, if only for a moment, and a moment was itself too long. Two of the hoplites trained weapons on the man, while a third circled round behind to check him for weapons.

"I'm not armed!" he said. By his uniform and the familiar gray metallic eyes, I took him for one of the magi. I should have stunned him then myself, but the time was fast coming when our clandestine effort must be transformed into a battle—and we needed answers.

Pushing round the research bench in the middle of the room—boots squeaking on the rubber mat—I peered down at the man. "What's your name?" I asked him.

"Abberton," he said. "I'm just a researcher—ah!" He yelped as Stas's man patted him down. "I said I'm not armed!" The soldier lifted a stylus off the fellow, tossed it aside before moving to secure the man's wrists with a length of cord.

Before I knew what I was doing, I'd crossed the last two yards between the magus and myself, hand drawn back. Without so much as a second thought, I smashed my armored fist into Abberton's face, striking him a backhanded blow that knocked him off his knees. Only the man holding him kept him from falling.

I towered over the researcher, blind to the trickle of blood that ran from one corner of his mouth. "What have you done?" I asked him, looming down. "What have you done to these people?"

To my astonishment, the little man did not snivel or cry. His eyes swiveled to look up at me, all sign of shock or pain erased. Some mechanism in his mind must have overridden his peripheral nerves. "Only what is necessary," he said.

"Are you attempting to replicate Mericanii life-extension techniques?" Valka asked.

"Life extension?" Abberton's eyes flashed. "Life extension? You Imperials . . . so small-minded."

I hit him again.

Abberton hardly blinked, all but confirming my suspicion that he had blocked all sensation.

Valka spoke again. "Are you developing neural substrate to implant an artificial intelligence?"

The magus hunched, spat red on the matted floor at my feet. I saw the yellowed glint of a broken tooth. He did not speak at once. His eyes flickered to the tumor under glass, to the polarized windows on the observation chambers. Despite his immunity to physical pain, I sensed a shadow of terror behind those eyes. "You didn't open it, did you?" He spit again.

Red on black.

I glanced at the *angu* melon–sized growth in the isolation pod. "Open it?" I asked.

We'd done nothing, opened nothing. There'd been no alarms, and Valka—a magus herself and demoniac versed in machine lore—seemed unafraid. And yet I sensed that to answer him would be a mistake.

My silence paid for itself almost at once.

"Fools!" Abberton lurched to his feet, heedless of the hoplite behind him. "You'll kill us all!" He made it half a pace before the soldier seized him, shoved him back to his bony knees, and wrapped one muscled arm beneath his chin for good measure. Abberton struggled a moment, but—realizing his efforts were futile—went limp.

"Kill us *how*?" I asked, still testing.

"The virus!" Abberton choked. "The virus is airborne! If you've released it!"

I felt a cold knife thrust deep into my heart. *A virus.* We were in a weapons manufactory after all, but it was not the chimeric army they built here, nor atomics or other machines of war. No. What they built in that terrible place was fouler by far, subtler and more evil.

Plague.

"A virus did this?" Valka asked, the numb shock apparent even through her helmet.

Abberton's eyes shone white in the dim, yellow light. "A retrovirus! I designed it! Me. The others. Built it for the Lodge."

"The Lodge?" I asked.

The magi's only response was to tap at the little plaque with the brass chevrons. MINOS.

"Cancer," Valka said into the stiff, unsteady silence, a horror in her voice unlike any I had ever heard there, ". . . as plague?"

The little man's eyes flashed, flat and as void of character as a shark's eyes. "LTH-81 is designed to incapacitate planetary populations. It targets the gatekeeper genes, excites the pituitary, encourages cell proliferation. Bone growth. If you've tampered with that sample . . ."

"Would there not be an alarm if we had?" I asked.

The magus blinked at me.

I grunted. "How do we get into the comms tower?"

"What?"

I drew my pistol, aimed it square between Abberton's eyes. "If I kill you, will your mind leap somewhere else?"

Numb to pain he might have been, and bleeding from his mouth, but the magus shook in the soldier's grip. "I . . . yes."

I pointed the gun at the tumorous mass in the isolation pod, saw Abberton's face go white. "My men are armored," I said. "Tell me how to get to the comms tower."

Abberton's eyes flickered from the isolation bench to my face, and he gurgled as the hoplite's arm tightened beneath his jaw. "Answer him," the soldier said.

But I had made a critical mistake.

Ignorance.

I could see the cogs turning in the little man's machine-addled mind, but I did not understand them. I had backed Abberton into a corner, trapped him between death and disease, or so I thought. He locked eyes with me, and to my surprise and confusion he smiled. "You . . . can't win." His words emerged crabbed and tense. "You dogs." Abberton spat again, pink sputum spattering my boots.

"I will not warn you again!" I said, primed the trigger.

"Death to the Empire!" the magus sneered, and tensed his shoulders.

And died.

No spasm, no poisoned tooth. He simply collapsed in the hoplite's arms.

An instant later, a siren wailed, and all throughout that hidden fortress its wraith-like cry resounded like the waking of the furies from foggy Tartarus to smite the damned Orestes. Abberton had killed himself, transmitted his mind to some receiver just as Kharn Sagara had moved from his failing body to those of his two children.

"He's gone!" I hissed, swearing, shouting over the alarm.

"He can't have gone far!" Valka said. "His neural lace won't have been powerful enough to boost him offworld!"

I swore, cast about for some sign, some clue, some form of guidance. Snarling, I aimed my pistol at the unconscious magus where she lay on the floor, squeezed the trigger. Valka flinched as the witch died. I did not look down. "The tower!" I hissed. "The tower!"

CHAPTER 24

IRON MEN

"SHARP!" I SHOUTED INTO the comm, following Stas and his troopers back into the hall. "Blow your charges!" With the pall of secrecy lifted, I had to hope the centurion had reopened his radio.

I needn't have worried. Quentin Sharp's gruff voice sounded over the line almost at once. "What happened in there?"

We didn't have time. Exposed though we were, an open radio was invitation to the magi to seize control of our suits, though the comms system was fairly isolated from air and water and the rest. Still, I had no way of knowing the full extent of the mischief these Extrasolarians might get up to if granted access to our hardware. "I said blow those charges, centurion! And get in here! They know we're here!"

I killed the line.

A trias of legionnaires rounded the corner ahead, lances bobbing as they hurried to regroup with us. My gun was still in my hand, my grip surprisingly steady. Killing the MINOS woman had felt like justice, had felt *righteous*, as though it were Urbaine himself or Severine I had slain. My mind was *horribly* clear, scoured as if by white flame, and I prayed that my actions meant that one at least of their vile number was dead for good and all. Clapping Decurion Stas on the shoulder, I bellowed, "Downstairs! Now!"

He nodded, pounded his chest to signal he understood, then pointed with two fingers toward the stairs whence we had come. He took up position by the door as the men pushed past, counting his soldiers for any strays. I could sense Valka hovering at my shoulder.

"Go!" Stas waved us on.

We went, followed the line of white helmets down the steps, their neck flanges catching the red light of the alarms. A moment later we burst out into the lower hall. The wall ahead was broken by deeply set windows, tall and narrow, that looked in upon the empty operating theater. More red alarms strobed across my vision, and more than once my suit's entoptics blacked out the glare as we pushed forward. Another of the cleaning drones moved ahead of us, its water-strider arms akimbo. The men ahead did not hesitate, but aimed their weapons at its domed carapace and fired.

Unarmored as it was, the custodial machine exploded in a nimbus of red flame.

A deep roar like the drum of distant thunder shook the corridor, its bass rumble rattling beneath the high, piercing wail of the siren.

"That was Quent with the shuttles!" Stas exclaimed, recognizing the explosions for what they were. "That should keep them busy!"

I could picture the burning shuttles clear enough, see the columns of black smoke rising in the poisonous air, flames fast dissipating for want of oxygen, everything stinking from the planet's elevated methane levels. "We need to get to that comms tower, quickly!" I said. Abberton had sounded the alarm, and I felt certain that even as we spoke the station's magi must be streaming toward the satellite uplink, preparing to evacuate like ghosts up a chimney.

"Move! Move! Move!" Stas waved at his men, several of whom had taken up defensive positions to either side of the hall. The corridor ahead ran straight back in the direction of the tower. The white walls gleamed dark and pinkly in the red glare of the emergency lighting, and for a time the only sound I heard beneath the sirens was the thud and rattle of my own armor carried through my bones to my ears. The research wing must have stretched nearly a quarter mile from end to end, and I thought that I could see a light at the end where the hall turned sharply right.

A white light split the red-lit gloom like a wedge, and it was only after it struck the shields of the men in front that I recognized disruptor fire for what it was. I threw an arm out to stop Valka's progress, pulled her into the dubious cover of a door.

"Taking fire!" called one of the men, himself folding into the opening of a side passage.

"I don't see anything!" cried another.

Down the corridor, perhaps half a hundred feet ahead, a black shape hove into view. At first I took it for a man, for it walked upon two legs. But its armor—if armor it was—appeared too tight to house any human body. Indeed, it seemed cast from the same mold as so many of the Cielcin chimeras, the arms and limbs too long, the torso foreshortened. But it was the head that betrayed just what it was we were up against: a shrunken turret half as high as the head of a man, flat-topped and featureless save for the collection of jewel-dark lenses that served the creature in place of eyes.

It was a golem, a creature of iron and glass wires, of silicon and ytterbium crystal. A puppet. A machine. Its clustered eyes picked out each of us, glittering as a spider's do. It fired again, disruptor bolts streaking up the hall. Then it was gone, blurring into motion faster than the human eye could track, visible only as shadows, as after-images caught in the strobing of the sirens. Two of the men still in the hall went flying as the creature slammed into them. It fired again, using the disruptors mounted to twin armatures on its shoulders to lay down suppressive fire, to keep our hoplites in their place as it turned and backed one of the soldiers into an alcove. Implacable as the tide, impassive as stone, the creature drew back its fist.

I had a clear view of the golem's back as it loomed over the man in the alcove. To his credit, the soldier fired, but the machine's ablative plating dispersed the plasma as easily as candle flame.

The monster's punch was perfect. The arm blurred almost to invisibility as it extended, shocking the soldier out of any hope of defense. It slowed for the microns necessary to cross the man's Royse barrier—a motion requiring precision to far surpass any human capacity—then accelerated again for a blow that shattered the man's ceramic armor like glass and staved in his ribs like the beams of a rotten door. The man sagged to the ground, feet slipping out from under him. A red stripe followed him down the wall.

"Do something!" Valka hissed in my ear. "Hadrian!"

What?

The golem spun round, spraying lightning in the faces of the two hoplites nearest it. I just stood there, mind blank, eyes stretched wide beneath my mask as I tried to shield Valka with my body. The machine flashed toward the nearest legionnaire, one hand slashing like a blade. It caught the soldier in his throat with such force that the man flipped over as he was tossed against the far wall, his neck broken.

"Hadrian!" Valka nearly screamed.

"Open fire!" Stas's voice was like a blast of lightning, and thunder followed.

The machine hunched, weathered the barrage. It was shielded, but shields were little use against the ambient heat of plasma fire, and its carapace glowed orange beneath the assault. Its shoulder-mounted guns fired, and when the light faded enough that my suit cleared my vision, I saw the golem had scattered two more of our men like dolls.

"Hadrian, *do* something!" Valka hissed.

What could I do? The crystal clarity that had come in the rush after I'd killed the captive magus had ebbed all away, and in its place a cold and filmy indecision lingered, like a sheen of oil upon a once-clear pool. The vision would not come, and I was only a man . . . small and weak and febrile, every inch the broken skeleton of a man I'd been in the dungeons of Dharan-Tun.

I wanted to run, but to where? There was no place any of us could reach that the golem could not reach faster.

Then Valka raised her gun over my shoulder—choosing for both of us—and fired.

The old Tavrosi service pistol thundered in my ear. Her aim was true. The plasma bolt struck the golem in the back of its shortened turret of a head. It stopped in its tracks. A moment later, the black eyes swiveled into view as the golem rotated its head full-round like an owl. Then limb by limb, the golem shifted each shoulder and hip, adjusting its posture so that by subtle flexion its back became its chest, and without having to turn round like a man, the beast reversed direction. The disruptors on its shoulders turned to face us, muzzle slits flaring red, preparing to fire. The grainy light of targeting lasers painted their beads across my chest. But I was shielded, and it was not the disruptor fire I feared.

For a moment—between beats of the siren and my heart—everything was still.

Silent.

I tried to reach for that silent place within me I once had known. Gibson's mantras echoed endless in the hollow chasms of my skull. *Fear is a poison. Fear is a poison. Fear is a poison.*

But the poison had taken root long ago, and though I scrambled for the power I had known, I could not reach it. Memory of the pit and the wall and the lash washed over me like a wave, until it was not the golem that strode toward us, but the very demons of the White Hand. It was Vati Inamna drawing near, towering over Valka and myself as it had in the arena of the Grand Conclave on Padmurak.

Shots caromed off my shield, and the light of those impacts flickered about us both. In the flashing of gunfire, the daimon drew near, flickering faster almost than sight. To this day I recall—sharp as Valka could—the hands like knives reaching out to seize me, a still image frozen in time by the quality of those strobing lights.

One iron hand seized my shoulder, and I saw the other fist pulled back, poised to strike through my shield as it had struck through the shield of the other man.

"*Du-mi kla!*" rang a clear bright voice, far too late—or so it seemed.

The golem's fist fell like a hammer blow, but its timing faltered, and the punch—faster than any bullet—struck my shield like the tolling of a great black bell. I felt it not, felt instead the adamantine spike of adrenaline and the shock of realization as I understood only one thing.

I had almost died.

The gun was still in my hand, and I clenched my teeth to raise it. One blade-like metal hand skated over my right shoulder, punched a hole in the dense plastic of the wall behind me and *stuck* there, caught by some spar or conduit buried beneath the surface. Awake and more alive than I had been for decades beyond count, I raised my own disruptor and jammed the muzzle into the joint beneath the iron golem's prisoned left arm.

My finger moved.

Dry lightning filled the air about us, conducted along the machine's endoskeleton and fried the delicate circuitry within. The black spider eyes sparked and went flat and dead as glass beads. Then the whole thing slumped in death.

I shoved the iron carcass off me and staggered clear, found Stas and several of the others staring at me. They thought it some trick, some miracle of Hadrian Marlowe's. But it wasn't.

Valka put a hand on my arm. "Good of you to show up," she said, squeezing my vambrace. "Welcome back."

It had been her voice I'd heard. Her words. *Du-mi kla* was Tavrosi Panthai.

Don't you dare.

Valka must have worked her magic on the golem, disrupted its timing just enough.

She could not see me smile at her—not through our helmet masks, black and white—but smile I did. "Thank you."

She'd forced my hand, forced me to wake up. To make a choice. To stand between her and the machine—or to let us both fall.

It was no choice at all.

Still, the old power had not come. Dorayaica had broken something in me, something not even Elkan's ministrations or years with Gibson upon Thessa could heal. The Quiet had not spoken to me in years, nor shared any vision. Even the gifts he had given me were gone.

When you call for it, the Prophet had sneered, *it will be Quiet.*

Had Syriani been right? Had Utannash the Deceiver deceived me? Abandoned me?

There was no time to think on it, no time to dwell. The sirens yet wailed, and the red lights flashed around us. But we were alive, and abandoned by the Quiet or no, we had a fight to win.

One last fight.

Only the past is written.

"Thank you," I said to Valka again, more quietly. Then turning to the group at large, I shouted, "We can't stay here!"

No sooner had the words escaped my lips than we heard the sound of feet in the hall ahead. No voices. Only the heavy tread of steel. I could imagine the color draining from Stas's face even through the helmet, and it occurred to me I was not wholly certain what the man even looked like.

Two more of the metal monsters rounded the corner ahead, head-turrets swiveling to take us in.

"Run!" I shouted, feeling the blood course into my limbs and fill my shriveled heart. "Run!" Trapped in that hall, we ran the risk of being boxed in, attacked from either side. Hammer and anvil. We had to move, to find a better position, and we stood little chance against those golems in an open hall.

Spurring Valka ahead of me, I looked back, saw three more of the machines emerge at the end of the hall, black eyes flashing white as the spinning lights of the sirens caught them. I gripped the baldric that held my Cielcin blade, tucked my chin as a bolt struck and crackled against my shield. Standing there amidst the rear guard, I felt as I imagined one of the soldiers of the God Emperor must have felt, facing down the soulless servants of the Mericanii at the twilight of the Golden Age. These were no chimeras—human or xenobite—but pure machines.

I am not a religious man, leastways not in any sense recognized by the ordinary man. I do not believe Mother Earth will return, nor that the God Emperor was a god at all. But the daimons he faced were demons in truth, inhuman terrors as deadly to man as the Cielcin and the dark gods they served. It may sound strange, but that sense of *continuity*, of connection to primordial man and his struggle against his own creations, grounded me and drove back my terror. I raised my pistol and fired.

To my complete astonishment, the shot struck true, and the foremost of the metal monsters fell in smoking ruins, its systems burned out.

"How on Earth?" One of the men looked around at me. "It's true! What they say about you."

"Go!" I shouted, and fired. The shot went wide.

"My lord?" Stas cut in.

Before I could reply, the noise of gunfire filled the air, and I threw a hand across my masked face to dampen the light as more disruptor fire peppered us from the golems' shoulder-guns. They could not have been a hundred feet distant by then, but still they did not rush as the first one had. Were these different from the first? They looked identical. Still they advanced, inexorably as the tide, their weapons flashing, chipping away at our shields. Perhaps they feared to collide with one another, rushing at high speeds—or perhaps some other factor gave them caution. Had they some human operator motivated by something other than reflexive security?

Did they know *I* had come?

"Take the doctor and go!" I said to the decurion. "Find Sharp! Go!"

"Hadrian, don't you dare!" Valka hissed. "This didn't work the last time!"

"What about you?" Stas asked.

"I'm right behind you!" I said. There wasn't time to argue or explain. "I'll draw them off, see if we can't split their forces. Get her out of here!"

I wasn't thinking clearly—but I had started to think. It was as if vessels long drained of blood were filled at last with a life new and raw and painful as new skin. Valka's cursing followed me up the hall in mangled Panthai as the Dragonslayers led her away. I grit my teeth. This was not to be Vedatharad a second time. I gritted my teeth, raised my pistol, and stepped shielded back into the hall.

Fired.

The prismatic flash of shields answered my paltry salvo, and my heart sank at once. Only then did I realize this second group of golems was not quite like the first after all. Burnished steel like silver decorated their shoulders and armored cores, and I thought I understood. Here were hoplites to the earlier peltasts. Heavy golems. Shielded.

"Noyn jitat," I swore under my breath.

All thoughts of splitting the enemy and drawing them off Valka and the others vanished. I turned and ran, chasing Stas and Valka up the hall, the golems hard behind.

They must be gaining.

The hall ahead ran straight for nearly a quarter mile before it took a sharp left turn to match the right at the far end, so that it formed half of a perimeter walk that boxed in the chambers in the middle of the level. The first of our men had already reached the end of the hall, and quickly I overtook Stas with Valka and the men of the rear guard, moving with palatine agility.

Seeing the decurion turn his head inquiringly, I shouted, "Nothing I could do!"

Stas said nothing to me, but turned his head to Valka. "Come on, doctor!" he exclaimed, tugging her by the arm. "Move it!"

"Go away!" Valka pulled her arm free. "Get off!"

A shot caught one of the light fixtures in the ceiling above, sending glass tumbling down upon us like snow. Another shot pinged off my shield, and again I gritted my teeth, risked a glance back over my shoulder. The golems were all rushing in perfect synchrony up the hall behind. There must have been a dozen of them, all told.

"Why aren't they on top of us?" Stas asked.

"Don't ask questions!" I hissed, rounding the corner at the end of the hall. The whole of Stas's division waited there, jammed into the atrium before a sealed door wide enough for five men to walk abreast. Two clustered by the security panel; one had the maintenance hatch beneath it open already. The other twenty or so were spread out, had taken cover behind the seats and the reception desk there. I marked signs of recent abandonment: a paper cup on the counter, a half-eaten lunch on one of the little tables in the sitting area. So close to the medical horrors upstairs, these little touches of humanity seemed all the more obscene.

Stas barked, "Vann! Get that door open!"

"Trying, sir!" said one of the men on the panel.

"Try harder!" The decurion wheeled about, tucking his disruptor rifle against his shoulder. "Rest of you, on me!" The others all pointed their weapons back the way we'd come, save a few who kept watch on the other two entryways. We could all hear the noise of the golems' advance, and I knew that at any moment the atrium would be full of fire.

"Get behind me," I said to Valka, loosening my baldric that I might draw my sword.

Stas's coarse voice slashed through the air. "Where are you with that door, Vann?"

"Nearly there. Forced a reset! There's a code!"

"Why don't you just blast it like the one upstairs?" Valka asked.

The man Vann did not look up. "Door's too heavy, ma'am. Never work, shit we packed."

"Then let me!" Valka said, shoving the man aside.

Behind us, Stas shouted for his men to form up. The enemy was nearly on us. "Open fire!" he roared, drowning out any objections from Vann.

Valka hunched over the keypad even as disruptor fire flooded the air around us and the golems reached the corner of the little lounge. I peered over her shoulder. The display shone a pale sky blue, five white squares gleaming in a row. Five digits. They were Mandari numbers. Nearly two hundred fifty thousand possible combinations.

"Can you open it?" I asked, shielding her with my body. In the corner of my eye, my suit's shield meter showed pale yellow, drained to some seventy percent of its full charge. "Valka?"

She raised a hand for quiet. Then worked at the clasps to undo the gauntlet on her right hand. She had it off in about ten seconds, and tucked vambrace and glove under her arm.

I know little of praxis, and less of the strange machines employed by the Demarchists of the Wisp. The nematodes that threaded Valka's brain and nerves had been there since she was an embryo, had grown with her like a parallel nervous system and brain. But for her mechanical eyes and a tiny core of ytterbium crystal sunk deep in the white matter of her brain, the machine parts of her were composed almost entirely of her own cells. Her perfect memory, her extra senses, her awareness of signals and of currents in the air, were all achieved by the novel arrangement of axon and dendrite.

She placed two bare fingers on the display, connected to the system beneath via the cells in her fingertips, nerves I did not have.

The whole panel flickered, and digits appeared in the white boxes, one after the next.

Three. Eleven. Seven. Nine. Five.

The door panel cycled blue, and the door began to open. Unable to stop myself, I laughed, and pressed her helmet to mine. The heavy metal portal split and slid into the wall at either side, opening on an airlock whose further door was heavy alumglass. Beyond it, golden sunlight streamed through the filtering of the geodesic, and I could see the swaying boughs of palm trees and the skins of bananas—and my heart fell. We were moving in precisely the wrong direction: *away* from the comms tower.

"Stas!" I called. "Fall back! Everyone, fall back! Into the airlock! Now! Now! Now!" We needed another way forward, another plan. If we could regroup with Sharp's unit—blast our way out through the dome and onto the flats outside, we might be able to come at the tower from some other route. Our initial scan had revealed no entry point on the tower exterior, but there had to be a way.

But more than anything, we needed to get away from the golems.

There was room enough in the airlock for all of us, and Valka and I led the charge. The rest came through in sections, the golems filling in the atrium as they gave way. Stas crossed the threshold last of all, backing up slowly to keep suppressive fire on the approaching automata.

"Loose!" he bellowed, the word clear and sharp above the sirens' wail.

Without hesitation a half dozen of the Dragonslayers hurled grenades into the lobby. Each pulsed with reddish light as they tumbled among the feet of our foes. Sensing their danger, several of the machines leaped back—moving almost like men in their haste to win clear. Valka found the airlock controls just as the explosives blew, and I felt myself hurled back against the glass door by the shockwave.

The inner door slammed an instant later, leaving us standing in smoky darkness, the muffled sound of the alarms bleeding through the sealed portal.

"Can they get in?" Stas asked the question on all our minds.

Valka shook her head. "I think not. Not quickly. Your doorman took the airlock off the datasphere before I cracked it. They'll have to open it manually." She made a gesture. "You should fuse the door."

Taking this for an order, two of the men nearest the portal raised plasma burners to the joint between door and jamb, wielding their weapons like welders' torches. As if in response to that very cue, the glass doors slid open, chiming brightly. The sirens resounded through the sealed door behind, muffled and far away. The glass garden dome greeted us with birdsong and the gentle music of running water.

"Wave the centurion," I said to Stas, shouldering my way out onto a paved, stone path that ran out through reddish, sandy soil and under the arcing fingers of the date palms. The dome must have been about a mile in diameter, and I could see the doors that led to the other parts of the base plain enough. We seemed to be alone. "Tell him what happened."

The decurion turned away to speak into his radio.

Thin tongues of black smoke coiled from the open airlock, rising from the work of the two men welding the door shut.

"How big is this place?" one of the others asked.

"You saw the scan," replied one of his fellows. "Goes on for miles."

I resisted the temptation to open my helmet. After the claustrophobic conditions of the airlock, I felt a great need to breathe the clean air, to smell the trees and the musk of vegetal decay. Life and death. But there was a chance—if only a small one—that we'd been exposed to Abberton's virus.

I relayed this thought to the others, ordered them to maintain suit discipline at all costs.

Suit discipline . . .

I stopped short, realizing that Valka had taken off her glove. But Abberton had said the virus was *airborne*, had he not? I told myself she was fine. She had only opened her suit in the hall, far from the virology labs.

"Any word from Sharp?" I asked Decurion Stas.

The other man shook his head, moving toward me. "Comm's off." Without warning then, the decurion seized me by the straps of my repulsor harness and nearly lifted me from the earth in the less-than-standard gravity. "Did you know about those things?" He shook me.

"What?" I almost mouthed the word, so taken by surprise was I.

"Let him go!" Valka snapped, brushing past two hoplites to reach Stas.

"Did you know about those damn machines?" Stas asked again, still shaking me.

"No!" I shouted, raising my arms to break the decurion's grip. "How could I?" I staggered back, adjusted my repulsor harness over my armor, steadied my alien scimitar in its scabbard.

Stas looked round at his men. Appealing to them and not to me—as though we were in debate—he said, "How did his woman know the door code? Eh?" He thrust a finger in my face. "How come those monsters went so easy on you two? Didn't even rush you when you stayed behind!"

"Don't be dim, Stas!" said one of the others. "She's a witch, ain't she?"

"And he's the bloody Halfmortal!" shouted another.

"We don't have time for this," I said, turning my back on the man to signal my lack of fear. "We have to get outside and signal the others, I—"

Boom.

The ground beneath us trembled, shaking dust loose from the frame that held the panes of the glass dome in place. I turned, seeking the source of that hideous sound, and found it almost at once. The hightower stood above the fortress like a skeletal finger, a great mast of aluminum from whose heights stretched the whiskered carbon cable that tethered the station in high orbit to the earth, taller even than the black spire of the comms tower.

As I watched, a secondary explosion shattered the delicate-looking struts that supported the mile-high tower. An instant later, a third blast fountained near the foundations, gouting flame and dark smoke against the sickly, orange sky. The black cable that tethered the station to the planet snapped and flew upward, yanked into the heavens by the centripetal force of the station's orbit. Without its anchor, the station would slingshot out of the planet's orbit, carried by the huge counterweight that secured the line at its far end.

Aron's unit had succeeded.

"That's got their attention!" I exclaimed, brushing the decurion's suspicions aside. "I can explain later, but we can't stay here." With a slashing gesture, I pointed to the wall of the dome. "We have to find another way into the tower."

Stas did not move at once, but stood studying me like a statue fashioned of ceramic plate. "Is this some kind of trap?" he asked.

"What?"

"You've led us a merry chase. Your woman knew the code, and that *thing* sure died easy when you got your hands on it." He stepped closer. "If this a game . . ."

"That doesn't make any sense!" Valka exclaimed, rushing forward.

Stas pointed his disruptor at her. A hollow threat—she was shielded—but a profound one. "Quiet!" he snarled. "She's one of *them*, isn't she? A magus?"

Valka froze, raised her hands, her Tavrosi service repeater dangling from one finger. "I'm Tavrosi."

Stas glanced from her face to mine. "Same difference. Head's full of that evil shit all the same." He brandished the weapon. "I lost good men in there! Good men!"

Some part of me had forgotten that these were not *my* men, not my Red Company. Stas and Sharp and the Dragonslayers had not fought beside me for years and decades. They did not know me, did not believe—and so did not understand. In my best *Lord Marlowe* voice, I said, "Lower your weapon, soldier!"

Stas did no such thing. "You're trying to pull the fleet into a trap here, aren't you?"

"What?" Valka and I both said in unison.

"They say everyone under your command died," the decurion said. "I heard the story. You're going to do it again."

"'Twas not the way of it!" Valka said, looking round her. The other men stood stunned, torn between support for their commander and their fear of me. Whether Stas was right or not, in their eyes I was still a palatine lord of the Imperium—and the Halfmortal besides. To throw their lot in with the decurion was to court death. If Stas was wrong—and he *was* wrong—they would all be blown out an airlock when we returned to the fleet.

Stas seemed to chew his tongue, thinking. Seizing the unsteady space, I said, "Stand down, and I'll forget this happened. We don't have time for this. We need to regroup and find another way into that tower."

"They ought to have some kind of tram system, base this size," put in one of the junior men, trying to defuse the tension in the air. "Underground, like."

The decurion's weapon wavered, half-fell from Valka's face.

Before he could respond, a shot split the relative calm of the garden. The bullet shattered against Stas's shield, but landed with enough force still to shock the decurion and make him stagger back. I whirled, trying to locate the source of this new devilry. "Guard yourselves!" I roared, reminding myself not to duck. Exposed as we were, it would avail nothing save to dishearten the men who followed me. There was no cover to hand save the trees, so I pulled Valka toward the nearest stand of date palms.

We didn't get far.

Tall and black as night, one of the turret-headed golems appeared between the trees. So cold and unfeeling a nightmare had no business beneath so warm and bright a wood, and starkly recalled the horror of the Cielcin in Kharn Sagara's gardens. It did not fire, but raised its iron palms outward, the red slits of phase disruptors gleaming from wrists and shoulders.

"Put your weapons down!" came a human voice an instant later, and a gray-armored man emerged from the trees behind the golem, his face concealed by a mirror-black visor, a plasma rifle in his hands.

I shot him instead.

The disruptor bolt cracked uselessly against the fellow's shield, and he replied with a gout of violet flame fired into the air above my head. A warning shot. Not heeding him, I launched myself in his direction, paying no mind to the hail of disruptor fire from my right that heralded the arrival of more of the enemy. We collided, and he fell with my weight atop him, his rifle trapped between us. I bashed the side of his helmet with the butt of my pistol, leaned into one knee to catch his arm. If I could just get the pistol in line with the soft part of his suit beneath his chin . . .

Fingers hard as old bone wrapped around my arms, clamped tight as pincers until I thought the titanium and zircon might break. *"Please do not resist,"* came a flat, almost reedy voice. My skin crawled at the hollow sound of it. *"Surrender your weapons."* The golem's hands tightened further still, and it lifted me as easily as a grown man lifts a child.

I tried to shake myself free, but it was no use. Looking round, I could see more golems and gray-clad men emerging through the trees. There must have been a hundred of them, all told, five men for every one of the machines.

Seeing that I was caught, Stas's men contracted into their triases, weapons bristling and primed. Valka had already holstered her weapon, and stood with hands upraised. "Stand down!" she shouted. "All of you! Stand down!"

I could feel the full weight of Stas's glare on me. If I had hoped to disprove his suspicions of me, I was not sure we had succeeded. I was caught, that much was true—but so were we all. The decurion was right, in a sense: I *had* led us into a trap. The golems in the hall had not slaughtered us in order that we might be driven to that place and into the waiting arms of these others. But why? The first machine that attacked us had had no compunction about slaughtering us intruders.

What had changed?

I had my answer a moment later.

"I could hardly believe my eyes when I saw you on the feed," came a drawling, nasal voice. "I said to myself, 'Self! Surely the Red Emperor would not be so foolish as to lose his favorite toy a second time!' But it appears I was mistaken."

Even ten paces distant, I felt Valka tighten and recoil. I felt it, too. I *knew* that voice. The lazy demeanor, the cold contempt.

Urbaine appeared an instant later, stalking out from behind his men and into orbit around Valka and me. I could not tell if he wore the same body he had worn on Dharan-Tun, but I thought it must be. Still tall and milk-pale was he, bald as an egg, his ears flattened and fused to his skull, his nose pointed and up-turned, halfway between a human nose and the slit nostrils of the Cielcin. As ever, he dressed in the styles of a Mandari businessman, long violet-gray *changshan* falling almost to his knees, white hose and matching slippers. "What a delight to see you again." He bowed mockingly, and turned to Valka. "To see you *both* again, that is. The Great One will be overjoyed to learn you are returned to us," Urbaine said, and gestured in the direction of Stas and the other men. "He has long lamented your escape from Akterumu. I thought we would have to burn half the planets in Centaurus to find you again—and here you come to us! And in such . . . meager company."

As he spoke, a dozen of the golems and their human douleters moved among Stas and the others, relieving them of their weapons. Recalling how the drones had dismantled shielded men in the halls of the medica, Stas and his men stood down. We were overmatched, well and truly. Our only hope was that Sharp and Aron were yet free and might signal the fleet.

For all I knew, they were on their way already.

Urbaine continued his orbit of us, circling nearer Valka and myself like a stalking panther. "What did you hope to achieve?" He stopped, turned on his heel, and took a mincing step toward me. Behind him, Stas and the other Dragonslayers were forced to kneel by the towering golems, hands on their heads. "Did you hope to stop the work that we are doing? With so small a force?" He crossed his arms, hands vanishing into his voluminous sleeves. "What do you think of our virus?"

"It's insane," I said, resisting the urge to flail in the golem's grip.

"What it *is*," Urbaine replied, "is beautiful." He smiled again, bowing his head like a shy boy flattered by his mother's compliments. "I must commend you on your timing, the—"

With a roar, one of the hoplites boiled to his feet, drawing a hooked *sica* from a sheath in his boot. The Dragonslayer leaped toward Urbaine's back, ready to slam the point of his knife in between the sorcerer's shoulder blades.

A black blur slammed into him, sent the hoplite flying half a hundred feet through the air. A golem stood where the would-be-assassin had been mere moments before. The hoplite had still been wearing his shield, but the automaton's sheer mass had been enough to hurl the man across the open meadow. Cocking one hairless eyebrow, Urbaine half-turned to watch as another of his iron men stomped after the fallen hoplite. "Miserable insects," he said, and turned back to me as his drone punched the soldier with enough force to turn bone to powder. Holding my gaze, the sorcerer cracked his neck.

As if that had been a signal, the disruptor muzzles of a dozen golems flashed at once, unloading rounds into the back of every kneeling man's head at point-blank range. Stas hit the ground, smoking where the weapon had fried both suit and nerve.

And then Valka and I were alone with Urbaine and his unholy little army.

"There," he said, and rubbed his neck. "That's much better."

CHAPTER 25

THE SERPENT
AND THE WITCH

"BRING THEM!"

At Urbaine's word, a golem seized Valka by the upper arm, and we were led from the garden via one of the other portals and down into the fortress's hypogeum. The sorcerer marched ahead of us, bracketed by soldiers in white and gray, leaving most of the guard in the dome above. They had work to do, gathering and disposing of the bodies. That necessity had reduced our escort from more than a hundred to a mere dozen—ten men and two golems. The machines marched in lockstep just behind Valka and myself, maintaining their grip on our arms, while the men were divided front and back, protecting Urbaine and any retreat we might attempt.

I could still hear the distant alarm blaring through the superstructure, and smiled. "It sounds like your people have their hands full."

"Do not flatter yourself," Urbaine said. "What remains of your embarrassing little band is of no consequence. Your antics have delayed us only marginally. Even now my people move to recover the upper section of the hightower. Once it is restored, we will resume normal operations. It will be as if you were never here." A door opened, admitting us to a subfloor corridor that doubled back in the direction of the medical wing, bypassing the ruined airlock. "I know you fancy yourself a great hero, my lord, but you have achieved only an act of petty vandalism here. Nothing more."

"We'll see!" I said, and hissed as the golem's grip tightened on my arm. "But you won't win, Urbaine. Even if Dorayaica does. It *will* kill you before the end, sorcerer!"

"Sorcerer?" Urbaine looked back over his shoulder, highlighting the alien flatness of his profile. Again he smiled, flashing shark-like teeth, and chuckled. "I have so missed our little talks, my lord." He turned away, continued his stately march along the hall. For a moment, the only sound was the iron tread of golem feet on the metal floor. Below ground, the halls were not the stark, sterile white of the medica above, but drab gray and canted inward so that the ceiling was narrower than the floor, lending the place the feeling of a starship or military bunker, lit by lonely lamps every half a hundred paces. "The Great One is no fool. It will not destroy us while we are yet of use, and our use runs deep." He tossed his head, the long, golden tassel of his cap snapping with the motion. "Even now, we are on the verge of delivering into his hands a weapon that will guarantee his victory in this war."

"The virus?" Valka said.

Urbaine chuckled. "LTH-81 is in production. Before long, it will be deployed across the galaxy. Nessus, Ares, Renaissance, Forum itself—even your precious Delos, my lord."

My blood ran cold at the words. "Delos?" It didn't feel possible. Somehow, my ancient home felt a part of another world. Another universe. I struggled to imagine Cielcin ships or Sojourners in the sky above Devil's Rest, but the image would not come. I shut my eyes, permitting the golem to escort me onward, pincers biting my arms. A hollow grief washed over me, and I struggled to master my breathing.

Grief is deep water.

It was not grief for my father that I felt, or Crispin—or this sister I did not know—but grief instead for the white streets of Meidua beneath our acropolis, for the common people and familiar sights and smells of home. For the mountains and the ocean and the fishermen who plied the river that ran between the two. It was grief for Hadrian Marlowe I felt in that moment, for the part of him that remained a part of Delos against all reason and the passing of years. It was a grief I felt in my bones.

"You know what Dorayaica intends," I said at last. I could not bring myself to say all the words, could hardly bring myself to *believe* them. Dorayaica's aim, to alter the course of time, to prevent the Quiet's birth— and thereby to prevent the very act of creation, and so unmake the universe entire—could hardly be believed. It sounded like something out of a fiction, out of the antique-most myth, a thing belonging to the age of Gilgamesh and Atrahasis, when giants walked the Earth.

And yet I believed it then, and believe it still.

"Abolition," Urbaine said. "Yes."

"And still you fight for it?" I asked.

"Fight for it?" he asked. "No! But you have not seen what I have seen!"

"I've seen enough."

Urbaine halted his progress up the hall, forcing the rest of our escort to stop as well. The golems towered over Valka and myself, silent and still as stone. "You have, haven't you?" He took a step toward us, guards rotating to track their master. "You know what the Great One is, what he is *becoming*, do you not?"

"What is he talking about?" Valka asked, speaking Panthai.

I did not answer her, but held Urbaine's gaze as suspicion and old fear rekindled to new horror. Every day I'd been away from Eue, away from the Cielcin, it had gotten easier to tell myself it had all been a dream, easier not to confront the truth I'd known all along—the truth I'd shared with the Emperor on Carteia, must share with Valka there in the hall beneath that dread compound.

In memory, I saw once more the headless corpse of the Prophet bleeding on the steps of Elu's temple, its silver blood pale as quicksilver in the gray light of the eclipse. And I saw again those pallid, long fingers snaking from Dorayaica's opened throat in my vision, and the one-eyed demon crawling forth. *That* had been only a dream, but I remembered, too, the milky tendril worming its way from the Prophet's wounded side.

And *that* had been no dream.

"You know." Urbaine was smiling his fangy, monstrous smile. "I see you do."

"The *Izhkurrah*," I said. "The Blood of Elu."

"Is the Blood of Elu's god!" Urbaine proclaimed. "Not a false god of the sort our primitive forebears embraced, but a *true* divinity. One real as you and me."

Valka strained against her captors, but the golems did not yield. "What in twenty-eight hells are you talking about?"

Urbaine raised a finger to his lips and shushed her, but turned his dead, metallic eyes on me. "You haven't told your little pet?" he asked, speaking as though Valka were a part of the furniture. "I see. But then, why would you?" He tittered, raised his hands in what seemed almost a shrug, as if his own words embarrassed him. "I serve a living god. Do you not know? Ours is a holy mission."

"A living god?" Valka scoffed. "A holy mission? You're wholly insane."

The dark magician snorted through his ruined nose. "Oh, she's funny! You're funny! And here I thought Lord Marlowe kept you around for one reason only . . ."

Again I tried to tear myself from the iron grip that held me, to hurl myself at the magus.

Again I failed, and settled for snarling, "I'll kill you, Urbaine."

"Stow the theatrics, dear lord!" the sorcerer said with laughing eyes. "No performance can avail you. The Blood of the Watchers flows in Dorayaica's veins. The Great One will become one of them, and we shall *study* him, and become like gods ourselves. We are humanity's future."

"What future?" I asked him. "If your master succeeds, if what Dorayaica says is true . . ."

"Then everything will end?" Urbaine completed my thought. "Lord Marlowe, you overvalue yourself. The Great One is deluded. You are not the center of universe, and nothing will end with you save you. These gods the Cielcin worship are simply organisms. Organisms greater than you or I, but organisms all the same. Higher-dimensional beings! Creatures that can walk light-years at a stride, or swim through time itself! Can you imagine? Imagine what *we* will do with such powers?"

I could, better than Urbaine knew.

Still in the grip of the machines, I shuddered.

Syriani Dorayaica was *becoming* one of them.

In its flesh the seed of some new and hideous higher being flowered. Dorayaica was but the soil, the sow. In its flesh, a newborn god was growing.

"We advise the Great One. In time, we shall come to direct his course." He lay a hand upon my shoulder, tried in his monstrous way to seem collegial and wise, but the effect was spoiled by his subhuman countenance. "You could yet join us. I know that Severine made her offer. You could yet live. We need not deliver you to the Great One. Think what we could do *together.*"

"You think you can control Dorayaica?" I asked. "*Direct* the Cielcin?"

"Why else should he trouble himself with us, if not to heed our counsel?"

"You're a fool," I said.

Urbaine's genial demeanor vanished behind a face new-pruned with half-constrained rage. "And you base apes, the both of you. You stink of rut." He drew a kerchief from one flowing sleeve and held it to his ruined nose. I thought of Gilliam Vas then for the first time in decades. "Have it your way. Remain animals. We shall unlock the Great One's secrets, with or without you, and when we do, we shall ascend. And *we* shall have the mastery."

Valka had been quiet for a long moment, but the comment about *apes* and *rut* had vexed her back to speech, and she said, "And here I thought Hadrian was histrionic."

That drew the attention of Urbaine's dull, flat eyes. "I do not jest. Laugh if you wish. Marlowe knows I speak the truth." His sly grin widened. "The Cielcin are primitives. Even Dorayaica. He thinks his gods have blessed him with fire. *We* shall steal it from him."

"Your reach exceeds your grasp," I said, knowing something of the transcendent myself.

"Says the ape," Urbaine said, all sneers once more. "You're like him, you know? Dorayaica. Both of you talk of *truth*, but you don't know it."

Behind my mask, I blinked. "And you do?" For myself, I could not say if Urbaine was right, if the Watchers were only another kind of animal, or something more. The creature whose bones I'd climbed within on Eue, the Dreamer, Miudanar, had been dead as the men whose funeral masks hung upon the arch of my father's council chamber, and yet some part of it had lived.

"There are no gods. No truth. There is only politics," he said, eyes flitting from me to Valka. "Only power." He licked his lips, and I felt a thrill of fury coil in my belly. "Dorayaica cannot unmake the universe as he believes, but he can unmake your Empire. And he will. He has the praxis, technologies inherited from the Enar and from his *gods*." The magus said that last word as though it amused him. "These Watchers."

"And you think you can take that power?" Valka asked.

"Direct it, for now! I told you!" Urbaine's teeth flashed, and he touched his silken cap. "Aristotle once said that with the right lever, he could move a planet. Dorayaica is the lever to move the whole galaxy."

"So sure of that, are you?" I asked, suppressing a secret grin.

"Dorayaica cannot rule forever, even with his mutations. He will be cast down like all tyrants. Like the Red Emperor. We have worked in the shadows of the Empire for millennia. We can continue our work under the Pale."

"You misunderstand me," I said. "It was Archimedes who said that about the lever. Not Aristotle."

Urbaine blinked at me.

"Makes you wonder what else you might be wrong about, eh?"

At some signal, silent and unseen, the golem that held me twisted my arm back, forcing me to my knees with a grunt of pain. "Will you correct my spelling next?" Urbaine towered over me. As thin as he was, he was nearly seven feet tall. He brushed a hand along the side of my masked face, almost a caress. "If it consoles you on your return journey to Dharan-Tun, I concede you win the trivia contest, my lord. But rest assured: you have won only in trivia."

"We'll see," I managed.

"So confident!" Urbaine looked round, as if expecting Valka and his men to laugh at some jape. "Do you believe the rest of your merry men can succeed?" He paused, letting the words drip like slaver before the coming bite. "Or do you think your *fleet* will save you?"

I was grateful for the mask, for it hid my surprise. It was only an educated guess, I told myself. Of course he must guess we had a fleet prepared to move in. Anyone would. I clamped my jaw shut, hissed as the golem twisted my arm.

"There is no point in denying it, Marlowe," Urbaine said. "You were sent to cause mayhem sufficient to serve as a distraction, hence the attack on the hightower. Your fleet was meant to find our defenses in disarray chasing after the station. I am afraid they will be disappointed." He made a claw-like gesture with one hand, twisted it in the air. The golem holding me twisted its arm, evidently under Urbaine's direct command. I told myself I'd not give him the satisfaction of hearing my pain, but the machine twisted until I thought Kharn's false bones would snap out of joint. "I'm afraid your friends will find mine waiting for them."

I did gasp then, and a strangled cry issued from my throat. Memory of my hanging returned, of Urbaine leering up at me where I dangled from the gates of the Dhar-Iagon.

Come down! he mocked from memory. *Come down!*

"I'll kill you!" I managed, wincing with each syllable.

"Let him go!" Valka exclaimed, voice slashing through the cloud that fogged my mind.

Urbaine let his hand fall, and he turned to Valka. "And you'll what? Let me in again?" he asked. The golem that held me relaxed its grip, and the pain in my shoulder ebbed. "Did you miss me that badly?" He sauntered toward her, smile stretching to inhuman widths. "Have you spent all these long years *dreaming* of me? Aching for my return?"

"Get away from her!" I found my voice.

Urbaine barely glanced at me, but wrapped one long-fingered hand about the back of Valka's neck, stared into her still masked and visored face as if they were lovers. Fury boiled red as suns in my chest, but I could not break free. "Ah," he said. "You've shut me out. I can feel it. Clever girl." His fingers trailed down her shoulder, down her arm.

Her *left* arm.

Valka slammed her head forward, cracking Urbaine in his snout-like little nose. The magus yelped and crumpled like cordwood. Valka's golem tightened its grip on her arm, and one of the guards stepped in and—raising the butt of his rifle—struck Valka across the face. I swore, and would have torn my own arm from its socket to reach her, but the golem that held me wrapped an iron arm beneath my chin and held me tight.

"Damn you! If you've hurt her!"

But Urbaine was laughing, a high, hooting sound like birdsong. He struggled to his feet, clutching his raw nose. "Ooh, I love *strong* women!" he cackled, swaying as he found his feet. "You remind me of myself, you know? Come here!" He grabbed Valka by the wrist. She tried to pull away, but the golem held her fast. She drew back so far as she could, turning her head away. I tried to shout, but the golem clamped down even tighter. Even with the suit, I could barely breathe.

A familiar pneumatic whine sounded, and Valka's helm opened and folded away from her face like a terrible flower. Even from my place on the floor, I could tell that she was seizing. Though the golem held her, her left foot had slid out from under her, and the muscles of her thigh and arm shook as Urbaine tugged the padded coif from her hair. Surely Urbaine could not have gotten through to her, not if she had locked down her neural lace. His mere presence had triggered the fragments of the program he had once injected into Valka's mind, and she was relapsing. Still, I guessed it was he and not Valka who had ordered her helm to open, overriding her suit's systems via its comms transceiver.

"You feel it, don't you?" Urbaine hissed. "That part of me that never left you?" His fingers wound through her hair, yanked her face up to look into his. "You tried to kill me, you *bitch*."

"'Tis . . . a pity Udax didn't shoot you instead," she managed to say, and the quavering quality of her voice smote my ear. "But I . . . know better."

Laughing through his nose, Urbaine kissed Valka on the brow. He drew back, admiring her at arm's length. Looking her up and down, he said, "I may keep you. You're of little interest to the Great One, and no use! But to me? Imagine what fun we'll have with that lovely neural lace of yours!" He leered, and with that he turned and resumed his course up the hall, passing his guards. He clapped his hands twice. "Come! We haven't much time!"

CHAPTER 26

THE LODGE OF THE SORCERERS

VALKA SAGGED IN THE arms of her iron captor, lifeless and still. I staggered after her, shoulder throbbing where the golem had twisted my arm nearly free of its socket. I cursed after Urbaine, but the magus pretended not to hear. I wanted to kill him, longed for the power to tear the machine that held me limb from metal limb, but even if I could find the vision again through the red haze of fury boiling in me, it would not have availed. As I could not break my chains on Eue, I could not break the golem's grip.

Why could I still not do it?

Had the Quiet truly forsaken me?

We emerged from the tunnel at last onto a lift lobby, all bare, gray metal and exposed duct-work. Urbaine's guards chivvied us into one of the large lifts—so large it might have carried Stas's whole unit with room to spare. The walls gleamed with pale, inset lights, horizontal black stripes strobing past as we ascended smoothly level by level.

"We shall watch the destruction of your friends in comfort, my lord!" Urbaine jeered as the concave arc of the door before us rolled aside, revealing a chamber of polished metal and black glass set high above the fortress and the umber desert above the ugly, green river. The ruins of the hightower smoked through high windows at our left, and I knew where we must be.

We were in the dark tower.

We had reached it in the end.

Men and women in the white and gray MINOS uniforms hurried about, while technicians similarly clad sat wired into terminal consoles, or wore entoptic headsets that hid their eyes and ears. These I paid little mind, however, and devoted my attention to the menagerie of strange, inhuman life that gathered about a holography well in the heart of that round chamber beneath a hanging structure that descended from the ceiling far above like a stalactite of metal and trailing cables. The ceiling itself stretched far away above our heads, level upon level of balconies that circled the outer perimeter of the tower above, and here and there a radial catwalk stretched from those outer balconies to the stalactite that hung in the tower's vast, hollow heart. Without having to be told, I knew that hanging spire housed the great matrix of the sorcerers, their vast computer and the transceiver system by which these magi traveled between the stars. The dish atop the tower outside was surely trained upon the Sojourner in orbit, or else upon some secret satellite in orbit deeper still, and was even then preparing to transmit the first of the magi's phantom intellects offworld. Their images. Their ghosts.

I had seen such a machine but once before. In the mountain fortress on Arae. That one had been smaller, but the shape was not so different. Somewhere in the levels above, I guessed, lay a chamber where the bodies of those sorcerers not at the terminals or gathered about the vast holography well in the center of the floor waited to transmit their false souls and die.

"That's *him*?" asked one of the strange men gathered about the holography well, a dark-haired fellow in a loose, Nipponese-style robe. He had the metallic gray eyes of all the MINOS sorcerers, but a diamond pattern of black lines like circuitry showed beneath the skin of his neck.

The woman beside him—her face concealed by a paper fan—spoke in a stage whisper. "The devil?" She let her hand fall, revealing a face concealed by an articulated ceramic mask in the style of Jadd, not unlike the one Rafael Hatim had worn, save that hers was white. I wondered at that, for in Jadd only the men of the *eali al'aqran* concealed their faces. Only the great princes and satraps of the realm and their sons, not the aryabite soldier caste or the other, lesser nobiles. Women were to be seen, and men invisible. Something about the inversion of seeing a woman masked Jaddian fashion disturbed me, as did her accent. She had none, nor did the man in the Nipponese robe. Their voices were flat, expressionless, more machine than human. Urbaine and Severine—even Iovan—still possessed the fingerprints of human feeling in their words. I wondered if these two were older, or if their hollowness of expression was a choice as well, an affectation like those dull, metallic eyes.

"He is shorter than I expected," said another, a very tall, rapier-thin man whose face lay hidden beneath a convex arc of gold mirror-glass from beneath the too-tall and narrow hood of his flowing gray mantle.

"And older!" chortled a being like a bloated infant seated on a floating palanquin, its metal eyes shining red almost as lasers as it smiled at me.

"He is our guest, Gaizka," said Urbaine, though whether he addressed the reedy giant or the infant I could not say. "We must be courteous!" At this, he raised one claw-like hand and spoke to the golems that held Valka and myself. "Release them!"

Valka hit the floor with a clatter, head striking the ground. Knowing I was alone and overmatched in a room filled with foes, I stifled the urge to fly at Urbaine, hurried to Valka's side instead. "Valka!" I rolled her over. "Are you all right?"

Her eyelids fluttered open, but only the right eye focused on me. "'Twas just a . . . just a memory." She blinked, left eye sliding into focus. "He didn't get in."

"Urbaine!" said the man in the Nipponese robe, the most commonplace of that ghastly congress. "There are more!" He gestured at the holography well, where three lozenges of red light had just winked into existence.

Still holding Valka, I stretched as straight as I could while still on one knee. The base of the well was filled with the green wire-frame shape of the planet, and green spheres and a yellow cylinder marked the location of the Cielcin vessels and the lone Sojourner in the sky above.

The red lozenges were *ours*.

Lin had come! Sharp had signaled the *Ascalon* after all. The word had gone out . . . and the cavalry had come.

But even as my heart rose it blackened, for if what Urbaine said was true, they were flying to face not an orbital defense scrambled by a surprise strike on the ground, but a combined Cielcin-Extrasolarian battle fleet armed and ready and spoiling for war. Doughty though Lin and the captains of the 409th were, they could not prevail against so terrible a force.

Even so, no sooner had the Nipponese man's words died than a flat, feminine tone filled the air, piped through hidden speakers on every level, confirming my guess. "Imperial forces have entered the system," it said, then repeated itself in Mandari, "Repeat: Imperial forces have entered the system."

I shut my eyes. Hope was not lost. Though hope was a cloud, I prayed silently then that Lin and Lorian and the lesser captains would prove a thunderhead indeed.

"We will have to abandon Ganelon," said the Jaddian woman with a sigh, naming that nameless world. "I was just getting used to this place."

"No matter," said the thin giant with the mirrored face. "Our work here is nearly done." He turned to Urbaine. "Should we prepare for broadcast?"

Urbaine shook his head. "No need, Gaizka. The Imperials cannot hope to win." He looked round the rim of the holography well, gestured at one of the others. "Vladilen. You must go to Dharan-Tun directly. Inform our client the security of this base is compromised."

The woman, Vladilen, paled and said, "Me?" She was one of the junior aides, not garishly dressed or altered like those gathered about the holography well, but one cut from the same drab, colorless cloth as Abberton and the woman in the lab had been.

"Need I repeat myself?" Urbaine asked. "Yes, you."

"But sir." The woman shuffled her feet, did not look up. "Dorayaica killed Nolwenn after the failure on Arae."

Urbaine dismissed this concern with a wave. "Then you had best prepare a new host, and pray the Great One is accommodating."

Vladilen did not raise her eyes. "But sir." Her nostrils flared, and she repeated herself with emphasis. "Dorayaica *killed* Nolwenn, tore him apart mid-transfer. Destroyed both transmitters, he—"

The pale magus raised a hand, and Vladilen made a choking noise, clutched her throat. "Then you had best pray hard, girl. Tell the Great One that we have recaptured Hadrian Marlowe." The magus looked down at me. "I am certain he will be overjoyed."

The woman, Vladilen, bobbed her head. Seeing this, Urbaine dropped his hand, and she sagged against the rim of the holography well while another junior man in unassuming white and gray patted her on the back. A cold dread spread throughout my chest, and never before had I been so glad to be born a man of the Imperium, without implant or neural lace. I glanced down at Valka, squeezed her hand. Urbaine had plunged his fingers into the woman's mind and stopped her tongue. Her breath.

"Earth and Holy Emperor," I murmured.

Some silent word must have passed between them, transmitted mind to mind, for—still shaken—Vladilen bowed and said, "I understand." She turned to go. Urbaine's suggestion that she should *prepare a host* resonated in my chest. It implied these undead magi did not necessarily have new bodies prepared. I looked round at the men and women in that high hall. Other than the eccentrics gathered round the well, they were to a man nondescript, unassuming, interchangeable. They might have belonged anywhere. Indeed, I felt certain I had seen many of those faces before, and shivered.

For they were not faces at all, but masks. Not bodies, but garments put on by deathless phantoms and set aside as an insect sheds its shell. By comparison, the garish inhumans about the well were a world apart, a class unto themselves, separated from the gray rabble by their modifications, their Exalted *abstraction*.

I studied them each in turn: the Jaddian woman in her ceramic mask and brightly damasked robes of red and gold; beside her the checkered Nipponese man in black and deepest blue. My eyes tripped over the towering Gaizka and the gimlet-eyed infant in its hovering seat. There were others: a squat dwarf wide as he was tall, evidently bred for some harsh, high-gravity world; a woman with another pair of arms where her legs should be, seated like the grotesque infant in a floating palanquin of wood and polished brass. And there was Urbaine himself, halfway between man and xenobite.

"Two more contacts," said the Nipponese man, indicating a pair of scarlet lozenges that flashed into being on the monitor. "They're deploying lightercraft."

"Direct Peledanu to engage the bulk of the fleet," Urbaine said lazily, and rounded on the creature that looked like a swollen child. "Captain Zelaz, can your ship intercept these newcomers?"

The little man floated toward Urbaine's face. "I am not yours to command, Elect-Master. You know whom I serve."

"I do," Urbaine replied, "and if Calen Harendotes wishes our continued help in his little vendetta, you will order your ship to fire on the Imperials."

The Exalted captain continued floating upside-down for a silent second, considering. Presently he flipped himself fully over in midair, so that he hung inverted, his flesh grafted or harnessed into the repulsor pod. "Very well!"

My mind was reeling, scrambling to catch up.

Peledanu. Urbaine had said *Peledanu*. Prince Gurima Peledanu had been one of the few aeta clan chiefs to side with Dorayaica at the Aetavanni. With Attavaisa and the others, it had gone down from the assembly in the innermost sanctum of Miudanar's skull to carry the body of Hasurumn down to be thrown to the mob as appetizer for the feast that was to come. Thus it had been spared the gas that had killed all the princes in the temples save Dorayaica and myself. Dorayaica's Watcher blood had saved it, as my human blood had saved myself.

I recalled Peledanu, a tall prince robed and armored in green. Silver caps had decorated its horns, and silver chains its throat and brow. Bits of jade had pierced its pale cheeks, and glittered as it knelt in obeisance to the prince who would be king.

Had it become a finger of the White Hand?

It must have done, if it indeed held the command.

Still kneeling beside Valka, I said, "Who are you people?"

The masked woman cocked her head at me, paper fan unfurled. "I thought he was supposed to be bright. Is not this the man who bested Kharn Sagara?"

"That isn't how it happened," I said.

"No indeed!" the little captain, Zelaz, cut in. "He saved Sagara! Ensured his reincarnation! It is because of him the Undying is of two minds about everything."

The Nipponese man spat, *actually* spat, upon the polished floor. "*Duplication!* Of all the Imperial Abominations, it is the only one true!" He shook his head. "To be in two places at once. The risks involved! The psychic drift! Synaptic incompatibility! What is divided cannot be brought back together!"

"Sagara has paid for his hubris, Takeshi," said tall Gaizka. "He has lost Vorgossos to himself."

"Herself," Urbaine said. "I heard the woman won."

Lost Vorgossos? My mind reeled. Kharn Sagara at war with himself? When I left the Undying, it had been as two people. His consciousness had duplicated, received by two of his clone children. They had elected to co-exist, to rule Vorgossos together. Evidently, that peace had not endured.

"*We,*" the Jaddian woman shaded her face with her flower-painted fan as she turned her flashing eyes on me, "are MINOS."

"A part of it," Gaizka amended. "We are the Elect-Masters of the Lodge."

"Sorcerers," I said.

"Scientists!" Urbaine sneered. "Your primitive Imperial superstitions have rotted your mind, lord. Not that it matters." He turned his back on me. "You will be dead soon."

"*Katsu!*" the man called Takeshi interjected, reprimanding his counterpart. "We need him alive. You saw Severine's report. He is needed for further study. He should not be given to the Cielcin."

I almost smiled at the sound of that interjection. *Katsu* was *kwatz* in the Nipponese.

Valka made a small, pained noise, and the sound of it brought me back into my body. Shutting out the sorcerers and the battle flashing on the monitor, I laid hands on her and whispered, "Are you all right?"

"I can stand," she said.

As I helped her to her feet, the high squeal of a new alarm sounded from one of the consoles against the outer wall. "What's happening?" Valka asked, permitting me to support her as we moved toward the central terminal where the Elect-Masters stood. Peering through the horizontal stripe of window that looked out on Ganelon fortress, I could yet see smoke rising from the landing field.

The coldly feminine voice that had filled the high hall minutes before sounded once again, first in Galstani, then Mandari as before. "Breach detected in Environment Dome Three."

Valka and I exchanged glances. "Sharp," I said.

The man named Takeshi rounded on the junior techs at their stations along the perimeter. "Deploy drone units!" He strode along the bank of terminals like Corvo along the catwalk on the *Tamerlane*'s bridge. Only then did I realize the techs were not moving, but leaned back in their chairs, glass wires coiling from shunts behind their ears. "Kill them all!"

Without motion or visible response, the command center gave the impression of eerie calm, like a temple or a tomb. On the monitor, the red lozenges of Bassander's fleet fanned out, tangling with the green points that marked the Cielcin defenders.

Peledanu had brought three worldships to what must at first have been a simple courier mission, for surely they had come to receive a shipment of MINOS's deadly creations. Three worldships. For much of the war, a single Cielcin moon was all that was needed to break the defenses of our colonies. Two had sometimes sailed together, surrounded by lesser ships in hollowed asteroids, or the crescent-shaped frigates and lightercraft and fanged spikes of siege towers that fell from the sky.

But three?

How much power could the Pale now bring to bear in one place, at one time? For now there was only one world-fleet. Only one blood-clan. Only one Prophet and King.

An Empire of the Cielcin.

"Come, Lord Marlowe!" Urbaine said, beckoning to us. "And you, my dear! Come! See how your friends die." Those dull, gray eyes of his lit up. "Again."

I lurched forward, hoping to reach the magus before his iron familiars could reach me, but Valka caught my arm. "Don't," she said, voice thick.

Urbaine's smile reasserted itself—but it had faltered, if only for a moment.

The giant, Gaizka, stepped aside to make room at the rim of the holography well. He peered down at me with his mirrored dome of a face, but said nothing. I caught a brief glimpse of his rope-like, gangling body, the legs like broomsticks and the silvery flash of a pistol wrought of the same polished electrum as his face. Valka gripped my arm.

"You were right, you know?" she whispered, speaking Classical English now in the hopes that *that* dead language might not be understood. "Give me your Empire over a universe of these . . . people." She swallowed, stumbled. I caught her. "Any day," she added. "Any day."

The old reflex welled in me, and the words formed themselves beneath my tongue.

It's not my Empire, I almost said.

I choked the words back down. To deny it was to deny Stas and the men who died in the dome below, was to deny Sharp and the others still fighting in the halls, was to deny Bassander and his fleet far above us.

Instead, I only nodded.

"I have ordered the *Melancholia* to engage," the floating Zelaz said, breaking a long silence. The little monster orbited around the well, surveying the gathered Elect-Masters, Valka, and myself. "It will cost you."

The Jaddian woman dismissed this with a wave of her hand. "We can pay."

The yellow cylinder that marked the Exalted Sojourner raced for higher orbit, lancing toward Bassander's fleet.

One of the red lozenges vanished.

"Target destroyed," said Takeshi.

I could say nothing. Do nothing. It was just like Eue, just like the Shiomu's coronation feast. I could only watch. Standing there by the well should have been easier than being chained to the altar. I did not have to hear the screams, to feel hot blood spray against my face, to scrabble through piles of limbs in the blood-soaked mud. But it wasn't. The quiet and the calm were horrors of their own. Have I not said that atrocity is writ in just such quiet rooms as that room, by just such bloodless men as these? Men who do not fear death—not because their art has rendered them immorbid—but because they never face the sword, the shot, or the cannon blast.

I almost would have preferred to face Syriani again. It I could respect, but Urbaine and his fellow *witches* gathered for their feast? They were a different species of devil: cowardly and venal, treacherous and cruel.

Clenching my jaw, I risked a glance toward Gaizka, to the light pistol strapped to his impossibly narrow waist. The golems still stood guard behind us, and a dozen common soldiers yet remained by the door. One had my scimitar. Agitated, I swept the room.

There was nothing I could do.

"That Imperial super-carrier is deploying landing craft," Takeshi said, raising a hand almost to his ear.

"Lin," Valka said, hand tightening on mine. That *super-carrier* was the *Gran Squall*, Simonyi's vessel.

Urbaine gripped the rim of the pit. "Shoot them down!"

The Jaddian woman snapped her fan closed against her palm. "We should prepare for broadcast. No sense in being caught unprepared."

"Whatever for, Samara?" Urbaine cocked one hairless eyebrow. "The Imperials are no cause for concern. Peledanu and the good captain here will soon pull their fangs."

"You are overconfident, Urbaine," said the Jaddian woman in her toneless voice. "And undercautious. Our continuity must be assured."

The giant, Gaizka, placed one attenuated, spidery hand on Urbaine's shoulder. "Our work is near finished. There is no sense in staying." With his other hand, he gestured to Valka and myself. "Nonessential personnel should beam offworld at once. We can resume manufacture at another site."

Urbaine seemed to consider this a moment, but shook his head. "There is no need! Our alien friend will soon crush the Imperials." He leaned over the projection, shouted at the bank of lesser men socketed into their terminals. "Deploy the garrison!"

The instant those words left his mouth, another alarm sounded from a console off to the right. The flat, feminine voice spoke again over the speakers, one language following the other. "Breach detected in Medical Zone B."

"This is getting out of hand," the Jaddian woman, Samara, said. "That's *two* now."

At a guess, both Sharp's and Aron's units had penetrated the facility. Briefly my eyes touched Valka's, darted once more to the silvered pistol strapped to Gaizka's side.

Samara peered up through the projection floating between us, eyes wide in her red ceramic mask. "Urbaine! If the virus gets out . . ."

"Very well!" the great magus groaned. "Go!" He waved dismissal.

The Jaddian woman turned and took her first step.

A flash of light filled the high hall, followed by a noise like the clap of thunder. Shattered glass. Beside me, Gaizka fell like a puppet with its strings cut, tumbling half into the ring of the holography suite. Only belatedly did I duck, forcing Valka down beside me. As I descended, I caught a glimpse beneath the Extra's tattered hood. The mirrored hemisphere that hid his face lay in a thousand shattered pieces along the floor of the holography well, disrupting the holographed image. The face beneath—if face it had truly been—was a nightmare of mangled flesh and twisted metal, dripping blood and the familiar white, milky fluid common to many among the Exalted. Light shone through the hole where his temple had been.

He'd been shot.

Panic bloomed all around. Captain Zelaz floated upward, vanishing toward the upper levels. Samara hurried for the lifts, more eager now than ever to leave Ganelon fortress. Takeshi had crouched just as we, but regained his feet, hand still resting on the catch of his shield-belt. Even Urbaine had drawn back in surprise.

Another shot exploded through the hall, punching clean through the outer wall of the tower before it struck its target: one of the techs wired into his machine.

"Where are the drones?" Urbaine yelled, rounding on the bank of supine technicians. "Find them!"

A third shot shattered one of the horizontal, slitted windows before burying itself in the central spire. From the noise of it and the way it penetrated the solid steel of the tower's superstructure, I guessed it was a MAG weapon, the bullets each solid slugs of depleted uranium, dense enough to penetrate even the hardened exterior of the fortress. One of Sharp's men—or Sharp himself—had gotten high enough to get a bead on the tower. They must have risked using their suits' comms to track mine and Valka's location.

Urbaine continued screeching orders at his subordinates. Takeshi prowled up and down the bank of consoles like a caged panther, unspeaking. From his demeanor, I guessed the Nipponese man was directing his subordinates' response to the attack. But I did not have time to wonder at the nature of Extrasolarian engineering.

Gaizka's gun lay within reach.

Snarling, I thumbed my shield back on and seized the weapon—fashioned for the dead chimera's inhuman fingers—and pointed it at Urbaine. The magus never saw it coming. My only thought as I pulled the trigger was that it was Valka's shot to take.

It didn't matter.

A wedge of violet light lanced from the pistol. No sound. No recoil. Only the faintly satisfying *click* of the trigger depressing beneath my finger.

Urbaine's head exploded like an overripe fruit, blood and brain and bits of metal spattering the holography well. The bastard had not even bothered to don his shield.

No last words from him. No quarter from me.

Before the magi's body could so much as strike the floor, something struck me in the back with all the force of a tram car. Only the shock absorption of my armor's gel-layer saved me from serious harm, and I skidded across the polished gray metal floor until a bank of consoles stopped me.

Already the golem towered over me, black as hell and pitiless.

"Please do not resist," it said, reaching down to seize me. It did not move fast. Even with Urbaine dead—or as near dead as such a creature might be—the golem did not wish to kill me. Its masters wanted me alive, wanted me for their own purposes, *needed* to take me to Dorayaica.

Certain the strange beam weapon would only glance off the machine's polished carapace, I aimed for the delicate instruments that served the monster for eyes, hoping at least to strike it blind. I fired.

A lance of violet energy shot forth and punched a clean and smoking hole through the golem's head. Blind indeed and sparking, its hand missed me by inches, and I scrabbled free, fired again. The shot pierced the golem's chassis and stopped its iron heart. I shot it again in the hip for good measure, half-severing its leg, and stood. The second golem had frozen, turret head swiveling between Valka and myself as if unsure how to proceed. I pointed the gun, fired.

In the instant between my pulling the trigger and the discharge of the fuel cell, the drone blurred to one side, outpacing not the laser bolt, but the finger that conjured it. I fired again, and again it moved, half-circling me, trying to get near enough to immobilize me without risk to itself. We stood there a moment, staring at one another, man and machine.

A shot caught me in the side of the face, turned back by my shield. One of Urbaine's human guards had fired on me, and the others were gathering their wits and fast. I recoiled from the shot all the same, and that moment was all my foe required.

The golem leaped toward me, faster than any human could respond.

I did not have time even to blink, though my eyes clamped shut in reflex, my shot thrown wide in panicked anticipation of the blow.

It never came.

I opened my eyes.

The golem had frozen mid-step, arms stretched out like some monster of childhood, eager to seize me. It shook, but did not move.

I understood at once.

Valka stood leaning against the rim of the holography well, gleaming eyes locked on the struggling golem, her face drawn and very pale. Before I could raise the gun to fire, the golem sparked and fell to one knee. Light left its glittering eyes, and the hulking thing struck the deck with a hollow sound like a bell ringing.

"Elect-Master Gaizka's image salvage complete," said one of the junior techs, voice flat, apparently indifferent to the chaos boiling around him, as though he lived in some other world. "Prepared to transmit."

"Prime transmission!" Takeshi bellowed, gripping the back of the junior man's seat.

Another of the depleted uranium rounds punched through the outer wall. It passed clean through the high hall and out the far side, letting the foul air leech in. Sensors had begun picking up the intrusion of Ganelon's poisonous atmosphere, and alarms were sounding all around. I fired uselessly at Takeshi. The Elect-Master grunted as the laser flash hissed against his shield. With Takeshi momentarily flash-blind, I rounded on the still-standing human guardsmen. It did not take long to find the one with my sword slung over his shoulder.

I raised Gaizka's gun and fired.

The violet beam cracked against the enemy hoplite's shield. Snarling, I shouted, "Valka!" She looked round, still clearly shaken from her seizure. Without warning, I tossed Gaizka's gun at her. The thing was no good to me, not against shielded opponents. The pistol struck Valka in the chest and clattered to the floor. As she bent to retrieve it, I turned back to the man with my sword.

There was nothing for it.

Letting out a cry polished in a hundred Colosso fights, I charged the hoplite. A shot from his lance pinged off my shield, but I hurried forward even as he pointed his bayonet at my face. I dropped my weight at the last minute, armor scraping along the metallic floor as I skidded into him, knocking his knees out from under him so that he tumbled over my head.

I wasted no time, turned back and kicked the lance from his hands. He'd fallen on his back, and the length of my Cielcin scimitar kept him from rolling to his stomach.

A shot from one of his fellows struck my shield just above my right ear, and I grunted in surprise as I clambered atop the downed man. All my weight fell behind my mailed fist as I struck the other man across the jaw. He lolled back, tried lamely to catch my arms and fend off my mad assault.

He wore a dirk in a sheath at his wrist.

I took it from him, and in a simple move drove the point up beneath his chin. He spasmed under me as the knife's point found his brain. Drawing back, I took up my alien sword, using the wicked thing as a prop for my tired weight. My own breath came out frayed in my ears, filled my helmet.

"Elect-Master!" one of the junior technicians half-shouted. "More ships detected emerging from warp!"

Takeshi's eyes were on me as he asked, "How many?"

"Unclear, sir!"

But I saw the holograph plain. The wire-frame face of Ganelon turned in the bottom of the well, the green sparks of the Cielcin fleet floating like motes above it, spread out against the half dozen or so red lozenges that marked Bassander's little fleet . . .

. . . they were not alone.

A red wave flooded the upmost regions of the projection, flashing into frame like a rain of blood. My heart flew to my throat, and I might have laughed had I the wind for laughter. Whoever they were—they were friend neither to MINOS nor the Cielcin.

The glass of one of the upper windows shattered above my head, and looking up I saw the red-and-white-clad shape of a Sollan legionary descending through the opening in suspensor harness, plasma rifle blazing. Another window shattered higher up and on the far side an instant later, and two more came falling in, drifting toward the floor like snow.

"Elect-Master Samara's image is ready to transmit," said one of the technicians. The Jaddian woman must have escaped to some higher level of the tower. I imagined her shunted into the dread engine in the spire hanging above, a braided glass cable thrust into her brain, just as the magi on Arae had done.

"Broadcast now!" Takeshi said, eyes still locked on me. He reached into his robe, drew forth a long knife. The magus sank into a two-handed guard, squared to face me. I studied the blade a moment. An ugly thing, perhaps a cubit long and squared, with no edge. "I understand you are quite the swordsman, Lord Marlowe," the magus said, and saluted.

I returned the gesture, sparing a glance for Valka. She crouched behind the holography well in the chamber's heart, safe for the moment from the lances of the guards. I said nothing. There was nothing to say. I knew Takeshi was playing for time, that as we stood there exchanging pleasantries, the images of Gaizka's and Samara's minds were being relayed—by tight-beam, I assumed—to some place off world. I prayed Urbaine was dead in truth, that I had acted fast enough to defeat his machines.

Eager to be done, I advanced on Takeshi. The Nipponese magus advanced, thrusting his weapon forward as he came. The strange knife hinged open like an arm unbending at the elbow, and an instant later a band of blue-white plasma blazed along its length, hot as the surface of a star and long as any sword. Cielcin ceramic parried the plasma blade, but I did not close. Fear of that strange weapon held me at bay.

Playing for time indeed.

Takeshi lunged again, blade gleaming blue hot. I turned the blow aside, felt the heat even through the layers of my suit. The thing would cut through flesh almost as cleanly as highmatter, I knew, and was grateful for the small protection offered by my armor. He pressed me back toward the lifts, and a shot rattled my shield. Remembering the hoplites at my rear and fearing a sneak attack, I circled right, swinging between the holography well and the line of consoles. The magus swept high, and the light off the blade whited out my vision. Red pain slashed my arm an instant later, and I staggered back. The armorweave alone had spared me a more grievous wound, and black smoke coiled from my wounded triceps.

"I expected better," Takeshi said.

Snarling, I pushed him back with a flurry of blows. The magus parried these effortlessly, laughing all the while.

"But you're only human," he sneered, and flicked his blade at my side, arm nearly vanishing with the speed of his strike. Mere chance saved me, but not from the second blow. The gleaming blade slashed my side, and I gasped, heard the sizzle of frying carbon where the suit underlayment melted and smoked. The blue-white blade descended from on high. I brought my own blade up to parry, gripping the Cielcin weapon with both hands. Our blades locked together. Takeshi sped forward on light feet, pressing me back. Before I could slip aside, my back struck something solid—one of the pillars that supported the walkways above.

I was trapped. Trapped with three feet of shining plasma inches from my face. Takeshi grinned. He might have made some move, but he didn't have to. The Cielcin sword glowed where the plasma bit into it. The alien material was strong, resistant to heat beyond the point of any metal, but Takeshi's blade was hotter still. The magus grinned through our crossed swords just as my blade began to crack. My heart leaped into my throat, but I knew what I must do.

Mad as it was, I tucked my chin and brought my forehead down and forward to headbutt Takeshi's blade. I wasn't sure if it would work, wasn't sure if I was ending my life by that action, but the ceramic in the crown of my helm was thicker than the face plate, and thicker by far than the nanocarbon armorweave that covered my neck—the armorweave that I felt certain had been the wizard's target.

Takeshi's blade struck my helm and *bounced off.*

My own blade fell shattered, but I did not care. I took one careful inward step and rammed the hilt with its broken shard of blade clean through the wizard's chest.

Takeshi's weight sagged against me, hot blood pouring from the wound. I shoved him away, trapping his sword hand beneath one foot. "I expected better," I said, but the man was already dead. It had happened too quickly, and I guessed that—as Kharn Sagara had triggered some failsafe when Bassander shot him dead, so too this lesser sorcerer had broadcast his evil will just as Gaizka and Samara had.

Just like Urbaine had done at Berenike.

Stooping, I snatched up the wizard's weapon, cursing as the heat of it boiled the air. I found the trigger and depressed it, cutting off the plasma supply. More of Sharp's Dragonslayers had found their way into the hall, were even then bursting through windows high in the tower walls. There was Sharp himself, distinguished by the gold medallions on his breastplate and the red paint on his shoulders, arms, and mask.

"We have to destroy the tower!" I said, almost snarling the words. "The magi are trying to escape!" I waved Takeshi's saber at the structure hanging overhead. "Sharp! Get your men up there planting charges! Fast!" The centurion tapped his visor with a fist to signal he understood as I hurried to Valka's side. "Get your helmet back on!" I said to her, flinching as another of the uranium rounds split the air. "The air's going bad!" On the monitor, the red wave had surrounded Peledanu's ships, and even the Sojourner—Zelaz's *Melancholia*—was encircled. The initial wave of landing craft Lin had launched were nearly on top of us, and an instant later I heard a roaring from the skies outside as lighters and landing shuttles fell from heaven trailing pillars of fire.

"Who are they?" Valka asked, voice flat and amplified by her suit speakers.

I gripped the rim of the holography well with my free hand. "I don't know." Shots rained about us, plasma bursts and stunner bolts as Sharp and his men chased down the surviving lesser magi and service techs. I moved my hand to Valka's shoulder. "But I think they're with us."

I could feel her smile even through the mask. "'Tis very nearly over."

I took her hand and squeezed it.

Then something bony and strong as the roots of an old tree twined about my ankle. The next thing I knew I was flat on my face, helm striking the lip of the holography suite as I went down. My armor squealed as I was dragged backward and hurled through the air. Takeshi's blade fell from nerveless fingers as I struck the wall and fell a dozen feet back to the polished metal floor.

"Twice!" came a polished, impassive voice. I lay on my stomach a moment, the whole world spinning, ears ringing, breath coming like knives in my chest. "Twice now you've gone for the head. Do you learn nothing?"

"Hadrian!" The sound of Valka's voice dragged me back to myself, and—grunting—I raised my eyes.

One of the golems was rising to its feet, limbs gouging the metal floor. Recognition howled through me like the wind out an airlock. "Urbaine?" It was the golem Valka had torn down, its suite of eyes glittering with sterile malice.

"Do you doubt it?" The machine-man's voice was utterly flat, without any of the magi's drawling venom. The hulking monstrosity clanked toward me, gait less steady than it had been before, as though the will that animated its iron carcass ill fit in its new shell. "We are not finished."

"Look around you!" I said, clambering to one knee. "The others are dead. Your fleet is lost! Surrender!"

"You think this a victory?" Urbaine asked.

"Peledanu's fleet is surrounded!" I countered. "The virus—"

"You think this was the first shipment of the virus we created?" the golem-Urbaine asked, and I think the creature would have laughed if it could. "We have been in production for *decades*, you fool!"

With my face concealed beneath my helmet, Urbaine could not see the blood drain away.

"Decades?"

"The great work cannot be halted," Urbaine said. "The Empire will fall! And when it has fallen, we will be there to pick up the pieces."

I searched for words to answer Urbaine, but the words would not come. With a tired groan, I heaved back onto my feet and stood there, unarmed and utterly spent. My whole body ached from my rough handling by the golems and Takeshi's burns.

Explosions rocked the world above, and debris came tumbling down from the upper levels, curtains of dust and chips of shattered glass.

"You're dead," I said at last, voice desperately ragged in my own ears. "You're trapped here."

The golem stood tall and thin and terrible between the well and me, flexing its long, grasping hands. "The *Melancholia* remains," the Urbaine-thing replied. "I will signal them when I have killed you."

Without warning, the golem flashed toward me, a black blur on the wind. Briefly I could see Valka still leaning—stunned—against the rim of the projection well. She had one hand—her left hand—wrapped about her own throat. Horror filled me, and I forgot myself—all concentration shattered to recall those horrid nights spent on Edda by her bedside while Tavrosi magi worked to exorcise the serpent from her mind.

The golem stopped inches from my face, and all time seemed to slow as it looked down at me. I can remember the dry rush of air as the sound wave caught up with Urbaine's movement, and I staggered back a step. Then the giant's knee slammed upward, caught me beneath the ribs. My armor took the brunt of the blow, but still the force of it lifted me from my feet and sent me tumbling through the air. Again I struck the wall above the lift doors, again I tumbled to the floor.

"Severine will be so disappointed," the golem-Urbaine declared. His footsteps clattered nearer, almost the clack of cloven hooves. "She so wanted to study you. Alas." A shadow fell across me. "But sacrifices must be made for the greater good."

The thought of Valka's own hand turned against her filled me with an animal fury, and I stumbled back to one knee. To stand once more. An iron hand clamped about my head and forced me back to the ground, to lie prostrate at the devil's feet. I scrabbled there, hands seeking some handhold, feet desperate for purchase.

But there was nothing.

Nothing.

Nothing.

"Dorayaica thinks killing you guarantees its victory," the machine said into my ear. "The Great One will thank me for this."

"It will kill you," I croaked, barely able to speak. The golem's fingers clamped tighter about my helm. I could hear the metal squeal and groan with the pressure, knew that soon Urbaine's fist would close and crush my brain between his fingers. "It told me . . ." But my words failed.

Urbaine made a small, curious noise. "Told you what?" It leaned its turret head lower, cocked as though bending an ear. "Speak."

Urbaine is a naked little climber, isn't he?

The Prophet's words resounded in my ringing skull, dry as old leaves.

"Men are weak," I said, repeating what Dorayaica had said. "*You* are the lever, Urbaine. It does not mean to conquer man. It means to destroy us. And you."

"You think I don't know that?"

I opened my mouth to tell Urbaine it didn't matter, that Dorayaica had anticipated his every move. I opened my mouth to tell Urbaine it was no praxis of the Enar that Dorayaica had inherited, that its transformation was not something the magus—for all his science—could control.

I never got the chance.

Where I lay with my face pressed to the metal floor, I could see the shining turret of Urbaine's head, the glittering black eyes, the iron length of the arm that pinned me to the floor. Above and beyond, the great spire was smoking in several places where Sharp's men had planted charges. Another explosion shook the hall even as I watched. And an instant later a spike of violet lightning tore through the golem, punched a hole clean through his armored head. Urbaine staggered at once, releasing his grip on me. I rolled away, wound up on my back even as another bolt of purple light tore through the black metal body. I saw the orange Ganelon sky through a gleaming hole in his chest. Still, the machine tried to rise, to round on its attacker.

A third bolt blasted it in the hip. A fourth in the shoulder.

"Stay down, *anaryan!*" Valka's voice was like a ray of sunlight after a month of heavy rain. My heart leaped, and she fired again. The golem-Urbaine's whole body groaned, lurched forward one agonizing step . . . and fell.

Valka did not stop firing until Gaizka's strange gun fired its last, advancing one ginger step after another toward the iron corpse of the nightmare that had haunted her for so many long and tired years. And when at last the trigger clicked lifeless in her hands, she snarled and hurled the inert weapon at the slag heap that was all that remained of the necromancer.

Then Valka screamed, and not the scream of a woman in pain, nor any cry of torment. Never had I heard such a sound—and never have I heard it since. So deep and primeval a sound it was that I felt the rawness in her throat as though it were my own.

The victory, the triumph, and the pain.

I knew them all in that moment.

In *her* moment.

CHAPTER 27

AN UNEXPECTED FRIEND

"IS HE . . . DEAD?" I asked, stumbling to my feet for what seemed the thousandth time that bloody day. I caught myself staring—not at the smoking hulk that had been Urbaine's final shell—but at the chairs where Takeshi's security techs had sat. Three of them were still there, bodies torn and bloody in their seats. Two more lay like cordwood upon the ground, caught by Sharp's men as they'd tried to flee.

"I think so," Valka answered, not taking her eyes from the smoking ruins of the golem. "But we can't be sure . . ." She blinked, and her eyes found me. "Why did he come back, Hadrian? He could have left with the others . . . why did he come back?"

The only answers within my grasp were ugly things, and I offered none of them to her. Instead I tried to solve the problem, to understand what had just occurred. "That woman, the junior one who left before the fighting . . ."

"Vladilen?" Valka's perfect memory conjured up the name at once.

I nodded. "She said they all had two transmitters."

"One in the brain, one in the chest," Valka said, pointing. "Just like Kharn Sagara. You got one when you shot him the first time. He must have used the other to jump to the machine."

Just like Kharn Sagara. Not for the first time, I wondered at the connection between the Undying King of Vorgossos and this lodge of lesser sorcerers. Gaizka had said Kharn Sagara had *lost* Vorgossos, said the Undying had paid the price for his *hubris*. They were not friends, that much was clear.

Had I not been told that the immortality enjoyed by the Elect-Masters was the sole province of Vorgossos? That Kharn alone held the keys to that half-life of immortality? That Kharn alone transmitted his thoughtform-image from host to host, moving like some mythic demon from antique fable? Was it possible that the magi of MINOS had come out of Vorgossos? That they had stolen fire from that dark lord?

Or was Kharn the usurper, outcast from their own vile order? Was MINOS *that* old?

"They took the tower down," I said, not without hope, and looked up at the ruined stalactite hanging above our heads. I could make out Sharp's men on the levels above by then. They were going level by-level, sweeping the catwalks and side chambers for survivors. I knew they would find none, would find only corpses. Master Samara had escaped, that much was sure. And Gaizka's image had been broadcast after I shot him. Of Master Takeshi's fate I was less certain, as I was less certain of Urbaine's. Several of the lesser magi would have escaped as well. The woman, Vladilen, would be on her way to Dharan-Tun and a meeting with the Prophet. Even the virologist, Abberton, must have escaped, relied on his suicide to transfer his thoughtform-image to the tower's transmitter. But the vast majority had not escaped, had been shot instead by Sharp and his men, or else burned out their own brains by some art embedded in their implants.

"They did," Valka agreed, and sagged against a pillar while she spoke. Using the column to guide her, she slid down the wall to a sitting position. As she did so, her left leg spasmed, and I moved to catch her, but she waved me back. "Don't touch me!" Her voice rose sharply, and she kept her hands up to keep me back. The left shook. After a brief pause, she said, "I'm all right."

I marked the still-shaking limbs, and a sorrow settled on my heart. Some part of me, I thought, had imagined that killing Urbaine might put an end to the last shadows of Valka's torment, that she might be free at last. I do not know why I thought it would be so. My own deliverance from the pits and lashes of Dharan-Tun had not taken away my pain. Why should Valka's justice heal her wounds?

Some wounds can never be healed, not by the powers of this world.

So I limped to a place beside her, set my own back to the pillar, and slid to the ground. I did not touch her, not at first. Not for many a count of seconds. Steadily I took her still-shaking hand, and so steadied it myself.

The ugliness of the world does not fade and pass away. Have I told you that? That fear and grief are not made less by time? All life is tragedy, for all life must end—and so no life grows stronger by its ending. Dorayaica was right about one thing. Time runs down into darkness. Even the stars burn out. And scars . . . there are scars that not even Death can wash away.

Valka would carry her wound for the rest of her days.

"I *am* all right," she said again, while the aftershocks of the battle faded and smoldered about us. Neither of us stirred. After another long silence, she said, "He could still have broadcast himself to the Sojourner."

"Did the golem have two transmitters?" I asked.

"I don't know," she said.

"You tore it to pieces!" I said.

"I know!" she hissed, hand clenching mine. "But we *don't* know. We may *never* know, Hadrian! He could be out there right now!"

How I wished I could truly see the future then, wished that I might chart our every possible course and know if Urbaine ever darkened our door again. I searched the howling warrens of those other memories, and found—as I had feared—encounters I was sure had never happened in waking life. Urbaine's throat was in my hand, flesh near hard as iron as he laughed despite my attempted strangulation. I faced him from the opposite end of a bridge over storm-tossed seas, the angry red face of a gas giant filling the skies as rain thundered down. A shot took me in the back, and the magi's ghoulish face leered down at me where I lay dying.

But were these memories of the numberless futures? Or of those pasts which would now never be?

I had no comfort to give Valka then, unless it was the warmth of my hand on hers.

"He's dead, Valka," I said, forcing it to be true. "And if he's not, we'll kill him again."

"You don't know that," she said, unwilling to be comforted. "You can't know that. But I could have! I could have read his mind, watched for a signal as I shot him! But I locked my implants down. I didn't want to risk him getting in. Not again! But if I'd been stronger, I'd know! I'd—"

"Don't talk like that," I said. "He's dead."

"Shut up!" She glared at me, and her hand shook in mine. "You don't know what it was like! You don't know what he's capable of!"

I only blinked at her. I knew full well what Urbaine and the magi were capable of. I had suffered in their grip for seven years on Dharan-Tun. It was Urbaine who'd designed the collar I'd worn, Urbaine who'd written the pain programs I'd been forced to endure when I was not forced to endure the more primitive but *real* torments of the Cielcin. I knew a part of what Valka must have felt when Urbaine invaded her mind. The degradations, the cutting, scratching, burning, tearing, the searing pain, the ceaseless violation of it all.

I knew, but my knowing did not matter. My empathy was neither requested nor required.

Only that I remained there, by her side.

"He could have reached the Sojourner," she said again. "He might have made it offworld."

"The Sojourner!" I exclaimed, and straightened. I had forgotten the Exalted captain, Zelaz. He was not of MINOS, and so might not have escaped the building, perhaps lacking their ability to travel as a creature of mere thought. I fumbled with the controls to reactivate my terminal and transmitted the news to Sharp. As I spoke, my eyes drifted to the holograph. The yellow cylinder that was the Sojourner *Melancholia* had vanished entirely.

And two of the three Cielcin worldships were gone.

The centurion replied almost instantly, apparently confident it was safe to use the comm once more. "If he's here, lord, we'll find him."

"Very good, centurion," said I, and killed the connection.

"The amount of data involved . . . a hard line would be preferable." Valka was still working through the question of Urbaine's death, and touched the spot on the back of her neck where the nematodes that formed the organic machinery in her brain converged above the atlas of her spine. "But Urbaine broadcast his image at Berenike. And Abberton and that giant, Gaizka, did as well. He could have done it."

"Kharn Sagara didn't need a line, either," I said, thinking of the bodies Siran and I had found plugged into the machine at Arae, still warm.

"No . . ." Valka agreed. "He could still be out there, Hadrian. He could have another body on Dharan-Tun or . . . anywhere. We might never know." She hugged herself, tried to hide the shaking in her left arm.

"We *might* never know," I said. "In which case he's as good as dead to us." I turned to crouch before her, resting on the balls of my feet. "But I don't think he made it out of here. I don't think he had a backup ready." Then I reminded her—whose memory was perfect—of what Takeshi had said about *duplication*, about the fear that one copy might attempt to usurp the place of the other, might grow so estranged as to become separate people entirely, as it seemed had happened to Kharn Sagara. But I allowed some safeguard might have been put in place, some measures taken to bind the after-image of Urbaine's tormented soul to our world. "I *hope* he's dead."

"He told me," Valka's voice broke, and a sob shook her and broke my heart. Her voice took on a cruel and mocking tone. *His* tone. "*A part of me will always be with you,* he said." She looked up at me, right hand massaging left. "I thought we got rid of it on Edda. But 'tis never going away, is it?"

I smiled at her—a useless gesture through the masks we both wore.

Beyond the windows of the tower, the air hummed with the noise of repulsors. Lin's landing ships had come, and not just Lin's. Amid the black and gold knife-shapes of the Imperial shuttles and landing craft, I spied the chromed and graceful fish-shapes of other vessels, the rigging of their solar sails like bony fins in the sun.

I knew their like, though I had not seen them since I was a boy on Emesh long ago.

They were Jaddian ships.

Marveling, I shook myself, turning away from the world and back to mine. To Valka. Carefully, I took her still-trembling hand in mine and held it fast as I shifted to sit beside her. "I'm not going either."

We were still sitting there when Sharp found us. The centurion saluted.

"No sign of the Exalted captain?" I asked, raising my eyes.

Sharp shook his head. "Gone, my lord. There was no sign of any shuttle."

"His flight pod might have been small enough to avoid detection," I said. "We must assume he escaped and the magi with him." I made to stand, swayed so badly as I did so that I braced myself against the pillar to steady myself. "What of the Cielcin?"

The command centurion appeared to gaze over my shoulder, but I guessed that beneath his mask the man was looking directly at me. Something in the tension of his shoulders betrayed him. "Two of their command ships escaped to warp. We believe their general was among them. Word is Captain Dayne and the tribune captured one of the others."

"Very good," I said, offering Valka my hand. "And the Jaddians?"

Leaning against me, Valka asked, "How did they know to find us?"

Sharp began a shrug, but stopped himself. "Your guess is good as mine, ma'am. Perhaps Mother Earth has smiled on us this day."

"Perhaps," I said. The Jaddian fleet had been sailing for the Centaurine provinces for decades, crossing nearly the radius of the galaxy from Jadd on the Rim of Perseus nearly to the Norman Expanse by the core. Evidently they had come.

"I've been asked to bring you both to the command post, lord," Sharp said, smashing through my consideration of astropolitics.

Valka and I looked at one another, hearts sinking behind faces impassive as stone. We both knew our fragile plan was crashing in around us. *The command post,* Sharp had said. That meant a frigate had already landed on the tarmac outside. Any request from us for the *Ascalon* would seem highly irregular, with a ship already on the ground.

And there were the Jaddians to consider.

How were we now to slip away? We could hardly take the *Ascalon* from its closed docking bay aboard the *Tempest* without violence, and so I would not take it.

We weren't going anywhere. Not that day.

"Who has command on the ground?" I asked.

"Tenavian," Sharp replied.

I could sense the grim tension in him. The grief. Neither Valka nor myself had told him what had become of Stas and the others of our party. Nearly forty men gone. Though the battle had been a success—and an astonishing one in light of the arrival of the Jaddian fleet—our incursion had been a costly one, our victory pyrrhic. I decided then and there I would not tell the centurion how Stas had turned against me. Let him die a hero.

"I am sorry," I said stiffly, "about your men."

Sharp bowed his head. "Thank you, lord," he said. "Come on. They're expecting you."

The hightower still smoldered over the sack of the compound as Sharp and what remained of his Dragonslayers escorted us from the fortress out onto the landing field beneath Ganelon's sickly orange sky. A myriad of Imperial and Jaddian vessels had landed on the tarmac, and already scores of legionnaires and mirror-masked Jaddian mamluks moved about the place. The Ganelon fortress had to be secured. Survivors would be captured—if there were any to be found—and would be killed or interrogated in accordance with their rank and import. Databanks would be secured, reports filed and transmitted to the Imperial fleet and to Forum—and to Jadd as well, I guessed. The bulk of Bassander's fleet would remain at Ganelon for months, I felt certain, scouring the facility for every gram, every drop of intelligence. If Urbaine was to be believed, the dread virus they had manufactured in the image of the Mericanii's ancient torments had already been given to the Cielcin and would soon be ready to deploy. We would need any scrap of data we could find if we were to develop effective countermeasures.

Captain Tenavian's command post was a hulking *Roc*-class lander, a little larger than the *Ascalon*, nearly two hundred yards from stem to stern, but blocky where the interceptor was sleek, its profile squarish and angular, its black surface bristling with comms equipment and gun turrets until it looked like a hedgehog wrought of ebony and brass.

Captain Sevim Tenavian herself awaited us in the command information center. The casual way Urbaine had opened Valka's suit told me we were not likely to have been exposed to LTH-81, but at my insistence Valka and I were subjected to a full examination and to decontamination in a mobile field unit outside the shuttle. My wounds were treated and—since my own armor was compromised—the now decontaminated suit was set aside, to be conveyed back to the *Ascalon*, which I was told had been restored to its berth aboard the *Tempest*. That boded ill for mine and Valka's half-formed escape plan. I had hoped to order the *Ascalon* to ground, had hoped Valka and I might simply slip away in the night, while Lin and the bulk of the Legions concerned themselves with the early stages of the mopup and interrogation.

But the Jaddian fleet and the discovery of the virus had changed all that. There were too many eyes and ears on the planet now, and the presence of the Jaddians meant there would be less time to ourselves and more security on the planet and in orbit and about the captured Cielcin worldship. The Jaddians were our allies, yes, but even allies cannot be blindly trusted in war. Besides, it would have looked odd for Lord Marlowe to send for his personal ship, rather than go to meet the arrival of the Jaddians.

We might have done, might have escaped indeed, but it would have been wrong.

Perhaps some part of me knew that. In my bones. In the deep structures of my brain.

Thus it was that Valka and I were admitted into the captain's presence clad only in unmarked suits of officers' dress black. Tenavian's batman had found a set of crimson silk aiguillettes, gold-tipped, and pinned them to the left shoulder of my tunic so as to distinguish me from a common officer, but I felt strange so under-dressed, like the boy I'd been on Emesh—without rank or mandate—advising Lin and the others in the matter of the Cielcin.

Sevim Tenavian stood and saluted stiffly as I entered. "My lord!" she said.

"Are you all right?" asked a familiar, polished voice. Lorian Aristedes's ghostly image flickered above the holography well in the center of the CIC, Tribune Lin's image beside him. "Report said you were injured."

Self-conscious, I touched the corrective tape on my arm hidden beneath my sleeve. "I've had worse."

"The Cielcin commander escaped to warp," said Bassander Lin's spectral image. "But we captured one of their worldships. I'm not sure if you were told."

"I was," I said. "We lost the magi as well. Nearly all of their leaders escaped."

"Nearly?" both Lin and Tenavian said. Lin's response came with a few seconds' lag, the cost of communication from orbit.

Glancing at Valka, I said, "We killed at least one of them."

"Or so we believe." Valka spoke over me, voice hard and heartbreakingly brittle. "You may find fragments of their thoughtforms on what's left of their mainframe. If there are, you must take care to isolate them. They may still be . . . aware."

Captain Tenavian made a warding gesture with her first and final fingers. "O Mother, deliver us," she said.

"Have you an Inquisitor on staff?" I asked the room at large. "We should be on guard against *infestation*." .

"We do," Lin said. "Thank you for the warning, Doctor Onderra."

"What of this . . . *djerm*? This virus?" asked a man I had not noticed, seated as he was in a chair before a console by the far wall. He wore the azure dolman and pale trousers of a Jaddian military officer, a red silk sash about his waist. His gilt highmatter sword, sidearm, and shield-belt denoted him as a high officer, one of the aryabite military caste, not quite one of the eali. In Sollan terms, he might well be considered patrician, though I saw no mark of surgical uplift on his unremarkably handsome face. He was pale for a Jaddian, though his hair was black almost as mine, oiled and perfectly combed back from his high forehead. I ought to have noticed him sooner, for a pair of mamluk clone-soldiers stood at attention, striped blue and orange cloaks hanging from too-narrow shoulders, sculpted mirror masks wholly without expression.

Captain Tenavian said, "Lord Marlowe, this is Commander Afsharirad, one of the prince's counselors."

"Captain," Afsharirad said, rising from his seat to bow. "Captain Fadroh

Afsharirad, *JNS Albaspatha*. It is an honor to be meeting you, Lord Marlowe. They are singing songs of your deeds in Jadd, songs of *Al Neroblis*, the Black Devil."

"It's *black* in Jadd, is it?" said Lorian a moment later, once the signal lag from orbit had caught up. I did not have to look at him to hear his smirk.

My long years of practice ignoring Lorian's jibes were still proving useful. Exhaling, I returned Afsharirad's bow. "An honor, captain. But it is your deeds they should sing of! I am in your debt. We all are." I gestured to Valka. "Were it not for your fleet's timely arrival, we would now be in the hands of the Cielcin." That brought the most pertinent question bubbling to the surface of my mind. "But tell me! How did you know to come here? Now?" I looked round at Tenavian, at Lin and Lorian's holographic projections.

Captain Afsharirad's gaze turned from me to Lin. "After we crossed the Gulf at Gododdin, we stopped at Nennoed to refuel. My royal master had word of your efforts here direct from your Emperor." The captain bowed his head. "It is only by God's justice that we arrived when we did. But Ahura Mazda destroys all who do not respect his creation, and these *davoi,* these Cielcin . . . they are the very worst." Afsharirad lifted his eyes, turned once more to me. "When my royal master heard *you* were leading this assault, Lord Marlowe, he bent the stars to come here with all due speed."

I blinked at this, surprised not by the reference to the Jaddian fire god, but that my presence had played some part in the great prince's desire to come to our relief at Ganelon. "Your master . . . Prince Kaim du Otranto?"

The Jaddian captain raised his hands as if offering a bowl to me. "I have that honor," he replied. "Indeed, that is why I am here. My royal master wishes to meet you, and asks that you join him on his ship to celebrate this victory. I am sent to escort you." That said, he pressed his hands to his breast and bowed low.

While the captain bowed, I glanced at Valka, then up at Lorian and Bassander Lin flickering above the holography suite's central plinth. I supposed that I should not be surprised so august a personage as the Darkmoon Prince of Jadd—the man who, it was said, would one day take his grandfather's place as First of the Princes of Jadd—would wish to see me. Had I not been a guest of the Grand Conclave on Padmurak? And of the Emperor himself more times than I could count? Yet here was a man I knew only by reputation. Great among the great of the galaxy. A peerless warrior, they said, as fierce in debate as he was in battle. A great patron of the arts, they said, and a greater lover of women.

A poet, a priest, and a prince in one.

One of the more amusing stories I heard oft repeated of Prince Kaim praised his piety and restraint for reducing his royal harem to a mere one hundred twenty-five bound concubines. That was a holy number, and struck a balance between the opulence expected of a man of his station and the self-restraint admired in a servant of his god.

I had also heard it said by certain, less charitable sources, that the prince was a fearsome drunkard with a temper like the sun, that he kept the company of boys as much or more than that of his women, and—most sordid of all—that he had conspired to murder his own father, Prince Osroes, the former heir presumptive to the high throne of Jadd.

I was not sure what to believe, and had until that moment little cared. Prince Kaim had been almost unreal, a figure on the edge of the map, little more than the dragons painted there by the superstitious cartographers of old.

Now he was as real as those dragons had proved to be, and present.

"There will be time for that," said Bassander Lin, drawing my attention back to his ghostly visage. The tribune fixed his flinty eyes on me. Leaning on his cane, he reminded me powerfully then of Raine Smythe, his old commander. "Hadrian, are you certain this . . . virus is still a threat?"

"Even if we stopped distribution of the virus here," I said, careful to weigh my words as precisely as I could, "with most of the magi escaped, we must assume they have the means to restart production elsewhere. We should assume the worst. The Emperor and LIO must be informed at once. I recommend the Emperor remain aboard the *Radiant Dawn* with all possible security measures taken. We should set sail for Siraganon at once." An idea occurred to me, and I looked to Valka. "We will take the *Ascalon*. We'll be faster alone."

Valka had moved to one side of the well where Lin and Lorian floated, and her eyes found mine. She did not need to ask the question for me to hear it. Did I truly mean it when I said we would fly to Siraganon?

I had no answer for her. We *could* telegraph the Emperor from anywhere in the galaxy as easily as we could fly to him. More easily. To make the rendezvous at Siraganon and return to the Emperor's side was to accept only another order, another mission, another impossible task. The Emperor would continue to spend my days like coin rather than address the vipers in his midst and family, and drive me as he drove himself: to the uttermost end of my strength. He would push me until at last I found myself unequal to the challenges set before me, and I gave up my last measure of devotion.

Valka was right. I could not keep doing it.

But what choice did I have? The *Ascalon* was safely stowed away in the *Tempest's* hold, and with the Jaddians coming it would be difficult finding an excuse to have it brought down. I had hoped to summon it in the wake of a successful mission, to use it as camp while our people picked over the ruins of the MINOS fortress. But there were shuttles aplenty on Ganelon's surface already, and we were being summoned to meet the Prince of Jadd.

There would be no chance to escape, no chance to call for the *Ascalon*. We would be taken to orbit to meet the Prince, then returned to the *Tempest* when that meeting was done, and stealing a ship from the hold of an Imperial battleship was quite different than setting out from the surface under clear skies.

The surface-to-orbit lag elapsed, and Bassander Lin shook his head, responding to my suggestion. "No need for that. Captains Tenavian and Dayne will remain here and collect all possible intelligence. LIO must be alerted—they will want to send teams of their own. This is no small victory. We've captured a worldship . . ."

He petered out, knowing as we all did that *captured* was premature. *Crippled* was the more appropriate term. There would be hard fighting in the caverns and trenches of the alien moon, but Tenavian and Dayne would be up to it. With the worldship's great engines disabled, there would be no escape for the Pale stranded beneath its surface.

It would be the Cielcin's turn to be besieged.

Lin continued speaking. "In the meantime, we will escort our Jaddian friends to rendezvous with the Emperor at Siraganon. We go by way of Fidchell. The Emperor should have reached Perfugium by now."

The thought of the Emperor continuing his tour despite my warning that his movements were known and safety compromised spoiled my blood, and I looked down at my hands. The silver scars Irshan had left on my left fingers and palm shone up at me, a reminder of the dangers of the Imperial court. Clenching that fist, I addressed Sevim Tenavian. "The Chantry will need access to whatever you find, captain." The words stuck in my throat. Much of the Chantry's power over the lesser houses on the Imperium—and indeed beyond the Imperium—came from its command of weapons not unlike the virus the sorcerers of MINOS had wrought, and to extend even the smallest shred of information to them felt like a betrayal of everything I had done thus far. It was the Chantry who had backed the Empress and Augustin Bourbon in their attempt to murder me, and the Chantry who had tried for years to execute me for witchcraft at Thermon.

But for all I hated them, their knowledge of such things might prove invaluable in combating this new threat, and I said as much. "Many of the finest bloodworkers in the galaxy are Chantry," I said. "Let them do some good for once."

"You must look the prince in the eye when you address him," Fadroh continued, speaking quickly as he escorted Valka and me along the hall of his master's ship. "You are *not* to look directly at any of the women, or to address them." He had been rattling off line after line of court etiquette since Valka and I emerged from the shuttle and hurried from the docking bay along corridor after corridor and up a lift tube to the more formal parts of the Jaddian flagship, the *Mnemon*.

The great ship was even then in high orbit above Ganelon, and the rusted, ugly world had been visible from more than one window as we followed the captain along hall after all, past masked and armored mamluk clones and aryabite caste officers in the same blue dolmans and white trousers that Afsharirad wore. Many of the latter bowed or saluted as we hurried past, and more than one whispered *Al Neroblis*.

The Black Devil.

I smiled blandly through it all and nodded, recalling similar conversations before my earliest meetings with His Radiance the Emperor, or with the Imperial Council, or even before my trial before a panel of Chantry praetors. "You will speak only when spoken to, and you will address the prince only as *Your Highness*, though *Dham-Eali* and *Domi* are both acceptable should you falter."

"Will he ask us to kiss his feet as well?" Valka asked dryly, still the Tavrosi underneath it all.

Captain Afsharirad was not amused. "If he does, you had better do it."

Eager to head off a confrontation, I said, "Please forgive my paramour, aryabite. She is Tavrosi."

Again, Fadroh made the gesture he had made aboard Tenavian's command post, as though he were offering a bowl with both hands. "Let each choose his creed," he said, though I sensed his words were not wholly without judgment. "You are Imperial, but you are a knight. So you may approach on your feet. You must not raise your eyes until you reach the dais and bow, and not until His Highness permits you."

"Si fueris Romae . . ." I said, looking at Valka, who was familiar with the Latin from her centuries of tolerating me.

Afsharirad blinked. "Forgive me, lord. I was told you spoke Jaddian . . ." The captain trailed off, dismay on his face. Evidently he thought I had attempted his language and failed.

That brought a smile to my face. "It's Latin, aryabite." Jaddian was—in a sense—a Romance language, a bastard descendant of the almost-forgotten Latin, offspring of Spanish mingled with Arabic and the Persian whose speakers crowded together in the mad scramble from Earth. The forefathers of the men who would become the princes of Jadd had retained their ethnic fraternity against all odds, against light-years of distance and millennia of time, and time and blood and toil had declared their independence from the culture of the greater Imperium.

The first princes of Jadd had done the impossible. They had cracked the genetic mysteries of the High College, wrested control of their generations back from the Emperor and the Council, so that the eali—their palatines— might give themselves heirs, and not beseech the Solar Throne for progeny. For six thousand years our two cultures had grown apart. While the Empire remained more or less centralized, the palatine houses dependent upon the Emperor and Imperial bureaucrats for heirs, the Jaddian principalities competed with each other, stretching the bounds of human potential. The porphyrogeneticists of Jadd had elevated eugenics to an art form, while we Sollans considered it a mere science.

Evidently disinterested in my linguistic digression or its meaning, Fadroh said, "My royal master is awaiting us in his audience chamber. This way." He ushered us through a gilded door and into the gondola of a tram that ran along the spine of the great ship *Mnemon.* Velvet cushions festooned the benches that ran along the wall, and the carpets beneath our feet were more than an inch thick. The walls about the narrow windows were padded in wine-dark tufted leather, and everything from the window frame to the handlebars by the doors was chased in gold.

A quartet of mamluk soldiers in blue and orange approached, and for the second time Valka and I were searched for weapons. When they found none, we were permitted to take our seats along the far wall. The faint aroma of jubala smoke hung on the air. The smell made me think of the winesink in Karch where I had chartered passage with Demetri Arello so very long ago. The places could not be more different, and yet . . .

Something moved in the corner of my eye, and all thought of Demetri

and of Karch vanished in an instant. Seated amid the wine leather and gold
at the fore of the gondola was one of the most beautiful women I had ever
seen, beautiful and terrible as the Empress herself. Her skin was a deep,
dusky olive, her hair black as oil and so long and braided that it coiled on
the seat beside her, its tresses hung with fine gold chains and tinkling medallions. She wore little save those chains, which draped across her forehead, her throat, her full breasts, and the flat plane of her stomach. Rubies
glinted amidst all that fine gold, and gold too was the embroidery on the
scarlet silk of her skirt. Almost I thought I knew her face, but told myself
that was impossible.

Remembering Fadroh's instructions, I averted my eyes almost at once.

That she was one of the concubines of Prince Kaim's piously shrunken
harem I had no doubt. Captain Afsharirad was silent then, remained by the
door opposite Valka and myself, one hand on the support rail as the gondola began to accelerate smoothly along the tube toward the rear of the
mighty ship. I risked a glance again at the concubine. Why was she here?
Why had she not spoken?

She was clearly an eali woman, tall at least as I was, and that was without the help of her tall gilt shoes. Legs crossed, she bounced one foot lazily, sending distracting tremors up her body. Had I seen her once at
Forum, perhaps? A friend of the Empress?

Her black eyes caught mine, and she smiled a tight and knowing smile,
moved one ringed hand to her breast.

I averted my gaze, placed a hand on Valka's knee beside me, a reminder
of who and where I was.

After mere moments the tram slid to a halt, and the door slid open.

Apparently blind to the concubine's presence and state of dress, Fadroh
Afsharirad spun on his heel and stepped out onto the new platform, the
mamluks right behind. Valka and I followed, and were ourselves followed
by the concubine, whose pointed shoes rang sharply on the tile. More
mamluks stood posted ahead along either side of a blood-red-carpeted
marble staircase that ascended perhaps three levels to a circular door of
polished brass.

"Remember to keep your eyes down until you are addressed," the captain said. "My royal master is a man of remarkable tolerance, but he will
permit no familiarity."

Agitated and exhausted by the long and horrible day, I replied, "He
invited *me*, captain."

How I longed for sleep!

But there would be no sleep, not until this prince of Jadd had his meeting, his chance to gawp at the Emperor's pet sorcerer, the Black Devil of the Imperium.

Afsharirad had no reply as we reached the top of the stairs. The inmost guards were not mamluks, I saw, but wore instead the crimson half-robe of the Maeskoloi swordmasters—the *mandyas*—belted at the waist. Beneath those, their tunics were azure as the captain's jacket, and highmatter swords waited in holsters at their right sides, swinging from their shield-belts. They wore no helms, no masks—though each was clearly of the eali caste, for none but those of that exalted lineage could be enrolled in the great Fire School of the Swordmasters of Jadd. One nodded at Fadroh as he passed, and all six stared at me.

The round door rolled aside.

I had a brief image of a man in black seated on a gilded dais beneath a blue silk canopy, then I remembered Fadroh's instructions and hung my head.

A nuncius spoke then to herald our coming, voice clear and sexless. *"Dom Hadrian Anaxander Marlowe-Victoriano, Faram du Seira Vasilko Victoriani e scortara!"*

Unlike the Emperor's audience chamber, the room was mostly empty. A stretch of red carpet ran from the entrance to the base of the dais, a crimson river on that floor of polished onyx black as space. No swarm of courtiers attended the Darkmoon prince, though the music of a lute issued soft from some unseen corner. Nor did I see the nuncius, and but for the two Maeskoloi who stood at the base of the dais ahead, the room was empty save for the man on the dais and the three women who reclined about his feet, each dressed as the one who accompanied us on the tram in a constellation of jewelry, fine silk, and empty air.

Eyes downcast, Valka and I approached the throne. I bowed graciously as I could in my bruised and battered state. I wished I had not left Gibson's cane aboard the *Ascalon*, for I might have used the support. Beside me, Valka bent only slowly.

"Rise! Please!" came a deep voice lilting with the accents of Jadd.

Looking up, I beheld a man lean but powerfully built. Clad all in black was he, arrayed not as a prince, but as a swordmaster, his half-robe *mandyas* a jacquard of gold on crimson, belted at the waist and secured by a fine gold chain beneath the opposing arm. His hair, too, was black, and hung down his masked face almost to his chin. The mask itself had been fired of the finest Jaddian porcelain, a polished black mirror of intricately crafted plates that moved with his every expression, flexing with the movement of mouth and jaw.

"When the Emperor said he had sent his pet demon to this place, I knew the time had come," said Prince Kaim du Otranto, Darkmoon of Jadd. "I was pleased to find we arrived in time."

"As am I, Your Highness," I said, unable to shake the feeling of unease that settled over me. "Were it not for your timely arrival, I fear the day would have been lost." As I spoke, the concubine who had followed us from the tram sauntered to the dais and sank onto the cushions, reclining at her master's feet. She placed one jeweled hand on the calf of Prince's Kaim's boot, gripped it possessively.

"I see you still undervalue yourself, my lord," the prince replied, his smile very white beneath the black ceramic of his articulated mask. "You would have found a way, I am thinking. I understand you have slain *two* of these Pale princes now. That you have crossed swords with the Scourge of Earth himself. Who would have thought these things possible of a rat from Emesh, mm?"

I took a step back, not quite understanding. The reference to Emesh of all things shocked me into higher alertness.

Valka understood. Her memory was perfect, and what had dulled for me across the centuries was to her yet sharp as highmatter. "Sir Olorin?" she said.

My eyes darted to the familiar concubine lounging at the prince's feet—Fadroh be damned. Some forgotten piece snapped into place. "Lady Kalima?"

The woman smiled, but said nothing. It *was* Kalima di Sayyiph, the Satrap of Ubar. I should have known her at once, but Emesh had been . . . so long before.

Prince Kaim laughed. "What was it you said, Doctor? That the galaxy is curved? That if you travel far enough and fast enough, you return to where you began?" He turned his masked face to me. "I told you, Hadrian, that in Jadd men would know your name." As he spoke, Prince Kaim lifted gloved hands to his face, undoing the clasps that fastened the porcelain contrivance in place. It clattered as he drew it from his face, and an instant later, Sir Olorin Milta was smiling where Prince Kaim had been a moment before. He set aside the mask and paused a moment to smooth his mustache and pointed beard, then smiled and said, "I *am* Jadd."

CHAPTER 28

THE SECRET PRINCE

"ALLOW ME TO INTRODUCE myself properly," Prince Kaim—Olorin—said, "I am Kaim Sanchez Cyaxares Nazir-Vincente Olorin ban Osroes ban Aldia du Otranto." The prince stood, extricating himself from Kalima's grip, and bowed. "It is exceedingly good to be seeing you again, my old friend!" He hurried down the steps and grasped me by the shoulders. "When I left you on the strand at Borosevo, I little imagined you would become *this*!" Before I could respond, the great lord of Jadd embraced me like a brother. "You are like one of the old stories!" he exclaimed, drawing back. "If William the Great and Prince Katanes and all the Fathers of Jadd were here, you would not be lost among them!" He laughed, and laughing he rounded on Valka. "And you, Doctor!" He took Valka's hand and kissed it. Still holding her fingers, he said, "The stars shine brighter to have you among them! Come, my friends, come! Let us sit a while."

The prince clapped his hands, and at once two men appeared from arras in the walls of the chamber, each porting a bloodwood chair intricately carved. These they set before the dais as Prince Kaim resumed his seat.

Neither Valka nor I had moved. Nor had Captain Afsharirad. I thought the young aryabite would die of shock to see his exalted master embrace Valka and myself, or to see the prince's face. Fadroh looked down at his feet, shaded his eyes as though he were a boy who had stumbled on a woman bathing and feared embarrassment might burn his retinas like the sun. So much for all his courtly etiquette and diplomatic procedure.

"I . . ." The words came thickly. Only slowly did I rediscover the use of my tongue, for I was as shocked—more shocked, even—than the Jaddian captain. "You were not a Maeskolos."

Sir Olorin—Prince Kaim—relaxed in his gilded seat. "Not *only* a Maeskolos," he said. "I must be begging your forgiveness, Lord Marlowe. In

Jadd it is said a man must do three things: *Fight well, seek beauty, and speak truth*. With you I failed this third charge. But in this at least I spoke truth: I *am Maeskolon*, a Swordmaster of the Second Circle. But I was not *sulshawar*—not lictor, you would say—to my Kalima." He smiled down at his concubine. "She is my *alkidar*, my paramour."

"You were not her servant," I said, making straight matters in my head.

Kalima di Sayyiph sat a little straighter, for in Jadd it was a high honor to be so bound to such as the prince. "I am his," she said.

"It was necessary to tell this lie that I might move freely amongst you Imperials."

"Why?" Valka asked.

I already knew the answer, and said, "To see with eyes unclouded." Traveling as a servant, Prince Kaim—Olorin—would have been able to see things, to go places he would never have been allowed to go as a prince. What lord of the Empire could risk harm befalling the grandson of Prince Aldia du Otranto? Balian Mataro could never have afforded to let *Prince Kaim* crawl through the tunnels of Calagah, or to see the truth of his world. The diplomatic implications of an accident shivered my blood.

"Just so!" Olorin said. "You know so well as I that we men of rank are bound tight as any prisoner. I could not see the truth because your lords would not permit me to look low enough, as they say. Prince Kaim might visit your Empire, yes, but he would be shown only what your Imperial masters wanted him to see. But *Sir Olorin*? Him they might permit to mingle with the soldiery, to rub elbows with a certain young myrmidon and his lady doctor."

Valka shifted in her seat beside me. "So you switched places with your servant."

Kalima's smile flashed again. "We did what was necessary."

"Many of the *Domagavani* believed this war was an Imperial matter only. But my grandfather was not so sure." Prince Kaim's fingers drummed against the arm of his chair as he spoke. "The worlds of Jadd are far away, but if your Empire were to fall, the monsters would darken our skies before long. Such was my thinking as well, and so Prince Aldia tasked me to see—as you say—what I could see. It is because of what I saw that he commissioned this army." He spread his hands, as if that gesture might encompass the entire *Mnemon* and all the Jaddian fleet as well. Olorin let his hands fall, and we were all silent then a moment. "It took much to convince the lesser princes of the need . . . for which reason we are come so late. But we have come."

A question occurred to me then, stirred by old, vague memories. "Did Count Mataro know who you were?"

"He figured it out *after* the attack on Emesh, once we returned from Calagah," the prince said.

Kalima di Sayyiph smiled. "His husband, the Mandari, realized how uncommon it is for a woman to be a satrap in Jadd. It is a vulgar profession. Man's work. Fit for an aryabite woman, perhaps. But no woman of the *eali al'aqran* would so sully her hands." As if to emphasize this point, Lady Kalima wrapped her jeweled and enameled fingers around her prince's leg once more and raised her chin. "They started asking questions."

Concubinage may have been a low profession in the Empire, but it seemed I knew less of the Jaddians and their ways than I believed.

"That put an end to our little tour," Kaim-Olorin added.

I felt realization like the flash of dawn. "You pressed them into sending me on my mission," I said, shaking my head. "They were afraid of you."

Prince Kaim grinned. "I applied only the slightest pressure, I promise you!"

"Why?"

"I believed as you did—or *hoped*—I suppose," the prince replied. "I *hoped* that peace might be possible between our people and the Cielcin."

"It isn't," I said, voice so dark that Valka reached out and gripped my leg for support. Remembering where I was, and that I spoke to a Prince of Jadd, I continued, "You gave me an impossible task." I bowed my head, the special irony of those words known only to me. I studied my scarred hands and Valka's tattooed one where it remained on my knee, possessive as Kalima's talons on Olorin's boot. "Perhaps you were wrong to put your faith in me."

Olorin laughed again, a warm and easy sound. "I am thinking not," he said. "It seems to me that—if there were a way—you would have found it, if even half the songs they sing of you be true. That you did not find it tells me no such way exists."

"It doesn't," I said, voice growing darker still, such venom on my tongue that I thought I might spit.

"So sure, are you?" Kalima asked.

Valka's hand tightened on my knee. She and Lorian alone in all the universe knew how sure was my conviction, and how sharp that truth. So she replied, paramour to paramour. "'Tis true." And there was a sorrow in her voice to match the acid in mine. "The Cielcin cannot be reasoned with. They do not want peace."

"Neither do these *jitaten* sorcerers that have allied with them," I added. "And the Cielcin do not know the meaning of the word. Peace to them is humanity destroyed." I did not add that peace to the Cielcin was *everything* destroyed. Somehow, to talk of the Watchers and the Quiet, of Utannash and the Iugannan and Iazyr Kulah was not possible. I could not bring myself to do it, could not bring myself to speak so openly of such things. They sounded mad, even to me.

Prince Kaim leaned back in his seat, stroked his pointed beard with one silk-gloved hand. "It is a pity," he said. "Nearly twenty thousand years since our forefathers first wet their feet in the ocean of stars. In all that time, *nothing*. No race like ours! I had hoped we might find brothers."

"The Cielcin are no brothers of mine," I said. "I shared your hope. Once. No more." I had to shut my eyes, as if by doing so I might extinguish the screaming of my men in my ears. Miudanar's hollow eye loomed large in the darkness of my mind. "There will be no peace unless we *take* it." Even with my eyes shut, I could feel Valka's gaze on me. "And I'm not sure I'm the man to do the taking." A thought occurred to me, and I opened my eyes, found Prince Kaim leaning forward in his seat, chin resting on one fist. "I lost your sword!"

The words sounded small in my own hearing. Pathetic. Trivial when measured against all else we had discussed. But the sword had been a princely gift, and I had been a poor steward to let it so drop from my hand. Prince Kaim but laughed again. "How did you come to lose it?"

Memory of that last, desperate scramble with Aulamn—of Pallino's death—spasmed across my face, and Olorin smiled in sympathy to see the pain writ there. "Slaying one of the Prophet's generals," I said at last.

"Ehpa!" he exclaimed. "Then you have not dishonored it!" Olorin leaned forward until he sat on the edge of his gilded seat. "Hadrian, it was a gift! And it would be no gift had I expected its return. I have lost nothing! And we have gained the death of an enemy. Though I see it was hard bought."

I tried to reply, but found my tongue had swollen in my mouth. Valka spoke for me. "Our whole company was lost," she said. No *sir*, no *highness*.

The prince did not rebuke her. "I had heard. I am sorry." He bowed his head. "These are grievous times. But perhaps so great a darkness calls for even greater light. It is written that no guide is known that can shelter the world from grief, for no man knows what God intends."

"I do not believe in your god," I said sharply, reflexively.

"That does not matter," Olorin said. "God does not need us to believe.

He does not need us at all. But we each have our part to play in what He intends."

Looking up at the prince, I spoke bitterly. "We are all chosen for something, eh?" They were my words, words I had spoken to the soldier at Berenike. What had her name been? Rian? Rhianne? Renna. That was it. But where those words had on Berenike been uttered fervently, above Ganelon they tasted of ashes. Of iron and blood.

"You think not?" Olorin asked and made a gesture to some unseen servant at the periphery of the room, then looked down at the four women lazing about his feet. *"Tiada, Belit, Sanazi, yamkinah piganeis,"* he said, dismissing them. The women—two darker even than Kalima and one white as snow—rose from their cushions and left the room in a haze of perfumed hair and tinkling bangles. It took all my power not to watch them go. When they were gone, Prince Kaim asked, "Is it true what they say? That you died and were reborn?"

How could a man answer a question like that?

I reminded myself that I sat before a Prince of Jadd, that though he had been my friend once—briefly—that had been hundreds of years ago. And Sir Olorin was not Prince Kaim. I had no notion who might be listening at the keyhole, or to whom the prince might one day relay my words.

"Fight well, seek beauty, and speak truth . . ." I repeated into the tense silence. My eyes went to Olorin's face, my lips pressed together. Here was a man who had saved my life, not once, but *twice*. Not only by bringing his fleet to Ganelon against all hope and chance, in the nick of time, but on Emesh long ago. If what he said was *truth*, then his word and secret name may very well have been the factor that tipped the balance between Raine Smythe and Ligeia Vas in the contest for my soul and fate. Young as I was then, had I appreciated how delicate my situation in Borosevo had been? Did I then know how slender was the thread from which I hung? Valka and I had cheated palace security, deprived the Chantry of a prisoner, defied the count's men and the whole damned Empire, and for what?

A little mercy, and a name.

We had wrung the name of Vorgossos out of Uvanari at the last, and with it a faint and desperate hope. A dream of peace. Smythe had believed that dream, and Olorin, too. They had vouched for me and my mad expedition, and in so doing had set me on my path—the path that brought me through Vorgossos to that mountain on Annica where the Quiet poured all of time through my head. Olorin had played his part—unknowing—in the Quiet's cosmic plan. Perhaps he was right. Perhaps I could trust him. Perhaps I had to trust him, and yet . . .

I looked round the chamber, as if expecting some sinister figure in a hooded cloak to vanish behind one of the pillars when he caught me looking. *Ten thousand eyes.*

Recognizing this paranoid gesture of the elite for what it was, Olorin said, "We are alone."

"Valka?" I turned to her.

Valka's Tavrosi implants might not find *everything*, but if there were microphones or hidden watch-eyes embedded in the baroque filigree on the walls or among the tapestries and hanging carpets, she might find enough to change my mind. Those golden eyes of hers swept the room, and she tilted her head, as if listening. Her lips parted, brows furrowed, and at last she shook her head. "'Tis nothing."

Nothing was a good sign. *Nothing* meant that either what devices were present were so subtle as to escape even Valka's detection—unlikely, given her skill—or that the prince had spoken the truth.

"The truth . . ." I said, and letting out a long and ragged breath I stood, turned from the prince and his paramour to circle behind my bloodwood chair. I smiled down at Valka as I passed her, pressed a hand to her shoulder. I had told the Emperor nearly all. I could tell this prince, this man who'd saved my life.

"They say you perform miracles," Olorin said to my back, and though his voice remained warm, I sensed a tension in it. "That you are a magician. That you rose from the dead."

I did not turn back, addressed the gilded circle of the door to the audience chamber. The faint scent of jubala hung on the air, and the thick carpets and bright tapestries depicting scenes of ancient battle lent the chamber a deep and warming quiet. "I am not a magician." Unconsciously, I gripped my left forearm, felt the ridges on the artificial bone through the muscle and the scars.

"You do not deny the rest?"

"I am not sure that they are miracles," I said, still speaking to my blurred reflection in that golden door. "I am not sure I know what a miracle is. If god exists—yours or any other—then surely, though he seems supernatural to us, his nature is to himself as natural as breathing. If that is so, then there are no miracles. There is only . . . what is."

Kaim was silent for a beat, processing. Apparently not defeated by this bit of philosophy, he pressed the point. "But you did rise from the dead? Is that truth?"

I made a gesture, unclenched my hands, as though the truth were some golden bauble I might simply let fall upon the carpet without remark.

"He did." Valka's voice shattered the quiet stillness of the chamber, though she did not shout. "I was there. I saw it."

The prince and his paramour both were silent. Until Kalima was not. "You expect us to believe this?"

"You expect us to come before a Prince of Jadd and *lie*?" Valka replied. She stood as well, and I flinched, fearing that some praetorian might emerge from the shadows and strike us both down in defense of his lord. But no such champion appeared. We were alone. "I know 'tis unbelievable. I would not believe it had I not *seen* it with my own eyes!" As she spoke, Valka peeled out of her officer's dress black tunic. She wore only a form-fitting white shirt beneath, and the fractal intaglio of her clan showed upon her arm and back and flank, even through the pale cotton of the garment.

I had turned from the gold door by then, and reached toward her. "Valka, what are you doing?"

"Be quiet, Hadrian," she said, slapping her tunic down over the back of her seat. "'Tis been a day, this! And I've no time or patience left for argument. Here: I'll show you." And then she did something I had never seen her do, not in all our decades together. Not once. She fiddled with something on her wrist-terminal—which alone among her effects had passed through decontamination in Tenavian's command shuttle—and unspooled a length of hair-fine glass wire from behind a small hatch. This she stretched a couple of cubits and—reaching around behind her head—attached it to the shunt at the base of her skull.

I knew why she hadn't done it before, leastways where I might see her. I winced and turned away, and the prince's *alkidar* asked, "What sorcery is this?"

But I could guess.

A moment later, the little projection lens in Valka's wrist-terminal gleamed to life, and a cone of light sprang forth in the air above her terminal. Within that cone of light, an image—not quite two-dimensional—sprang into being, facing the prince so that Valka and I looked *through* it like a window. It wavered and shook, swaying with the movement of whatever device had recorded that image. An instant later, the whole image flickered, then *blinked* in the next instant, and I knew.

We were looking through Valka's eyes.

Those golden Tavrosi orbs forgot nothing. All they saw was etched indelibly in the organic circuitry that threaded Valka's brain. I saw it then as I had never seen it—as I had tried to forget.

Aranata Otiolo stood like a mountain of black stone, snow-crowned and adamant, Smythe's sword like blue fire in its fist. Against it stood a figure terribly small, clad in the ill-fitting white and scarlet of a common legionnaire. I did not know him at a glance, so *young* was he: his hair untouched by frost, his face unmarred by claw. I might not have known him at all, were it not for that look of final exhaustion in his face—*that* I knew too well. *That* and his violet eyes.

"*Tuka ujanyn,*" the Pale prince exclaimed, fangs gnashing. *You are tired.* "You are weak like all your kind!"

"Strong enough," I murmured from my place behind the bloodwood chairs, and saw Olorin's face darken as he watched. Aranata's stolen blade clashed with my Jaddian one, but it was plain for all to see that I was failing.

The Cielcin prince seized me by the hair, tearing my scalp with its talons. Blood ran down my face, and Valka's hands shook in the recording as she aimed and fired to no good effect. Valka herself stood stonily by, holding the holograph steady, the wire connecting her head to her terminal agleam.

The younger Hadrian had fallen to the ground by then, and Aranata Otiolo stood over me.

I shut my eyes.

I did not want to see it. Not again. Not so clearly. Not as Valka had seen it.

Pallino's old recording had been a distant and murky thing. This was too sharp, sharper even than my memory.

From the image Valka gasped and whispered, "No!" An instant later she shrieked my name. "Hadrian!" she cried out. *That* word, and the way her voice broke—that I have never forgotten. She had started crying then, and the whole of her vision blurred until the window she projected for the prince and his concubine shimmered in the air before us four.

"Marlowe!" a distant voice rang out, the voice of Bassander Lin.

I knew what happened next, did not need to see, and yet I could not stop myself, and opened my eyes a slit.

Against the overhanging wall of stone beside that cursed lake, a tall, red fountain played.

Valka tore the wire from her skull, and the image snapped away.

"It's a trick," Kalima said. "Tavrosi magic!"

"No," I said softly, more than loud enough.

"You lie!" Kalima tossed her head.

But Olorin—Prince Kaim—stood and raised a hand for silence. His eyes were shining, and he shook his head. "You say you do not know miracles," he said. "Are you blind?" He shook his head again, more violently. "You do not believe in God, but I do." He descended the dais as he spoke and drew level with me. "And I believe *you*." His eyes flickered from Valka to myself. "In your Empire, they say you are the Earth's Chosen. I say you are a gift. God has sent you to us, and sent me to you." Prince Kaim extended his hand to me, as he had once upon the airfield in Borosevo when I was just a boy. "We will fight these monsters, and by Ahura Mazda, we will win."

CHAPTER 29

PALE FIRE

"IT'S ALMOST . . . BEAUTIFUL, ISN'T it?" remarked Bassander Lin. The tribune sat rigid in his seat at the head of the long conference table that dominated the *Tempest*'s ready room just off the bridge. I regarded him in silence, marking the way the holographed images shining above the projector in the center of the table glistened in his black eyes.

Above the table, DB-639D was burning. The white blossom of nuclear fire flowered from the ocher soil of Ganelon. Its petals spread, flattened against the roof of the planet's poisonous atmosphere, smeared and cooled from white to red to a pillar of black cloud. How small it seemed—that devastation—from so high and far away. And yet that cloud would linger, its ash and radiation both, and in a thousand years or ten, when man or her successors found the world again, its memory would linger still in the strange death of moss and grasses where the radiation fell. They would know—without knowing who or why—that men had come to that place before.

It was better that they did not know or guess the evils done on that world by the sorcerers that once had called it home.

We were nearly three years out from Ganelon by then, at the end of the first leg of our journey. Prince Kaim and the Jaddian fleet—along with the great part of the 409th—had all powered on, setting their oars for Siraganon by way of Fidchell. We had paused. Lin had ordered the *Tempest* to drop out of warp on the prearranged date to receive our scheduled telegraph drip from Captains Tenavian and Dayne, who had remained behind at Ganelon to secure the planet and pacify the captured Cielcin moon.

Instantaneous the quantum telegraph might have been, but it could only send us one bit of data at a time. The telegraphs aboard the *Tempest* and Tenavian's ship, the *Fearless*, shared only one bonded pair of electrons between them, and so *everything*—raw text, audio, video, phototype, even full tri-D holography—had to be drip-fed to us one datum at a time. Zero. One. Zero. Zero. One.

The report began simply enough: with a solitary line of text: *Fortress on DB-639D destroyed. Report to follow.*

The report had followed, bit by precious bit, for the better part of two weeks. For two weeks the *Tempest* sat alone at anchor in the midst of the blank Dark of space. A long time, but far shorter and faster than the years it would have taken for a signal to reach the nearest datanet relay at mere light speed.

Tenavian and Dayne had been thorough. With the remaining Cielcin worldship crippled, they had rounded up the survivors of the MINOS team on Ganelon itself, destroyed their golems, and either executed or interred their mercenary guards, forcing them into fugue to be dealt with at a later date. With the planet pacified, they'd turned their attention to the marooned Cielcin in deep orbit, having already repelled a trio of desperate sorties launched by the enemy against their portion of the fleet in space and on Ganelon itself.

Tenavian spoke of bitter fighting in the sky above the planet and in the trenches and tunnels of the Cielcin moon. The Jaddian captain who remained behind, Serenelli, had led a force that found the command center not far beneath the surface, and broke their resistance in pitched battle. Word had been sent to Nessus of the captured worldship, and I did not doubt that soon the Chantry and men from HAPSIS would be sailing for the DB-639 system. I almost wished that I could have stayed behind.

Reams of video and still images had followed. Interviews with captive magi, with mercenary guard officers, pages and pages of scientific data lifted from the memory banks of the fortress's computers, records of samples taken and experiments performed by Tenavian's science officers . . .

There had been no one left alive on Ganelon itself when the atomics rained down. Neither the magi nor their golem familiars, neither the technical staff nor the poor, hapless patients Tenavian's people had euthanized one by one. Now not even a single tree or blade of grass remained in the garden domes.

Only glass and ashes remained.

"Beautiful." I repeated the word like a curse, not certain if it was agreement or bitterness that edged my voice. Beauty is Truth, the poet once observed, and I have said it is not so, for there are hideous truths. But Truth is *good*, I thought then—and think now—even when it is hideous, and the atomic light and fire of the devastation playing out on the screen before Bassander and me was *good*, for it destroyed much that was evil.

"They still got away. Their leaders," said Lorian from his place beside me, ever the little devil in my ear. "And if MINOS has one such base in the galaxy, you can be certain there are more. Remember Arae?"

I had not forgotten Arae, nor had I forgotten Iovan on Padmurak, hiding in plain sight. It was not hard to imagine there might be more of the sorcerers lurking behind the faces of our ministers, or among the aryabites of Jadd. Never before had I been so grateful for the Chantry and its Inquisition. They at least would not suffer such witches to live.

Bassander Lin crossed his arms. "How do you think they mean to deploy this plague?"

"I'm sure it must be in Tenavian's report," I said. "But if it were me . . . I'd use drone ships, maybe even light-probes. Something that small could bypass orbital defenses. If the virus is truly airborne, they need only introduce the virus to a planet's atmosphere. If they can target the air above our cities . . . it'll spread soon enough." I found myself remembering the Gray Rot that had plagued Borosevo when I was young. Talk in the streets had been that the plague had been of extraterranic origin, the result of some foreign animalcule like a bacterium. I wondered if it, too, had been developed in some Extrasolarian lab and sent against the hated Empire.

But I shook myself. There was enough ugliness in nature without my resorting to such baseless speculation.

Lorian sucked air in through his teeth, was already shaking his head in disagreement. "Too high a risk of failure. I'm no medical doctor, but viruses wither in the sun, they say. They can't live forever. If it were me, I'd use fugue pods. Infect some poor bastards and load them onto passenger liners like . . . like timed explosives. Migrant workers, free traders, mercenaries . . . whatever they can get." He raised his shoulders defensively as Lin turned to look at him. "It's how many interstellar plagues spread. Commercial starports are cesspits, especially on the bigger worlds. You get folks from all over that close together . . . drinking, fucking, doing whatever it is people do . . . besides, port security's never so tight as they advertise. Most worlds'll let anyone land at least, so long as their paperwork's in order."

Remembering my youth on Emesh and the way the salvage workers had pulled me out of fugue and hurled me half-dead into the gutter to better lay uncontested claim to Demetri's ship, I nodded. "You're probably right."

"I wish we'd caught one of their leadership," Lin said, and cursed. "If we'd but secured the tower ten minutes sooner . . ."

"They would still have their other sites," Lorian observed, sober as can be.

"The great work cannot be halted," I murmured.

Both men looked at me, but Lorian asked, "What?"

"Just something Urbaine said," I answered him. Talk of Urbaine blackened my mood. I had been out of the freeze then for a little less long than we'd been at anchor receiving Tenavian's telegraph drip, and the memory of the Battle of Ganelon was still sharp and cold in my breast, Valka's cry of victory and unvanquished pain still raw in my ears. "It would have been better to catch one of the Elect-Masters, yes—and better still if we had stopped them. But we struck a blow all the same. At least Urbaine is dead."

"Are you sure?" Bassander asked, composing his blunt face and blunter manner into something like a conciliatory mask. "We thought that twice before."

"I am sure of almost nothing," I told him—told them both. "But I have to believe this was all *for* something."

"The battle?" Lorian asked. "We captured a worldship! And at least we caught wind of this virus before it was deployed! This *is* a victory, Marlowe."

"I know it is a victory, *Aristedes*," I said, unable to keep the snarl from my tone. I could not think of Urbaine without thinking of Valka, without remembering her own hand crawling to strangle her in the night, without seeing her seizures and the subtle ways her torment would reoccur for her anew even after her ordeal on Edda, when her people treated her as best they could before they tried to destroy her themselves. "I meant Valka. I meant what *she* has suffered. I have to believe all *that* was for something."

"Oh."

"Oh," I said, and felt myself deflating. Lorian had done no wrong, and it was wrong to turn my pain upon him. I squeezed my hands together on the tabletop, felt a strength like their old strength in them again. "He's dead. He has to be."

At my side, the intus had gone quiet and very still. He put a silver-braced hand upon my shoulder. It was light almost as paper. "I hate that bastard for what he did to Valka," Lorian said. "It's enough to make a man pray there is hell . . . even at the risk of ending up there himself."

I felt myself offer a thin and crooked smile.

"Is she all right?"

"She was," I said, finding that I couldn't look into other man's eyes any longer, "when we went under the ice. As good as I'd seen her in . . . since . . . since before . . ." I wanted to say *since before Padmurak*, but the words choked me. Maybe they were not even right. Maybe I should have said *since before Berenike*. Since before that day upon the Storm Wall.

My fingers found her phylactery through the soft fibers of my shirt.

At length I swallowed, bobbed my head. In pursuit of a new subject, I turned to Bassander and asked, "Was there word from the Emperor?" We had signaled the fleet before we left Ganelon ourselves, and again when we had stopped to receive Tenavian's signal. The Emperor's party had reached Perfugium, where they had been welcomed by the ruling duchess, Saskia Valavar. The planet had celebrated the Emperor's arrival with a month of festivals and games, and the itinerant court had set about reviewing the planet's colonial stores. Perfugium had been a hub of ancient Imperial expansion, in millennia past when man had rapidly spread across the Centaurus Arm, and though colonial settlement had slowed with the onslaught of the Cielcin Wars, still the planet kept millions of sleeping colonists in fugue beneath the capital city of Resonno.

"Nothing of note," Bassander said. "All is going according to plan with the Emperor's mission." He turned his face from mine to watch as Tenavian's holograph replayed the atomic destruction of the MINOS base from orbit. "Legion Intelligence congratulated us—and Prince Kaim—on our victory, and has directed Captain Tenavian to remain in-system and await relief." He shrugged, adjusted his cane to keep it from falling where it leaned against his chair. "Beyond that, they simply reiterated our orders to make for Siraganon."

"They said nothing about the virus?" I asked, and felt a frown deepen.

"Tenavian telegraphed Forum and the fleet both at the same time as us," Lin said. "The Emperor knows all we know."

I had no reply for that. I should not have expected some editorial from the throne or Legion Intelligence, and yet I had. "How long until we reach Siraganon?" I asked instead.

"Not long," Bassander said. "Another five years. We have to stop at Fidchell to refuel. We'll be there in a few months. Prince Kaim will beat us there by a couple weeks. He's agreed to wait for us, that we may all arrive at Siraganon together."

I had not told Lin much of my meeting with Prince Kaim du Otranto—with Sir Olorin Milta. I had not shared the prince's true identity with him, or the fact that we three had stood together against the Cielcin at Emesh, in the darkness at Calagah. Olorin had not asked Valka and me to keep his secret—as the Emperor had sworn me to silence—but to tell even Lin who lay beneath the Darkmoon Prince's mask seemed a betrayal. And at any rate, Lin had not asked.

"Fidchell?" Lorian repeated the strange name. "I've never heard of it."

"And with good reason," Lin said. "It's an iceball. Petroleum mines, mostly. Just a Guild outpost, but the Legion keeps a fuel depot there. We burned more AM fuel short-jumping round DB-639 than I'd have liked, but it's no trouble. Fidchell is not far out of our way, and the fleet knows we're bound there. We may yet reach Siraganon before His Radiance, depending on how long he remains at Perfugium."

My chair squealed as I leaned back. "Does he expect to be detained?"

Lin opened his hands. "Have you been to Perfugium?"

"I have," said Lorian, before I could answer. "Back when I scribed for Strategos Beller. Before I joined the Red Company."

The words *Red Company* burned me, but I smiled to remember my long-ago meeting with the junior Lieutenant Aristedes, chained to a desk in the office of Strategos Amalric Beller on Forum.

Lin fingered his cane, made a face to suggest some conflict on the subject of Lorian's commission. If Bassander had an issue with the intus, he had never voiced it. But he said, "There are millions of sleepers on Perfugium, in the old storehouses beneath the city. Miles of catacombs. Cubicula, I mean. Not just the typical bunkers you find under castles or cities. There was talk of relocating some of them. The Emperor wanted them carried off and resettled in the Perseus, far from here."

It was Lorian's turn to make a face. "I'd heard that," he said. "If it's true, he'll be stuck on Perfugium a long while. Those old colonial stores had their own starports built in back in the day, but it would take months to move that many people."

"Still, Caesar may try," Lin said.

"He will," I said. "If the Cielcin come to Perfugium, those catacombs will be nothing but meat lockers."

"Likely he *is* arranging some form of exodus!" Lin chewed his tongue as if it tasted foul, and thumped his cane twice against the ready room's metal floor, its brass nib ringing in the still air. "Whatever happens happens, as they say!" He made to stand and stretched his shoulder, and a shadow of pain flickered over his face. The tribune leaned heavily against the table, did his best in the process to stifle a groan.

My hand went sympathetically to my mended shoulder as I rose to help him, and asked, "Are you well?" I had forgotten that here was a man whose injuries ran deep. General Bahudde had fractured nearly every bone Lin had. He had survived Berenike only thanks to the timely intervention of my Irchtani, who had rushed him to fugue in the Storm Wall with all haste. He had had good surgeons, but even the likes of Doctor Elkan could not have made him good as new.

"I need a drink," Lin answered, surprising me with his venom. He stiffened suddenly, embarrassed, as if he'd been caught in some innocent lie. "It's easier up here. In the Dark. I hate going planetside anymore. The higher gravity's hell on my bones." As if to underscore this admission, he took up his cane.

"What a trio we make, eh?" Lorian exclaimed, pushing his own chair back from the table. His own feet barely reached the ground, and when he stood he was little taller than a boy of twelve. "Marlowe's spare parts, you're falling apart, and I!"—he bowed, one braced hand on his chest, "am a *mutant*."

Standing myself, I leaned forward and switched off the holograph. I could not bear to watch the image of the bombing cycle a fifty-second time. Struck by the realization that I was the halest of the three of us, I murmured, "When old age shall this generation waste . . ."

"Is that more poetry?" Lorian asked, recognizing the Classical English. "Do you have a line for everything?"

"Almost everything," I allowed, and translated:
When old age shall this generation waste,
Thou shalt remain, in midst of other woe
than ours . . .
"You're a cheery sort, Lord Marlowe," Lorian said.

"No, I'm not," I said, and clapped the smaller man on his thin shoulder. "That's why I have you, Aristedes. Every great lord deserves a proper jester!"

Lorian emitted a burst of nearly mirthless laughter. "And as you're not a *great* lord, *my lord,* you must settle for me!"

Waiting for us both by the exit back to the *Tempest's* vast and mostly silent bridge, Lin allowed himself a rare smile. "Each of the three of us should by rights be discharged—"

"—or never admitted, in my case," Lorian interjected, having evidently noted Lin's earlier reaction to his words and presence.

Lin continued as if the good commander had never interrupted. "We are what the Empire has."

I bowed my head to hide whatever must have flickered on my face.

Exhaustion. Shame. I had no hope of waking Valka from her sleep and stealing the *Ascalon* while we waited all at anchor, and it would be suicide to attempt any escape while the *Tempest* was at warp. Worse, it would be homicide. Any attempt to breach the bigger ship's warp envelope would destroy the *Ascalon*, but the resultant explosion caused by any breach in our fuel containment would annihilate the *Tempest*, too. The *Tempest* and the tens of thousands of souls aboard her.

Besides, I had stolen a ship from Lin before.

I could not ever do it again.

"Earth help the poor bastards, if we're the best they have!" said Lorian, laughing, blind and deaf to my turmoil. "Three cripples! Well, two and a half—Marlowe got over it!"

I tried to smile at the good commander, but I sensed the expression came out soured.

Aristedes looked up at me, and I marked the shadow of concern behind his pale, bloodless eyes. "Are you staying awake a bit? For the trip to Fidchell?"

Hands deep in my pockets, I thought it over. It was less than a year to Fidchell, then five to Siraganon. After a moment's thought, I found myself shaking my head. "I've had my fill of space travel," I said, in direct contrast to Lin. "Soon as medical clears me to go back under, I think I'll sleep."

CHAPTER 30

THE CALL

SINCE THE DAY I ordered this cell and requested ink and parchment from the archivists, I have feared to come so far. You have heard how Hadrian Marlowe slew the Cielcin at Gododdin, how he tore the Pale King from its throne and set the heavens on fire. You have heard how he slew the demon princes Aranata and Ulurani; how he battled the iron devils of the White Hand; how he riddled with daimons from the ancient world, the bastard offspring of Felsenburgh's thrice-damned daughters. You have heard how he loved his lady, his witch doctor of the Tavrosi clans—though they were forbid to wed and to conceive. You have heard also how he defied Death itself, and Time, and spoke with he who might be, who *must* be: the Hidden One who sits above all things at the ragged end of Time.

You have heard tales of how he suffered—and of how he failed. How *I* failed.

Ever since the day I began my work in this cell, I have known I must come to this pass, and have daily dreaded it. Whole months I have passed in the archives, or in the grottoes far below—where Gibson dwelt in happier days—or worked with the brothers in this athenaeum, rather than go on. I am old now, far older than any man who has lived and *died* a man.

I will grow older, still.

Centuries have gone by since that day on Gododdin, since our new Emperor ordered me slain. Centuries more have passed since that bloody victory on Ganelon, since the call found us on Fidchell. It was not the call I'd been told to expect.

But it was the call I feared must come.

Since the day I began this account, I knew I must endure many things anew.

Vorgossos. Padmurak. Dharan-Tun.

Perfugium.

Whole drafts I have written and abandoned—or burned—before this point. So much easier to begin again than go on. I have but to start over to have my people—my friends—alive again. In starting out afresh in scholiast vermilion, I meet Pallino and Switch, Siran and Elara again in the fighting pits of Emesh. I meet Valka for the first time upon the balcony in Castle Borosevo. I see Corvo again through the bars of my cell in the dungeons of Marius Whent. I see the *Tamerlane* rising above the skies of Forum like a new sword shining in the sun!

So many beginnings . . . so much easier.

But there are endings, as you and I well know.

Once more I find I wish to throw my work into the sea—so inadequate a document it seems! So feeble and blinkered by my merely human hand and eye, so poor a testament to the people I have known.

To my people.

I have no wish to continue, even alone.

But I had no wish to answer the call then, either.

Yet answer I did.

And as I did then, I shall try now.

CHAPTER 31

THE MESSENGER

THE FIRST FRESH GASPS always brought pain. Fluid in the lungs, in the nasal passages, the mouth. No matter that it was oxygenated. The animal mind still panics, still believes it is drowning. The medtechs had turned me on my side, and I retched cerulean fluid on the white plastic of the examination table. The process was no less violent, no less demeaning than it had been on Dharan-Tun. How could it be? Naked and pissing, shivering with cold.

Then darkness.

Light.

"Where?"

"Steady now, my lord," came the voice of the medtech, soothing and maternal. "Steady now."

"I can't see."

"It will pass."

I was in a bed. Cleaned. Dry. Dressed in a white medical gown. I could feel the linens weighing on me. Blindness was not uncommon after fugue. The eyes often deformed in the freeze, but already my vision was blurring, darkness tending toward light. Soon I would be able to discern the shape of my caretaker, and of the instruments in the *Tempest*'s medica looming like statues through a mist. Then would follow the cognitive tests and the customary glass of imitation orange juice.

New life.

Turning my head in the direction of the gray shape I took for my nurse, I asked, "Siraganon?"

I expected her to nod. She shook her head. "Fidchell."

"Fidchell?" I had left orders to leave me until we arrived at our final destination. A blackness darker than my bruised vision filled my mind. "Why?"

No one would explain anything to me, but I thought I could guess what had happened. One dour medical officer administered a stimulant via atomizer and ordered me to get dressed. When I questioned him, I was told that Valka was still under ice, and that Bassander Lin and the other bridge officers were still being roused, but that orders had come from Fidchell station that I was to tender in from the *Tempest* to the station itself as soon as I was able.

"Rouse Doctor Onderra," I said to the man.

"Our orders were for you only," the officer replied.

"And I am giving you a new order!" I said. The adrenaline cocktail he'd given me was in full effect. "If I must go alone, I'll go alone, but *you* will wake the doctor. Am I understood?"

The medical officer swallowed. "My orders come from higher than you, my lord."

"Where's Tribune Lin?"

"In medica," the man said, speaking with the air of one who had just answered the same question minutes before. "He's not sensate yet."

I growled, searching for words. I was not commandant of the Red Company any longer. This was not my man, nor my ship. "We'll speak when I return," I managed after a tense silence.

Before long I'd dressed and armed myself as best I could with dagger and sidearm. A quartet of white-masked legionnaires met me in the hall, and escorted me—boots ringing—along black corridors and brass lift carriages to the launch flume where a shuttle waited.

Time seemed to pass in a gray haze, and the medication they'd given to wake me and combat the headaches and nausea of fugue sickness left me strangely decoupled from my body. I felt as though I watched Hadrian Marlowe—that absurd, corvine figure with his black-and-white-streaked mane—as he strapped himself into the crash webbing of a short-range *Heron*-class shuttle.

We fell away from the *Tempest* at once, the running lights on the inside of the launch flume flashing past before the stars appeared, white and silver and red against the blackness, like glittering jewels.

Fidchell itself shone white and pale blue—a frigid snowball of a world in orbit about a distant yellow star. The sparse lights of mining settlements glowed on its night side, but the day showed little signs of human habitation. Only limitless tundra.

Fidchell Station, on the other hand, gleamed ahead like a topless tangle of silver towers, some rising, some falling, some proceeding at right angles from the equatorial band where—like a mighty wheel—ships smaller than our *Tempest* lay at anchor.

The men of my guard spoke little as we descended toward the station. Following their lead, I sat quietly by the porthole and watched the approaching station. Too well I knew the dark lozenges of Mining Guild vessels and the long-masted ships of the Consortium, their silver sails all furled. Many ships there were of other shape, some lesser, some greater, though their markings and heraldry were strange to me.

We did not—as I had expected—pull in to dock along the station's equatorial ring, but diverted instead toward a black vessel moored not far from the station itself. It was not properly docked, but hung connected to the rotating station by an armature housing a shielded fuel line. Even at a distance, I recognized the matte black of a Legion ship.

It wasn't large. I counted her engines on approach, the two-and-one-and-three configuration, fusion torches and warp slit and ion drives, and took her for an interceptor, possibly one of the smaller destroyers, perhaps half a mile from bow cluster to stern. I had seen many such ships in the camp at Carteia. They tended to have smaller crews, not being intended for use as troop carriers, as the *Tempest* was and *Tamerlane* had been.

As we drew alongside her, I marked the brass apertures of cargo bays, lit by the glow of Fidchell and the torch-beams of our own shuttle. Squinting, I saw the remnants of a gun emplacement on a spar overlooking those shuttered gates. It had been blasted off, and the bones of broken metal stood out twisted and torn, as if the turret had been ripped off by some mighty hand.

The black dread that had taken up residence in me since waking yawned wide.

At last we reached an open hold. Attitudinal jets fired, and we were inside.

In minutes the airlock cycled open, and I was greeted by a haggard man with heavy shadows beneath his eyes. Seeing his face and his scarlet uniform, I knew all.

This was not the man from HAPSIS I had been ordered to expect. This was not *the call*.

"Lord Marlowe?" His voice was rough as the living rock, exhaustion thick in every syllable. He thumped his chest with a fist, bald head bowed.

"I am, chiliarch," I said, acknowledging the man's salute and his rank. "What's happened? What's going on?"

"I'm to take you to His Highness at once," said the chiliarch, adjusting his tunic. His uniform was not the Legion black, but red and white, with the Imperial sunburst on one collar tab and the white-capped red planet of his home on the other.

He was an officer of the Martian Guard.

"What's happened?" I asked again, taking him by the elbows. "What's become of the Emperor?"

Still the man was silent. He only shook his head.

Undaunted and buoyed up by my stimulant, I continued pressing. "Why was I sent for alone? Tribune Lin at least should be with me. And what of Prince Kaim and the Jaddians? They should have arrived ahead of us."

"The prince has already spoken with the men of Jadd," the Martian chiliarch said. "Please, come."

My four guards followed me and the Martian out into the sealed shuttle bay and through another open airlock into a corridor that ran the length of the destroyer. Here the halls were narrower than I was used to, but the look was the same: black metal and black glass, brass fixtures and the omnipresent banks of red and gleaming blue lights on doors and on control panels. The convex arc of a lift door rolled aside, and the six of us rode the tube up two levels.

More men in Martian uniforms—none of them armored—hurried along this upper hall, moving away from us on some errand of their own. That these men had come from the Emperor's own fleet was certain as the dawn, for the protection of the Aventine House was the sole charge and province of the Martian Guard, and but for the Emperor, there were no members of the House Imperial this far from Forum and the core worlds in Orion.

"In here, sir," the Martian said, pausing by a sealed chamber door. Two lesser Martians in full plate and long white gambesons stood at either side of the door, each with a plasma rifle tucked into the crook of his arm. "Your guards may remain in the hall. The prince will explain everything."

"The prince?" I echoed the words, dumbly.

Perhaps you see already, Reader, what my disoriented and unprepared mind and ears had missed. No members of the House Imperial but the Emperor, indeed! The Emperor . . . and Alexander.

The doors slid apart, revealing a close, windowless chamber whose only furnishing was a long table of black glass at whose head a white figure was seated, a black shadow at his left hand, four armed and armored Martians behind.

The white figure looked up abruptly as I answered. His face had been in his hands, and his eyes—Imperial green—were red and shadowed even as the chiliarch's had been. Seeing me, Alexander let his hands fall. "Hadrian . . ."

"They have your father," I said, knowing in that moment that my fears were all true.

The prince nodded. "Yes." He inhaled sharply, looked round at the little conference chamber like a man seeing it for the first time. "Yes."

The shadow beside him—Archprior Leonora—shifted where she stood but did not speak.

Alexander fixed his gaze on me. Too well I knew the pain in those green eyes, had felt it myself aboard the *Ascalon* when Valka and I fled Eue. "Ours was the only ship to escape. The whole fleet . . . they caught us. I'd never seen anything like it. There were *seven* of their moons, Hadrian. They tore the fleet apart, nearly tore the planet. Captain Thuva said the tidal stresses drowned nearly half the planet. Earthquakes did the city in before they even started shelling . . ."

Only slowly did I realize my hand was on my knife, for from the moment the chiliarch had said the word *prince* my body had gone on high alert. Perhaps it was the result of my stimulant, but I feared some trick, some trap. I had been brought alone from the *Tempest*, stripped of my guard.

"How did you escape?" I asked, stepping cautiously to one side of the door so at least to have my back to a wall.

If Alexander saw my caution for what it was, he gave no sign.

"I was in orbit when the attack came. Father sent word that I should transfer here and flee. We knew you were coming to Fidchell before . . . before Siraganon." His eyes were shining. "They destroyed the *Radiant Dawn*. The whole fleet!"

Steadily I relaxed my grip on the knife, shifted my hand instead to the catch on my shield-belt—a more practical, less paranoid posture, that. "Your father . . ." I said, hardly daring to breath the word. "Dead?"

The prince swallowed, and after an eternal instant, he shook his head. "No. He was on the planet when they came, overseeing the transfer of the colonial stores. We were going to take them back with us . . ." Abruptly he fell silent, hung his head.

Leonora placed a reassuring hand on his shoulder as the prince pressed the heel of one hand to one eye. Such human warmth from the old bat astonished me, and in a soft voice, she said, "His Radiance is alive. We telegraphed him when we reached this system. He replied."

"I warned him," I said, halting, not seeing the chamber myself. "On Carteia. I warned him. Him. Nicephorus. The whole damned security council. I warned them all." The sense of dislocation I'd experienced on the flight over intensified, and through the stimulant I felt I watched Hadrian Marlowe feel around with his scarred left hand for the smooth metal of the wall. "I told them: the Cielcin knew his movements. They tortured the coordinates out of my men. Out of *me*."

Perfugium. Vanaheim. Balanrot . . . Aulos, Carteia, Siraganon . . .

I was sure I had shouted the name of Perfugium myself, a dozen times about the churning waters of the pit as blood dripped from my temple, when not even the oblivion of unconsciousness would come to relieve me.

The prince seemed not to notice my admission—the admission I had never managed to make to the Emperor himself. "We've been nearly a year getting here," he said, raising his eyes to me once more. "That's nearly a year *my father* has lived like a rat in those tunnels. We *must* rescue him, Hadrian."

I found myself nodding in slow agreement. "We have the fleet," I said at last. "The Jaddians are here, are they not?"

"They arrived two weeks ago," said Leonora. "We urged them to go on, but their prince refused to depart without you."

"He said it would be disaster not to coordinate our assault," the prince said, rather lamely.

"He's right," I said. "I would very much like to speak to him."

Alexander nodded. "We'll need a council. Today. Tomorrow at the latest."

"Why did you send for me?" I asked, hand still on my shield-belt. "Before the others? Tribune Lin is not even out of the ice yet! What do you want of me?"

The young prince—not so young, not anymore—flinched at the harshness in my voice. Had he been awake for the entire trip from Perfugium to Fidchell? His red hair was longer even than it had been at Fidchell, fell now past his shoulders in untidy curtains. He had a sailor's pallor, and he seemed to me like a man long bereft of sleep.

"I . . ." Alexander faltered, and he seemed to see his hands on the tabletop for the very first time. He clenched them. "I don't know . . . I . . . I don't know what to do, Hadrian."

I took one halting step from the wall, and for a moment considered moving to the prince's side. But I stayed where I was, beside the door, some part of me still cautious, still weighing the possibility that this was all some sick joke, some trap. Part of me said that I was being too suspicious of the prince, that for all the harm he'd done me or tried to do, he would not go so far—was not capable of so supreme an act of deception—as this.

"If my father is dead . . ." Alexander choked.

"Then you are the Emperor," I said.

"No," Alexander said. "No. Father will have left his will with the Council. They will have to read it, execute it. There are protocols."

I gripped the back of a chair for support, leaned over it for emphasis. "You are the only one of your family in the field," I said. "The only one here. In Centaurus. If your father is dead—or worse—taken, then it falls to you to avenge him. You have a fleet, Alexander. The Jaddians are here. You have to act. *We* have to act."

The prince did not respond, but twisted the ring on his first finger.

"I asked you once," I said, "if you thought the road would be easy? If you thought it should be? Do you remember?" Alexander only bobbed his head. "This is your road, Highness. *Our* road." I fell silent for a beat, watched the prince staring at his reflection in the black glass. "But you said your father is *not* dead. Something about the tunnels?"

Alexander didn't move.

Leonora spoke. "His Radiance secured himself in the colonial stores. The catacombs are shielded, reinforced against orbital bombardment. He has the duchess of House Valavar and most of the court safely underground."

I shut my eyes, picturing what it must be like in those bunkers. The low light, the close air, the smell of unwashed bodies. How many battles on how many worlds had come down to such last redoubts? Nearly every Imperial world had its bunkers, built in the age when interhouse warfare was the rule of law.

"When was his last message?" I asked.

"Right after the Jaddians arrived," the prince said.

"Two weeks ago," said Leonora.

"You've signaled to say we've arrived?" I asked, trying to orient myself. "How long since we made it in-system?"

The prince and the priestess looked at one another. "A few hours only," said Leonora. "But yes, we sent word."

"They still have telegraph capabilities, then?"

"It's all they have," Alexander said. "I told you. The fleet's lost, and not just the fleet. All the Valavar forces are gone, everything on the surface."

I could only blink at him. "Everything on the surface?"

"Hadrian, you weren't *there*," the prince said. "They didn't raid anything. It wasn't like Berenike. They didn't try to take the city, they hit us with *everything* they had. You saw the fleet we had at Carteia. More than a hundred ships! We didn't last two days! And these were no common legions! These were the Martian Guard! We only survived because we *ran*!"

I gripped the back of the seat before me more tightly still. "You were right to run," I said, and stopped, who would not say as much to myself. After a thick pause, I added, "And right to come here. Had you gone instead to Siraganon we would have lost precious time, and who knows how long your father and his men may hold out. Do you know how many others survived?"

Alexander shook his head. "Only those on the surface with him," he said. "Thousands. Ten thousand at the most."

Against seven worldships.

I was not a religious man. Still my fingers jerked to form the sign of the sun disc. "Holy Mother Earth bless him and keep him," I said, hollow words from me, but well meant.

"That isn't all," Alexander said. "Hadrian, the *Prophet* was there."

My blood went all to ice, and I staggered leftward, chair by chair, until I had traveled half the length of the table. "The Prophet?" I repeated the prince's words. "You're sure?"

Alexander nodded. "I saw some of the footage from the surface during the initial assault. He projected his image—just like he did at Berenike, a mile high. He appeared after the first bombs fell . . . ordered Father to surrender."

I hardly heard the prince's words, and screwed shut my eyes. So clearly I saw Syriani Dorayaica, clad in striated black, its horns all silver-sheathed, its forehead dripping with fine chains of silver and sapphire, jeweled as the houris of Olorin's harem. Azure and sable, its robes of state hung from one shoulder, secured by a pin fashioned in the shape of a grasping hand. It spread its own white hands—six-fingered—as the drape of its garments blackened the sky and the bombs and siege towers fell.

"*Down!*" it roared, voice like the thunder. "*Down to dust, mankind!*"

I could picture it forcing the Emperor to kneel as it had forced Prince Iamndaina. I saw William stagger, try to rise—saw him forced to kneel again. A vision? A memory? The Emperor's face was slashed, and one eye ruined, red weeping down one cheek as the Prophet-King forced His Radiance to kneel still yet a third time.

Down!

"Hadrian?"

I blinked. I was standing halfway down the left side of the conference table, hands each gripping the back of a chair.

"You're sure?" I asked. "You're sure it was Dorayaica?"

"I was at Berenike," the prince said. "Or had you forgotten?"

Was it my imagination, or had a bitter edge crept into the prince's tired tone?

At once, I remembered where I was, and with whom—and that I was alone and friendless. Standing, I drew my cloak about me, and let my hand find the shield controls once more. I cannot say why—save rank suspicion only—that I expected to find some lesser shadow lurch from behind an arras with drawn sword and fury.

None did.

"I remember," I said. I had not expected Dorayaica to come itself, and the thought of facing it again—and the beast that grew inside it—was more than I'd prepared for in the stark light of the conference room. "But there must have been a dozen worlds left to search. More! The Prophet would have had to send its forces to them all—to track the Emperor across the frontier. What are the odds it choose rightly?"

Neither the prince nor Leonora spoke for a long time. Eventually, Alexander did. "I don't know," he said, simply. "But I know Dorayaica. It was him."

"If the Prophet wanted to destroy your father, it would have," I said. "They could have split the planet in half if they'd a mind. But they haven't, and therein lies our hope." My fingers played with the shield catch, nails clicking. Old reflex reached for my sword, found the hilt and hasp absent. "Dorayaica will want to make an example of your father. It will humiliate the Emperor if it can." I released my shield-belt, massaged one wrist, recalling the binders that shackled me to Elu's altar. "It knows the power of a symbol. Killing your father will make a new Emperor, but humiliating him will destroy the *idea of emperor* . . ."

Half-formed, I recalled a passage I had read—I think from Impatian—that spoke of a captured king of Earth, and of how his conqueror had humbled him, forcing him to serve as a footstool for the new king. What fate the Prophet intended for our Emperor I dared not guess, I who had seen the black city of Dharan-Tun and feasted in the halls of the Dhar-Iagon.

Alexander was nodding. "I understand."

"That means we've a chance," I said. Not knowing what I was doing, I advanced to the prince's end of the table. The prince's Martians—long forgotten like statues behind his seat—tensed at my approach. So I went to one knee, not in obeisance, but to put my face near a level with the prince's own. "Call the captains."

The prince inhaled sharply, pushed his fall of crimson hair back from his face. "You don't . . . think we should run?"

"Why would I think that?" I asked, looking up at Leonora. The Archprior pursed her lips.

"Should we not . . . abandon my father?"

I felt my mouth open, but for a moment, no words would come out. "Your father is the Emperor of Mankind. We cannot abandon him to the enemy." Alexander's lips moved without sound, as if old thoughts were working in the dark manifolds of his brain. "If he is fallen," I said, "then we will do what we must. You and I." I caught his wrist, caused the Martians to tense, but Alexander raised his free hand, eyes locked on my face. "If he is fallen," I said again, "you must take the throne."

"Unhand His Highness!" exclaimed the Archprior shrilly.

"That isn't how it works," Alexander said. "I told you."

I shook my head. "If your father is dead, *you* must avenge him. Press your claim. Return to Forum an avenger and victorious. None would deny you."

"So you can rule at my right hand?" the prince asked. "And marry my sister?"

"I do not want *your sister*," I said. "I do not want power. Or the throne. I want . . ." I choked. I wanted my family back. *Pallino and Elara. Ilex and Crim. Corvo, Siran, and Durand.* But that was beyond the might of our holy Emperor, beyond the might even of Kharn Sagara and his black sorcery. Time does not turn back, and not even the gods of night our pale enemy worshiped could grant my dearest wish.

"What?" Alexander asked, shifting in his seat to better look at me. "What do you want?"

"You must unhand His Highness!" Leonora barked again.

A long moment then I held the prince's hand and eye. Neither one of us moved. Not even Leonora stirred from her place behind the prince. "I want . . ." I swallowed, eyes going first to the black-robed confessor, then to the tense Martians in red and white.

Red. Black. White. Like labyrinth chess. Like my own colors.

"I want my freedom," I said. "If we reach Perfugium and find your father dead. If we return to Forum and press your claim . . . I want your leave to go."

"To leave?" Alexander echoed the words as if they were of some ancient tongue unknown to him.

I looked long and hard at him, up at Leonora. "You want the throne," I said, and when Alexander moved to deny it, I spoke again more loudly. "You want the throne, and so you cannot imagine that any man might *not* want it." Glowering at Leonora, I continued, "They say I am the Earth's Chosen, but I have never said that."

"But Berenike!" the prince said. "I saw what you did! What you can do!"

"What I *could* do," I countered, refusing to elaborate. "I am *not* the Earth's Chosen. I'm something else."

"What then?"

"I don't know!" I hissed. Tightening my grip, I seized the boy's eye once more with my own. "Alexander! Alexander, I swore to serve your father. I will. We will save him. Call the captains."

"You want . . . to leave?" Alexander's words came as if from the bottom of a well, and his head shook minutely. "I thought . . . I thought you believed you were the God Emperor come again."

I shook my head, released his hand at last. "I am only a soldier of the Empire. These stories are stories *other men* have told." Again I glared up at Leonora. "I have never wanted power—unless it was the power to end this war." I stood and withdrew a pace, letting my hands fall back to my sides beneath my white cloak. I had to remember that I was not before the Emperor then, not before William the Twenty-Third, William the Great, the Sun of the Millennium. Alexander was a boy, a young man of some forty years, I guessed.

I had to shock him. To push.

And so I opened my mouth, chose my words deliberately. "I know it was you, Alexander . . . behind that poor Urslicman on Carteia."

The prince looked up, eyes at once sharp and hard.

"I know you tried to kill me."

"You dare!" Leonora rounded the prince's chair, her robes secure in her fist. "You dare accuse His Highness of! Of!"

The word she sought was *murder*, but the holy woman could not find it.

"I accuse him of nothing, Your Reverence," I said, hoping her honorific might calm her down. Turning once more to Alexander, I continued, "I know it was you."

All at once, it seemed the prince found he could no longer look at me. His hands were in his lap.

I took a further step back. "You still think I mean to challenge you?" I asked. "To steal your throne?" I almost laughed, and a fey mood settled on me. "Then do it, Alexander. Kill me. Order your men to kill me." I knew he would not, and yet knew fear as I spoke. If I was wrong—if I had misread the boy's intentions in sending for me, his fears—I could not fight four Martians, not as I was. Nor could I win free of that chamber, and even if I could persuade the four guards that had come with me from *Tempest* to fight in my defense, we would never reach Bassander's ship. I would never reach Valka, nor we the *Ascalon*.

If I was wrong, I had reached my final page.

"Guards!" Leonora jabbed a finger at me. "Arrest this madman!"

"Do it," I said, and threw back my cloak to reveal my empty hands. To Alexander himself I said again, "Do it."

The Martians tensed, anticipating the order.

But Alexander didn't move.

In the new and more tense silence, I kept talking. "You sent for me. For what reason, if not to kill me?"

Again Alexander's lips moved, but his words did not come at once. "I . . ." he croaked at last. "I want to save my father."

An intense relief swept through me. And I realized with sudden, painful sharpness . . . that I had not wanted to die. A strange warmth suffused me as I stood there beneath the buzzing sconces. For how many years had I lived life a walking shadow, waiting to die?

Standing there, I felt as I imagined the condemned man must feel upon the gallows when the magistrate orders the carnifex to halt. It was as though the clear, golden sun of Earth fell upon my face, and I learned—discovered—that life was still precious and sweet.

The Martians had not relaxed. Their hands were still upon the hafts and firing stocks of their lances, and by their posture I knew they were ready to bring their bayonets in line at a gesture from their prince.

It never came.

"I want to save your father, too," I said, not daring to move my hands from sight.

"How do we do it?" Alexander asked. "That's why I called you here. For counsel."

"For counsel . . ." I echoed the words in whispers, studied my black boots on the polished metal floor. "You have not denied my charge."

Alexander looked up at me, and his eyes were like chips of raw jade. Not answering my words, he said, "You swore an oath to my father. Will you swear one to me?"

With excruciating slowness, I lowered my hands. "If I can."

"Do you swear to serve me in this?" he asked. "To save my father? If he can be saved?"

"I am a soldier of the Empire, my prince," I said.

"That isn't what I asked," he said.

He's afraid, I realized. Afraid of me. Of what I would do to him now that the truth was out.

He had reason for fear, and better reason than he knew. I had killed Augustin Bourbon, had seen Lorcan Breathnach sentenced to Belusha, had defied even the Empress when she turned her knives against me. What, then, did Alexander of the Aventine House fear Hadrian Halfmortal would do to him for no lesser evil than those of Bourbon and Breathnach?

"Alexander . . ." I began.

"Swear it!" he almost shouted, none of his father's cold temper in his mettle. Fragile as pig iron. He always was.

"I forgive you, lad," I said. "I will help you save your father. I swear it."

The prince's eyes were shining then, and he seemed to quake, a faint tremor hardly to be noticed. I felt for him, then, the survivor of a day of horrors nearly so evil as the one I'd endured on Eue.

I chewed my tongue, unsure if I should proceed.

I chose silence instead.

Alexander did not stand, but began nodding his head, brushed back his fall of hair, and looked round like a man seeing for the first time. "All right," he said. "All right then. Good enough. I've no stomach to argue with you." He risked a fragile smile. "I'll take what I can get."

"I would have us be friends again," I said, advancing half a step to offer my hand.

"Friends?" The prince regarded my scarred and half-healed hand with a mixture of skepticism and disgust. "I am a prince of the Sollan Empire, the blood of the God Emperor himself. I do not have friends, Marlowe."

I withdrew my hand at once, and muttered a half-formal apology.

"We have work to do," he said, and looked round at Leonora. "Have

Lord Marlowe returned to his ship. And call the captains. We will have our council as soon as may be."

Understanding that I was dismissed, I turned to leave. The door at the end of the conference chamber slid apart at my knock, but I stopped in the doorway and turned back. "I'm glad you're all right," I said. "Please tell me the minute you get a telegraph response from Perfugium. If your father is alive, we'll save him, and if not . . ."

"Fire," Alexander said. "Fire and vengeance will do."

CHAPTER 32

THE PLAN

I WAS RETURNED TO the *Tempest*, shaken somewhat by my confrontation with the young prince and by his tidings, but alive. True to his word, the medical officer had not awakened Valka, and when I cornered Lin—barely restored to consciousness—in the officers' medica, he refused to waken her as well. "We will not be here long," he said. "A day or two at the most. We must take council quickly, and she is no Imperial officer."

When I tried to protest, he raised a hand. "Hadrian, I know she is important to you, but this is a matter for the princes and myself. We mustn't waste time."

In the end, I relented. He wasn't wrong. Valka and I were accessories, each without command. The Red Company was gone, and the *Tamerlane* with it. I was a passenger in all but rank. There was nothing to do but wait: for the other captains to rouse themselves from icy sleep, and for tidings from Alexander's ship about the state of things on Perfugium.

Neither of us dared ask what might happen if no reply came. My words to the young prince echoed in my ears.

Avenge your father. Press your claim. Return to Forum an avenger and victorious.

None would deny you.

Despite my assurances, did Alexander yet fear that I intended much the same? Did he still think I wished to return to Forum with Dorayaica's head to claim his sister and his throne?

Could I blame him? Had I not seen myself enthroned in countless aspects, Selene seated at my feet like one of Prince Kaim's *alkidarae* in a gown of living flowers?

But I had spoken truth to the young prince.

And in any case, it did not matter.

The Emperor's reply came swiftly, within hours of my return to *Tempest*.

"I told His Radiance this would happen," I said for the ten thousandth time since I returned to Colchis, twisting my hands in my lap. "I told him his movements were compromised. I *told* him. But he would not listen."

"But he is alive," said Alexander at my right hand.

The last notes of the distress call still lingered on the air of the meeting room, the noise of it hanging like the smoke of burning cities above our heads. Holographs of the ruined city of Resonno—taken by the planet's satellite grid in the first days of the assault, or by brave souls who dared the surface between Cielcin raids—gleamed white and ash-gray above the table, reflections in the black glass below like ghosts.

A simple text message had preceded the telegraph drip.

Perfugium is besieged, it had read. *His Radiance lives.*

"They're dug in beneath Resonno," Bassander Lin informed the meeting, hands pressed flat against the conference table, his shoulders hunched as though he bore a heavy load. "Have been for nearly a year . . ." He glanced at Alexander. "Orbital defense is gone. The fleet. Local forces. All of it."

The prince spoke up, saying, "The fleet was lost in days. There were just too many of them."

Lin's gloomy first officer, the giant Commander Astor, shook his massive head. "It's a miracle they've held out so long."

"Those bunkers were dug six thousand years ago," said Captain Simonyi, physically present for the first time. "They're half a mile underground in places, ray-shielded, with geothermal sinks down into the core. The Pale aren't getting in without excavators, and so far it seems the Emperor's men have been successful holding them off." I could picture Martian strike teams emerging through hidden doors to undermine Cielcin dig crews, vanishing back beneath the surface.

Astor leaned forward, his frown growing deeper still. "Looks like they raided the city from orbit, burned all the ships the Emperor brought to ground." Satellite images showed on the holograph display in the center of the table, papered the plates on the various walls. They showed the bombed-out skeleton of a city, black scars and glassy pits where plasma charges hollowed the earth. I could remember my first look at such a battlefield, on Rustam so long ago. "I'd reckon there's nothing spaceworthy within a thousand miles of what's left of the city. And even there we can bet the Pale have torched most everything."

"How many people were there living in this city?" Prince Kaim's voice had a tinny, distant resonance, and came after several seconds' delay. The Jaddian prince and his officers had declined to tender over to the *Tempest* for reasons of their own, and the prince's ghostly form sat and flickered alongside Kalima and Afsharirad and an admiral called Serpico. His beetle-black mask was firmly back in place.

"In the city?" said a flat-faced scholiast in the customary green. "Three million." His eyelids flickered as he recalled some bit of information. "But the colonial stores house as many as nine."

"Twelve million people," the prince replied, his spectral image shaking its head.

"We must assume everyone in the city is dead or taken," said old Captain Simonyi by Bassander's side. He rubbed his eyes, clearly still working off the fatigue of fugue sickness. "They've had the run of the place for months. It's too much to hope anyone's escaped this long."

About the table, several of the men and women made the sign of the sun disc, touching forehead, heart, and lips. "Earth and Emperor protect us," muttered one more junior man, apparently unaware of the irony.

It was the Emperor who needed our protection.

"It's not just the capital," Alexander said. "It's the whole damn planet."

"Delphard. Romance. Port Almavera. All the major population centers." Commander Astor swept a hand over the glass tabletop, forcing the holograph to cycle through more and more satellite images that had been waiting for us in the hands of the Imperial Datanet Courier Service when we arrived in Fidchell system. "You can bet they hit the villages, too."

"They need to eat," Bassander said darkly, drawing the eyes of the table. Still the doughty tribune had not moved. Like Prince Kaim, he might have been graven from stone.

I turned my face away as Prince Kaim and Bassander and the other high officers debated what must be done and how.

The icy face of the planet Fidchell shone through the conference chamber's one genuine window, white as diamond and cold, half-veiled by the ribbed struts and whiskered carbon cables of the fuel-station superstructure to which the *Tempest* had at last docked. Something of that cold—of the icy cold of space, and of the snows of that alien world—seemed to penetrate that window, my uniform, my soul.

It reminded me of Dharan-Tun.

Presently, Prince Kaim spoke again, asking the question I was surprised none had asked already. "Is it the Scourge of Earth?" Almost it was possible to forget it was Sir Olorin Milta beneath that mask. His whole demeanor had changed. Gone was the affable swordsman, the swagger and easy laughter of the Maeskolos I'd known as a young man, transmuted into a creature of silk and black marble with eyes like distant stars.

Still bent over the head of the long table, his face lost in shadow, Bassander Lin raised his eyes, first to me, then to the young prince. I had told him all I knew, all that Alexander had told me.

"We think so," he said.

"You think so?" The prince's eyes widened behind his Jaddian mask.

Alexander scowled at him. "Dorayaica appeared in holograph to demand my father's surrender after the initial assault. I saw the footage with my own eyes before we made the jump to warp and came here."

"But there's no sign of its ship," said Simonyi, waving a hand through the holographs displayed before us. "That big moon."

Dharan-Tun, I meant to say, but could not make the sound.

"This does not mean the Scourge is not present," said the Jaddian Admiral Serpico, a severe-looking aryabite man whose image flickered at the prince's right hand. From the prince's left, Lady Kalima—evidently still more than a concubine—voiced her agreement.

"According to the report, Dorayaica appears almost daily to demand the Emperor's surrender," the scholiast said, tapping a printed copy of the report before him for illustration.

Bassander's eyes caught mine, and I knew we were remembering the same thing, the Prophet's image shimmering taller than the mountains, its ghostly feet astride the shattered starport that stretched before the Storm Wall. "Just like Berenike," he said.

"The same demand?" asked Captain Simonyi, as much a ghost as the Jaddians, and looking a little worse for wear for having been wrenched—like nearly all of us—from fugue.

"Does it matter?" Kalima di Sayyiph's rich tones contrasted with the all the masculine rasp and harshness of the other voices, drawing the gaze of nearly the whole table. Only the scholiast and I were immune. I had returned to watching the planet Fidchell through the window, turning slowly against the iron bristles of the station. More than anything, I wished that Valka were by my side.

Lin's voice had gone black and heavy as he threw the *alkidar's* question back at her. "Does it matter if it's him?"

"It's *all* him," I said, speaking for the first time in minutes. "It. The Prophet. There are no other princes. No other blood-clans. Don't you understand? There are *two* Emperors in the galaxy now. One red, one white." I ticked them off on my fingers for emphasis. "Dorayaica intends to make a spectacle of our Emperor," I said, speaking to Alexander as I had the day before. I massaged my throat, recalling the collar I'd been made to wear. The chains. Turning to address the whole council—and the scholiast in particular—I continued, "The Cielcin are not beasts, and their Prophet . . . counselor, the Prophet could match wits with the very best of your order." I let my hand fall, shut my eyes. "I was its prisoner for *years*. It might have killed me any time, and nearly did. But it did not want to kill me, it *needed* to kill me in the sight of all its kind." I did not know if Dorayaica believed killing me would usher in its paradise, or if it truly believed it could abolish the universe itself, or if that abolition were some kind of metaphor for the Cielcin Empire it meant to build. It didn't really matter. Gathering my words, I continued, "The Prophet meant me to be the rock on which it built its new dominion. It means William to be the rod that breaks our own."

"It would never work," the scholiast said. "A new Emperor could be crowned."

"The holy bloodline is immortal," Simonyi said.

"But the Emperor is *not!*" I scoffed at both of them. "You think Dorayaica does not know this? You think it does not know how many heirs the Emperor has?" I swept my gaze over the entire council. Over Lin looming like a colossus, over his scholiast and first officer, over Simonyi and the other captains, over Kaim and the Jaddian contingent—all flickering like candle flames. "It knows. It knows it can't simply decapitate the Empire. It knows that if William has not already selected an heir, the Council and Chantry will elect one from among his children. But it isn't trying to decapitate the Empire. It's trying to demoralize us."

I did not stand, but hollow-eyed held Lin's gaze across the table—and no fire held between us, only cold regard and understanding. I realized I had crossed my arms, was holding myself close as I was able. It was all I could do not to shake, to recall the horrors of Dharan-Tun. Not releasing myself, I felt the scar behind my right ear. "If Dorayaica captures His Radiance, his pet magi will broadcast whatever humiliation it has planned to every human world in the galaxy. When we have all seen Caesar tortured, raped, used for a footstool—his belly slit open and his innards tossed to its servants . . . no one will *want* the Solar Throne. No one will believe in it. The Empire is a belief! A commandment! What is Caesar if not a man who can command that he is Caesar? Who can prove it by the sword?

"The Emperor is a symbol," I continued. "Kill him and you kill the man, yes. But capture him? Humiliate him—and more—let all know he is humiliated? You kill the symbol. Combine that with any succession crisis that might occur if the Council and Chantry don't like William's choice of heir, if he has one . . . the Empire will shake itself to pieces, never mind how many legitimate heirs there are. Each heir may become an emperor to *someone*."

That brought the entire gathering to silence—the Imperial contingent, at least. I could feel young Alexander's eyes on me, recalling our conversation of the previous day. "My father is alive," the prince said again. "I will not discuss the fallout of his death while he yet lives. Am I clear?"

I bowed my head, but said no further word.

Perhaps sensing the tension between us, Lady Kalima spoke up. "We should count ourselves blessed," she said, words breaking the cloud I'd cast over the proceedings like the sun. "It seems the enemy has gone to great pains to keep your Emperor alive. In this, even the Cielcin share our goals. It may be their undoing."

Prince Kaim agreed. "We have our chance," he said.

Captain Afsharirad interjected. "It is one hundred and ninety-seven light-years to Perfugium. That is nearly eighteen months' travel by our slowest ships."

Lin looked at me, anticipating my thoughts. "We have ships that could be there faster. Lord Marlowe, you could take the *Ascalon*."

"And slip through the Cielcin blockade unaided?" I felt my frown deepen. The notion—once uttered—seemed madness in my ears. "Maybe. But even if we reached the surface, the city must be crawling with Cielcin. You saw the dig teams on holographs. We might join the Emperor in his bunkers, but we're not like to make it out. It would only take one scout to see us and shoot us down. The *Ascalon* is not invisible. Without support from the fleet, we'll be picked off the minute we land." And we would have to land. For the *Ascalon* to remain in the air was to increase the risk of detection. We had evaded capture on Ganelon, yes, but the *Ascalon* had been in-system for less than a couple hours. It could not leave us to find the Emperor and return. We would have need of haste, and need it nearby.

"And if you're caught," Simonyi said, "the Cielcin may opt to destroy you and the bunkers alike. Antimatter *could* penetrate to that depth."

"You think they would do that?" Kalima di Sayyiph asked. "Even if they want the Emperor alive?"

"They will kill him rather than risk losing him, I am thinking, *mia qal*," said Prince Kaim.

I flinched at the Jaddian term of affection. *My heart.* Jinan Azhar had called me that. I did not like to think of Jinan Azhar, and wondered briefly what had become of her. For all I knew she was in the fleet alongside us. On the *Mnemon,* perhaps, or on Afsharirad's *Albaspatha.* She might be dead, killed in battle or by Ever-Fleeting Time.

I did not ask.

The prince steepled his gloved hands. The gold filigree about the eye-holes of his mask twinkled, even on the projection. "We will take the whole fleet, then."

Lin's gaze snapped toward the prince then, daring to hope. "You will come with us?"

"We came to fight," the prince replied, turning his eyes to me. "Against such demons as these, all men are brothers."

Returning the prince's gentle nod, I said, "Would the Lothrians felt the same."

"The Lothrians!" Admiral Velkan Serpico nearly spat. "We heard word of their betrayal."

Kaim raised a gloved hand to silence his subordinate. "The Lothrians are nearly demons themselves." The prince stood straighter then, directed his words to Bassander Lin. "We will fight with you."

One could almost feel the spirits of those in the room rally. I studied Prince Kaim then, Sir Olorin behind his mask. I told myself not to forget that here was a prince of Jadd, and no mere friend—of the Empire, and of mine. He had said it himself. Should the Empire fall, the Cielcin would come for Jadd next. The Principalities shared a border with the Common-wealth, whose black allegiance with the Pale spelled only future war and turmoil for the men of Jadd. It was in Kaim-Olorin's interest to defend the Emperor and Empire.

At length, Alexander turned and inclined his head to Kaim's projection. "My family is in your debt, Prince of Jadd. Your fleet will help us break their own." He turned his face to the projections, to an image of the clustered Cielcin moons shining above the face of the Perfugium, an image his own destroyer had taken as it streaked toward the edge of Perfugium system.

Seven moons.

I thought of the hundreds I had seen above Eue, some near, some remote. Some had been vast almost as Dharan-Tun, while some were little more than asteroids. Many showed the scars of old fighting, black craters and deep canyons where plasma fire had cracked and melted the deepest ice. Others bristled where the machinery of vasty engines hollowed their icy surfaces, while others were smooth as glass.

"So many together . . ." the young prince said.

"It is as I said," I whispered. "They are an *empire* now. One clan. One tribe." I shook a finger at the holograph. "This will be the way of things from now on. We will have to defend our core worlds. We do not have the ships to defend the colonies. The battles will be greater, but fewer in number. Mark my words."

"Then it is well we have come!" said the Prince of Jadd.

"It is," Lin agreed, and bowed his head once more. "You honor us, Highness."

"It is necessary," the prince replied, made a gesture of acknowledgment with one hand. "What is necessary is right." Kaim du Otranto rose from his seat, and extending a hand toward me, he said, "Rescuing your Emperor must be our highest priority. If Lord Marlowe's ship can indeed slip the blockade, I suggest he do so." I flinched, but Prince Kaim was not quite finished. "I shall accompany him."

In unison, Serpico and Afsharirad turned toward their master. "Highness, you must not! It is too dangerous."

More Olorin than Kaim for a moment, the prince waved the admiral and captain down. "I will be in no more danger than the Sollan Emperor."

"That is precisely the issue!" Serpico hissed in Jaddian.

"*Silencios, Velkan!*" Prince Kaim commanded, and the admiral bowed his head. "*Tu parolla ati domi tuo.*" Mollified, the admiral bobbed his head and drew back. Returning his focus to the room at large, the prince said, "I will accompany Lord Marlowe and rescue your Emperor."

My own heart was suddenly light. I did not wish to enter the labyrinth again, to go into the net of battle and the trenches. And yet to do so with Olorin once more by my side! It was as if I were a boy again on Emesh, off on that first adventure.

Kaim-Olorin laid a reassuring hand on the shoulder of his admiral. "Serpico, I shall take Tiada and Baraz with me, and as many of my guard as may be." His image appeared to lean over the table, holographed elbows touching the glass, hands steepled. "Lord Marlowe, how many will this ship of yours hold?"

"Half a hundred in fugue," I said. "We can load a hundred for a short journey."

"Just like at Ganelon," Bassander said.

Disbelief coloring my voice, I said, "Just like at Ganelon." I was never going to get away, would never be free of the curse and burden of duty. Again I looked to Kaim. Did this prince of Jadd hope to curry favor with the Emperor by riding personally to his rescue? What did he stand to gain?

For the second time in my life, Olorin Milta had recruited me, and this time I could not run. On Emesh, I had leaped at the chance to seek for Vorgossos, to make a difference in the world. There, on Fidchell, I wanted nothing more than to take Valka and run, to live as we had lived on Colchis—without a care.

But Fate had spun its net, and we were caught in it. Our chance to escape on Ganelon had evaporated with the coming of the Jaddian fleet—our salvation and our doom.

We would go to Perfugium.

Our only route out was *through*.

"All right," I said, and rounded on Lin. "All right then. But I want Valka. And Commander Aristedes. And I want your man, Sharp." Without warning, my fist acted on its own and pounded the tabletop, making the scholiast jump. I chewed my tongue, held my breath as Gibson himself had taught me oh so long ago.

Rage is blindness, he always said.

"Done," Lin said. He turned to his captains and to Serpico and Afsharirad. "We'll strike them from orbit and buy Marlowe and His Highness the opportunity they need to slip down to Resonno and make contact with the Emperor. With any luck, the Pale will be too distracted to notice."

"And if they are not?" Serpico asked.

"We must clear the field for a landing party," Lin said. "Captain Simonyi's ship carries sixty thousand men on ice. If it comes to it, we will meet on the ground and in the air." He turned from me to the prince and his admiral as he spoke. "I will have Fidchell Station telegraph Perfugium and let them know that we are coming."

I laid my hands flat on the table, unconsciously mirroring Lin's posture from my seat. Unheard by the others, I muttered, "Lorian isn't going to like this."

CHAPTER 33

THE CITY OF BLACK SEPULCHERS

"I DON'T LIKE THIS," Lorian said. "What happened to *Lin needs you, Aristedes. You're wasted on ground engagements?* I ask you!" The small man peered nervously around the corner of the crumbling tower that marked the end of a once-handsome boulevard. He looked absurd in his undersized skin-suit. The form-fitting garment—padded though it was—only enhanced his resemblance to a child. *To a scarecrow,* I corrected myself, so thin was he. No armor had been found to fit him, and the red tunic he wore over the environment suit was several sizes too big.

Hauling him back around the corner, I said, "*I* need you. Someone has to organize the retreat. Get back!"

The curving blade shapes of inhuman fliers slashed across the heavens. Safe in the shadow of what once had been the arched entrance to a hotel, we watched them go a moment, slicing across the blue-gray sky. Rubble and the slag of fallen buildings blocked the roads, and but for the whine of those fliers, the world was strangely silent. Fires still burned in places, rising from ruined townhouses and blasted streets, or from the edges of the vast and craterous desolations where the Pale had shelled the city from orbit.

But the battle—the real battle—had happened long ago.

"Another patrol," said Quentin Sharp near at hand. "They must be onto us."

"If 'twere onto us," Valka replied, "surely we'd be dead."

"Is it always like this?" Lorian asked lamely, turning his white-visored head from Sharp to myself. "I don't like this."

Glad my mask hid my expression, I said, "Weren't you all ready to fight at Ganelon?" I had to remind myself that for Lorian, war had been the bright lights of a ship's console, schematics and statistics, readouts and data.

"That was different!" Lorian protested. "That was an Extrasolarian fortress with a light garrison! This is . . ."

"War, lad," Sharp said. "It's fucking war. Has been for centuries. Where've you been?"

Lorian bristled at being called *lad* by a plebeian doubtless less than half his age—or by a mere centurion—and instinctively Valka put a hand on his shoulder to stay his riposte. It wasn't the time. "Do you see the Jaddians?" she asked.

"They can't have landed far," Sharp replied, adjusting his MAG rifle on its shoulder strap. We'd dropped in two groups, spread out to minimize our chances of turning up on Cielcin sensors. A large, dense cluster of falling men might appear on scan as a smudge or blur, where smaller, sparser clusters might slip through unnoticed.

A flash of light filled the sky above, for a moment washing out the optics in my suit. Beside me, Valka and Lorian each shielded their eyes. "Them's our boys, boys!" Sharp called softly to his men. About half a hundred of Sharp's Dragonslayers hunkered in the bombed-out opening of the hotel behind, apparently at their ease. I glanced back at them as the light of the silent blast cleared, each man waiting patiently for the signal from the Jaddians. Turning away, I shaded my eyes—a pointless gesture. My suit's optics had adjusted to the ambient light of the blast above, polarized to levels my merely human retinas might endure. Beyond the sky, Lin and Serpico had engaged the enemy, and the coming of their twin fleets was like the dawning of new suns above Perfugium.

"We haven't far to go," Valka said. "The hippodrome's just over that hill. This gate the Emperor's man spoke of should be below." She had studied what plans of the city were available on the voyage from Fidchell, and so had slouched into the role of guide. Valka spoke like one born to that place.

Sharp eyed her warily. "Sure of that, are you?"

Valka glared at him, and though I could imagine her face through that visor plain as daylight, the centurion could not, and was not cowed. "'Tis *your* intelligence," she said coldly. Sir Gray Rinehart had managed to get a signal through as we arrived in-system. A short message. The Emperor and his people had survived—against all hope—in the bunkers beneath the city of Resonno. All that remained of the ducal palace was a ziggurat of white stone rising cracked and burned black by the touch of high explosives. The stone itself had bubbled and run like wax in places, and the buildings above were nothing more than fingered shadows of metal beams and iron skeletons of fallen towers.

Nothing grew in Resonno anymore. It was not snow that fell upon the broken city, as had fallen on Carteia, but ash. Gray ash coated everything, lending its deadening hush to the world. Though it was summer, the empty streets reminded me of nothing so much as a winter wood, as the English garden at Maddalo House when Sananne was lost in snow. How I longed for that old place then. Maddalo House had been a prison, but it had been *mine*, and a place where Valka and I had lived in peace.

I would never know peace again.

Should we save the Emperor, my reward would be only another impossible task. To kill a god—if the Emperor had his way—and then what? Unable to keep me at court for fear the Chantry or his own wife would attempt to finish what they'd begun, Caesar would be forced to drive me ever before him—like a dog—until I died in harness.

And if he died in our attempt . . . did I truly believe Alexander would let me go?

"We should try calling them again," Sharp said.

Lorian snapped, "There's too much interference! You'll never get a message through, even tight-beam. Besides, those bunkers are hardened against *atomics*. You think your dinky little radio's going to penetrate all that lead?"

"They got a message out," he said.

"By *telegraph*!" Lorian hissed. "A telegraph would have reached us if we were halfway to Andromeda!" The commander looked away, disgusted, said again, "I don't like this."

Eager to make peace, I laid a hand on Lorian's shoulder. Affecting an ease I did not feel, I said, "You just don't like it because it's not your plan."

"I don't like it because it's not *a* plan," the intus replied. "Where are those bloody Jaddians?"

In answer, I turned to Valka. "Can you get a sense of their location?"

Valka cocked her head, as if listening for some disturbance on the wind. "'Tis too much static. I'm not sure if 'tis radiation left over from the bombing or some device of the enemy . . ." Her words drifted far away. My own suit's instrumentation had offered no warnings about radiation. The Cielcin did not often use atomics. They favored plasma fire or kinetic weapons, more often than not simply dropping great rocks—pieces of their own worldships—from orbit. But there was a first time for everything. At length she shook her head. "'Tis nothing."

"We should get moving," Sharp said. "Mads! Teren!" The centurion sketched a circle in the air, the sign for his men to make ready.

"Shouldn't we wait for the Jaddians?" Lorian asked.

"They're not—" *coming,* Sharp might have said, but at that moment a peal of terrible thunder rent the sky, stopping the centurion short. The shadow of another patrol ship passed before the sun.

Valka's hand seized me by the shoulder, and her voice came out a hushed gasp. "Hadrian!"

It was not thunder.

It was a word.

"Humans!" it said, and despite the unnatural depth of that voice, I knew it, recognized the high coldness, the flat affect, the erudition. The inhumanity of it. Adrenaline slammed through my chest like the point of a frozen knife, and I felt every vein in me constrict. Valka gripped me even harder then, willing me to be calm, to master the panic pounding through me with every newly ragged heartbeat.

It all came back to me in an instant. The cave. The wall. The pit. Adric White's head on its platter, the tables laid with rotten meat; white-faced courtiers with blood dripping from inhuman mouths; all the horrors and demonic decadence of Dharan-Tun came flooding back from the depths of my tormented mind. I put my hands to my helmet as if to cover my ears, but the voice got in still, conducted by my armor's audio system.

It was the Prophet's voice.

"Your world is lost! Your armada scattered! Surrender!" Syriani roared, words beating like the distant dropping of bombs on the margins of that ruined city. *"Surrender your Emperor and I will spare all that remain!"*

"What's wrong with him?" Sharp asked Valka, peering down at me. "What's happening?"

Her arms around me, Valka hissed at the centurion to shut up.

"It's here," I managed through clenched teeth. "It's *here.*"

As if to explain my answer, the great voice boomed again, *"I am Shiomu Elusha, King of the Cielcin, Scourge of Earth. Surrender your Emperor to me, and I will spare what remains of your world. You will be allowed to live as slaves. You will pay tribute to my legions. But you will live."*

Lorian peered out from the shadow of the colonnade. "I can't see it. The holograph."

"Breathe, *anaryan,*" Valka said into my ears. "Just breathe." She had endured decades of my nightmares, and so could handle these waking terrors.

Wrapping an arm about her, I willed myself to stillness. *Fear is a poison,*

I thought, feeling that poison at work in my veins, in my ragged breathing. "Fear is a poison."

"He was seven years a prisoner of the Cielcin," Valka said to the centurion, answering his question at last. "Did you not know?"

Sharp did not reply, but took a step back.

"It's here," I said, and shook my head, holding Valka tighter. "If it's *here* . . ." I could not bear the thought of facing Syriani Dorayaica again. Silver blood glistened on its face, dripped from crooked fingers, from severed neck. Again I saw the vision I'd seen that one dark night at Akterumu, the slender hands prising themselves free of Dorayaica's headless corpse. Again I shook my head, attempting to banish the gray fog that muddled my mind. Finding a thread, I seized it. "If it's still demanding the Emperor, they don't have him." I let Valka go. My chest was heaving. "We're not too late."

Boom!

The distant blast of some explosive charge knocked ash free from the capitals of the pillars over our heads, dislodged too that foggy piece of my soul. "We have to go!"

"But the Jaddians!" Lorian said.

"They know to head for the hippodrome!" I said, reaching for my sword. My hand found the pistol I'd brought instead, and I drew it forth. I had not replaced the scimitar I'd lost to Takeshi on Ganelon. I had but the pistol, my knife, and my shield. There had been no time to send for a smith from Elos or Phaia to craft a new hilt for the old highmatter core, and the ceramic blade had been as much liability as boon in the battle against the sorcerers—leastways in the hands of one so used to highmatter.

I prayed we would not come to pitched battle. Our mission was to find the Emperor and escape *before* the Cielcin even knew we were there. Let them think Serpico and Lin intended to burn their fleet before so much as attempting a landing on Perfugium itself. Let them think that we were natives, survivors picking the city's bones.

We hurried up the street, feet kicking up little clouds of soot. Seldom had I been so glad of my suit and of my respirator. I was the certain the air must be a terror, thick with ash and stinking of the sack of cities and of burned men. At every cross-street, every shattered window, I expected to look in upon a tableau of horrors: on mangled corpses half-eaten and despoiled. I never did. Signs of habitation there were, and of violence. Burned-out homes and storefronts—tables overturned in what appeared to

have once been a winesink; wrecked fliers and groundcars parked or abandoned in the streets; windows boarded up to defend against the Cielcin,
against human looters. Words and symbols daubed in ash marked still-
standing walls, threatened the invaders or else warned scavengers against
trespassing. It broke my heart to think of men turning against men in the
desperate struggle to stay alive. On our approach, I'd seen the highways
leading out of Resonno choked with vehicles fleeing for the countryside.

They hadn't made it out.

"Imperial Command, this is four-oh-nine Centaurine," Sharp spoke
into his comm as we hunkered in the shadows of a line of stone houses.
"Imperial Command, do you copy?"

"You won't get anyone," Valka told him.

Sharp waved her to silence a moment. Nothing. "Have to try." The
pale shape of a skull glowered down from the tumbled-down wall of a
Chantry sanctum, leering up the street. The words XENOS GET OUT
showed beneath it, white on black stone. Pointing up at it, the centurion
said, "There's someone alive out here."

Another loud explosion rocked the city a few blocks distant, and an
instant later I caught the sound of gunfire, the shout of human voices.
"Olorin?" Valka asked.

"Who?" one of the men asked.

"The Jaddians," I said. "Should we help them?"

"This'll all be wasted if we don't make it to the bunkers," said Lorian
Aristedes.

The top of the hill lay just past the crumbling sanctum. Reaching
the crest, I stopped, pausing a moment beside the petrified trunk of a tree.
The bomb that killed the Chantry had turned the wood to stone. The
hippodrome—what remained of it—stretched out below us like the rotting carcass of a whale. The gutted remnants of colonnades and vomitoria
looked like so much exposed bone, and the huge clockwork mechanisms
that hoisted the pillars and rings atop and between which the gladiators
and myrmidons had fought shone in the wan sun. It was longer, narrower
than the arena in Borosevo, designed more for horse races than ritual combat, but standing beside the stone tree, I could almost hear the cheering as
we staggered out to fight for our lives and coin.

The tree above my head exploded.

Sharp tackled me to the ground an instant after. Too late. We were
lucky, each of us was shielded, but all the same . . .

"Taking fire!" one of the others shouted. "On the right!"

"Where?"

"Open fire, you dogs!"

"Get off me, centurion!" I growled, turning my head to find our enemy. I saw a flicker of white on the rooftops to the right, a blur of motion. "Demons . . ." Sharp offered a hand, and taking it, I bellowed the word. "Demons!"

The chimeras had come. Inhuman brains in iron casings, bodies of ceramic and steel. I saw one bound from one rooftop to the next, loping like a wolf. Sharp wasted no time. The centurion slung his MAG rifle from his shoulder, aimed, fired in less than two seconds. Only then did I realize it had been he who had saved us with Urbaine in the tower. The depleted uranium shot tore through the demon just below its lone red eye. It tumbled as it fell, hit the street with a terrific sound.

"Bastard wasn't even shielded," Sharp said with a satisfied jerk of his head, lifting his rifle.

"Loose!" shouted one of the others, and an instant later three grenades arced through the air and connected with the downed monstrosity. Sharp's men hadn't hesitated a second.

Lorian grabbed my arm. "We have to move!" he said.

In a second, I outpaced the small commander. Valka at my side, we led the way down the sloping avenue toward the craggy facade of the hippodrome. If Rinehart's telegraph could be believed, there was a hatchway in the building's hypogeum—one of many yet unfound by the Cielcin—that fed into the city's network of underground bunkers and the catacombs which housed the sleepers in the colonial stores. The telegraph had said Rinehart would station men at the hatch and have them ready to bring the rescue team to the Emperor. In theory then, we would not have to find the hatch, only to get close enough for the Imperial Guard to find us.

"What happened to the Jaddians?" Valka gasped, hot on my heels.

Another explosion shook the air, and the brown stone facade of a house to our right exploded into a billion tiny fragments. I had a momentary, horrible vision of one of the chimeric demons standing amid that devastation like the idol of some pagan cult, four-armed, dog-legged, white as snow. The ash billowed about it in thick clouds, for a moment veiling all but its lonely red eye. It raised one taloned hand and fired.

The plasma bolt cracked against my shield, and I turned away. Kept running.

Somewhere in the city, above and behind me, a Chantry bell began. Was it in the little sanctum we'd passed? No, it could not be. The sound was too far off. The lonely beauty and the purity of that sound—the sound of home, of countless towns and villages on countless worlds—smote my heart. It was the sound of man, of the Imperium I both loathed and loved. How small it sounded! And how defiant!

"Do you hear that?" called one of Sharp's troopers.

"Someone's seen us!" Lorian gasped.

"A signal?" Sharp asked. "The Jaddians?"

I did not answer. I did not think it was the Jaddians pulling that chain, nor would any of the Pale have rung such a note. No. We had been seen, were even then being watched by what few survivors remained in that wretched place. They knew we had come, had found a way to signal even through the jammed comms.

The bells.

A hundred yards of open ground separated us from the outer wall of the hippodrome. The blackened fingers of burned-out trees lined the open laneway with the hulks of blasted cars. The avenue descended into a cutting as it curved left to encircle the arena, and on the right a retaining wall reared up, hugging the bend of the road. Ahead, I could see where the high and narrow arches stood above the entryway, the door glass blown out, the gray dust piled in great drifts about the gates.

Not far!

The adrenaline still resounding in my veins, breath ragged and gritty, I spurred myself forward. If we could just get out of the open . . .

Another shot struck the earth not three yards to my left. The blast wave lifted me from my feet and sent me tumbling through the ash across the broad avenue. Landing on my belly, I managed to get a knee under myself and half rose. "Valka!" She'd fallen just beside me, and rolled onto her back.

"I'm all right!"

The crack from Sharp's rifle split the air, and staggering to my feet, I saw the line of his men streaming down the slope from the ruined sanctum, half-turned to return fire on the chimeras that had hounded us up the street. Even as I watched, one of the monsters leaped down from the flattened rooftops and fell among the men. A grenade went off, blasting the creature's arm out of joint. Still it raged, its white scimitar sketching a crimson maze among our men.

"Get down!" Valka's words sliced across my mind, and an instant later she was on top of me, knocking me back to the earth. A beam of blue-hot light slashed through the air where I had been a moment before. Rolling out from under her, I saw our new enemy.

At first, I thought it was Teyanu. The hulking *vayadan*-general was the size of a tank, death on six legs. This chimera was smaller, but of similar build, not crab-like as Teyanu was, but spidery, the chassis that housed what remained of the Cielcin brain smaller and bulbous, swaying as it scuttled forward on legs like saber blades. Its single eye gleamed bright as a dying star in the smooth orb it called a head, and upon its back the turret of its weapon shone brighter still as it swiveled to face me.

"*Iukatta!*" I said, lurching to my feet, hoping the sound of its own language in the mouth of mere humanity might give the creature pause.

The spider plunged one claw-tipped foot into the pavement at its feet, stomping closer. If my words had caused the beast to hesitate, it was only for a second. The lens of its beam cannon flared, targeting laser painting my chest. Shielded as I was, it would not be enough. So great an energy weapon was sure to drain the battery.

There was nowhere to run, and no time to run in. I threw up a hand in vain attempt to shield myself from the coming blast, straining as I had strained at the altar before Miudanar's skull, searching for a light from that higher world I had once possessed the art to see. As the world slowed about me in what I knew must be my final instant, it shimmered, rippling as it had a hundred times before, across time's limitless possibilities.

I *saw*. Or thought I saw.

The demon's fell machinery whined as it primed itself to fire, and I realized the light was only that of the demon's target laser painting my suit's optic sensors.

I clenched my teeth.

But the shot never came.

Through the clouds of drifting ash, a strange, ululating cry rang out. "*Alala! Alala!*"

Something struck the spider-thing in the side of its metal body, slow enough to penetrate the chimera's shield. I heard the *clink* of metal on metal, saw the faint red flashing, and knew it was a magnetic grenade. A second later, the chimera's side erupted in violet flame, one of its legs torn clean off. It staggered, but did not die.

Again the strange, musical cry. "*Alala! Alala!*"

Through the dust, a fey light appeared, not red, but crystal blue. Blue as moonlight.

A trio of hooded black shapes sliced through the haze, shards of crystal in their hands. Blades of highmatter. The weapons flashed, severing blade-edged limbs, carving the body of the chimera open.

Black-masked, black-armored beneath the traditional crimson *mandyas*, Prince Kaim raised his sword in greeting. I raised my hand to match him. We looked strangely kin to one another, red and black, though the prince's armor glittered with golden filigree, the eyes outlined, the brows and sculpted mustache gleaming in the light of his sword. How he and his two companions—a woman and a man—moved in the cumbersome half-robes, I could not imagine.

But move they did.

The woman flowed like water, dashing away across the flat yard to rejoin the Dragonslayers. She leaped, and such was the strength of her eali blood that she soared nearly two dozen feet through the air—over the heads of the legionnaires—and struck down one of the lesser demons with a single blow. A hail of plasma rained from across the avenue, and turning my head I saw the Jaddian mamluks—homunculi all—moving through the ashen fog like the tide.

"You're just in time!" I said to the prince.

"Indeed!" The prince bowed his head, and sparing a glance for Valka, he carried on, "I had hoped to see one of your miracles, my friend."

A stiff wind raked the street alongside the hippodrome, pulling my cape with it. "They don't come easy," I said. Since Akterumu, they had not come at all.

"Perhaps not," Kaim said. Had he been watching us? Lying in wait to see if something might happen? I looked at him sidelong, no longer sure I should trust him as I had been. "But this day will be long. There may yet be—"

The crack of Sharp's MAG rifle brought us both back to our place, and the centurion wheeled round. "That's the last of them!" The centurion paused long enough to pull back the slide on his weapon and insert another of the uranium rounds. "Your Highness, my lord, we can't stay here. We're too exposed."

As if to underscore his point, a shadow passed overhead with a noise like the growl of some tiger in the jungles of Earth's forgotten past. "Fliers!" shouted one of the men.

"Into the hippodrome!" I said, drawing my pistol and brandishing it in lieu of the sword. "Take point, centurion!" Sharp thumped his chest in salute and barked commands to his men, shouting for Mads and Altaric. As the Dragonslayers pushed past to take the lead into the ruinous coliseum, Valka took my hand. She did not speak, but squeezed it, held it fast.

One last fight, I told myself. *One last fight.*

I would beg my leave of the Emperor, as I had of Alexander. That was what I'd do.

But I knew he would never let me go.

"Are you all right?" Valka muttered in my ear. "You froze up, *anaryan*."

"I thought I could see it," I replied to her in Panthai. "Just for a moment. I thought I could *see* again."

"Din chaksyn?" she asked. *Your vision?*

I nodded stiffly.

Prince Kaim stood by all the while, listening beneath his mask and hood, looking like some gilt- and silk-wrapped executioner in his blacks and damasked scarlets. I got the sense that he and the Jaddians had been watching our battle down the avenue from the crumbling sanctum, waiting, their prince hoping to see precisely what I had showed him. Had they held back until the final moment?

Perhaps sensing some fragment of my disquiet, Prince Kaim du Otranto said, "My soldiers will cover our retreat. Tiada! Baraz!" His voice rang out like the bells, attracting the attention of the two other Maeskoloi. He made a tight gesture with his free hand, thumb and last finger hooked. I did not grasp its meaning, but the others did, and raised their swords in acknowledgment. "Your man is right, we must not linger." That said, he bowed slightly, gallant as anything, and indicated that Valka, Lorian, and I should move on ahead.

I had forgotten Lorian in the chaos. The little man limped on beside us, fell behind as Valka started to jog, pulling me along with her. I shook her off, and turning back asked, "Are you all right?"

Faceless behind his helmet mask, the intus shook his head. "I'm fine." But I marked the way he held his arm as he brushed past me, stiff and awkward. He grunted sharply as he took a step, and I heard a faint *snap* as he tugged his left arm back into joint. I reassured myself that the commander's bones were no more brittle than mine, but his limbs slid out of joint and his nerves went numb without warning. How much pain must young Aristedes endure on a daily basis? As much as I had? More?

And mine had ended.

The gray shadows of the coliseum arch seemed almost to grasp at us as we drew near. Logic said the door we sought must be in the hypogeum, beneath the level of the killing floor. Beyond that great entrepot, the lobby sang of past greatness. The marble floor lay chipped and gouged where the metal claws of inhuman feet had marred the once-lovely surface, half-obscured by drifts of ash. Here and there mighty columns lay like the trunks of felled trees, and the broken windows of the ticket station between the security scanners watched like the empty eyes of dead men.

All was silent but for the noise of our feet echoing off the barrel vaults above. Sharp's men had leaped the turnstiles and were already climbing the steps to the ring that surrounded the stands.

"Strange there are no bodies," remarked one of the prince's *sulshawar*-protectors in Jaddian.

"Non, es nonna," I said in the same language. "They'll have rounded up the living and the dead alike and taken them all back up to space. This siege has gone on a long time."

"An army marches on its stomach," Lorian said, speaking perfect Jaddian. I looked sharply at the little man. I'd not realized he knew the language. The intus stopped and leaned against a column. Switching pointedly back to the standard, he said, "There was a bloody bit of fighting here. See those plasma scores?" He pointed at a set of deep, black scars on the inner wall where the gray stone had melted and blistered.

Kaim looked round at the devastation, highmatter blade still gleaming in his hand. "This is the worst I have seen," he said, speaking Galstani for the benefit of Sharp and his men. "This world. There is almost nothing left."

"Through here!" cried the centurion in question, red helmet reappearing around an arch to our right. "We can get down!"

Valka helping Lorian, we caught up with the command centurion. Sharp had found one of the vomitoria that passed from the arena's perimeter concourse through to the stands. In times of peace, the commoners would pass through the hall and—turning left or right—mount the steps that led up into the stands, there to watch their violence and their sport.

All was empty now, the echoing of feet the only sound.

We climbed *down* instead. Some blast had shattered the rail ahead and collapsed a portion of the wall beneath it, so that a rough slope of masonry descended some half a hundred feet to the killing floor.

Coming out behind me, Lorian cursed.

We had all seen something of the devastation from the hill above, but to stand inside it was something else entirely. The Cielcin had shelled the great building in their initial assault on Perfugium. One blast had torn a corner off the far end of the circus, and the space inside the orbit of the racing track was a horror of pits and broken masonry. I could see the levels of the hypogeum below the killing floor exposed like the bones of a rotting carcass, level upon level where the beasts and prisoners were held awaiting their day of execution.

Sharp's men had already made it to the rail and were picking their way down the slope to the exposed hypogeum.

"Hadrian!" Valka grabbed my arm.

I froze, looking round to see just what it was that had put such fear into Valka's voice. There was nothing.

Nothing to *see*.

Had you stood beside me, you might not have noticed it at first. None of the others had. A faint, soporific droning, as of the whir of a trillion insects far and far away, or of the thrum of engines through yards of tempered steel. Nothing to be frightened of, save that the city had been silent before.

I tipped my head, listening.

Valka's ears were no sharper than mine, but her memory was. It was a sound I had not heard since that black day on Eue, and seldom so far off—or in such number.

"*Nahute,*" she breathed, and seeing that I then heard what she heard, shouted, "*Nahute!*"

CHAPTER 34

THE WEEPING WALL

"FOS!" **BARAZ WAS SHOUTING,** calling for light. The gray sun of Perfugium fell through in places, illuminating the dusty halls, but if we were to find Sir Gray's hatch and access the catacombs, I suspected we would need to delve deeper than the sun had gone.

The mamluks, ever silent, activated suit lamps in near synchrony. The homunculi clone soldiers were perfectly obedient, programmed—in a sense—by RNA indoctrination whilst still growing in their tanks. Their beams and the crystal glare of highmatter led the way.

"Hurry!" one of Sharp's men called back.

"Try calling again!" Sharp himself.

I heard the comm whine and the distinctive crackle of static from the suit speakers of a man ahead. "Imperial Command, this is four-oh-nine Centaurine. We are here for evac. Imperial Command, do you copy?"

Nothing.

"Stairs here!" announced another of the Dragonslayers.

Sharp made a slashing gesture. "Check it out!" I could hear the tension in his voice. "We can't have more than two minutes before that swarm is on us. We've got to get deeper! Shut the doors if we can! Do we have any idea where this fucking gate is?"

"Rinehart said it was in the hippodrome subterrane," Lorian said, rubbing his bad shoulder. Again, he cursed. "This is suicide! Why in Earth's holy name was I not at the briefing? I could have talked some sense into all of you maniacs!"

"Take it up with Lin!" I said, moving toward the stairs Sharp's man had found. Looking back over my shoulder, I found Olorin standing a short distance back up the hall. "Your Highness! We've your safety to think of as well!" I gestured at the door.

Olorin glanced back up the hall toward the surface, shouted an order to Baraz in lightning-fast Jaddian. The junior Maeskolos bowed his hooded head and took a step back. "Your Highness!" I shouted again.

As if jolted, Olorin sped toward me, placed a hand on my shoulder as he passed through the door, the third swordmaster, Tiada, following him close as his own shadow. "Baraz will hold the way for us," he said, and hurried down the stairs after the first of Sharp's men, a line of the mamluks following in his wake.

"Hadrian!" Valka had gone after Olorin, but had stopped at the first landing. Lorian was still beside her. "Come on!"

I glanced back at Baraz. The Maeskolos stood ready in the hall, so still even the golden tassels of his *mandyas* might have been carved from stone. "Get *this* door between you and them at least!" I shouted at him, speaking Jaddian to be sure he understood.

Baraz gave no sign that he had heard me.

Hissing, frustrated, I turned and slammed the door. Sharp appeared at my shoulder. "Thought you went on ahead?" I said.

The centurion shook his head. "Mads took point. Here." He raised his plasma burner to fuse the door shut.

I slapped his hand down. "The *nahute* don't have thumbs!" I growled, following Valka and Lorian down the stairs. "And that mad Jaddian will want to follow as soon as that swarm hits!" Welded shut or no, the *nahute* drones would drill their way through the door in time, but assuming the lower levels of the hypogeum were yet more or less intact, the door would at least bottleneck the evil machines, give them but one avenue of pursuit.

Memory of the long stairs aboard the *Tamerlane* came rushing back, and once more I felt my chest constrict, but I forced myself to breathe, and choked back the old memory. Fear was a poison, had poisoned me.

Before I'd made it round the first landing, the high, piercing scream of inhuman sirens went up from the city above, and the roar and whine of engines.

"Shuttle!" Sharp said. He stopped, listening, adjusted the drape of his rifle on his shoulder. "Not a drop tower from the sound of it."

"It'll be more chimeras," I said, stopping as well, my hand on the rail. A terrible thought had just occurred to me. "If their comms are still operable . . . if the ones we fought outside got a message out to command . . . they know I'm here. They'll send whatever they've got." I pounded the rail with my fist. "I've endangered the whole mission."

Sharp almost shrugged. "No time for that, sir."

The centurion and I emerged through the door at the bottom of the stairs one after the other. Above, I heard a shout and the noise of gunfire. Baraz and his mamluks had engaged the enemy.

"Imperial Command, this is four-oh-nine Centaurine. We are here for evac, do you copy?" Sharp tried the comm again, swore. "Dead as dirt!"

"Rinehart!" I shouted, drawing abreast of Lorian and Valka as I hurried up the hall. "Rinehart, it's Marlowe!" I had to hope that wherever this hatch was, the director had posted sentinels, and they were listening. The hall was solid stone plastered over and painted white, deep enough on this lowest level and solid enough to have survived the bombing overhead. Glowspheres still shone embedded in intervals along the apex of the rounded ceiling and at the intersections where other halls diverged. Too well I knew that sort of hall, the wiring concealed by rubber molding that ran along the ceiling, the gummy feeling of the stone where hundreds of coats of new paint had been artlessly sprayed down to cover up years of human abuse.

At one busted door I stopped, marking the flattened cots, the metal bedframes, the peeling pinup of a nude dryad woman with flowers in her hair. A pair of boxing gloves lay on the nearest cot, abandoned by their owner. There were still cards set out on the common table.

Sharp nearly collided with me in haste. "What is it?"

"Myrmidons' quarters," I said, swallowed, shook my head.

"Hadrian! Come on!" Valka shouted.

I shook myself. Lorian was yelling. "Aren't you able to . . . sense them? Or something?"

Valka was dragging the little man by the wrist, her gun drawn and raised in the other hand. "Or something!" she replied, voice taut. "Where do you think they are?"

I shook my head, stopping at the next door to peer inside. Nearly all the great Imperial cities had some manner of catacombs. Sewers, steam tunnels, and the like. There were always bunkers to which the nobiles might flee in the event of a planetary siege. Perfugium had been settled in the last great wave of Imperial expansion, before mankind began pressing into the Expanse about the galaxy's core. More than bunkers lay beneath her city of Resonno. The great cubicula, the catacombs of ice where slept our waiting millions: colonists awaiting the trumpet and a new home. I never saw a complete map. Passages such as the one we sought were not kept on official records. Such postern gates were often built in by the nobiles seeking an escape should it be the Inquisition or the Emperor's own Legions that came calling. There were other reasons.

"Gilliam Vas," I said. I hadn't thought of the priest in decades, hadn't said his name aloud in even longer.

Valka flinched. I had killed the priest in her name—and for myself. It was an ancient wound between us, a wound not properly mended, one that ached with old age. "What about him?" she asked, and I was glad the helmet hid her golden eyes.

"Who?" Lorian asked.

Ignoring Aristedes, I brushed past them both on my way to the next door, unable to endure even the shadow of her glare. "He brought that Cielcin prisoner into the Colosso. I always thought he must have used some secret tunnel from the bastille—do you remember?" I hurried down the hall, shouting to the men. "Find the dungeons!"

Sharp's voice intruded. "You think Rinehart's door is in the dungeons?"

"Where would you put it?" I asked. "If you needed to be sure of a steady supply of men?"

"*Anaryoch,*" Valka spat, employing her oldest, most favorite curse. "You're not saying they pulled colonists out of fugue for the fighting?"

I didn't answer her. Some old debates were not worth having. She was right, but I could not change the worlds, could not right every injustice under every star in the galaxy. No man can.

"That makes sense," Lorian said.

"What is wrong with you people?" Valka exclaimed.

"Contact!" came a voice from ahead. "Open fire! Open fire!"

The sounds of plasma discharge and flashes of violet light blossomed up ahead. Not from the stair behind. I felt my pulse quicken, saw two of Sharp's Dragonslayers back into the hall. One wielded his plasma burner like a scythe, slashing at the air, his weapon at full bore, not shooting but spraying an arc of superheated plasma, blue as the hottest stars. He stopped, shouted something to his companion, who leaped back toward the door. A third man staggered out, stumbling, struggling with a rope of braided silver. Hot blood sheeted down his breastplate, soaked the crimson tunic. The metal snake had drilled its way through the exposed underlayment and the gel-layer at the man's neck, and though he had stopped the vile thing boring its way through meat and sinew, the damage was done.

The second legionnaire attempted to tear the drone from his companion's neck, but even as he did so the dying man's grip slipped, and the *nahute* slithered deeper, chewing the man's insides as it made for center mass.

Highmatter flared, fell, and the dying man fell in two pieces. Sir Olorin stood masked and hooded in place. The *nahute* inside the corpse sparked as the body hit the floor.

"You killed him!" the man who'd tried to save his brother said.

The prince waded past him into the room whence the *nahute* had come. "He was dead already." A moment later I heard the flash of highmatter and the clatter of steel. Olorin emerged into the hall a moment after, tugging the door shut behind him. Turning to me, he said only one word. "Vents."

"We're running out of time," I said. "We need to find the dungeons. If I'm right, that's where we'll find Rinehart's gate." With that, I hurried down the hall after Sharp and his men, pushing past a pair of mamluks. "Valka, Lorian! With me!"

The door leading back to the stairs banged open, and the swordmaster, Baraz, appeared. He'd lost his *mandyas*, but his sword was still in his hand as he slammed the lower door shut. An instant later, a series of metallic *thuds* struck the steel door like heavy rain, denting the surface.

Olorin shouted something in Jaddian, faster than I could track. Baraz waved his master on. "Snakes!" he said. "Go!"

The prince gestured at a number of the mamluks close about him, and wordless they obeyed, moving to join the swordmaster and hold the inner door. *"Deu abarrah, Baraz!"* the prince said. *God bless you.*

"He already has, lord!"

We did not stay to watch the confrontation, and before we had even reached the end of the hall there came a crashing loud as thunder as the door was blasted inward. No *nahute* could have done such a thing, and looking back I caught of glimpse of a demon armored in white.

The dungeons were not far. Sharp's men had already prised open the heavy doors—there would be no shutting them again. Only the faintest light of glowspheres illumined the cramped confines of the lockup. Empty cells yawned at us as we all hurried inside, and Sharp's men scrambled to form a primitive barricade using the heavy lockers that stood against the inner wall.

There was no other way out.

"Humans!" The word resonated from above, faint, far away, but still

discernible through the levels of concrete and living rock. *"Your world is lost! Your armada scattered! Surrender!"* It was the same message, the same recording of the Prophet broadcast over the city, booming like the thunder. *"Surrender your Emperor and I will spare all that remain! I am Shiomu Elusha, King of the Cielcin, Scourge of Earth. Surrender your Emperor to me, and I will spare your world."*

Syriani had given the same speech, made the same demands in the same way. *A recording,* I told myself, relief opening like a chasm in me. *It's just a recording. It isn't here.*

"Help me with this!" cried one of the soldiers. I recognized the voice of Altaric, whom Sharp had berated before the siege of Ganelon. Shaken from my search, I turned and helped him use a steel bench to brace the lockers against an inner wall.

Straightening, I said, "This won't hold them long."

"Neither will that mad Jaddian bastard!" said a man with decurion's stripes. "He's worm food."

"He bought us time, Aron!" Sharp said. "Have a little respect."

Boom.

Dust shook from the lights and the wire molding overhead. Behind the stacked lockers and supply crates, the heavy doors squealed. "Hold!" Olorin shouted in Jaddian, brandishing his sword at the barricade. Thirty mamluks leaned their weight against the pile, chromed sabatons grating against the scratched tile.

Boom.

A second blow struck the barricade, knocking a crate loose from the top. The mamluks hastened to restore it.

"You said the door was here!" Olorin rounded on me, and he was *Prince Kaim* again, cold and imperious.

"I said I thought it was!" I said, spinning about. The room was gray shadows in my vision, the contours of cells and walls and rounded ceiling amplified by my suit's sensors. "It has to be here!" Leaving the men to hold the barricade, I rushed back along the row of cells, shouting, "Rinehart! Rinehart! It's Marlowe! Let us in!"

While Lorian sat on the floor, his voice floated up in the darkness. "I told you this was suicide."

"You're very smart!" I hissed back down at him. "Now be silent!"

Boom.

"There has to be something *here*," I hissed, reaching the far wall. Once more dust snaked from the roof overhead, and a fell, hellish light shone through a chink in the barricade. Like a madman I scrabbled at the cement wall. No plaster here, only cubits of damp and sweating stone.

Shots rang out behind me, their violet radiance throwing hard shadows on the wall, the shapes of men—of me—of iron bars closing in.

"Rinehart!" I hammered on the wall. "Damn you! We're here!" Exhausted, I pressed my forehead to the stone. My helmet rang.

Something caught my eye by the light of the guns. Something green.

"Hadrian!" Valka's voice was far away. "They're getting through!"

Moss.

There was moss growing on the wall, fed by the weeping moisture. Like the flower of that other world growing on the mountaintop on Annica, bleeding across time.

Whence came that water?

Ignoring Valka, I found the controls for my helmet and took it off. My breath frosted the air. "It's cold." Something *cold* was on the other side of the wall. The catacombs! The fugue pods! Again I hammered on the wall. "Rinehart, you stuffed-shirt Imperial bastard! In the name of God, open this door!" Growling, I turned back. "Olorin! Your sword!"

The knight-prince left the defense of the barricade, leaped toward me. I showed him the weeping wall. "Here!" I said.

"The door?"

Boom.

"I don't know where the door is, just cut the wall!" I said, ordering the great prince of Jadd.

Kaim du Otranto raised his sword to pierce the wall.

"Stop!" A strange voice spoke from the darkness to my right, and turning I saw two troopers in Martian red. The Emperor's troopers. They were standing in the mouth of a tunnel that had appeared swiftly and silently in the back wall of the last cell. "This way!"

"Where were you?" I snarled, rounding on them.

"This way, sir!" they said again, waving us on with rifles in hand.

Kaim whirled back toward the barricade. "Tiada!" He waved his sword in the direction of the Martians. *"Alle!"*

The other Maeskolos turned and ran toward us, shouting orders to her mamluk slaves.

"Valka!" I waved my arms. "We found it!" But she had already seen, was already helping a limping Lorian back to his feet. Holding my pistol high, I pushed them past, called for Sharp and his men. The command centurion emitted a shrill whistle and turned aside, leaving the mamluks to hold the barricade. Beyond the piled lockers and heavy crates, the metal squealing stopped.

Boom.

The barricade flew to pieces in an instant, heavy boxes hurled inward like a tower of wooden blocks blown apart by an angry child. I saw two mamluks flattened in an instant, smashed dead by the barricade. A pack of *nahute* twisted in, soaring through clouds of ash and dust. As they retreated, Sharp's men fired, purple plasma and the white lightning of disruptor fire thickening the air. Stray shots caught against the shield curtain of the *thing* that waited outside the last door, shimmered as it ducked its three crowned heads to fit beneath the lintel.

"You still live!" came the familiar high, cold voice. "You still live!"

Tall they were—taller than the greatest lords of men—and straightened until their thorn-crowned heads scraped the roof of the dungeon overhead. Pale white were their iron carapaces, and skeletally thin. They had no faces. The blank emptiness of each mask was relieved only by the presence of a single electric eye. These focused on me, and on me alone. "Iubalu! Bahudde! Aulamn! My sister-brothers! You killed them!" They spoke in unison, all animated by the same puppetmaster will. As one they stepped forward, the leftmost firing at one of the still-living mamluks as they came, moving casually, not breaking stride. "I'll kill you! Damn the Prophet's orders! I'll kill you here and now!"

Behind it, a dozen *scahari* berserkers stood ready and waiting, scimitars held at the ready. I understood then, understood just whose shuttle we had heard landing on the killing floor above our heads. The creatures that had attacked us in the streets *had* recognized me, and had sent their orders straight to Cielcin high command—the very highest. The *vayadan*-general Hushansa itself had come, had sent its puppet bodies.

For me.

"*He* wants you alive! But he is not here!" The central body advanced, drawing a blade from a compartment in its thigh. The ceramic blade unfolded, clicked into place. "I will enjoy *feeding* him your heart, *yukajji!*"

The panic I expected to feel did not come. In the moment, at the last, I was calm.

I fired the handgun.

The shot pinged off Hushansa's shield. Useless.

The *vayadan* laughed from all three of its bodies.

Something flew over my head, and once more I saw the telltale red blink of a grenade. Someone had thrown one from the mouth of the secret passage. I barely had time to drop my hand in surprise.

The blast lifted me from my feet and hurled me back against the damp dungeon wall. I struck my head and, dazed, felt hands on me. Long, pale hands dragging me down through dark water. All sound faded, swallowed by a tinny ringing that drowned me as sure as the darkness.

I knew no more.

CHAPTER 35

APOLLO UNDER ICE

"HE'S AWAKE!" SOMEONE WAS shouting. "Commander? He's awake!"

"Get the director!" a familiar, drawling voice replied. "Double quick, man!"

The ceiling slid into bleary focus, and the world with it. A solitary strip of cold light ran along the apex of the low-ceilinged room, illuminating the rounded, Roman arches and concrete pillars that marched along the far wall, beneath each of which a black sepulcher stood, a fugue creche rimed with frost.

Valka's face swam just above me, brows contracted in concern. She still wore her suit's coif up over her head—to guard her ears from the cold, I guessed. Her pale cheeks flushed, and her breath went up in a white mist as she let out a laughing breath of relief.

Tongue thick and fuzzy in my mouth, I said, "What happened?"

"You nearly died is what happened," said Lorian Aristedes, stumping into view. He'd removed his helmet, but likewise still wore the elastic coif tight about his face. He still looked strange without the familiar silver-white tangle of hair. At once younger and aged. "The hell were you thinking? You should have run with the rest of us."

Valka put a hand on the intus's shoulder to calm him. "One of Sharp's men threw a grenade to stop those chimeras. You hit your head." She combed her fingers through my hair. "The Martians dragged you through."

"Just in time, too," Lorian said. "They had the whole passage mined. Collapsed it soon as we were clear."

I just lay there a moment, coming to grips with the situation. There was no getting out, no going back. But then, there never had been any going back. Not since I climbed up the steps to Nov Belgaer on Colchis, seeking

after Gibson's true name. Not since I climbed down the steps to the hypogeum gaol beneath the coliseum in Borosevo to meet the Cielcin prisoner
Makisomn. Not since I left the Colosso in Meidua in disgust and out of
shame.

I was on the path. The *shortest* path.

I had lost control of my fate, and lost it long ago.

"Can they get through?" I asked.

"They know where to dig now," intruded a flat, surprisingly calm voice.
Sir Gray Rinehart appeared over me. He looked dreadful, almost like one
of the slaves I'd seen in the warrens of Dharan-Tun. So thin he was! And
the beard that grew from his square chin had paled from steel to snow, and
his flinty eyes were deep-sunken in a face made craggy by long care. "You
left us no real choice."

Seeing the director, I was at once acutely aware of my position: lying
on the floor, my head cradled in Valka's lap. I did not get up. "You would
have left us to die." It was not a question.

"You led them straight to our door," the nobile said, eyes flitting from
me to the legionnaires and Martians gathered about. From the way four
men were sitting, I guessed they'd been playing at dice until the director
appeared. There was something sheepish in their posture that ill-fit the
Martian Guard. They had been so long at their posts. Who could blame
them? "And for what? Now you're trapped here with us."

I blinked at him, and did sit up then. "You sent the telegraph. We came."

"You were meant to bring a fleet, not imprison yourself."

My head pounded as I wavered to my feet. "I brought the Prince of
Jadd!" Did he not know that Lin and Admiral Serpico were at that very
moment attacking the Cielcin fleet in orbit? But no. Olorin—Prince
Kaim—would have demanded to be taken directly to His Radiance, would
not have bothered explaining himself to a mere servant like Rinehart. And
they had no radio, no satellite feeds, no datanet access. Hushansa's men had
destroyed Resonno's infrastructure in the attack, and in the eighteen months
of siege had progressively blinded, deafened, made mute the survivors in
the icy catacombs beneath the once-proud city. Only the QET remained
to them.

"You did," Rinehart said, eyes narrowing.

Valka steadied me with a hand on my leg, but did not rise herself. "And
with luck, this cave-in of yours might have killed a number of their general's bodies."

The director blinked at me. Seeing he did not comprehend, Valka said,

"Machines. Their master is elsewhere controlling them. In the city perhaps. Possibly in orbit."

"Their *general*?" Rinehart repeated.

"It came for me," I said, tugging my own coif back from my face to free my hair. I combed it loose, looking round at the long, narrow chamber: the black sepulchers of the fugue creches in their niches, their bodies blurry, pale shapes floating quiescent behind a layer of frost; the men sitting or standing about, leaning on lances or against pillars. "More even than the Emperor, their Prophet wants me."

"You?" I could hear the skepticism in the director's voice without needing to see his disbelief. "Why?"

I only looked at him. Rinehart blew air past his lips. "You don't mean to tell me the Pale King believes this Chosen-of-Earth bullshit, do you?" he laughed, but when I did not at once join him, he stopped. Flint eyes sparking, he asked, "Do you?"

The words I'd spoken to Olorin aboard the *Mnemon* floated back to me, the words I'd spoken to Renna before the Battle of Berenike, but I did not speak them.

We're all chosen for something.

By something.

"Do I believe the Earth chose me for some special fate?" How could I possibly explain the Quiet? Explain Utannash and the Lie? And do so in a way that fit comfortably inside that cramped, long, narrow room beneath the ground? "No."

Rinehart visibly relaxed. Did he think—like Alexander—that I had come to stake some claim, to stage a coup? To emerge from the catacombs, William dead, with the circlet of Empire bright upon my brow?

Did he think I could?

"But I am a useful symbol, just like His Radiance. The Prophet means to humiliate Caesar. To broadcast that humiliation across the galaxy. It will use that to press *its* claim as Emperor."

The director blinked. "*Its* claim?"

"To the strongest! Yes," I said. "An empire of the Cielcin." I did not say, *And if all it believes is true—as I suspect—there will be nothing left.* Staring at Rinehart, at the darkness of that low chamber, I could see only the darkness of Miudanar's hollow eye.

Arkam resham aktullu. Arkam amtatsur.

I shook myself. "How much better if Marlowe were crucified beside Caesar in that broadcast, eh?" The implications were working themselves out on Rinehart's face, etching the lines of grief and care a micron deeper. "Humanity would kneel in an instant. It *is* our way." The pathos; the sheer, sepulchral doom in my voice was enough to cut the heart from my chest. "Where is the Emperor?"

"I'll take you to him," Rinehart said, drawing back a step. "He's with your prince of Jadd in the command post."

My hands found their customary place tucked into my belt. Someone—Valka perhaps, or Sharp—had located my gun and restored it to its holster on my right leg. "Very good," I said. I looked round, marked Valka's place on the floor, Lorian leaning on the wall beside her. I found Sharp a moment after, further down the hall. It had taken me a moment without his helmet, but the burn scar on his forehead and bald scalp glowed red and furious in the sickly gray light. "My companions will come with me."

Ghostly faces peered at us as we followed Sir Gray along corridor after winding corridor. The sleepers stirred not in their icy tombs, but floated naked and mostly unseen behind glass dark enough to guard their nudity, neutrally buoyant to defend against cryoburn, saddled with hoses and blood-lines to keep the bodies cold and the lungs filled.

"We loaded so many of them as we could onto the shuttles," Rinehart said, knocking on the lid of one as we passed. "Too few. His Radiance wanted the whole of the stores packed and transferred core-ward. To Nessus or Gododdin."

"Gododdin?" Valka asked. "Why Gododdin?"

"It used to be a colonial store," Rinehart replied. "Back in the old days, when the Centaurine Provinces were new, and *this* was the final frontier." He led us round a corner and up an arcing corridor, his words tinged with ironic futility. Here men in Martian red and others in quartered gray and gold I took for the arms of Perfugium stood watch about an open set of blast doors two cubits thick. The gate captain—a hard-eyed woman with a pointed jaw and dressed in Perfugium livery—saluted the director and myself but did not speak. "We'd hoped to deploy them to re-seed the worlds devastated by the invaders, but now . . ." There was genuine sorrow in the logothete's voice. "Now they'll be lucky to escape at all."

"Did you get any of them offworld?" I asked, pausing beside the man as a column of soldiers hurried along a cross-corridor, armor and sabers rattling off the stone walls.

Sir Gray chewed his tongue. "To the fleet, aye."

"The fleet . . ." Lorian's words floated up from some place below my shoulder.

The fleet was gone. Every man, woman, and child the Emperor had moved to orbit for conduct back toward the heart of the Imperium was dead. Every one.

"How came you to be trapped down here?" I asked, swaying a little as I hurried to keep up with the director's pace. My head throbbed painfully, and I held a hand to the back of my skull. "Why did you not flee?"

Rinehart turned and looked at me for a long moment, as if he could hardly believe I had asked so inane a question. "We were down here when they arrived." With that he turned, his next words drifting back to me with his smoky breath. "His Radiance insisted on overseeing the evacuation himself."

"He *what?*" Valka could not help herself. "Truly?"

I raised a hand to head her off.

"Surely you told him it was too dangerous," I said, trying to keep up. I still felt sluggish from my brush with unconsciousness, though I understood Valka's incredulity all too well. Despite centuries beside me, she was yet enough the Tavrosi to act surprised whenever one of the nobility displayed anything resembling her foreign virtues. For myself, I was surprised not by any display of civic piety or care, but because Caesar was *Caesar*. He was simply *too* valuable. He was the axis about which all our worlds turned.

Echoing my thought, Rinehart replied, "He is *Caesar*, my lord. I cannot *tell* him to do anything." Chewing my tongue, I let my gaze fall to my feet. Rinehart wasn't finished. "He said it was what you would have done."

"Me?" I looked sharply up, choking down confusion, surprise.

"Black planet!" Lorian breathed, words floating up from some point below my shoulder. "It's catching."

"So 'twould seem . . ." Valka's voice dripped tired amusement.

I wanted to deny it, to protest.

I had given Syriani the names of the planets on the Emperor's itinerary. I had failed to convince the Emperor to call off his tour of the provinces, had inspired him to take this foolish risk.

Perfugium. Vanaheim. Balanrot.

It was my doing. My fault. Mine.

What matter it that Dorayaica had gotten the names of those planets from other lips than mine? I had delivered those other lips to the Prophet's dungeons by my failure—my inattention—at Padmurak. I had led us into the Lothrian net. I had failed to lead us out again. All my faculties, all my *power*, and it hadn't been enough.

Rinehart turned and resumed his pace up the hall, skirting a knot of men in the gray and gold of House Valavar, the Lords of Perfugium. I heard the whispers chasing up the hall.

"That's him?"

"The Halfmortal?"

"How many are left here?" I asked.

Not looking back, Rinehart asked, "On ice? Eight million, seven hundred thirty thousand." His voice quavered slightly as he added, "We had nearly three hundred thousand aboard the . . . aboard the fleet when the attack came. We'd hoped to have about two million with us for the return to Nessus."

"I am sorry," I said.

Ever the pragmatist, Lorian asked the question I had intended. "How many defenders?"

The Intelligence Director did not at once reply. "Six thousand."

"Six thousand?" Valka echoed, aghast. "So few?"

There had been millions in the Imperial entourage. The eunuch homunculi in the Imperial household alone—his butlers and batmen, his chefs, tailors, cleaners, barbers, coaches, scribes, and pages—numbered more than ten thousand, each vat-grown and woven from genetic looms not so unlike the ones that wove us palatines. And all the men I'd seen in the bustling camp upon Carteia—and Prince Rafael Hatim and his women, I would later learn—all the courtiers and hangers-on that orbited the Emperor as planets about a star . . .

All gone.

"Just those of us on the ground when the attack came," Rinehart said. "Lord Bulsara, myself—some of the other high officers. Duchess Valavar is with us. Her and her family. We saved everyone we could." He paused to catch his breath, to master some emotion rolling, whale-like, against the surface of his face. "There are other boltholes throughout the city. Ones not connected to the colonial stores. And we've reason to believe there are hundreds of thousands still free across the countryside. Before the Pale cut all the hard lines, we were in contact with a couple cells in the Torvic Basin out west." He seemed to deflate as he spoke, steadied himself against one of the icy fugue creches that lined the wall to our left. "It's all gone silent. The whole planet's dead and gone, I'll warrant."

"Not so!" I told him. "There were bells in the city!"

Rinehart looked back, a light in his pale eyes. "Don't give me hope."

I—who had no hope left to give—said, "Oft hope is born when all is forlorn."

"Is that . . . English?" Rinehart asked, clearly not understanding.

"It is," I told him, and translated the words.

The verse was very old, born of the Golden Age before the Advent of Man, before the Foundation War, before even the death of Felsenburgh. Whence had it come to me? When had I read it?

"I pray you are right, Marlowe," Rinehart said, and turned. "It is good the prince at least escaped. He is with your fleet?"

"He is," I said.

"And he's well?"

"He would have come had I not argued it against it," I said. "He misliked being left behind while the Prince of Jadd flew into battle." I was exaggerating, but Rinehart did not seem to notice. Alexander had never volunteered to join us, but Rinehart had the look of a man in need of building up, and Alexander had at least yearned *for* the rescue of his father.

Rinehart was nodding his approval, and wiped his tired face with one hand. "It was good of you to persuade him to remain in space. The situation is dire without bringing His Highness back into the fire." He straightened suddenly, the old soldier reasserting his control. "Come," he said. "The Emperor is not far."

The heart of the catacombs, the chambers to which Caesar and the Duchess Valavar and all the nobiles of Perfugium's lost capital had fled, sat above a deep cistern warmed by the very geothermal sinks that drew heat from Perfugium's core to power the sleepers' icy beds. Rinehart acknowledged the salute of the captain at the inner gate; led Valka, Lorian, and the rest of our little band up a short flight of steps and past vault doors fully five cubits thick.

Within, men and women sat in tight groups or huddled beneath heavy coats. I caught the scent of burned coffee and the acrid tang of verrox stimulant on the air. Wide eyes turned to watch us, and I had to remind myself that ours were the first strange faces these men and women had seen in more than two years of agonized waiting.

The director led us up three short steps onto a circular promenade that overlooked the cistern in the center. Following him, I peered over the rail at the black water a hundred feet below.

"Lord Marlowe?" a voice called from behind, and turning I saw a thin woman in the grays of the diplomatic corps. "They said you were dead."

"Not yet," I said, unthinking. "Not again."

The woman stepped back, mouthing the word *again*. Her face had gone white at my words, so casually had I spoken them. The stories dropped like grain from my hands.

"Have you come to save us?" asked another.

"Come, my lord," Rinehart said, and laid a hand on my arm.

The director led me through a side door and along a passage that radiated from the cistern and its promenade like the spoke of a wheel. Someone had unrolled a rich carpet of Tyrian purple to decorate that rough, cramped space. The richness of that rug contrasted with the chipped paint and molded wire of the bunker in a way that spoke to me of the empty, iron halls of Vorgossos, and of Dharan-Tun.

"I hate it underground," I said to Valka, and once more touched the bruised portion of my skull.

"I know," she said, laying on hands to steady me. In her native Panthai, she whispered. "Are you going to make it?"

Hand still on my wounded head, I offered a weak, faltering smile. "One last fight?"

She matched my smile.

Six Excubitors waited by the round door at the end of the hall, high-matter blades drawn and ready. They did not so much as blink as we approached—or so I guessed, for their eyes were black almonds in their mirror-polished faces. How like to the mamluks of Jadd they seemed to me then. Homunculi, not fully human. The door dropped an inch in its jamb and rolled ponderously aside.

The men standing gathered about the holograph all looked up and turned at our approach. I recognized Prince Kaim readily enough, glittering in his Jaddian blacks and gold, face still hidden behind the segmented porcelain of his mask, though he had lowered his hood. His *sulshawar* Tiada stood beside him, unmasked—for she was a woman—and seeing her not in the chaos and context of battle, I recognized the deep olive face and high cheekbones of one of his concubines. More than a concubine, it seemed.

But it was the man beside them, the man who turned steadily to face me, that drew the whole of my attention. How many years had Caesar aged since last I'd last seen him? It might have been only two or three in truth, depending on how long he'd slumbered under ice traveling from Carteia to Perfugium.

It might have been three hundred.

Though he wore an enameled white breastplate with pteruges of crimson and gold and heavy cape of samite red as his hair, that hair was going gray at the roots. The thick, square beard that now coated his jaw had rusted in places and begun turning white. New hollows had carved themselves in his cheeks and beneath his eyes, though the eyes themselves yet flashed with emerald fire. He was undoubtedly still *Emperor. Commander.* Still William of the Aventine.

Still Caesar, but a Caesar aged by months of hard campaign.

Without preamble, he asked, "You were successful?"

"Yes and no," I replied, knowing my reply was unhelpful. "We destroyed the fortress, but many of the magi escaped." Remembering my place, I knelt, and felt Lorian and Sharp kneel behind me—though Valka remained on her feet. "Radiance, they have a new weapon. A virus they mean to deploy across the Imperium. I believe . . . I believe it to be derived from an ancient Mericanii bioweapon."

The Emperor blinked, and I bowed my head. "Mericanii?" He repeated the hateful name. "Mericanii . . . by Earth . . ." A shadow stirred, and glancing up I saw Lord Nicephorus rise from its seat at one of the nearer consoles. If anything, the Lord Chamberlain looked even more haggard and careworn that Caesar himself. "But you destroyed the fortress?"

"Yes, Honorable Caesar," I said, and lifted my eyes. "We've come to rescue you."

"I know," the Emperor said, and gesturing to Olorin, said, "Prince Kaim was just telling me you brought the Jaddian fleet." He nodded slowly, seeming almost to chew the words as he turned, placing a steady hand on Nicephorus's shoulder as he circled the holograph. Only as he did so did the whole of the room heave into focus: the low strip lighting, the logothetes hunched at their various displays, fingers tapping at keys, muttering information to one another. "We cannot go yet."

A knot formed in the pit of my stomach. "Radiance?"

His back now fully to me again, Caesar replied, "You may stand, Hadrian."

Valka advanced to help me stand, but I waved her back. "Radiance, we cannot stay! Tribune Lin and the Jaddian admiral are not certain they can hold the Pale at bay indefinitely—and we have no way of knowing how many ships the xenobites have held in reserve. I have a ship standing by. There must be other ways out of these tunnels the Pale have not yet found. We have to go now." On my feet again, I hurried toward the Emperor by the holograph.

"And what of my people?" asked a thickly accented voice strange to me. A gaunt woman in gray military dress sat on a velvet-cushioned stool on the far side of the holograph, her curling black hair pinned back at the right to fall over her left shoulder in what once—in better days—might have been a glorious display. The gold threads of epaulet and aiguillette marked her for a nobile—and her face was undeniably palatine.

Turning to her, I asked, "You're Lady Valavar?"

"I am the Duchess of Perfugium," she answered in lieu of *yes*. "I ask again: what of my people?" She gripped the edge of the holograph table before her. "There are thirty million people on Perfugium. You would abandon them?"

My mouth opened to reply, but no words came out. I studied the lines of care etched onto Saskia Valavar's face, the distress. That she cared for her world and all the people in it was undeniable, and very, very sad. "There is nothing to be done for them. If we cannot break their fleet—"

"We have already lost millions," the Emperor said, his baritone slashing across mine like a riposting sword. "I will not allow them to take millions more."

"And how will you stop them?" Valka asked, leaping to my defense. "Emperor! There are thousands of people dying right now to buy us the time to save you! What of them?"

Silence greeted her words. No one dared speak the truth: that those thousands were soldiers, that soldiers died by definition. Died according to plan. No one dared speak at all, for she had challenged Caesar himself.

To his credit, William himself was silent. A lesser Emperor might have raged, fumed, ordered her taken from his sight or shot. A lesser Emperor might have feared such a challenge. But William was no lesser Emperor, nor even a merely good one. William was a great Emperor, the greatest perhaps since the first. But he was Emperor in an age that begged more than greatness of its lords.

And he was *only* great.

"I will not leave this place." He stopped on the far side of the holograph beside the Duchess Valavar. "Not until we have saved everyone we can."

As if to compensate for Valka's challenge, I bowed my head. "Radiance, if it is known that you have fled the planet, the Pale may break off their assault. They have sucked the cities dry. It is for you they stay."

Sensing the tension between us, perhaps, Prince Kaim said, "Your man speaks sense, cousin."

"This is no common *scianda*, Radiance," I continued, advancing until I leaned over the holograph well opposite the duchess and Caesar. "This fleet is under the command of one of the Iedyr Yemani, the White Hand of the Prophet."

The Emperor blinked. "Not the Prophet himself?"

"No, my lord. I do not believe Dorayaica is here," I said, with a side-long glance at Rinehart. "They know *I* am, however."

The director stepped forward. "They made a damned mess getting in here. The hippodrome gate is lost to us." Rinehart stood straight as he was able, flinty eyes sparking. "Honorable Caesar, I . . . agree with Lord Marlowe. We should leave by one of the other gates while we still have them open to us. The guild house door is still free, and the one in the Sanctum of the Blessed Wisdom in Belhaven."

The Emperor raised a hand for silence, and silence fell. "I shall hear no more of this," he said, eyes sweeping the room. Pointing at the image on the holograph, he continued, "See this here?" It was a tri-D map of the bunkers, showing the spider's web of corridors, chambers, vaults, and halls, the power conduits and the intricate plumbing that served to keep the sleepers on ice. There must have been hundreds of miles of catacombs criss-crossing and spiraling beneath ruinous Resonno. I picked out our location—highlighted in blue—near the very bottom, more than half a mile beneath the surface. The Emperor's gloved finger showed where the halls connected to a series of what looked like silos high above.

They were hangars, I realized. Blast pits.

"These transports are each fitted to carry five hundred people. Each one," the Emperor said. "We had them loaded for a second wave when the attack came."

"How many are there?" I asked. It looked like dozens. Hundreds. They were distributed in tight clusters about the perimeter of the city, not in any centralized starport. From the maps on the displays about the walls of the Emperor's war room, I guessed the actual starport had been one of the earliest sites devastated. The landing field was too large an area to shield effectively, and had fallen in the initial invasion, taking the *Radiant Dawn* and the rest of the Emperor's grounded navy along with it. The ducal palace's private launch bays had been destroyed when the Cielcin landed troops to destroy the shields. *That* offensive had been what had driven the defenders underground, through hidden ways in the white ziggurat beneath the citadel itself.

"Nine hundred seventeen," replied the Duchess Valavar.

"'Tis nearly half a million people," Valka said, voice thin.

"We know," Rinehart said.

Again Caesar raised his hand. "Peace, Sir Gray." He folded his arms, cape draping to cover his armored core. "We lost dozens in the bombardment. The Pale dug up a hundred more. He stared unblinking at the display, and for a moment I thought I might perceive the weight of the worlds bearing down on him, at Atlas shrunken and aching from centuries of near-ceaseless labor.

Moving to my side, Valka asked the next obvious question. "Are they not warp capable?"

Caesar did not move anything but his eyes, which hooded as a lantern turned on Valka. "No. They're common freighters. In-system. Sublight."

The Duchess Valavar said, "They were only ever intended to ferry the sleepers to a carrier in orbit."

Prince Kaim—forgotten a moment in the midst of our Imperial concerns—raised his lilting voice. "Our fleet would be willing to carry them."

"With respect, Your Highness, we can't coordinate with your fleet," Rinehart said. "Our comms are down."

"There's the telegraph," the prince replied, taking one cock-footed step toward the holograph.

Rinehart's eyes narrowed. "It's too slow! We could never coordinate orbital extraction with the fleet! Besides!"

Kaim made a dismissive gesture. "Then don't coordinate. Tell them what you intend and trust them to respond."

"You would have us launch half a million men and women into orbit *blind and deaf* in the hopes that your people can salvage them before the enemy?" Rinehart was aghast as he rounded on the Emperor. "Your Radiance, I must protest! This is madness! It's suicide!"

Calm as a still pool, the swordmaster prince replied, "Do they have a better chance here on Perfugium?"

"We don't have the pilots!" Rinehart replied.

"Of course you do!" came a high voice from behind me.

All eyes turned on the frail little man in the shadows at the edge of the holograph's pool of light. Lorian Aristedes had remained by the door, had remained kneeling when Caesar had ordered me to rise. He rose then, holding his aching shoulder with the opposite hand. "Among the sleepers. Eight million? You must have a thousand licensed pilots. You must have ten thousand!"

Rinehart blinked, as if astonished my diminutive companion had spoken at all. I felt a strange coldness settle over the chamber, and had to remind myself what Lorian was. He was clearly an intus, one of the misborn, a palatine bastard and reminder of just how precarious a thread the double helix was. Caesar's face was impassive, closed, unreadable.

One of the other logothetes, a short woman in Perfugium livery seated at one of the perimeter consoles, broke that brittle silence, saying, "It'll take at least a day to find them and thaw them."

"Then do it!" Lorian said, and bowing awkwardly with his injured shoulder, the good commander said, "Honorable Caesar, permit me the use of the telegraph. I can contact Tribune Lin and the Jaddians."

Another voice boiled up from one corner in protest. "They'll be shot out of the sky!"

Something familiar in that voice caught my ear and turned my head. Leonid Bartosz—*Sir* Leonid Bartosz—stood silent in the corner, dressed in the long tunic and white *lacerna* of a naval strategos. He still wore the pointed beard, and on his vulpine face the haggard look of exhaustion worn by all in the Emperor's bunker took on a strangely furtive cast.

"You!" I said.

"I can hear no more of this!" Bartosz said, "Majesty! You are ill advised! Don't listen to this charlatan—" he gestured at me, "—and his toad! Those ships will be blasted out of the sky!"

Valka's fingers tightened just above my elbow. "We don't have time for any of this."

"I know," I said, placing my hand over hers.

Lorian was shaking his head. "We need to call in air support. Divert the fleet's aquilarii, use lighters to cover the transports."

Bartosz advanced into the pool of light about the holograph. "And expose the fleet to boarders?"

"Is this not war?" Lorian asked, rounding on his superior officer.

Marking the intus's advance, the vulpine strategos took a step backward. "Stay back, *inmane*!" It had been a long time since anyone had dared to use the word of Lorian in my presence, and the sound of it was like gunfire in my ears. "You dare question me?"

Lorian raised a hand, as if to touch the strategos. Bartosz flinched away. "Keep your distance, sir. Your cowardice might be catching. I was at Berenike, too. I was the one who picked up your mess—or have you forgotten?" I had to admire the way Lorian had turned the man's disgust back on himself. He had a good teacher.

"Marlowe, who is this man?" Caesar's voice cut across Lorian's antics.

"He is the last survivor of my company, Radiance," I said—and fearing some reprisal from Bartosz, I added, "and he is my armsman." Lorian's head snapped round to look at me, but he said nothing. Lorian had not sworn personal allegiance to me or to my own House Marlowe. He was simply a legionary officer under my command. It was a lie I told, but a lie that might have saved his life.

"He is an intus," the Emperor said, speaking as though Lorian were not present.

I stiffened, and fixing my gaze on a point over the Emperor's shoulder, replied, "He is a fine officer."

Bartosz sniffed. "You must punish him."

Eyes flicking shut, open again, I focused on the strategos. "If you have a problem with my armsman, sir, you may bring it to me. I've no sword, but perhaps one could be found for me."

The strategos paled.

Coward.

"I too was at Berenike, strategos," I said. "Perhaps you remember?" I had ordered Bartosz removed from his command, packed into fugue to prevent his killing himself in his despair and fear.

Leonid Bartosz was silent. "Radiance." I turned to face the Emperor. "If you will not come with us, please permit my man access to the telegraph."

CHAPTER 36

THE VAYADAN

"LIN SAYS THE FLEET'S holding," Lorian said, peering up the slope of the launch silo toward the armored door hundreds of feet above. "The Jaddians launched an assault on their worldships out beyond the farthest moon. Lin's group smashed the fleet in geostate above the city. They're chasing them round the planet as we speak."

I paused to take a deep breath, hoping for something like fresh air. I hoped in vain. The air of the launch silo was stale as a tomb, and damp from the sweat and breath of the men laboring to ready the ship before us. It was but one of nearly a thousand such vessels lying in wait beneath the surface of Perfugium, primed and ready to go.

"How long can they hold?" I asked.

"Long enough," the little man replied. "Lin at least is only in danger a few minutes every orbital cycle. His ships and the Pale are taking potshots at each other, counter-orbiting." He wound his fingers in circles through the air to illustrate his point—a rather awkward gesture. "They can hold." He sounded like a man trying to convince himself.

"Clear!" came a voice from behind, and I had to usher Lorian aside as two men advanced, dragging the fuel line to connect it to the waiting vessel.

The commander winced as I touched his bad shoulder, and I asked, "Are you all right?"

"I will be," he said, but gave the lie to his words as he sank and sat upon the first of a flight of thin metal steps bracketed to the wall of the launch tube. He rubbed his shoulder. "I've had worse. Wasn't built to be running around like a common foot soldier." He bit the words off with his staple irony, turned where he sat to look up the sloping track of the silo.

The builders long ago had hollowed out a channel twice as wide as a tram tunnel—perhaps sixty feet in diameter and nearly a thousand feet long—carved into the living rock at a steep angle. A track ran along the bottom of the shaft, allowing the shuttle to accelerate along the slope and so launch itself tangent to the planet's curve. It was hard to imagine hundreds of such shafts built beneath the planet's capital, their caps concealed in the hills and ridges that rose about bleak Resonno. I had to remind myself that the city had been built *for* these catacombs, for the conquest of Centaurus so very long ago. Resonno had been a colonial *machine*, constantly shipping men and women on ice by the thousand, receiving new blood all the while as serfs signed their futures for a new life.

In the distance, the noise of thunder rolled.

"Another bombing," Lorian said, lifting his eyes as if to pierce the roof of the world above. "Rinehart sent men to reinforce the door to the hippodrome. He said the Cielcin have been in there clearing the rubble away. They're trying to fuse the passage shut."

"It won't hold," I said, darkly. "We don't have time."

"We might have time," Lorian said. "The pilots are coming out of fugue now. Imagine what that's like: waking up to find William Caesar breathing down your neck."

I felt my eyebrows rise involuntarily. "It's a pity we can't just stun him and haul him out to the *Ascalon*."

"Ah!" Lorian managed a weak smile. "Had I a hurasam for every time Corvo or the doctor said that about you, I could buy a palace on Jadd and the harem to go with it." His smile faltered. "I could *buy Jadd*."

Not amused, I half-turned away, and for the ten-thousandth time checked my wrist-terminal. "Nine hours already."

Lorian hauled one ankle up over the other knee with a pained expression, began kneading his calf. "Nothing for it. Nothing to do but wait." He made a sharp, pained sound. "Besides, you're missing the good part of all this."

"There's a good part?"

The commander pressed his lips together. "This little, ah . . . *sideshow* of the Emperor's will provide the perfect distraction for us to get him away to safety." When I blinked down at him, not fully understanding, he said, "We can make a break for it while the Pale are distracted by the refugee transports."

Something cold and oily clamped itself around my heart. "Don't let Valka hear you say that."

"I don't have a death wish."

"Are you sure of that?" I asked, watching as the techs affixed the fuel line to the shuttle. One signaled his fellow back by the door of the silo. We were—for a brief moment in that cramped space—truly alone. "What were you thinking? Challenging Bartosz?"

Lorian held my gaze for only a moment, his pale, colorless eyes shining in his bloodless white face. He deflated the instant after, said, "I suppose I should thank you."

"You never have to," I said. "Just be careful. You and Valka are . . . all I have left." I turned my head away, studied the blunt, ugly shape of the transport ship. "Don't go risking your life like that, mouthing off at strategoi in front of the Emperor."

"You do."

My eyes slid back to the commander's face. "You're not me."

"I know that," Lorian said, "but they were . . . wasting time."

"Weren't you the one just telling me there was nothing to do now but wait?" Another distant blast of thunder shook the roof of the world above, as if to underscore my point.

Lorian let his leg drop. "That was before we were committed to this farce. It was clear to me the Emperor had no intention of changing his mind. Bartosz and Rinehart were wasting time dithering."

"They're tired," I said, "and scared."

"Bartosz was born scared," Lorian said. "Bastard should have killed himself after Berenike."

Looking to be sure none of the technicians had overheard him, I said, "That's not for you to decide. Most of the court have never seen a battlefield, Lorian."

"No," he agreed, "they just send us to them."

"I think the Emperor realized the problem with that now," I said. "That's why he's here. That's why he's fighting."

"Aye," the little man agreed. "But his way of fighting is going to get him and us all killed."

What could I say to that? Had not Rinehart said that it was I who had caused the Emperor to take this foolish risk? Was it not then my way of fighting that would get us all killed?

As if in answer, the thunder of the bombs rolled once more. "Was there any luck getting through to Lin?"

"You mean on the comm? No." Lorian rubbed his eyes with one long-fingered hand. "Valka said she'd try and boost the signal, but there's not much to work with. The city grid's gone. Lines are cut, and even if they weren't, the Pale are drowning all comm frequencies. We're as mute as we are deaf." Eyes focused on a patch of the ceramic-tiled floor, the commander pressed on. "But the telegraph's still good. Lin knows what we're up to and when. He's ready to drop the lighters on us on my mark, but I'll say it again: I don't like this. It's like playing druaja by shouting orders to a man in the next room. Can't see the board."

"We can trust Bassander," I said. Unbidden, a laugh escaped me, short and flat, but true. What a change that was, *trusting* Bassander. After Rustam. After Vorgossos. After the Battle on the *Demiurge.* "We can trust Bassander."

"Lord Marlowe!"

Turning, I saw a bald young man hurrying through the blast doors from the terminal. I blinked. Not a man. It was a homunculus, one of the Emperor's pages, the genetic eunuchs that surrounded and served the Solar Throne. I had never seen one without the traditional powdered white wig before. I had always assumed them hairless, but two years in the bunkers had given the lie to this perception. Without the careful grooming and maintenance of court protocol, the fellow's eyebrows had grown in, and a fine stubble of hair stood out upon the bare scalp.

It was red as dying flame.

Almost I took the creature for one of the Imperial princes. It had the hair, the emerald eyes, the alabaster complexion of Alexander and his siblings. I wondered at that. Were the Emperor's servants all grown from the same stock as the Emperor himself? Abruptly I recalled old Saltus, the long-armed sailor I'd known but briefly aboard the *Eurynasir.*

We are both homunculi, he'd said to me. *Both sticky drafts from the same old bottle.*

"My lord," it said, having regained its breath. "My lord! Master Nicephorus sent me to find you! You must come quickly! The war room! The holograph!"

Raising both hands for calm, I said, "Speak, sirrah."

The homunculus nodded swiftly, swallowing hard. "The Pale, lordship! Their master! It's on the comm!"

"Where is the Emperor?"

"In the war room, lordship—but it won't treat with him!" the page stammered, eyes darting to the men still fueling the transport. They had stopped to listen, looking on. "It's asking for you!"

Dread led me by the hand as I followed the genetic eunuch back through crowded corridors and down spiraling ways to the core of the bunker, to the cistern and the war room that lay beyond. With every step, I felt the crawling sensation of eyes on me, heard the whispers of the soldiers and surviving courtiers in the soiled finery chasing Lorian and myself in our haste. Once or twice, hands reached out to touch my armored shoulders, my flank, the trailing hem of my torn cape.

I could hardly stand it.

They thought me their savior, but my arrival in that dank darkness had only hastened their doom. If what the page said was true, if Dorayaica *had* come . . . I could not finish the thought, or suffer the hope in so many eyes.

The door to the Emperor's war room rolled aside, and glancing to the Excubitors on my right as I entered, I saw my black figure reflected in their chromium armor, their white capes gone gray from their long months underground fluttering like moth's wings. I held one violet eye reflected in the knight's sculpted cheek guard, for just a moment.

How hollow it seemed to me, how drained of life and color at the thought of facing Dorayaica again.

But it wasn't Dorayaica whose image turned to receive me, hovering spectral above the holography plate in the center of that dim chamber. Nor was it Hushansa, red-eyed and legion.

Prince Ugin Attavaisa sat upon its many-legged iron chair. No more did it wear the cobalt-enameled armor it had worn to the Aetavanni, but dressed instead in armor of fleshy, striated white, the six-fingered hand bright upon its chest in black outline, fingers taloned and outstretched, for it was *prince* no more. Aeta no more.

It was *vayadan*: warrior and concubine, general and slave. Finger of the White Hand of the Prophet.

"*Daratolo!*" it said as I approached. "You live! I thought for certain Hushansa was mistaken." As it spoke, it twisted a gilt chain in its hands. Something groaned at the Cielcin's feet and moved, and it was with horror that I recognized the shape of a man, his face bruised, one eye swollen shut and leaking pus, his bare abdomen horribly bloated, black and yellow with contusion.

I looked away from the half-naked slave, clenched my fists beneath my cloak. *Fear is a poison.* I said nothing, did not trust myself to speak. Looking through the image, past the horned back of Attavaisa's seat, past the windows and the stars behind it, I saw the Emperor standing on the far side of the room, Nicephorus beside him, his eyes terribly intent. The whole room seemed frozen about me, as if every man and woman, every soldier and minister from the lowest technician to the duchess and Caesar himself, were waiting to see what I would do.

I did nothing.

"The gods, it seems, have preserved you for their purpose," Attavaisa said, lips peeling back from glassy fangs. Its tongue slid out, hooked upward with vicious anticipation. "And they have brought you to me."

"Where is your master, slave?" a calm voice spoke, and several long moments passed before I recognized those measured tones as my own. "If your gods have brought me here for a purpose, it is not to treat with the likes of you."

Attavaisa flinched, yanked the chain that held its human slave. The man fell at the former prince's feet, and Attavaisa rested one taloned foot on the poor fellow's back as though he were a foot stool, just as I'd imagined Dorayaica doing to the Emperor. "We know you have reached your *Emperor*," the *vayadan* said, using the Galstani word.

All the fear I'd expected to feel was gone. I knew the answer to my question without having to be told. Dorayaica was not in the system. I felt clear, cold as the wind upon the mountain on Annica.

"If you surrender yourself, your Emperor may go free," Attavaisa said.

The words washed over me like lightning, and I looked round, seeking a scholiast, some lay adviser translating in the Emperor's ear. But Caesar was alone, though his eyes were still on me. Would he take such an offer? Could he refuse?

"What is it saying?" asked one of the more junior naval officers in the Emperor's train, a tribune—I thought he was.

Opening my mouth to speak, I found Valka in the gathered crowd, her eyes almost glowing in the dim. She twitched her head almost imperceptibly, side to side.

No.

Once upon a time, a very brave, very foolish boy had been forced to stand as translator while a Chantry Inquisitor named Agari questioned a Cielcin officer in a torture cell on Emesh. He had very foolishly lied. Lied to the Inquisitor, lied to humanity, lied to the Cielcin captive in the hopes of winning some victory, some progress in the endless, bitter war between human and inhuman. He had won a narrow victory, and earned for himself a quest. But he had hardly once contemplated the danger he put himself in with his lies.

I knew better.

"It says that if I surrender myself to it, it will permit Your Radiance to go free."

The words had Attavaisa's desired effect. At once the chamber erupted in a tumult of shouts, suggestions, commands. The *vayadan's* teeth shimmered in the holograph, bright as the stars through the windows at its back.

"He must do it!" shouted one old minister.

"It's a trick!" said an officer.

Duchess Valavar was shaking her head, her magnificent hair floating about her face, a striking contrast with the humble gray fatigues her long internment in those tunnels had reduced her to. "It makes no sense," she said. "Why would they want Marlowe more than you, Radiance?"

Still William's eyes had not left me. He raised a hand, and one of the Excubitors slammed the floor with his fasces, the ringing of metal on stone an inescapable call for order. When order came, the Emperor repeated the duchess's question. "Why do they want *you* so badly?"

His Radiance knew the answer. We had discussed it on Carteia.

Had he not believed it?

I looked once more to Valka. She'd bowed her head, was chewing her lip—never a good sign, that. *Because of the Watchers,* I thought, and held once more the Emperor's eye. *Because of the Quiet. You know this.* But I said, "They don't recognize blood as we do. I slew two of their princes, and so to them I am a kind of prince. I am the only *man* who is." When the Emperor did not at once reply to this, I hedged my words. "They believe I am the only one of our commanders who constitutes any serious threat. Meaning no disrespect to Your Radiance or to the other worthies here, but they know me. They do not know you."

This seemed to satisfy the Emperor.

Attavaisa, on the other hand, tugged on the heavy chain. *"Netotta tikoun!"* it barked. The legs of its iron seat twitched, and the poor fellow slipped as the contraption unbalanced him, knocking him on his distended belly. "Answer me!"

Still strangely calm, I shook my head. "We must discuss it."

"Veih!" it said. "No! The Elusha has warned me of your games. I will have your answer now!"

My eyes slid from the prince to my Emperor. "It says we must decide."

Still Caesar's eyes had not left my face. I was not certain he had so much as blinked. Nicephorus leaned in and whispered something in his ear, but the Emperor waved his servant off. Into the crackling silence, the Emperor spoke, words calm, almost halting. "If I order it, will you go?"

My heart plummeted from my chest, fell rapidly as a neutrino through the floor and deep, deep into Perfugium's molten heart. Ducking my head to hide my expression, I went unsteadily to one knee. *We're all pawns, my boy*, Gibson—who had been a prince himself—had once said. Almost it seemed I heard him once again, as though he were one of the Imperial retinue, Prince Philippe again among the palatine lords of Empire. *But your soul is in your hands,* he whispered.

Choose.

I had never understood what choice he meant. What could I say but *yes*? Kneeling there before the Emperor, I understood. I had no choice but to obey, but I could choose *why* I obeyed.

And how.

"If you ask it of me, I will, Radiance." The Emperor gave the minutest of nods, and I let my head droop. "I have given my life already in your service. Can I do less now?"

No reflection, no shadow peered up at me from the rough stone floor. *There,* I thought, *there. Let them all think I meant only that I have lived my life in service.* Looking up, I could see that Valka caught the double meaning, and there was a curious tilt to Prince Olorin's head that said he got it, too.

"*Netotta ti-koun, Aeta ba-Yukajjimn!*" Attavaisa said. *Answer me!*

"No," came the Emperor's answer, sharp as a ray of sunlight after a night of storm. "No, I think not." Caesar half-circled the holograph, hands clasped behind his back. "Not one more life, I said. Not one more will they take from me!"

"But Majesty!" said Lord Haren Bulsara, Director of the Colonial Office. "He is only one man! The xenobites offer reasonable terms!"

The Emperor was shaking his head. "I do not believe it!" he said, jerking his head in the direction of Ugin Attavaisa. "I do not believe it! They will take Marlowe, and take this fortress the next day!" He rounded on Bulsara and the rest of his counselors, on Saskia Valavar and all the rest. "I am scion of the House of Windsor, of the blood of the God Emperor himself! I do not accept *terms*. I am not some border-world baron to be cowed and broken!" He slashed a hand in the direction of the console. "I will not surrender even the meanest slave to these curs from outer darkness! They shall have nothing of me!"

"Nietiri mnu dein ne?" Attavaisa asked, not understanding the Emperor's words. Unlike the first generation of the White Hand, Attavaisa was still organic, still Cielcin, and so lacked Vati and Hushansa's facility for human speech.

Acting as translator, I said, "He says *no*."

Attavaisa hissed and stood, hauling its bloated slave to his feet. The fellow gasped and shook as the prince-turned-*vayadan* drew that man close, yanking the man's head back by the hair. "This man is known to you?" it asked.

I could only shake my head. *"Veih*. No."

"What is it saying?" the Emperor asked, unwittingly mirroring the *vayadan*'s own question.

"It asks if we know him."

Caesar's face revealed only vague puzzlement. Nicephorus squinted at the display, its head cocked to one side.

We had our answer the next second.

Duchess Valavar stumbled forward. "Gaspard?" she said. "Gaspard? Is that you?"

The slave opened his one still-working eye. "Saskia?" The eye watered. "Saskia?"

"Black planet," Nicephorus whispered, barely to be heard. "It's the duke."

The *vayadan* Attavaisa made a deep hissing noise, wrapped one ringed hand around the man Gaspard's throat. By his accents I guessed that beneath the crusted eye and vile contusions the man was palatine, and by her tears and the way her voice shook, I knew Lord Nicephorus had the right of it.

"Oreto oyumn o belutono ti-tajun!" Attavaisa's ink-black eyes flashed as it adjusted its grip on the Duke of Perfugium. *I see you know him.*

The former duke was naked but for a tattered breechclout. By his build and the lean muscles of his limbs I could tell he was not a fat man, which made the grotesque swelling of his belly all the more horrific.

"Turn it off!" I said. Attavaisa meant to terrify the Emperor and the other nobiles and patricians in the room.

Nicephorus said, "Caesar, that is Gaspard Llewellyn-Valavar, of a certainty."

At his chamberlain's prompting, Caesar raised a hand for silence and to draw Attavaisa's attention. "That is the Duke-Consort of Perfugium," he said to the *vayadan*. "What will you accept for his return?"

I did not translate Caesar's question. I had been here before, arguing with a very different Cielcin across a different holograph. "Radiance, you cannot reason with it."

"Ask it what it will take in trade for Duke Gaspard," the Emperor insisted.

"Radiance, it is trying to frighten us into capitulating. This is not a negotiation—there are *no* negotiations—this is a dominance display! It's a threat!"

William Avent's emerald eyes flickered to my face and back to the display. "Do as you are told, Marlowe!"

There was no easy way to ask the Emperor's question. As I had learned so long ago, one could only respond to the Cielcin as a king responds to his slaves, and one could only intimidate a Cielcin from a position of strength—and we had none. Only a desperate hope. "Give us the duke," I could only say.

Attavaisa's black tongue lashed. "His fate will be the same as yours."

True to my fears, the *vayadan* produced a knife, a wicked, curved thing the same shape and style as the weapon Dorayaica had drawn to slash its own hand the day of the Black Feast. This it drew without hesitation along the underside of Duke Gaspard's bloated stomach.

"Turn it off!" I shouted again.

Too late.

Too late I understood what it was we were seeing. The duke was not bloated, not swollen.

He was gravid.

Pregnant.

The *child* spilled from Duke Gaspard's torn bowels amid blood and dripping ichor, black and red. Already I could tell the thing was dying. Born too soon, its too-long limbs folded tight against its thin core. The first growth of horns showed on its high forehead, and its eyes were closed. Attavaisa let Gaspard fall, and in the bunker the Duchess Valavar screamed words I could not hear. Seven years in Dharan-Tun, and here was a horror I had not witnessed.

"Turn it off!" I said again, voice flat and far away. I had lost my mettle then, and felt like a man grasping, pawing about in the dark for a switch or sign.

No one heard me, and even the Emperor recoiled as Gaspard Valavar's Cielcin *child* twitched and went still. Its human parent—its host—went still a moment after, and Saskia Valavar sank—still howling—to the stone floor.

Prince Kaim had appeared from nowhere, placed himself between the woman and the projection, shielding her vision with the flowing sleeve of his *mandyas*.

Seeing the distress it had caused, Attavaisa laughed. The high, piercing sound of its inhuman laughter scratched like nails along the stone of our cavern. *"Raka si emumen ba-okarin iyad e ba-tajarin,"* it said. Its face was all teeth. Glass in black gums.

"Turn the damn thing off!" I was shouting. "Now!"

But Attavaisa had done its damage. Failing to secure what it wanted by coercion, it meant to have what it wanted by terror. And it *had* brought terror. I thought back to my gaoler, the Cielcin Gurana, about what it had wanted to do to me. And I thought back to the torn and headless corpses I had seen mounted on hooks outside the mouths of tunnels in the great cavern city before the doors of the Dhar-Iagon. It was not only to work as slaves that the Pale kidnapped entire populations, nor only as food—but as hosts. Incubators.

On the holograph, the black-clad *vayadan* stooped and seized Duke Gaspard by the hair, dragged his lifeless corpse up into the light again, that we might see him more plainly. The red ruin of his abdomen glistened wetly, and there was no light in his one clear eye.

"Vateba dein vatatha, eza ioman," the slave general declared, shaking Gaspard's lifeless form. *"Raka si emumen ba-okarin iyad e ba-tajarin wo!"*

"Turn it off!"

This time it was the Emperor who spoke the command, and at once the connection shattered. Darkness and silence ruled the war room, and for a moment no one moved except the Duchess Valavar. "I thought he was dead," she whispered into the Jaddian prince's shoulder. "All this time . . . I thought he was dead."

I could feel how brittle was that stillness, that quiet, could almost taste the tension and the horror on the air. Many of the logothetes and high officers knew what the Cielcin were capable of. I had known, had seen the signs on Dharan-Tun, had seen various reports in my long years of service. But to know a thing and to see it, to experience it, are as different as the moon and the finger pointing to it. Knowledge is not truth, only the apprehension of it. Experience is something else entirely.

"What did it say?" the Emperor asked. His hand was on my shoulder. For support? "Marlowe, what did it say?" I shook my head. To answer the Emperor's question was to do Attavaisa's work for it. To spread terror. But Caesar was insistent. "What did it say?"

I turned to hold the Emperor's gaze. "It said our fate will be the same as *his*," I said. "The duke's."

The door rolled shut behind me on a room filled with terror and doomed men. Lorian had remained behind to coordinate the evacuation, and I had half a mind to hurry back up to the level of the hippodrome door to help rally the defenders. Dazed, I had nearly cleared the long, purple-carpeted hall before a series of chimes sounded and a strained, feminine voice rang out.

"All Alpha Flight transport pilots and escorts to silo muster stations. Repeat. All Alpha Flight transport pilots and escorts to silo muster stations."

We were still besieged, and there was yet work to do. Despite horror, despite . . . everything. Time does not stop. Not ever. Not even once. The future comes, whatever it may hold. Alone of all the things and forces in the universe, Time will never end, and will remain—ticking on—after even Death has died and the universe lies dark and cold.

Hearing the order, I drew to one side of the hall as a runner hurried up the passage toward the war room with a message from one of the perimeter stations. He glanced aside at me, but did not stop. *He* had not seen a man disemboweled, had not seen a Cielcin spawn fall from his torn body. He had not dwelt seven years on Dharan-Tun, had not watched the slaughter beneath the black sun upon the black sands of Eue. His life moved on.

I checked the timepiece on my wrist-terminal. Eleven hours had passed since Rinehart had brought us to the Emperor, nearly half a standard day. When had I last slept? Before the descent into Resonno, but how long had that been? I needed to lie down. An hour. An hour would be enough, just enough to keep me on my feet. If the pilots were just then answering the muster call, there should be time—three hours, maybe four—before the first wave launched.

We had to time the operation perfectly. The launch of the first wave had to coincide with the arrival of Lin's air support, which meant his fleet in orbit must deploy the wings of aquilarii as they soared back over Resonno in their loop around Perfugium. The Cielcin defenders no longer held position in geosynchronous orbit above the city, having been chased to higher orbits by Lin's and the Jaddians' arrival, but the lighter wings would need a great deal of luck to penetrate whatever ground defenses remained in and around the city.

And once the silos started opening, revealing themselves across the city, the whole of the colonial storehouse complex would be compromised. Dozens of new gates would be opened, whole wings would need to be collapsed and sealed off to permit the defenders in the core to survive in the darkest depths above the cistern. Once done, there would be only three routes remaining to us for use in the event of escape. One lay through the Sanctum of the Blessed Wisdom, another of the many Chantry buildings in the heart of the ruined city. That was a dangerous road, for the inner parts of Resonno were still patrolled by the chimeric demons of Arae, still scouring the city for insurgents. The second ran through the sub-basement of the Agriculturalists Guild hall; while the third, and in many ways the least desirable path, descended to the level of the water far below and followed the track of a canal cut into the very rock of Perfugium. Thus it ran for miles before at last emptying into the River Deste, where it fell into the low countries on its way to the sea.

"Hadrian!" Valka pushed past the runner and into the hall, hurried after me. "Where are you going?"

"I . . ." I didn't have an answer. "Back to the hippodrome door. *That's* where they'll make their push."

She seized my wrist. "Let the soldiers do their job. We need you here."

"I'm wasted in there," I said, inclining my head toward the door. "That's why we brought Lorian." I tried to pull my hand away and go, but Valka held me fast, squeezed until I felt the ridges of my hollow bones pressing through my skin. "Let me go, Valka."

But Valka stepped in instead and wrapped her arms around me. She did not speak for a long moment, but pressed her head to my chest. Slowly, I felt the grip of the horror of the holograph loosen on my heart. My arms rose, one after the other, and encircled her in return. "I'm sorry," she said, still pressed flat against me. "I wish we could have saved you sooner. On Dharan-Tun, I mean. I wanted to. Otavia wanted to." I felt her head shift and found one golden eye peering up at me. "Was it like that all the time?"

"Like that," I agreed. "And worse."

"How do you think it will end?" she asked.

My eyes had locked onto a point on the wall opposite where a white scratch marred the gray cement like a scar. Holding Valka close, I glared at it, still half-frozen by the memory of Duke Valavar's vivisection. "There are only two ways it can," I murmured, grip tightening. I did not want to let her go. "Us. Or them." I forced my eyes shut, extinguishing the hall. "They've given us no other choice."

"We're never getting out of this, are we?" Her own hands tightened against my back.

She was afraid.

I could hardly remember ever seeing her afraid before. Startled, yes, and distressed. Even broken. But afraid? Truly afraid? Nothing we had experienced, nor anything she'd endured, had made her seem so small, so shrunken as she seemed in that quiet, lonely moment in the hall. Her left arm trembled as I held her tighter, wanting never to let go.

"I wish none of this had happened," she said. "This isn't the life I wanted. When I left home, I . . ." She pressed her forehead against my chest. "I wish we'd never gone to Padmurak. Or Vorgossos. Vorgossos is where it all went wrong." I could feel her fingers tighten, gripping my cloak. Her left arm shook, and I held her shoulder to keep her steady. "I wish none of this had happened to you. Or me. And I wish you weren't . . ." She stopped short, seeming to hold her breath. "Whatever you are."

"So do I," I said, pressing my cheek to the top of her head. I shut my eyes, and for a moment neither moved nor spoke. The strange calm that had settled over me in the war room returned then, a stillness like air expanding to fill a vacuum.

She was afraid.

She needed me *not* to be afraid.

The horrors of Dharan-Tun: the pit, the wall, the whippings, beatings, and broken bones, the starvation, the cold, and the white-hot agony of skin peeled off . . . these I could set aside. They were a poison, sure as fear. But I had suffered all any man had to fear, had come face to face with a deathless god old when the universe was young, and I was alive. And Valka was alive, and she needed me.

I said once that women sit in judgment over men, our judges, jurists—our executioners, if they judge us wanting; our patrons if they do not. In the Golden Age of Earth, ladies tied their favors to the lances of great knights before they rode their destriers to war. Men knelt to beg marriage and offered women a ring and their swords, and the woman—if she were worthy in her own way—kept the ring and restored to the man his sword.

Valka had given me her favor long ago, on a battlefield, on the Storm Wall above the plains of Berenike. I wore it still, had never taken it off since I found it again in the dust and desolation of Maddalo House where it had waited for me all those years.

She fished it out then, working the silver pendant on its chain out from beneath the collar of my armor. It clattered against the ceramic plate, and it took Valka a moment to seize it in her still shaking hand. "I watched you die," she said. "I saw it. We never talk about it, but I know what I saw."

I looked up, glanced briefly aside, afraid that some page or common logothete had overheard her. But we were alone. Dust trickled down from the concrete overhead, knocked loose by another bomb.

"I know." I laid my hand over hers to stop it shaking.

Her nostrils flared. "I can't keep doing this," she said, "I can't. *We* can't." Valka pressed her forehead against my chest. The scent of smoke and sandalwood still lingered in her hair, masked but not wholly obliterated by the day's exertions and the chemical tang of fear. "I can't lose you again." She thumped me with the hand clutching the phylactery pendant.

"I know," I said again, not letting her go.

"We should use this," Valka said.

Drawing back just enough to see her properly, I found her stroking the pendant, staring at her reflection in its silver surface, not really seeing it. She was seeing something else, something I could not quite see.

But I knew, and suddenly I couldn't breathe.

"You're not serious?"

"I think I am," she said, and nodded.

I almost laughed, would have, but all my air had left me.

The Tavrosi did not wed. To wed was to privilege one person—one partner—above the rest, and in their strange, unnatural view, such privilege was discriminate. Children were purchased from the clan, the *state*, by credit and standing—and purchased by an individual, not by a couple. Each clansman was expected to raise one, perhaps two children, and to do so alone. Valka's father had raised her. She had never known her mother. Often the clan itself provided the donor cells, though on occasion one clansman might request donation from a friend or even a lover.

My phylactery contained a preserve of Valka's blood, and its twin—about her neck—held mine. Valka's compromise. She was too much the Tavrosi to wed in the Imperial fashion, but Imperial enough to break her people's law. It was forbidden for the clansmen of the Demarchy to exchange phylacteries, for no clansman should have a sibling, or know two parents. To have such bonds was an unjust privilege to the Tavrosi mind.

But Valka had done it. For me.

"I want a child," she said. "I think. Our child."

I couldn't speak. Our whole life she had resisted. Maybe her Tavrosi upbringing just made the thought impossible for her even to consider. I didn't know, and after years had given up asking. It was enough that we had our life together, enough that she was not Lady Marlowe, but Marlowe's lady. Enough.

The centuries, it seemed, had worn her down at last, and at the last she had found in the bottom of her soul a wish and want she'd never known was there.

"I . . ." My tongue had dried, had filled my mouth. "You're sure? But I'm palatine." Any child we had without Imperial approval, without the Emperor's stamp and the oversight of the High College, would be an intus, misborn as Lorian was misborn. As Gilliam Vas.

It didn't really matter.

Again Valka thumped me in the chest. She had not released her grip on the phylactery. "We are saving your damned Emperor *right now.* I don't want to hear a word about palatines or High Colleges or any of it, *anaryan.* He owes you! Us! And he knows it! Once we're out of here, you make him give us what we want."

I did laugh then, and kissed her. "All right!" I said, and found tears in my eyes. "You're really sure?"

She bit my lip, moved her hand to the back of my neck and held me there, alone, the two of us at the end of the world. "You doubt me?"

"No," I simply said. "No."

I kissed her again in the dim light of that bunker while the violent thunder rolled, and the earth shook with the tramp of fire. None of it mattered. None of it could. We had each other—if nothing else—and that was enough.

It was all.

CHAPTER 37

THE RISING TIDE

EVEN THROUGH THE THICK concrete walls and steel blast doors and thousands of feet of bedrock and raw earth, the noise and force of ignition shook the world. Instruments rattled on the holograph display tables or tumbled from the desks that stood beneath wall consoles. Hand-in-hand, Valka and I watched from one edge of the central holograph as the various transport silos glowed red.

"Alpha Flight doors opening," announced the flight director, a scarfaced Martian officer in full crimson plate, turning to address the Emperor.

Among his retainers, Caesar nodded but did not reply.

"Gating error on A-17 and -19, sir!" announced one of the technicians seated about the perimeter. "The flumes won't open."

"Abort those launches!" the flight director replied, striding along the bank of consoles like a sea captain along the deck of his ship. I almost expected the man to brandish his saber. "Report."

The technician shook his head. "Unclear, sir, could be the flume's blocked. No fault in the electrical."

"Sir!" shouted another. "I'm detecting similar gating errors in A-41 and -46."

"They have to be buried," said Lord Haren Bulsara to the Emperor. "There are hundreds of launch bays dug across the city, Radiance. It's only natural we should lose a few. The bombings . . ."

The Emperor ground his teeth until I thought they must crack beneath the strain. "Rinehart! I want teams sent to those launch bays to ascertain the nature of the problem and get those flumes cleared!"

The Intelligence Director nodded and withdrew.

I could understand the Emperor's frustration. Each ship that made it free was another five hundred lives saved, and every blocked flume was another five hundred buried. And more than five hundred, for several of the launch tubes were track-fed, with second and even third transports chambered like the bullets in a gun.

"Prepare for burn!" the flight director exclaimed.

At the same moment, the same strained, feminine voice that had summoned the first wave of pilots said, "Countdown to ignition. Twelve, eleven, ten . . ."

Lorian caught my eye across the tri-D map of Resonno and the colonial store complex that shimmered between us. He had seated himself on a high seat, drawn one knee up to his chin. He pressed his lips together and bobbed his head.

". . . three, two. Go."

Red light flickered blue across the board before us, and glancing to the displays about the wall, I watched from a hundred different angles as the transport craft flared and rocketed up their slanting trackways toward the opened sky.

"Alpha Flight is away!" the woman said, and I picked her out, an older woman in the charcoal and gold of House Valavar, one hand to the earpiece and wire she wore. "Repeat: Alpha Flight is away!"

A strangled cheer went up in the room about us, a sound strangely muted and reserved. Lorian marked it, too, and moved a hand away from his mouth. "None of them are getting out of here. They all know it." He combed his hair back from his face.

"There's no way out but through," I agreed.

Lorian shook his head fiercely, eyes darting toward where the Emperor surveyed Alpha Flight's escape. "There's no way out for most of them. We can't take much more than His Radiance. The rest have to stay here, and they know it."

I followed Lorian's watery eyes toward the Emperor, who had turned from the map to watch the flight of the transport shuttles. I understood him perfectly then. They had to know—every one of them not in the Emperor's immediate circle of retainers and guards—they had to know they were to be left behind. The *Ascalon* would not carry more than a hundred, and there was no cavalry, no other chariot coming to rescue them. Some would find their places on the last wave of transports to leave the catacombs, but the men and women in that room? The ones coordinating the evacuation? They would not leave Perfugium, would be forced instead to remain, to fight to the last in darkness beneath the earth, or to attempt a last desperate retreat by one of the few passages remaining to them.

"Lin?" I asked.

"Sent the message," Lorian said, again taking his hand away from his mouth. "We have to trust him to do his part."

Valka squeezed my hand. "He will."

Several of the displays along one wall showed views from cameras mounted to the exterior of the shuttlecraft. Through one, I could see the mouth of one silo flume yawning from a bluff overlooking the city. Still more emerged from points along the base of the castle ziggurat, heretofore undetected by the Cielcin invaders amidst that castellated ruin. Through them all, I could stitch together a vague impression of the entire city.

A misery of ash.

The skeletal remains of sky-spires fingered the colorless sky, rising like the bones of leviathans from a desert of gray sands. But for the lines of shops and apartment buildings and the cracked domes of the city's sanctums—the commonplace humanity of those forms—almost it might have been the dull face of Eue I looked upon, and shuddered.

"'Tis like the end of the world," Valka said.

"It's the end of *a* world," Lorian said through his hand.

Silent and watchful, I turned from the topographic map to join the Emperor by the displays. I could not shake the thought that men were not meant to witness armageddon and live. How long would it be before flowers and green grass took root again atop the ruins of Resonno? How long before the ringer of the bells walked once more the dusty boulevards without fear of the sky? Would any live to do so?

As if in answer, two of the displays winked out.

Caesar turned toward them, his whole body going tense. Before he could ask the question, one of the techs spoke up. "We lost A-49!"

No sooner had those impacted the lords and officers than another flight tech spoke up. "A-12 is gone!"

The flight director rounded on his subordinates, roaring, "Where is the air support?"

Already the video feeds from the transport ships were beginning to fade, the images crackling, lost in snow.

"We're losing contact with the transports," said another technician.

"Get me eyes from the surface!" the commander said.

The images on the display wall began to change, cycling from the dead feeds from the transport cameras to watch-eyes embedded near the flume mouths. Half a dozen clouds of black smoke trailing shrapnel hung in the air above Resonno, but more than half a hundred columns of golden fire rose into the sky. The transports were flying, clawing for altitude and escape.

"Where are they?" the Emperor asked, half heard at my side. I swept my gaze over the dozens of angles, saw no sign of aircraft, of lighters or swarms of *nahute*.

Looking over my shoulder, I saw Lorian tapping his wrist-terminal, his wrist bent back to read the chronometer on the device's underside. He muttered something to Valka, shook his head.

"Your Radiance," I said, leaning to whisper in Caesar's ear. "We must get you to safety." The Emperor raised a hand to silence me, but I continued, "Radiance, the evacuation is underway. Please, leave the rest to your Martians. Permit me to summon my ship. We must get you to safety while we still can."

As if to punctuate the urgency of my words, another bomb shook the earth above our heads. The lights flickered, dimmed, flared back to life. I saw the black knife-shape of a Cielcin flier streak across one of the ground cameras.

"Alpha aught-one through aught-five are dark, sir," one of the techs announced. "There's too much static!"

On one of the screens, a yellow-white nimbus flared, overwhelming the camera a moment.

"Which transport was that?" the scar-faced director asked.

"I think we lost Alpha two-niner, sir!" replied one of the women at the consoles. "Confirmed. Alpha two-niner is down."

"Seven of them now," the Emperor said, and made the sign of the sun disc—prompting several about him to do the same. "May their souls find peace on Earth." Three and a half thousand of the refugees dead and gone in instants. "Thoras! What of those blocked flumes?"

The scarred flight director, Guard Captain Cedric Thoras, turned to bow and shake his head. "Nothing yet, Mars!"

"I want those ships free and clear!" Caesar barked, rounding on the holograph table behind us as an alarm flared.

Following him, I said again, "Caesar, please! Permit me the use of the telegraph. The *Ascalon* can be here in minutes!"

Again, the Emperor brushed me off. "Report!"

One of the Valavar officers minding the map of the tunnels jerked his head up. "One of their fliers dropped a charge down the silo at E-34. The launch sledge is shot."

"Have the garrison reinforce that position!" I said, drawing the Emperor's eye. "They'll try and force an entry, sire. If they can't dig out the hippodrome gate, they'll enter through any of the launch tubes they can."

The Emperor nodded slowly, rounded once more on the Valavar man. "Can you collapse those tunnels?"

The Valavar man had gone white, clearly petrified to be speaking with William Caesar. "We can, but not without cutting off the farther launch bays." He pointed at the map, showing passages that would be cut off from the greater tunnel network if approach to the compromised launch silo was collapsed. "The launch teams would be trapped."

The Emperor nodded again. "Send runners. I want those men told to take shelter on the transports. As many as the vessels will bear!" The man bowed in obedience and fled for the doors, already shouting for runners to dispatch to the higher levels of the catacomb complex. The Emperor turned to the rest of us, apparently satisfied. "The poor bastards will stand a better chance against the Cielcin guns in the air than they will in those tunnels."

As he spoke, he glanced back at Guard Captain Thoras and the bank of wall displays. The blue light of the holograph map lit his face with a spectral, deathly glow, hollowing his cheeks and highlighting the white gold in his red hair. I saw in that moment a shadow of the man's true age, fine shadows tracing their lines across the oft-unseen crags in that Imperial visage. William was old, older than me by centuries, and had for centuries borne the weight of Empire on his shoulders.

"Radiance, please," I said, and laid a hand on the lip of the holograph table. "Please, we must get you and the Prince of Jadd to safety." I looked round as I spoke, found Prince Kaim and his remaining Maeskolos standing nearer the display wall. "We may not have much time."

The Emperor pounded the rim of the table, rounded on me like a lion, roaring, "Enough, Marlowe!" I stepped back. "Do you think my life means more to me than the lives of all the millions on this world?"

"Of course you don't!" I said, regaining my footing. "Each life matters, Radiance. *Each*. But I have a mind also for the trillions of lives across our Empire to whom your life matters! You are not only a man, sire, but *Caesar*, and *Caesar* is a symbol. Of stability! Of civilization! Of *everything*!"

His Imperial Radiance William XXIII, King in Avalon and Guardian of the Solar System, stepped back, shock writ on his chiseled palatine features. The emerald eyes were wide. How long had it been since any in all the cosmos had spoken to him in such a tone? Not since his mother, the late Empress, died, I guessed. For who under all the stars of heaven would be so daring, or so foolish, as I?

"Have a care, Lord Marlowe," said bald Nicephorus from not far off.

William himself did not even know how to respond. His brow furrowed, mouth worked like that of an infant struggling for words. Like a drowning man myself, I reached out and began that day's long slide downhill.

I placed a hand on the Emperor's shoulder. "You have them to think of as well," I said, pressing the juice of sympathy into each syllable.

The Emperor recoiled from my touch. "Unhand me, Marlowe!" he said, and thrust a finger at me. "You overstep yourself! Not one more life, I told you. Not one more!" He turned away, turned back, teeth clenched. "More than two years I've been in this hole. Two years! While they butchered *my people* above. Every one of them under *my* protection! How many died? How many were eaten? How many met the fate of Duke Gaspard? Answer me that!" When I did not—could not—he bared his teeth at me. "Speak not to me of *symbols*. Not when there are men dying!"

He turned away, leaving me alone by the console's rim with Lord Nicephorus. The homunculus was silent, stood watching me with hard eyes. I glowered at it, breathed the words, "You know I'm right."

Valka stood silent over the Emperor's shoulder, her eyes very wide. All her life she had ridiculed the nobility, dismissed them as craven, as eaten out with greed, with cruelty. And here at last she saw the Emperor of Man himself moved to fury at his inability to save the lives of the very lowest. Farmers. Settlers. Pioneers.

"Thoras!" the Emperor bellowed. "I want the second wave ready to go, as many ships as you can launch! We haven't much time. Flood the skies above Perfugium. They can't kill them all!"

The Martian Guard captain acknowledged this order and turned back to his ranks of ship technicians. "Prime Beta Flight for liftoff!" The techs bent to their tasks, but Captain Thoras hurried about the perimeter, barking orders. When he reached the end he wheeled back and shouted, "Where is that damned air support?"

Lorian raised a hand, two fingers extended. He said nothing. I alone saw him at first. Even Valka did not; she was beside him and still watching me. Presently he dropped one, eyes glued to his chronometer.

Unable to help myself, I asked, "Lorian?"

The little man offered no reply, only glared down at his watch. Valka put a hand on his shoulder, but Lorian shook her off, darted a glance at the display wall. His lips moved.

He let his hand drop.

Nothing happened for several tense instants, and still the commander did not move, his brows furrowed. "Did I count it wrong?" he muttered, checked his wrist as Prince Kaim came up behind him.

A gasp rippled through the chamber an instant later, followed by an eerie stillness as the soldiers and technicians, the nobiles and logothetes all processed precisely what had happened.

The sky on the display panels had filled with starships.

Our starships.

Lin's aquilarii had come, and the shadows of their black wings filled the airs of Perfugium like a murder of crows, streaking down amidst the rising transports, all guns blazing as they picked their targets among the enemy aircraft and gun emplacements. In that moment, a great cheer went up from the men and women manning the terminals, and even Captain Thoras permitted himself one triumphant clap of his great hands.

The Emperor's jaw had gone tight again, but there was a smile on his usually impassive face.

Lorian Aristedes tapped his watch, confused. "Three seconds off," he remarked, obviously displeased. "I'm slipping."

Looking down at the good commander, Valka matched my grin. "Lin?" she asked.

"Lin," Lorian confirmed. "He telegraphed his launch."

The tribune had deployed his lightercraft at precisely the right moment as his fleet orbited the planet in its running gun battle with what I was sure must be Hushansa's portion of the fleet, had pointed them—per Lorian's plan—right at the city. Lorian knew the technical specifications of the Sparrowhawk- and Peregrine-class attack ships, knew the mass and circumference of Perfugium itself, and from that deduced to within a matter of seconds the precise moment in which Lin's men would arrive.

We may have been blind, deaf, and nearly mute in the bunker, but Lorian's one quantum telegraph had been enough. We had put our faith in Bassander Lin, and the Mandari officer—solid and dependable as ever—had not let that faith fall from his hands.

The aquilarii dove through the columns of smoke left by the rising transports and slashed them all to ribbons, tearing through the sky like a hail of arrows. On one display I saw a Cielcin bomber blown to pieces by an invisible ray of energy. On another, I saw one of the spider-tanks vanish in a burst of violet plasma. The white flash of teeth filled the war room as men and women dared to smile at one another, dared to hope.

"Burst transmission received!" one of the techs exclaimed. "Captain?"

Cedric Thoras hurried to the technician's side. "Put it through, man!"

The incoming voice was garbled, buried by the ocean of noise the Cielcin had pumped out to flood the airwaves, but he was close enough and his signal boosted enough that words still came through. *"Imperial Comm— . . . —ord Flight. Repeat . . . Sword . . . here to assist. Over."* A bright whine followed by the hiss of static played from speakers in the man's console.

It was enough.

Imperial Command, this is Sword Flight. Repeat. Imperial Command, this is Sword Flight. We are here to assist. Over.

Captain Thoras must have pieced the broken Standard together as well, for he leaned over the tactical display and half-shouted, "We read you, Sword Flight. This is Imperial Command. Guard the transports. Repeat. Guard the transports. Over."

"Copy tha— . . . —mmand. Over."

Satisfied, Thoras straightened and was heard to mutter, "We may just get out of this here yet." He rubbed his neck, then moved back toward the display wall. "Is Beta Flight primed for liftoff?"

"Not for another . . . six minutes, seventeen seconds, sir!"

Thoras barked an order for the men to hurry things along. The arrival of Sword Flight had eased the pressure of the moment, but standing in that dim and low-ceilinged chamber, one still felt the sensation of the walls closing in.

"Where is Lady Valavar?" Prince Kaim asked, coming to stand opposite us across the holograph, his warrior-concubine Tiada close at his elbow.

Valka and I looked round, as if expecting to find the proud duchess curled up beneath a table or in a corner between two of the consoles. She'd have had every right to be. The mere mention of the name *Valavar* sent flashes of Duke Gaspard's death crackling across my brain. "I don't know," I said, grimacing.

Kaim lay a hand on Tiada's arm, and, in Jaddian, ordered her to find the Duchess. "She should be on one of these transports at least. The next wave, perhaps." By the shape of his eyes in the holes of his mask, I guessed the prince arched his steep brows. "Any of these nobiles not needed for the defense should go, and should go now. We haven't the room for them aboard your ship."

"I know that," I said. "But the Emperor won't go yet."

"He will, I think, agree to save these." The prince gestured to the room at large.

I opened my mouth to reply, but at the same moment another alarm sounded. Still in his seat overlooking the map of the tunnels, Lorian said, "Looks like they breached the blast doors at silo E-34!" He pointed to a reticle flashing on the spider's web of tunnels, side chambers, and launch flumes.

"I thought they collapsed the tunnel?" I asked, looking to the Emperor.

William snarled, cloak falling across his snowy armor as he pushed back from the table. "Thoras! Send Belman to deal with the intruders! I want that tunnel sealed and the flight crews packed onto the next ship out of here!"

"Send a runner!" Thoras bellowed.

Stepping forward, Nicephorus pointed to one of the Emperor's pages, a homunculus like itself, and nearly twin to the one that been sent for Lorian and myself. "Maurice! You go! Find the lieutenant, double quick!"

Belman. May whatever powers that be curse the fool unto the last unkindling of the stars.

The androgyn leaped to its feet and ran fast as its slippered feet would carry it, yellow light streaming in from the hall as the Excubitors rolled the heavy door aside.

The Maeskolos Tiada appeared a moment later, leading a disheveled and shaking Saskia Valavar from some side chamber I took for a lavatory. Her once-luxuriant hair had transformed into a hideous snarl, and deep scratches marred her alabaster face where she had torn at her cheeks. And her eyes! Hollow as the abyss were they and swollen, red as dying stars.

Valka placed a reassuring hand on the duchess's shoulder, but Lady Valavar seemed not to feel it. Prince Kaim raised his voice, black eyes picking the Emperor out of his place across the holography table. "Emperor!" he said, no *Radiance,* no *Caesar.* "Permit me to escort the duchess and your ministers to the transports."

"What?" His Imperial Radiance looked round, settled on the prince. He looked almost surprised to find the Jaddian standing there. "Prince Kaim?"

The prince said, "We can load all the nonessential members of your court onto the transport shuttles. Please."

Steadily, the Emperor nodded, raised a permissive hand. "As you will," he said, eyes shifting to the duchess. "Saskia, I am sorry." Her eyes shifted to his for a moment, and in them there was no light. They flickered away.

Kaim turned to go, whistling to his mamluks. The Emperor raised his voice. "Marlowe, accompany him."

I blinked, looked round to find His Radiance stooped over the tri-D projection, studying the image of the catacomb system as though it were some biological sample on a slide. He did not look up.

"Radiance?" I asked.

"You are so eager to save our life, my lord," he said, and I caught the return to the Imperial *we* and felt my blood cool. "Perhaps you had better direct that energy to save these others. Go. Make yourself of use."

I bowed and—sensing it was best not to speak—for perhaps the first time in my life, said nothing. Wordless, I placed a hand on Lorian's shoulder. He gripped my arm briefly, and I touched Valka's arm. "I'll be back," I said softly, and pushed past her to join Kaim by the door.

"What's this, then?" The Emperor raised his head, and his eyes—which had before been hooded and veiled with labor and pain—were clear as green glass. "No parting remark?"

A spasm crossed my face, somewhere between a smile and a grimace. I was glad that neither the Emperor nor Valka could see it. As though my spine were a rod of iron, I turned and bowed again. "I am your servant, Radiant Majesty."

"Good," the Emperor replied. His voice faltered then, and those glassy eyes narrowed. "Do you remember your oath?"

"I have never forgotten it," I said, staring at a spot of the cracked concrete floor. About me, the technicians readied the second wave for launch, and the din of Thoras's shouting and the flight controllers' replies were like the distant crack of gunfire.

"See this course to its end, then," he said, citing a piece of that oath. The Emperor then threw back his cape and—to my astonishment—unhooked his sword from his belt and tossed the gilded thing to me as though it were a trifle. I caught it.

"Radiance!" Nicephorus gasped, is disapproval obvious.

I paid the chamberlain no heed.

The Emperor's sword was heavier than the Jaddian weapon I'd grown used to, doubtless the cost of all that gold. Her inlay was mother of pearl, and rubies shone in the pommel and at the hand guard by the emitter. The gold work was exquisite, but I had little time to admire the carved lions and delicate filigree.

I did not kindle her blade, but bowed my head. "I will," I said, and turned to go, reaching up to tear my cape away. Torn already, it would be more a hindrance than anything in the catacombs of the colonial store. I cast the garment—the white cape of the Imperial service—over the back of an empty chair by Lorian's side and hurried to join the prince. "Where's Sharp?" I said.

"Your man?" Kaim asked. "We left him by the cistern."

"Very good," I said, not sure Sharp was *my man*. My men were all dead—but for Aristedes. Sharp was Lin's. But I did not belabor the point.

The sound of a chair striking the cement upset the world behind me, and looking back I saw Valka leaping free to save herself from a fall. I caught her, realizing as I did that she'd upset the seat in her haste to catch up with me.

"Careful!" I said automatically.

"I'm coming with you," she said.

"I'll be right back!" I said.

She shook her head. "For the last time, Hadrian. You're not leaving me behind." She extricated herself from my grip and tugged her coif up over her red-black hair. Switching to her native Panthai, she said, *"Kar lasu braiyot, khwa?"*

One last fight.

CHAPTER 38

THE LABYRINTH AGAIN

IT IS PERHAPS STRANGE to speak of hope in so desperate an hour, and yet it was hope that filled my chest as Olorin and I escorted the Lady Valavar and a column of the Emperor's own ministers from the war room. Though the earth shook beneath our feet and dust fell like snow from the battered mold overhead, beneath my helmet, I almost smiled. I stopped and let the two Maeskoloi take the lead, and Valka passed me, guiding the shattered duchess with kind hands.

A child. After all our years.

The thought alone shed centuries from my shoulders, and I felt as though I walked upright once more for the first time since Padmurak, since Thermon, as though I was not the man who had suffered on Dharan-Tun, not the man who had died aboard the *Demiurge.* The boy I'd been was gone, replaced—renewed—by that thought and promise of a new tomorrow. A new future. A new life. Gone too was the woman I had met on Emesh, cold, cruel, and quick to judgment. I had changed so much since I left Delos, but I had little marked the changes in Valka. Not her wounds—invisible to many, if not to me—but as I had grown beyond my frame, so had she, abandoning her demarchist prejudices, if not the iron in her spine and jaw.

I loved her then, as well and truly as I ever had.

"We need to hurry!" Valka said to the other woman. "Come now, let's get you and your people out of here."

There was no reply as we passed into the crowded cistern chamber and Olorin's remaining mamluks began to force a path through the huddled masses. These were mostly patricians, I realized. Valavar palace staff and members of the Imperial retinue ill-suited to the task of running the defense. I shouted for Sharp, waving my arms as we advanced.

"To me!" I shouted, the Emperor's sword unkindled in my fist like the lord's scepter. "To me! Come on!" The centurion sprang toward me, slinging his rifle back over his shoulder, his men fast behind. "We need to get the duchess and the rest to the transports!" I said, indicating Haren Bulsara and the others who had come with us.

Sharp tapped his forehead twice to signal he'd heard over the noise of crowd and bombing, relayed the order to his men with a series of tight gestures. Our column thus assembled, we hurried back toward the outer gate of the cistern complex and back into the catacombs proper. As I ushered the last of the Emperor's surplus ministers over the threshold, the address system screeched, and when it had quieted, the brusque feminine tones of the flight controller rang out, *"Beta Flight is away! Beta Flight is away!"*

About me, the patricians massed about the rim of the cistern drew their neighbors to themselves. No cheering here, only tension and quiet prayers. I could read the lips of a woman near to me.

Bless me with the Sword of your Courage, O Fortitude . . .

Unconsciously, I curled the thumb and first finger of my free hand into the sign of the sun disc, a wordless prayer to a god in whom I did not believe. And the god in whom I *did* believe was silent, too.

We moved out into the tunnels, spurred forward by every alarm, every muffled blast of artillery and crash of dying vessel from the surface up above. Though I saw none of it, I could picture the carnage overhead as plain— more plainly—than the cramped and frigid corridors through which we weaved. How well I saw gray Resonno beneath its pall of smoke and swirling ash! How clear were the Sparrowhawks and Peregrine lighters to me in that moment, wings tacking against the wind, guns shouting fire!

Lin's ships had dropped from low orbit, streaking toward Resonno from the west like a charge of cavalry down the green slopes of Earth. The blast of their lances had broken the artillery emplacements and circling bombers of the Pale, and chaos reigned in the airs above our heads. Beta Flight was rising into a charnel house of falling lighters, of particle beams, and of churning shoals of *nahute* deployed to darken the sun like the locusts of lost Egypt.

"This way!" Prince Kaim said, leading us round a bend. Tired soldiers drew aside as we hurried past, shouting questions and asking for orders.

"Hold your positions!" I said to one shaggy officer, pounding the fellow on the arm. "We're getting the duchess aboard the next wave out of here!"

A sign done in luminous paint glared from the wall ahead. *BAYS*

E21—E40, it read, with an arrow pointing right. Last of the company I rounded this bend, driving a pair of timid logothetes ahead of me like cattle.

"Lord!" shouted one of the sentinels guarding the passage door. "What's going on? A column of the Emperor's lads ran through not ten minutes back, didn't say a word!"

The Emperor's lads. That would have been Martian Lieutenant Belman on Thoras's orders. Did the man not know? I hesitated only a minute. "The Pale breached at Bay E-34!" The man blanched, took a step back. "Reinforce this position, hold until we get back! Is this the only route to these terminals?"

The man blinked. "There's another way up near E-41." He pointed. "Martians went on thataways. Didn't say no word!"

"You hold until we get back!" I said again, and hurried after Valka, the Dragonslayers, and the Jaddians.

We hadn't to go far.

The path ahead wound in a broad corkscrew by several turnings up and up toward the surface and the level of the launch bays. Doomed sleepers watched through black glass from fugue pods to either side, and here and there the crunch of frost sounded underfoot where our boots disturbed the heavy rubber mats that protected us from a fall.

"All Gamma Flight transport pilots and escorts to silo muster stations. Repeat. All Gamma Flight transport pilots and escorts to silo muster stations."

The announcement chased us up the ramp, and as we rounded the last spiral I knew we were close. Smoke filled the air and clouds of rock dust, and I tugged my coif back up over my head and punched the controls for my helmet. I pitied the duchess and the ministers, who could not so protect themselves.

"We have to move fast," I muttered to no one in particular.

Something small and shining snapped out of the fog ahead. Tiada's blade rose to meet it, and caught it mid-flight. The two pieces of the hurled weapon fell like stones, sparking to the catacomb floor.

"Nahute!" I cried, seeing the shining thing land at my feet.

We had found the Cielcin.

An instant later, the sounds of gunfire echoed from the hall ahead. Belman's men? And a horned and fangy devil leaped from the cloud of dust and smoke ahead. The Cielcin had to stoop in the cramped confines of the tunnel, but its kind had been born below ground, in the lightless caverns of Se Vattayu. It was made to crouch. It roared at us—a high, grating sound like iron on glass—and smashed one of the fugue creches with the heavy mace it wielded. Cryonic fluid blue as royal blood spilled out onto the rubber matting, mingling its mist with the smoke and dust as it heated rapidly, cooling the air. The body within the creche sagged, and the instrument panel beeped and blared red.

A piece of the old fear thrilled in me once more, and I felt my feet waver. But for Attavaisa, I had not seen one of the xenobites since that black day on Eue, and Attavaisa had been but a holograph. The reality was something else, something wicked, the noseless, wide-eyed face like a skull crowned with fingers of bone. The slitted nostrils flared as it bellowed another war cry and charged.

I needn't have feared.

Olorin leaped forward himself. Highmatter shone milk-white in the gloom, its radiance catching on the spilled fluid and filling the dusty air. In a single fluid motion, the Prince of Jadd parried the monster's mace and struck the horned crown and head from its neck. Olorin shoved the body aside just in time to strike another of the *nahute* from the air.

More were coming. I could see their shadows boiling ahead. Three more of the *nahute* sprang forth, and though the Maeskoloi ahead caught one between them, two rushed by, seeking the throats of the men in our column.

"Guard the duchess!" Sharp shouted, pushing forward. One of the mamluks kicked off one wall and snatched the silver serpent from the air. It fell to the ground amidst the rapidly warming cryonic fluid, wrestling the snake-thing to the ground. The mamluk held it away from its body while another of the Jaddian homunculi shot the machine near its head. Elsewhere, another of the things had grappled one of the Dragonslayers, wound its tail around his arm while the drill-bit head ground against the ceramic of his armor.

The *scahari* fighters who had hurled the deadly things appeared an instant later, pouring out of the fog. Sharp's men surged forward, forming a solid block between the xenobites and the unarmed nobiles we escorted. The first rank of the Cielcin fell like chaff beneath the shout of the legionnaire's guns, but those behind them jumped over their fallen allies, maces flashing.

These had been Attavaisa's warriors, I guessed. They dressed strangely, not in black with the white masks I had come to associate with the Prophet's army—and thereby with the Cielcin as a race—but in grays like dry bone, their faces bare, teeth snapping as they roared and laughed and smashed their maces through the glass of fugue pods to either side. A few still wore the cobalt badge of Attavaisa's *scianda* and *itani*, its world-fleet and blood-clan. So much had changed in what was—for the xenobites at any rate—so little time.

"Hold!" Sharp could be heard bellowing. "Hold the line, lads!"

So ferocious was the attack of Attavaisa's berserkers that but for the mamluks of Jadd they might have pushed through. One huge fighter brushed past Tiada and Prince Kaim-Olorin and swept three mamluks from their feet at a single blow. Then fully half a dozen of the Jaddian homunculi surged forward—no thought of safety or fear of death in their vat-grown hearts—and leaped upon their foe, knives drawn. The massive Cielcin's knees buckled, and it crashed to the ground, weeping blood from dozens of puncture wounds.

Prince Kaim himself, undaunted by his brush with the behemoth, advanced like the swell of a riverbank with the first snows of Delos's brief spring. His blade moved effortless through three of our attackers, leaving the Cielcin to litter the floor in grisly pieces.

"*Empras!*" he shouted to his mamluks, brandishing his sword. And again he shouted, "Forward!" for the benefit of my men. My eyes followed the direction of his blade to where another phosphorescent sign said *BAYS E21–30,* with an arrow pointed left, and *BAYS E31–40* leading right.

"Olorin!" I shouted. "Left!" If the Cielcin were coming from E-34 as Thoras and his flight controllers surmised, then we needed to move *away* from them. Each of the launch bays housed multiple shuttle transports, some as many as five, each chambered like the bullets of an antique gun and ready to slot into place once the launch tube cleared.

Olorin saluted awkwardly with his left hand to show he'd understood, then spun round, *mandyas* fluttering like a lonely wing. Sharp and his men turned right, holding the corridor against any threat that might be coming as Valka and I ushered Lady Valavar, Lord Bulsara, and the rest forward.

"Earth and Emperor protect us," Bulsara muttered. He too was shaking.

"First time, my lord?" asked one of the Dragonslayers, helping the Director of the Colonial Office over the body of a fallen *scahari.*

Bulsara shook his head, not in denial, but because he feared to speak. The director had gone pale as milk, and his heavy mustache trembled. How well I understood.

"Hadrian!" Valka's voice shocked me as I rounded the corner, turning left to follow the Jaddians and the stumbling courtiers. She caught my arm and dragged me back a step. Just in time. The mace descended with all the finality of a headsman's axe, striking the stone floor with a mighty clangor. I whirled to face my assailant. The berserker had punched its way through Sharp's line, its sheer mass and ferocity overcoming the fire of their guns.

And it was shielded.

But the Emperor's sword sang in my hand. I depressed the twin buttons that conjured the blade. The weapon's weight balance shifted in my hand as the exotic highmatter streamed out, turning from a heavy ingot to a thing supremely balanced and sharp as cutting light. The blade caught the berserker's left hip as it extended, and I dragged it upward as it turned to strike at me with its heavy club. The point slid cleanly upward, cutting through bony armor and the supply hoses that paralleled its ribcage so that it exited via the left shoulder. Desperate to parry the still-swinging mace, I slashed *through* the monster's torso to sever the arm above the elbow.

Ichor black as ink spilled from the ruined xenobite as it fell in pieces to the floor. Ahead of me, Sharp's men had reformed their line and were pulling back, firing with every step. "Go! Go!" I shouted to Valka, urging her ahead. I lingered only a moment.

A single red eye floated through the mist and smoke over the heads of the Cielcin opposite Sharp. A chimera, a demon of Arae. One of the Iedyr? I could not say. Had Vati come as well? Or were Attavaisa and Hushansa alone in leading this fight?

I shifted Caesar's sword in my hand, unable to help but admire the feel of it, the perfection of its craft. It was a thing honest and clean, a piece of human ingenuity at its finest, a triumph of mortal consciousness and art over the laws of physics.

A fierce, concussive *boom* filled the tunnel then, and over the heads of the Dragonslayers and the Cielcin I saw a flash of white light and a rush of wind as a shockwave shook the catacombs. Someone had let off explosives further up the hall. Belman and his men, I guessed. Had they collapsed one of the tunnels?

"Damn!" I cursed to myself. What I would have given for reliably working comms.

The red eye turned away, drawn off, I guessed, by this new and greater threat.

"Hadrian! Sharp!" Valka called from the shaft behind. "Move it!"

I hesitated only a moment before turning to chase after her.

"Enemy troops have entered the base!" came the voice of the chief flight

controller again. *"Enemy troops have entered the base! All gate teams to high alert! Repeat! All gate teams to high alert!"*

Olorin and Tiada had reached the gate that led to the cluster of launch bays we sought. The guard checkpoint was empty, though whether the men had been forced to flee or deserted was any man's guess. There was a map of the launch terminal pasted on one wall, and Valka glanced at it, the inhuman processors in her mind subitizing the information at more-than-human speed.

"The tunnel dead ends here!" she said. "Launch flumes are just ahead! Centurion!" She looked back and called to Sharp, "Hold the gate!"

Sharp did not reply, but with his men dug in about the cyclopean masonry and metalwork of the gate.

"Centurion!" Valka said.

"I heard you!" Sharp shouted, holstering his short plasma burner to tug the rifle from his shoulder. "Just go!"

Side-by-side then, Valka and I hurried after the Jaddians and our charges.

Tiada was already banging on the first door, shouting for the men within to open it.

"Let me by!" Valka exclaimed, shouldering the Maeskolos woman aside. She stooped over the door panel, cursing in Panthai and Nordei without distinction. *"Khun!"* One-handed, Valka tapped at the controls. "I can't *hear* anything," she growled. I knew the neural lace in her head relied on her sensory cortex, mingling the higher, computational functions of her implants with her ordinary senses. She could *hear* these devices, *feel* them, even *see* their transmissions on the air. "Too much damn noise. *Khun!* Ah!" The panel lights cycled red to blue, and the door opened.

The three men within raised guns to greet us, but seeing we were human dropped them. One still had his hands on the controls. "Sorry," he said. "Thought you were them at first." Two wore Valavar fatigues, and the third an unmarked black jumpsuit, an oxygen mask strapped across his lower face. One of the sleepers, I realized, one of the pilots Lorian had convinced the brass to rouse from his frigid slumber. The fellow looked half-ready to fall over where he stood.

"How long until you can launch, man?" I asked, looking past the trio and through the little airlock to where the new transport waited on the rails. The mouth of the launch tube stood open, and beyond its aperture I saw a patch of grayish sky, heard the scream of Peregrine engines as Lin's aquilarii tore overhead. To the left, the hangar door stood open, and I could see the ship of the fourth wave already waited to roll out onto the launch rails. Fuel hoses still ran to the ship, priming for launch. Ice was forming on the line and on the exterior of the ugly transport's fuel tank.

"Ten minutes?" the pilot mumbled. I had to get him to repeat it.

"Good!" I said. "How many of these can you take?" I asked.

"Five?" the pilot said. "Maybe six? It'll be cramped."

"It'll have to be. Lady Valavar, here!" I snapped my fingers, summoning her as she herself might have called a common serving girl. Bulsara brought her forward. The duchess still seemed like one far away. As if none of what was happening were real to her. How well I understood that feeling. "Not you, my lord!" I held Bulsara back. "We'll want you in another ship. Valka, Tiada. Try another of these doors. Go!" I shoved Bulsara toward the Jaddians. "Pilot! This woman is Duchess of Perfugium. Treat her with all due respect and courtesy, but her safety comes first. Get her to orbit and signal the fleet. Ask for Tribune Bassander Lin. Tell him Hadrian Marlowe sent you, and you have the duchess in your charge." I gave him the frequency to hail the *Tempest*, made him repeat it. "Go!" I shoved the duchess through the portal. "Take her! And you four!" I brandished the Emperor's blade in the direction of four courtiers, three logothetes and one of the androgyn pages. "Go!"

They went.

"And seal the door behind you! Don't open it for any reason! Even for us!" When the pilot and his two technicians just *stood there* unmoving for half a second, I screamed, "Now!"

The door slammed. With Saskia Valavar gone and Haren Bulsara on his way, I hurried back toward Sharp. "Any sign?"

"They've gone up the other way, lord," the command centurion said, still sighting through his rifle scope.

"Good." I leaned against the wall beside him, winded from all my shouting, and looking back saw Tiada ushering Bulsara and a half-dozen others through the doors. "Good." That was another weight lifted. With the duchess and Director of the Colonial Office safe and much of the court offloaded, that left only the Emperor and those few closest to him—Rinehart, Captain Thoras, his Excubitors, and Lorian, of course—to worry about bringing to the *Ascalon*.

Prince Kaim came running back down the hall, a quartet of mamluks in his train. "We should collapse this tunnel behind us when we go!" he said, pointing up at the roof beyond the guard station. "Can you close this gate?"

"Are the pilots all here?"

"I think so," the prince replied. "They were in the bays we opened."

I chewed my tongue then, watched Valka press a pair of Legion Intelligence boffins over the threshold into Launch Bay E-26. "I don't want to strand any one of these ships without a pilot," I said, thinking of the five hundred sleepers left aboard.

"Nor I," Kaim-Olorin replied. "But better stranded and sealed in than prey for these *davoi.*"

It was hard to argue with his logic. Fully fueled, the transports might sustain the fugue creches for days, even weeks—long enough to perhaps excavate the tunnels and save them if saving the Emperor meant drawing off the Cielcin assault. If the Cielcin remained, on the other hand . . . if they stayed to starve or smoke the survivors out of the catacombs and colonial store complex, it would mean hundreds, thousands more dead than might have been had we not secured this branch of the tunnel system.

"*Noyn jitat,*" I swore.

"Indeed," the Jaddian agreed. "My friend, I fear we have no choice."

"You may be right," I allowed. Valka and the others came running back. How small our party looked stripped of our courtly charges! A mere fifty-some of Sharp's Dragonslayers and perhaps half as many mamluks. Maybe fewer. "Who has the charges?"

"That'd be me," said Aron, one of Sharp's decurions. The man produced a pair of shining metal pucks about the size of tea plates from a sabertache strapped to his dinted armor.

"I cannot make the decision, my friend," said Prince Kaim, eyes on me.

"We'll do it," I said, after only a moment's deliberation.

The blast wave chased us back down the spiral ramp toward the men who held the lower gate. Aron had placed his charges right where the tunnel branched, where I had slain my first enemy of the day. Belman's men would have to circle back by their other route once they secured launch bay E-34.

"What news?" asked the captain of the guard station.

"They won't be getting in this way!" I said, seizing him by the shoulder. "No one will. Seal the gate here and draw back to the cistern. If the Pale get in some other way, I don't want you lot cut off."

The captain's brows drew together, and he pointed. "But the gate!"

"They'll have to dig through ten tons of rubble to come at us this way!"

I said, looking round the twenty or so men of the guard. "Which of you is fastest?"

"My lord?" The captain blinked, uncomprehending.

"Send a runner back to the Emperor. Tell him the duchess and Lord Bulsara are away. Tell him to launch Gamma Flight as soon as possible."

One man—hardly more than a boy—leaped down from a ledge high in the wall to our right. "I'll go!" he said, hiking up his shield belt. He wore no armor, only the drab fatigues of House Valavar. He would move faster than the lot of us could together.

"Good!" I said, seizing the lad by the shoulder. I made him repeat the message, spurred him up the hall. "Go now! Tell His Radiance we're on our way back!"

CHAPTER 39

MARS

OUR LITTLE EXCURSION TO deliver the nobiles to safety had not cost us too dearly. We staggered back through the main gates to the cistern and the command center with only a few fewer men than we'd departed with. A handful of Prince Kaim's mamluks had fallen, and a couple of Sharp's men. But we had saved the Duchess of Perfugium and much of the Emperor's surviving court—and though they were common bureaucrats like Bulsara, they were something.

Waving Olorin and the Jaddians on, I stopped in the mouth of the tunnel back to the Emperor's command center and put out a hand to stop the centurion. "I am sorry," I said, "about your men."

With his helmet on and face obscured, I could not tell if Sharp was looking at me or not. He did not turn his head. "That's the job, lord."

"All the same, I am sorry." Sharp's unit had—like the Irchtani before them—lost around half its members between the battle on Ganelon and the siege on Perfugium.

"That's the job," Sharp said. "They did what they had to do. Same as you and me." He turned his back, shrugging his shoulder to resettle the long and cumbersome rifle. "Worse ways to die than saving the Emperor."

"We haven't saved him yet," I said.

The centurion did not turn back. "Then we'd better. Else the lads will haunt me from here to Earth." He held his right hand up, thumb and forefinger curled in the sign of the sun disc.

I opened my mouth to reply, but one of the other Dragonslayers called out, "Oi, Quent!"

The centurion did not wait to be dismissed. He hurried to his men, and I turned, found Valka staring at me from the doorway. "What?" I asked.

She shook her head. "Come on."

The whole planet shook beneath us, and Valka staggered into me. I caught her, peered up at the roof above our heads. "That was too close," I said, not taking my eyes from the roof. *Bomb or lighter crash?* I remember thinking.

The war room was a fury of tension and shouted orders as Valka and I joined the prince and the Emperor at the holograph table. "The duchess and Lord Bulsara are safe aboard their transports!" I said, still holding the Emperor's sword hilt in my fist.

Caesar looked up at me. "We know. We had your runner, and the prince here was just explaining the details." He raised a hand to Kaim, who stood with Tiada by Caesar's side.

"Gamma Flight, two minutes to ignition!" the flight controller said.

Captain Thoras's response cut over the flight controller. "Any luck with the commsat?"

"What's going on?" I asked, aiming my words at Lorian.

The Emperor answered in his place. "Your man here telegraphed the fleet. They're trying to float a frigate above the city as a comm buoy."

"Will that work?" I looked at Lorian.

The good commander's colorless eyes found mine, and he made a curious, shrugging expression with his mouth. "The Pale have blocked every radio frequency I can think of, but Lin's fleet has a couple old *Gorgon* interceptors. They've got high-energy maser projectors, should be powerful enough and tight enough to bypass all the Pale's noise."

"But I thought all your receivers were shot?" Valka asked the table at large.

Unseen in the Emperor's shadow, Director Rinehart said, "The station's all are, but if we ground one of the transports and hard-line it into the storehouse datasphere, we can use the ship as a transceiver. Communicate with the fleet."

"They're above the noise?" I asked, picturing a cloud of interference like smog blanketing the world. But the radio waves the Cielcin had pumped into the air above Resonno would be caught against the planet's ionosphere, and low orbit beyond the Heaviside layer would be clear of their interference. If Lorian's plan was successful, if Lin could float a frigate above the ionosphere and the city alike, and we could rely on tightbeam from one of the intact colonial transports . . .

"Seems like," Lorian answered. "Lin didn't mention any trouble in his telegraph." He lifted an actual sheaf of paper printed from one of the wall consoles. Valka took it from him and started reading.

"Won't you have to leave the silo open?" I asked. "To receive the maser bursts?"

"Yeah," Lorian said, "but they're open already. What we really have to hope is the Pale don't catch on to the fact that one silo's not firing. Otherwise we'll have to block up another launch flume grounding the transport if we want a clear beam."

"Gamma Flight ignition in one minute."

I ran the numbers. There had been just under one hundred and fifty active launch silos when Alpha Flight had taken off. That meant a little more than six flights were needed to evacuate all the transports the Emperor had on-station when the attack had started. Nine hundred seventeen transports. Four hundred fifty-some thousand men. Millions more remained on Perfugium, would likely die there, never to wake from their icy slumber.

At my back, Thoras was shouting orders to the flight controllers.

"Which ship is in E-22?" I asked, pointing at the bay where we'd left the Duchess Valavar.

Lorian squinted over my shoulder at a wall display. "Gamma aught-seven."

"G-07 is the duchess," I said to the Emperor and to his staff, relaying Lorian's words. "Caesar, I implore you. Let me summon the *Ascalon*. Your men can to see to the rest here."

I had timed the question almost perfectly, better than Lorian had timed the coming of the aquilarii. The instant the words left my mouth, the chief flight controller's voice sounded throughout the bunker's internal address system. *"Gamma Flight is away. Repeat. Gamma Flight is away."* Deep as we were beneath the earth, the churn of so many engines was like the gallop of a hundred thousand horseman over our heads. Again the cry of relief and hope went up through the chamber, and again the shape and fire of rockets rising through smoking air and combat filled the monitors on all sides. Numbers flashed red and the Cielcin shot the rockets down.

Lorian bit one fingernail and tucked his legs up under himself in his high seat.

But the Emperor ignored me. His gloved hands gripped the rim of the table, but his eyes were on the list on the wall display opposite. G-04 went red. G-16. G-29. 31. 44.

"They're dropping like leaves," William said. How clearly I remember the pathos in his voice, the utter weariness. "Is the air support not holding?"

But the Martian captain did not hear the Emperor. Cedric Thoras was shouting for the flight controllers to move Delta Flight into position, his words punctuated by the insensible fragments of comm chatter from the aquilarii in Sword Flight bursting over the comm line.

"What is happening up there?" the Emperor bellowed at his captain.

"Radiance!" The door to the hall slid open, and a man staggered over the threshold to fall ten paces from the Emperor's feet. Four Excubitors stepped reflexively forward to defend Caesar from this new threat, and Lord Nicephorus moved to stand between the Emperor and the runner. But there was no threat. By his red plate and white tunic, he was one of the Martian Guard. His helm was gone, and his face—when he raised it to implore the Emperor's attention—was smeared with blood.

Red. Not black.

"Radiant Mars!" he said, one hand pressed to his wounded side. He was struggling to breathe. "The . . . lower gate. The lower gate is overrun! The Pale made it through. Used some kind of plasma . . . plasma bore. Didn't stand a chance."

Breaking every protocol I thought I understood about the Imperial person, the Emperor pushed Nicephorus gently aside and knelt before his wounded man. Taking the Martian by the shoulders, the Emperor asked, "The lower gate?" He spoke smoothly, calmly, trying to soothe the wounded man. "Do you mean the hippodrome access?"

The Martian nodded, gasping. Blood dripped from his wound onto the stone floor. "Came as fast as I could. We're overrun."

"Where is Commander Votta?" the Emperor asked.

"On Earth, Mars."

Dead. I circled round behind the Emperor as the Martian spoke, trying to get a sense of the poor fellow's wounds. One bloodied hand gripped his side below the ribs. His right side, right above the liver.

William Caesar froze for only the barest instant, said, "So he is."

You have heard stories of the Emperor and his Martians. Everyone has. They say—though I had long suspected it was not true—that they were all taken as boys from the prison slums on Mars in the very shadow of Old Earth herself. That they were reared on stories that they were a chosen people, so close to Mother Earth and so long suffering. That they were trained in fanatic devotion to the service of the Emperor. That it was hoped such devotion might prevent them—like the Praetorians of ancient Rome—from asserting control of the Throne and of Caesar himself.

But watching the Emperor with his Martian, I almost believed the tales were true.

Some tales are.

"Someone fetch this man a medic!" the Emperor snarled.

"At once," Nicephorus said, already running.

Rinehart hurried forward to help the Emperor with the wounded man.

With tender care, the Emperor helped to roll the man onto his back and stood. Red blood marred the Imperial breastplate, but bubbled and rolled from the fabric of the Emperor's cape and would not stain it. Turning, Caesar's eyes found mine. "You!" he said, and thrust a wet finger at me. "You led them to the hippodrome!"

"You summoned me!" I did not bow my head. "I came!"

"Go!" Caesar pointed toward the open portal whence came his wounded man. "We are not finished here! I will not leave this place until we have done all we can. Go and hold the gate *you opened*, my lord!"

Again I did not bow. I did not protest. I looked to Valka, to Prince Kaim. Beneath the mask, Olorin nodded.

"So be it," I said, adjusting my grip on the Emperor's sword. "So be it."

CHAPTER 40

THE GATES OF THE UNDERWORLD

IT WAS HARD NOT to admire the man. I could find no fault in him I had not found once—more than once—in myself. The sight of blood and his people's death had him in a rage. I see now that he was on Eue himself, living his nightmare. Caesar meant what he had said to me on multiple occasions. He *was* humanity. Its guardian. Its servant. He felt each death as I had felt the deaths of my Red Company on the sands beneath the walls of Akterumu, though the men and women of Perfugium and the store-house were all strange to him. Thirty months the Emperor had been trapped beneath the surface of that world, forced to watch his cities burn, his people suffer. Gaspard Valavar had done for him what Adric White's head had done for me on Dharan-Tun, what Prince Aranata's pet translator had done aboard the *Demiurge*: had made the Cielcin utterly beyond good and evil, beyond the border conditions imposed on petty human morality by millennia of acculturation and pursuit of all that was good and true. He had known the duke, and so his death and humiliation had lit a fire and a fear in Caesar's belly hot and white and quenchable only by the blood of victory or abject defeat . . . and though Caesar was himself on Eue in his way, all was not quite lost, however desperate the hour.

How could I, who had abandoned hope and found it again in Valka's love, fault a man who'd yet to stumble?

I could not. Or should not, at least.

Valka at my side, the Jaddians ahead, Sharp and his men at my back, we hurried to the relief of the lower gate. Other soldiers rushed ahead of us while the remaining logothetes and members of the Imperial court and Valavar retainers dragged and carried wounded. No man or woman was idle, and the cramped corridors made going slow, even when Kaim and Tiada brandished their swords to clear a channel for us.

There would be chaos in the tunnels behind. With the Cielcin penetrating the base, the Emperor was sure to lose control of the huddled masses about the cistern soon. If he was not careful, His Radiance would soon have a riot on his hands. With the fortress breached, the Cielcin would not stop their onslaught, even if we were to escape with the Emperor. They would pillage and rape and slaughter until every man and woman—awake or sleeping—was carried back to Attavaisa in chains. Perfugium would be made an example of, a horrid cinder and a warning to all who looked upon it or upon the footage of its ruin: defy not the Great King, the Pale Prophet of the Cielcin. *He* is your master now.

Even without the Emperor in chains, the sack and loss of so great a bastion of Empire would strike a blow to every human heart. As sure as the loss of Marinus and the Veil, the destruction of Perfugium would send its message: man is not the master of the galaxy. The Centaurine provinces would start to fracture. The Cielcin would come screaming into man's void, would assail Vanaheim, Salamass, Siraganon—would assail Nessus itself, and move beyond Nessus to Gododdin, and from Gododdin to the topless towers of Forum itself and tear the Eternal City from the skies.

That, doubtless, was what the Prophet foresaw. Perfugium was to be but the first link in the chain that hanged mankind. Whether I was killed or not, whether the Emperor was killed or not, it didn't matter.

The campaign was on.

I told you once that the universe has no center, and thus every point is its center, and it is so. If I have strained you, reader, by my repeated insistence that every action matters, that every moment of every life is *the* moment, the axis about which all things turn, understand that I say these things because they are true. Every step, every turn, every refusal to step.

Everything matters.

The cosmos is not cold or indifferent because *we* are not indifferent, and we are a part of that cosmos, of that grand *order* which has dropped from the hand of He who created it. Every decision creates its ripples, every moment burns its mark on time, every action leads us ever nearer to that last day, that final last battle and the answer to that last question:

Darkness? Or light?

Perfugium was only one link in that great chain, but still Perfugium *mattered*. Mattered indeed *because* it was a part of that chain, a part of the Quiet's shortest path to that rocking cradle. The gates that had been opened in the belly of the world were the gates of hell itself, and the Cielcin who came pouring in were demons then in truth, servants of the Watchers who would answer *Darkness!* and make all forever silent.

Every moment matters. Every battle. Every step.

"Delta Flight is away!" The message echoed above even the sirens as we reached the level of the gate, clear as the ringing of bells had been in the city above. *"Delta Flight is away!"*

Two flights left, I remember thinking. *Only two.*

"Shouldn't we reinforce the guard posts between here and the Emperor?" Sharp asked. "Seal the doors?"

"No!" shouted Martian Lieutenant Belman, who had returned from his sortie just as we were departing and who had been drafted as our guide. "That'll leave us unable to reinforce the launch flumes in the south terminal complex."

"But those bays are all locked from the inside."

"They only need to blow one to turn this whole tunnel complex into a blast furnace," the lieutenant replied.

That was an unpleasant thought, and for the first time I realized that the system of locks and foot-thick titanium doors were designed not as fortifications to repel an invasive enemy, but as barriers to protect against the fusion torches on the transport rockets in the event one of the launch bays suffered a containment breach.

The entire design of the colonial store complex and starport, the long tunnels, the sharp turns, the tightly spiraling ramps to reach higher and deeper levels, all had been designed with exquisite care to best attenuate the fire of those sublight fusion drives. So vast, so extensive had been the great building, the hollowing out of the bedrock beneath Resonno, that it had been deemed more reasonable and prudent to use the corridors themselves as overflow vents than to try to dig separate exhaust flumes.

The builders had not foreseen that any defenders should attempt a full-scale launch operation while under siege from the air and space *and* via one of the postern gates. Or if they had, they had decided that any survivors trapped in that last, nightmare scenario were as good as dead anyway.

"Enemy troops have entered the base!" the call rang out once more. *"Enemy troops have entered the base!"*

"We need to collapse the tunnels farther in!" Belman had to shout over the alarm to be heard. "If we block them nearer the outer gate, it'll buy us the time we need to prep Epsilon Flight." He stopped, signaling that Olorin and I should draw nearer, and pointed along the tunnel ahead. About us, men were shouting, and whole decades of legionnaires in Martian scarlet pounded past us, segmented armor rattling as they moved with plasma rifles gleaming ready in their hands. "Path forks ahead. Right leads to half the launch flumes! Other half's left! Hippodrome access is past the flumes on the left. We need to get *past* them and bring this tunnel down."

"What about the flight crews?" Valka asked, pressing up against me to be close enough to hear over the tumult.

"Depends on how long we tie the Pale up with another cave-in," Belman replied. "If they're still trapped near the hippodrome, they can retreat back to the main bunker, no problem. If they get pinned down behind the gate checkpoints by the terminals, they'll have to ride out with the last wave!" He paused to let a line of soldiers rush past, gave their decurion the time he needed to bark a set of orders.

Seizing the silence, I leaned in and clasped Belman by the back of the neck. "Is this the only way?"

Belman seemed to think about his answer for half the life-age of the universe. Trying to trace a map of the tunnels against the inside of his skull, I guessed. "There's a fork a little past the left launch bays, runs through medical. One of the recovery wards. But if we get past that, we're clear!"

I let him go. "Lead the way, Martian."

Belman did just that, moving with his men off ahead. Sharp and I followed with the Dragonslayers, pushing our way through the garrison that held the checkpoint gate, the Jaddians close behind.

"We cannot hold much longer!" Kaim shouted after me. "Hadrian, when we return, your Emperor must depart."

"I know!" I called back, trying not to curse. My head throbbed where it had struck the wall of the dungeon during Hushansa's attack. I thought I recognized parts of the tunnels ahead, vaguely remembered the guide-posts painted on the walls to either side. The words SOUTH TERMINAL with an arrow leading forward were stenciled in red high to our right, above the words EAST TERMINAL and CENTRAL CONTROL with an arrow pointing back.

The fork Belman had spoken of waited just ahead. More stenciled words loomed on the chipped concrete wall. Beneath the words SOUTH TER-MINAL, a signpost read: BAYS S01—S30, left, and BAYS S31—S50, right.

We turned left.

The air thickened as we went and the torch-beams of weapons and of suit-lights caught on billowing waves of dust. Gunshots and the shout of voices human and inhuman echoed from up ahead. When we had first passed this way, following Rinehart, the tunnels had been packed with soldiers and other personnel. Now they were empty, the soldiers having pressed forward to meet the challenge at the gate, the noncombatants retreating back to crowd the cistern in central command.

A scream resounded from ahead, and a legionnaire in Martian plate flew from around the bend ahead and struck the wall of the corridor. In the next instant, a trio of silver *nahute* streamed into view and latched lamprey-like to the fallen man. Muddied by his fall and the blow to his head, the Martian fumbled at one of the iron serpents, but he never stood a chance. Drill-teeth whined and scratched through ceramic and carbon armorweave and an instant later the hall rang to a screeching unlike anything I'd heard since that day at Akterumu.

I thought that I would freeze.

I ran faster, conjuring the Emperor's blade in my fist.

A moment later, the downed Martian and the three serpents tearing at his flesh vanished in a nimbus of blue fire. We all stopped short, surprised, each of us realizing in his turn what had happened. In his dying moments, the Martian soldier had crushed the tab on one of his own plasma grenades, taking what little was left of his own life to destroy the Cielcin drones. In his place, a heap of carbon and smoking metal smoldered at the epicenter of a great black mark.

His killer—the owner of at least one of the *nahute*—appeared from around the corner. The Cielcin looked down at the corpse. I can remember the speculative way it tipped its head, as if wondering if the Martian's corpse might leap up and keep on fighting.

It never saw the shot that slew it.

One of Belman's men avenged his fallen brother with a plasma bolt that blackened horn and reduced the creature's face to a pitted, bubbling ruin. Then Belman and his people surged round the corner, firing all together. Valka and I followed them at once, Sharp's men and the Jaddians right behind. Just ahead, a knot of the Pale had won through the human relief and stood among the bodies. Still shouts and the noise of battle sounded from ahead, and at the sound of our first assault the Pale turned.

"Fire!" Belman cried, and plasma streaked up the hall.

The unshielded Pale fell in an instant, joining their victims on the floor of the hall.

"This way!" Belman yelled, waving us forward.

Ahead, the main hall branched, side passages angling out like the ribs of a fish from its spine, each dead-ending a thousand feet in and lined with fugue creches. They angled sharply away from us, providing us with a clear view down each aisle as we approached and ensuring the men ensconced along each remained unseen by the attackers advancing from deeper inside.

There must have been a dozen aisles to either side, each connected to one another by a series of hatchways in the middle and at the extreme end. They had been cut at angles—like so many of the branchings in that awful maze—to protect the sleepers stored along them from any blast or heat wave that might have come down the tunnel from the launch bays up ahead, and the mouth of each aisle housed static field generators to aid in just such a purpose.

It was here the fighting seemed thickest, and the corpses of men and Cielcin alike lay thick as carpet on the cracked cement. I was glad of my helmet, for I was certain the air stank of ozone and iron and of the carbon musk of seared flesh. Here and there the pale, fleshy shape of a sleeper lay bloodless and torn to ribbons in a pool of his or her own suspension fluid, and ice formed on the ground where the coolant met blood.

"There's another set of these laneways up ahead," the Martian called, drawing to one side to get out of the central avenue. "We have to push through, past control and maintenance, past medical! Launch bays are past that and left!"

"Then more of these aisles?" the prince asked.

"Then the aisles!" Belman agreed.

Pressed in beside me, Valka squeezed my arm. "Then we're back where you woke up. The gate's just a little farther."

A little farther was, in this case, more than a mile of tunnel, more than a mile of tunnel brimming fit to burst by then with the foot soldiers of the enemy. I counted it a small blessing that the larger of the chimeric machines could not fit in the cramped spaces of the catacombs. Indeed, almost I might at any point have reached up and touched the arched ceiling with my outstretched hand.

In this, at least, the advantage was ours—if only just. Tall as the Pale were, they had to fight stooped in the cramped confines of the hall. Like beasts on all fours they charged us, horns pointed to gore a man or pin him down.

"We must find this plasma weapon of theirs!" the prince was shouting. "Destroy it before we bring the tunnel down!"

The muffled blast of a grenade sounded from the next aisle up, and a man shouted, "The sleepers! Watch the sleepers!"

Another man yelled, and the low, croaking sound of inhuman laughter sounded from not three yards away. Heart hammering in my chest, I gripped the Emperor's sword more tightly. Valka's fingers tightened on my arm in sympathy. She looked up at me, and I fancied I saw her sad smile and the light of her eyes through the faceplate. She nodded.

With a snarl I hurled myself around the corner ahead of the other men, the Emperor's sword a pale fire in my fist. Twice the blade flashed. Left. Right. Two Cielcin fell to pieces, joining their human victim on the bloody ground. My boots splashed in mingled blood and coolant, and I could feel the very blood shaking in my veins as my mind recalled the blood-soaked sands and the shoals of ruined corpses in Red Company dress that rose all about me. I stepped over the pallid body of one of the sleepers and thrust the point of the Emperor's blade between the shoulders of a Cielcin who had leaped upon the fallen form of a Valavar trooper. Seizing the xenobite by its horn, I pulled it off the man and tossed it aside, blade carving through one of its black hearts as I did so, cutting without resistance.

"Are you hurt?" I said, again astonished by the terrific calm in my voice despite the galloping of my heart.

The man shook his head, but did not dare speak.

Shots filled the main hall behind, and glancing I saw Centurion Sharp and two of the Dragonslayers at my back like faithful shadows. Shaking the blood from my tunic, I said, "Find a weapon, then. Fight, if you think you've anything worth fighting for!"

Following the sounds of fighting from the next aisle, I hurried up and through the midway hatch, trying not to look too closely at the undead men and women slumbering in their black and frozen sepulchers. Plasma fire streaked past, right to left, and glancing I saw a knot of Martian legionnaires pinned down further up the aisle. I turned left, found myself facing five of the Cielcin dressed in the gray armor of Attavaisa's former *itani*, wielding the maces I had seen in the east terminal. Even as I rounded the bend, one smashed another of the fugue creches.

It was the last thing it ever did.

Twin rays of moonlight shone behind the enemy and fell, twisted, spun through a dervish that tore the Cielcin apart.

Olorin and Tiada stood above their ruin. The prince's mask glowed blue in the light off his blade. He did not speak, but raised his sword in salute, then darted back into the main hall, his mamluks close behind.

"Black planet," Sharp said behind me. "Never seen fighters like them."

"I have," I said, and started after the Jaddians. "Long ago."

The main corridor was awash with battle, with our people entangled with the Cielcin foe. The fractal glimmer of shields deflecting impact lit the cracked concrete walls, and ahead another of the stenciled markers read *BAYS S01—S30* and *MEDICA*. The main hall itself was wider here, wide enough that five could walk abreast.

At length we reached the end of the aisles, the mamluks and Martians alike carving their wedge against the advance of the enemy. The two Maeskoloi formed the point of that wedge, the flash of their swords tossing black blood upon the walls like ink from the brush of a Mandari calligrapher. I followed on, blood yet rattling in my veins. One Cielcin in the gray of Attavaisa leaped from the aisle on our left. Valka shot at it, plasma bolts striking wide. One took it in the ribs, but the behemoth kept coming, carried by the momentum of its attack. Its mace descended even as the Martians ahead turned.

Sharp's rifle cracked with a noise like the breaking of ice even as I rose to parry and slash the alien weapon in two. The mace fell in two pieces as its owner flew back and struck the corner of the aisle.

We found ourselves then in one of those strange islands of calm which form in the heart of battle.

Belman's voice drifted back from the hall ahead. "Form ranks!" he shouted. "Guard the sappers! Move it! Move it!" The Martians did just that, forming themselves into columns as the hoplites moved to bar the hall, their short lances thrust forward.

Seeing what the lieutenant intended, I shouted to the Jaddians. "Olorin! Fall back!"

The prince turned and shouted something to what few clone slaves remained him. The mamluks fell back as ordered, with Tiada and the prince last of all pressing through the Martian line. Five wide then and nearly a dozen deep, the Martian block advanced, the men behind bracing the men ahead with hands gripping their shoulders. The sounds of further fighting came from the hall ahead, where—if I'd understood Belman correctly, and if memory served—the labyrinth split again, with a path to the left leading to another guard post and the lower-numbered portion of the south terminal launch bays.

We passed a series of doors on the left and right that opened and led away to more dead ends and branching corridors where still more of the sleepers dreamed, awaiting the day their number was up and their pod installed on a ship bound for the next chapter in their long-paused lives.

Down many of those avenues I saw the flash of plasma fire and heard the shouting of men and of Cielcin.

"Launch terminal's just ahead!" Belman shouted, pointing to another marker on the wall that said *MEDICA* along one rightward branch. The minute he spoke, his front line opened fire on three Cielcin who clambered around the bend ahead. One of them threw its *nahute* the instant before plasma fire felled it, and the drone sped toward us faster than the Martians could track. The snake battered against the shields of the first men in line, and the formation faltered as two of the Martians wrestled the weapon to the ground.

Shots rang out behind, and looking back I saw a pair of Valavar men stumble back out of a side passage marked off limits to unauthorized personnel. One clutched his wounded shoulder, and they broke and ran back up the hall, ignoring Sharp's shouted orders for them to hold their ground.

"Should we go back?" he asked. "What's through there?"

Belman didn't hear him. The Martians had pressed ahead, had nearly reached the bend in the corridor where the three Cielcin lay dead. Shots rang out as a *nahute* rose from beside its master's corpse. I looked forward and back.

Always forward.

"Leave it!" I said, gesturing with the Emperor's blade. "There can't be that many of them left that way. Come on!"

"Marlowe!" Prince Kaim called. "The Martians!"

I hurried to join the prince, and together we reached the bend. Again the hall broadened, and we came upon one of the gatehouses. The vault doors were easily a cubit of solid steel, their surfaces protected with ceramic tiles designed to withstand the heat of the exhaust in the event of a breached launch bay. The bodies of men and Cielcin alike lay everywhere. The gatehouse stood at a T-shaped junction; the path ahead presumably led on to more catacombs and the hippodrome gate. I remembered following Rinehart this way. We *were* close.

Valka stopped in the archway. "Can't we just seal them off?"

"This isn't the only way back. We have to get past the medica, elsewise they'll be able to circle round," Belman said. "And there are men up ahead. Fighters and sleepers alike!"

My eyes went to the leftward branching path. "Is that the way to the transports?"

Belman rounded on me, leaving his men to guard the far door. "It is!"

he said, slapping the concrete frame of the mighty gate. "But if the Pale could cut or dig their way through what our men did by the hippodrome, two feet of heat shield won't stop them long. We need to go further in. We can't collapse the tunnel just on the far side. It's too close to the sleepers."

Again I gripped the lieutenant by his shoulder. "We don't need to buy much time!"

"I know!" Belman shook my hand off. "Just a little farther, my lord."

"Marlowe!" Sharp's voice slashed across our arguing. The centurion inclined his head up the hall, over the heads of the ranked Martians, and pointed with his gun. "Listen!"

Belman and I both broke off our argument, peering through the ranked men of the Martian Guard.

"'Tis gone quiet," Valka said, craning her neck to get a better view.

The sounds of fighting from ahead had ceased, and no more did the faint flash of fire echo back from the tunnels ahead. For a solitary instant, there was nothing but the faint thunder of the battle overhead. Nothing moved but the falling dust and the men it fell upon.

"So much for your men ahead," I said to Belman.

I thought I could sense the lieutenant scowl through his faceplate at me as he turned away, white pteruges clacking against his crimson armor. He did not reply, but raised his voice to his troopers and said, "Steady on, men!" He passed his short lance to his left hand to kindle his own sword in his right, a short, leaf-bladed weapon of the sort favored by Martian officers. "Stay in formation!"

Crack.

The sound of iron striking stone echoed from up ahead, and the Martians shifted in their line. "Steady!" Overhead, the lights sputtered, leaving only the phosphorescent paint lines on the walls ahead and the narrow beams of our suit lamps to light the corridor.

One of Sharp's men muttered a prayer behind me.

Crack. Crack. Crack.

"The hell is that?" asked Sharp himself.

In the Dark, my mind raced to thoughts of Hushansa, or of Vati. Almost I expected either of the great generals to emerge from the dark ahead, as Hushansa had in the hippodrome dungeon, as Vati had behind the thrones of the Grand Conclave.

A single Cielcin emerged from the gloom ahead, its white face green in the faint illumination. In its hands it twirled its *nahute*, scraping the quiescent drone across the floor with a noise like a length of chain.

"Open fire!" Belman yelled.

The Cielcin hurled its charge as the Martians attacked. By the flash of lance fire, I saw that *this* one of the Pale wore not the grays of clan Attavaisa, but the blacks and White Hand of the Shiomu Elusha, of Dorayaica itself.

And it was shielded.

The *nahute* struck the shields of the Martian front line, and its owner lunged toward us, knowing it must die, perhaps, urged on by the masters it would not dare to disobey. Belman's men dealt with the *nahute*, and fired on the lone xenobite. Its stolen shield flickered as their shots broke against it, but it did not slow. Behind it, in the darkness, more Cielcin were coming. I saw their faces green-white in the dark.

"*Teke! Teke!*" the alien cry went up, just as I had heard it on Berenike so many lifetimes before. There must have been dozens of them streaming toward us, shielded and screaming, scimitars in their hands. I saw their aim plain as starlight. They meant to use their shielded berserkers as a ram, meant to push through Belman's line like cavalry on the green hills of Earth, to trample us like the very grass.

"Steady on!" Belman shouted. The lieutenant emitted a shrill whistle, and his hoplites braced one another and checked their lances, bayonet heads glittering white as the inhuman faces. As the xenobites closed, our lancers let out a cry like the raw throat of hell, and so mighty a sound was it that I think the Pale faltered, if only for a moment. The fire of their lances spat like the strobing light of cameras, and one of the berserkers fell, its shield overwhelmed, body smoking where the laser smote it.

"Stay with me," I said to Valka, and looking to Sharp I said, "Eyes out behind, centurion."

Sharp tapped his forehead twice with his fist. "You heard his lordship, dogs!" he barked. "We're to cover the asses of the boys in red!"

"We need to close the gate," Olorin said, leaning down to hiss into my ear. "We will not get farther."

Belman whistled again, and as a single organism the Martians pushed forward. The whole world shook about us as yet another bomb struck just above our heads. But the Martian line held. With nothing to do behind them but watch, I stood with Valka and the Jaddians.

"Advance!" Belman bellowed.

The Martians marched forward, pressing the enemy back. I saw one Cielcin fall with the point of a lance buried in its neck.

"Advance!"

"Dolá Deu di Fotí!" Olorin said. "Sweet God of Fire, they're doing it."

Step by grievous step, the Martians gained ground, marching over the bodies of their foes as they pressed on. Twice a man in the front was wounded, and his fellows pulled him back, expelling him from the rear of their formation to be set against the wall by the men behind.

Still on the Cielcin came, pressing against the block of men like a black tide.

Belman whistled twice, short blasts, and as a unity the front line of Martian fighters peeled back, slid between the ranks as the second advanced. They abandoned lances, opting for their short, ceramic swords, swords cut in the same leaf-bladed fashion as was Belman's. The Martians relied on heavy, segmented plates on their left arms to turn back the scimitars of the Pale, using their armor like shields.

A pair of *nahute* arced over the block of men, tearing into the gatehouse. Undaunted, Tiada advanced and struck them both down with a flash of her blade. "I do not like this," she said, whirling to face her prince. "We can do nothing."

"Patience," Kaim-Olorin said, but I sensed the unease in the man as well. His eyes kept darting left to the passage that ran to the launch bays.

Seeing this, Valka said, "They should have the next flight ready any minute."

Belman's whistle blasted twice again, and again the ranks rotated. Half a dozen wounded Martians slumped against the walls of the tunnel behind. One tried to help another stand. Two more, I thought, were dead already.

I ran forward. "Valka! Help me!"

She joined me, and together we helped the two men to stand. One of them between us, the other limping alongside, we reached the threshold of the gatehouse again, and helped them to rest against the wall. Seeing me at my task, a trias of Sharp's men joined in in salvaging the rest. Two were indeed dead, and a seventh man staggered back from Belman's unit and fell, one hand still pressed to his torn throat. He was gone before we could reach him.

Still, Belman's soldiers pressed on, fighting with a cold ferocity I had seldom seen, but then, I had seldom seen the men of the Martian Guard in battle, and, Reader, I tell you the stories of their prowess and the songs of their valor are not overstated. Against all odds, Belman's men had reached the end of the short tunnel.

"Hold the gate!" I said to Sharp, and leading the Jaddians forward, I negotiated the carpet of bodies—Martian and Cielcin—that lay thick in the hall. More aisles opened to either side, pointed sharply back from the main corridor like the first to spare them in the event of bad launch.

Belman's whistle shrilled twice, and again his shrunken force rotated. "Stay in formation!" the lieutenant yelled, driving his men out under the arch. "Advance, men! Advance! Hold tight!"

Almost at once, things began to go wrong. The Martian formation, which had proved lethally effective in the cramped confines of the hall, where it had only one direction to defend and only one way to go, was not prepared for the assault that closed in then from all sides. It was as though the wall Belman had built to stem the tide were only a little thing. A child's dike dug upon the seashore, sufficient to hold the tide back only at its lowest ebb.

But that tide was coming in.

The Cielcin crashed in from the aisles to either side, and Belman's men—though they had known what to expect—were wholly unprepared for the ferocity of that onslaught, and at once I got the sense that the Pale had *planned* this, had sacrificed their own in the hall to draw the Martians into their waiting jaws.

And then there was the *chimera*. It wasn't Hushansa, or Vati, or any of the great captains of the Pale, but one of the more common horrors of the sort I had first battled on Arae long ago. It swept three men aside with a contemptuous motion of its arm and leaped on Belman himself like some terrible hound. The lieutenant's highmatter was no good measured against the adamantine plate the monster wore over its iron bones, and the next instant the beast drew back its heavy fist and hammered Belman's helm with all the force of a steam hammer.

Belman didn't stand a chance. Damn fool that he was, he little deserved his fate. The iron fist fell twice, three times, four, and when the chimera at last was done, the lieutenant's head and chest were smashed flat as paper, his armor crushed and shattered as food cans beneath the tread of a tank.

The Martians broke and ran, pouring back up the tunnel they had so lately won. Seeing this, Valka and I halted and turned, pushing the Jaddians back toward the gate. "Move!" I shouted, fearing for the stampede that was forming. "Go back! Back!" And then, "The gate, Sharp! Close the gate!"

The centurion turned from his place by the far door and stumbled to the door controls. Holding Valka's hand in mine, I plunged with her back across the threshold, the Jaddians right behind. Once clear, I unkindled the Emperor's blade and turned back to watch the retreat of the Martians. The chimera led the charge, trampling over the men in the rear. One or two turned back to hurl grenades. The blast of one rocked the chimera as it came, but the monster shook itself and kept coming on.

"Niko, the charges!" shouted a Martian in the gate beside me. "Drop the fucking charges!"

One of the Martians slowed, glanced back over his shoulder.

"They don't have time!" Olorin hissed, then shouted something in Jaddian.

Half a dozen mamluk homunculi sprinted past me, their azure cloaks streaming behind them like wings. Olorin himself drew up beside me, his guard reduced to Tiada and a mere quartet of clone slaves. He did not speak, and despite his mask I knew the great prince held his breath.

The mamluks threw themselves at the chimera, firing past it at the *scaharimn* close behind. One of the clones leaped within range of the monster's arms and thrust its lance up into the common metal beneath the armored breastplate, while two more seized on one of the giant's metal limbs. Then all six of the mamluks were on it, their inhuman arms shaking as they held the machine back, boots sliding on the blood-slicked floor.

"Drop the charges, Niko!" the Martian said again.

The Martian who had hesitated near the mouth of the tunnel did just that. Fumbling at his pack, he let the sapping charges he'd carried from the cistern fall just as the chimera seized one of the mamluks by its head and slammed it into the wall. Three *nahute* streamed from the crowd behind and fell upon the mamluks. The chimera surged forward, dragging the remaining Jaddians in its wake.

"Close the gate, Sharp!" I yelled.

The man Niko had nearly reached the threshold when the chimera seized him. One iron claw grabbed the man by the ankle and pulled him down.

"Close the gate!" I yelled again—though I am not proud to write it.

Sharp found the control at last. I watched Niko dragged back and slammed against the floor as the heavy door rolled shut. I shut my eyes, struggled to master my breathing as I staggered back from the sealed door.

The Martian had done his job. A moment later there came a blast like the noise of mountains falling. The great door shook in its frame . . . and held.

All then was silent, and I knew that at least the chimera was dead.

I slumped against the wall. Overcome by a sudden need for air, I keyed my helm to open. Sucking at the free, damp, and metallic air, I looked round at Valka, at Kaim and Sharp and the few remaining Martians.

When Valka spoke, it was to say the thing we all were thinking.

"We did not make it far enough," she said, voice flattened by her suit speakers. "They can still cut through the medica. They'll find their way round."

CHAPTER 41

BY INCHES

"WE HAVE TO CUT them off!" Valka exclaimed. "We can beat them back. Close the other way to the medica. If we're fast." She pushed her way through the Dragonslayers back toward the hall we'd come from. "Come on!"

Alarms blared as I staggered after her. I knew we'd passed the other route that led to the terminal's medica, but the whole dense tangle of tunnels and chambers was turning into a haze behind my eyes. But I put my trust in Valka's instincts, in her perfect memory. As she had led us rightly through the labyrinth of Vedatharad, she led us through that labyrinth too. More fortunate than Theseus was I. Theseus had only the thread which Ariadne had given him. I had Ariadne herself.

"All Epsilon Flight pilots to silo muster stations. Repeat. All Epsilon Flight pilots to silo muster stations!" The flight controller's voice was frantic on the comm.

"They're only just now prepping the next wave?" one of Sharp's men asked, armor rattling up the corridor behind.

As if answering his question, the flight controller's voice sounded over the comm. *"Attention. Attention. All noncombat personnel. Retreat to central command. Repeat. All noncombat personnel retreat to central command. The east terminal is breached. Repeat. The east terminal is breached."*

Jogging along beside me, Prince Kaim asked, "Does that mean all the ships in the east terminal can't get crew?"

"I don't know!" I shouted my reply. "We have to seal off the medica and get back to the Emperor. I don't care if we have to drag him out of here. There isn't any more time!"

Kaim said nothing, a response I took for quiet agreement.

We met no resistance in the tunnels behind, though twice men emerged from side passages ahead and—seeing us—bolted up the hall to reach central command. The first were Valavar troopers, but the second were cryonics technicians in white fatigues.

"You there, hold!" I shouted, running ahead of the others to wave one down. The woman looked at me, wide eyes rolling, and I knew she wanted to do anything but stay. Still, I caught her arm and held her. "Go to command!" I said, and again the world shook above our heads as another bomb fell. "Go to command! Tell the Emperor the tunnel to the hippodrome is closed. Tell him Lieutenant Belman is dead. Have you got that?"

She nodded, but I could not be sure she truly understood. Only then did I see the blood on her white uniform, and marked the way her hand shook in mine. "Go!" I said, letting her go. Too late, I realized I should have told her that *I* was still alive. That the Jaddian prince, too, yet lived.

She stumbled into the wall as she wheeled about and ran on.

As she did, a column of Martians rounded the bend ahead, escorting a column of men and women in the unmarked black fatigues of Legion recruits.

Sharp shouldered his way up beside me as I jogged toward them. "Where are you taking these men?"

The Martian at the head of the column said, "Epsilon Flight pilots, lordship. Is the way to the terminal clear?"

I stepped aside to let them pass. "We collapsed the tunnel just beyond the junction."

Sharp bellowed, "Clear a path! Everyone clear a path!"

The Jaddians and the remainder of out motley contingent pressed aside to let the pilots and their escort through. They hurried by, and every instant we were forced to stand aside felt like a hundred years. I counted thirty pilots and as many men to guard them.

"How long do you think we have?" I asked Valka.

She shook her head. I could sense the tension in the poised way she held herself. "Minutes," she said. "Minutes."

"Martian!" I shouted after the column. They didn't stop. "Stay and reinforce the terminal. There may yet be Pale about. The side passages aren't all clear, and they may work their way around. Protect the transports!"

The commander shouted back. "I've orders to return to command!"

"Belay that! Comms are down. Command doesn't know the situation down here."

"My orders are straight from Captain Thoras."

"I don't care if your orders are from Caesar himself! Guard those blasted transports! They'll have your head and mine if anything happens to the sleepers."

But the Martian officer was gone, carried away by the press of his column.

"'Tis not far now," Valka said, pressing by me. "Up ahead on the left!"

With Sharp's men and the Jaddians hard behind, we disentangled ourselves from the pilots and their escort and continued our scramble up the hall. Valka was right. It wasn't far. Another T-junction lay not three hundred feet ahead. A glowsphere embedded in the ceiling fell as we approached, shattered on impact as the world shuddered once again. The fateful word gleamed on the wall in the typical phosphorescent paint beside its arrow.

MEDICA.

Two of Sharp's men reached the turning before me and raised their lances at once. My heart sank, for but one thing in all the cosmos would have made those men react that way.

"Open fire!" the Dragonslayer shouted.

The energy-lance flashed blue-white, its beam for a moment visible in the dust and vapors that filled the air. Cursing myself, I thumped my chest to re-engage my helmet and skidded to a halt at the juncture in the hall, the Emperor's sword springing to life in my hand once more.

I had expected to meet Cielcin troopers, maybe even one of the chimeras—guessing that the hybrids would move faster through the medica complex to find the way through.

Instead I found a cloud of *nahute*. A dozen. Two dozen. More. Though the lance-fire had blown a handful apart, they overwhelmed the two Dragonslayers in an instant, worming slowly through their shields and shredded suit underlayment and the flesh beneath. The men were dead in instants, their insides churned by the mouths of the vile serpents.

The next instant they were on me. Bouncing off my shield as their slow daimons worked out how to slide through. I was glad of the Emperor's blade then, and slashed wildly about, cleaving the weapons in two, in three. But there were still too many. I felt the clamp and grip of suction as the head of one attached lamprey-like to my ribs. My breastplate vibrated as it began to grind away the fine ceramic.

Seizing the tail of the weapon with my free hand, I punched my sword through, careful not to cut my own arm. I staggered back into the main hall, toward Valka and the rest. Lance-fire flashed about me, and my suit's entoptics darkened to save my eyes. I was well aware of drones dying all about me, and when I felt another socket to my flank below the liver I struck at it.

A little too late.

Alarms blared inside my helmet, and the words *SUIT INTEGRITY COMPROMISED* flashed in the corner of my display, and though I tore the dead drone from my side, I felt the cold of the catacombs seeping in.

"Alala! Alala!"

In leaped the Maeskoloi, Tiada and Prince Kaim, blades flashing like sheets of lightning in the dark. Together they drove the torrent back, cut the cloud to ribbons. I stumbled back against the wall, having claimed a dozen of the things at least for myself.

"Are you hurt?"

Valka came up beside me. I felt the spot on my side, felt her fingers join mine in the wound. "No," I said, wincing as she pressed.

"'Tis not deep," she said. I could feel my suit constricting to stanch any flow, but by my examination I guessed it was little more than an abrasion. Skin-deep. "You got to it in time."

Nodding, I wrapped my arm around her, pressed the forehead of my mask to hers. I said nothing, but came off the wall as the Dragonslayers and surviving Martians alike rounded the bend, lances and plasma burners snapping to the ready.

"Set the charges!" I said. "Down the passage! Double quick!"

One of Lieutenant Belman's men came forward, clambering over the wreckage of the *nahute* that littered the floor. Like the ill-fated Niko, he wore a heavy pack slung over one shoulder, and the armor he wore had a heavier, more solid build to it, the usual Martian refinements sacrificed for a style more angular and austere. He unclipped the bag as he advanced, shouting for us to make way.

Kaim and Tiada—who had traveled farthest up the passage toward the medica—checked their advance, their twin swords gleaming like spikes of sunlit ice. Their few remaining mamluks gathered about them, a knot of Martians behind, their guns at the ready.

"Olorin!" I shouted, pressing my left hand to my wound. "Come back here."

The prince half-turned back to look at me, one black eye glistening in the light of his sword. "Someone must hold the way!" he said.

The next instant, the noise of shattering glass and crash of metal on stone rang down the hall, carrying with it the hoot of inhuman voices. In the hall just behind the Jaddians, the Martian sapper and another of his fellows finished affixing the first of his charges high on the wall to the left.

Ahead, a hellish red glow suffused the farther stones, issuing from around a bend farther up the passage. The clangor of destruction drew nearer. I could picture the Pale breaking medical cabinets, shattering any fugue creches along the way, and clenched the Emperor's sword more tightly in my hand.

"*Na es jahizya!*" Prince Kaim called to his coterie. "Be ready! They come!"

"Eyes forward, lads!" Sharp's voice boomed up and down that narrow space. The men about us adjusted their weapons in sick anticipation, trained their weapons up the hall. As ever, the *nahute* had been only the vanguard of the main host.

The sapper and his assistant hurried to the right wall, moving back a dozen paces to stagger their explosives. "Come on," I muttered to myself, blade bouncing in my grip. "Come on. Come on. Come on."

A terrific scream issued from around the bend ahead, and we defenders all braced ourselves as something huge and hideous rounded the corner. The chimera was far larger than any ordinary Cielcin, and so crawled on all fours like a beast. Its bladed talons tore long scratches, razor thin, in the walls and floor, throwing sparks. If it was surprised to find so many of us arrayed against it, the beast gave no sign. Its solitary red eye contracted in the unmarked orb it called a head, and again unleashing its grinding, metallic scream, the beast of MINOS launched itself at the foremost of our defenders.

The swordmasters did not back down, flowed instead like water to meet it even as the Martians and Dragonslayers both recoiled at the horrendous sight. Tiada went low, skidding across the floor as Olorin went high, springing off the wall like a gymnast. The woman's blade rose, and as she slid between the demon's legs, highmatter bit deep into the common alloy between the adamantine plates on calf and thigh. The demon lurched, fell against the left wall such that the slashing blow it had aimed at the prince fell short.

Olorin's sword fell like an avalanche, molecule-sharp edge striking hard at the joint between neck and shoulder. The smooth orb of the monster's head—like a great eye, it seemed—fell from the bunched shoulders. Olorin seemed to fall in slow motion as hydraulic fluid white as milk sprayed from the severed neck.

Headless, short half a leg, the chimera struck the floor. Tiada and her prince had taken the thing apart in seconds.

But it was not dead.

One hand with fingers like long knives thrust at Olorin, and he caught the blow on the edge of his sword. But as I caught Irshan's blade in Colosso, the giant caught Prince Kaim's. The Maeskolos slid backward, knees bending beneath the tremendous weight and force of the machine. Appearing from behind the monster, Tiada speared the chimera's wrist, twisting through the titanium bones, tearing hydraulic lines and cables until the hand went limp and struck the floor.

Behind them, the noise of clawed and armored feet drew nearer, and a red glow cast horned shadows on the wall. White masks hove into view, and the one in front hurled a *nahute* down the hall toward us.

The sappers finished with the second charge, raised a thumb for confirmation. The man with the bag shoved his partner back along the tunnel, and Sharp's men picked their shots past the Jaddians and their hulking quarry. I saw one of the *scaharimn* fall dead of a lance blast, but its fellows trampled its body in their haste to come near.

"Olorin!" I shouted, pushing past Sharp and his men to get into the hall. "The brain's in the chest cavity!"

"Hadrian, come back!" Valka called after me. "The bombs!"

As Valka spoke, a hatch opened in the shoulder of the wounded chimera, and a fusillade of flare rockets—each no larger than a pen—tore from the aperture. A noise like the cracking of a thousand tiny bolts of thunder filled the air with a light like stars. Men screamed, and I threw an arm across my face to shield my eyes as the blast wave took me and hurled me back against the far wall of the main corridor.

Groaning, I put my legs back under me. "Valka?"

She had pressed herself against the near wall left of the corridor. "I'm all right."

A few of the defenders—those whose shields had saved them—regained their feet, trained weapons down the hall at the approaching horde. The Cielcin were nearly on the broken body of the chimera, and a few *nahute* streamed toward us.

"Olorin!" I shouted, but of the swordmaster there was no sign, nor of his concubine. "Damn it." He could not be dead. He had been shielded. "Olorin!"

Incredibly, neither of the planted charges had gone off in the blast. I guessed the computers that MINOS has slaved to the Cielcin brain within the chimera's twisted form had picked its targets with care. Picking out the soldiers to clear the way before it for its companions.

And where were the sappers themselves? I could see neither the bag man nor his companion, nor indeed the bag itself.

"Olorin!"

"My lord!" Sharp called from the left by Valka. "Get out of there!"

I ignored him. The Emperor's sword flared in my hand. My ribs ached as I lashed out to slice one of the *nahute* in two. "Olorin!"

A hand thrust out from the tangle of bodies and dust and broken masonry, and a man followed. Prince Kaim's mask was gone, and a fine stream of blood ran from his temple, so dark it was almost purple against his olive skin. I felt my spirit rally at the sight of him. He looked round, scanning the carnage about himself, eyes wide and white in the dim.

Looking for his sword, I realized. *Or for his woman.*

The first of the Pale had reached the ruined hulk of the chimera and leaped upon it without so much as slowing down. Unarmed and alone at the end of that long hall, the Prince had nothing. He caught his attacker in the chin with a vicious uppercut, his own momentum staggering him back. The Martians close about me fired on the horde, and at last Olorin turned and began stumbling back along the hall.

"Tiada!" he shouted, tearing the ruined *mandyas* from his shoulder.

"Here!" the answer came at once.

Another of the Cielcin slid down over the hunched back of the dying machine and hurried toward Olorin, its scimitar pulled back to stave in the prince's head. Olorin could not have seen it; he was too busy helping Tiada out from under the torn ruin of the chimera's leg. I didn't have time to shout a warning, trapped as I was by the dazed men ahead of me. I recognized another of Sharp's decurions dead on the ground.

The Cielcin made its move.

How he did it—how I knew—I cannot say. But somehow he did. Olorin raised his arm over and behind his head to block the blow upon his vambrace. The ring of ceramic on steel sounded in that dark and dismal place. The Maeskolos grimaced, teeth flashing as he turned. He hadn't even looked.

I had forgotten something, something that had struck me as so very strange when first I'd met the man as a boy on Emesh.

He wore more than one sword.

A second highmatter blade burst from his clenched first as he spun and dashed his assailant to pieces. So sudden and startling was that blow, and so grievous the injury, that the foremost of the Cielcin recoiled.

"*Taal tora!*" the prince said in Jaddian. To his enemies? To his *alkidar*?

Tiada wavered to her feet, her own *mandyas* torn at the shoulder. Kaim shoved her forward, turned back to cover her retreat. Behind, the Cielcin had recovered their courage and streamed back at the prince. Several fell as the Martians and Sharp's men picked careful shots over the prince's shoulders. Olorin slew two as they flew at him, striking their scimitars in two. He shouted something in Jaddian, daring the monsters to attack.

The Jaddian woman reached me, and I pulled her past the Martians at my side. "Turn left!" I shouted after her. "Back to the cistern!"

"Hadrian, get the hell out of there!" Valka called.

Olorin parried a blow from one of the *scaharimn*, turned his blade to cut through a *nahute* as it flowed past. Having cleared a little space he turned, and leaping like a panther over the bodies of the men behind he hurried back down the hall.

"What about the charges?" I asked, pushing back myself to where Sharp and Valka waited at the right of the juncture.

To underscore my question, the Jaddian prince slid to a halt beside me, moving to the corner opposite Valka and the centurion. "We can't hold them much longer!" he said. "We have to close the tunnel!"

"My lord," Tiada said, "your face."

The prince ignored her. "Where is the detonator?" He turned back to the tunnel, scouring as I had scoured for the sapper in all the wreckage. But one dead Martian legionnaire looked much like another, and the bag I guessed was buried.

"There's no damn time," Sharp said, shouldering past Valka. "Pull back, men! Pull back! Where's Altaric?"

"Here, Quent!" The lesser Dragonslayer pressed forward from where he'd been holding the rear, watching over the path that led back the way we had come.

"*Marlowe!*" a high, thin voice wailed. "*Marlowe!*"

It was Hushansa. The *vayadan*-general's voice rose above the hall, and at the sound of it the Cielcin drew back. With a start, I realized the voice was rising from the ruined chimera whose bulk blocked half the hall. That should not have been. I knew the style and manufacture of the machine body. It was not one of the general's puppets. But as Urbaine had ridden in the heart of his iron golem, so too the general had hijacked the body of its slave. "*Surrender!*" it said. "*Surrender and your people may live as slaves.*"

I met the single red eye of the machine's severed head, but said nothing. With its hydraulic lines cut, the chimera was as good as dead. Crippled. *"It is the only way,"* Hushansa said, *"the only choice you have to save them."*

"Centurion, shut it down!" I said.

"Aye, sir." Sharp raised his rifle to his shoulder and fired.

His shot struck true. The damage Kaim and Tiada had done to the chimera had compromised its shield, and the bullet tore through the exposed neck, banishing Hushansa's shade back whence it had come.

Sharp's shot had given the men all the encouragement they needed to vacate the tunnel. The last Martians retreated backward, firing as they pulled back into the corridor.

"What are you going to do?" Valka asked.

"Altaric!" Sharp exclaimed by way of answer. "Grenade!"

The junior man understood just as I did. Without the detonator, without the sapper, our only hope was to set the charges off.

It was the only way.

Altaric didn't hesitate. Moving with casual confidence, with the ease of long practice, he drew a plasma grenade from his belt and threw it, shouting, "Clear!"

How well I remember the sound of it. The clear, metallic *ping* of it as it bounced off one of the bodies, rolled among the onrushing foe, and vanished amid the chaos. I could not have heard it, not in all that noise, and yet I feel it—even now—as one feels the pealing of Chantry bells in the narthex of a sanctum.

In my chest.

My heart.

"Get back!" Sharp called.

Olorin grabbed my shoulder, pulled me back around the corner on the cistern side of the main tunnel.

Violet flame flowered down the hall just below the nearer charge. I turned and looked at Valka—or think I did. I do in memory, looking left to where she stood safe behind Sharp around the corner opposite. In my memory, she wears no helmet—and I know that can't be right. But I see her, eyes wide, lips parted as if, as if to speak some word. Had she been but one step closer, I might have reached out and touched her then.

One step.

Altaric's grenade set off the sapping charge, and deep explosion tore the catacomb apart.

Boom.

Valka's eyes were like twin suns as the second charge—the one further down the hall—went off as well. Olorin dragged me back farther, shouting something about keeping my head down, and so I could not see if Sharp's man had succeeded in his task.

Boom.

I heard the fall of stones and screams of surprised xenobites as the roof and walls came crashing down, and I knew that we had succeeded, and sagged against the wall. Still Olorin held my arm.

Boom.

A *third* explosion cut the air and earth alike. The initial blast wave knocked me from my feet, and I took one of the Dragonslayers down with me. There shouldn't have been a third explosion. They had only planted two charges.

But the bag. *The bag.*

We had forgotten the bag.

I could hear nothing, nothing save a high, vibrating ring. The blast had stunned my ears, and I looked round in blurry confusion from my place on the floor. From that unexalted vantage, I had a perfect view of the ceiling in the instant that it fell. I had no time to react, no time to think, no time to call upon my vision—for all the good it would have done.

Even I could not stop the avalanche.

And then again, for the second time in those terrible halls beneath Perfugium, all I knew was black.

CHAPTER 42

NEVER

"MARLOWE! MARLOWE, DAMN YOU! Wake up!" a familiar voice resounded in my ear.

"He's coming round." Another voice, deep and lilting. Olorin's.

"Tell him to hurry it up!" the first voice replied, its aristocratic drawl tightened with strain. "We all want to sleep, but he has to wait same as the rest of us."

"Lorian?" I opened my eyes. Still inside my helmet, my entoptics fizzled and spat where the cave-in had done its damage, and so my view of Olorin and Tiada peering down at me was interrupted by darkness lit by the tiny internal lamps—cold and blue—that shone down by my chin. "Where? How?"

The commander spoke over my confusion. "Lin's men found the beachhead the Pale'd set up to jam surface comms. Blasted it from orbit. You missed it while you were napping."

"How long was I out?" I asked, wincing as I fumbled for the controls to unseal my helmet.

"Not five minutes," the prince said. "We were about to move you. I sent some of the men ahead."

The delicate clockwork mechanisms that served to open and fold away the sculpted mask and cowl of my helm jammed half-open, whined. Cursing, I reached up and twisted the whole thing off manually, hurled it away. I was lying on the floor of the corridor not ten feet from the juncture that led to the medica, or what was left of it.

The tunnel was blocked, and the main corridor too, the whole thing lost behind blocks of torn concrete and tangled bars of steel, beneath broken conduits and bedrock and raw earth. A water pipe leaked from high up on the left, forming puddles at the base of the wall. Olorin stood smoothly, stooped to offer me a hand up.

"Can you stand?"

I looked around, still taking in the horrors that had come in after the blast. The corridor I had known was gone, transmuted into an alien landscape. Not a corridor at all, but the bowel of some stone giant, the guts of the planet itself. Here no man had gone before, for the landscape which arises after cataclysm and carnage is always a new world, and undiscovered country from whose bourn no traveler returns unchanged. A few of the remaining Martians and Dragonslayers had removed their helmets, and sat tired and wide-eyed, clutching their guns. I marked that but two of the Jaddian mamluks remained, and perhaps a dozen of the soldiery.

My mouth opened and formed the words before my conscious mind was really aware of them. "Where's Valka?" Sharp, too, was gone, and most of his men with him. "Olorin, where is she? And the centurion?"

"I'm here!" Her voice sounded near at hand, and I looked desperately round, as if expecting to see her seated on the rubble. But she was nowhere. "I'm with Sharp. We're on the other side."

The other . . . My eyes went to the devastation that blocked the hall. All Perfugium shuddered then, and I took Prince Olorin's hand. "The other side?" I said, stumbling to the rubble. Without so much as a second thought, I pried one stone away and tossed it aside. My wounded flank burned, and I gasped.

Someone had put the Emperor's sword into the hasp at my belt, and I drew it, cut a metal beam even as one of the Martians shouted, "Don't!"

The whole thing spilled down without the beam to hold it, earth and rubble tumbling like a waterfall toward my feet. I jumped back. Olorin caught me. "We can't clear it."

"We have to!" I said. "Valka's on the other side. There are people on the other side!"

But Olorin shook his head. He was *Prince Kaim* again. "We don't have the proper equipment. Even if we did, the Cielcin will start digging soon."

Unkindling my sword, I wrested myself from the prince's clutches, hurried back to the fallen stone, began moving it again, stone by stone. I could do it, I knew I could. If I could just *see* a path through, choose those actions which could keep the wall from falling, however remote. I was Hadrian Marlowe, by all the gods of Earth. I had endured the guns at

Berenike, had survived on the surface of Annica without a helmet. I could move some bloody stones!

But still the vision would not come.

Tears blurred my eyes, but they were *only* tears.

Even if I had summoned up the vision, I could not have hoped to succeed. There were too many stones, too many twisted beams and torn conduits. Too many variables. And we had too little time.

"The fortress is lost," Prince Kaim said, gesturing at the ruin before me. "We have but bought a little time. We must hurry."

"We can still get out!" Valka said. "Sharp sent men ahead to see if the way to the terminal is still clear. They just called in. Epsilon Flight will hold for us."

"Epsilon Flight?" I said. I had almost forgotten the transports. Pressing a finger to the spot behind my ear to ensure the comm patch was seated properly, I asked, "Is Sharp there?"

The centurion's flat voice came back at once. "Aye, lord."

"How many are with you?"

Sharp didn't reply at once. "I count two dozen and five. Plus the three I sent on to scout the terminal."

So few.

"I'm sorry," I said.

"I told you, lord. That's the job," he said. "Save the Emperor. That's why we're here."

Unseen behind the landslide between us, I beat my breast in salute. "We will."

I winced as a burst of comm chatter crossed the line. Heard Lorian's voice. "—need to send all we can along the river passage. Hadrian! Get your ass up here! It's time!"

Not responding, I seized one last little stone and lifted it. "Valka," I said. "I'll see you in orbit."

"I know," she said.

"I love you," I said.

"I know that, too, *anaryan*," came her reply. "You're not wrong."

Sheepishly, I tossed the rock aside, embarrassed to have so old a private joke played out before any audience. Hissing as another flash of pain striped from my wounded side, I took a step back. I didn't fancy the long run back to the Emperor's war rooms, not in my state. "Centurion!" I said, limping past Prince Kaim and the waiting soldiers.

"Sir?" came Sharp's reply.

"Get her out of here. Keep her safe."

"Aye, lord," the centurion said. "We'll be on the comm."

The chaos in the Emperor's command post had risen to a fever pitch. We had had to fight through tides of survivors and the walking wounded through the space above the cistern just to reach the purple hall. Some of the remaining Valavar troopers had opened the postern gate that led to the stair that spiraled down the rim of the cistern to the level of the water, and a torrent and terrible crush of humanity was flowing in that direction, shoulders pressing for advantage and access to that narrow stair.

"Your Radiance!" I shouted, hand pressed to my side. "We've stalled the Cielcin, but half of the southern terminal is blocked."

"I know!" the Emperor said, not turning from his study of the wall displays.

Captain Thoras spoke across us. "T-minus six minutes to burn, Caesar."

The Emperor only nodded. He folded his arms and watched. Beside him, Nicephorus turned to look at us. The homunculi's face went white to see our wounds, but it said nothing, pressed its lips together.

Lorian raised his head from the map of the catacombs; his watery eyes found me. "Epsilon Flight just signaled. Valka and the Dragonslayers reached the terminal."

With the Emperor stoic, still fixated on his task, I moved to join the intus. My cape still hung over the chair beside him, and though I gripped the back, I did not take it. "What ship is she on?"

Lorian looked back down at his display. "E-17." He indicated the bay in question, far out on the end of the south terminal. The launch silo looked like it opened on one of the bluffs overlooking the hippodrome. "Are you all right?"

His eyes flitted from the wound on my side to my face and back again.

"It's nothing serious," I said. "Hurts, but it's hardly more than skin deep." In truth there were likely millions of tiny pieces of ground ceramic and armorweave in the abrasion, and though the *nahute* had failed to penetrate very far, the wounds dealt by such things were ugly and difficult to mend. "How is your shoulder?"

The junior man massaged his shoulder speculatively. "It's betrayed me, but hardly for the last time." He cursed. "Damned inconvenient time to go hurting myself."

"Hadrian!" Prince Kaim was moving toward me. Someone had affixed a white corrective to his torn brow. "You must call your ship! With the comms restored they can track your terminal."

"We won't have to rely on the telegraph," Lorian said, audibly relieved. "I was starting to worry about that part of the plan."

Raising my wrist-terminal, I opened its holograph interface, slid my fingers through the ghostly display that drifted along the inside of my forearm. "How soon can we leave?"

Lorian hesitated before saying, "As soon as His Radiance allows. There's a passage through here that leads to a sanctum on the edge of the city."

"Blessed Wisdom, I remember." I'd found the call frequency, broke off to speak into my wrist. "Marlowe to *Ascalon*," I said, "Marlowe to *Ascalon*, do you copy?"

Seconds passed. That was not unexpected. Wherever the *Ascalon* was, parked in high orbit and dark, it would take several seconds for the comms wave to reach her. Eyes shifting from Olorin to Lorian, I waited.

The hiss of static filtered over the comm patch behind my ear, and I felt a wave of relief wash through me. "Good to hear your voice, sir!" came the voice of Lin's pilot officer. "This is *Ascalon*. We read you."

Unable to suppress a grin, I looked to Lorian and said, "*Ascalon*, we have the Emperor. Repeat: we have the Emperor. Requesting evacuation."

Another pause. Signal delay. Silent tension. "Understood. What are your coordinates?"

Again, I looked to Lorian. The good commander bent over his console, adjusted something with his controls. "North thirty-seven dot one-three-five-nine. West seventy-six dot oh-two-oh-four."

I repeated the numbers, and added, "Track my beacon. We need to get the Emperor clear of the bunkers. How quickly can you make planetfall?"

The reply was a moment coming. "We can make the rendezvous in forty-nine minutes."

I mulled that a moment. "Best make it ninety. We may be delayed in leaving." I glanced to where the Emperor stood surveying the displays. Several of the feed had fallen dead, I saw, and guessed the Cielcin had made successful bombing runs on many of the launch silos. If so, each dead screen meant five hundred dead, more if they caught them with the extended bays open.

There were thousands.

A Martian came running through the door and stopped to salute Captain Thoras. "The last of the refugees have taken the river exit, sir."

Thoras nodded. "Very good, Jon. Take ten men and ensure they make it clear of the waterway. Mine the stairs. Prepare to collapse the tunnel as soon as flight control makes it clear. With luck, the Pale won't notice the tunnel until you've reached the river."

The junior Martian saluted and turned to go. "Jon!" the Martian Captain called after him. The junior man turned. "Perfugium may be lost to us. We may not be in a position to return for you."

The Martian officer called Jon nodded stiffly. "I understand." He thumped his chest in salute, directing his gesture toward the Emperor, whose back remained turned. "Hail Mars."

"Hail Mars," the captain replied, and waved the fellow off. Jon turned without complaint, his dedication, his faith a miracle to see. Like as not, the young Martian and his fellows marched off to die. Apocalypse had fallen on Perfugium. If the Cielcin remained, hunting the survivors for sport, theirs would be a life of desperation, scrabbling in the ruins of the world for some mean form of survival. Even if the Pale departed, life would be hard, and it might be decades, a century or more, before relief came to Perfugium system. Perhaps the duchess would return to rebuild her world. Perhaps not.

I never knew nor learned what became of Jon and the other survivors of armageddon, nor learned who it was who rang the bell in Resonno in defiance of all that was evil and inimical to human life.

As Jon turned to go, the flight controller's strained voice cut in. "One minute to burn on Epsilon Flight."

I pushed my way round the table to the Emperor. "Radiance. We must go at once. I've signaled the *Ascalon*. Please. We can do no more here."

"In a moment." The Emperor raised a hand. "Zeta Flight is the last we have prepared."

"Caesar, *please*. Trust your people. We have to go." My side flared, and wincing I drew back a step.

"William," came a calm, quiet voice then. "We should go." It was Lord Nicephorus who had spoken. The bald homunculus placed a hand on the Emperor's shoulder, and smiled when Caesar turned to look it in the face. "You've done all you can here."

I was glad of the chamberlain's intervention, for Caesar's nostrils flared, and his eyes were chips of agate sharp as glass. "You too, Nic?" he said, coolly.

"It may already be too late," the homunculus said. "Your son is in orbit, Radiance. And your people are out *there*." It pointed heavenward. Well I marked the return of the Emperor's honorific. He was *Radiance* again, not *William.*

But dogged as ever, William shook his head. "One more!" he said. "One more, Nic! Let me at least stay and ensure the last wave is sure to fire! Too many have died here. Too many!"

Transforming my rising curse to a hiss, I left the Emperor and his chamberlain by the displays and rounded back on Lorian. "Get me Valka!" I spat, and the little intus tapped his console, gave a sign. "Valka!" I said, finger to the patch behind my ear. "Are you all right?"

Her voice came in clear over the line, as though she were right beside me. "We made it to the ship."

"I know," I said, pacing along the long edge of the table. "Lorian told me."

Hearing his name and divining the identity of my conversation partner, Lorian said, "Is she in the cockpit? I should be able to put her on screen now."

"Are you with the pilot?" I asked.

"E-17, yes," she said. "Sharp's with me."

I hurried back to join Lorian. The intus toggled a control, and a holograph panel snapped into existence in the air to the left of Lorian's seat at the head of the table. It showed the interior of Valka's transport cockpit: the frightened, fugue-sick pilot officer blue-faced in her seat. The transport was clearly of older make than I had at first imagined. Imperial designs tended to waver between cramped, mechanical control boards and smooth holographic displays. Valka's ship was of the former variety. Every surface on the cramped bridge bristled with control switches and blinking buttons, red and blue and green.

Valka turned the instant the feed clicked on. I wasn't sure if she could see me, or if her implants or some instrument informed her of my presence. I never learned. But she smiled. "Are you leaving?" she asked.

I nodded. "After you. The Emperor wants to see the last wave off."

Valka's brows contracted. "Maybe I was wrong about all you *anaryoch.*"

"No." I shook my head. Even after all our years, it felt *wrong* for her to concede anything, to give an inch. To say that she'd been wrong. "Not all."

"Thirty seconds to launch!" the flight controller interjected.

I'd glanced in the direction of Thoras and flight control, returned my attention to Lorian and to Valka on the display. "Tell Lin—when you see him—that we'll see him at the rendezvous," I said at last. We were to take the *Ascalon* and warp directly to a point in space several light-years outside Perfugium system, there to rendezvous with the *Mnemon* and the bulk of the Jaddian fleet that had engaged the Cielcin worldships in deep orbit. They would break off the engagement as soon as we were free, would move to cover Lin's smaller Imperial force as they collected the refugee transports in low orbit.

"I will!" Valka said. "I'll see you soon."

Unspoken between us was the understanding that we were not getting away, not from the Emperor, not from service, not *to* any sort of new life. I might ask the Emperor for leave, but he could never let us go. But still I smiled at her. "See you soon."

We hadn't been apart since Akterumu. Not for any length of time. Watching her go felt . . . *wrong*. Like misplacing a limb. Still, I smiled, gripped the back of the seat where my cape still hung, stinking of the ash of Resonno.

"Ten seconds. Nine. Eight . . ." The flight controller began her count of the final seconds.

Behind Valka, Quentin Sharp undid his helmet. His bare, burned face downcast, he shifted in his seat to look out the viewport ahead. They were seated at an angle, I realized, the whole transport slotted into place on the flume rail, ready to launch. There was a string of prayer beads hanging from an overhead console. They weren't Valka's. The pilot's, perhaps? They had the look of a Cid Arthurian *malaros*. I could not recognize the knight on the medallion.

"Seven. Six. Five. Begin ignition sequence."

"Ignition sequence: engaged!" replied a flurry of voices from the men on the lower terminals. The distant drone of ceaseless thunder shook the planet again. I glanced at the flight status board. One hundred twenty-three ships were rising. The board was blue, all clear save the yellow break-ages where flumes were blocked or utterly destroyed. All about us, in every terminal and every launch silo still operable, the great fusion rockets burned like tiny stars. The cramped bays at the base of each silo filled with fire hotter than the surface of Earth's sun.

"Four. Three. Two."

Valka turned from the holograph plate, settled her head back into the seat. My heart leaped, half-expecting itself to feel the bootheel of hard burn. *I* never felt it. Valka and Sharp and the pilot all sank into their seats. Through the little stripe of window visible on the far side, I saw the flume wall streak past in an instant.

Then open sky.

Valka's hands gripped the arms of her seat. The transport shook, *malaros* beads swaying from the console above. I marked the knight then. It was Sir Tristan on the medallion.

An alarm blatted on the holograph table, and Lorian said, "They're bombing the west terminal." I glanced up at the control board. Flights winked red, transports pounded into the earth before they hit the sky.

"Where's Sword Flight?"

"Ragged as hell," Lorian answered. "Lin's boys got their asses kicked covering Delta Flight." He glanced to the next holograph table, where a glittering projection showed a render of Resonno on a curving slice of the planet's surface. Epsilon Flight rose like a forest of new shoots sprouting from the ash, blue vectors growing. Lin's fleet gleamed high above, chasing the scattered remnants of the Cielcin force that had remained in geostationary orbit above the city. I saw the scattered clusters of Lin's aquilarii wheel about to engage the Cielcin ships.

How little I grasped the mechanics of the whole. The shoals of fighter craft moving like phalanxes of geese across the sky, the rockets rising, the fleet high above, circling round to catch the survivors in orbit. Valka went to join the earlier waves of transports in orbit. The little rockets sat like barrels floating in the sea, like flotsam hoping some fishing boat might chance by and salvage them. I was living well out of my time. I was meant, I think, to live in an age when men walked the Earth and did not fly.

I was useless in naval engagements. I had always been useless, powerless as a father at birth. I looked to the Emperor then. Caesar stood with head bowed, arms crossed, before the wall of monitors. Sharply then, in that moment, did I understand his fever, his fury and drive to save these people. There was nothing he could do himself, either. Nothing but command, nothing but make his wishes known and move the lesser pieces on the board. For all his power, all his station, his breeding and command, the king could move but one square at a time.

One step through the labyrinth.

I felt his fury, too, and his desperation.

I was old then, and tired of war. Of death. I wanted nothing more than our quiet home on Thessa and seagulls crying in the morn. But Thessa was behind us, and Time, Ever-Fleeting—though her faces peer in both directions—runs only in one.

Time runs down.

"Hadrian!"

I do not know what made her call out then, her voice strained by the force of her acceleration. Turning from the display of the aerial battle, turning my back on the Emperor, I returned to Lorian's side. To Valka. Finger pressed behind my ear, I asked, "What is it?"

She never answered.

I gripped the back of my seat, glanced away an instant to Lorian. The intus was looking up, bereft as I was of any task. Valka shifted in her seat. Her ship shook around her. Sir Tristan's medal gleamed. Her lips parted, shaping the unheard word. "I—"

The holograph went dead.

Every cord in me contracted, and my heart collapsed like a dying star. "What happened?" I asked, seizing Lorian by the shoulder. The intus winced, and I recoiled, rounding on the display board. "Bring her back!"

E-05. Red. E-09. Red.

E-17.

Red.

"Lorian, bring her back!" An abyss vast and empty as all the plains of Eue howled dark through my soul. Lorian's lips pressed together, and over his shoulder the whole board began turning red. *Bring her back . . .* This time the words would not leave my throat. They have never left me.

Lorian could not bring her back. Nothing could.

Hand still on the back of my chair, grip broken, I sank to the floor.

"No," I said, a little, useless word. Too small for any use. "No . . ."

But all my denials could avail nothing. Change nothing.

Only the past is written.

Time runs down, and what once was never comes again.

Never, never, never, never.

Never.

CHAPTER 43

BROKEN AGAIN

VALKA IS DEAD.

The words hung in the air before me like the dead holograph, like the smoke of her murdered transport drifting in the gray-lit sky. I stared numbly at the display, a black panel dark and silent, a window opening . . . opening on nothing. About us all, alarms blared, and the purple glow of the displays—mingled blue and red—shaded red and redder still, as though a sea of blood were rising incarnadine about the war room.

I hardly noticed, nor heard the panicked shouts of Thoras and the flight controllers.

"We lost E-35 and -36!"

"E-67 and -69 are gone!"

"E-13, -16, -17, and -20 are down!"

Nearly all of Epsilon Flight had vanished in seconds, the status boards clicking red one bar at a time. The wall of displays before the Emperor turned black as ship cameras went dark like eyes closed forever.

Valka is dead.

"Where did they come from?" Thoras shouted. "Where did those ships bloody come from?" More alarms flashed on Lorian's table, adding their cries to the monstrous din.

I hardly heard them, could hear only Valka's final word, could see only her face. Her lips parted, eyes shining, golden as the old sun of vanished Earth.

I . . .

We were too late, had wasted too much time.

A gulf had grown between me and the men and women in that bunker, a difference of category deeper than the abyss which separates man from Cielcin. They hardly seemed real, not men at all to me in that moment, but shades, shadows on the wall of the cave that was the world. Or it was as if they were all actors, holographs—and I alone was real. Still they moved, not realizing the light had gone out, not knowing the crowds were gone.

Valka is dead.

How could they play on, actors and shadows moving, everything moving? How could they still be moving? Did they not know the world had stopped? That it had ended mere minutes before?

"I'm not sure, Captain!" replied one of the more junior flight controllers.

"They came in from the south!" another interjected. "Got them on scan!"

Hardly heard by me, Thoras grunted. "Must have diverted them from one of the other cities. Pale must have ground bases elsewhere on the planet. Camps."

"Sir, Epsilon Flight! It's . . . it's gone."

Though I did not stir from my place on the rough stone, though I did not look—I remember the reddish hell-glow of the status boards, all flights lost.

"Get me First Sword," the captain said, meaning the commander of Sword Flight.

"First Sword's not responding!" came the voice of one comms officer from the table with the projection of the aerial combat. "They're scattered, sir. Awfully scattered."

Thoras cursed.

I did not see William Caesar in that moment—my eyes were for the black square that had taken Valka from me, still hovering in the air beside Lorian in his chair above me—but I imagine him standing before his displays, head bowed, face lost in shade crimson as his hair. All eyes save mine must have moved to him, for it was in him and on his shoulders that the final decision rested.

A slim, tired figure approached His Radiance, his logothete's suit grubby from the long months underground. Sir Gray Rinehart cleared his throat and, head bowed as the Emperor's, the Director said, "Radiance, we cannot launch Zeta Flight now." Rinehart inhaled sharply, stood straighter. "The transports will be torn apart."

I did not see, but guess that William raised hooded eyes to peer into the face of his servant. He did not speak.

Somewhere in the dimness, a message bell chimed.

"Knight-Captain, sir!" cried one of the techs. "Incoming message from Tribune Lin!"

Sir Cedric Thoras responded first. "Put him through!"

At the sound of Bassander's name, I glanced up at the primary display. The Mandari officer flickered into view, strapped into his captain's chair aboard the *Tempest*, his face gray with the strain of battle and gravitation. The bridge of the great warship gleamed about him, black and bronze.

Before Lin could speak, Thoras bellowed, "What in Earth's holy name is happening up there, Tribune?" Thoras was only a captain, and should have been Lin's junior, but he was captain of the Emperor's Martian Guard. "We lost the refugees! All of them!"

I turned away from Lin's face on the screen, turned back to the dead panel above me, a window into endless night. "The Pale launched a new force from the planet forty degrees west of the city! They must have been holding them in reserve!"

"You didn't see them?" Thoras barked, incredulous.

"No!" Lin made no excuses. "And it's not just the new assault on the city. They've launched cruisers to intercept us in orbit."

"Move to counter!" Thoras said, but his orders were blind. "Destroy them!"

I didn't have to look to see Lin's stony face, the ashen expression. "Captain, the first assault scattered my fleet across orbit chasing the Pale. We're holding the GEO point above Resonno alone. We can't hold!"

"What about the Jaddians?" Thoras asked.

"The Jaddians drove against their worldships!" Lin said. "They're out beyond the moons! It would take hours to get them here!"

"Can you save the refugees, Tribune?" came the Voice Imperial. I heard the sound of feet, guessed that the Emperor had moved to stand beside Thoras. "The ones that made it to orbit?"

Lin's reply was a second coming. "Some of them. Possibly, if . . . Radiance, I must abandon the defense of geostate above Resonno."

"See it done, Tribune!" the Emperor said.

See it done, barked Captain Corvo from some aching cavern in my mind.

I am no longer certain what happened first. Perhaps it was the monitors. Every video feed showing a view of the surface went white. Several went dead. Then the earth convulsed, and alarms flared, and even I stirred upon the floor, shaking Olorin's hand from my shoulder.

When had he come to stand at my side?

"What the hell happened?"

It was an officer unseen aboard the *Tempest* who answered. "AM burst detected in the city! Launched from the new ships."

Light. I could see the blast clearly in my mind's eye. A white light annihilating everything it touched.

"Antimatter?" the Emperor said. "Where?"

"Northeast terminal complex!" Lorian said, hunched over the display. Under his breath, he said, "*Cid Arthur . . .* they're desperate."

Antimatter. The word was almost enough to shake me from the sea of ink I was drowning in. If the Pale had resigned themselves to antimatter bombardment at last, they had abandoned all hope of taking the complex, of taking the Emperor alive. Truly desperate, General Hushansa must have thrown all caution and its master's orders to the wind. Better to kill the *Uganatai* and the *Utannashi*—the False King and the Champion of the Lie—than to let them escape. The Shiomu Elusha would forgive it, would it not?

Some part of me smiled—even then—to think of the mixed welcome the *vayadayan* Hushansa and Attavaisa would receive upon returning to Dharan-Tun after such a poisoned victory.

Another of the junior men about the holograph exclaimed, "The northeast tunnels are breached!"

"Can we collapse those tunnels?" Thoras asked.

He never got an answer to that question—or if he did I never heard it. "They're hailing us!" shouted another of the flight controllers, voice shrill. "Caesar, they're hailing us!"

A cold knife—a blade of ice, or so it seemed—plunged between my shoulder blades. I did not need to be told who *they* were. The Cielcin had come to talk. To gloat. To order our surrender. They had taken Valka from me, and the Emperor had taken Valka from me, and I had nothing. Nothing but a cold, clear rage unlike any I had ever known.

"Put them through," the Emperor said. "Wait." William paused a moment. "Tribune Lin," he said, and I did not have to look to imagine the way Bassander's posture straightened. "Save all you can."

"At once," Lin said, and vanished.

"On the holograph," the Emperor said, his red cape floating into the edge of my sight.

The black window through which Valka had vanished had closed—was gone forever. The whole map of the fortress went with it as the Emperor moved to stand before the holograph.

The *Vayadan*-General Ugin Attavaisa appeared in Valka's place, still seated on its iron throne. Duke Gaspard's body and that of his stillborn Cielcin child were gone, and in their place two white-armored chimeric soldiers stood guard to either side of the general on its throne, the badge of the White Hand in black outline upon their left shoulders. Looking up from the floor, I saw plainly the great windows behind the Cielcin and the shining face of Perfugium beyond and beneath the alien ship.

"Emperor!" the xenobite growled, teeth tripping around the human word. *"Raka vaayu ti-taadyr! Svassaa ti-wetidiu! Iamamarra o-yukajjimn ba-okun ieturi!"*

Attavaisa was still all Cielcin, was not machine like the older fingers of the White Hand. It did not know our words, had not had them dripped into its brain, did not pass its thoughts through MINOS's filter.

"What did it say?" the Emperor asked, looking round for a scholiast, for someone—anyone who could translate. "What did it say?"

But there was no one to answer him. No one . . . save me.

"Marlowe!" The Emperor's eyes had seized on me. "What are you doing on the floor?"

"They killed his woman," Tiada said, just behind me. "She was on the ships."

My eyes found the Emperor's green ones. Caesar's face was empty, placid as that of any pharaoh. "I see," he said, eyes flickering back to Attavaisa. Lips pressed together. A frown. Of sorrow? Of pity? Of only frustration?

They killed his woman. Tiada's words echoed in the cavern of my skull, too sharp to be real. *Valka is dead.* Valka was not dead. Could not be . . . dead.

"Junne!" the Cielcin general said, gesturing at the floor with one claw.

"Marlowe, what is it saying?" the Emperor asked.

"Junne!" Attavaisa said, the same word Syriani had said to Iamndaina when the Prince of Princes forced its enemy to its knees.

Down.

My eyes left the Emperor, turned back to Attavaisa grinning from the comfort of its ambulatory throne. It was Attavaisa who had ordered the attack on Delta Flight, Attavaisa who had led the Cielcin siege of Perfugium.

Attavaisa who had killed Valka.

I could feel the blood rushing in me, hammering in my ears. The general had not seen me, huddled as I was upon the rough stone of the floor, *down* already. Its lipless mouth parted, glass snarl of teeth flashing in the ghost-light of the projection. "You thought you could endure," it said, "thought you could stand against the might of the *Cielcin*. You had your chance. You could have surrendered, could have offered yourself for your people. Now none shall live. I shall peel their hides for cloaks, and wring their blood to fodder the worms! Their offal will feed my slaves, and their meat will sate my armies. And you! You I will bring before the Shiomu Elusha in chains. He will break you. You will be his slave. His pet. His plaything!"

Attavaisa found its feet as it shouted, and spit as it cursed and stepped down from its throne. Though its threats fell hollow on uncomprehending ears, still it fumed and beat its breast. Alarms still flared about the hall, and still the flight control displays glowed Death's dull red.

"Junne wo!" it hissed, and again, *"Down!"*

"Marlowe, answer me!" the Emperor said. "What does it want?"

As if he could not guess.

Slowly, as though I shouldered an immeasurable weight, I found my knees.

Still Attavaisa had not seen me. *"Down!"* the Cielcin general commanded. "On your knees! Down! Down!"

I stood up, swaying. My head was swimming then, throbbing with the music of blood and breath, and I gripped the rail at the edge of the holograph table to stop myself from falling. Only slowly did my eyes focus and settle on the image of the Cielcin general. Armored all in white it was, and stood before its throne. Evidently surprised, the whiteless black eyes of Ugin Attavaisa found my eyes glaring back.

I did not speak, did not look away.

"Aeta ba-Yukajjimn!" the *vayadan* said. "The King of Rats! You live! Hushansa failed, then! No matter! I will bring you to the Great One myself!"

Still I did not speak. The general's image shimmered above me, its guards like porcelain statues gleaming to either side. Perfugium shone behind them, cloud-bound and gray, her terminator just coming into view. There, on that world below—the world where my world ended—I still stood. A thousand miles or more from the general.

So far.

Too far . . .

"Perhaps he will share you with me, when he has taken your life."

The general's words spread on the air and died. All fell silent then, quiet as I. Alarms and other indicators still beeped and screamed from the consoles all around, but even Thoras had turned from his task to watch.

Valka is dead.

That single thought ran through me like a bolt of lightning, like a beam of killing light. As I had grasped Irshan's sword in Colosso, I grasped that thought in my mind, held it until I felt my hands both bleed. All unknowing, I had made of my hands twin fists, and the nails had cut my palms.

Still I did not speak, did not take my eyes from Attavaisa.

Rage is blindness. Gibson whispered in my ear, admonishing. *Grief is deep water.*

But I was beyond rage. Past grief. I stood upon a mountaintop in the grip of a fury cold and clear as ice, but the grip was itself my own. My blood hammered in my ears, and my eyes stretched wide open, so wide I thought I must weep. The men about me drew away, save Lorian, who reached out one uncertain hand.

"What?" the *vayadan* jeered. Not familiar with the faces of man, the beast had mistaken my fury for fear, and it smiled. "Have you nothing to say?"

How must I have seemed to the Pale general? A little man, wounded, haggard, hands at his side—silent and frozen with fear? For it smiled, and its black tongue tripped over the points of its teeth like a diner at a feast. I clenched my own jaw in answer, held it until I thought my teeth must shatter like chalk.

Slowly—micron by micron, degree by degree—my eyes left the general's face, slid instead to the windows, to Perfugium beyond. So peaceful it seemed, as if war had never touched her old, gray face. But I had walked upon her surface, had battled monsters in the ruins of the city above, where fire rained that very moment, where before the ashes fell like snow.

Then Attavaisa *fractured*, and two generals stood before its throne. The blood thrumming in my ears fell silent. My breathing stopped. I stood once more between two moments in time, between heartbeats. Nothing moved. Nothing but me.

Nothing but my vision.

I looked at the general and saw it in innumerable aspects, repeated in subtle variation across infinite potential time: its teeth bared, its head cocked at a slight angle, its crown of horns banded silvery and glittering on the holograph. I saw Attavaisa victorious, mocking, and cruel. Time stretched, smeared and fractured until it seemed I saw the world through a kaleidoscope of red lights and glass fangs.

But I had seen *more* than Attavaisa.

Glass . . .

I looked upon the glass windows behind the Pale general's throne, and—looking—chose.

Silent was my fury. A silence *beyond* words.

Nothing endures, nor lasts forever. Not stone, not empires, not life itself. Even the stars will one day burn down—as I have seen and know perhaps better than any other man. Even the darkness that comes after all will one day pass away to new light. This record, too, and this warm scribe—my hand—perhaps, will fade. The stones here on Colchis shall fall into the sea, and the sea dissolve to foam. The stars shall burn the worlds to ash, and cool themselves to cinders.

All things fade. Fall. Shatter.

I raised a bleeding hand.

"Dein?" Attavaisa asked, cocking its head. "What? Speak!"

A thin line traced itself along the pane of glass behind the general, faint and silver as a spider's thread. I smiled, watched it fork and propagate throughout the pane—

—precisely as our actions propagate throughout time.

I bared my teeth in a Cielcin's feral smile.

The windows behind the general shattered. Attavaisa's eyes went wide as the wind rushed past it, tugging at its white braid. Its mouth opened, but its curses and its threats were forever silenced as Ugin Attavaisa and its guards were pulled from their feet and thrown into the black heart of space beyond.

The holograph plate cracked itself an instant later, banishing the image entire.

In the sudden dark that followed, I screamed, and the noise of it tore from me and through me as I fell once more to my knees. It was a scream to rival Valka's in the dark tower of Ganelon, a scream of triumph and pain both—and of power returning. The lights in the ceiling above my head burst like ripe fruit, plunging the space at hand into darkness total and absolute.

Silence then.

Whispers.

"Was that?"

"Earth and Emperor!"

"Did he . . . kill them?"

"It isn't possible."

"But . . . how?"

". . . only stories. I thought they were only stories."

I looked up. The Emperor was looking down at me, his eyes very wide. I tried to read his face, but I saw too many emotions, each standing in the place of the other, each vying to come forth.

I knew what I had done, and knew also what I had to do—what was *expected of me*. The eyes of the court were on me, of the Martians and of Jadd. The eyes of the Emperor were on me, also. I was already on my knees. I had only to bow and submit myself to the will and rule of the Emperor, to reassure His Radiance and all that the natural order of the world would be upheld.

I was already kneeling . . .

But I would not bow.

I shook my head instead. "She would be alive," I said, heedless of all consequence. "If you had but listened to me."

The Emperor's mask faltered, and William peered out. Was that awe in those emerald eyes? Was that triumph . . . or fear? The Halfmortal could no longer be mocked as rumor, no longer dismissed as legend. The Emperor had *known* before that moment, but he had *seen* me then with his own two eyes.

"I . . . I'm . . ." he said, and shut his mouth. The *Emperor* reasserted himself. "We must go."

All that happened next passed in a kind of haze. Olorin and Tiada helped me back to my feet. I remember shouting voices, remember the Emperor barking orders to the Martians and the remaining flight controllers alike. The Excubitors moved ahead to secure our exit. Too late—and nearly too late—Caesar had decided that it was time to flee. The *Ascalon* was to meet us in the Sanctum of the Blessed Wisdom in just over an hour's time.

We could make our rendezvous.

Olorin laid a hand on my shoulder, tried to move me.

I shrugged him off.

How well I remember my reflection in that broken holograph, that table of shattered glass. Jari the Seer had spoken of my broken road, my ruined path through time. Brethren, too, had seen it, had marked the ways in which the Quiet had interfered with me, had moved me to his purpose. He had shifted Demetri's ship from Teukros to Emesh, had traded my right arm for my left, had brought me to that mountaintop on Annica, and from Annica to . . . where?

To Eue? To Perfugium? To hell itself?

And for what? I had seen that Black Feast and sacrifice in memories of the future a thousand times in as many nightmares, but never once had I seen *her* death.

But it had happened.

Was I beyond my visions? In escaping the net of Akterumu, had I gone beyond the Quiet's sight? He had said I would, had he not? Upon the mountain on Annica?

Or had the Quiet withheld Valka's fate from me? Kept her death a secret to steel me to my purpose, to hold me to the mark? These thoughts warred in me, droning beneath the wailing emptiness of the pain and terrible truth.

That Valka was dead.

Ask me how we escaped the catacombs, and I will tell you that Olorin and I followed the Emperor and his guards through a door in the back of the control room. Great gearworks moved plugs of stone and steel ten cubits thick, opening a passage just wide enough for two to walk abreast. I can see the passage if I try, hear the rattle of those cyclopean mechanisms turning, shaking off the dust of millennia, for they had not had cause to move since the first dukes of Perfugium set them in their places. I remember the wavering of suit lamps and the echo of shouting in the dark. One of the Dragonslayers—Mads, I think—followed close behind, his breath ragged in my ear.

But I did not see them then, not really, nor did I see the bravery of Lin's last stand in orbit. I was only a kind of beast, herded with the other beasts by those men who had not lost all. How well I understood the Duchess Valavar, and thanked whatever gods there are—the Quiet perhaps among them—that Valka at least had not suffered as the duke had suffered. Tears stung my eyes, blurred the tunnels to smears of formless gray.

I do not remember entering the sanctum, emerging into the undercroft and climbing the polished stairs. I *do* recall the altar, however, and the statue of the God Emperor crushing a square pyramid to symbolize the machines. I stood before it for several long minutes while we waited. The dome above had shattered in some earlier bombing, but still the statue stood victorious in its battle with that old enemy. William Rex, King of Avalon, Conqueror of Earth, Chosen of the Hidden One—of the Quiet Himself.

Ashes lay in drifts about the ruined splendor of the sanctum, mounded against the altar and about the feet of my divine ancestor, triumphant beneath the oculus far above. I wore no helmet then, and heard with my naked ears the roar of engines approaching. I felt the dead wind in my hair, and smelled the foul burning of the ashes of man.

"The ship, Marlowe!" Director Rinehart gripped my shoulders. "Where's the ship?"

"Coming," said some man with my voice. I held my terminal weakly up. "It's coming."

Rinehart did not move. I found him peering into my face, a strange look in his grave and distant eyes. "I am sorry," he said, and gripped my shoulder, "for your loss."

His words were like splinters of broken glass, each a spike pushed into me. Her death had reached the lips of other men. Tiada had spoken of it to the Emperor not an hour before . . . but Rinehart? Rinehart was the first to grieve with me, if only to offer a token.

It had happened. It was real.

Red lightning flashed beyond the sky as the great ships burned their courses through orbit. "Is that our ship?" one of the remaining ministers asked, eyes wide.

"That's the fleet in orbit," Rinehart said, shading his eyes as he stared up through the shattered dome.

Those red flashes are all I saw of the great rescue of Perfugium. I have heard versions of the story where I was in that battle and not on the ground at all. There are tales told—started by the Chantry, I don't doubt, and by the Ministry of Public Enlightenment—that I was there, on the bridge of the *Tempest,* or that I had the command. In the years since, I have heard it said that I faltered in my command, that it was for that failure that the Emperor exiled me, banished me from the Imperium.

It isn't so.

My crime was something else. Something smaller . . . and more foolish. So foolish.

But there is yet truth in their stories. Namely, Bassander Lin.

The Phoenix of Perfugium.

I was not with him in his hour of glory, whatever the stories say—nor was his victory my failure. I did not even see it, unless it was in those red flashes in our sky. As I stood there, hollow and broken again, Lin pulled off one of the most stunning rescues in Imperial naval history. His fleet scattered, his ships outgunned, Bassander Lin managed to intercept and salvage the refugees who had escaped Resonno and Perfugium's gravity entire.

Six hundred twenty-three ships had made it into orbit in those first four waves.

More than three hundred thousand people.

Lin saved six hundred and six.

So many. So few.

Nine million had slumbered beneath Perfugium. We had saved fewer than one in thirty, though the Emperor was one. But Perfugium was no victory. I saw reports later, heard stories, of how the Cielcin had cracked open the catacombs behind us, of the millions drained of cryonic fluid, killed, and hung upon the walls of Resonno. Attavaisa was dead, but Hushansa's men feasted on all of those we could not save.

Perfugium was no victory. It was a holocaust. And for me?

It was the end.

For there are endings, Reader, have I not said? All that follows here, all that *must* follow, that *must* be, happened to a different man. A lesser man. I have consoled myself on sleepless nights—and there have been thousands—that she did not suffer, that she felt no pain. More, I have consoled myself that *they* could not have found her body.

There must have been nothing of her left.

CHAPTER 44

REQUIEM

AMONG THE EXTRASOLARIANS, THEY say, there are men who take memories, who siphon them away in crystal phials and stopper them like djinni. But I could not seek their services, not and remain myself. I said once that a man is the sum of memories, and it is so. Thus, to discard those memories—however terrible—is to discard a part of ourselves. A part of me had died and so remained on Perfugium with Valka, will remain there until its sun swells and swallows that miserable world, but the scars left where she once dwelt are a part of me, too, and worth the price and privilege of knowing her.

Of our life together.

I would not cut them away.

In Tavros, in the Demarchy, they take memories as well. When I had taken Valka there after Urbaine wounded her on Berenike, her clansmen tried to heal her, to cast out the worm that had entwined itself around her brain. As I have here written, they failed, succeeded only in crippling Urbaine's virus. Valka had been saved, but not without symptoms, not without scars herself.

They had offered another solution, had offered to overwrite her lace entire, to destroy all she was and ever had been, to rebuild her anew and let her live free and healthy—but as someone else. Some new woman would have walked away with Valka's body.

She had refused, rebelled when they attempted to compel her. She had chosen to live with her pain, with the memory of all Urbaine had done, with her seizures and her own hand strangling her in the night.

How could I do less?

But how could I do anything?

We made our rendezvous with the Jaddian fleet and docked aboard the *Mnemon*. The Emperor and his court all left the *Ascalon* in short order and left me alone, almost forgotten. Even Prince Kaim had left me. He had matters of state to attend to. He had, after all, played his part in the rescue of the Emperor, and Jadd had its hopes and interests. Only Lorian would not depart. Not at first. Not even after I hurled a bottle of wine at him. I had to drive him off at last, and hurled him bodily down the ramp and sealed the airlock doors behind him.

Alone. I was alone.

I left a trail of armor behind me, vambraces, manica, and greaves. My cuirass I let fall as I had that terrible day on Eue, and barefoot—clad only in my torn skin-suit—I found our chamber again and, still bloody and stinking of sweat and soot, I sank onto the bed.

The scent of smoke and sandalwood perfumed the bedclothes, as if she sat beside me. It burned my eyes—or was it only grief?

Tears.

My mouth opened, forming words that would not come. A thin, weak sound escaped me, fingers finding the silver chain about my neck. How cold the phylactery seemed in my hand, its hard, defined edges biting the palm, sharp ás truth. It was all that remained of her, a single drop of blood made crystal, preserved against the ravages of time.

A half-moon. A broken circle.

The pendant would never be whole again.

One last fight, indeed.

I knew . . . I knew when I started this account I must return to this, my blackest day. I thought I would be ready, thought that after all these years and centuries, after so many false starts, that I could write of her. Of her end. I thought that now, perhaps, I could say something of that bleak silence, that total silence in the *Ascalon* then.

But there is nothing.

Nothing.

No words can enclose that silence, or capture the blackness on the holograph where she had been. I can write of that day only as a terrible emptiness, a void blacker than space. Mere words are insufficient, are too small to capture the chasm that had opened beneath my feet.

I remember blood on the bedsheets from my wounded hands and side, and soot and cinder and the stink of wine. I would sooner relive every hour on the walls of the Dhar-Iagon, every night in the pit, blood dripping from my ear, would sooner stomach the blood and screaming of the Prophet's coronation feast than endure that terrible silence.

And yet it is ever by my side.

I can hear it even now. It is with me always. If I but set down my pen and call her name . . . she will never answer me.

Not ever again.

CHAPTER 45

THE DEMON AND THE KING

THE BATTLE WAS OVER. The world was lost—and mine with it. The *Tempest* and the remainder of Lin's fleet caught up to the greater Jaddian force in the deep of space light-years from Perfugium. We needed time to collect ourselves, to determine which ships could yet make the journey back to Fidchell, and from Fidchell to Nessus. The Emperor's expedition to inspect the outer provinces had ended in disaster. An entire fleet destroyed, a planet lost and millions of lives with it.

Perfugium was not simply a defeat, not a strategic retreat and heroic rescue. It was a blow. Far more than a key colony on the border between Centaurus and the lost Norman territories, it represented the first great loss in Centaurus itself. And more, it was the first great battle conducted by the *imperial* army of the Shiomu Elusha against the Legions of Man. The Cielcin were one tribe, one blood-clan then. At Akterumu, Dorayaica had forged its people into one, uniting for the first time since the days of Elu nearly all the warring tribes.

And those tribes had spilled into the provinces of Centaurus. Word would come in the years ahead of sacks across the provinces. Nessus would burn in time, and the Lothrians would pour across the Rasan Belt into the upper Sagittarius, and we would be beset at both ends. Spread thin by the needs of defending the broader realms of Centaurus and Sagittarius alike, our Legions would find themselves outgunned in battle after battle, and too late besides.

How clearly I could see it, remember it as I remembered wandering the halls of Echidna with Valka—where we had never gone in waking life.

How little I cared.

"Hadrian?" The knock sounded again. "The Emperor is waiting for you!"

I stared at the airlock door. It was the same airlock at whose gate Valka had met me in the bowels of the *Tamerlane*. I had been standing in the airlock itself for perhaps two minutes. I couldn't bring myself to open the door, no matter how Bassander hammered. A week had passed since the battle ended, three days since the rendezvous with the Jaddian fleet, six since the *Ascalon* met the *Mnemon* at the edge of Perfugium system. An eternity, and no time at all.

"Hadrian!" Bassander's voice grew sharper. "I know you can hear me."

I must have opened the door. To this day I cannot remember doing so, can remember only the somber, tired face of Bassander Lin peering in at me where once there had been only the padded inner face of the airlock's outer door.

The tribune—the knight-tribune, for the Emperor had elevated him to knighthood for his service in the great rescue of the three hundred thousand—leaned heavily on his cane. His uniform was perfect as ever, and the copper sun of the Order of Merit he'd been given glittered proudly on his chest, its white and scarlet ribbon pinned to his tunic front. It was identical to the medal I'd received for my defeat of Aranata Otiolo so very, very long ago. I remember thinking it strange that I had been so honored as a boy, while Lin—the faithful soldier and the professional—had lived so long without order or knighthood.

What Lin saw in the airlock door doubtless beggared description. I had washed the day of the battle, sat I think for hours in the mist of the shower stall, just as I had done after Akterumu, only I had done so alone. I had not washed since, and my hair clung to me in a greasy snarl, and I was certain the smell of me was a horror in itself. I remember chewing my tongue. The new teeth that had grown in during my time on Colchis had not done so neatly, and my breath stank of the poor wine I'd sent a man to liberate from the *Tempest*'s commissary, the same case as the bottle I'd hurled at Lorian to persuade him to leave.

Bassander Lin took in my disheveled appearance without comment, and he reached out to steady me. "You've been drinking," he said, dark eyes peering up into my face.

I could sense the faint judgment in his tone, the concern. Bassander never drank, or if he had, he had long ago given it up. There was fear for me in his dark eyes, and pity. I did not *want* his pity, I could stomach it less well than so much wine.

"She's gone," I said, and fancied I could *feel* how deep-sunken were my eyes. The words rang unreal in my own ears, voice ragged. I had not spo-

ken for days. Not since I drove Lorian from the *Ascalon*. "She's gone, Lin."
So few were the friendly faces left me in all the universe that I settled for
Lin's. Like a tower falling I folded toward him. The knight-tribune dropped
his cane in his haste to catch me. He did not speak at once, but leaned
against the wall to take my weight from his aching bones. "She's gone," I
kept repeating.

Unsure what to do with himself, Bassander patted me on the back. "I
know, Marlowe. I know." He pushed me back, staggered against the wall
of the airlock. "I'm sorry."

Stumbling back to stand against the inner wall, I said, "My fault. It's all
my fault."

Lin went to one knee to retrieve his cane. Ignoring me entire, he said,
"The Emperor is waiting for you. Let's get you cleaned up. We're nearly
late already. I've brought a shuttle to ferry you over to the *Tempest* . . ."

"Let him wait!" I hissed, practically spitting, and wheeled away, retreating deeper into the ship. The bottles I mention—what remained of them—
lay shattered in the hall. The bridge lay dark, and beyond its windows the
great bay of the *Mnemon* shone brightly and inviting. It wasn't right. There
should be no light. No light anywhere. Somewhere in the gloom, my terminal was reciting Orodes.

Despite my objections, I moved toward our cabin—my cabin, I supposed, and shuddered—to quickly wash and prepare myself. I knew I could
not truly keep the Emperor waiting.

I knew this audience must come.

I cleaned and dressed in short order, slamming the cabin door in Lin's face.
Not wanting to waste time on the luxury of a shower, I used the sonic
scrubber in the shower pod and scraped myself with the strigil. Raw and
dry I saw myself in the mirror. Long gone was the young athlete from the
pits of Emesh, long vanished the proud knight of the Emperor's own. A
revenant stared at me, hollow-eyed and undead, his skin like old parchment. The mark of the surgeon and bite of the lash were everywhere in
evidence upon his flesh, and the stripes of the Prophet's claws glowed on
his left cheek. His hair had gone white at temples and at forelock and ran
along his crown like lightning—just like his father's—and his eyes! His
eyes were the bottoms of deep wells untouched by any light.

But the phylactery at his throat was mine. I lifted a hand—the hand

Irshan had scarred, the hand the Quiet had granted me to save my life in
the arena—and touched the half-moon pendant.

The revenant's hand moved with my own.

The *Tempest* had no throne room, no receiving hall, and lacking for a court,
the Emperor had installed himself not in one of the officers' conference
rooms, but in one of the cargo holds. Thusly ordered, Lin's men had duti-
fully moved the crates to either side. Officers and the surviving members
of the Imperial court—logothetes and androgyns alike—sat upon the tiered
boxes as though they were the terraced benches of a coliseum.

More like jurists than spectators they seem to me now, by the light of
memory, for jurists they became.

Haren Bulsara and Director Rinehart stood to one side of the throne
with Lord Nicephorus. Archprior Leonora—reunited with the court—
stood in her customary place beside the seated Emperor, a black-robed
reminder of the Chantry's eternal presence. Prince Alexander sat upon a
lesser seat at the foot of his father's makeshift dais, just as Crispin and I had
sat beneath our father to welcome Director Feng so many lifetimes before.
Was that sorrow in the young man's eyes? Or something else?

Lorian Aristedes—his arm in a sling—half-made to join me as I passed,
but I forestalled him with a discreet hand, guilt filling the hollows of my
belly. Had his injury on Perfugium called for that sling? Or had I put him
in it when I threw him out of the *Ascalon*? Beside him—masked once
more—stood Prince Kaim Sanchez Cyaxares du Otranto, and beside him
was the Lady Kalima in cloth of orange and gold, and Admiral Serpico,
and Captain Afsharirad, and a selection of still more Jaddian officers in
white and blue. The prince's eyes met mine, bright in the polished black
mask that hid his friendly face. I paused for the space of a step and looked
up into the makeshift gallery—and saw seated above the rest a woman in
the black of mourning. A veil of delicate black lace concealed her face, but
I knew from the quartered heraldry of the men about her that she was
Saskia Valavar, once-duchess of Perfugium.

Catching me looking, she gave me the smallest of nods, and I realized
that—more than any other in that echoing hold—she most understood my
pain. The crooked smile I gave her returned that pain, and I turned my
head away, for in her half-concealed eyes I sensed the vanished light I'd
seen in the revenant that had glowered at me from my mirror.

Caesar himself was seated not upon the Solar Throne, but upon a common camp stool. His royal armor had been taken away for cleaning, and he sat sans cape, sans coronet, sans even the red velvet of his gloves. No raiment of the proper white was there to be found for him aboard *Tempest*, and he wore the dress blacks of a Legionary naval officer, with a red sash about his waist.

Gone was the blast of silver trumpet, gone the wailing strains of "Far Beyond the Sun." The pomp and circumstance of the Imperial court had all been blown away, etched by the scouring winds of war until only the ivory remained in the form of one reedy androgyn, whose clear castrato rose to announce the coming of some absurdly styled chevalier I slowly came to realize was myself.

I had not heard the nuncius's words, but I knew the style well.

"The Lord Hadrian Anaxander Marlowe-Victorian, Supreme Commandant of the Imperial Red Company, Knight-Commander of the Royal Victorian Order, Bearer of the Grass Crown, Holder of the Order of Merit, Hero of the Empire!"

. . . and escort, I thought. But I had no escort.

She was gone.

Many of those seated stood, and the surviving Martians—those few who had clambered aboard the *Ascalon* or aboard the ships launched from the catacombs—thumped the ground with the butts of their lances. Only the Excubitors that guarded the Emperor's dais seemed unmoved.

If I was expected to bow, I disappointed. I'd worn no finery, nor pinned any medals to my chest. Without even the white cape of my knighthood, I stood before the throne in the dress blacks I'd been given on Ganelon— very like unto those Caesar wore himself—with only the red aiguillette at the left shoulder to distinguish me from some common ensign. Only the aiguillette—that is—and the Emperor's sword, which I carried tucked into my right boot.

I'd had no opportunity to return it.

"Lord Marlowe," Caesar said, eyes downcast. "We are with you in your grief. The loss of your paramour is a great personal tragedy against the background of these evil times. Were it not for you—and for her sacrifice in the tunnels of the colonial stores—the fortress might well have been overrun, and our person and indeed our Empire would even now be in the grip of the Cielcin."

Caesar's words hung above me like a stone swinging on a line. Unreal. It was all unreal, could not be real. Hanging my head, I wished for nothing so much as the wine-soaked gloom of the *Ascalon*, for the quiet dark of the necropolis beneath Devil's Rest, for the oblivion of my cave on Dharan-Tun. I longed to be alone, to be away from those pitying, prying eyes, to escape the nervous whispers.

Could they not all leave me be?

But the Emperor was unfinished. "But your actions . . . your actions are in keeping with the very highest traditions of service. Let no man question what we have long known." His pause for effect was perfect, the result of centuries of training and fine practice. I looked back up, just as doubtless he'd intended me to do, so that I might see him turn and direct his words to the black shadow named Leonora, and to young Alexander at the foot of the dais. Caesar's air was almost casual, his pitch perfect, yet final as the fall of the White Sword. He continued, "That you are our servant, loyal and true."

I had not prostrated myself before him in the bunker, after I had slain Attavaisa, as I knew I ought. Nevertheless, it seemed, Caesar intended to renew his hold over me, to stake his claim and so cast his cloak of protection over me once more in the eyes of his more-than-decimated court.

Politics . . . The word boiled in my chest. How could they still be playing *politics* after everything that had happened? After *all of it*?

Valka is dead . . .

Rage is blindness, Gibson cautioned deep within. *Rage is blindness.*

But I was blind already, and spoke. "Are you?" I asked, unable to help myself. The words fell like corpses loosed from the gallows. I heard discomforted whispers from the galleries to either side, saw confusion color the Emperor's pharaonic mask. He didn't understand the question. None of them did. Had Mad Marlowe just asked the Emperor if he were *his* servant?

"Are you?" I asked again. More bodies fell from the gallows, legs breaking upon the hard ground. "With me? In my grief?" A weak laugh escaped me, and my vision of the Emperor seated on his stool blurred, though whether it was with second sight or with tears I could not say. I turned my head away.

"Order!" shouted Nicephorus, raising its hands for calm.

The Emperor raised one bare hand. "Peace!" he said. Still holding up his hand, he continued, "Yes, cousin. I am. I did not know your woman, but yes—I grieve with you." The royal *we* had vanished, the Emperor became the man.

That shook the tears from me for true, and I raised one scarred hand to shade my eyes. For a moment, I did not dare move, aware at once that I was thrust upon the highest stage, and naked stood upon it, unclad in the eyes of history, for this moment—whatever it was—would be remembered by men until the stars burned down.

Tears in my eyes, I shut them, and let my hand fall.

Grief is deep water, I told myself. *Grief is deep water.*

No, I heard Gibson say, and almost I thought I felt his hand upon my shoulder. *It is human. Have you forgotten? To be human is the greater thing . . .* Eyes still closed, I felt though I had only to turn my head and see him standing there, and not just him. For a moment I felt I had only to turn and see *her* standing there beside me, and Pallino with her, and Elara, and Ghen and Siran, Ilex and Crim and Corvo and all the rest . . .

Maybe I was mad at last, as so many doubtless whispered.

The Emperor's voice rose once more. "More than any other of our servants, you have suffered in our name."

I did not contest this, though none of what I had done I had done for him. Why had I done it? For the Empire? For its men and women? That its children might not know war? No. I had wanted adventure, had felt a longing deeper than any since Alexander to see the world and shape it. I had dreamed of peace, and found none, and dreamed of Quiet thereafter.

Quiet.

Had they, had it, had *he* done all this to me? Had the Quiet set that very longing—that *dream*—in that black organ I called a heart and so spurred me to his purpose?

You are a lever pulled by your genes, Brethren once had told me.

I am a puppet pulled by some eldritch thing, I answered in my heart, though some other voice like mine responded, saying: *Though he slay me, I will trust in him. Have you forgotten?*

How could I forget . . . or trust . . . when all trust had won me was pain?

The Emperor was still talking. The world kept on turning, always turning. "More than any other of our servants, too, we are in your debt. You saved our life."

"I did nothing," I said, summoned back to myself.

"It was *your* ship," the Emperor said, "*your* men in the catacombs, *your* efforts that held the way."

I shook my head. "It was the Jaddians, Radiance, and your Martians."

"And they shall have their rewards as well, but you will have yours. It was you who slew their captain! I *saw* it, Marlowe. With my own eyes, I saw it."

My shaking head had become something of a nervous tic, and I stepped backward. "No," I said, denying myself, denying what I had done and the god who had placed such gifts into my hands. "No."

"That is three of the Prophet's captains you have undone. Who here—who under all the suns of Earth—can say the same?"

Four, some part of me replied. I had slain four. He had forgotten Aulamn, though I had told of its demise in my reports. Hushansa was not dead, of that I was certain, and Vati and Teyanu yet lived, and Peledanu. But I did not doubt the Shiomu Elusha would soon replace its lost fingers, as I had regenerated mine.

One, said another part of me. Udax had done as much to kill Iubalu and Bahudde as I, and Aulamn's death had been Pallino's doing. Thinking of Pallino and Udax only made it worse, and again I drew back a step, still shaking my head.

"For your suffering and your service, cousin, you may now ask of us whatever you wish." The words were spoken with the formality of ancient script, of rite and rote. "Our dominion stretches from sun to sun, and our generosity is deep as the space between." This pronouncement hung above me less like a stone and more like incense, but just as deadly.

Whatever I wish . . .

I managed to stop my head from shaking then, and looked to Alexander on his little stool beneath the Emperor. He knew what I wanted.

These royal scripts were all of a type, and after so many years, I knew them all. Some piece, some forgotten memory of childhood etiquette lessons and of decades at court on Forum and on Nessus moved me as sure as any lever. "Your Radiance," I said, choked. "Your generosity extends from sun to sun. But there is . . . nothing—" A murmur of approval rippled through the crowd behind, as though some breeze pushed the surface of a mirrored pool. They thought me pious. The perfect knight, denying reward as if the service itself were reward enough. Their soft remarks made me choke a second time.

I could not *lie* to them, would not let them lie to themselves.

"There is nothing," I said again, more loudly this time. "Nothing you can give me to replace what I have lost. Valka—" My tongue caught a third time. I was not sure if I had said her name since the holograph died—and found I could not say it without pain. A racking sob shook my shoulders, and I bowed my head in grief and—I think—in shame.

Distantly, as though I heard it from miles away, Rinehart whispered, "Perhaps we had best adjourn this, Caesar. The poor man is in no state . . ."

Something cut him short. The Emperor, I guessed. I did not see.

"Radiant Majesty?" the Archprior's voice rose in question.

Hard footfalls could be heard on the hollow ground, armored boots on metal.

I must have fallen to my knees, for a pair of boots—bearing ceramic greaves and sabatons whiter than white—appeared in my view. Dressed the Emperor might have been in the blacks of a common soldier, but his boots were yet his own. Few memories are to me as clear as those boots, though why they should remain so sharp when so much else from . . . before has gone to rust I do not now know. Yet they remain. How exquisite their craftsmanship! Grave and graven faces peered out from sunbursts at the knee, and a pattern of wings enameled golden—the wings of seraphim—radiated from those faces with the rays of the sun. And so bright, so reflective was their substance that the light of it caught in my tears. Hardly ever had I seen so pure a white, the argent which only the Emperor might wear, which I had briefly worn as a god in triumph, that substance which reflects all light.

They vanished as the man knelt, and laid his hands on my shoulders.

I froze, forgot even to cry.

For the second time, then, William XXIII of the House Avent, Firstborn Son of Earth, Guardian of the Solar System, King of Avalon and Prince Imperator of all the realms of Man, embraced me like a brother. In my ear he said, "*I am so sorry, cousin.*"

"Had you but left when we arrived," I said, not knowing what I was saying. "Had you but listened. She would still be alive. Why didn't you listen?" The Emperor drew back. I dropped my eyes, afraid to see his face. "Why didn't you listen?"

"You dare!" exclaimed a distant voice. Nicephorus, maybe. "You address the Emperor!"

My attitude alone—the accusation in my voice—was itself enough to condemn me. But William brushed my words away, and when Leonora's shadow loomed above, he stood, and raised an open hand to still her tongue and proclaim. "I am *the Emperor*," he said, simply, reminding all present at once.

"Release me," I said.

Not looking, I almost heard the Emperor blink, peering down at me. "What?"

"You asked me what I want," I said, not taking my eyes from the Emperor, though his face was like the sun. "I want to be released from your service. I want to *go*."

Silence. Total and absolute.

It was . . . the very worst thing I could have said. Had the Emperor not minutes before stressed the totality of my devotion? Had he not tried to renew my fealty to him in the eyes of all?

And there I was . . . breaking it.

Sensing how treacherous were the waters of the freedom I begged, I scrambled to my feet, scrambled to justify my words. "Have I not given *all* to this fight? All my life? All my people? Even *her*?" Again my voice broke, and I held the muscles of my jaw and neck taut to stop my voice from shaking. "What more can I give?" I had half a mind to rend my uniform, to bare my scars and catalog them—though the worst of them were all invisible.

Caesar had not moved. His mask was firmly back in place. I fancied I could hear his thoughts—schooled as mine were schooled by the arts of Imore and the *Book of the Mind*.

Rage is blindness, the Emperor must have thought. *Calm is sight.*

"Coward!" a raw voice intruded.

Like a man electrocuted, I lurched, identified the speaker at once.

Alexander had found his feet, and seized his chance in the same moment.

Fear moved him, I see that now, but then confusion filled my heart. Had we not discussed this very thing? On Fidchell before we sailed? Had he not himself agreed, assented, to free me from my charge?

But Alexander only wanted me gone, and saw his chance to make it so. He had no need of assassins in that instant, of knives and knife-missiles, myrmidons or poison.

A single word was enough.

"Coward!" he said again. "You would abandon us now? When the need has never been greater?" The prince thrust a finger at me, advancing a step or so. "Father, I told you: this man cannot be trusted. Whatever he was, he is no more! Give him what he wants! Send him to Belusha! Let him *go* there, and live out his days!"

The crowd shifted uncomfortably, whole pockets of it holding their collected breath. The Emperor turned on his heels to regard his son. "That is enough, Alexander," he said, hand raised once more for calm. Returning his attention to me, he said, "Director Rinehart is perhaps correct. Lord Marlowe is tired, and grief clouds his heart. We shall adjourn."

"No!" I said, raising my chin. "You asked what I wanted, Caesar. I want an end to this. Release me. Please."

The Emperor lifted his own chin, addressing not me alone but the whole of the congregation. "This we cannot allow!" he proclaimed. "Perfugium must be avenged!" he decreed to the remaining court. To me, he said, "Your woman must be avenged! Help us to do this thing, my lord! Help us set the stars to rights!"

"I have helped you," I said, and did not bother to disguise the bitterness and the venom in me, "and lost all."

"For all that you have lost, I will repay you seven times over!" Was that desperation in the Imperial tone? He had seen my power, my gift from the Quiet, and he had not forgotten that snowy day on Carteia—as I had not. How could he let me go? I was only safe in his service, only useful as his tool. Freed of that service, I was a danger, must be branded an enemy. I understand him now, his desperation.

He was trying to save my life.

The Chantry had wanted me destroyed—dissected, possibly—since my knighting after Vorgossos. In anointing me one of his Royal Victorians, the Emperor had cast a cloak of protection over me the Chantry might challenge only in private. Though proof of my resurrection had never come to light, though all evidence had been lost with the loss of the *Tamerlane* and with Valka, still the stories had spread. Like sand in the tracks of pilgrims' feet, like pollen on the wing. By witnesses like Bassander Lin, by believers like Carax of Aramis. Those stories had condemned me, had followed me for centuries. Only the Emperor's countenance had shielded me, only my usefulness had spared my life. William had brought me forth that day to reinforce that countenance, to shield me even from those who knew beyond all doubt—by the evidence of their own, unlying eyes—that all my stories were true.

And I refused him.

"How?" I asked, incredulous. What could he offer? What could I ask for that could amount to so much as a steel bit measured against the oceans of gold that were less to me than the barest instant with her? Voice shaking with anger, with disbelief, I pressed on. "How could you *possibly*? How little do you think she was worth?"

The Emperor blinked. "She was only Tavrosi," he said simply, totally ignorant of his crime. "We would make you our son. Our daughter, Selene, is yet unwed."

She was only Tavrosi.

Only Tavrosi.

"Only Tavrosi?" I said. *Never* had I known such a rage . . . or such a blindness, and never had I cared less. The boy from Emesh stepped forward—the proud knight stepping with him—and struck the Emperor full across the face. The crowd gasped and cursed behind me as Caesar staggered back against the crate upon which his makeshift throne had stood. He managed better than Gilliam had. The rotten priest had fallen. Six Excubitors streamed toward me, highmatter gleaming in their hands. Martian lances lowered, aimed, primed.

The Emperor's sword—which I had so little used—thrummed to life in my hand, and I thrust its point at the first of his Excubitors. "Try it, you bloodless *slaves! Try it* and by all the gods of Earth, I swear I'll tear you each apart!"

"Stop!" the Emperor exclaimed. "Damn it, Marlowe! Stop! Stand down, all of you!" He clutched his bloody nose, just as Gilliam had done. *Gilliam . . .* There was no ring to save me this time. No title, no rank, nor any duel to fight.

The bell was rung, the die cast.

I didn't even care.

The Excubitors obeyed instantly, drew back, the light of their drawn swords blue against their dispassionate, mirrored faces. The Martians followed suit more slowly, raising their lances. Snarling, I circled, point still thrust out in the hanging line my fencing master had taught me to command the space between me and the knights. Shadow that I was, I knew I would die there, even with my vision returned. There were too many! Simply too many!

"Put the sword down, Marlowe!" the Emperor said, still clutching his broken nose. He waved Rinehart and a pair of androgyns back. "I'm fine!" He screwed his eyes shut, cleared his head before saying. "I'll not let you suicide yourself by my men, Sir Hadrian! Put the sword down!"

There were perhaps thirty Martians at my back. The Excubitors made nearly forty. Even with the Quiet's blessing, I could not hope to win. The Emperor was right. I wanted to die.

Knowing that, I still did not drop my sword.

"Try it!" I said, seeing one Martian step forward.

I turned to face him.

It wasn't a Martian at all.

It was Lorian.

The intus held out his hands, cane secure in one fist. His eyes were very wide, his silver-white hair glowing in the harsh lighting of the hold. "Hadrian," he said, "please put the sword down."

I did not move. We were alone, Aristedes and I, the only survivors of Akterumu, the last of the Red Company. We were each—in a sense—all the other had left. "Please," he said. "You told me you didn't have a death wish, remember?" Behind him, Olorin and Bassander both moved into the aisle, the latter limping as he came. Lorian's almost lisping aristocratic voice hardly rose above a whisper. "Hadrian, this isn't what she would want."

The hand that held the Emperor's sword wavered. The point fell. The blade unkindled, turned to smoke. "I am finished," I said, every word sharp as glass, two-edged and double-meaning. I was through with Imperial service, and I was dead, I knew. Turning back to face the Emperor, I cast the gilded sword down at his feet. "Kill me. Send me to Belusha like your son wants. I care not. I am your man no more."

The Martians were on me in instants, many hands restraining me. A swift kick to the back of one knee collapsed me, and a fist tightened in my hair. Memories of Dorayaica's throne room came back to me, and my veins constricted, heart hammering against my ribs. The room erupted in paroxysms of fury. The courtiers all rose, bellowed suggestions unasked for, each shouting over each. Olorin stood nearby, head down, eyes closed behind his mask. Neither Bassander nor Lorian moved. Alexander and Leonora had hurried to join the Emperor. The prince had his father's ear, and once more jabbed a finger at me.

I could make out no words in the tumult.

Nicephorus—silent through it all—met my gaze and held it while the court boiled and seethed. The old androgyn shook his hairless head, only once, and broke the thread our eyes had made between us. The chamberlain had seen what I'd done to Attavaisa, just as the Emperor had. It had not believed me, that day on Carteia, as William had. It knew better then, and knew that my foolishness and my fury had undone much of the plans laid that cold day.

I did not have it in me to care or feel ashamed.

Above it all, Saskia Valavar sat, a motionless black spot in the colored sea of motion that was the upper galleries, a mirror on myself.

Wounded in pride and still clutching his dripping nose, William Caesar looked down on me. "I would have made you my son," he said once more, and there was sorrow—not rage—in his voice.

"He must die for this!" Leonora exclaimed. "Radiant Majesty, he *must* die for this!"

"Quiet, Leonora!" the Emperor said, smearing blood across his face with the back of his hand. But she was right. Caesar could not tolerate such an insult, such defiance. He was untouchable as a god, and I had struck him. "You have left me little choice," he said, and lifting his eyes, found something behind me. "Knight-Tribune Lin!"

I heard Lin's boots squeak as he squared himself and offered salute. "Honorable Caesar!"

"You have a brig aboard, I trust?"

"Yes, Honorable Caesar." Lin's voice came out flat and colorless.

"Take him away," the Emperor said. "I can no longer bear the sight of him."

CHAPTER 46

THE GOOD COMMANDER

ALONE AGAIN.

Of the many cells I have known, the one they found for me aboard the *Tempest* was far from the foulest. Where my cave on Dharan-Tun had been all dark, the little cell was forever trapped in a vague, gray twilight. The room was almost perfectly cuboid, with a dry toilet and sonic hand basin in one corner opposite the bare cot with its flattened mat of gray foam. If you have yourself languished in any cell aboard any Imperial naval vessel, you will have seen it, and well know the black of the walls, the narrow vents, the bronze fittings on the tap and about the door.

They are all the same.

Stripped of everything but my clothes and Valka's phylactery—stripped even of my boots—I lay on the bed. The colorless illumination never dimmed or changed its shade, and without my terminal to mark the passing hours, I could only guess at the passage of time. But a gaoler brought a meal tray thrice daily—or so I guessed. Not ration bars. Proper commissary, from the officers' mess, to judge by the quality. A prisoner I might have been, but I was a palatine prisoner.

They left me there for days, and by something like the fifteenth meal, I began to thank the man who brought the meal trays, began to remember something of the essentials of human decency and human function.

Valka was dead, but the shock of that horrific blow had begun to ebb enough that I could see the bottom.

The Emperor had summoned me not merely to express his gratitude, as I have said. He was himself trapped by the conventions of society and the expectations of rank. Since the day I first arrived on Forum, he had shielded me, served as my protector and patron both. I had been a useful tool and symbol to him, the hero who had slain a Cielcin prince. The more cautious of those who surrounded the Solar Throne—the Empress, the Chantry, Bourbon and Breathnach and the other Lions—had always whispered that my risks outweighed my uses, especially as a symbol. For many of the soldiery, I had become the focus of religious awe, an almost anti-Emperor to some, and intolerable thereby.

Berenike had only made matters worse. Where before my legend had been only legend, the miracle at Berenike had sent a bolt of lightning through those who had ever opposed me. Where before the Empress had tried to kill me for an upstart, the Chantry's move against me had come out of fear. Only my close association with the Emperor and the Emperor's men had kept me safe in Maddalo House for so many years. A gaoler Venantian might have been, but he was the Emperor's man, and so long as I was on Nessus, in Sananne, I had been squarely in the Emperor's keeping, and needed to be. After Berenike. After Thermon, where the Chantry failed to kill me. That was why he had summoned me to the cargo bay. I had performed another miracle, one witnessed not by the ragged defenders of Berenike, but by survivors of the very Imperial court itself. No excuses could be made, no webs spun, no stories told. The truth would out.

Hadrian Marlowe is the Trueborn Son of Earth, they would say.

That was why the Emperor had again offered Selene, as he had once so very long ago. By binding me again to his persona and his throne, he not only held my enemies at bay, preserving my usefulness to him and to his war—he held off another war entirely.

Hadrian Marlowe is the God Emperor Reborn.

For seventeen thousand years—at least since the Great Charters and the constitution of the palatine caste—the Aventine House had been engaged in a genetic program with the stated goal of recreating the genetic patterns and fabled powers of the God Emperor. They had failed, but believed that in me the God Emperor's gift had recurred. I was a cousin—however distantly—of the Emperor himself. That blood ran in my veins, however thinned. But thinned it had flowered to new strength, as if by sheer statistical anomaly.

But I knew better.

Blood was not the way of it. That I shared the God Emperor's blood and his gift was mere coincidence. I had inherited nothing. Like William Rex I was simply *Chosen*—not by Earth, but by the Quiet One, the Hidden One. Chosen to serve his purpose: to shepherd mankind toward that cradle and the egg in the age of dying stars.

How many us have there been, in how many ages? How many links formed the chain by which the Quiet yoked his future to our past?

I know not.

But the Emperor saw me as the fulfillment of his prophecy, the completion of his family's own private program, that much was plain.

But what could he do for me now?

And what was to be done with me?

I knew not.

I counted nineteen meals by the time the door opened, making it, I think, the seventh day of my imprisonment. I sat up from my bed, expecting Bassander Lin and a guard, expecting perhaps the Emperor, or a Chantry confessor—perhaps Leonora herself. I expected even a Chantry assassin not unlike the one who came for me on Thermon, or another friend of Alexander's, and half-leaped from listless half-dreams of darkened windows, ready for any of these.

But it was Lorian.

The good commander still wore his arm in a sling, wore his jacket over his shoulder like a matador's cape. He looked better rested than when I'd last seen him, but there was a bone-deep exhaustion in the dulled gleam of his eyes I knew too well. Still, he seemed to me a living man, not at all akin to the revenant that still watched me from the cell's little mirror.

The gaoler, a thick-set man with the customary shaved head of a legionnaire, eyed my sudden move speculatively over Lorian's head, his dark brows contracting.

"Did he really strike the Emperor?" the big man asked. From the way the words burst out of him, I could tell that he'd been dying to ask that question for days. Such guards were forbidden to ask questions of political prisoners like myself. Doubtless the poor fellow would be in for a caning and reassignment to sewage processing for the infraction.

That it *was* an infraction seemed not to bother Aristedes, who nodded wearily. "That he did."

"Shouldn't have done that," the big man said, rather stupidly. "It ain't done."

"No," Lorian agreed, a sour expression on his thin-skinned and pointed face. "It ain't."

"Shall I stay, commander?" the gaoler asked.

"No," Lorian said. "I'm in no danger, thank you."

The gaoler saluted. "You just knock, commander, when you're ready to come out." Then he withdrew, door hissing down like a guillotine behind him, trapping Lorian in with me.

"They took my cane," the younger man said, rather sheepishly. "Seemed to think you'd beat me with it and make your daring escape." His pale eyes raked over the narrow ventilation shafts, and with an almost wistful sigh, he said, "Foolishness."

Returning myself to the edge of the cot, bare and callused feet on the cold metal, I said, "They have to take anything that might be used as a weapon."

The little man turned from his examination of the vents, brows lifted. "Not that. You." He thrust a bony finger in my face. "What in Earth's name were you thinking? You don't *break the Emperor's nose*, Hadrian!"

For the first time in what felt like a life age of the universe, I smiled. Unable to stop myself, a short, bitter laugh spilled out. "I did!" I said, and wiped my face with a hand to drag the smile down. "I did, didn't I?"

Lorian's nose wrinkled, and I knew the man well enough to know it took every ounce of his composure not to smile himself. I was a dead man. Living men did not laugh at the Imperial person. "Black planet! But it's rank in here. Have they not let you wash?"

Suddenly conscious of the film of oil on my face and of my greasy hair, I looked away. "I've been in here the whole time." Changing tack, I gestured at his sling. "I'm sorry about your arm. It's not broken, is it?"

"This?" Lorian bent his hand at the wrist and waggled his fingers at me over the lip of his sling. He was still making a face at the doubtless hideous smell in that little room. "This wasn't your doing. Tore a couple ligaments on Perfugium. They sewed in correctives. I'm just waiting for them to knit."

"Still," I said, not totally convinced, "I'm sorry. I shouldn't have thrown you like that."

"The throwing didn't help," he said. Only slowly did Lorian relax his disgusted expression. "Why did you do it?"

"You know why," I said.

"I know why," Lorian agreed, leaning against the wall opposite. He looked like a child, strangely out of place in his dress blacks. "Only I can't believe you'd be so damnably . . . stupid! Hadrian, you punched the *Emperor!*"

My arms crossed themselves, or so it seemed. "I know, Lorian! Damn it!"
She was only Tavrosi.

I shut my eyes.

"I'm sorry," Lorian said, voice very far away. "I just can't believe it. I
can't believe she's gone."

Eyes still shut, I inhaled sharply. "They all are," I said at last.

"Except me." Was it my imagination? Or did Lorian's voice shake as he
bowed his head. "Why did you choose me? You might have saved Pallino,
or one of the women. Why me?"

The iron and sulfurous stink of Eue returned in my nose, and I turned
my head away, stared at the bronze tap that dispensed water. Small though
my cell was, its walls seemed the borders of infinity in that instant, so very
far away. "You were the ranking officer," I said shortly. "Durand was dead.
It should have been you or Halford."

Lorian was already shaking his head with a fury. "That's why I should
have stayed. Those were *my* people, Hadrian! I should have died leading
them, for all the good it would have done!"

"You would have died!" I said.

"You don't know that!"

But I did. We both did. He reached up and massaged the shoulder still
in its sling. "If I were better," he said, "stronger. *Normal.* I could have
stayed. I could have done something. Why did you pick me?"

"Don't talk like that!" I said, still staring at the tap. "If you were any
different, you wouldn't be what you are." But could I fault him in his
thinking? Had I not thought much the same of myself, a hundred hundred
times? Do we not all think this way sometimes—whatever our condition—
and in a sense is it not true? Evil occurs because we are insufficient to
challenge it. Too weak to stop it at the gates, too blind to see it bubbling
within. Were we all angels in our virtue and heroes in our capacity, we
might hold all chaos at bay, might stop even the unkindling of the stars.

Yet we are but men. Even me.

"And what am I?" Lorian asked.

I did turn and look at him then, found those milk-pale eyes glaring
back at me out of the cloud that had settled on the other man. Seeing his
pain, I offered what smile I could. "My friend," I simply said, and laughed.
"My last friend. Unless one counts Lin and the prince—and I'm not sure
either of them can afford to count me under the circumstances."

"I'd not be so sure of that," Lorian said shortly, dropping his gaze. He
pressed his lips together, like a child who'd said almost too much.

The silence rolled like waves between us, crashing against the walls of that cell. We stayed that way a long while, neither moving, neither speaking, two of the last few pieces on the board, gulfs between us, each alone. "You've always told me the truth," I said at last, eyes returning to the tap. "Always. Even when it was hard. Even when I couldn't hear it. And I thought . . ." I struggled for the words. "I thought of all of us you might best avenge us. You are one of the finest officers I have ever known."

The little man straightened, almost, *almost* saluted on the spot. But he stopped himself, looked back at his shoes. "I never thanked you."

"For what?"

"For your faith in me," he said, and shrugged. "Until you came along, it was just desk work. Back room, out of sight. Or following Beller around like his personal court jester. You let me be . . . *more*."

"I did no such thing," I said, shrugging myself.

"You did," he countered. "I'm a bastard, Hadrian. An intus. Your friend Lin doesn't think I'm fit for service, did you know that? I'm only here because my father's Grand Duke of Patmos, not that he'll admit it."

My lips pressed together, and thinking of my own father, I said, "I know what it's like not to want the future we're given." Lorian's gratitude— the naked honesty of it—stung my hands like antiseptic. Another unsteady silence washed over us both, and when its wave had broken, I asked the question I most wanted the answer to. "What's to be done with me?" Lorian did not answer at once. His jaw clenched as a man attempting to crack some shell between his teeth. "Do you know?"

Running one silver-bracketed hand through his nimbus of short hair, Lorian said, "It isn't right." Realizing he'd criticized an Imperial decision, he glanced at the black hemisphere of the watch-eye embedded in the ceiling, flinching the while. I waited him out. It was easier that out-waiting the Emperor. Or Kharn Sagara. Lorian opened his mouth. Shut it again. After a short breath, he said, "You're being sent to Belusha."

"Belusha?" I felt my blood run cold. The Emperor's favorite prison planet. The latest in a long line stretching back to ancient Mars. Gibson— Prince Philippe—had been sent to Belusha. I was following him, after all, if not to athenaeum. "So Alexander got his way. I'm to die in exile."

"I don't think so," Lorian said. "If it were me, I'd put you under, freeze you until all this blows over." He fidgeted with the cuff of his shirt where it had caught on one of his hand braces. "What did you do to piss off that princeling, eh? I thought he was your greatest admirer."

I flashed Lorian a sharp look. I did not want to talk about Alexander, not then. "He was," I said, "until he wasn't." I had insulted him only, but that insult had come from the man the young prince had most admired, and so crushed him. Spurned, he had fallen into his mother's perfumed clutches, and she had persuaded him of the grave danger I posed their house.

"All right then, have it your way," the good commander said with a tight smile. Apparently unwilling to *let* me have things my way, he appended, "Break his heart, did you?" When I only gave him another sharp glare, the commander raised both hands like a man at gunpoint. "I surrender!" he said, laughing. "But the Emperor knows how valuable you are, Marlowe. He won't let you live to death on that snowball, I promise you that."

Head in my scarred hands, I stared at the smooth floor. "I see." I understood perfectly. "He won't even let me die."

"You may not even *serve* your sentence," Lorian said, attempting jocularity. "You won't even know you've been."

How clearly I saw the road ahead. I would be escorted from my cell to the medica, or to a shuttle for transfer and processing—it was possible the Emperor would remand me to the care of his few Martians to get me away from Leonora and Alexander all the sooner, and not let me molder in a pod aboard the *Tempest*. Frozen, I would be delivered to the prison planet, and frozen brought down its solitary hightower. Frozen still, I would find my way to some remote lazaret where—never once awoken—I would be interred like the undead in the catacombs of Resonno.

Thus undead, I could never escape.

There, perhaps, I might be forgotten, along with my offense. His Radiance would save face, and I might elude the Lions and the wolves of the Chantry. So hidden, I might escape the Cielcin leopard, too.

And undead, I might be recalled at any moment, by any word of the Emperor. Should the men of HAPSIS ever find what it was they sought, I would be recalled, and brought as a prisoner to serve far from the Imperial court. The Emperor would get his use out of me, and save face. He was not a man to waste his tools, or to let them go to rust.

On Belusha, I would be safe and unseen and preserved against the hour of uttermost need.

It would be like my exile on Nessus, only more extreme. I would be utterly at the Imperial mercy, and utterly in its power, a slave in all but name, my chains no more gilded. And frozen, I wouldn't even be allowed the time to grieve.

Let the punishment fit the crime.

"Damn it!" I said. Shutting my eyes was just enough to stop the tears again. There were too many tears. I hadn't known I had such water in me, and was ashamed.

"I asked to be the one to tell you," Lorian said, shuffling nearer. "I wanted to say goodbye."

"What of Lin?" I asked, shoulders bunching. "And the Jaddians? What happens now?"

"Back to Nessus with all haste. I don't know about Lin. I assume he's in for a promotion with Massa dead. Knight-*Legate* of the 409th, I reckon. Haven't heard . . ." He trailed off. "The Emperor sent to Forum. One of his daughters is to marry the prince."

"Olorin?" I asked, looking up, genuinely shocked. No member of the Imperial house had married into the Jaddian bloodlines since the romance of Cyrus and Amana in the time of the Jaddian Wars. "Prince Kaim, I mean? To which princess?" I felt a strange and perverse pang of jealousy at the thought that it might be Selene. Or was it outrage? Disgust that her father should so casually trade one prospect for another?

Lorian cocked his head. "How do you know him?"

"I met him when I was a boy. He gave me my sword, the . . . one I lost." I shook my head. "A marriage between du Otranto and the Aventine House . . . God and Earth and Emperor, what times are these!"

Eyebrows raised, Lorian nodded. "I know!" He chewed his lip. "I want to say it was . . . Viola? Vivian?"

"Vivienne!" I said. I remembered her, one of the youngest, I thought she was.

"That was it!"

I wondered what the excitable young princess might think of life among the Jaddians, or about the prince's piously shrunken harem. But thoughts of women pained me, for the chief of all the women of the daughters of Earth was dead. Setting all such thoughts aside, I said, "Really I should be the one thanking you," I said, and stood, and offered Lorian my hand. "You saved my life, once. I'm not sure I ever thanked you."

Lorian Aristedes reached up and clasped my scarred hand with his fragile one. "More than once, I think. But you did thank me," he said, "though you never had to." Our hands separated, and stepping back, he bowed. His eyes were shining. "I may never see you again," he said, straightening and moving toward the door. The words struck like lightning. He was right. My sentence on Belusha, however short it may seem in icy dream, would doubtless be long enough to spend whatever years remained to the younger man, and who could guess at the count of years left an intus? He might have centuries, or solitary years. He did salute then, as crisp and as formal and as unlike himself as anything I had seen. "It was an honor and a true privilege, my lord."

I returned the gesture as sharply. "The honor was mine."

The smaller man chewed his tongue—himself again. He was working himself up to say *something*. He found his words seconds later. "I thought I would die where you found me, sir. Chained to a desk. I'd given up hope." His tone had taken on a sheepish, almost childlike quality.

Embarrassment? From Lorian Aristedes?

"Don't give up hope," he said, lamely. "Way I see it, we've still some avenging to do, you and me. For Lady Valka . . . and for the rest."

Choked, I could not answer him. He turned and banged on the door to be let out.

"Lorian!" I called, voice raw.

The good commander turned, eyes raw as well. "Hadrian?"

"How did you do it?" I asked. I'd always wanted to know, and now it seemed I'd never have another chance. "Rescue that lieutenant from the Chantry and reach the Council?"

The door opened, and the big, bald gaoler appeared.

"How did I save your ass, you mean? Was that the *one time* you meant?" and he grinned wolfishly despite the water in his eyes and tapped his nose with a finger. "I'll tell you another time."

CHAPTER 47

ANOTHER TIME

THE SOLDIERS WOULD NOT answer my questions when they came, nor speak to me beyond the perfunctory orders to stand and present myself. Ten legionnaires had come for me, a full decade, each masked and armored not in Martian red, but in common ivory. These were not the Emperor's personal guards, as I'd expected, only ordinary soldiers. Men from the *Tempest*. Lin's men, at least officially.

"Who sent you?" I asked.

"Put on your boots," their decurion said, voice flat and inhuman through the suit speakers. He proffered the footwear with one hand. When I had donned them and their calves had tightened about my own, he said, "Hands."

For the thousandth time in my life, I offered my wrists for binding. The electromagnets whined and snapped shut.

"What's happening?" I asked. "Are you taking me to medica? Am I to be put under?"

"Quiet!" the decurion said, and struck me across the face. I should have been expecting such treatment, but the blow had caught me by surprise, and I staggered against the cot. Standing over me, the decurion gestured to two of his companions. "Bring him. And be careful. He's supposed to be dangerous."

"Folded pretty easy, though."

Of all the men in that cell and in the hall beyond, I alone had a face. With Lorian having said his goodbyes, I was truly alone, and alone permitted myself to be led from the brig and through receiving where a bored woman sat and out via a short, broad stair to the tramway platform. The guard had not looked up from the yellowed pages of the folio she read, had not asked for papers or discharged me. Perhaps that had all been taken care of.

There were no other guards.

The tram platform was similarly deserted. On a ship so large as the *Tempest*, with tens of thousands aboard—and most of those still awake following the Battle of Perfugium—there ought to have been *someone*. Evidently the Emperor had not wanted a spectacle.

I felt a thrill. Was this LIO's doing? Special Security? Even HAPSIS?

"Where is everyone?" I asked.

"I said *quiet*," the decurion said. "They said you were supposed to be smart."

"They say a lot of things," I said tartly. I expected the fellow to turn and strike me again, or for one of my companion bookends to do it for him. The decurion only snorted.

They marched me right up to the edge of the platform. There we waited.

Silent as a gondola on black water, the tram car slid into station and came to a stop. For the three seconds or so before the hatch slid open, all was totally silent. Even the omnipresent white noise of the ship was muted, as if the very engines and reactors had fallen all asleep.

The hatch opened, and I was chivvied onto the tram. There were no seats, were not even the rails to which personnel might cling as the tram slid on its way. It was a freight car.

That was my first indication that something was wrong, and the light of it shone back on those earlier things. Cuffed as I was and in their power, I asked, "Who sent you?"

The decurion whirled and struck me in the belly as the doors closed. I doubled over, gasping, leaned against the wall of the freight car as it began to slide on magnetic rails above and below.

They ignored my groans and my questions alike, and after five minutes of silent tension—during which the tram underwent a track change and descended several levels before arcing back toward the aft of the great ship—the doors opened.

"This isn't medica!" I said, stepping out onto the platform.

"You're being transferred," the decurion said.

"Transferred?" I echoed. "Transferred where?"

I wasn't to be placed in fugue aboard the *Tempest* then, but shuttled over to some lesser ship in the fleet and sent directly to Belusha. The Emperor wanted me gone then, as quickly as possible. That was probably wise. The Emperor had found a way to maintain his cloak of protection, though only its fringe obscured me.

"You're for Belusha," the decurion said. "Ship's waiting."

But something was wrong. I could taste it. The woman at the guard post should have sealed release forms, given handling orders to my guards. *Especially* if the transfer were so clandestine. Orders for pedestrian prisoners were simply broadcast to the far end.

Had the Chantry sent these men? Was there no shuttle? Only an empty airlock lurking up ahead? Or was Lorian mistaken about my future on Belusha? Were the decurion's words a lie? If there *was* a short walk out the airlock awaiting me, was it the Emperor's orders that sent me to it? Light-years from any system and alone in the Dark of space, Hadrian Marlowe's body would never be found. How easily he might be assumed into heaven! Gone to stride the Elysian hills of Earth with all the other great heroes of man!

An airlock *did* await me at the end of the cramped hall, but a shuttle waited on the far side. I felt my fear ebb a little to see the cramped compartment just beyond the outer door. The decurion ducked through the umbilical ahead of me, and the other men filed in behind. I could sense the tension mounting in the men about me. Surely they would not fly me out in a shuttle just to kill me? Why bother? The man on my right wore a sword, a common ceramic gladius. I could seize hold of it, but the men had not restored my shield-belt with my boots. And I did not like my chances unshielded against ten armed and armored legionnaires.

It is hard to live. Easier perhaps to die. Easier at least to be dead, though the gate is harder won when one raises the portcullis himself than those who have not tried it believe. And yet I found I did not wish for death, though neither did I wish for life. I would fight—when the time came—as an animal fights, wild and without plan.

My companions strapped me into my place and strapped themselves into the places opposite me, their invisible eyes on mine. One man bounced his feet in agitation. Impatience. Fear?

"Seal the door," the decurion said.

One of the others did just that, and the indicator by the door cycled blue to red. Locked.

The man tapped his helmet twice with a balled fist, signaling his commander to go ahead. I looked up at the man, mouth open, and turned to sight through the open hatch into the cockpit.

There was no pilot officer.

"What's going on?" I asked.

The decurion reached up and put his hand on the striped yellow-and-black lever to release the clamps that held the shuttle pod in place.

"On three, Mads," the decurion said.

"Mads?" My heart leaped in my throat as I turned to the man in the rear. The legionnaire put his hand on the release.

"One," the decurion said, heedless of my shock. "Two."

Three.

A deep *clang* resounded through the shuttle as we fell away. The shuttle pod lay dead and silent all around. No thrusters, no life support. Dead as Death herself.

"Think we tripped their sensors?" Mads asked from the rear.

"Not if the little man did his part," the decurion said, and undid the seals that fixed his mask. The whole cowl and baffle folded back, revealing a flat-faced, serious man with black skin. "Reckon he did."

I looked at him, remembered him from our brief meeting in the *Ascalon*'s hold before the siege of Ganelon. "You're . . . Aron, right?"

Sharp's junior man nodded. "Sure am. Sorry about the licks, lordship. Didn't want you asking too many questions. Didn't have time to explain."

"Didn't want to run the risk the cameras were still working, you mean," said one of the other Dragonslayers.

I looked round at them all. They'd traded their uniforms for those of common soldiers, no mark of special detachment or rank. The suits looked new. I realized my mouth was hanging open, closed it sufficient to get my bearings, and asked, "What's going on?"

"Jailbreak," Aron said. "What's it look like?"

"Why?" I looked round. "Where are we going?"

"Didn't tell us that part, case we got caught," the decurion answered. "We were just meant to take you out. Tribune's orders." As he spoke, he thumbed the controls that deactivated the electromagnets that secured my wrists, and bent to undo the binders entire.

"The tribune's?" I could hardly believe it. *Bassander Lin?* But no, no it couldn't be. Not alone. This was too devious, too clandestine. Remembering what Aron had just said about *the little man*, I said, "This was Lorian's doing, wasn't it?"

"He the little man?" Aron asked.

"Yes."

"Then yes."

I sat back in my seat, mouth again falling open. I stayed that way a long moment. "Earth and Emperor," I swore. "He did it again." Had he been trying to tell me, there at the end?

Another time.

"Where are we going?" I asked.

Aron shook his head. "Best not to talk, lord. Life support's out. We've got our suits, but you've only got the air in this compartment. It should last you, but best not to stretch it. Besides, I don't rightly know myself. Tribune said there'd be a pickup." He looked round, pointed at something in the netting under the bench opposite. "Cal, pass over that EmKit. It's gonna get fucking cold in here fucking fast with the engines off, and his lordship's not dressed for the weather."

I accepted the thermal blanket Aron's man produced from the emergency kit gratefully, and wrapped myself in it—though I didn't pull the heating tab just then. It was possible we'd be stuck waiting hours in the wild dark, and the field blankets only carried so much charge.

"How long?" I asked.

Aron shook his head, pressed a finger to the spot on his mask where his lips should be. "Best you try and sleep, lordship," he said. "You want water? We got that and some rat bars."

I accepted the water gratefully, but was not so hungry then to want another damned ration bar. I stared out the window instead, thought I could see the black shape of the *Tempest* lost against the darker black of space, her running lights like ordered stars. Aron had said it was a jailbreak, which dashed all thought of HAPSIS and Imperial conspiracy to pieces. If Lin's hand and Lorian's were behind this . . . this was something else.

"Nothing is finished," I breathed, remembering Gibson's words.

"What's that?"

"Nothing."

It was hours before they found us. I could hear their harpoons *clank* against our hull. Minutes passed before I heard—before we felt—the clangor of hands and feet on the exterior of the pod. I could not make out the armor of the men swimming in the black outside the cockpit glass, but time after time their torch-beams tracked across the opening and illumined the pod.

It was getting cold, and I alone of the shuttle's occupants had no suit, and shivered despite having pulled the tab on the thermal blanket many hours before. We were being hauled up through the darkness on a line like a box of Spanish gold from the abyss. The men about us were like divers swimming for the sun, and above—a sun appeared—a white light shining through an aperture like the beam of some unshuttered eye. The hatches of a cargo bay.

I felt the pull of a suppression field a moment later, heard the grinding of metal at my back as the winch dragged us over the floor. They'd hauled us in on our side, disorienting my earlier conception that we were being dragged *up* into the light. I'd the good fortune to find myself lying on what had become the floor. Aron—who alone had remained not belted into one of the seats, stepped carefully over to me and bent to undo my straps.

But I had already undone my restraints, and he offered me a hand up instead.

I took it, and he moved ahead to join Mads by the rear hatch. We could hear shouting from outside, but I did not at once recognize the language, muffled as it was through the thick metal of the hull. Someone banged on the hatchway three times.

"I hear you!" Mads grumbled, punching the controls on the wall above his head.

Cold light streamed in through the open door. After so many hours in near darkness inside the pod, I shielded my eyes, permitted hands to guide me out and into the light.

"I confess," a familiar, lilting voice began before my eyes could adjust to the sudden glare, "I did not believe your friend the *cacogenos* could do it, but it seems you are not the only one who is full of surprises."

Blinking back the harsh illumination, I could a see a figure in black with a red toga standing before me. I blinked again. Not a toga. A *mandyas*.

"Olorin!" I said, aghast. "How?"

"Your friend, the dwarf," he said. "It was his idea. I did not think it could be done, and yet . . ." He put his hands on my shoulders to steady me. "You are well?"

"Cold," I said. "But how?"

Bassander had been in on it, Aron had said as much. Someone had minimized the guard on the brig, cleared the tramway, arranged for the freight tram pod and not the typical one. Did the freight pods have cameras? Had the cameras been powered down? The feeds doctored? Sharp's men had used the manual release to unmoor the shuttle, so there'd be no detecting heat signatures or even the faint burst of hypergolic thrusters. There'd been nothing, nothing but the magnetic push as the shuttle's plates repelled against the short launch tube. Leaning on the prince, I recalled the way the *Tempest* had fallen away as we fell into darkness, like a lump of coal lost in a bucket of ink.

Lorian, you've done it again.

"He did not tell us," Olorin said. "Only where we might find you."

The Jaddian prince sobered. "I believe he intends to take full responsibility for your escape. To cover my tracks and those of your tribune."

"No!" I drew back from the prince, looked back at Aron and Mads and the other Dragonslayers who were—I guessed—to be my companions in exile, as if one of them might gainsay the Prince of Jadd. "They'll kill him! Why would he . . ."

Behind his black porcelain mask, Prince Kaim's eyes shuttered like dark lamps. "He said he owed you his life, and that you would have done the same."

"Damn him . . ." I raised a hand to shield my eyes. "Lorian, you idiot!"

"Perhaps they will not execute him," the prince said, voice as reassuring as he could make it.

But I shook my head. "He's an intus. They won't hesitate."

"They may but imprison him. He is perhaps of use."

I swallowed, accepted these words as the comfort the prince intended. When I lowered my hand, I found us standing on the floor of a narrow hold. Two Maeskoloi stood guard five paces behind the prince, both men, both masked. A number of mamluks and human *aljanhi* soldiers stood behind, along with the armored dockworkers in their spacesuits of dull gray and brass. Ever present, Kalima di Sayyiph stood to one side, watching me in silence. Tiada stood with her, dressed as the former in the translucent silks and gaudy chains of an *alkidar*, though I marked her glittering sword hilt among the bangles at her slim waist.

How little I knew of Jadd, and of this prince.

Realizing this, I moved back a step, and asked the better question: "Why would you help me?"

The great prince blinked. "Because God has sent you. How could I not? I have seen the Truth! Both in the eyes of your woman and again, on Perfugium. Your Emperor fears you, fears you mean to supplant him. He casts you aside because you are like highmatter with no handle, and he lacks the art or courage to understand. I lack only the art."

"You want me to fight for you?" I asked.

"If that is your wish," the prince said. "I wish to offer my protection. Imperial knives are against you, but I told you once that you have friends in Jadd. That is ever true."

"Fight well, seek beauty, and speak Truth, is that it?"

"Just so."

I saw the prince's offer plain enough. "Sanctuary," I said, "and in exchange, your bonecutters and porphyrogeneticists will want to study me, is that it?"

Prince Kaim du Otranto did not reply, neither did he deny it. I held my own counsel a moment. MINOS had my blood already, my brain scans—that meant the Prophet had them. And Kharn Sagara. Those bells could not be rung back. Time runs but forward. There was wisdom, then, in trusting Kaim. In trusting Olorin. Whatever they were—friends or opportunists—the Jaddians were men, not demons or demoniacs, and I did not think them enemies like Alexander and the Chantry . . .

. . . or like the Emperor himself. For I was a fugitive from the Emperor's justice already.

There was no going back.

Besides, Lorian had trusted them enough perhaps to die for this deal he'd struck.

"Sanctuary," the prince agreed.

"Will this not mean war again between the Empire and Jadd?" I asked.

The prince made a negating gesture, throwing some invisible trash away. "We do not wish war, and your Emperor needs our ships, our soldiers. It may be some years before he discovers we have vanished you, and more before he finds you."

"Lorian will take the blame," I said.

"Yes," Olorin said, a touch of sorrow in his voice as he looked to his women. "He has accepted this. It was—as I am saying—his plan."

The great doors of the bay still stood open behind us, and not even the brightest stars were visible against the light of the hold. Only a static field held back that void, the outer Dark and cold of eternity, the nothingness to which the Watchers drove all ends. I could see nothing in it. Not the *Tempest*, not the *Gran Squall*, nor any ship of the fleet.

"Have they gone?" I asked.

"No," the prince replied. "We will go with them when they do, but your ship is here, and you will leave on it when we depart. My people will convey you to Jadd in secret and in safety. You will be safe there."

"On Jadd?"

"On Jadd."

Again I shaded my eyes. My hand fell to the phylactery, which hung outside my unbelted tunic. I held it in my fingers, the last piece of *her* in all the universe. The only piece.

Prince Kaim reached up and unclasped his mask, handed it to one of his guards. Olorin Milta smiled sadly at me. "I wish I had known your doctor better," he said, and—placing a hand on my shoulder—came to stand beside me in contemplation of that bottomless void. "I will order our priests to pray for her. There will be a fire burning to honor her on Jadd. Depend on it."

There was nothing I could say.

"It is said that all spirits leave God of their own will to come here and fight for the good, even if they do not know it in this life," he said. "Her spirit chose this fight." I could feel his face turned toward me. "This is comforting, I hope?"

I nodded, though I did not understand, or truly care.

Instead I said, "There is so much darkness." And inclined my head toward those open gates.

"Once, there was nothing, if the magi are to be believed. All of this—all creation—was hard won. By God, and by us. Besides!" The great prince again placed a hand upon my shoulder. "There is much light you cannot see."

There are endings, Reader, and this is one. Of all the wounds I have suffered, the marks of sword and lash and claw—the very worst left no scar. The greatest part of me, my very heart, will forever lie scattered with the ashes on the winds of Perfugium. With her. The empty silence where she used to be is with me still, even as I mark this parchment.

It will never leave me, though I drive it back with a word. Always it returns.

Valka is dead.

You see, Dorayaica was right, and Gibson, too. Time runs down. The past is written. Perfugium was very long ago, and the ink not five lines above these words is itself already dry.

Time runs down, and leaves no man unscarred . . .

. . . leastways until the world is changed, and its god returns with new light.

If what I have suffered, if what I have done disturbs you, Reader, I do not blame you. If you would read no further, I understand. You have the luxury of foresight. You know where this ends.

I shall go on alone.

Dramatis Personae

THE MEIDUA RED COMPANY

WHILE IT WAS NEVER formally dissolved, the Meidua Red Company—or the *Imperial* Red Company, as it was officially known, effectively met its end at the Battle of Akterumu in ISD 17061, when the *ISV Tamerlane* was destroyed with nearly all hands. Of the ninety thousand men and women that crewed the *Eriel*-class battleship, only three people escaped: Commander Lorian Aristedes, Doctor Valka Onderra Vhad Edda, and Lord Hadrian Marlowe himself. While Lord Marlowe would participate in several more battles—most notably at Perfugium and Gododdin—he would never again do so as a great captain of men. The Red Company died on Eue, at Akterumu, its defeat a crushing blow for the Imperium, and for Lord Marlowe personally.

Here follows a list of those members of the Red Company mentioned in this volume of Lord Marlowe's account:

LORD HADRIAN ANAXANDER MARLOWE, Supreme Commandant of the Imperial Red Company, Knight-Commander of the Royal Victorian Order, Bearer of the Grass Crown, Holder of the Order of Merit, Hero of the Empire. The Halfmortal, the Sun Eater, Starbreaker, Palekiller, Deathless. Notorious genocide responsible for the death of the entire Cielcin species.

—His paramour, **VALKA ONDERRA VHAD EDDA,** a Tavrosi demarchist and xenologist interested in the Quiet phenomenon, afflicted by an Extrasolarian mind virus.

—His armsman and friend, **LORIAN ARISTEDES,** commander and former tactical officer for the *ISV Tamerlane.* The bastard son of the Grand Duke of Patmos and one of his knights, a palatine intus plagued by idiosyncratic pain and connective tissue disorders.

The Fallen:

—{OTAVIA CORVO}, former captain of the *ISV Tamerlane*, slain at Akterumu.

—Her first officer, {BASTIEN DURAND}, commander, slain at Akterumu.

—Her junior officers:

—{RODERICK HALFORD}, commander and so-called *night captain*, slain at Akterumu.

—{KARIM GARONE}, called CRIM, lieutenant commander and former security officer for the *ISV Tamerlane*, slain at Akterumu.

—His paramour, {ILEX}, lieutenant commander, former ship's engineer. A dryad homunculus. Slain at Akterumu.

—{FELIX KOSKINEN}, lieutenant and former ship's helmsman. Slain at Akterumu.

—{ADRIC WHITE}, lieutenant and former ship's navigator. Slain at Akterumu.

—{JULIANA PHERRINE}, lieutenant and former ship's communications officer. Slain at Akterumu.

—{LUANA OKOYO}, lieutenant commander and former ship's chief medical officer. Slain at Akterumu.

—{TOR VARRO}, Chalcenterite scholiast and scientific advisor. Slain at Akterumu.

—{PALLINO OF TRIESTE}, former chiliarch and Hadrian's bound armsman raised to the patrician caste. Slain at Akterumu.

—His paramour, {ELARA OF EMESH}, former quartermaster for the *ISV Tamerlane* and Hadrian's bound armsman. Raised to the patrician class. Slain at Akterumu.

—{LEON}, an ensign. Slain at Akterumu.

THE IMPERIAL COURT

Dating back to the House of Windsor and Earth's Golden Age, the Aventine Dynasty has ruled over the Sollan Empire and mankind since the defeat of the Mericanii in antiquity. The reigning Emperor of Lord Marlowe's day, William XXIII, took the throne as a young man in ISD 15826 after the passing of his mother, the Empress Titania Augusta, and ruled for an unprecedented thousand-year reign—spending much of his time in transit around the Imperium, unlike most of his predecessors. He began one such tour in ISD 16989, sailing with a Legion fleet from Forum to Gododdin to Nessus, and then in a circuit about the Centaurine provinces to assess the damage dealt by Cielcin invasions and the general war-readiness of the provinces. This tour required the uprooting of much of the Imperial court, as well as an escort of several Martian Legions.

Here follows a list of those members of the Imperial Court mentioned in this volume of Lord Marlowe's account:

His Imperial Radiance, the **EMPEROR WILLIAM THE TWENTY-THIRD OF THE HOUSE AVENT;** Firstborn Son of the Earth; Guardian of the Solar System; King of Avalon; Lord Sovereign of the Kingdom of Windsor-in-Exile; Prince Imperator of the Arms of Orion, of Sagittarius, of Perseus, and Centaurus; Magnarch of Orion; Conqueror of Norma; Grand Strategos of the Legions of the Sun; Supreme Lord of the Cities of Forum; North Star of the Constellations of the Blood Palatine; Defender of the Children of Men; and Servant of the Servants of Earth.

—His wife, **EMPRESS MARIA AGRIPPINA AVENT,** Princess of Avalon, Archduchess of Shakespeare, and Mother of Light.

—Their children:

—**AURELIAN,** Crown Prince and firstborn child.

—**RICARD ANCHISES,** forty-seventh-born child. Conspired to kill HADRIAN MARLOWE.

—**PHILIP,** fifty-second-born child, a notorious gambler and womanizer. Conspired to kill HADRIAN MARLOWE.

—His servant, {**IRSHAN**}, a Jaddian swordmaster of the Fifth Circle. Tried to kill HADRIAN MARLOWE.

—**SELENE,** ninety-ninth-born child, potentially betrothed to HADRIAN MARLOWE.

—**ALEXANDER,** one-hundred-seventh-born child and former squire to Sir HADRIAN MARLOWE.

—**VIVIENNE,** one-hundred-twenty-sixth-born child.

—His ancestor, {**KING WILLIAM VII WINDSOR**}, called **WILLIAM THE ADVENT,** the God Emperor, Emperor of Avalon and Eden, Last King of the United Kingdom of Great Britain, King-in-Avalon, and Lord Sovereign of the Kingdom of Windsor-in-Exile. The first Sollan Emperor, deified by the Chantry.

—His paramour, {**CATHERINE**}, called **HOLY CATHERINE** or **CATHERINE THE WHITE.** Author of the *Acts of Will*, mother of the second emperor, {**VICTOR SEBASTOS**}.

—His predecessor and mother, {**TITANIA AUGUSTA**}, whose reign first brought humanity into contact with the Cielcin. Fondly remembered for her hawkish response to the crisis.

The Imperial Council:

—**PRINCE HECTOR AVENT,** Supreme Chancellor of the Imperial Council, Prince of Aeolus, a brother of the EMPEROR.

—**LORD RAND MAHIDOL,** Minister of War, a member of the Lion Party.

—His subordinate, **SIR GRAY RINEHART,** a Director of the Legion Intelligence Office.

—**LORD ALLANDER PEAKE,** Minister of Justice, a member of the Lion Party.

—His son, **LORD GARAN PEAKE,** a courtier. Not a member of the Council.

—**LORD PETER HABSBURG,** Minister of Works, a member of the Lion Party.

—**LADY LEDA ASCANIA,** Minister of Public Enlightenment, a member of the Lion Party.

—**LORD HAREN BULSARA,** Director of the Colonial Office, a member of the Lion Party.

—**LADY MIANA HARTNELL,** Minister of Welfare.

—**LORD NOLAN CORDWAINER,** Minister of Revenue.

—**LORD CASSIAN POWERS,** Special Advisor on the Cielcin Question and Baron of Ashbless. The so-called Avenger of Cressgard, formerly a strategos in the Legions who led humanity to their first victory against the Cielcin in the Second Battle of Cressgard. A member of the Lion Party.

—His Holy Wisdom, **VERGILIAN XIII,** Synarch of the Holy Terran Chantry, First-Among-Equals of the Synod and the Choir, Grand Prior of Forum, Metropolitan High Priest of the Eternal City, and Speaker for the Vanished Earth.

Unnamed members of the Council:

—The **LORD MINISTER OF RITES.**

—The **DIRECTOR OF THE HOME OFFICE,** a member of the Lion Party.

{**LORD AUGUSTIN BOURBON**}, former Minister of War and member of the Lion Party. Son of the late Prince PHILIPPE BOURBON. Killed on HADRIAN MARLOWE's orders in retribution for his role in a failed attempt to assassinate Lord MARLOWE.

—His ally, **SIR LORCAN BREATHNACH,** former Director of the Legion Intelligence Office. Convicted for conspiracy to murder HADRIAN MARLOWE and sentenced to life on the prison planet Belusha.

SIR CEDRIC THORAS, a Captain of the Martian Guard sworn to protect the EMPEROR.

—His subordinates:

—**SIR ELMON VOTTA,** Martian Guard Commander.

—**TITUS BELMAN,** a Martian Guard lieutenant.

—His subordinate, **NIKO,** a common guardsman.

—**JON OF MARS,** a Martian Guard lieutenant.

—**ELAN,** a centurion.

—**WILLEM,** a common Martian legionnaire.

—**THUVA,** a ship's captain.

LEONORA, an Archprior of the Holy Terran Chantry. The EMPEROR's personal confessor.

TOR XANTHIPPUS, a scholiast and military security advisor.

PRINCE RAFAEL HATIM BAN ONOPHRE DU LURASH, a Jaddian courtier and son of the Prince of Lurash. A guest of the EMPEROR.

—His *alkidarae,* his concubines: **ARIANNE** and **TULA.**

NICEPHORUS, the EMPEROR's butler, an androgyn homunculus.

THE LEGIONS

There are thousands of legions constituted under the Imperial banner, broadly divided by geography, with the various Perseid, Orionid, Sagittarine, and Centaurine Legions comprising the bulk of the force, in addition to the Norman Legions (greatly reduced in number due to the fighting with the Cielcin) and the Martian Legions tasked with the protection of Forum, Avalon, and the various other estates of the Aventine House itself. The smallest legion may number as few as thirty thousand men—naval officers, flight crewmen, and troopers—or as many as three hundred thousand. These legions are loyal to the Emperor, and are composed primarily of recruits raised on direct Imperial holdings (those with Governor-Generals and not under the auspices of a feudal lord), although in wartime levies have been extracted from feudal demesnes. The Legions are not to be confused with the private armies of said lords, who are not answerable to the Emperor in themselves.

Here follows a list of those members of the Imperial Legions mentioned in this volume of Lord Marlowe's account:

{**LORD TITUS HAUPTMANN**}, Duke of Andernach and former First Strategos of the Legions of Centaurus, killed in action at the Battle of Berenike.

SIR LEONID BARTOSZ, strategos and military advisor to the EMPEROR. Former legate of the 437th Centaurine Legion.

SENDHIL MASSA, legate of the 409th Centaurine Legion.

BASSANDER LIN, a tribune in the 409th Centaurine Legion and captain of the *ISV Tempest*, formerly attached to the 437th Legion. A longtime associate of HADRIAN MARLOWE, present at his death in the battle against ARANATA OTIOLO.

—His first officer, **LUCIUS ASTOR,** a commander.

—His captains:

   —**MATTIAS SIMONYI,** captain of the *ISV Gran Squall*, a super carrier. A veteran of the Battle of Senuessa.

   —**SEVIM TENAVIAN,** captain of the *ISV Fearless.*

   —**AUSRIC DAYNE,** captain of the *ISV Thunderhead.*

—His former commander, {**DAME RAINE SMYTHE**}, a tribune of the 437th Centaurine Legion, killed in action by Prince ARANATA OTIOLO.

QUENTIN SHARP, First Centurion and commander of the 409th Legion's Ninth Special Detachment, the so-called Dragonslayers.

—**ARON** and **STAS,** two of his decurions.

—His soldiers, **ALTARIC, MADS, TEREN,** and **VANN.**

SIR HECTOR OLIVA, commander, a young knight attached to the Legion Intelligence Office. Future captain of the famous *ISV Siren* and commander of the defense at the Battle of Taranis. A hero of the Cielcin Wars.

—His companions, **CIPRIAN KARRAS** and **SOPHIA MAGARYAN,** both lieutenants.

—His soldiers, **LORAS** and **ALLEMAN.**

LUKE, PAUL, and **SEV,** three soldiers from the Emperor's camp on Carteia, tasked with guarding Lord Marlowe.

IN THE SOLLAN EMPIRE

By the dawn of the seventeenth millennium ISD, the Sollan Empire stretched across much of four of the galaxy's spiral arms, half a billion habitable worlds, and billions of airless moons and station outposts. Comprising innumerable ethnic groups, countless religions, hundreds of thousands of nobile families—palatine and patrician—and tens of millions of soldiers, its total population cannot be counted, but the best estimates put the number at more than one quintillion human souls.

Founded approximately two thousand years after the development of space travel, the Sollan Empire began when William, King of Avalon, defeated the last bastion of the Mericanii Empire at Earth. Crowning himself Emperor of Man on the Aventine Hill in Rome, William Windsor launched the greatest dynasty in human history. The renamed Aventine House has ruled for sixteen thousand years in line unbroken, maintaining its control of the lesser nobility through a careful breeding program that has wrested reproductive control from the nobile houses and placed it in the hands of the Imperial Office. His line and Empire have endured several threats throughout its long history, none greater than the invasion of the Cielcin.

Here follows a list of those people appearing in various settings throughout the Sollan Empire mentioned in this volume of Lord Marlowe's account:

ON NESSUS:

Conquered by the Sollan Empire late in the ninth millennium, the planet Nessus has remained under the direct control of the Imperial House through the person of the Magnarch, an appointed representative of the Emperor. A pastoral world, Nessus was originally settled by the ancestors of the Normans, among them a devout Cid Arthurian community, who trained warrior monks in the highlands. Since falling into Imperial hands, it has been an agricultural and industrial center, producing starships and provisions, as well as a training ground for Legionnaires in the region. Through Nessus and the Magnarch of Centaurus, the Emperor has exerted his control over the far provinces, and even pressed into the Norman Expanse, but that control has for centuries been jeopardized by the arrival of the Cielcin.

LORD KAROL MARCUS VENANTIAN, Magnarch of the Centaurine Provinces, Viceroy of Alicante Province, Governor-General of Nessus, Archon of Sananne Prefecture, appointed by His Radiance, the EMPEROR.

—His subordinates:

—**SIR KOLOMAN LYNCH,** Commandant of Alden Station in orbit above Nessus.

—**SIR DAVETH KARTZINEL,** Commandant of Fort Horn on Nessus.

MARIUS, an Inquisitor.

VIETOR ELKAN, a surgeon and porphyrogeneticist from the Durantine Republic.

{**ANJU**}, chief of HADRIAN MARLOWE's domestic staff at Maddalo House.

KAFFU and **GREN,** both groundskeepers at Maddalo House.

ON COLCHIS:

The primary moon of the planet SAG-8813D, called Atlas by the locals, Colchis was settled in the fifth millennium ISD, then the furthest settled world from Earth. Following the Hundred Year Terror of Boniface Grael, Emperor Gabriel II ordered the Imperial Archives moved from Avalon for safekeeping. Despite this critical function, Colchis is largely underdeveloped, with the majority of its population—primarily members of the Legions and Imperial civil service—living in the capital city of Aea. The remaining locals are primarily fisherfolk descended from the original colonists.

LORD VELAN DORR, Governor-General of Colchis, an Imperial appointee.

—His chief counselor, **TOR NUMA,** a scholiast.

—His secretary, **ADA.**

—**MODANPOTRA,** an agent of Legion Intelligence attached to the Governor-General's office.

TOR ARRIAN, formerly **LORD MARCUS AVENT,** a cousin of the EM-PEROR. Primate of Nov Belgaer athenaeum and master of the Imperial Library.

{SIRAN OF EMESH}, formerly a companion of HADRIAN MARLOWE, one of his myrmidon companions. Retired to Colchis. First Keeper of Thessa. Deceased.

—Her husband, **{LEM OF COLCHIS},** once eolderman of the village of Racha, a native Sevrastene.

—His former apprentice, **EJAZ,** an elderly fisherman.

—Their descendants:

—**{ELARA OF COLCHIS},** named for the Elara of the myrmidon companions, Second Keeper of Thessa.

—**{AMARTA OF COLCHIS},** Third Keeper of Thessa.

—**{BAGOS OF COLCHIS},** Fourth Keeper of Thessa.

—His children:

—**IMRAH OF COLCHIS,** Fifth Keeper of Thessa.

—**ALVAR OF COLCHIS.**

—Their cousin, **GINOH.**

{TOR GIBSON OF SYRACUSE}, a scholiast. Born **PRINCE PHILIPPE BOURBON** of House Bourbon of Verehaut, disgraced during the Septembrine Revolt and stripped of his titles. Former tutor to House Marlowe of Delos and something of a father figure to HADRIAN. Banished from Delos for abetting HADRIAN's escape from his father.

{HORIZON}, a Mericanii artificial intelligence found beneath the Great Library at Nov Belgaer. Officially dismantled on the orders of the Emperor.

ON CARTEIA:

Colonized in the late thirteenth millennium, Carteia already possessed an atmosphere and native flora-culture conducive to human settlement, but no advanced life, and indeed little developed fauna. This made it a prime candidate for annexation, and the title was sold to House Bampasis, who held the planet as its demesne until it was besieged by the Cielcin in the early eighteenth millennium, during which House Bampasis was annihilated and the capital city of Rothsmoor burned. The title of baron passed to Sir Caedmon Brandt, previously a mere archon, and at the order of the Emperor in ISD 17125, the new capital city of Bennu was built not far from the desolation of the old.

{LORD ARLAN BAMPASIS}, last baron of the House Bampasis. Killed in the Cielcin invasion of Carteia along with the rest of his kin.

LORD CAEDMON BRANDT, formerly **SIR CAEDMON BRANDT,** the titled Archon of Urs, made Baron of Carteia by the decree of the EMPEROR WILLIAM XXIII.

ON PERFUGIUM:

First colonized in the mid-twelfth millennium, Perfugium was established as a beachhead for Imperial efforts at colonizing the outer Centaurus. Perfugium was given quickly into the hands of House Valavar, previously the Marquises of Danne, who administered the demesne until the Battle of Perfugium in ISD 17136, after which the planet was broadly abandoned due to the devastation and the Cielcin horde's pouring into the Centaurine provinces, making it impossible to launch salvage and reconquest operations.

LADY SASKIA VALAVAR IV, twenty-seventh and last Duchess of Perfugium and Archon of Resonno Prefecture.

—Her husband, **LORD GASPARD LLEWELLYN-VALAVAR,** Duke-Consort of Perfugium, disappeared in the Cielcin invasion of his world.

THE CIELCIN

According to this account and their own legends, the Cielcin were delivered from their homeworld, Se Vattayu, to the planet Eue by the High King, Elu, who with its adherents, the thirteen Aeta, constituted a kind of Cielcin Empire on the far side of the galaxy. After Elu's death, the various Aeta turned on one another, their armies fracturing into tribes. Each Aeta, or clan-chief, could at one time trace its lineage by blood or conquest back to one of the original thirteen. By Hadrian's day, those thirteen had fractured to more than a thousand different clans, each calling home a fleet of interstellar ships, some large as moons, and all distributed across the galactic volume in the Norman Expanse and the farther regions beyond the galactic core. Following the events of the Aetavanni, the great Prince Syriani Dorayaica unified nearly all the various tribes and factions under its banner, declaring itself the Shiomu Elusha, the Prophet-King of the Cielcin.

Here follows a list of those Cielcin mentioned in this volume of Lord Marlowe's account:

THE SHIOMU ELUSHA, formerly **SYRIANI DORAYAICA,** the Prophet-King of the Cielcin and Prince of Princes. Aeta-ba-Aetane and Aeta-Prince of the Itani Dorayaica. Supreme Ruler of Dharan-Tun. Blood of Elu. Blessed of Miudanar. Master of the Thirteen Tribes of Eue. Called the Scourge of Earth by the humans.

—Its generals, the **IEDYR YEMANI,** or White Hand:

—**VATI INAMNA,** the First Sword. Closest companion of the Prophet. One of SYRIANI's vayadan, its servant and concubine. Converted into a half-machine chimera with the aid of MINOS. Chief Admiral of the Prophet's forces.

—Its lieutenant, **GORRE.**

—**HUSHANSA,** the Many-Handed. One of SYRIANI's vayadan, its servant and concubine. Converted into a half-machine chimera with the aid of MINOS. Capable of occupying several bodies at once.

—**TEYANU,** the Unbreakable. One of SYRIANI's vayadan, its servant and concubine. Converted into a half-machine chimera with the aid of MINOS.

—**{AULAMN},** the Wings of Despair. One of Syriani's vayadan, its servant and concubine. Converted into a half-machine chimera with the aid of MINOS. Slain at Akterumu.

—**UGIN ATTAVAISA,** the Blue. One of SYRIANI's vayadan, its servant and concubine. Formerly the Aeta-Prince of the Itani Attavaisa, joined SYRIANI at the Aetavanni on Eue. Commander of the fleet at the Battle of Perfugium. Replaced IUBALU.

—**GURIMA PELEDANU,** one of SYRIANI's vayadan, its servant and concubine. Formerly the Aeta-Prince of the Itani Peledanu and Lord of the Fiftieth Branching of the Line of Imnun. Joined SYRIANI at the Aetavanni on Eue. Commander of the Fleet at the Battle of Ganelon. Replaced BAHUDDE.

—**{IUBALU},** the Four-Handed. One of SYRIANI's vayadan, its servant and concubine. Converted into a half-machine chimera with the aid of MINOS. Slain at the Battle of the Beast.

—**{BAHUDDE},** the Giant. One of SYRIANI's vayadan, its servant and concubine. Converted into a half-machine chimera with the aid of MINOS. Slain at the Battle of Berenike.

—Its slave, **GURANA,** a common soldier.

{ARANATA OTIOLO}, Viudihom, Aeta-Prince of the Itani Otiolo, Lord of the Seventeenth Branching of the Line of ZAHAKA. Slayer of and former vayadan to UTAIHARO. Once supreme ruler of the worldship *Bahali imnal Akura.* Killed by HADRIAN MARLOWE in the battle aboard the *Demiurge.*

—Its child, **{NOBUTA OTIOLO},** killed by HADRIAN MARLOWE in the battle aboard the *Demiurge.*

—Its former master, **{UMNA UTAIHARO},** last scion of the Line of Utaiharo, a branch of the Line of ZAHAKA.

—Its servants:

    —{CASANTORA TANARAN IAKATO}, a baetan, priest-historian of its clan.

    —{ITANA UVANARI AYATOMN}, ichakta, captain of the ill-fated Cielcin expedition to Emesh.

{VENATIMN ULURANI}, former Aeta of the ULURANI clan, killed by HADRIAN MARLOWE in single combat at the Battle of Aptucca, allowing a nearly bloodless human victory.

{ELU}, a mythical figure. According to legend, the Cielcin High King who brought its tribe through space to the planet Eue. Blessed of MIUDANAR.

    —Its mate, {AVARRA}, sacrificed to Miudanar according to Cielcin legend.

    —Their offspring, {UMNA}, the First Aeta.

    —Its followers, {DUMANN}, {IMNUN}, {ZAHAKA}, and {IN-UMGALU}, among the first Aeta, and the progenitors of various lines of Cielcin succession.

{ARAXAIKA}, the Almost-Blessed, another mythical figure. Brought an end to the Kinslaying, a civil war between the Cielcin clans attested to in this account. Failed to unite the tribes.

THE EXTRASOLARIANS

For as long as the Sollan Empire has existed, there have been those eager to escape it. Tracing their descent back to survivors of the Mericanii and of the Mandari corporate clans, the Extrasolarians are not truly a people. The term is rather an umbrella capturing innumerable disparate factions dwelling in the spaces between the stars, on asteroids and rogue planets, on black-site stations and on huge migratory starships called Sojourners. They may be part of microstates or planetary kingdoms, or part of no state at all, many being anarchists and economic adventurers. They are united only in their opposition to the Sollan Empire and in their willingness to use technologies forbidden by the Chantry.

Multiple factions and agencies among the Extras are referenced in Lord Marlowe's account; here follows a list of those described:

ON VORGOSSOS:

According to legend, the planet Vorgossos was settled in ancient times by the ancestors of the Extrasolarians fleeing the early Empire. Lord Marlowe's account indicates that the settlement of the planet may go back even further, and that the city he visited may have been an outpost of the Mericanii Empire during the Foundation War. What is more, Marlowe's account insists on there being some truth to the legend of Kharn Sagara, insisting that the ancient warlord found a manner of immortality by relying on abandoned Mericanii technology and has ruled the planet since antiquity, providing a hideaway for pirates, mercenaries, and for all manner of unsavory activity, notably the black-market genetics and cybernetics trades.

KHARN SAGARA, called the **UNDYING,** King of Vorgossos. Presumably the same Kharn Sagara from ancient legend, a man more than fifteen thousand years old. Last seen divided into two bodies.

—His children: **{SUZUHA}** and **{REN}**, both clones. Dead, the mind and personality of Kharn Sagara has possessed both of them.

—His servants:

—**BRETHREN,** a Mericanii artificial intelligence composed of human tissue confined to the underground sea beneath Vorgossos.

—**CALVERT,** Exalted magus in charge of the cloning program and body farms of Vorgossos.

—**YUME,** a golem or android.

OF MINOS:

Virtually no reference to an Extrasolarian organization called MINOS exists in the Imperial record outside Lord Marlowe's account, casting some doubt as to whether or not they are another of his inventions. It is the case that the Cielcin Prince Syriani Dorayaica contracted various Extrasolarian agencies during the wars to construct equipment and soldiers for its armies, but Marlowe's claims of an order of magi capable of traveling between bodies and across light-years cannot be corroborated.

The Elect-Masters of MINOS, comprising several magi, their total number unknown:

  —**URBAINE,** Elect-Master of MINOS, nominally an advisor to Prince SYRIANI DORAYAICA. Infected VALKA ONDERRA with a dangerous mind virus at the Battle of Berenike.

  —**SEVERINE,** Elect-Master of MINOS, also nominally advising Prince SYRIANI DORAYAICA. Encountered HADRIAN MARLOWE at the Battle of Arae.

  —**IOVAN,** Elect-Master of MINOS, serving as an agent among the Lothrians, disguised as the man in the Ninth Chair.

—**TAKESHI.**

—**SAMARA.**

—**GAIZKA.**

  —Their subordinate, **VLADILEN.**

  —Their subordinate, **ABBERTON,** a research virologist.

  —Their former subordinate, {**NOLWENN**}, killed by SYRIANI DORAYAICA.

ON LATARRA:

Reports reached the Sollan Empire in ISD 16551—shortly after the Battle of the Beast—that a new Extrasolarian warlord, Calen Harendotes, had emerged on the planet Latarra in the Norman Expanse. Not much is known about Harendotes. Legion Intelligence reports from the period indicate him to be some sort of renegade palatine nobile, but no House Harendotes exists in the High College registry, leading this translator to conclude it must be an assumed name. Further record exists of several efforts on behalf of the Imperium to variously recruit and assassinate Harendotes, whose army of Norman and Extrasolarian interests constituted an item of interest to the Imperial office. Per Marlowe's account, the Monarch had dealings with agencies aligned with the Cielcin.

CALEN HARENDOTES, the so-called MONARCH of Latarra, an Extra-solarian warlord gathering power in the Veil of Marinus.

—His servant, **ZELAZ,** the Exalted Captain of the Sojourner *Hermetic Melancholia*, a small, posthuman chimera.

THE PRINCIPALITIES OF JADD

The Jaddian worlds were settled along a broad swath of the Perseus Arm near the outer rim of the galaxy during the eighth millennium. Due to the region's remoteness, the palatine families there tended to intermarry rather than connect back to the broader Imperium, which—coupled with a shared Zoroastrian heritage dating back to the time of the Foundation War and the Exodus—created a racialized subculture among the region's elites and led to the formation of a local identity separate from that of the broader Imperium.

This separation reached a turning point in the twelfth millennium, when the Imperial Prince Cyrus absconded with his Jaddian lover, Princess Amana di Jadi, scandalizing the Jaddian lords. The Jaddians maintain to this day that Amana was raped and kidnapped, while Imperial accounts attest to a romance between the pair. What is beyond dispute, however, is that Amana was recovered by the Jaddian Duke Katanes du Otranto, who recovered not only her, but the High College genetic codex tied to her, which contained the intelligence necessary to free the Jaddian palatines of Imperial control. Though Amana died and her house was destroyed in the wars, the eighty-one remaining palatine families took her name as their own, becoming Jaddians in ISD 11466, after the Battle of the Encircling Moons, when Duke Katanes bested the Imperial Legions with the first Jaddian mamluk clone army.

The eighty-one Jaddian families took the title *shahdom*, meaning *prince*, and have ever since elected one of their number to rule from the planet Jadd, formerly the home of Amana's family. Katanes's house, House du Otranto of Laran, have made up the majority of all High Princes in Jadd in the millennia since. Relations with the Empire—initially strained—relaxed in recent millennia, as the princes and the Emperor were forced into an uneasy alliance against the Commonwealth in the Persean Wars.

Here follows a list of those people of the Principalities of Jadd mentioned in this third volume of Lord Marlowe's account:

PRINCE ALDIA AHMAD DATAPHERNES RODRIGO-PHILIPPE ALDIA BAN ALDIA BAN GOBRYAS DU OTRANTO, High Prince of Jadd, Prince of Laran, First-Among-Equals of the Princes of the Principalities of the Jaddian Peoples, Chief of the Dham-Eali, Lord of the Encircling Moons, Keeper of the Planet of Fire, and Beloved of God.

—His grandson, **PRINCE KAIM SANCHEZ CYAXARES NAZIR-VINCENTE OLORIN BAN OSROES BAN ALDIA DU OTRANTO,** called the **DARKMOON** and known to HADRIAN MARLOWE as **SIR OLORIN MILTA,** a Maeskolos of the Fire School's Second Circle.

—His *alkidarae*, his concubines:

—**KALIMA DI SAYYIPH,** of House Sayyiph, his closest companion and confidant.

—**TIADA DI UMAZ,** of House Umaz, also a Maeskolos of the Fire School's Fifth Circle.

—**BELIT & SANAZI.**

—His bodyguard, **BARAZ DU SIMAR,** of House Simar. A Maeskolos.

—His late father, {**PRINCE OSROES DU OTRANTO**}.

—**ADMIRAL VELKAN SERPICO,** supreme commander of the Jaddian armada dispatched to assist the Sollan Empire in the war against the Cielcin, captain of the flagship *JNS Mnemon.* An aryabite.

—His subordinate, **CAPTAIN FADROH AFSHARIRAD,** a close friend of Prince Kaim's and captain of the *JNS Albaspatha.* An aryabite.

—His subordinate, **CAPTAIN SERENELLI.**

—**LIEUTENANT JINAN AZHAR,** an officer in the fleet and former lover of HADRIAN MARLOWE. An aryabite.

{**PRINCE KATANES DU OTRANTO**}, first High Prince of Jadd, Duke and later Prince of Laran, and the man who won Jaddian independence in the Jaddian Wars and brought House Otranto to supremacy amongst the Jaddian houses.

THE WIDER WORLD

A small number of the persons mentioned in Lord Marlowe's account are difficult to group with the others due to their remoteness from the events he describes.

Here follows a list of all those persons mentioned in this volume of Lord Marlowe's account:

LORD ALISTAIR DIOMEDES FRIEDRICH MARLOWE, Archon of Meidua Prefecture and Lord of Devil's Rest, former Lord Executor of Delos System, and Butcher of Linon. HADRIAN's father.

—His wife, {**LILIANA KEPHALOS-MARLOWE**}, a celebrated librettist and filmmaker, deceased.

—Their other children:

—**CRISPIN ORESTES MARLOWE,** presumptive heir to Devil's Rest.

—**SABINE DORYSSA MARLOWE,** a daughter born to replace HADRIAN after his exile.

—His late parents, {**LORD TIMON MARLOWE IV**} and {**LADY FUCHSIA BELLGROVE-MARLOWE**}.

—His castellan, **SIR FELIX MARTYN,** Commander of the House Guard and Master-at-Arms in charge of instructing the Marlowe children.

—His counselor, **TOR ALCUIN,** a scholiast.

LORD BALIAN MATARO, third Count of Emesh, Archon of Borosevo Prefecture and Lord of Castle Borosevo.

TOR PSELLOS, an Imperial scholiast working at the Echidna dig site.

EDOUARD ALBÉ, an Imperial intelligence officer.

THOSE BEYOND

Lord Marlowe's account makes frequent references to entities not attested to by science or the historical record. These may be broadly divided into two groups: the Quiet, previously described as an extinct race of xenobites of great antiquity, and the Watchers, initially assumed by Lord Marlowe to be the pagan idols of the Cielcin people. Lord Marlowe's account claims both these groups are real, and that their reality is common knowledge among the Cielcin. It is impossible—from studies of Cielcin writings and artifacts—to conclude that both the Quiet and Watchers are anything but religious fetishes promulgated by the Cielcin faith. That there are the ruins of many ancient races across the galaxy is not disputed in athenaeum. The ruins on Emesh, for instance, exist as Lord Marlowe describes. That these ruins are related to sites on other worlds—such as the Marching Towers of Sadal Suud—has never been corroborated by scholiast research, though I grant this may be the result of Chantry interference in our work. The so-called *Quiet* hypothesis has existed for thousands of years, but cannot be examined due to Inquisition censors and oversight of our colleges. In any case, Lord Marlowe's claims that the Quiet is a singular entity, and that the ruins on these worlds are anti-entropic structures traveling backward through time, likewise cannot be corroborated. Further investigation is needed.

As for the Watchers, the names of these various deities do appear in numerous Cielcin sources captured during the war, but no artifacts have been positively identified as confirming the existence of these creatures. The planet Eue, attested to in this account, has—to the knowledge of the Imperial Library—never been located, nor the bones of Miudanar found. These Watchers are therefore, in the opinion of the translator, wholly fictional, and Marlowe's account is to be regarded as highly fanciful and mythologized. Nevertheless, their names and roles are recorded here:

THE QUIET, called **UTANNASH,** the **LIAR** by the Cielcin, believed by them to the be the author of the universe itself and eternal enemy of the

Watchers. An entity of pure will aligned with humanity, protector of HADRIAN MARLOWE. Previously assumed to be an extinct species of ancient xenobites.

MIUDANAR, the **DREAMER,** chief god of the Cielcin pantheon, a massive one-eyed serpent with many arms, once worshiped by the Enar. Gave technology to the Cielcin and brought Elu to Eue. Apparently dead.

—The other Watchers:

> —**IAQARAM,** whom it is said hears all things. Occupies a place of honor in Cielcin worship second only to dead MIUDANAR.

> —**SHAMAZHA,** Father of Giants.

> —**NAZHTENAH, PTHAMARU, SHETEBO,** and **USATHLAM,** of whom little is known.

INDEX OF WORLDS

HEREIN IS APPENDED A list of all those worlds referenced by Lord Marlowe in this volume of his account. The purpose of this list is simply to remind the reader which world is which. For detailed notes regarding astrography and planetology, please refer the Vandenberg Catalog. What information I have provided here is sufficient to understand Lord Marlowe's text.

—Tor Paulos of Nov Belgaer

Annica   An airless world orbiting a red dwarf somewhere on the far side of the galactic core, apparently connected to the Quiet.

Aptucca   An Imperial colony in the Veil, site of the defeat of the Cielcin Prince Ulurani in single combat by Hadrian Marlowe.

Arae   Site of a battle in the Cielcin Wars where Hadrian Marlowe discovered evidence of an alliance between the Cielcin and Extrasolarian humans.

Ares   One of the oldest Imperial worlds in the Spur of Orion, site of the Ares Command School, where the best Legion officers are trained.

Ashklam   A former Norman kingdom in the Veil of Marinus, conquered and annexed by Calen Harendotes, the Monarch of Latarra, during the Cielcin Wars.

Athyras   An older Imperial world, home to the predatory xanarths.

Aulos   An Imperial colony in the Centaurine Provinces, one of the sites on Emperor William XXIII's tour of the frontier.

Avalon   One of the original human colonies, site of heavy European colonization by generation ark. Birthplace of the Sollan Empire.

Balanrot   An Imperial colony in the outer Centaurine provinces, part of Emperor William XXIII's grand tour.

Belusha   The most infamous of the Imperial prison planets, the last destination of many political prisoners. A dismal, cold world.

Berenike   A former trading hub and mining colony on the Centaurine frontier on the border with the Veil of Marinus, site of a major battle in the Cielcin Wars.

Carteia   An icy world in the Centaurine provinces, devastated by the Cielcin in the war. One of the sites on Emperor William XXIII's tour of the frontier.

Centaurus Arm   The innermost and farthest of the four arms of the galaxy colonized by the Sollan Empire, north of Sagittarius, Orion, and Perseus. Most Centaurine provinces are clustered near the heart of the galaxy, just south of the Veil of Marinus and the galactic core.

Cidamus   An Imperial demesne in the Centaurine Provinces, ruled by the counts of House Volsenna, sacked by the Cielcin in the Battle of Cidamus in ISD 17064.

Colchis   The first Imperial colony in the Centaurus Arm, named for the garden at the end of the world, a moon of the gas giant Atlas. Never an important colony (it was eclipsed quickly by its neighbors), it is known for the massive scholiast athenaeum of Nov Belgaer.

Comum   A Centaurine demesne, site of the Battle of Comum, one of Lord Marlowe's many battles.

Cressgard   A lost Imperial colony in the Veil of Marinus, site of the first contact with the Cielcin at the Battle of Cressgard in ISD 15792.

Delos   Birthplace of Hadrian Marlowe and seat of the duchy of House Kephalos in the Spur of Orion, a temperate world with wan sunlight, famed for its uranium deposits, which made it extremely wealthy.

Dharan-Tun   A Cielcin worldship larger than some moons, the seat of Prince Syriani Dorayaica.

Echidna   The first Cielcin worldship captured and impounded by the Sollan Empire for study. A dwarf planet converted into a starship by the Cielcin Prince Laramnaina. Captured by Imperial forces under the command of Lord Cassian Powers after the Second Battle of Cressgard in ISD 15797.

Edda   An arid, windy world in the Demarchy known for its canyons, sinkholes, and subterranean oceans. Its people are primarily ethnic Nordei and Travatskr.

Eikana   An airless, desert world in the central Centaurine provinces, noted for its antimatter fuel manufactory, operated by Yamato Interstellar. The primary fuel supplier for Nessus.

Elos   A world renowned for its particle foundries.

Emesh   A watery world in the Veil of Marinus, seat of House Mataro. Home of the coloni Umandh and the subterranean ruins at Calagah. Originally a Norman colony.

Eue   A planet belonging to the Vaiartu and later to the Cielcin, the site of Cielcin migration from Se Vattayu and the seat of their early empire. Resting place of the Watcher Miudanar.

Fidchell   An icy world in the outer reaches of the Centaurus Arm and site of an Imperial fuel depot.

Forum   The capital of the Sollan Empire. A gas giant with a breathable atmosphere in whose cloud belt are several flying palace cities that serve as the administrative hub of the Imperium.

Ganelon   VA-639D in the Vandenberg Catalog, a semi-habitable planet in the Centaurus Arm of the galaxy, used as a base by the Extrasolarian company MINOS during the war.

Gododdin   A system between the Centaurus and Sagittarius Arms of the galaxy, famously destroyed by Hadrian Marlowe during the final battle in the Crusade.

Hermonassa   An Imperial world in the Sagittarine provinces, the site of a major Red Star Foundries Legion shipyard. Destroyed by Syriani Dorayaica in the Cielcin Wars.

Ibarnis   An Imperial colony in the Centaurine provinces. One of the sites on Emperor William XXIII's tour of the frontier.

Idu   An Imperial colony on the borders of the Veil of Marinus.

Jadd   The planet of fire, sacred capital of the Jaddian Principalities, on whose soil none shall tread without the express permission of the High Prince.

Latarra   A former Norman Freehold in the Veil conquered by the Monarch, Calen Harendotes, an Extrasolarian warlord.

Lurash   The capital of the Jaddian Principality of Lurash, seat of House du Lurash, one of the great families of Jadd.

Marinus   The first Norman Freehold seized by the Imperium and amongst their first colonies in the Expanse. The Imperial capital in the Veil of Marinus.

Mars   One of Old Earth's sister planets and the site of the first major offworld colonial efforts during the Exodus but before the Peregrinations.

Nairi   An Imperial territory in the Outer Perseus, never formally settled, the site of certain Vaiartu ruins investigated by Sir Damien Aradhya of Hapsis and the *Atropos* expedition. Purportedly the resting place of one of the Monumentals.

Nemavand   An Imperial colony in Rammanu Province on the Centaurine frontier.

Nennoed   An Imperial military depot world along the Centaurine trade lanes between Gododdin and Nessus.

Nessus   Seat of the Centaurine Magnarchate, famously the site of Hadrian Marlowe's nearly 100-year exile following his arrest and near assassination by the Holy Terran Chantry.

**Norman
Expanse**   See VEIL OF MARINUS. The terms are used interchangeably, though the Veil moniker is more common in the Empire, while the Normans refer to it as the Expanse.

Old Earth   Birthplace of the human species. A nuclear ruin and victim of environmental collapse, she is protected by the Chantry Wardens and none may walk there.

Padmurak   Capital of the Lothrian Commonwealth, a frigid, airless world in the Upper Sagittarius, on the far side of the Rasan Belt.

Perfugium   A colonial distribution center in the Centaurine provinces, the home of billions of sleeping human colonists. The site of a major battle in the Cielcin Wars.

Perseus Arm   The outermost of the four settled arms of the galaxy, comprising most of the outer-rim territories. Variously settled by the Sollan Empire, the Principalities of Jadd, the Durantine Republic, and various freeholder colonies and smaller states not annexed or allied with a greater power.

Phaia   A world renowned for its highmatter sword craftsmen.

Pharos   A Norman freehold ruled for a time by Marius Whent, an ex-Imperial legate defeated by Hadrian Marlowe during his time as a mercenary.

Rasan Belt   A broad swath of unsettled space, one hundred light-years across, that stretches across the Upper Sagittarius between the Sollan Empire and the Lothrian Commonwealth.

Renaissance   One of the most populous worlds in the Empire, located in the Spur of Orion. A cultural center almost entirely covered by urban development. Formerly a Mericanii colony called Yellowstone, located in the Epsilon Eridani system.

Rustam   An Imperial colony in the Norman Expanse, site of a minor engagement with the Cielcin that culminated in the destruction of its capital city.

Sagittarius Arm The second arm of the galaxy colonized by humanity, north of Orion but south of Centaurus. Comprises the core of the Sollan Empire— along with Orion—but the Lothrian Commonwealth constitutes a large portion of its western frontier.

Salamass   An Imperial colony in the Centaurine Provinces, one of the sites on Emperor William XXIII's tour of the frontier.

Second Gulf   The vast emptiness between the arms of Sagittarius and Centaurus.

Se Vattayu   The mythical homeworld of the Cielcin, its surface apparently honeycombed with labyrinthine tunnels like those the Quiet dug at Calagah on Emesh.

Senuessa   A Sagittarine world, site of the Battle of Senuessa, one of the bloodiest in the entirety of the Cielcin Wars.

Siraganon   An Imperial colony in the outer Centaurine provinces, one of the sites on Emperor William XXIII's tour of the frontier.

Small Kingdoms   Any of the countless independent human polities in the Lower and Outer Perseus not aligned with or subject to Imperial rule, considered too remote to easily annex by Imperial forces and treated as little better than Extrasolarians.

Sybaris   An Imperial colony in the Centaurine frontier, site of a major battle in the Cielcin Wars. It was at Sybaris that Hadrian Marlowe was arrested by the Chantry's Inquisition and taken to Thermon to stand trial.

Syracuse   A temperate world in the Imperium, notably the site of the scholiasts' athenaeum at Nov Acor.

Taranis   An Imperial demesne in the Centaurine provinces, site of a battle between the Imperial Legions and Syriani Dorayaica, one of the Cielcin prince's rare defeats at the hands of Sir Hector Oliva.

Teukros   A desert world in the Imperium, notably the site of the scholiasts' athenaeum at Nov Senber.

Thagura   An Imperial colony in the Veil of Marinus, formerly the demesne of House Malyan. Site of a major battle in the Cielcin Wars.

Thermon   A Chantry stronghold in the Sagittarine Provinces, famously the site of Hadrian Marlowe's twelve-year-long trial for witchcraft.

Tiryns   Seat of the Persean Magnarchate.

Typhon   The second Cielcin worldship captured and impounded by the Sollan Empire, dismantled for study.

Ubar   An arid Jaddian satrapy loyal to the House du Otranto, who have been the High Princes of Jadd for generations. Begs loyalty to the Prince of Thessaloniki.

Vanaheim   An Imperial colony in the Centaurine Provinces, one of the sites on Emperor William XXIII's tour of the frontier.

Veil of Marinus   The region of space at the base of the Norma Arm of the galaxy where it joins the galactic core. Formerly a colonial expansion region dominated by the Sollan Empire and Norman Freeholders, it is also the site of most Cielcin incursions into human space.

Vorgossos   A mythical Extrasolarian world orbiting a brown dwarf, said to be a mecca for the black-market genetics trade. Formerly a hideout for the Exalted, presided over now by a warlord known as the Undying.

LEXICON

HEREIN IS APPENDED AN index of those terms appearing in this fifth volume of Lord Marlowe's manuscript which are not easily translated into the Classical English, or which bear a specific technical or cultural definition requiring clarification in the opinion of the translator. For a more complete explanation of the methodology employed in devising these coinages for this translation, please refer to the appendices in volume one.

—*Tor Paulos of Nov Belgaer*

abstraction   The process by which members of the Exalted remove themselves from humanity through technological modification.

adamant   Any of the various long-chain carbon materials used for starship hulls and body armor.

adorator   A member of any antique religious cult maintained by the Empire and tolerated by the Chantry.

Advent   The destruction of Old Earth by humanity at the end of the Foundation War.

Aeta   A Cielcin prince-chieftain. Appears to have ownership rights over its subjects and their property.

aljanhi   A human Jaddian soldier, distinguished from the clone mamluks.

alkidar   In Jaddian culture, a woman—almost always of the eali caste—bound to a eali man in formal concubinage.

alumglass   A transparent, ceramic form of aluminum, stronger than glass, which is common used in windows, particularly in ship design.

androgyn   A homunculus exhibiting either neither or both male and female sex characteristics.

angu   A species of large, faintly sweet melon popular in the Iramnene desert region of the planet Delos.

aquilarius   A fighter pilot.

Archprior   Within the Chantry clergy, a senior prior, usually one entrenched in the Chantry bureaucracy.

armsman   Any individual—usually patrician—sworn to serve the person of a palatine lord or his/her house in perpetuity.

aryabite   Any member of the warrior middle class of the Jaddian principalities. Roughly equivalent to the role of patricians in Imperial society, comprising genetic uplifts and their offspring, but no pure-blood eali.

athenaeum   Any of the research compounds/monasteries of the scholiastic orders.

backspace   Any territory within Imperial space not formally colonized by the Empire. Often a refuge for the Extrasolarians.

baetan   In Cielcin culture, a sort of priest-historian of the scianda.

bonecutter   Slang. Any black-market geneticist or surgeon not sanctioned by the High College.

bromos   A protein-rich strain of engineered hyper-oat that serves as the basis for ration bars and as protein base for artificial meat production.

cathar   A surgeon-torturer employed by the Holy Terran Chantry.

centurion   A rank in the Imperial Legions, commands one hundred men.

chariot   A flying personal vehicle in which the pilot stands vertical and changes directions by leaning and via the hand controls.

chiliarch   A rank in the Imperial Legions, commands one thousand men.

chimera   Any genetically altered or artificially created animal, usually by blending the genetic code of two or more animals.

Cid Arthurianism   A syncretic religion founded late in the fourth millennium as an offshoot of Buddhism recognizing the British King Arthur as a Buddha, emphasizing chivalric virtue as a means of pursuing enlightenment.

Cielcin   Spacefaring alien species. Humanoid and carnivorous.

Colosso   A series of sporting events held in a coliseum involving professional gladiators, slave myrmidons, animals, races, and more.

colossus   Any huge mobile artillery unit, especially those designed to walk on legs. May be several hundred feet tall.

consortation   One of the Twelve Abominations. Conversing with or having similar contact with artificial intelligence, even unknowingly.

Consortium   The Wong-Hopper Consortium. The largest of the Mandari interstellar corporations, specializing in terraforming technologies.

consul   A type of Imperial apostol formally installed in a consulate among foreign powers, a permanent ambassador.

cornicen   In the Legions, a soldier tasked with playing the horn or trumpet at parades.

cothon   A starport launch terminal, especially one of the toroidal sort with the launch pit in the center of the ring. Usually built just below ground level.

cryoburn   Burns incurred as a side effect of improper cryonic freezing.

daimon   An artificial intelligence. Sometimes erroneously applied to non-intelligent computer systems.

datanet   The loose association of all planetary dataspheres connected by quantum telegraphs and inter-space satellite relays.

datasphere   Any planetary data network. In the Empire, access is strictly restricted to the patrician and palatine caste.

davoi   The Jaddian word for the Cielcin, literally "demons."

Deeps   A species of possibly artificial and intelligent microorganisms found on several worlds, capable of digesting and altering other living creatures.

Demarchy of Tavros A small interstellar polity far from Imperial control. Radically open to technology, the people vote on all measures using neural lace implants.

Domagavani In Jadd, the legislative and elective body composed of all eighty-one Jaddian princes and the ranking religious clerics, especially those of the Zoroastrian faith.

douleter A slave overseer or trader.

druaja A board game, sometimes called labyrinth chess.

dryad Any of a species of green-skinned homunculi capable of photosynthesis, designed for work in outer space.

duplication One of the Twelve Abominations. The copying of an individual's genetics, likeness, personality, or memories through cloning or related practices.

eali The Jaddian ruling caste, product of intense eugenic development. Practically superhuman.

Elusha The Cielcin word for "king," a title granted to Syriani Dorayaica, previously held by the semi-mythical Cielcin ruler Elu, whence comes the word.

Emperor The supreme ruler of the Sollan Empire, considered a god and the reincarnation of his/her predecessor. Holds absolute power.

Enar The Cielcin name for the Vaiartu civilization. See VAIARTU.

entoptics Augmented reality device where images are projected directly onto the retina.

Exalted A faction among the Extrasolarians noted for their extreme cybernetic augmentations.

Excubitor The innermost circle of the Emperor's guard, comprising 108 of the finest knights and fighters in the Empire.

Extrasolarian Any of the barbarians living outside Imperial control, often possessing illegal praxis.

extraterranic In terraforming and ecology, refers to any organism not of Old Earth extraction. Extraterrestrial.

Feni A fermented liquor made from cashew apples.

Firstborn The label used by the Empire to refer to the civilization known colloquially as "the Quiet," as a means of distinguishing them from other extinct galactic civilizations, namely the Vaiartu.

fordgron In the Cid Arthurian religion, a temple or abbey, especially one focused on the training of warrior monks.

Foundation War The war between the early Empire and the Mericanii, in which the Mericanii were destroyed and the Sollan Empire founded.

fravashi In the Zoroastrian religion of Jadd, the spirit of a person, specifically the part of one's spirit who remains with their God in the spirit world.

fugue The state of cryonic suspension induced to ensure humans and other living creatures survive the long journey between suns.

Galstani

The common language of the Sollan Empire, descended from Classical English, with heavy Hindi and Franco-Germanic influences.

glowsphere

A spherical, bright light source floating on Royse repulsors, battery or chemically powered.

golem

A mechanical being fashioned in the shape of a man, containing no organic parts.

governor-general

The ruling executive officer of an Imperial planet or territory (as opposed to a palatine lord), appointed by the Emperor, may rule for a term or for life, but may not pass the title on to an heir.

Grand Conclave

The ruling bureaucratic organization of the Lothrian Commonwealth, led by the thirty-four members of the Bench, but containing several hundred functionaries and Party members.

Great Charters

Ancient collection of legal codes imposed on the Empire by a coalition of the houses palatine. Maintains the balance among the houses and between the houses and the Emperor.

groundcar

An automobile, usually powered by solar or by internal combustion.

HAPSIS

The semi-independent, secret division of the Legion Intelligence Office tasked with managing contact scenarios with alien civilizations, especially first contacts, and most especially with regard to matters relating to the Firstborn, Stonebuilder, and Monumental species.

High College

Imperial political office tasked with reviewing palatine requests for children and with overseeing the pregnancies of same. Prevents mutations.

highmatter

A form of exotic matter produced by alchemists. Used to make the swords of Imperial knights, which can cut almost anything.

hightower

An elevator designed to lift cargo from the surface of a planet to orbit and vice versa.

Holy Terran Chantry

State religion of the Empire. Functions as the judicial arm of the state, especially where the use of forbidden technology is involved.

homunculus

Any artificial human or near-human, especially those grown for a task, or for aesthetic purposes.

hoplite

A shielded foot soldier. Heavy infantry.

hurasam

Gold coin used among the Imperial peasant classes, worth its mark-weight in gold. Print notes for various denominations exist.

hypogeum

The underground maintenance complex beneath a coliseum. More generally, any underground complex.

Iedyr Yemani

The six vayadan-generals sworn in fanatic servitude to Syriani Dorayaica. The so-called White Hand.

Imperial Council   The ruling and advisory board of the Sollan Empire, headed by the Chancellor and comprising the lords of the various ministries, the Synarch of the Chantry, various legionary strategoi, and certain special advisors. Advises the Emperor, but also runs the various executive offices of the Imperium.

Imperium   See SOLLAN EMPIRE.

indoctrination   The process by which a person is treated with specially tailored RNA packets to learn and absorb new information and skills quickly.

infestation   In Chantry religious law, the state in which a computer system may contain elements of artificial intelligence or the precursors to same, often leading to possession.

Inquisition   The judicial branch of the Imperial Chantry, primarily concerned with the use of illegal technologies.

Inquisitor   A Chantry official tasked with conducting judicial investigations and overseeing the torture of criminals.

intus   A palatine born outside the oversight of the High College, usually possessing several physical or psychological defects; a bastard.

Irchtani   Species of coloni xenobite native to the planet Judecca. Bird-like with massive wings. Considered an exemplar of coloni assimilation.

itani   Pl. itanimn. A Cielcin family unit, especially the extended clan.

Jaddian   The official language of the Principalities of Jadd, a patois of ancient Romance and Semitic languages with some Greek influences.

jubala   A powerful and popular pseudonarcotic. Can be inhaled or ingested in a kind of tea.

knife-missile   A kind of drone, little more than a remote-controlled flying knife. A favorite of assassins.

Legion Intelligence Office   The Empire's military intelligence, espionage, and foreign intervention agency.

legionnaire   Any soldier in the Imperial Legions, especially the common foot soldier.

lictor   A bodyguard for a nobile or other dignitary. Usually a knight.

lighter   Any starship small enough to make landfall on a planet.

light-probe   Any of a class of very small, ultralight reconnaissance devices propelled by ship-board laser to nearly the speed of light.

logothete   A minister in any of the governmental agencies of any palatine house, used colloquially of any civil servant.

Lothriad   The legal text of the Lothrian Commonwealth, in two volumes: the first containing the laws of the Commonwealth, the second a dictionary of all approved words and phrases, constantly revised.

Lothrian Commonwealth The second largest human polity in the galaxy, a totalitarian collectivist state. Longtime antagonist of the Empire.

Maeskolos Pl. Maeskoloi. Any of the legendary swordmasters of Jadd, drawn exclusively from the eali caste. Credited with superhuman speed and skill.

Magnarch The chief Imperial Viceroy in each arm of the galaxy: Orion, Sagittarius, Perseus, and Centaurus. Essentially co-Emperors.

Magnarchate Region of the Empire ruled by a Magnarch, comprising several provinces.

magus An intellectual, most especially a scientist or natural philosopher.

malaros In the Cid Arthurian religion, a necklace of prayer beads— usually 108—with a medallion of one of the Holy Knights and a tassel at the end.

mamluk Any homunculus slave-soldier of the Jaddian Principalities.

Mandari An ethnic group semi-detached from Imperial society, most commonly found staffing the massive interstellar trading corporations.

mandyas Traditional garment of the Maeskoloi. Half a robe with one flowing sleeve worn over the left shoulder, cinched at the waist.

Martian Guard The Emperor's palace guard, an elite corps of soldiers raised from the population on Earth's nearest neighbor, Mars.

medica A hospital, typically aboard a starship.

Mericanii The ancient first interstellar colonists. A hyper-advanced technologic civilization run by artificial intelligences. Destroyed by the Empire.

MINOS An Extrasolarian organization or order specializing in biomechanics and technological research and development, apparently aligned with the Cielcin Prophet.

Monumentals Another name for the Watchers, used by human scholars prior to first contact with the Cielcin.

Museum Catholic Church An adorator cult centered on the planet Caritas, believed to have existed since the Golden Age of Earth and protected on reservations by Imperial decree.

myrmidon In the Colosso, any contract or slave fighter not a professionally trained gladiator.

nahute Pl. nahute. A Cielcin weapon. Resembles a flying metal snake. Seeks out targets and drills into them.

nobile Blanket term referring to any member of the palatine and patrician castes in the Sollan Empire.

Nordei The principle language of the Demarchy. A patois of Nordic and Thai with some Slavic influences.

Norman — Anyone native to one of the planets of the Norman Expanse, particularly those not under Imperial control. A so-called Freeholder.

Norman Expanse — The frontier of human settlement in the Norma Arm of the Milky Way, near to the galactic core.

nowoyuk — In Lothrian society, any hermaphroditic homunculus grown by the state, or the hermaphroditic offspring of one such homunculus and a natural-born human. All nowoyuk children are genetic hermaphrodites as well. Part of a mostly failed attempt by the Lothrian government to abolish the natural sexes.

nuncius — In Imperial society, an announcer or herald.

Old Lions — A coterie of traditionalist, hyper-monarchist lords in the Sollan Empire close to the throne. Nominally supporters of the Emperor against the bureaucracy.

palatine — The Imperial aristocracy, descended from those free humans who opposed the Mericanii. Genetically enhanced, they may live for several centuries.

Pale — The Cielcin. Slang, considered offensive by xenophiles.

Panthai — A Tavrosi language descended from the Thai, Lao, and Khmer-speaking peoples who settled the Wisp alongside the Nordei.

patrician — Any plebeian or plutocrat awarded with genetic augmentations at the behest of the palatine caste as a reward for services rendered, or descendants of same.

phase disruptor — A sort of firearm that attacks the nervous system. Can stun on lower settings.

phylactery — A device for storing the genetic and epigenetic information of an individual for the purposes of artificial reproduction.

plagiarius — A smuggler, fence, or other black-market salesman.

plasma burner — A firearm which uses a strong loop of magnetic force to project an arc of super-heated plasma across short to moderate distances.

plebeian — The Imperial peasantry, descended from unaltered human stock seeded on the oldest colony ships. Forbidden to use high technology.

poine — A structured, small-scale war carried out between Imperial palatine houses. Subject to the scrutiny of the Inquisition.

porphyrogeneticist — A geneticist employed in the creation of palatine or eali children, usually by the Imperial High College or by one of the great houses of Jadd.

primate — The highest administrative office of a scholiasts' athenaeum, akin to a university chancellor.

Principalities of Jadd — Nation of eighty former Imperial provinces in Perseus that revolted over palatine reproductive rights. Heavily militaristic and caste-driven.

Quiet The hypothetical first civilization in the galaxy, allegedly responsible for several ancient sites, including those on Emesh, Judecca, Sadal Suud, and Ozymandias.

repulsor A device which makes use of the Royse Effect to allow objects to float without disturbing the air or environment.

Rothsbank An ancient, privately owned banking house tracing its roots back to the Golden Age of Earth.

Royse shield Any force field making use of the Royse Effect to stop high-velocity objects from penetrating its energy curtain, especially those worn at the belt for personal use.

satrap A planetary governor in the Principalities of Jadd, subordinate to one of the regional Princes.

saylash Among the Tavrosi clansmen, a fractal tattoo covering large portions of the body, containing the history of the clan back several generations.

scahari Pl. scaharimn. In Cielcin culture, any member of the warrior caste.

scarab A small colossus used for urban combat, a six-legged mobile artillery platform crewed by half a dozen men.

scholiast Any member of the monastic order of researchers, academics, and theoreticians tracing their origins to the Mericanii scientists captured at the end of the Foundation War.

scianda Pl. sciandane. A Cielcin migratory fleet, comprising several *itanimn* and presided over by a single aeta.

Septembrine Revolt A poine civil war fought in the sixteenth millennium between two factions of House Bourbon of Verehaut, started by Prince Philippe Bourbon, who attempted to claim the title of prince, but was blocked by his brother, Prince Charles. Ended with Philippe's exile to Belusha.

Shiomu The Cielcin word for "prophet," a title granted to Syriani Dorayaica.

Sojourner Any of a class of massive Extrasolarian starship, often hundreds of miles long, especially those crewed by the Exalted.

Sollan Empire The largest and oldest single polity in human-controlled space, comprising some half a billion habitable planets.

SOM The lobotomized shell of a human being animated by machines, used for slave labor and as soldiers by the Extrasolarians.

Special Security A division of Legion Intelligence interested in matters of high Imperial security; that is, in situations and persons affecting the integrity and security of the Empire as a whole.

spydust Any microscopic surveillance device, be it a camera, microphone, or other sensor. May be airborne.

Stonebuilders An earlier name for the Vaiartu civilization used by human scholars. See VAIARTU.

strategos   An admiral in the Imperial Legions, responsible for the command of an entire fleet, comprising several legions.

Stricture   The formal rules governing the lifestyle and behavior of those members of the scholiast order as outlined in *The Book of the Mind* and the rest of Imore's writings.

sulshawar   In Jaddian culture, a warrior who serves as bodyguard to a prince, satrap, or other important personage. May also represent that person in legal duels. Comparable to a lictor.

swordmaster   See MAESKOLOS.

Tavrosi   Any of the languages from the Demarchy of Tavros. Typically refers to Nordei.

Telegraph/QET   A device which uses entangled quantum particles to communicate instantly over vast distances.

terranic   In terraforming and ecology, refers to any organism of Old Earth extraction. Not extraterrestrial.

trias   A unit of three legionnaires, usually two peltasts and one hoplite.

triaster   The commander of a trias, usually a shielded hoplite.

Udaritanu   A complex, nonlinear writing system used by the Cielcin. Pl. udaritani, referring to the individual glyphs used in same.

Umandh   A coloni species native to the planet Emesh. Amphibious and tripedal, they have an intelligence comparable to that of dolphins.

Vaiartu   An ancient and extinct species of xenobite who, according to Lord Marlowe's account, ruled much of the galaxy and destroyed millions of planets and races several million years ago, and whose legacy explains the relative emptiness of the universe.

vate   Any preacher or holy man not formally a part of the Chantry clergy.

vayadan   In Cielcin culture, the bound mates and bodyguards of an Aeta.

verrox   A powerful pseudoamphetamine derived from the leaves of the verroca plant. It is taken by ingesting the leaves, which are usually candied.

Vigran Huaxia   A Mandari banking house with deep ties to the Extrasolarians.

Watchers   According to this account, a species or collection of powerful xenobites, possibly worshiped as gods by the Cielcin and other alien races.

watch-eye   Any flying camera drone.

worldship   Any of the massive Cielcin vessels—some as large as moons—which make up the core of their fleets.

xanarth   A massive land predator native to the planet Athyras.

xenobite Any life form not originating in terranic or human stock, especially those life forms which are considered intelligent; an alien.

xenologist A scholiast or lay magus specializing in the study of inhuman beings, especially those rising to the level of sentience.

zuk Any of the working class of the Lothrian Commonwealth.

zvanya A cinnamon-flavored distilled alcohol popular in Jadd.

ABOUT THE AUTHOR

CHRISTOPHER RUOCCHIO is the internationally award-winning author of the Sun Eater, a space opera fantasy series, and the former Junior Editor at Baen Books, where he edited several anthologies. His work has also appeared in Marvel comics. He is a graduate of North Carolina State University, where he studied English Rhetoric and the Classics. Christopher has been writing since he was eight and sold his first novel, *Empire of Silence*, at twenty-two. His books have appeared in five languages.

Christopher lives in Raleigh, North Carolina with his wife, Jenna.